# THE WARRIORS

☆

## JOHN JAKES

### THE KENT CHRONICLES
#### VOLUME SIX

NELSON DOUBLEDAY, Inc.
Garden City, New York

Produced by Lyle Kenyon Engel

For my mother

# CONTENTS

BOOK THREE

*The Fire Road*

BOOK FOUR

*Hell-On-Wheels*

## BOOK FIVE

### *The Scarlet Woman*

*And I saw askant the armies,*
*I saw as in noiseless dreams hundreds of battle-flags,*
*Borne through the smoke of the battles and pierc'd with missiles I saw*
*   them . . .*

*I saw battle-corpses, myriads of them,*
*And the white skeletons of young men, I saw them,*
*I saw the debris and debris of all the slain soldiers of the war,*
*But I saw they were not as was thought,*
*They themselves were fully at rest, they suffer'd not,*
*The living remain'd and suffer'd, the mother suffer'd,*
*And the wife and the child and the musing comrade suffer'd,*
*And the armies that remain'd suffer'd.*

   1865:

Walt Whitman,
in the
*Sequel to Drum-Taps,*
written in the summer
and published in the autumn
following Lincoln's death.

# THE WARRIORS

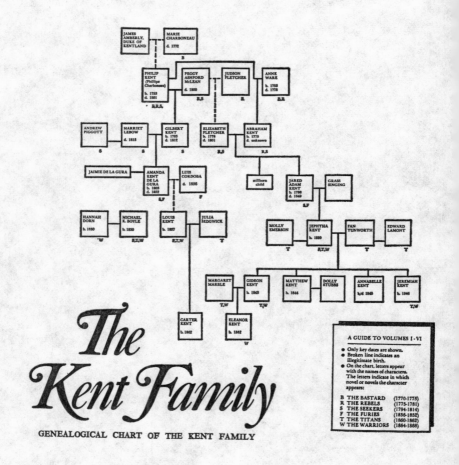

# The Kent Family

## GENEALOGICAL CHART OF THE KENT FAMILY

## Author's Introduction
## to this Special Edition

WHEN the first volume of The Kent Chronicles appeared in October, 1974, its publication could have been likened to the dropping of a small pebble into a huge pond. Few people connected with the project, I think—and certainly not the author—believed there would be more than a modest ripple created by THE BASTARD and its successors.

But in one of those genuinely unplanned and unplannable miracles which occur now and then—miracles which help make the publishing business a sort of Monte Carlo of words, ink, and paper—the ripple effect grew larger with each succeeding book. Within a relatively short time, many readers began to adopt the Kents as their second family—just as I had.

It seems to me there are two main reasons why this happened:

Although readers are often told by pundits that there's something slightly shameful about enjoying an old-fashioned *story*, those same readers, bless them, continue to ignore the message. Any writer has to be grateful for that.

But the gratitude is doubled because the Kent saga is not only the continuing tale of a family, but the story of our country's beginning and growth. That story can't be re-told too often; especially in these times when we often founder in pessimism, forgetting that Americans have overcome enormous obstacles in the past, and steadfastly continued to perfect a form of government which, with all its faults, remains a beacon of hope for the world.

I've received many a letter complaining about the dullness of history as it seems to be taught in school. The letters often ask rhetorically why the colorful, human side of that history seldom appears in conventional texts. I've never quite figured out a satisfactory answer for the question. But this series, in its own way, is an attempt to help remedy the apparent deficiency.

It's been interesting to travel around the country, talk with readers, and watch another developing aspect of "the ripple effect." In the beginning—

and this is a completely subjective, unscientific analysis!—the series seemed to attract mainly those people who liked historical novels and couldn't find a sufficient quantity of new ones; in other words, the first readers were dedicated readers.

Of late, though, I've begun to encounter a different kind of Kent fan. Typically, he or she will start a conversation by saying, "I don't usually read books, but—" Or, "I only read a couple of books a year, but—" That too adds to a writer's satisfaction, which, contrary to popular belief, isn't really derived from gloating over sales figures, but from knowing a given book has touched an individual human being on a one-to-one basis.

So if the series has attracted readers who might not normally have turned its pages even a year ago, so much the better.

Many people have repeatedly asked for more permanent versions of the novels. Consequently this special edition fills a genuine need, and its publication provides just one more opportunity for men and women to watch the unfolding drama of America through the eyes of the Kents—a family, by the way, that I never intended to be made up entirely of successful, flawless paragons. Real families are seldom like that.

My thanks, then, to the publishers of this edition for their willingness to present the times, triumphs and travails of the Kents—and the canvas of our common past—to yet another segment of the American reading public.

JOHN JAKES

*July, 1976*

Prologue at Chancellorsville

# The Fallen Sword

MAJOR GIDEON KENT was worn out. Worn out and plagued by a familiar edginess he only permitted himself to call fear in the silence of his mind. The feeling always came on him during a battle.

About six o'clock that afternoon, he'd witnessed more than the beginning of a battle. He'd seen the start of a slaughter. Thousands upon thousands of his Confederate comrades had gone charging out of the second-growth timber called the Wilderness, bugles blaring, bayonets shining.

Noisy blizzards of wild turkeys fled before the howling men and their streaming battle flags. The surprise attack had caught the Dutchmen—the German regiments in Von Gilsa's brigade—taking their evening meal in Dowdall's Clearing, most of their arms stacked.

The Germans were manning the end of General Howard's exposed flank. The Southerners tore into them. Stabbing. Screaming. Blowing heads and limbs away at point-blank range. On horseback, the commander of the II Corps, Army of Northern Virginia, had closely followed his charging lines, his eyes blazing with an almost religious light. Now and then the commander's hands rose to the thickening smoke in the gold sky as though thanking his God for the carnage.

The general's outrageously risky attack had succeeded. That much had been evident while Gideon observed the first few minutes of the engagement. Then he was summoned away. His own commander, the restless Beauty Stuart, saw that the terrain and the element of surprise made cavalry not only unnecessary but useless. So he requested permission to take a regiment and a battery up to Ely's Ford on the Rapidan River, where some worthwhile damage might be done to a Union wagon park. Gideon, assigned to General Stuart's staff, had gone along.

Around eight o'clock Stuart had sent him back to deliver a report to the general commanding II Corps. Some Union horses had been discovered— part of Stoneman's elusive force. Stuart's message said he was preparing to attack, though he stood ready to swing about if the commander of II Corps needed him.

That the commander needed no one had become clear to Gideon as he'd maneuvered his way south again through almost impenetrable woodland to reach the Fredericksburg Turnpike, where he was now riding, armed with saber and revolver.

The surprise attack had rolled the enemy back for a good two or three miles. Gideon could dimly see the evidence: hundreds and hundreds of blue-uniformed dead sprawled in the lowering dark. To the east, the battle was still raging. Artillery had joined the combat, and shot and shell had ignited stands of timber along the fringes of the Wilderness.

By now the sun had set—it was Saturday, the second day of May, 1863—and Gideon was moving toward the center of the fighting. He had begun to wonder if he'd been given the right directions by some officers he'd met a ways back. Was II Corps' commander really somewhere ahead? Impossible to tell on this increasingly black road flanked by stunted trees and thick underbrush.

His little stallion, Sport, had trouble keeping his footing on the rock-studded highway. The wiry long-tailed Canadian horse—Canucks, the Yank cavalrymen called them—had fallen into Gideon's hands after Fredericksburg. It was a short-legged shaggy prize, coveted and cared for almost as attentively as Gideon looked after himself.

But the damp, hard winter at Camp No-Camp—the name was another of Jeb Stuart's whimsies—had taken its toll. A week ago, despite Gideon's best efforts to keep the captured horse on firm, dry footing whenever possible, he'd discovered the telltale signs of greased heel. Sport's front hoofs had suffered too much mud. They were rotting.

Still, the animal was game, moving steadily if not rapidly through the tunnel of trees. Somewhere not far ahead lay that white-columned farmer's manse at the crossroads dignified with the name Chancellorsville.

The road had grown dark as the devil. But above, there was an eerie light compounded of the glow of the rising full moon, the pulsing glare of the Federal cannon to the east, and the sullen red of burning woodlands around the horizon.

Gideon speculated about whether the fighting might go on throughout the night. Perhaps not. For some reason unknown to him—but evidently clear to the generals—the Yanks commanded by Fighting Joe Hooker had failed to commit their admittedly superior numbers to the battle. Old Marse Robert's mad double gamble seemed to be on the point of succeeding.

Gideon started. On his left—to the north, where smoke drifted through the gargoyle tangle of tree trunks—he thought he heard infantrymen moving.

He reined Sport to a walk. Whose troops were those?

He immediately decided he'd go only another quarter mile or so in his search for the leader of II Corps. The lines were obviously still shifting. And he couldn't be positive the information given him earlier was correct —that the general and a small party of officers, couriers, and Signal Corps sergeants had ridden east on this same turnpike to scout ahead of the re-forming lines. If he didn't soon locate the man his father had known in Lexington before the war, he'd turn about and seek better guidance. Beauty Stuart didn't like officers on his staff to be tardy delivering reports on the cavalry's position.

He started and gasped as an artillery barrage exploded a half mile to his right. He heard the crash of falling branches. That patch of sky was now something out of an artist's conception of hell. It flickered and shifted through every shade of red. It seemed the whole Virginia countryside below the Rappahannock was afire.

Again he heard screams—distant but unnerving. In the dark to his right, beyond the road's south shoulder, he sensed more men moving.

Were they Yanks caught behind the forward sweep of the Confederate ranks? Or were they friendly reinforcements being brought up; responding to the general's favorite command—*"Press on! Press on!"* The general drove his men so hard and fast they were sometimes called the foot cav-alry.

Gideon didn't like not knowing who was out there. His hand dropped to the butt of the Le Mat revolver tucked in his sash as he nudged Sport forward with his knees. He began to be quite concerned that the general might have advanced well beyond the point of safety.

All day an unconfirmed story had circulated among Stuart's staff members. The story ran that the commander of II Corps had risen after a bad sleep and sipped some cold coffee before starting his men on the audacious flank march that culminated in the charge at Dowdall's Clear-ing. While the general drank the coffee in the cold dawn air, his scab-barded sword had been standing against a nearby tree. And then, with no one touching it—no one even near it—the sword had suddenly clattered to the ground.

Gideon didn't count himself especially superstitious. Yet, that story bothered him more than he liked.

And there *was* reason for worry. He'd ridden quite a ways down the Fredericksburg Turnpike.

Why hadn't he found General Stonewall Jackson?

ii

He tried to push the worry out of his mind. In a moment it became easy. Another shell arched overhead. Gideon ducked as it blew up trees about half a mile behind.

He wished to God he could see more clearly. Even if there were men on the road ahead it would be almost impossible to detect them from a distance. Pressing his threadbare gray trousers against Sport to urge him on, he strained to see through shadows and drifting smoke now tinged red by the fire glare, now yellow by the full moon.

To counter his weariness and fear, he again reminded himself that the battle seemed to be going favorably. By all logic it shouldn't have been going that way at all.

Estimates said Hooker had brought down between a hundred and thirty and a hundred and fifty thousand men—including Stoneman's cavalry, which had disappeared somewhere further south. The Union commander was desperate to give Lincoln a decisive victory after the debacles of McClellan, the political general who'd dawdled and ultimately failed on the Peninsula, and Burnside, of the formidable side whiskers, who'd been routed at Fredericksburg.

Fighting Joe's gigantic Union force was faced by less than half as many Confederates. And few of those were in good shape after a winter of privation in the camps around Fredericksburg. Gideon remembered all too well the pathetic sights of the cold season:

Young boys, most of them barely fifteen, their uniforms in tatters, their mouths scurvy-rotted, grubbing in the forests for wild onions—

Feet wrapped in scraps of blanket leaving scarlet tracks in the mud as men filed out of the religious services held to keep their spirits up—

The round, alarmed eyes that first glimpsed the curious bulb-like bags carrying men in big baskets and bobbing on anchor ropes in the blowing mists north of the river—

Gideon himself had been one of those startled and worried watchers. He had never before laid eyes on an observation balloon, but he'd heard about them. The balloons were a disheartening sight. They were more evidence of the superior resources and ingenuity of the industrial North. Against it the South could only muster dogged courage and the spirit epitomized by Jeb Stuart's baritone voice bellowing *Jine the Cavalry* as he led his brigades into a fire fight.

Finally Hooker's onslaught had come. He'd hurled his columns over the Rappahannock on pontoon bridges. General Lee had then done the unthinkable—split the outnumbered Army of Northern Virginia into even smaller components. First he'd left ten thousand under Early at Fredericksburg. Then he'd sent twenty-six thousand with Jackson. That left fourteen thousand Confederates to confront the Union center, which consisted of three entire corps; something like seventy thousand men.

Lee's division of his strength was deliberate. By taking a supreme risk, he hoped for a supreme triumph. Stuart's riders had spotted a weakness in the Union plan. Hooker's right wing straggled out southward, unprotected.

Only last night, Major Hotchkiss, an engineer, and Reverend Lacy, both of whom knew the countryside well, had located a route through the tangled woods along which Jackson might march down, around, and behind the exposed Union right. And so, after his sword had fallen, Stonewall had buckled it on, and with Lee's approval, started at seven this very morning, urging his twenty-six thousand men to *"Press on!"*

Toward the close of the day, the stern, curious soldier who resembled some Old Testament prophet, had ripped into Howard's encamped Germans, the surprise march a complete success.

Gideon, a tall, strong-shouldered young man who would be twenty next month, took a fierce pride in that kind of daring. He found it in Jackson, in Marse Robert, and in his immediate superior, General Stuart, to whose staff he'd been assigned just after the Fredericksburg triumph. Again outnumbered at Chancellorsville, the Southern commanders had had to strike more boldly; gamble everything. Only a general whose military skills approached genius would have agreed to dividing inferior manpower not once but twice, in the faint hope of turning what appeared to be almost certain defeat into possible victory. Only other generals of equally incredible vision and audacity could have executed such a plan.

Moonlight through a break in the trees lit Gideon's tawny hair for an instant. He'd lost his campaign hat around six o'clock when a Yank ball had blown it off. As he thought of brave, imaginative Lee and the hard-driving Jackson, he barely heard another rattle of brush on his left.

Vaguely he realized the turnpike was dipping downward. The soft *chock* of Sport's rotting hoofs changed to a mushy sound. There was swampy ground at the foot of the little hill. But Gideon paid only marginal attention to the terrain. He was happily bemused by the real possibility of a victory. With a few more decisive routs of Lincoln's procession of inept or hesitant generals, the Confederacy might be able to negotiate a peace. Then he could go back to Richmond. Back to his wife and their infant daughter. It was time. Of late he'd been bothered by a feeling that his luck was playing out.

A year earlier, when he had been chosen as one of the twelve hundred men to ride with Stuart to scout McClellan's Peninsular army, he'd nearly lost his life at Tunstall's Station. He'd been leading a detachment burning the rolling stock on the York River Railroad. Some of his men had started firing revolvers to celebrate. Some corporal's careless shot had blown Gideon's beloved roan Will-O'-the-Wisp out from under him.

Stunned, he'd lain unnoticed while the freight cars crumbled around him like fiery waterfalls, setting his uniform afire. Somehow he'd found enough strength to crawl to a ditch and roll frantically until he'd put out the flames. He'd spent the night in that ditch, half conscious and hurting. At dawn he'd discovered that Stuart's horsemen had all ridden on and the district was swarming with Yanks.

He'd crawled out of the ditch, limped into some trees, and hidden out all day, delirious with pain. After dark he'd managed to rouse himself and move on, finally blundering into the dooryard of a small tobacco farm. The farmer had put him to bed, and the farmer's wife had dressed the worst of his burns with poultices.

The family tended him for over five weeks. At last the itching tissue had sloughed off his arms and chest, leaving only faint scars.

Then Gideon had disguised himself in country clothing and slipped back into Richmond to find his wife—who had feared him lost forever.

That sort of brush with death—his first had come at Manassas in '61—had relieved him of all conviction that this war was glorious. Stuart still fought with zest, and Gideon still joined the cavalry's singing as they rode. But his emulation of his commander's spirit was forced. He now found the war a necessary but filthy business. He wanted it over; settled with as much advantage to the South as could be gained.

Perhaps that was why he felt so strangely euphoric just now. If a victory could be wrenched out of the night's confusion it might lead at long last to the European recognition Jeff Davis sought for the government. It might lead also to a negotiated peace, with the South once again prospering as a separate nation on the American continent. But most importantly, it might lead him home to Margaret and little Eleanor.

Gideon's head jerked up. Musketry rattled ahead. He reined Sport to a dead stop. The fire-reddened moon hung above the trees but did little to relieve the gloom on the turnpike.

The firing died away. Gideon scratched his nose. The air stank of powder—and worse. Hoof thrush wasn't his mouth's only affliction. Too many hours of a saddle on Sport's back had opened one of the familiar and nauseous sores that plagued cavalry horses. Gideon could smell the fetid ooze beneath him; the sore ran constantly. It pained him to think he was only worsening it by riding his spunky mount so hard.

But he only had one horse. And he also had a very important dispatch in the pouch thrust into his frayed, dirty sash.

Now that the muskets were silent, he could hear a party of horsemen approaching. He quickly swung the stallion to the north side of the road. The moon glinted cold and hard in Gideon's blue eyes as he scanned the turnpike.

The small arms fire from the direction of Chancellorsville started again, then gradually died away beneath the rhythmic plopping of hoofs. The horses were coming up the slight incline from the low place.

Next he heard voices. Did they belong to friends, or to enemies?

### iii

Gideon drew his Le Mat. He thought briefly of heading Sport into the brush beyond the flinty shoulder. But then he heard more sounds of movement and decided against it.

Dry-mouthed he waited. Should he hail?

No, better wait and see whether the broken moonlight revealed gray uniforms—or blue ones.

A horseman materialized, followed by several others. The leading rider, thin to the point of emaciation, turned his head at the sound of another shell bursting south of the road. Gideon saw the rider was wearing gray. The man had a straggling beard, eyes that glittered like polished stones, and an unmistakable profile.

Relieved, Gideon holstered the revolver. He'd found Jackson.

He touched Sport gently with his spurs. The stallion started forward. Behind the general, Gideon thought he saw six or eight mounted men in a double column. There could have been several more; it was impossible to be sure in the bad light. He headed the stallion back across the turnpike, moving toward the general at an angle.

As he opened his mouth to hail, someone hidden in the woods to Jackson's left let out a shout. From the same spot a horizontal line of flame flashed. Rifled muskets roared, volleying at the road.

### iv

The general's horse reared. Gideon crouched over Sport's mane just as a ball whizzed past his ear. To Jackson's rear, men yelled out as he fought to control his alarmed mount.

"Who's there?"

"Damn Yanks!"

"No, those have to be our men, Morrison."

"No firing! *Cease firing!*"

In answer to the last cry from the road, the unseen riflemen volleyed again.

Sport shied, neighing frantically. Over the roar of the guns, Gideon heard a fierce, familiar wail from the dark trees—

The Rebel yell.

The men in the woods weren't the enemy. Perhaps they were from A. P. Hill's division. The officers Gideon had met earlier had told him the division was supposed to be advancing somewhere in this area. With visibility so poor, Jackson and his party had been foolish to push out so far ahead of the Confederate lines.

Gideon kicked Sport forward, realizing from the rising clamor of voices that soldiers were crashing through the trees on his side of the road as well. He'd evidently escaped an attack because he was a single rider, proceeding in relative quiet.

The voices on the turnpike grew louder, creating confusion as horses screamed and reared:

"*Who are you men out there?*"

"Hold your fire! You're firing at your own officers!"

"Damned lie!" a Southern voice howled from the blackness. "It's the Yank cavalry we was warned about, boys. *Pour it to them!*"

"General!" Gideon shouted, riding toward Jackson, who in turn was spurring his horse toward the side of the road Gideon had just left. Gideon let go of the reins in a desperate attempt to reach for Jackson's shoulders and drag him out of the saddle. He touched the fabric of Jackson's uniform. Then his hands were pulled away as Sport's right foreleg went into a hole.

The stallion careened sideways, almost fell. Gideon tumbled from the saddle, landing hard as a new volley boomed from the thickets toward which Jackson was riding.

Sport clambered up, apparently unhurt. On hands and knees Gideon blinked and gasped for breath. He saw Jackson's tall figure stiffen, heard him cry out.

Jackson's right hand flew upward as though jerked by an invisible rope. Then his left arm flailed out. Gideon scrambled to his feet, realizing from the way the general was swaying that he'd been hit. And not just once.

Another howl of pain from the tangle of men and horses told him someone else had taken a ball. "Boswell's shot!" a man cried, just as another volley roared from the road's north side.

The turnpike was bedlam. Wounded men slid from their saddles. Terrified horses bolted.

Gideon staggered toward Jackson. The general was still in the saddle.

With both arms dangling at his sides, Jackson had managed to turn his horse's head away from the direction of the last volley. Gideon still hoped to reach the commander and pull him down before the concealed soldiers fired again.

A riderless horse crashed into him from behind, spilling Gideon on his face. A rock raked his cheek. He yelped as a hoof grazed his temple. Instinct made him cover his head with both forearms.

Just as he did, he had a distorted view of the bearded general being carried forward by his plunging mount. A low-hanging branch bashed Jackson's forehead, knocking him to the ground.

Still more shouting:

"Sergeant Cunliffe?"

"He's down too. Dead, I think."

From somewhere in the trees, a strident voice:

"Who's there? *Who are you?*"

An officer bent low and running toward the fallen general screamed, "Stonewall Jackson's staff, you goddamn fools!"

Gideon heard Jackson's name shouted out in the dark on both sides of the road. Then he heard cursing; accusations. Finally a voice identified the unseen marksmen as part of the Thirty-third North Carolina—General Hill's division.

On his feet again, Gideon lurched toward the half-dozen shadowy figures clustering around the fallen commander. A sudden memory gave him a sick feeling:

*The sword fell.*

*No one touched it.*

A hand seized his shoulder. Whirled him. A revolver gouged his chin:

"Who the hell are—?"

"Major Kent, General Stuart's staff," he panted. Shock became rage. He slammed a fist against the revolver muzzle and knocked it aside without thinking that a jerk of the soldier's finger could have blown his head off. "I've dispatches from—"

The man paid no attention; spun back toward the general.

"How is he?"

"A ball through his right palm."

"He took another in the left arm. No, looks like two."

*"Don't move him!"*

The voices sounded childish in their hysteria. In the woods on both sides of the turnpike, men began to hurry toward the road, heedless of the noise. An officer in gray confronted one of the first infantrymen to emerge from the trees. With a slash of his revolver muzzle, the officer laid the soldier's cheek open. Moonlight shone on running blood as the rifleman reeled back. The officer brandished his revolver at the other ragged figures beginning to creep into sight:

"Fucking careless butchers! *You shot Stonewall!*"

Somewhere a boyish voice repeated the name. Someone else began crying.

How many Confederates had been hit in those volleys? Gideon had no idea. He counted three sprawled bodies on the turnpike—perhaps a fourth part way down the slope of the little hill. A party of riders clattered up from the west, was challenged, then told the news. The new arrivals joined the men already kneeling around Jackson. One bearded fellow with a heavily braided sleeve thrust his way through the group. With a start, Gideon recognized A. P. Hill, three staff officers right behind him.

The stunned Hill dropped to his knees, gently lifted, and cradled Jackson's head in his arms. One of Jackson's aides pulled a knife and began to slit the general's left sleeve from shoulder to cuff. Blood leaked out of both of the general's gauntlets.

Like most of the rest, Gideon stood staring, overwhelmed by the tragic accident. He caught an occasional glimpse of Jackson's stern face. The eyes were open; shining in the moonlight. The branch that had struck the general's forehead had opened a cut. Trickles of blood ran in his eyebrows.

Beyond the southern shoulder of the turnpike a tumultuous shouting had started. Men relayed word of the shooting. Even further out, Gideon caught the sound of horsemen cantering. More Confederates moving up? Or the enemy cavalry for which Jackson and his party had been mistaken?

A man who identified himself as Morrison, the general's brother-in-law, crawled to Hill's side.

"For God's sake, sir, let's get him into the shelter of a tree."

General Hill raised an anguished face. "Send a courier for the corps surgeon."

No one moved.

"*Do you hear me, fetch McGuire at once!*"

"And an ambulance!" a second voice bawled.

"We've got to move him," Morrison insisted. "Captain Wilbourn?"

"Here."

Another man pressed through the group around the fallen general. Laboriously, Wilbourn and Morrison lifted Jackson and dragged him toward the shoulder, ignoring the protests of several others about possibly worsening the injuries. In the forest the shouting and the drum of hoofs intensified.

Gideon wrenched his head around and called, "They're making so damn much noise, the Yank outposts will hear!"

No one heard him. Everyone was shouting at once. Wilbourn and Morrison seemed the only men sufficiently self-possessed to do what had to be done; the others kept yelling warnings, orders, questions.

Someone ran up to report that at least two men were dead for certain. A courier snagged the reins of a horse—Sport, Gideon saw with consternation—mounted, and galloped off before he could protest.

He turned back, tense and still shaken. Wilbourn propped Jackson against a roadside tree, gently pulled off the blood-soaked gauntlets, then carefully unfastened the general's coat. Jackson was still conscious. He groaned when Wilbourn found it difficult to free his right arm from the sleeve.

"Kerchief!" Wilbourn demanded.

A. P. Hill produced one. Wilbourn knotted it around Jackson's upper left arm, then asked for another. He used it to tie a crude sling. Gideon thought he saw bone protruding through the mangled flesh of the general's arm.

Breathing hard, Wilbourn leaned back on his haunches.

"General? We must see to your right hand."

Jackson's lids fluttered. His voice—so often stern—was a mild whisper: "No. A mere trifle—"

General Hill stamped a boot down, hard. "It's too dangerous to wait for an ambulance here. Rig a litter. Use my overcoat. Branches."

Trying to banish the persistent image of the fallen sword, Gideon darted toward the brush on the north side of the road. A private, a starved-looking boy whose ragged gray uniform was powder stained, leaned on his rifled musket, staring at the wounded man. In the smoky moonlight the boy saw Gideon's enraged face. He seemed compelled to plead with him: "Don't blame us, Major. Jesus, please don't blame us. We heard the Yankee horse was movin' this way. We thought it was them—"

"You didn't think at all!" Gideon cried, raising a fist. The boy cringed away. It was all Gideon could do to keep from hitting him.

Finally, muttering a disgusted obscenity, he shoved past the boy, dragged out his saber, and began cutting a low branch. More of the damn fool North Carolina troops were drifting out of the woods. They stood like silent, shabby wraiths, gazing at Jackson. Gideon hacked at the branch with savage strokes, as though it were a human adversary.

When the branch dropped, he started to chop off a second one. He grew conscious of a faint whistling, coming from the east and growing louder. He glanced up, his palms cold all at once. Whether it was coincidence or the result of all the noise in the wood, the Federal gunners had chosen that moment to open a new bombardment.

He flung himself forward against the trunk as the Tarheel soldiers scattered. The shot burst at treetop level, almost directly above him. The shock wave slammed his cheek against the bark.

Bits of metal and wood rained down. None struck hard enough to hurt him. But the explosion and fall of debris touched something raw in him—something abraded by the months of separation from his wife; by the wretched conditions of the winter camp where the brave songs had begun to sound hollow and infantile. He was suddenly gripped by a paralyzing panic.

He broke it with an enraged yell. He snatched up the first branch, yanked the second off the trunk by sheer force, jammed his saber under his arm, and stumbled back toward Jackson.

A shell exploded close by. The road lit up momentarily. Crouched over with the branches in his hands and the saber jutting from his armpit, Gideon dodged a shower of burning twigs while his mind reproduced the dreadful image again:

*The untouched sword scabbard slowly, slowly toppling—*

At First Manassas, Jackson had stood like that stone wall and earned his famous nickname. He was more than a master tactician. He had become a legend to thousands of Confederate soldiers who'd never even seen him; a name in newspapers that gave hope to those at home when hope seemed futile. He was the supreme example of the South's one matchless weapon —raw courage in the face of superior numbers and industrial strength.

Gideon's panic became almost overwhelming. The Confederacy couldn't afford to lose Stonewall Jackson. General Lee couldn't afford to lose him. The survivors on the road *had* to save him!

Even if they died doing it.

v

The Yank bombardment became almost continuous. Shells were being lobbed in every few seconds. Exploding shot spattered the turnpike like metal rain. Gideon reached the group of men around Jackson and began to jab the two branches into the sleeves of Hill's gray overcoat. He worked with desperate haste, driven by the conviction that Jackson was the only man who could execute Lee's most daring strategies and win victories that textbooks said were impossible.

"He's not that badly hurt," Morrison breathed. Whether it was true or only a prayer, Gideon didn't know. But he tended to believe Morrison was right. The greatest danger to Jackson at the moment was the shelling.

An eighth of a mile east, another charge blew a huge pit in the turnpike, raising a cloud of dirt that sifted down on the men a moment later.

Captain Wilbourn leaned over Jackson's head to shield him from the falling earth. As the upper limbs of a nearby tree caught fire, he jumped to his feet:

"Get that litter up and carry it out of here!"

Gideon and three other men grabbed the cut limbs with the coat stretched between. The men at the bottom end had the hardest job—holding the branches and the skirt of the coat to keep it taut. Jackson was lifted onto the litter, then cautiously raised.

Gideon tried to walk steadily—ignoring the detonations, the glaring lights; the flaming trees; the hissing grapeshot. Through the woods on both sides of the highway, bugles pealed, officers bellowed orders, men crashed through the thickets. Occasionally a piercing scream signaled the killing or wounding of one of those men by artillery fire. Gideon breathed hard, the dispatch from Stuart entirely forgotten as he concentrated on one simple but immensely important task:

Getting Jackson to the rear. Out of the shell zone. Getting him to a place where he could be treated. Saved.

*He's only wounded in the forearm,* Gideon thought. *If he doesn't bleed to death—if we can reach the surgeon in time without all of us getting blown up—he'll be all right.*

He ducked his head as another shell burst. A flaming limb just missed his left side, the heat scorching for a moment. He tried not to think about how desperately the Army of Northern Virginia needed this peculiar, unkempt man who had once taught at the Military Institute in Lexington, where Gideon had been raised. He just kept walking, lifting one foot carefully after the other, trying not to jostle the litter.

Steadily, they bore Jackson westward. The cannonading never stopped. One litter bearer went down, hit by a piece of shot. A major from Hill's staff reached out to catch the branch as the wounded man let go.

But the major wasn't quick enough. The litter tilted. Jackson rolled off. When he struck the ground, he uttered no sound.

The general's brother-in-law, Morrison, knelt beside him, tears in his eyes:

"Oh, Lord, General, I'm sorry."

Smoke drifted away. The moon appeared again, lighting the bearded face. Jackson's tongue probed his lips, as if he were thirsty. His eyes looked bright, fierce.

"We'll be on our way again within a minute—" Morrison began.

"Never mind," Jackson whispered. "Never mind about me."

"Come on!" Morrison exclaimed. "Lift him!"

They carried the general for another eight or ten minutes, until they reached the ambulance that had been summoned. Once Jackson had been laid inside and the vehicle turned around, Gideon trotted along behind—it moved slowly to avoid sudden jolts—and presently the ambulance and the men accompanying it reached a hospital tent in a dark field out of range of the Union artillery.

Without his horse—God only knew what the messenger had done with Sport—Gideon had little choice but to remain outside the tent for an hour. And then another. Finally Dr. Black, the surgeon, came out wiping his hands on a bloody apron.

Lantern light shone on the faces of the dozen or so men who'd been waiting for word. The surgeon glanced from face to face while the cannon continued to rumble beyond the burning trees on the eastern horizon.

"I have successfully amputated the general's left arm," Dr. Black said. "The bone was beyond repair. If there are no complications, he'll soon be back to lead his men again."

Gideon shouted like a boy. So did the others. Hats sailed into the air as the weary doctor turned, gave a faint smile of satisfaction, and stumbled back into the tent.

Gideon sank down on the ground, incredibly tired. While a few of the men continued to whoop and dance around him, he leaned his forehead on his knee and thought:

*At least I've helped do one thing in this war that I can be proud of.*

After two years of fighting in which he had changed from a cheerful, contentious young man eager to see battle to a weary professional who now knew the dreadful cost of the South's principles, it was good to be able to single out even one such accomplishment.

He yawned. Closed his eyes. It was good.

Though he knew he should get up and hunt for Stuart, he didn't. He was too tired. He sat upright in the glow of the lantern outside the medical tent, struggling to keep his eyes open.

It would soon be Sunday, he realized. Maybe it was Sunday already.

Would Margaret be going to church in Richmond? *Must write her*, he reminded himself. *Write to tell her how we saved old Stonewall—*

Eight days later, before Gideon found the spare moments to put his thoughts to paper, Thomas Jonathan Jackson lay abed in a small house at Guiney's Station—

Dying.

vi

*—It was pneumonia, they say. Jackson was making a good recovery. Then, quite abruptly, Wednesday I believe it was, he began to sink.*

I've been told it was a relatively peaceful death, though the general suffered periods of delirium near the end. His wife Mary Anna was among those at the bedside. They sang a hymn he requested.

According to what we've been told, the general spoke twice, once to issue an order for A. P. Hill to "come up" with his infantry, the second time to utter a most peculiar remark—"Let us cross over the river, and rest under the shade of the trees." Some claim the word was "pass," not "cross." But no one knows what he meant.

I didn't realize he was so young; he had observed his thirty-ninth birthday only in January.

I've considered trying to write my father in New York where he is once again preaching. I wanted to tell him Stonewall has died. But I am sure no letter of mine would reach the North, and he will doubtless read of the passing, since Jackson's exploits were so widely discussed.

In Lexington, the general was a friend to my father when he had no others. He will mourn the cruel accident, I am sure, even though he believed his friend had given his loyalty to the wrong side.

It is hard for me to express my feelings just now, Margaret. We won a sound victory at Chancellorsville—though at a high cost. I've heard there were as many as 13,000 of our boys killed, maimed, or lost. We would have made the success an even better one if Fighting Joe had not lost his taste for fighting—something it appears he never had to begin with!—and got away across the Rappahannock pontoons before we could catch him. And the loss of Jackson has robbed the victory of all sweetness.

Even General Stuart, with whose command I was reunited before the fighting ended, seems in poor spirits. He is being praised in some quarters, and d——d in others, as a result of his handling of Jackson's infantry. He took command when A. P. Hill fell wounded the same night Stonewall was shot.

You may say I place too much importance on Jackson, but I do not believe so. It's the common feeling that, between them, Lee and Jackson would one day have pounded the Lincoln crowd into submission to our point of view. Lee was like an anvil and Jackson a hammer, and whenever the Federals were caught between them, they were lost. Now Lee's hammer is gone. He is reportedly grieved almost beyond consolation, though outwardly maintaining a show of courage. Men claim—rightly, I think—that when we lost Jackson, we lost the irreplaceable.

I even sense a new attitude among those on our side. I can't quite put it into the proper words, but there is not much talk of winning now, only of a long hard fight with a truce the most we can hope for, and defeat being more likely. The feeling did not seem present a few months ago, and certainly not a year ago. I hope the mood will pass, but I wonder. Something has changed.

In truth, I have changed too. I am ashamed to put unmanly thoughts on paper, but I cannot help them. I was never before afraid that we would lose, but I am afraid now. I am even more afraid of what will happen to us—you and Eleanor and myself—if the worst comes to pass. The last time I saw father, he quoted Scripture and stated that the Kent family need not forever be harmed by the war. But what of we three?

I never felt strongly that the nigras should remain perpetually enslaved—the plain truth is, I never thought much about their condition at all; a mistake, I am beginning to believe.

But my doubts about certain aspects of the war do not alter the fact that I have taken part in what the North calls the rebellion. Will I or any other soldier on this side be easily forgiven for that? I doubt it. Of more importance is this question. Even if I am forgiven, how will we make a life for ourselves when peace comes again?

You know the many, many hours I have spent during the winter studying the books you have sent, trying to teach myself to put words down in a proper order, and with some intelligence, because a good officer—especially a staff officer—must have that skill. But I am a grown man, and I still lack a decent education. War is the only trade I know.

You must forgive much of what I have written. I am caught up in the sad spirit of these days, and should not pass my gloom along to you. I love you with all my heart and pray for your safety and that of our dear child there in the capital which the enemy wants to destroy so very much.

Will write again the moment I can. Let us hope God and the circumstances of the war enable me to do so in a more cheerful spirit.

Give the baby hugs and kisses for me.

Your husband,
G. K.

# BOOK ONE
## *In Destruction's Path*

# CHAPTER 1

## *Soldier Alone*

SLOWLY, SO HE WOULDN'T make a sound, the kneeling Confederate corporal stretched his right hand between the slats of the corn crib on the small Georgia farm.

The interior was black. He couldn't see what he was after, but he was determined to find food. His belly hurt, though he didn't know whether it hurt from hunger or from the onset of another attack of dysentery.

*Better get hold of something to tide you over,* he thought. All he'd had to drink for the past two days had been creek water; his only nourishment a few berries. If he starved he'd never reach Jefferson County. And he had to reach it. That was why he'd risked sneaking the quarter of a mile from a clump of pine woods to the back of this crib on a small farm in Washington County. While he'd crossed the open ground, he'd kept the crib between himself and the run-down house, which appeared to be deserted. From the safety of the trees, he'd watched house and crib for a quarter hour before venturing out.

He couldn't find any corn in the crib. He pressed his right shoulder harder against the slats, stretching and wiggling his fingers; groping. He was a lean young man of eighteen. His face, which always tended to a gauntness inherited from his father, looked even more bony than usual. He had his mother's fair hair, but accumulated dirt had given it a dingy brown cast. Large dark eyes and a straight well-formed nose were spoiled just a bit by a mouth that took on an almost cruel thinness when he was determined.

The Georgia twilight had a curious, cold quality despite the huge red ball of the sun dropping over a patch of woodland where leaves were changing to yellow and vermillion. Or perhaps he only thought the oncoming dusk seemed cold because he was alone. It was Sunday, the twentieth of November, 1864; the eve of winter.

Grunting softly, his hand searched to the right; to the left.

Nothing.

He jammed his eye up next to an opening between two higher slats but saw only darkness. *Lord, was the crib empty?*

He looked disreputable, kneeling there. His cadet-gray tunic, designed to cover his trousers to a point halfway between hip and knee, was torn in five places. From the two rows of seven buttons, just four remained. His point-down chevrons had come half unsewn, and the light blue trim that edged the tunic and identified him as an infantryman had almost raveled away. Dust and weather had soiled the light blue collar and cuffs as well as the matching sides and crown of his kepi-style forage cap that hid the white streak in his hair. A duck havelock hanging down from the back of the cap to protect his neck from the weather had turned from white to gray. A canvas shoulder sling held his imported .577-caliber Enfield rifled musket upright against his back.

Like any good soldier, he had strong personal feelings about his weapon. It was his companion; his means of survival. And he was good with it. That was a surprising thing he'd discovered during his first weeks of service. Perhaps it was his upbringing—his grandfather had taught him how to shoot. But whatever the reason, he'd quickly become a proficient marksman. He was fast at reloading, with an instinctive feel for the intricacies of handling firearms—such things as wind velocity and tricks of sun and shadow that could affect accuracy. He'd been complimented more than once on being a fine shot. The compliments helped develop a conviction that, without a weapon, he was not complete. His gun had become an extension of himself.

Straining to find something inside the crib, he failed to hear the footsteps. The farmer must have slipped out of the house in a stealthy way, somehow spotting him on his passage across the field. His first warning was a shadow that fell over the side of the crib.

"Y'all get up from there, you damn thief."

He jerked his head around; saw the man. Paunchy; gray-bearded. Old, weather-worn clothing. Filthy toes showing at the tip of one worn-out boot.

Thick-fingered hands clasped the handle of a pitchfork. The tines caught the sundown light and glittered like thin swords.

"I said get up!" the man yelled, lunging from the corner of the crib.

The soldier reared back. The tines of the pitchfork stabbed into the slat where his cheek had been pressed a moment before.

The man yanked the pitchfork loose. The corporal steadied himself, feet spread wide, hands held up in front of him:

"Look, I only wanted a little food—"

The pitchfork flashed red. The corporal eyed the points. Would they stab at him again, without any warning?

The man's slurry voice showed his fury:

"What corn I got belongs to me and the missus and my two little girls. You ain't gonna touch it."

"All right." The corporal backed up a step. "Just be careful with that fork. I still have a ways to travel."

The man squinted at him. "Where you bound?"

"Home," the corporal said, resorting to an evasion he'd used before. He was thankful he'd ripped the Virginia regimental emblem from his cap, in case the man could identify the insignia of state units.

"Where's home?"

"What's it to you?" the corporal shot back, resenting the man's hostility to someone in Confederate gray.

The farmer came forward again, the fork held horizontally, the tines a foot from the younger man's belly.

"Goddamn it, boy, *you answer!*"

"That's a hell of a way to talk to a soldier from your own army!" He tried a bluff; lowered his left hand to touch the brown-spotted bandage knotted around his thigh. "I got mustered out. I was hit."

A gumble of doubt: "That a fact. Listen, I know they're sending boys back to service shot up a lot worse 'n you. You ain't tellin' me the truth."

The corporal was angry. This ignorant clod couldn't begin to understand his concept of devotion to duty; could never understand why he was traveling alone across central Georgia; hiding out during the daylight hours; stealing and getting shot up for trying to pilfer a chicken to eat.

"You say you're goin' home—"

"That's right."

"What's your name?"

"Kent. Corporal Jeremiah Kent."

"Well, now, Corporal Jeremiah Kent, you just tell me where your home's at."

"Mister, I don't mean you any harm. You wouldn't miss an ear or two."

The pitchfork stabbed out, the tines indenting the fabric of his tunic just above the belt:

"Boy, answer the question. *Where's home?*"

Alarmed, he risked a little of the truth:

"I'm headed for Jefferson County."

The farmer's face twisted in an ugly sneer. Very softly, he said:

"Then you're tellin' me lies. You ain't no Georgia boy, I know by the way you talk. You come from someplace up north. Carolina, mebbe. Virginny. But not Georgia. You run away?"

The tines poked deeper. Jeremiah felt one pierce his tunic; prick his skin.

"You're a goddamn deserter."

Furious, Jeremiah didn't know how to answer the accusation. In a way it was true, yet he'd traveled for miles with no sense of dishonor. Traveled with pride and purpose, in fact.

"I sent two sons to Mississippi and lost both. *Both!* I ain't feedin' or shelterin' no damn runaway coward!"

The last word exploded in a rush of breath. At the same instant, the farmer's hands jerked back at his right side. Then with full force he rammed the pitchfork forward. Jeremiah jumped sideways. A tine slashed another hole in his tunic. The points hit a crib slat so hard they hummed.

Jeremiah's mouth looked thin and white as he laced his fingers together. Color rushed into his cheeks. While the farmer struggled to wrench the tines loose, Jeremiah slammed the back of the farmer's neck, using his interlocked hands like a hammerhead.

The farmer staggered. Jeremiah struck again, ruthlessly hard. *Time to quit fooling with this old man.*

The man dropped to his knees, his palms pressed against the slats of the crib as he gasped for air. A little of the harshness went out of Jeremiah's eyes as he whirled and dashed toward the pines, hoping the farmer had no firearm within quick reach.

Short of breath and dizzy—the sickness seemed to be coming on again—he slowed at a point halfway across the field and turned his head around.

Lord God! The damned lunatic was chasing him! The raised pitchfork shimmered in the red light. Despite his age, the man ran with powerful strides.

Jeremiah bolted for the trees. How could you explain anything to a father who'd seen two sons killed in a war that was ending in failure? How could you make such a man comprehend that you were out here alone because you believed, above all else, in honoring promises and obeying orders? Especially orders from someone who'd saved your life?

Eyes slitted, head back, mouth gulping air, he drove himself. Reached the sanctuary of the sweet-smelling pines and kept going, brambles slashing at his legs, needles on low branches raking his cheeks.

Finally, deep in the woods, he leaned over to catch his breath, near fainting from the aches in his chest and midsection. Somewhere behind he heard the farmer thrashing in the brush.

"Yellabelly! They gonna catch you! They gonna *hang* you! You an' every other goddamn deserter!"

The thrashing sounds diminished. Presently the woods fell silent except for the shrieking of a jay. He'd eluded the man. But he couldn't elude the accusation. It enraged him.

He started on, mentally minimizing the failure of his raid on the crib.

He probably couldn't have kept corn kernels in his stomach anyway. He was undoubtedly getting sick all over again. He'd just keep moving.

His fury toward the farmer abated slowly. A man like that wouldn't understand what he was doing; no one could understand except a dead Confederate officer, and two women Jeremiah had never seen.

As he limped from the woods and angled toward a dirt highway in the deepening darkness, his heartbeat slowed. He climbed the shoulder of the road and turned in the right direction after a backward glance to assure himself the farmer hadn't taken to horseback after him.

No, he hadn't. The road stretched silent, winding into the black and scarlet autumn sunset.

He swallowed, concerned about being sick again. Sickness would only delay him further. Was there anyone left in the whole damn world who'd understand what he was doing? What if those women called obeying an order desertion? If they did, his flight and all its perils would count for nothing.

Just like the war itself.

ii

A mile or so down the road Jeremiah began pondering a question he'd asked himself many times, without finding an answer. What really had become of the war he'd gone to fight? That brave, honorable war for the St. Andrew's cross of the Confederacy and all it represented?

He thought he knew part of the answer. The bravery had been rendered worthless by military routs, and a widespread sense of impending defeat. The honor had been turned into a mockery by behavior he'd witnessed among the men on his own side.

Gradually, the shock of his encounter with the farmer passed. He honestly couldn't blame or hate the man now that he'd escaped him. The beautiful night soothed the anger and brought understanding.

A high-riding white moon blazed then darkened as thin clouds sailed past. The color of the countryside changed from moment to moment; silver to sable to silver again. A breeze rustled the branches of a plum orchard to his left, out there past a little brook that ran beside the road. He heard the sound of rabbits hopping in the orchard. Somewhere, late-blooming wild roses fumed their sweetness into the air.

His belly began to growl again. His intestines seemed to be clutched by a strong hand, then released.

The sickness had left him helplessly weak for half a dozen days at Lovejoy's Station where he'd rested in early September, recovering from a light wound. At Jonesboro a Yank ball had sliced the flesh of his left upper arm. The ball would have killed him if it hadn't been for Lieutenant Colonel Rose.

Rose had been trying to rally the troops under his command during the Jonesboro action. He'd seen the Union sharpshooter take aim at Jeremiah, who was kneeling and loading with frantic speed. Rose had lunged and knocked Jeremiah over—again demonstrating that he was the kind of man Jeremiah wanted to be himself—

An honorable soldier.

Scarcely eight hours later, Rose lay beneath the lantern of a field hospital, mortally wounded.

That night he revealed a side to his personality Jeremiah had never seen before—deeply hidden bitterness and pessimism. Pain destroyed his pretense when he gave Jeremiah a letter to his loved ones. Rose had written the letter a few days earlier, using the only material available—brown butcher's paper.

Jeremiah could still vividly recall how Lieutenant Colonel Rose had looked in those moments before his death. The field hospital lantern lit the sweat in his beard like little jewels. He grimaced; summoned strength as best he could; whispered to his orderly:

"Take the letter home for me, Jeremiah. My wife and daughter—they'll need you more than this pitiful army needs you. My God, you know we're done for. Have you counted—"

A violent, prolonged fit of coughing interrupted him. Jeremiah stayed rigid, not wanting to turn and see why a man on another of the plank tables was shrieking. The rasp of a saw told him why.

"—counted the numbers we're losing every day? Some will go back where they came from, but some will turn into scavengers."

Jeremiah had seen it already. Enlisted men disobeyed their officers, slipped out of camp after an engagement and prowled among the Union dead, stripping them of personal effects, prying loose gold teeth, even stealing uniform buttons.

"They'll be roaming all over Georgia soon. I don't care what others tell you, war—war ruins some men. It ruins land but worse, it—ruins people. You've seen what's happening. Desertions. Profiteering. Brutality to prisoners. Andersonville—"

Another spasm of coughing. Rose went on, more faintly:

"—Andersonville! Right here in Georgia—an affront to God and everything that's decent. It's no different on the other side. And now there's Sherman to fret about. I fear for my wife's safety. Go to her. Don't let anything stop you—or turn you into what some men in this army have become. You're better than that. Any man—" he grimaced. "—would be proud to call you his son. I would. I've never had a son."

Jeremiah's eyes filled with tears, but he felt no shame.

"I did you a service," Rose whispered. "So you must do one for me. As soon as you can—promise?"

The sight of the officer's pain nearly broke his heart. But he had to answer truthfully:

"Sir, I—I couldn't. That'd mean deserting."

Rose's eyes opened wider, resentful. He clenched his teeth. Raised himself on one elbow:

"Then I—I order you to go. You understand, Corporal Kent? I'm your commanding officer and I'm *ordering you*."

Ordering him? That tangled the whole request so fearfully, he didn't know how to deal with it. He stood mute while Rose glared:

"You will carry out the order?"

"I—"

"You will." It was no longer a question. "Promise me." The harshness became pleading. "Please promise me—"

He whispered it:

"Promise, sir."

Rose fell back, his chest heaving as he labored to breathe. Almost before Jeremiah realized it, a surgeon was covering Rose's face. Then men wrapped his corpse in a bloodied canvas and carried it outside to dump it beside three dozen others. Hardly aware of the throb of his bandaged arm, Jeremiah wept.

The order he'd promised to carry out lingered in his mind. He'd promised. There was no question of *when* he'd leave; only of how. He had to get away without being caught.

It took a while. The combination of his none-too-serious wound and the chronic intestinal ailment of the army put him out of action for six days, forcing him to stay at Lovejoy's Station while General Hood moved most of the troops further west, to Palmetto—hopefully out of Sherman's range.

Eventually Jeremiah was ordered on to Palmetto with a dozen other men who'd recovered from injuries. He remained at Palmetto during most of September, waiting for orders. He saw Jefferson Davis from afar when the president slipped in to confer with Hood over problems plaguing the disintegrating command structure.

Jeremiah's promise to Rose became an obsession. Quite often he was tempted to read the letter he guarded so carefully. But he felt that would be a dishonorable violation of Rose's confidence. Even though the concept of an honorable war had become almost a joke, he clung steadfastly to the belief that he must continue to behave in an honorable way at all times.

Yet watching desertion-ridden companies at Palmetto shrink to half a dozen men made it hard. So did the loss of all the little amenities he'd taken for granted when he was younger:

The way your hands felt clean after scrubbing with harsh yellow soap. There was no longer any soap.

How your mouth tasted better in the morning after using salted water and a toothbrush. He'd lost his toothbrush through a hole in his tunic pocket. The whole Confederacy was short of salt. He had resorted to a twig and his own stale spit.

Food had grown progressively poorer and scarcer. There was usually soup, if you could dignify it with that name. Water thickened with some corn meal. Occasionally he'd get potatoes, which he'd mash up and cook with a precious bit of meat. He'd learned to save the chunk of meat, wrap it in a scrap of cloth and re-use it the next day. He'd cooked one such chunk of pork over and over until it was black and smelled like garbage.

It was no wonder the dysentery felled him again, this time for nearly three weeks.

When he recovered, it was already mid-October. He was glad he hadn't tried to get away yet. Some of the deserters had been caught, brought back, and sent to prison. But he was growing fretful; impatient.

*I am ordering you—*

*Promise me—*

*"Promise, sir."*

General Hood had taken the army and disappeared into the northwest, hoping to cut Billy Sherman's supply lines from Tennessee. Since Jeremiah's unit was gone, he was ordered out with a contingent of Georgia Militia to find and join Hood. He was still physically weak. Couldn't keep up—or at least had an excuse for pretending he couldn't. One dawn, the militiamen left him behind.

He was free.

He rested three days in a glade above Atlanta, then headed southeast to deliver the letter. Technically, he supposed he *was* a deserter. But not in his own mind.

He circled wide around besieged Atlanta and crossed the shell-blackened, trench-scarred fields with caution. With one expert shot he bagged a wild turkey, then gutted and roasted it. He had no salt to add as a preservative, but the meat would still last him a while.

Careful as he was to avoid being stopped or questioned, he was defenseless against one threat: the disease in his system. He lost four more days in another patch of forest, lying on the ground hour after hour, wracked by fever, and bowel trouble. It was from those woods, a week ago, that he'd seen more evidence of how ruthless the conflict had become.

He'd seen a sky blackened by fire-shot smoke. Heard thunderous rever-
berations from dynamite charges. The South's transportation center and
major rail junction was being systematically destroyed by men who didn't
give a damn about fighting honorably, only about winning their war to
free the nigra and crush the rebels. He remembered wondering, hatefully,
how many noncombatants had been blown up along with the rolling stock
and roundhouses in Atlanta.

Now, a good two miles from where he'd encountered the farmer, he
was forced to stop. Out of breath. Lightheaded.

The darkness of the countryside oppressed him. The moon was temporarily hidden. Perhaps it was the lonely dark that made him think of his
mother, Fan Lamont.

She'd sent him off to this failing war with a curious and contradictory
set of admonitions:

She'd hated to see him go. Expressed grave concern about his safety.
Warned him to be as careful as he could.

Yet she was proud of his enthusiasm. Didn't refuse when he begged to
enlist. And, at the last moment, urged him to fight well and—most importantly—*honorably*.

He suspected that the fervency that had finally overcome her fear had
had something to do with his stepfather's mysterious death in Richmond
in 1861. It seemed that Edward Lamont, the actor, had tumbled down a
flight of stairs in the building where he and Fan had been living. Jeremiah had been in Lexington at the time, staying with Fan's father, Virgil
Tunworth. The boy had heard the account of Lamont's death from his
grandfather.

When Fan returned to the little town in the Shenandoah Valley after
the funeral, Jeremiah began to have a feeling the accidental fall wasn't the
whole story. Based on the somewhat nervous way Fan answered his questions, he had decided there must have been something disgraceful about
Edward's death. Something Fan was desperate to counterbalance by giving
reluctant permission for the last of her three sons to risk his life for the
cause.

*Fight well and honorably.*

Jeremiah soon became thankful he had never told the entire truth about
the war in the few letters he had sent home. He'd said nothing about the
spoiled meat dishonest suppliers sold to the army; nothing about the
wretched living conditions; nothing about the men who fled under fire at
Chickamauga, and the wholesale desertions later. He hadn't wanted his
mother to know how bad conditions were. She had enough to fret about
with her home threatened and the well-being of Jeremiah's two older
brothers constantly in doubt. Everyone in the Confederacy knew the risks

taken by General Stuart's regiments. And Matthew—who was too easygoing to bother with more than one or two letters a year—was somewhere on the Atlantic between Liverpool, the Bermudas, and the Carolina coast, serving as supercargo on a blockade runner.

In Jeremiah's opinion, that was both honorable and dashing. Typical of Matt, too. Jeremiah had always admired and envied Matt, even though their times together had been few. Fan's second son had been away at sea since Jeremiah was a small boy.

If it had been possible, he'd gladly have exchanged places with Matt. His brother had a naturally happy disposition. Loved games, particularly baseball, a game he and thousands of other boys and young men had created in parks and fields and dusty lots, adapting it from an old English game Matt called rounders.

How vividly Jeremiah remembered the sweaty excitement on Matt's face one autumn afternoon years ago—he could recall the color and texture of the sunshine, though not the date—the ebullience with which Matt whooped and pranced when he came home, celebrating the way he'd pounded out three aces with his bat, and singlehandedly carried his ball team of five black boys and four white ones to a victory.

Matt possessed a talent for drawing that he'd somehow discovered in himself when he was young. In his imagination, Jeremiah could still see some of the charcoal sketches Matt had sent home occasionally after taking his first berth on a Charleston cotton packet. The style of the drawings was bold, personal, and unforgettable. Though Jeremiah had seen less of Matt than he had of Gideon, he felt a closer bond with Matt, and prayed he was safe.

The cloud drifted away from the moon. He drew deep breaths. The Enfield on his shoulder actually weighed only eight pounds fourteen and a half ounces, but it seemed ten times heavier tonight.

He pulled the canvas sling off and laid the piece in the dirt, shutting his eyes until the attack of dizziness passed.

While he stood swaying in the center of the road, his right hand strayed to his belt; closed unconsciously, protectively over the piece of oilskin containing the precious letter he'd promised to deliver.

He opened his eyes. The small animal noises had stopped in the plum orchard. Or perhaps he didn't hear them because of the ringing in his ears.

He licked the dry inside of his cheek; sniffed his own abominable, unwashed smell. He wanted to stop awhile but felt he shouldn't. What if the farmer was hunting a horse, still intending to chase him?

Well, if that happened, let it. He'd just take to the fields, where he could easily elude one pursuer. He'd make faster progress if he had a short rest.

He sank down on the shoulder, the Enfield near his feet. For a brief moment a shameful despondency swept over him. Everything was failing. The war was lost, or would be soon, now that Lincoln had been returned to the Presidency of the North just a couple of weeks ago.

Lincoln hadn't run as a Republican, but under some new label—the National Union party, Jeremiah thought it was. As his running mate, Abe the Ape had chosen a damned, ignorant Tennessee politician named Johnson who'd betrayed his own kind and sided with the North, claiming the Constitution forbade any other decision. The bottle forbade any other decision, Rose had commented a day or two before his death. Johnson, he said, was a drunkard.

Johnson would have no hand in carrying the war forward, though. Just as Jefferson Davis did, Lincoln personally picked and supervised his generals.

At first he'd chosen poor ones. The pompous Democrat, Little Mac McClellan. Old Burnside. Hooker, who had inexplicably lost his nerve at Chancellorsville and squandered a chance for a stunning victory.

But Jackson had been accidentally shot by men on his own side at Chancellorsville, and that battle had turned out to be less of a Southern triumph than it might have been, even though J. E. B. Stuart had led the infantry from horseback, flourishing his saber, jumping his stallion into enemy cannon emplacements, and creating on the spot, to the tune of *Old Dan Tucker*, a derisive song urging Old Joe Hooker to come out of the Wilderness and fight.

But then Jackson had perished of pneumonia. His presence had been missed when Lee made his bold foray into Pennsylvania a month later. Even Meade, who'd defeated Lee in the North, wasn't merciless enough to satisfy Lincoln. The Yankee President wanted, and ultimately found, a supreme commander who fought like a madman:

Unconditional Surrender Grant. Another drunkard!

But he'd been sober enough to crush Vicksburg in the west. Sober enough to take charge of the Army of the Potomac in March of this year, and begin to spend his soldiers by the thousands, the tens of thousands, as though they weren't human beings but manufactured parts in a grinding, unstoppable war engine lubricated by blood and more blood.

The zest, the zeal that had led the South to stunning successes early in the war had all but vanished.

Jeremiah could recall one or another officer speaking with sad pride of Pickett's rush up a gentle hillside toward a clump of trees on the final day at Gettysburg, where Lee had ultimately failed in his attempt to reprovi-

sion his army with Yankee grain and Yankee meat, win a daring victory on
enemy ground, prove the folly of Davis' policy of only fighting a defensive
war on Southern soil, and perhaps frighten the enemy into suing for peace
—all at one time!

The heroes such as Pickett were still praised, but few of the living pretended their heroism had made much difference. If the Confederacy
hadn't surrendered in fact, it had surrendered in spirit. Even the most ardent patriot now had trouble believing otherwise.

That the South was indeed facing defeat had been borne out by Fan's
last letter, written late in June and weeks in transit. The fury of the war
had found Fan at last. But that hadn't been the only sad news.

The letter contained tragic tidings about Gideon.


### iii


Having escaped death on the Peninsula in '62, Jeremiah's oldest brother
had ridden unscathed through action after action—until chance took him
to a place called Yellow Tavern on the eleventh of May. There, he and
General Stuart had met Union horse soldiers of a kind they'd never encountered before.

Even a year earlier, under Pleasonton, the Yank cavalry couldn't match
the South's. But it had been growing steadily—dangerously—better. Now,
led by Sheridan, it had turned into a scythe sweeping across Virginia. At
Yellow Tavern the blade had struck and killed Jeb Stuart.

Stuart's men had run into fierce, competent opposition. The most dangerous Yanks turned out to be Michigan men, riders who sported red
neckerchiefs, and whose regimental band played them into the charge
with *Yankee Doodle*. They were commanded by an officer almost as flamboyant as Stuart himself—twenty-four-year-old George Armstrong Custer,
the "boy general," who led them, screaming, *"Come on, you Wolverines!"*

Custer wore gold spurs, slept with a pet raccoon, and dressed his long
curls with cinnamon oil. Jeremiah had read occasional newspaper accounts
describing him as a man who expressed no great personal animosity toward Southerners; he was just out to whip them.

Like Stuart, he thrived on being called a daredevil. The personal motto
he'd brought with him from West Point was "promotion or death"—
though from the way he often defied caution in battle, the motto apparently meant *his* promotion would be earned by the deaths of others. A
Democrat, he still managed to remain the darling of the Washington Republicans, the public, and a press that eulogized him as Napoleon's suc-
cessor.

At Yellow Tavern one of Custer's Wolverines had shot Stuart out of the saddle. Another had engaged Gideon—or so his immediate superior wrote Fan the following week. During the combat, horseman against horseman, Gideon had reared back in his saddle to dodge a saber stroke, lost his balance, and tumbled to the ground. In a matter of seconds enemy troopers had swarmed around him, taking him prisoner.

So now Gideon was either dead, or alive and rotting in one of the prison pits of the North. Fort Delaware, or possibly Elmira in New York.

And as if that loss hadn't been grievous enough, Fan's letter also reported that Hunter's cavalry had swept through the Valley to Lexington. In the surrounding countryside, the Yankee horsemen had burned mills, granaries, farm implements—then buildings in the town, including the Military Institute, Governor Letcher's residence, and other private homes. Only old Washington College had been spared at the last moment because some of Hunter's men refused to torch an institution honoring the nation's first President.

Fan tried to conceal her sadness when she wrote her youngest son. But it came through clearly in the final paragraphs which spoke of the privation sweeping the Confederacy as the enemy blockade bottled up port after port.

Profiteers had driven prices out of the reach of ordinary people. Fan commented that she had no good cotton stockings left, but would make do with old ones since she couldn't afford eight dollars for a new pair.

She'd forgotten what coffee tasted like, she said. Southerners who had cornered the existing supply demanded up to forty dollars a pound.

And when her doctor had prescribed a dose of calomel, it was unaffordable at twenty dollars the ounce.

Even the physical look of the letter was testimony that the end was coming. There was no more writing paper to be had in Lexington, Fan noted. So an enterprising merchant had devised some from an old roll of wall paper. Inside the envelope, and on the back of each sheet, was a crudely printed floral pattern.

It was almost over.

Rose had been right. His wife and daughter undoubtedly needed Jeremiah's help more than the army did. With the Rose women, he'd find a place where his presence would make a difference again.

But if he was going to find them, he couldn't sit in the moonlight. Weary as he was, he had to keep moving.

With effort, he stood up. Reached down for the Enfield. When his fingers were an inch from the weapon, he heard a sound on the road behind him.

He straightened, searching the shifting silver shadows of the landscape.

He couldn't see them; they were too far away. But he heard them.

Mounted men. Coming fast.

That farmer. *That damned, vengeful old man!*

He hadn't been satisfied to locate one horse and ride after Jeremiah alone—he'd had to roust out his neighbors and lead them in pursuit.

Jeremiah shivered, remembering the farmer's warning.

As punishment for his desertion, he'd hang.

# CHAPTER 2

## "Sixty Thousand Strong"

ALMOST AS SOON as the appalling thought struck him, Jeremiah began to question whether it made sense. How the devil could an old man muster a party of neighbors in a rural area? There were damn few males left on homesteads anywhere in the South, unless you counted boys and old men. Horses were equally scarce, that much Jeremiah knew for certain.

Still, those *were* horsemen hammering toward him. Who could they be?

Georgia Home Guards? No, he'd heard they couldn't find mounts either.

Enemy cavalry, then? Some of the ruffians who rode with the blond-bearded Yank, Judson Kilpatrick?

He didn't know. But he didn't intend to linger in the middle of the road and find out. The riders were coming faster than he'd anticipated. The moon's whiteness lit a rolling, phosphorescent cloud of dust at the crest of a hill he judged to be no more than half a mile away. Figures that seemed part man, part horse, appeared and vanished in the swirling dust.

Jeremiah grabbed the Enfield and sprinted for the ditch to the left of the road, where the brook ran. A small boulder hidden in the long grass tripped him. With a curse, he went tumbling down the incline. He splashed into the shallow water, remembering at the last moment to twist his body to keep the oilskin pouch and his cartridge box dry.

The dust cloud rolled toward him, the hammer of hooves growing steadily louder. As he lay with his right side in water that felt incredibly cold, he realized he'd dropped the Enfield when he fell.

He raised himself a little—the movement seemed to create a noise loud as a waterfall—just as the first of the horsemen thundered by. Once more a cloud cleared the edge of the moon. There, plainly visible on the shoulder, his piece shone bright.

Someone saw it. Yelled. The horsemen reined in, the leading riders turning back. As he sank down and lay still, Jeremiah tried to count the looming figures. A dozen; maybe more.

A man dismounted, cocking a pistol. He reached for the Enfield. He wore a forage cap much like Jeremiah's.

"Enfield, Captain." The man raised the piece to his chest. "I can feel stamping—C.S.A."

Another man pointed:

"Weeds are matted down right there. Whoever dropped it may be hidin'."

Two more pistols were cocked. The horses fretted and stamped. A tall man rode through the group to the side of the road nearest the brook. He leaned over his horse's neck, as if studying the ground. Then he called out:

"You down there. You better come out."

Jeremiah thought the voice had a soft, relaxed sound. A Southern sound.

The tall man drew a carbine from a saddle scabbard.

"*I said, come out.*"

Soaked, Jeremiah staggered to his feet and clambered through the grass to the road, his hands raised above his head.


ii


The barrel of the tall man's carbine glowed in a spill of moonlight. Water dripped from Jeremiah's fingers, from the bandage on his thigh, the torn hem of his tunic, the havelock attached to his cap.

"Captain?" one of the men exclaimed. "He looks like one of ours!"

They *were* Southerners. The moon showed him dusty cadet-gray sleeves and trouser legs that matched his own, except for the yellow trim. This wasn't as bad as being caught by Yanks—unless the men were as ferocious about desertion as that old farmer.

The captain waggled his carbine. Jeremiah glimpsed a double line of gold braid on his cap as he asked:

"Who are you?"

Jeremiah pivoted slightly so the moonlight would show the chevrons on his sleeve:

"Corporal Kent, sir."

"Turn. I can't see the badge on your cap."

"I lost it, sir." He'd learned a lesson from the farmer. He tried to sound calm, as if he had nothing to hide. "I'm from the Sixty-third Virginia, last with Reynolds's brigade, Stevenson's division—"

A horseman further back growled, "Didn't know they was any Virginny boys with the Army of Tennessee, Cap'n."

"Two or three regiments, I think." The captain was a heavy man, with jowls. Moonlight on one cheek showed a scattering of pox scars like miniature black craters. "Corporal, give me the name of your corps commander."

Cautiously, Jeremiah said, "You know we were Hood's Corps, sir. But General Hood was leading the whole army, so our actual commander was General Lee. General Stephen D. Lee," he added for authenticity.

The mutter of a couple of the men said they recognized that he was telling the truth. The captain raised the carbine to quiet them. Then, sharply:

"Were you with Bob Lee in Pennsylvania?"

"No, sir, I mustered in a month afterward."

Another voice; suspicious:

"Didn't your regiment lose a flag at Gettysburg?"

"Not to my recollection." He'd heard enough of the history of both Virginia units that had been transferred to the west to recognize the trap. "I think it was the other bunch in the Army of Tennessee. The Fifty-fourth. When I joined up, my regiment belonged to the Second Brigade, Department of Western Virginia. But we were put on the cars along with the Fifty-fourth and—"

"You detached from service?" the captain interrupted.

Jeremiah's hands grew colder. He struggled to keep his voice level:

"Yes, sir. I was invalided out at Palmetto, after General Hood left for Tennessee."

He lifted his leg to show the bloodied bandage, even though the pain grew ferocious when he bent his knee. But maybe they'd be less suspicious than the farmer. Blood was blood. They couldn't tell he'd gotten the wound from another of those damned old country boys who didn't want soldiers, *any* soldiers, prowling around their property.

The last of the turkey meat had run out when he was near Milledgeville. On the outskirts of Atlanta he'd slipped into a chicken house after dark. In spite of his efforts to keep quiet, he'd roused the flock. Wakened by the squawking, the poultryman had come charging from his house. He hadn't even issued a challenge or asked a question, just blasted away with a shotgun as Jeremiah dashed off. Once out of danger, he'd cut four buckshot out of his leg with a sheath knife he kept in his right boot. Then he'd cleaned the wound as best he could and bandaged it with his torn-up underdrawers.

The captain wanted to know more about the wound:

"In what action were you hit?"

"Jonesboro," Jeremiah said promptly. "Afternoon of the last day of August."

The dismounted man holding the Enfield said, "Well, I know Steve Lee was there, all right."

The captain: "Last day of August, you say. Sure as hell taking a long time for that to heal, isn't it?"

"Infection set in. For a while the doctors thought I might lose the leg altogether. Got knocked down with dysentery at the same time. Actually I had two wounds. The one in my shoulder's come along just fine. This one, though—doesn't seem to want to mend right."

While the captain digested the information, Jeremiah decided he'd better tell as much as he dared. These men sounded more persuadable than the farmer. He might be able to outwit them. But not if he seemed reluctant to talk.

"My commanding officer, Lieutenant Colonel Rose, he came out of the Thirty-sixth Georgia in Cummings' brigade. After Chickamauga he was assigned to division staff for a while. I was picked to be his orderly and courier. He got shot at Jonesboro too. Died the same night. Before he passed on, he ordered me to go to his plantation if I got out. He said only his wife and daughter were left to run it." He added an invention he thought sounded logical, and might divert their suspicion even more:

"The colonel told me his nigras were getting fractious because of Old Abe's proclamation—"

"Yep, that's sure as hell happening," someone agreed. "All over."

"Where's this plantation?" the captain asked him.

Jeremiah began to feel a little less tense; maybe the issue of desertion wouldn't come up at all if he kept trying to convince them he was doing what he thought to be his duty.

"Near Louisville, across the Ogeechee River in Jefferson County. Seems like I've been walking for days to get to it."

"Well, you have thirty or forty miles still to go," the captain informed him. "More or less due east." A hand scratched at the pox scars. "I gather you felt this personal business more important than returning to your unit?"

Jeremiah scowled. To help them see his anger, he yanked off his forage cap. The sudden movement shied a couple of the horses.

The moon struck his dark eyes and matted hair as he straightened to his full height. In the light, the white streak showed plainly, starting at the hairline above his left brow and tapering to a point at the back of his head.

Honesty had failed him with the farmer; he didn't intend to repeat the mistake:

"Sir, I told you—I was invalided out! It was either head home for Virginia—too blasted far away—or stay in Georgia and do what the colonel asked of me while he was dying. My unit had already moved out north again. I felt I owed the colonel's womenfolk some protection—'specially since the colonel saved my life at Jonesboro."

"Oh?" The captain cocked his head. "How'd he do that?"

Jeremiah told him the story.

"You have any proof to support what you're saying?" the captain asked.

Jeremiah almost reached for the oilskin pouch. He held back; the contents of the letter were still unknown to him. What if Rose had written his wife saying he intended to urge his orderly to desert?

"No, sir, I'm sorry, I have nothing."

"What's the name of this here plantation?" the dismounted man with the Enfield said.

"It's called Rosewood. After the colonel's people."

"I've heard of it," the captain told him. "I come from near Savannah. My papa was a cotton broker before he died. I believe he did business with the Rose family at one time—" All at once he sounded more tolerant. "If your unit's gone to Tennessee and you were pronounced unfit to serve, I suppose you made the best choice."

Jeremiah breathed a bit easier. The captain went on:

"And those women you mentioned—they're liable to need all the protection they can get. All of Georgia's liable to need it, matter of fact."

"What do you mean, sir?"

Hunching forward, the captain said, "Corporal, do you have any notion as to who we are?"

Jeremiah tried to smile. "I know you're on the right side. And those yellow facings say you're cavalry."

"My name's Dilsey. Captain Robert Dilsey. We're with General Joe Wheeler. Scouting Sherman."

"*Sherman!* But he's back near Atlanta!"

Dilsey shook his head. "Not any more. Fact is, we're about all that stands between that son of a bitch and the seacoast. Excepting of course, the Home Guard that Governor Brown's trying to turn out." One of Dilsey's troopers snickered contemptuously. "But old men carrying rakes and hoes aren't going to be worth a hoot against Billy Sherman."

Thunderstruck, Jeremiah gasped, "You mean he's on the move?"

Dilsey sighed and nodded. "Started last Wednesday. Marched out in two columns, sixty thousand strong. Slocum has two infantry corps on the left wing, Howard two more on the right. And that Kilpatrick's riding along with them."

"Where's Sherman going?"

A shrug. "Appears he's headed straight across the state to the ocean.

Looks like he's just said to hell with maintaining supply lines and is poling off in this direction to do any damage he can."

Another caustic voice:

"Mebbe he's tired of fightin' men. Mebbe he wants to fight females and young 'uns for a change."

The captain didn't take it as a joke. "Certainly possible. He's got a reputation for being half crazy sometimes. A move in this direction violates every sound principle of strategy. But he's coming—along with that blasted butcher, Kilpatrick. You know what they call Little Kil's riders, Corporal? The Kill-cavalry. We're moving southeast to stay ahead of them. Trying to find out for certain where they're actually going. Harass them, if we can."

The announcement of the sudden advance by the general who'd captured and burned Atlanta still sounded unbelievable. Jeremiah groped for words:

"But—but I don't think there are any troops left to fight in this part of the state!"

The man with the Enfield said, "Well, there's you."

He puzzled over the laughter the remark produced as Dilsey said:

"There *is* plenty of food in Georgia for a change. Finest crop in years, I'm told. And Bob Lee's army still depends on what comes out of this breadbasket. So if you look at Sherman's move in that light, it makes more sense. I'd guess he's after the food, though he may be after Savannah as well."

"That's crazy!" Jeremiah cried.

"Any man who burns damn near a whole city doesn't fight like a gentleman, Corporal—or by the book. You'd better keep on toward Jefferson County and tell the Rose ladies Old Billy's probably coming their way."

The man with the Enfield spat. "Goddamn soon."


iii


Despite the stunning news, Jeremiah felt oddly elated. He'd convinced Dilsey of the authenticity of his story; done it just right, too. The word desertion hadn't even been uttered.

One of the cavalrymen spoke:

"Captain, we ought to be movin'."

"Agree," Dilsey said. "Kent, we'd fill your canteen if you had one. We've fetched along some goobers to eat. Hand him some, Mullins."

Jeremiah raised his arm to accept the handful just as Dilsey uttered a hard, peculiar chuckle that chilled him. Again Dilsey scratched his face.

"You're lucky to be alive, Corporal, you know that? We stopped at a farm a few miles back. Watered our horses from the well. We heard about you."

Jeremiah closed his fist on the goobers; almost dropped them slipping them into his pocket. What a fool he'd been. What a damn fool. He hadn't tricked Dilsey for one minute.

The captain pointed at Jeremiah's leg.

"That injury may hurt. But as the old farmer said, lots of boys shot up worse than you are still with their regiments. So I don't expect you were invalided out. I expect you up and left. As for the rest—I'm willing to accept it. Strikes me it has too many warts to be an outright lie. I don't know what persuaded you to tell me the truth—or ninety percent of it, anyway. You didn't tell the farmer. But as I say—you're lucky you changed your mind. If you'd just handed me that tale about going home—"

Dilsey rammed his carbine in the scabbard. Reached down and snatched the Enfield from the dismounted trooper. Aimed it at Jeremiah's chest, his smile humorless:

"—I'd have used your own weapon on you. Killed you where you stand."

He flung the Enfield. Jeremiah barely managed to catch it. Dilsey laughed at him; a hollow, unfriendly laugh:

"As things worked out, however, you're going to find yourself smack back in the war. Why, you may turn out to be the only young man within forty miles of that plantation. Commander of the whole resistance! Hope you can handle that. After running away, seems fitting you should be required to try."

Seething, Jeremiah watched Captain Dilsey and his men re-order themselves into a column of twos. Moonlight spilled across the officer's back; his face was hidden. When he spoke, he sounded cheerful and cruel at the same time:

"Good luck to you, Corporal. I hereby promote you to general in command of Jefferson County."

He wheeled his mount with a ferocious yank of the rein and galloped off along the country road, his men right behind. Their passing left another phosphorescent dust cloud that soon hid them from sight.

iv

*Sixty thousand,* Jeremiah thought, the barrel of the rifled musket shaking in his hand. *Sixty thousand led by the wickedest soldiers in the whole damn Union army!*

By letting him go on to Rosewood alone, Dilsey had punished him. He too had failed to understand Jeremiah's sense of duty and loyalty—

How that soft-spoken man must have been laughing to himself all during Jeremiah's babble about Colonel Rose. For a moment the humiliating anger was almost beyond bearing.

It began to pass when he reminded himself that he *was* still alive. And Sherman's coming would indeed give him a chance to fight again. All in all, despite thinking he'd fooled Dilsey and the shock of Dilsey's announcement that he hadn't, he concluded that things could have been a devil of a lot worse. The hand clasping the Enfield grew steadier.

Jeremiah laid the weapon down, shelled and swallowed four of the goobers given him by the cavalrymen. They settled hard in his stomach, producing almost instantaneous pain. He was forced to sit down on the shoulder of the road, clutching his middle, praying for the pain to ease.

It didn't.

A bird shrilled in the plum orchard. But miserable as he felt, he still believed his luck had taken a better turn. One Enfield would make no difference in Tennessee. It could make a lot of difference in Georgia.

Under the black and silver sky, he jammed the butt of the Enfield into the grass and literally climbed hand over hand to get to his feet. He still felt shaky and frightened. Tortured by spasms of pain, he stepped onto the road, hurrying—

He went only a quarter of a mile before he began to stagger. The goobers came up in a retching heave. He was forced to unfasten and drop his trousers and crouch dizzily awhile.

Covered with cold sweat and aching from his breastbone to his groin, he eventually managed to start walking again. He passed another ramshackle farmhouse. A cow lowed in the vast dark. Pushing himself with every bit of his remaining strength, he kept trudging on.

Toward Jefferson County.

Toward two women he'd never met.

Toward a chance to fight honorably again—

*Sixty thousand strong,* he kept thinking. *Jesus Almighty!*

Yet in spite of the terrifying numbers and his physical agony, his spirit wouldn't break. Mentally, he felt stronger and more determined than he had in weeks.

*I'll get there.*

*I'll get there before Billy Sherman—if I have to crawl every foot of the way.*

# CHAPTER 3

## *The Slave*

THE FIRST SENSATION was heat. Stifling heat; too intense for November.

An insect whined at the back of his neck. With his eyes still closed, he tried to raise his right hand to swat it. He couldn't seem to summon enough strength to draw his hand from what felt like mud.

The insect landed on his havelock, then on exposed skin. He clawed his hand out of the mud as the insect bit—a faint, nearly painless sting. The whine diminished.

Panicky, he tried to recall where he was. That is, where he'd been when he sprawled on the ground at twilight on—

Tuesday. Yesterday had been Tuesday.

Late in the day he'd forded the Ogeechee River, bypassed the little town of Louisville, and tried to follow directions given him by a farmer's boy. Somehow he'd taken a wrong turn at a crossroad. The road he was walking had petered out in brambles at the edge of a bare cotton field near the river.

Still sick, he'd blundered ahead—straight into a maze of little tributaries of the river, a place of rank water and steaming gloom produced by huge cypresses and live oaks. He'd slopped across one shallow backwater and up the far bank, intending to lie down and rest only a few moments. That was all he remembered until now.

He grew alarmed by a weightlessness in two places where there should have been weight. The precious Enfield no longer pressed against his shoulder; his cartridge box was missing from his belt.

His face felt scorching; oily. He knew he had the fever again.

He dragged his left hand back. Fumbled at his waist.

The oilskin pouch was still there, thank God.

He heard a foot squish down in mud. Heard a man breathing. His teeth started to chatter as he opened his eyes.

Ten inches from his nose a small turtle lay upside down on the curve of its shell. The turtle had withdrawn its head and legs. He couldn't tell whether it was alive or dead. A short distance beyond the turtle he saw a man's feet, calves, and the bottoms of tattered trousers. His panic worsened.

Thick, horny toenails were half hidden in rust-colored mud. But Jeremiah could see the skin well enough—

Black skin.

ii

He heard a heavy, mellow voice, neither friendly nor hostile:

"You 'wake, mister soldier?"

Jeremiah's head jerked up. His temples throbbed from the sudden move. His lips compressed, he jammed his fists into the red clay bank where he'd slept. Doubled his knees. Eventually staggered to his feet, his uniform filthy, his face and hair caked with mud.

"Who are you? Where am I?"

The black man was superbly built, with a slender waist and a broad chest. A ragged shirt cut off at the shoulders exposed thick arms. He was about thirty, Jeremiah guessed. His skin was so dark it had a blue cast.

The man's eyes were almost perfectly oval, with huge brown pupils. He stood in a placid, relaxed pose. Yet Jeremiah couldn't escape an irrational feeling that the Negro was simmering with hostility.

"Which question you want me to answer first?"

Jeremiah saw a double image of the black's curly head. He squeezed his eyelids shut and spread his feet, hoping to keep his balance.

"Tell me where I am."

"This here's a swamp down by the acreage we call the bottom."

"Who calls it that?" The black's lackadaisical air angered him. "Don't you know how to be civil to a white man?"

"Why, 'course I do." But Jeremiah thought he saw a corner of the man's mouth twitch. "The bottom land belongs to Rosewood."

"Rosewood," he repeated. "Colonel Henry Rose's place?"

The black licked his lips. Staring into those round brown pupils, Jeremiah thought, *My Lord, he hates me. Or he hates the uniform I'm wearing, anyway.* He was increasingly aware that he lacked any weapon except the sheathed knife in his boot. Without the Enfield he felt naked.

"Reckon there ain't another Rosewood in the county."

"It's the place I've been hunting." Fingers plucked at the pouch on his belt. "I'm carrying a message for the colonel's wife."

The black stared, as if he didn't comprehend.

"Is this Wednesday?"

It took awhile for the black man to decide to reply:

"That's right, Wednesday. Every Wednesday Miz Rose gives me an hour in the mornin' to come catch cooters." His glance flicked to the turtle. "Can't abide 'em myself. But I sell 'em to Miz Rose for soup. She's real kind, lettin' us niggers make a little money of our own." The last words carried a faintly caustic edge.

"Then you're from the plantation. One of the slaves—"

A quick, adamant shake of the head:

"No more."

"Oh?"

The man smiled. "Year ago January, Linkum said I wasn't property. Jubilee's come, mister soldier."

Yet he spoke the words joylessly; sounded angry. Jeremiah was growing increasingly angry with the man's quiet arrogance:

"If you think you're free—"

"I *know* I'm free."

"Then what the hell are you doing around here?"

A shrug. "Waitin'."

"For what?"

"To see who wins. If you boys lose, I can go off anyplace I choose. But if you win, an' I leave ahead of time, I could be in a peck of trouble. Don't appear likely that you're goin' to win, though. Still—can't be too careful. Isn't that right?"

*Smart bastard*, Jeremiah thought. *Smart, wily bastard. Getting out of this swamp alive may take some doing.*

He scanned the area; saw nothing but narrow watercourses winding between mud banks and the great trees. Sunlit insects flitted over green-scummed water like flakes of living gold.

"What's your name?"

"Price."

"Which way's the house?"

"Yonder," Price told him, with such a faint inclination of his head that he might have meant any point on a whole quarter of the horizon.

"Your overseer anyplace close by?"

Price smiled. "Don't think so. He went off to fight jus' like the colonel. Ain't come back. Any overseein' to be done, Miz Catherine does it."

"That's the colonel's wife—"

" 'Pears you know a lot about the Rose family, mister soldier."

"My name is Kent. *Corporal* Kent. You call me that, hear?"

Silence. The black's eyes wandered down to the turtle, which appeared to be dead.

Even more sharply, Jeremiah said: "And lead me up to the house. I told you I have an important paper for your mistress. The colonel gave it to me before—"

Abruptly, he held back from breaking the news of Rose's death. The colonel's wife and daughter deserved to hear it first.

Price looked indifferent. God, what were those wicked Yanks in Washington City thinking about, granting freedom to men like this?

Of course Jeremiah knew very well what they were thinking about: the possibility that the blacks might rise up against their masters and aid the Northern war effort. Lincoln's detested proclamation in the first month of 1863 hadn't been so generous as to free every black man in the land; not by a damn sight. The President and that vicious pack of Republicans he served had only declared blacks were free in the rebelling states. Lieutenant Colonel Rose had commented caustically on that limitation one time:

"Old Abe has enough trouble on his hands without antagonizing the border states. Besides, I've read some of his speeches. He doesn't believe nigras are the white man's equal. He'd just as soon ship them all to Liberia and be shed of them. He's freeing *our* nigras to make it hotter for us, that's all. He's no humanitarian, he's a cheap politician who'll use any available trick to beat us down."

Jeremiah had accepted that as gospel; it jibed with all the anti-Northern talk he'd heard as a boy. Lincoln's proclamation was merely one more example of how dishonorably the enemy was conducting the war. Let the North—and nigras like this one—praise Abe Lincoln as a high-minded emancipator; Jeremiah knew that wasn't the truth at all.

With a move that rippled the muscles of his right forearm, Price reached up to flick sweat from his shiny blue cheek. He grinned, his eyes still mocking:

"You don' finish a lot of your sentences, mister soldier."

*Sentences?* That was a mighty fancy word for an ordinary field hand. The realization confirmed his feeling that this was a dangerous man. Price probably knew how to read and write—had no doubt learned in secret, in defiance of the law.

"That's my business."

The smile remained fixed. "Guess it is. You say you got a paper from the colonel 'fore somethin' happened to him?"

"Before I left him. Also none of your affair. You take me to the house— right after you tell me something." He swallowed hard, trying to stand steady. Price cocked his head, waiting.

"You tell me what happened to my musket."

Price blinked twice, his expression deliberately blank. Jeremiah wanted to hit him.

"Musket?" Price turned his head right, then left. "Don't see no musket anyplace 'round here—"

"I had my Enfield and my cartridge box with me when I passed out! They're gone."

"Can't help that. I didn't spy any such 'quipment when I come onto you lyin' there. Guess somebody must have stole it during the night."

"Who the hell would wander through a place like this during the night?"

"Oh, mebbe some of the other niggers from the neighborhood, mister— ah, Corporal," Price corrected himself with an obviously forced politeness. "No, I surely can't tell you what happened to that gun and that box. You didn't have 'em when I found you, and since I was the only one awake right about then, guess you'll just have to take my word for it."

Jeremiah took a step forward, almost falling:

"You stole them. You hid them someplace. *Didn't you?*"

Price's gaze admitted it. But his face grew pious:

"Now that's a frightful thing to 'cuse a man of, Corporal. Me, a field buck, steal a white man's weapon an' hide it? Why, I could be whipped half to death for such a thing, if Miz Catherine was the kind who whipped her niggers. No, sir, I jus' don't know what become of those things you're talkin' 'bout. You'll just have to take my word."

Price's dazzling grin scorned him as a fool. Jeremiah concluded he might have been wrong about the cause of Price's insolence. The man's pigmentation might have nothing to do with it—

*I wouldn't trust this son of a bitch if he were as white as me.*

Price leaned down to scoop up the dead cooter. He sounded almost obsequious:

"Care to hang onto my arm, Corporal?"

"No, thank you."

"You sure lookin' poorly. It's 'bout a mile to the house—"

"I'll manage!"

The black watched him, the smile gone. Jeremiah felt increasingly threatened:

*He's taken the Enfield and hidden it where he can go back and find it. Use it.*

"This way, then."

Jeremiah staggered after him, wondering whether Lieutenant Colonel Rose's widow knew exactly what sort of treacherous rascal she was harboring. As if things weren't bad enough with those sixty thousand bluebellies somewhere to the northwest and no male overseer on the place, the two women he was going to meet were threatened by a mean, devious nigra who now had a gun.

Jeremiah's head pounded. He was shivering uncontrollably. The path out of the swamp seemed an endless maze.

He forced himself to keep up. Price might be older, but Jeremiah realized he couldn't let the black man think he was stronger or smarter—even though Price had already outfoxed him by purloining the musket and ammunition.

Price cast a quick glance backward. Jeremiah looked him straight in the eye. The black pretended to study a wild turkey roosting in a live oak, but Jeremiah thought he heard the man snicker.

*Got to watch out for that one,* he thought.

*Walk behind him all the time.*

Behind *him. Never ahead.*

# CHAPTER 4

## Rosewood

PRICE AND JEREMIAH approached Rosewood from a gently sloping cotton field that had been harvested earlier in the autumn. Though he was dizzy and hot—particularly now that he and the black man were into the full glare of the sunlight—he felt a peculiar sense of happiness at the sight of the plantation. To him it was very nearly a second home, so often and so lovingly had the slender, courtly Henry Rose described it.

Rosewood's land, accumulated by the colonel's father and grandfather, totaled about a thousand acres. Something like sixty-five slaves had worked the property, three-quarters of which the colonel had put into cotton, the remainder going into corn.

Originally Rosewood had been a rice plantation. But in the past two decades cotton had proved a far superior cash crop, even though the product of Rose's fields never commanded the premium prices of the cotton grown in Alabama, Mississippi, and Louisiana.

The plantation had a prosperous, if oddly deserted look this Wednesday morning. Directly ahead stood two large, immaculate barns. Beyond them Jeremiah glimpsed the end of the white-painted three-story manse that faced a dirt highway on his left. A half-mile road led from the highway to the house between rows of live oaks Rose's grandfather had planted. Festoons of tillandsia hung from the branches, providing extra shade all the way to the white-painted fencing, the gate, and the bell with a rope pull.

As he and Price approached, more of the house came into view. He saw the front piazza, shaded by lattices twined with cypress vines. Square pillars reached up to a second-floor gallery running the entire length of the house. Starting near a well at the back of the building and running away from it at a right angle stood two long rows of slave cottages. The paint on the cottages had peeled in a few places, but otherwise they looked well kept. Directly behind the last two was a small picket-fenced burial ground.

Black men, women, and children idled in the dirt lane dividing the rows of tiny houses. An elderly slave tending a garden patch turned to stare at the gray-clad stranger and Price as they rounded the barn and passed three large hog pens. Magnolias had been planted near the perimeter of the pens. Rose had told Jeremiah he'd done that so the smell of the blooming trees would partially mask the stench of pig manure. This morning the stench was overpowering.

Past the manse Jeremiah saw the large gin house and two equally big corn cribs. Several blacks hailed Price from the cabin street. He acknowledged the greetings with little more than a curt nod. His arrogance told Jeremiah the man was someone special among his own kind.

A crowd had gathered near the stone well at the head of the lane, plainly curious about Price's companion. But Price's erect posture and steady stride seemed to preclude interference.

"Reckon we might find Miz Catherine in the office," the big man remarked as they walked onto the rear piazza. The cooling shade made Jeremiah feel better. But not much.

Price tossed the dead turtle onto the ground beyond the piazza. A naked tot darted toward it from the well. One swift glance from Price sent a young woman dashing out to pick up her child before he could touch the prize. She had a frightened look on her face.

Jeremiah leaned a sweaty palm against the side of the house, struggling to catch his breath. He felt close to passing out again:

"Give me a minute—"

Price folded his arms, waiting. The black's silence seemed a condemnation of Jeremiah's weakness.

Voice rasping, Jeremiah said, "Pretty quiet for a weekday."

"That's true. Cotton's all baled. Corn's in. We're waitin' to see what's goin' to happen."

"What do you mean?"

"Judge Claypool's nigger, Floyd, he come rammin' over in the judge's buggy yesterday. He said there was Yanks on the march from Atlanta. A whole lot of Yanks."

The unblinking eyes fixed on Jeremiah. "You see any Yanks while you was comin' this way?"

Jeremiah shook his head. "But I met some cavalrymen. They said General Sherman's left the vicinity of the city with sixty—with some men."

"Well, now!" All at once Price seemed quite interested.

"Don't get your hopes too high. The cavalry boys didn't know which route the troops were taking."

"Judge Claypool's Floyd, he said Mr. Doremus of Louisville rode back from Milledgeville, an' when he left, the Yanks was almost there. That was Monday. Could be a mighty interesting Thanksgiving."

Thick-tongued, Jeremiah repeated, "Thanksgiving?"

"That's right." The corner of Price's mouth quirked up again. Damn the black thief for treating him like a slave instead of a master! "Didn't you 'member Thanksgiving's only two days away? We usually have a mighty big dinner for Thanksgiving. Maybe this year, the Yanks'll roast us instead. What d'you think?"

"I think you better shut up with jokes like that."

Price chuckled. "Yes, sir."

Jeremiah had completely forgotten the holiday. The amused gaze of the slave irritated him. He was willing to bet Price would love exactly the sort of Thanksgiving he'd described. Price would probably help the damn Yanks overrun Rosewood—using the Enfield he'd stolen.

The brief happiness he'd felt at finally reaching his destination was fading, driven from his mind by the black's silent contempt and the knowledge that he still had to inform the colonel's wife about her widowhood. He assumed she didn't know, and he didn't look forward to telling her. It would require tact; the proper words; a clear head. And his head was anything but clear. His ears buzzed; his eyes watered; his legs felt boneless. He wondered how much longer he could stay on his feet.

"My," Price murmured, evidently still thinking of Sherman. "We could sure have a real jubilee of a Thanksgiving 'round here—" Then, with a touch of impatience: "We can go inside whenever you feelin' up to it."

He wasn't, but he said, "I'm feeling up to it."

Price bobbed his head, leading him to the rear entrance.

As they stepped across the threshold, Price underwent an abrupt and noticeable transformation. He seemed to lose two or three inches in height. He bent his head forward slightly. His step became slower. The buck was trickier than old Billy Sherman himself!

They walked down a cool, dim hall smelling of furniture oil and more faintly of roasting sweet potatoes. Price's posture gave him an almost servile look. He knocked at an open doorway on the left. Immediately, Jeremiah heard a firm feminine voice:

"Come."

Dreading the encounter with Mrs. Rose, Jeremiah walked unsteadily toward the door as Price disappeared, scraping his bare feet in what was almost a shuffle.

ii

The light in the small, cluttered office had a hazy quality. The polished oak floor seemed to tilt. Price stood between Jeremiah and the woman at the desk. He couldn't see much of her except for a skirt, but he did glimpse objects on the desk. Open ledgers. A pen laid aside. A large ring with a dozen or more keys on it. A cut glass goblet half full of something that looked like fruit wine. Blackberry, he decided.

"Yes, Price, what is it?"

The slave deliberately thickened his speech:

"Miz Catherine, I found this yere officer lyin' sick down in the swamp beyond the bottom. He come to find you—"

Blinking to clear his vision, Jeremiah quickly took in the details of the office. Two walls were entirely covered with shelves crowded with books. On the spine of one he recognized a design his mother had shown him once. A gold stamping of a partially filled and stoppered bottle; the mark of the publishing house of Kent and Son, owned by the despised Northern branch of the family.

Near the ledgers on the desk stood a small oil painting depicting a sad-eyed, sandy-bearded man. Rose. Beside it was an even smaller frame with a curling lock of bright red hair sealed under glass above a small square card. On the card in ink that had long ago faded, someone had written:

*Serena, 1846*

Serena was Rose's daughter by his first marriage. The colonel had alluded to the marriage several times, but never discussed it in any detail—nor his former wife. Jeremiah had gotten the impression that Serena's mother must have been the wrong sort. Rose was closemouthed about her, in contrast to his constant praise of Catherine.

He'd said Catherine was a woman of warm, loving temperament—the closest a gentleman ever came to admitting his wife had a passionate streak. He described her as intelligent and trusting of her fellow human beings, willing to believe only the best about them—including the slaves—but not lacking the strength to take action if her original opinion proved wrong. Jeremiah was going to have to warn this paragon of womanhood about Price.

Dimly, he realized Price was still speaking with a slurry politeness quite different from his earlier rude mockery.

"—poor officer, he lost his gun during the night. Those trash niggers of Judge Claypool's who fish 'round here probably picked it off him. I think we ought to report it to the judge right quick. We sure don't want no niggers with muskets runnin' loose—'specially with them Yanks on the way like this officer says."

*Damned liar,* Jeremiah thought. But his throat was too dry to utter the accusation. Besides, the most important matter at the moment was the news about Rose and the letter.

Price stepped back politely as the woman stood up.

"Good morning, young man." Catherine Rose extended her hand, unconcerned about the mud on Jeremiah's fingers.

The colonel's widow was a handsome woman in her forties, with broad hips, a slim waist, and full breasts tightly bound by a faded gingham dress. She had a generous mouth set in an oval face, and intelligent, direct gray eyes. On her cheek just to the right of her lips was a tiny mole, like a punctuation mark. Her light-brown hair was beginning to whiten.

The hand grasping Jeremiah's was neither soft nor smooth. "Price says you want to see me?"

"Yes, Mrs. Rose. My name's Corporal Kent—"

Recognition widened her eyes. "Henry's orderly! He wrote about you once. And in a highly complimentary fashion. You don't look well," she added with a quick frown.

"I'm fine, ma'am."

"But Price said he found you unconscious."

"Just sleeping, that's all."

Skeptically, she surveyed him. The odor of fruit wine was unmistakable. "You're pale as death. Skinny, too."

"I was hurt in action near Atlanta."

"Good heavens, you've come all the way from *Atlanta?*"

"Yes." His hand groped for the oilskin pouch. "Before I left, your husband gave me a letter to deliver. My home's Virginia, but I promised him I'd bring this to you."

He handed her the pouch. Tears filled her eyes.

Then Catherine Rose seemed angry at her own weakness. She dashed a hand against her cheek. She began to examine the pouch as if it were some kind of holy article. A wistful, affectionate smile softened her face. Jeremiah could understand why Rose had spoken highly of her.

Come to think of it, Rose had been lavish in complimenting both his women. While Mrs. Rose opened the pouch, Jeremiah recalled a rare moment of comradeship when Rose had rambled for a while about his daughter's relationship with her stepmother.

Rose had said his wife lavished every attention on the child of that first marriage. Yet the colonel believed his daughter somehow considered herself Catherine's rival for his affection. She was a good child, Rose said. High-spirited, but with a certain reserve that made it extremely difficult for him to ever know what she was thinking. The rivalry between mother and stepdaughter was only suspected, never overt or disruptive. Catherine's affection and forbearance prevented that.

One other detail about Mrs. Rose slipped into his mind—the woman was a transplanted Yankee. It was apparent after she glanced briefly at the letter without reading it. He detected a faint nasal quality in her voice that was distinctly un-Southern:

"You were very kind to bring me this, Corporal Kent. You've seen my husband recently?"

Jeremiah's forehead burned.

"Yes, ma'am. Fairly recently. He gave me the letter at Jonesboro, before General Sherman took Atlanta."

"Jonesboro?" She whispered it. "Jonesboro was in late August."

"Ma'am, haven't—haven't you received any word about him yourself?"

"Not for weeks. And we've had only scattered reports of the disasters the armies encountered." A tolerant smile. "Henry was never too faithful about writing letters home. Sometimes, before he left, I practically had to force him to pick up a pen to write someone on business. Or when a special occasion absolutely demanded a letter. A birth in the family of one of his relatives. A death—"

Her hand closed on the pouch and letter. She looked at Jeremiah:

"Oh, dear Lord in heaven. He's dead. That's why you're here—"

"I—" Somehow he couldn't get the words out.

"That's why you've traveled so far."

Overcome, Jeremiah could only swallow and nod.

Catherine Rose dropped the letter and pouch. She walked around him, unsteadily, but without hurrying. At the door she called:

"Serena?"

"He wrote the letter a night or two before he took a ball in the Jonesboro action—" Jeremiah began.

Clutching the doorframe, Catherine Rose raised her voice slightly:

"Serena? Come down!"

"—he saved my life. After the—" Jeremiah realized he was rambling, but he couldn't help himself. "—after the surgeons said they couldn't do anything for him, he begged me to bring that letter to you. I swore I would."

"*Serena!*"

She struck one frustrated blow on the jamb of the door. Then she clenched her fist and lowered it to her side as if it were a separate living organism she had to fight. The ringing in Jeremiah's ears turned to a high, windy whine. Without warning, his legs gave out.

He started to tumble forward. With quick action, Price could have caught him. The black didn't move.

Arms folded across his huge chest, Price watched the young soldier fall. Jeremiah had a swift impression of Price's eyes. Malicious. Amused. But the slave's "Oh, my!" had had an appropriately alarmed sound.

Jeremiah's jaw slammed on the polished oak floor. He heard an exclamation from Mrs. Rose. Running footsteps—Serena hurrying to the office?

The footfalls grew softer instead of louder. The roar in his ears drowned them out. Gasping, he flopped over on his back, his mind a jumble of frantic thoughts:

*Sherman's on the way.*

*That black bastard's got my Enfield.*

*She'll be too upset to pay any mind.*

*But I've got to warn—*

Darkness cut off the rest.

# CHAPTER 5

## *The Women*

HE WOKE AT TWILIGHT, in a bedroom at the second floor front.

He lay awhile in the high bed, reflecting that perhaps he was beginning to mend. His belly didn't ache quite so badly. The ear trouble and dizziness had left him. Best of all, he felt clean.

His filthy uniform had disappeared. He wore a man's flannel nightshirt which because of his height reached only to his knees. A flush burned his cheeks when he realized someone had undressed and washed him and rebandaged his leg wound with new, spotless linen. He hoped it had been one of the nigra women he'd seen around the place.

Downstairs, voices murmured. He swung his legs off the edge of the bed, stretching luxuriously. He was stiff. Still a mite feverish, too. But he was astonished to discover he was hungry.

When he stood up, barefoot on the smooth, pegged floor, he felt a familiar pressure. He located the chamber pot in a corner. The china surface was decorated with a hand-painted scroll bearing the words *A Salute to Old Spoons.*

Spoons? He studied the pot, then recalled the man to whom the word referred. He laughed for the first time in longer than he could remember.

He picked up the pot, lifted the lid and looked inside. On the bottom, the artist had enameled a man's portrait. Jeremiah recognized the puffy cheeks, drooping mustache, and cocked eye of the infamous Beast Butler, the military governor of conquered New Orleans. Butler had earned the South's hatred with a regulation specifying that any New Orleans gentlewoman caught showing disrespect to the occupying troops would be dealt with as if she were a prostitute. Sometimes the Beast was called Old Cockeye. He'd also been called Spoons because he'd reportedly plundered silverware from the city's finer houses. Jeremiah replaced the pot on the floor, pulled up his nightshirt, and cheerfully pissed on old Spoons.

He was just replacing the lid when he heard steps in the hall. Hastily he clambered back into bed. A knock was followed by a respectful, "Sir?"

"I'm awake. Come in."

A small, fragile black woman appeared. She was barely five feet tall, with wrists no thicker than both his thumbs put together. She must have been seventy, but the eyes in the dark, lined face sparkled. She glanced at the white streak in his hair as she set a mug containing a steaming drink on the table beside the bed.

"You feeling any better, sir?"

"Much, thank you. By the way, my name's Jeremiah. Jeremiah Kent."

A nod. "Miz Catherine told me. I'm Maum Isabella." She touched the mug. "I brought you this to see if you could keep something down."

"Smells first-rate. What is it?"

"One of my toddies. Peach brandy laced with white sugar. If it sets well, I've got ham in the kitchen. Ham and hominy."

Jeremiah sipped the sweet beverage and found the first taste not only bearable but delicious. He wiped his lips with his wrist and smiled at the diminutive black woman who stood with her hands folded at the waist of her patched skirt. There was nothing servile about *her* speech or demeanor; no pretense of the kind he'd seen Price indulge in. The woman obviously occupied a position of importance in the house and knew it.

"That's damn—that's very good, Maum—"

"Isabella, sir."

He gestured at his nightshirt. "Who fixed me up this way?"

"Miz Catherine did. Soon after you passed out downstairs."

Blushing, he said, "You mean she didn't go to pieces when she learned about the colonel?"

The old woman shook her head. "Miz Catherine knew the risks when he went off to serve. She's mighty grieved, of course. So's everybody on the place—excepting two or three bad niggers."

He presumed Price was included in that last group.

"Miz Catherine's a mighty strong lady—for a Yankee woman," Maum Isabella added, allowing herself a small, wry smile. "Also, we have a house to run. Chores to do. She allowed herself 'bout a half hour of crying, that's all. She'll be up to see you soon, I imagine. Serena too."

The mention of the younger woman seemed to carry less enthusiasm than the reference to Mrs. Rose. Then, sympathetically:

"You must have seen some hard fighting."

He didn't understand the reason for the question, so he only nodded.

"What I mean—" A frail hand pointed. "You're mighty young to be turning gray."

"Oh, this—" He ran his fingers through the white streak. "That's from Chickamauga. A Minié ball knocked my cap off—grazed the top of my head. The ball was almost spent, so all I got was a good thump. Guess it did something to the hair, though. A surgeon said it would grow back the right color, but it hasn't."

"I see." Her curiosity satisfied, she started for the door. "Well, you want anything, just stomp on the floor and someone will come up right quick. Oh, I nearly forgot. Tomorrow morning—"

"Thanksgiving."

"We don't have a lot to say thanks for this year," the little black woman declared. "The colonel's gone. Those Yanks are coming out from Atlanta."

"So the word's gotten around?"

"Yes, sir. I heard about what you told Price. By now most everyone on the place knows."

"Maum Isabella, may I ask you a question that might not be any of my business?"

"You can surely ask, Mr. Jeremiah. I'll decide about a reply when I hear the question."

"Where'd that buck come from? Price, I mean. Has he always been on the plantation?"

"No. The colonel bought him five years ago in a batch of half a dozen niggers Mr. Samples owned. Mr. Samples had the next farm over from this one. He went to his reward very suddenly. Had no kin to take over the property, so the colonel picked up part of the acreage and some of his people too. All good people except that Price. He came from Louisiana when he was young. He was raised by a man who treated him bad. Maybe that explains why he acts mean. But it doesn't excuse it. I've always had a queer feeling about Price."

"What sort of feeling?"

"He could have been raised in a pig lot or a palace and he'd still have come out mean." She smiled. "The Yanks don't have a corner on meanness, you know. Fact is, there ain't a single group in all God's creation dares claim their baskets are free of bad peaches."

"Price sure strikes me as one."

Maum Isabella didn't disagree. "Most of the niggers on the place can't abide him. There *are* a few who encourage him on the sly. They like to see him get away with being uppity. Miz Catherine should have sold him off long ago. Well, I got things to do. I expect the mistress will be here soon. We'll have dinner tomorrow afternoon, late. In the morning there's to be a memorial service in the parlor. For the colonel. Most everybody'll be there."

The sentence implied a question about his presence. Jeremiah nodded, his dark eyes shining in the candle glow. The toddy had warmed and relaxed him. The scent of roses and dahlias drifting in from the bluish dark was like a balm after the stenches of war: pus; dirt; offal; powder; blood—

"So will I. The colonel was a good man. He saved my life."

At last Maum Isabella looked as if she approved of him.

"I'm happy to hear you'll be able to pay your respects," she said as she opened the door. She marched out as Jeremiah reached for the toddy.

He was incredibly content. He savored not only the drink but the comforting feeling of being halfway well again. Well; clean; and in a safe haven.

A *temporarily* safe haven, he reminded himself. Out there in the Georgia dark, Sherman's soldiers were marching relentlessly. Rosewood might lie directly in their path.

He finished the toddy. He couldn't pretend he wasn't frightened by the possibility of Sherman's approach. But the idea brought a touch of pleasure as well. After too long a time, he might again be called to do something worthwhile in this war.

ii

Catherine Rose looked in about twenty minutes later.

She was dressed more formally than when he'd first met her. She'd changed from her faded gingham to a full-skirted black gown with rustling underlayers that bulked the skirt into the fashionable hooped shape.

Her bodice looked different than before. Her breasts were pushed up higher; were more pointed and prominent. He assumed she was wearing one of those steel-boned corsets. The kind he'd seen in his mother's empty room in Lexington one time, and stolen in to touch with a feeling of experimentation and acute embarrassment.

Even though Jeremiah was eighteen, his knowledge of the intimate details of a woman's life were limited. In the army he'd often bragged about visiting a lady of easy virtue when he was only fifteen. It was the typical young soldier's lie. He was totally innocent—and ashamed of it. Now the sight of Mrs. Rose's figure generated a lewd excitement all the more thrilling because it was shameful.

Clad in black as she was, the widow's only concession to her duties as mistress of a household was a lace-edged apron of white lawn. Even the heavy crocheted net holding the large chignon at the back of her head was black. She'd dressed her hair since he'd last seen her.

"Corporal Kent." She greeted him with a small, strained smile.

"Evening, ma'am."

"Maum Isabella reports you're feeling somewhat better." She stood at the foot of the bed, composed but pale.

"Thank you, I am. Please call me Jeremiah."

"Of course. I'm truly sorry you had to suffer so much to bring that letter to Rosewood."

"Why, that's all forgotten, ma'am," he fibbed. "You're the one who—" Caught in an awkward trap, he didn't want to finish.

The mole beside her mouth lifted as she tried to smile with greater warmth. Her eyes were puffy. Otherwise she was in perfect control. He admired her courage.

She finished the sentence for him:

"—who has suffered? I'll admit I did let down for a little while. But the truth is, even before you arrived, I was beginning to think something had happened to Henry. He usually forced himself to write a letter every three or four weeks. A few lines. But I hadn't received one in two and a half months."

She drew a cane chair to the bed and sat down. He smelled the fruit wine again; strongly.

"Besides, there's no time for excessive indulgence in grief. With all those stories of Yanks loose around Milledgeville, we must get busy. I need to make a list of what we should hide—food, furnishings, valuables— in case Sherman does come this way."

"I want to help any way I can," he said, suddenly self-conscious about being alone with a woman in this flower-scented bedroom. It hardly mattered that the woman was at least twice his age. "I'll be out of bed before you know it."

"Very kind of you, Jeremiah. I appreciate your willingness. I'll feel free to call on you. Some of the bucks on the place may not stay."

"Not stay? Why?"

"Judge Claypool's boy, Floyd—he came over yesterday—he told me a great many nigras are running away from their masters to travel with Sherman's army."

An awkward pause. Jeremiah felt compelled to say something more about her husband. He struggled—not at ease with sentiments appropriate to such a moment:

"Whatever happens, you must let me help. I wouldn't be drawing a breath if it wasn't for the colonel. I'm truly sorry he—"

A red-knuckled hand lifted:

"Not necessary, Jeremiah. Your feelings for him are evident. And your loyalty. You got here."

Her eyes focused on the gallery, and the dark. "Henry was an excellent husband. I liked him from the first time he came to tea at Christ College.

That's where I was teaching when we met. I was an instructor in the classics. I'm originally from Connecticut."

"Yes, he told me."

"I came down to Georgia to accept a position at the female institute at Montpelier when I was twenty-two. Henry had recently—had lost his first wife—" Her voice trailed off. "His aunt was also on the faculty at the institute. She introduced us. She was an Episcopalian, but Henry was a Congregationalist, as I am. I never regretted my decision to marry him. Or to bring up his child."

Another pause. Then she asked how Henry Rose had died.

He described the circumstances in a guarded way, emphasizing the colonel's heroism and omitting the more gruesome details. He made no mention of the blood, the filth, the brutality of the field hospital—nor of Rose's despair about the course of the war. Catherine nodded from time to time. Once he thought he saw tears in her eyes.

She asked about her husband's body. Again he resorted to partial honesty. He cited the confusion that always followed a battle and took the blame for not keeping track of Rose's remains. He avoided any reference to the heap onto which those canvas-covered bodies were dumped one after another. He tried to finish with something positive:

"He was thinking of you right to the end, ma'am. Never a word about himself. Just about you. How you'd need assistance—"

A small sigh. "It appears we will. It pains me to say it, but over the last few months I've noticed a change in the attitude of a few of the nigras. They still do their duties, but they've become—" She searched for the proper term:

"—impudent."

He saw no reason to skirt the issue any longer:

"Is Price one of them?"

"The worst, I'm afraid."

"Well, then, I should tell you what I really think happened to my musket."

Before he could begin, the door opened. A girl walked in.

Her dress was as black as her stepmother's. But her bright red hair framing pale cheeks shone like a fire, so that she hardly seemed in mourning.

The girl was taller than Catherine, with pale blue eyes and a splendid figure. There was an astonishing perfection about her features. Together with her delicately white skin, it gave her an almost angelic air. But the liveliness of her eyes flawed the effect.

She came quickly to the bedside, her skirts gathered up in her hands. The older woman turned:

"I thought perhaps you'd forgotten us, Serena."

"No, not at all," the girl answered, ignoring the hint of criticism in Catherine's remark.

Serena Rose studied Jeremiah. She was a lovely creature, but plainly not the older woman's child.

"I do hope you're comfortable, Mr. Kent," she remarked with a smile that struck him as sweetly polite rather than sincere.

"Fine, thank you."

He knew the girl was two years older than he was; twenty. The difference seemed an abyss. And even before he'd spoken his three-word answer, she glided to a wall mirror to study her hair. Somehow that angered him.

### iii

"You could be a bit more cordial to our guest, my dear."

Serena spun around, her smile still ingenuous. "Was I being otherwise, Catherine? I'm so sorry."

She was hard to read. Reserved; every move studied. While Catherine's politeness masked feelings she felt it might be unseemly to reveal, Serena's behavior apparently concealed a lack of any feeling whatever. Or, if she did have feelings, she kept them deeply hidden. He began to suspect she'd come up to the bedroom solely because it was an obligation.

"I apologize if I was rude to you, Mr. Kent," she said. "The news about Papa, and all this talk about the Yankees—it's quite upsetting."

"I can certainly understand—"

"But now we have a trustworthy man to help us," Catherine said.

"That's reassuring," Serena replied, though a flicker of her eyes suggested she doubted *man* was an appropriate term for Jeremiah. He was both repelled by the girl's cool manner and attracted by her physical beauty—of which she was quite conscious. She stood so that he had a clear view of her figure—her bosom—in profile. In a perfunctory way, she asked:

"Where do you come from, Mr. Kent?"

"I was serving with the Sixty-third Virginia until I was reassigned as your father's orderly on the division staff."

"Virginia," Serena repeated. "That's a mighty long way from Georgia."

He decided he might as well get some of the details out of the way. He told them a little about his family. First his mother, still in the endangered Shenandoah. Then his brother Gideon, captured in the fire fight that slew Jeb Stuart at Yellow Tavern.

No, he replied in response to a question from Catherine, there was absolutely no word of Gideon's whereabouts, and he was worried. Men were known to be dying by the hundreds in the Northern prisons, now that Grant had put a stop to the exchange of prisoners in order to further deplete the South's manpower.

The account of his middle brother was only slightly less grim. For a few moments he spoke glowingly of Matt's sunny nature; his fondness for games; the memorable quality of his drawings. Then he told them Matt had been—and presumably still was—on a blockade runner, a fast, Liverpool-built steam vessel slipping back and forth between the Bermudas and Wilmington on the Cape Fear River. But Matt's last, badly spelled letter had been delivered to Lexington over eight months ago. There'd been no news since. Either Matt hadn't written again, or a letter from Fan with news of him had failed to reach Jeremiah. Whatever the circumstances, there was a question mark after Matt's name nearly as ominous as the one after Gideon's.

Jeremiah concluded with a brief mention of the other branch of the family: his father Jephtha, from whom his mother was divorced, and who was now a Methodist pastor again—this time in the Northern wing of the divided church up in New York. Jephtha had originally been an itinerant parson in Virginia before the Methodists split over the slave issue. Then he'd been a newspaperman on *The New York Union.*

"There's at least one more in the family up north, but I know even less about him. His name's Louis. He has a wife and a small boy, and he's a rich man. Owns that newspaper Jephtha worked for, plus part of a steelworks, some kind of cotton factory, and a publishing company in Boston called Kent and Son. I saw a book from the company in your office, Mrs. Rose."

Serena's blue eyes showed greater interest:

"So the Northern relatives are the ones with money, Mr. Kent?"

"Yes, Miss Serena, I'm afraid that's true for the present. Eventually, though, my brothers and I—"

Before he could finish, and tell them he and Matt and Gideon might one day be wealthy in their own right, Catherine interrupted:

"I think we've taxed Jeremiah quite long enough."

Serena pouted. He'd piqued her curiosity. She was gazing at him as if trying to guess the ending of his unfinished sentence.

"He was kind enough to describe how your father died—" Catherine said.

There was no response. If the girl felt any emotion she never showed it. Jeremiah was fascinated by her good looks, but he began to think he didn't like her much as a person.

"—and we were discussing the attitude of some of the nigras when you came in." Catherine swung back to Jeremiah. "I hate to tire you further. But you mentioned something about a musket?"

"The same one Price talked about in the office," Jeremiah said, nodding. "I slept all last night on the creek bank where he found me. When I woke up, the musket was gone. My cartridge box, too. Your nigra claimed someone else must have come along and taken it. But I'm pretty certain he took it."

Catherine frowned.

"I think he *hid* it," Jeremiah went on more firmly. "I don't believe it's safe to have a nigra you call impudent hiding a gun when the Yanks are on the way."

The discussion sparked a combative look in Serena's eyes:

"Now let me get this clear. Price claimed he *didn't* take the musket?"

"That's correct, Miss Serena. He said some nigras who fish down there must have pilfered it."

"And you have no evidence one way or the other?"

He admitted that was true.

Catherine Rose chewed her lip. "I hesitate to make an issue without proof. If the Yanks arrive we'll need the support of every nigra on the place. Price has a mean streak in him. But it's usually directed at the other slaves."

"He's been saucy to you lately, Catherine," Serena flared.

"I know. But I still don't think he'd do us any harm."

"Mrs. Rose, I beg to disagree." Jeremiah struggled to sit up straighter in bed, ignoring the way his nightshirt hiked over his knees, much to Serena's amusement. "I think that buck should be questioned until he admits the theft."

"So do I!" Serena exclaimed, the candles putting little reflections in her pupils.

Again Catherine negated the idea with a shake of her head:

"We have always conducted the affairs of Rosewood in a humane and Christian way. Right or wrong, we'll continue to do so. At this difficult time, I won't have the nigras losing their trust in me because of Price."

"I heard most of them hate him," Jeremiah responded.

Catherine sighed. "Maum Isabella's been talking again. She's right. But there are delicate balances on a plantation such as this one. If I accuse Price, he'll never admit the theft because there's no evidence against him. To force a confession, I'd have to punish him. Then the nigras might switch their loyalties—even if only briefly. I'd become their enemy. I don't want to be their enemy with Sherman on the loose."

"But Catherine—" Serena protested.

"Child," the older woman broke in, her voice soft but strong, "I have the final say in this. Even granted Price is lying, I don't intend to provoke more turmoil. We'll give him the benefit of the doubt and stay alert. That's enough for the time being."

Serena stamped her foot. "Stay alert till he breaks in one night and shoots us!"

"Serena, don't argue."

Red-cheeked, the girl blazed back, "Yes, I will! You're too easy on the niggers! Mr. Kent's warned us, but you won't pay any attention. You're always so blasted anxious to have everyone think you're a saint!"

The color draining from her face, Catherine whispered, "I try to behave in a Christian way."

"When the neighbors are here! They never see that blackberry wine you're always—"

"Be quiet!"

Catherine stared at Serena until the younger woman looked away.

Jeremiah was embarrassed yet morbidly fascinated by the sudden display of hostility between the mother and stepdaughter. Sensing his discomfort, Catherine stood up.

"It's no disrespect to Jeremiah if we don't press the issue with Price. We'll be careful."

*Careful isn't enough,* he thought. *I saw that buck's eyes down by the river—you didn't.*

Serena refused to surrender: "We should do more than that. We should force Price to admit he's lying. *Whip* him!"

*"I will hear absolutely nothing more on the subject."*

Catherine said it with such vehemence that Serena looked as if she'd been struck. She opened her mouth to retort, then noted the fierceness of Catherine's gaze and whirled away. Jeremiah thought the older woman's prudence was ill-advised. But it wasn't his place to enter into a family feud whose nature and origins he didn't understand.

Trying to take the sting out of the confrontation, Catherine walked over and reached for her stepdaughter's arm. Serena turned again, drawing back. For a moment the women faced one another.

Finally Serena stepped aside, her cheeks pink, her face far from angelic. Catherine walked toward the door. Serena hesitated, then followed.

"Good night, Jeremiah," Catherine said in a strained voice. "Maum Isabella will look in presently to see whether you need anything."

"I am feeling a wee bit hungry—"

"Then I'll send her up immediately."

Opening the door, she reached for Serena's arm a second time. The girl gasped as the older woman literally dragged her out.

Jeremiah sank back in bed, disturbed. In his opinion, Catherine Rose's ideas about handling the situation with Price were all wrong. He'd need to be watchful. Very watchful.

And those two women—they were certainly a puzzlement. They might be related by marriage, but they clearly weren't related by temperament.

Settling himself against the pillows, he inhaled the sweet scent of the blossoms outside the house. Just what kind of hornet's nest had he blundered into on this plantation?

# CHAPTER 6

## Shadow of the Enemy

*"MR. KENT?"*

The whisper brought him bolt upright in bed, surprised and terrified. Then the terror vanished as he realized who had spoken. But bewilderment lingered.

The candles had gone out. From the angle of the November moonlight falling across the gallery, he judged the hour to be very late. Serena Rose was kneeling beside the bed, her face no more than a blur in the silver-blue gloom.

She repeated his name. He mumbled, "I'm awake," although he was still drowsy. Turning on his side, he could feel the warmth of her breath on the back of his hand.

"Catherine doesn't know I'm in here. You won't say anything?"

"Won't say—?" He fought a yawn; knuckled his eyes. Answered more coherently: "No, 'course not."

"I wanted to tell you I went down to the cabins." Her voice was low, the words rushed. "I asked Leon to help me. Leon's a buck who was born at Rosewood, he's trustworthy. We talked to Price." Her tone hardened. "I ordered half a dozen laid on him out by the burial ground."

"Laid—?" His lethargy left him. "You mean the whip?"

She nodded. "We don't use it often, but we have one."

"You did the right thing," he said with conviction. His mouth had that bloodless, cruel look for a moment. "Did Price confess?"

"Not on your life! He just took the whipping without a word. But you should have seen the way he looked at me!"

She clutched his wrist. He felt something wet on her fingers when they brushed the cuff of his nightshirt.

"He stole the musket, Mr. Kent. I know he did!"

"What if your stepmother discovers that you—?"

"She won't. Leon won't say anything to Catherine, I forced him to promise. I doubt Price will say anything either. He's scared of me," she hurried on. "He understands I'm not soft the way Catherine is. And tattling, that's not his style. He'll wait for a chance to get back at me."

"Then you took a risk you shouldn't have taken. I'd have been on my feet soon, I could have—"

"I didn't want to wait a minute longer. I had to find out whether he was up to something. Now I'm sure he is. Catherine's wrong and you're right. But now there are two of us to keep a sharp eye on him. Catherine's too trusting, Mr. Kent. She still believes some of those pretty words they taught her in church when she was a girl. She doesn't realize how that nigger hates us!"

Her fingers closed tighter on his wrist. The tips still had that curious wet feel.

"I just wanted to say you're right—and I'm glad you're here to look after us."

He didn't quite realize what had happened until it was over. She came off her knees and leaned near, planting a quick kiss on his cheek. For a moment her breast brushed his forearm. Under the coverlet his body responded quickly and automatically.

He could see very little of her face in that moment when it was close to his—half of it was in darkness, half a pale blur. In the moonlight her red hair glowed almost white.

With a rustle of gathered skirts, she scrambled to her feet. Why the devil was she so interested in him all of a sudden? he wondered. The first time she'd come into his room she'd hardly paid any attention to him. Why had she reversed herself? Was it because she and her stepmother were at odds? Because she wanted to win him to her side?

Serena squeezed his hand. "I'd better scat out of here. I think Catherine's asleep, but I'm not sure. Her room's down the hall just beyond mine. I know some of the house niggers are still up. If one of them sees me, by this time tomorrow people all over the county will be calling me a scarlet woman." She uttered a low laugh, sounding more amused than worried.

He had no time to say anything as she hurried away. The door clicked shut before he knew it.

He was still mightily confused—downright stunned, in fact—by the swift secret visit. Of course he was gratified that the girl had swung over to his side of the argument about Price. But she'd indeed taken a scandalous chance—risked compromising her reputation—by slipping into his room. Apparently she wasn't afraid of such gambles.

Serena's eagerness to punish the black bothered him, too.

Not that Price didn't deserve punishment. He did—if only as a warning. What troubled Jeremiah was her tone of voice during parts of the conversation. She'd sounded as if she'd actually *enjoyed* ordering the man lashed. Puzzling over her curious nature, he drifted into sleep.

When he woke in the morning, he happened to glance at the sleeve of his nightshirt. He caught his breath.

He gazed at the brown stain on the cuff and realized why Serena's hand had felt wet. Leon hadn't been the only one who had touched the whip.

He spent ten minutes naked in front of the washstand, scrubbing at the stain. He couldn't get it all out because the blood had dried. A telltale blotch remained. Not too noticeable, he hoped.

He poured the discolored water into the chamber pot and hastily put the lid in place with a hand that shook just a little. He'd have whipped Price dispassionately, for the sake of prudence. She'd apparently whipped him for pleasure.

Lord! An angel face like that—what was behind it? Part of him was drawn toward discovering the answer. Another part warned he'd be into dangerous depths if he did.

ii

*"O God, our help in ages past,*
*"Our hope for years to come—"*

Jeremiah moved his lips, unfamiliar with the words of the hymn sung with such lusty confidence by the people in the sitting room of Rosewood just after eleven o'clock that same Thanksgiving morning.

Outside, a brilliant sun shone. During the past hour, some twenty white neighbors had arrived. The men were all elderly, the women of varying ages. Dressed in Sunday clothes, the visitors stood unselfconsciously among the plantation's blacks who filled the rest of the room. More of the slaves packed the entrance hall and part of the front piazza near the main door.

Even Price had come to pay tribute to the departed colonel. Jeremiah could see him just outside the sitting room arch, bellowing the hymn as if what Serena had described last night had never happened.

*"Our shelter from the stormy blast,*
*"And our eternal home."*

Noting Price's erect posture and cheerful expression, Jeremiah wondered if he'd dreamed the nocturnal visit.

Serena had again dressed like her stepmother—in black crepe. As the group sang, she played the London-made pianoforte. For a number of reasons Jeremiah was decidedly uncomfortable in the midst of the gathering.

Just after he'd washed out the blood, Maum Isabella had delivered a pair of the colonel's linen trousers and a luxurious white silk shirt, as well as underclothing. Everything was too small. He looked and felt like a bumpkin in the ill-fitting garments. Neither did he like wearing a dead man's clothes.

And before the service, he'd been required to meet all the guests and repeat an involved series of falsehoods about his wounds and fictitious discharge. Grave-faced people, among them a couple named Jesperson, had bobbed their heads sympathetically in response to his romanticized description of Henry Rose's death.

> "Under the shadow of Thy throne,
> "Still may we dwell secure—"

Pretending to sing, he found his mind returning to the crosscurrents that seemed to be aswirl in the house. There was a curious, secretive quality about them. For instance, while standing at Catherine's elbow and speaking with two of the visitors, he'd picked up the unmistakable tang of blackberry wine again. If she'd drink before company came, she was under greater tension than she permitted others to see.

The right hand of the Congregational pastor, the Reverend Emory Pettus, arced back and forth as he led the hymn to its loud climax. Pettus was an immense, paunchy man in a warm-looking black alpaca coat with a secession rosette in the lapel. He kept his eyes on the ceiling and sang in a bellowing baritone:

> "Sufficient is Thine arm alone,
> "And our defense is—"

Abruptly Serena lifted her fingers from the keyboard and turned toward the open front windows nearby. Her net-bound chignon glowed even with the morning sun muted by the gently stirring lace curtains.

The various singers straggled on to a weak finish. Pettus frowned as Catherine took her hand from the hymnal she'd been sharing with the minister.

"Serena, why did you stop?"

The girl pointed outdoors. "I heard the bell ring. Twice."

"Nonsense." Catherine smiled frostily. "No one would ring the bell and disturb—"

She was interrupted by a commotion on the piazza. A white-haired old fellow with palsy tottered to a window, mumbling complaints. Outside, a black shouted:

"Miz Catherine? Buggy comin' up the lane!"

"I told you someone rang the bell!" Serena was vindicated.

Catherine ignored her, looking concerned. A slave boy of fourteen or fifteen slipped through the crowd in the sitting room, an apologetic expression on his face.

"Who is it, Zeph?" Catherine asked.

"Marse Claypool, ma'am."

The one referred to as the judge? Jeremiah wondered. Catherine had already commented on the surprising absence of the Claypools.

Jeremiah heard a rattle of wheels and the sound of hoofs scattering small stones. The nigras outdoors shouted questions as the vehicle halted. The horses of the other rigs pulled up in front began to neigh and stamp. Catherine hurried to one of the open windows, thrust the curtains aside, and stuck her head out, not a little annoyed:

"Theodore, we're right in the middle of the service!"

"My profound apologies." The man had a wheezy voice; sounded out of breath. "I'd have been here sooner, but I was waiting for Floyd to come back from another trip to Milledgeville. Those folks indoors—all of you—better pay attention! The Yanks are in the capital!"

The guests all began talking at once. The slaves murmured among themselves. Over the noise, Catherine called:

"Are you sure?"

"Positive. The first of them arrived day before yesterday. Two whole corps of Union infantry, the Fourteenth and the Twentieth. Sherman's with their commander, General Slocum."

Absolute pandemonium then. A portly woman near Jeremiah gasped, closed her eyes, and started to faint. Her male companion tried to catch her, failed, and knelt beside her, chafing her wrists and whispering, "God preserve us. God preserve us."

Jeremiah shoved his way to the windows to hear the rest:

"—wouldn't believe what's happening in Milledgeville, Catherine. The Yanks are tearing up the railroad tracks! Heating the ties and bending 'em around trees. Sherman's hairpins, that's their clever little name for 'em. Floyd said he saw soldiers destroying books from the state library. And Secretary of State Burnett's wife—"

The unseen man paused to suck in another breath as the guests and the blacks fell silent.

"—she had to bury the state seal under her house and hide documents from the legislature in her pig sty."

Catherine leaned halfway out the window. "In heaven's name why?"

"Because that infernal Sherman has issued orders that his men can forage liberally on the country. Those were his exact words—*'forage liberally!'* Of course the sanctimonious devil's also announcing that he hasn't authorized his men to enter homes or molest citizens unless there's guerrilla resistance."

"But the Home Guards are mobilized!" someone exclaimed.

The judge snorted. "Precisely. That qualifies as resistance. So Sherman looks the other way while his scalawags rob private dwellings and burn farms and plantations where the owners have tried to hide some of their crops. Evidently *that's* guerrilla resistance, too! Believe me, Floyd saw barns and gins being put to the torch—houses being gutted in Milledgeville—he talked to one family whose whole place was torn down! They had to take refuge in an overturned boxcar in the rail yards."

Jeremiah pressed up beside Catherine and lifted the curtain. In the drive he saw a bony, perspiring old man seated in a two-wheeled hooded chaise. Red dust covered the man's frock coat and trousers.

"Can't the militia stop them?" Jeremiah asked.

"Old codgers like me? Boys? A few cavalrymen?" Claypool harrumphed. "I doubt it."

"Are they headed this way?"

"Well, they seem to be after rail junctions and the larger towns, so I expect they are. They'll probably come right past here on the way to Millen."

Consternation again.

The man whose wife had fainted helped her to her feet, muttering apologies to Catherine. She didn't hear, standing with one hand shielding her half-closed eyes. The man and his wife edged through the crowd toward the hall. Reverend Pettus announced that they'd better end the service and return to their homes at once.

The words were superfluous. A small stampede had already started, guests jabbering and pushing the blacks aside to get to the buggies and phaetons outside. Jeremiah was suddenly thankful he still had the sheathed knife tucked in his boot. Sherman's shadow was growing longer. Touching Rosewood now.

Still, he had a hard time believing the Yanks would destroy undefended private property on any large scale. Surely they couldn't be that dishonorable. The outbreak in Milledgeville must be an isolated case. Even the razing of Atlanta had had some strategic purpose. But the incidents the dusty old man in the chaise described had none at all, unless you counted the kind of thing Jeremiah was witnessing at this moment: the creation of utter panic among defenseless civilians.

One phaeton was already gone, clattering down the lane in a cloud of sunlit dust. The driver lashed his team as though Satan were three feet behind.

"Catherine? What are we going to do?"

Jeremiah and the older woman both turned at the sound of Serena's voice. The girl didn't appear worried, merely curious.

Judge Claypool came struggling in against the tide of the exodus, talking first to one person, then another:

"—swear to Jesus—oh! Excuse my language, Reverend—it's all true! They've got a flock of runaway niggers dogging 'em wherever they go. Disloyal, disreputable niggers, every one!"

The judge's announcement in the hall caused another, somewhat more restrained stir, this time among the blacks. Claypool fanned back his dusty coat to display a holstered horse pistol. "Thank God we have none of that kind around here. If we did they'd be candidates for shooting. And I don't mean by Yanks."

Serena prodded her stepmother:

"Well, Catherine?"

"If they come," Jeremiah said abruptly, "we'll stand up to them."

"Really?" Serena inquired. "How?"

"War or no war, they have no right to ruin private property. We'll make them understand that."

Serena's blue eyes grew amused. "My, you certainly have faith in the decency of Yankees."

The sarcasm rankled. He *had* to believe the cruelty of the battlefield couldn't spread into civilian territory. He had nothing else to believe in any longer. It was his last article of faith. He tried to justify it:

"I just don't think any army would go on burning and looting that way. Sherman's men have probably done it around Milledgeville because that's the capital."

Catherine took encouragement from the words:

"I'm sure he's right, Serena. Provisioning an army off enemy land's one thing. Ruining civilian property is another. They certainly won't continue—"

"Don't be too damn sure, Catherine," Judge Claypool warned.

"By God, we won't stand for it," Jeremiah blurted. "It's against all the laws of decency!"

Someone laughed.

He spun, his eyes locking with those of Price.

The slave's face was blank again. But Jeremiah was positive Price was the culprit. A young woman with her hair covered by a bandana was backing away from him. And Maum Isabella was staring at him too, lips pinched tight together.

Jeremiah glared at the slave but drew no response. Price's pupils might have been brown stones.

A few remaining guests clustered around Catherine, offering apologies and empty condolences before they departed. Jeremiah drew Serena aside:

"We'd better get your stepmother working on her list."

"What list?"

"The one she mentioned last night. Covering anything on the place that ought to be hidden. Are there firearms in the house?"

"No, none. Papa took everything." With her back to Price, who hadn't changed his position in the hall, she whispered, "There's a musket some-where—" She seemed to be goading him.

"We'll do the best we can without it," Jeremiah declared, even though the lack of the Enfield left him feeling less than whole.

The vehicles belonging to the guests rattled down to the highway one after another. Maum Isabella had put grief behind her and was shooing some of the nigras through the house toward their cabins. At last Price turned and strolled off in the same direction.

Dust boiled through the open windows of the sitting room, billowing the curtains and settling on the polished wood of the pianoforte. A last visitor tipped a table and spilled back issues of the *Southern Literary Messenger* in his haste to depart. As the copies plopped on the carpet, Jeremiah heard faint laughter again, then Maum Isabella's voice, loud and scolding.

"Jeremiah?"

He turned to Catherine.

"Serena asked a very pertinent question. We must plan what we're going to do if the enemy comes."

Remembering the laughter, Jeremiah thought, *He's already here*.

# CHAPTER 7

## *Warnings*

THANKSGIVING DINNER was a tense, joyless affair.

Jeremiah suspected it might turn out that way the moment Catherine appeared, bringing her cut glass decanter of blackberry wine out in the open—right to the table. As she set it down she murmured an excuse about needing a "medicinal tonic" after the strain of the service and Judge Claypool's arrival with the bad news from Milledgeville.

Maum Isabella hadn't stinted on preparing a good meal. But Jeremiah and the two women barely touched their food. Unpleasant questions seemed to come up almost at once. Would Sherman actually reach the Louisville district? Would his troops behave as badly as they had in the capital? Jeremiah gave encouraging answers, as much to reassure himself as to reassure them.

Catherine inquired about his initiation into the war. The words he used in reply automatically carried his thoughts to a place he preferred to forget:

To a hillside in the northwest part of the state. In September twilight a year ago, he'd gone up that hillside with his bayonet fixed and his palms sweating, ducking and starting at his first exposure to the whine of Minié balls.

The Confederates had been trying to take a position held by the Yank general, Pap Thomas. After the battle, Thomas came to be called The Rock because his lines held and blew back charge after rebel charge while, behind them, routed Rosecrans fled for Chattanooga. Jeremiah narrated an account of the engagement, but said nothing about how terrified he'd been at first.

He described the ball that had grazed his scalp and produced the streak of white hair. He told them how he'd shot his first Yank—the first one he was certain he'd killed, that is. But he didn't mention the disturbing feelings he'd experienced watching the young man fall.

He'd shot as he was supposed to shoot—obeying orders—yet his reaction to the hit had been a kind of cold joy. He tried not to remember the joy. It didn't fit with his concept of war honorably conducted.

He hated to admit there was an aspect of his nature, slowly strengthened as he gained proficiency with firearms, that could be termed ruthless. At times he even denied the trait's existence. But it was there, and he guarded against giving in to it.

Once in a while he did succumb. Before escaping from the farmer with the pitchfork, he'd struck the back of the man's neck and felt absolutely no pity. Nor had he experienced any qualms about the whipping of Price.

While Jeremiah talked, he noticed Serena picking at her cloved ham and glancing around the room in a restless way. She was certainly a creature of moods. Last night, she'd declared she was his ally. This morning he seemed to bore her. He concluded that her night visit must have been solely an act of defiance directed against her stepmother. His account of his experiences in battle didn't interest her. This afternoon he was merely a guest to be tolerated. A boy.

It was infuriating.

Yet he couldn't help being fascinated. The late afternoon sun haloed her red hair and profile, making her look like some beautiful image from a church window.

Catherine drank two goblets of blackberry wine during the meal. She didn't touch the quill pen, the inkstand, or the foolscap sheet in front of her place. One line was written at the top of the sheet in a delicate, slanting hand:

*To be done*

Somehow she seemed unable to get down to working on the list, or even to discussing it, permitting the conversation to veer off in other directions.

"Jeremiah." She refilled her goblet a third time. "How was the colonel's state of mind when—when he—"

She couldn't complete the sentence.

A black woman cleared the unfinished dish of dessert plums from his place as he answered, "Well, apart from fretting about you two, he seemed to be in good spirits the night before we fought at Jonesboro."

A lie. He balanced it with a truth:

"He was annoyed, though."

"Why?"

"There was something special he wanted to read. The next part of a serial story in a New York weekly. Someone had given him two old copies that contained the first two chapters, or whatever you call them."

"Installments," Serena said.

He felt humiliated again. "Anyway, it was some sort of spooky story by a writer named Wilkie—" Memory faltered a second time.

"Wilkie Collins?" Catherine asked.

"Yes, I think that's it. He said the two things he wanted most were to see you"—the remark was intended to include Serena, but she paid no attention—"and to finish *The Woman in White*."

Catherine sighed and dabbed her napkin against the corner of her mouth. "He had a fine mind. He was a literate, Christian man. We had good times just talking, or going over the ledgers. Small things."

"Small things were all he cared about," Serena complained.

Voice thicker, Catherine retorted, "You mustn't speak disrespectfully of your father."

"I'm not being disrespectful, I'm telling the truth!" At last she faced Jeremiah, who occupied a place at one side of the long table, between the women seated at the ends. "I don't know how many times I begged Papa to take us to Savannah so we could have dinner at the Pulaski House. Best food in the whole state, everyone says. Best in the whole South! But he wouldn't, he was always content around here. Do you know I've never been out of Jefferson County except for part of a year at Christ College where Catherine taught? I wanted to see New Orleans, Savannah—even Washington. And all I ever saw were silly books and silly women in a stuffy old lyceum!"

Catherine bristled, waggling her goblet:

"You also saw a few disreputable young men who took you buggy riding after hours. Who compromised you by bringing along spiritous liquors."

Serena glanced at her stepmother's glass. "You're a fine one to talk!"

Catherine scowled. "Serena—" The warning went unfinished because the girl spoke immediately:

"Well, you are!" She turned to Jeremiah: "Catherine's always been a pillar of the county temperance society. Of course none of those nice ladies has any idea there's always a jug of blackberry wine handy around—"

"*Enough, Serena!* When there's a war, things—things change. Your father's been gone a long time. Sometimes a person needs help to keep going."

Serena's laugh had a vicious sound. "And everything's fine as long as it's taken on the sly!"

Catherine set the goblet on the table and stared at it, sadly. Jeremiah wanted to run. Only politeness kept him there, caught in the hostility boiling beween the two women.

Although Catherine's unhappy concentration on the goblet was an admission of guilt, Serena didn't find that satisfying enough:

"I tell you, sometimes I just get sick to death of the way you look down on me! You act like Moses on the mount! One of these days—"

Flushed, she held back the rest. Catherine looked at her, half stunned, half furious:

"What, Serena?"

"Nothing."

"No, I insist. Finish the sentence. Did you mean to threaten me?"

"No, I—really, I didn't. I apologize." Her voice was flat; insincere.

Jeremiah grimaced. She obviously *had* meant the uncompleted sentence as a warning. But prudence—or a second thought that represented more deviousness than caution—had convinced her to keep it to herself.

Still, she wasn't through baiting the older woman, though she did it indirectly, speaking to him again.

"Catherine's always been just heartbroken that I didn't last the year at the institute. I was supposed to study for a degree in the arts, but one of the proctors smelled spirits when I came in ten minutes late one night. A whole ten minutes! That was the end of my grand education. Not that I cared! I was glad to leave that stupid place."

The colonel's widow picked up the quill and tapped the nib against the inkstand. "I don't believe we need subject Jeremiah to an account of your unfortunate record at Montpelier."

He tried to ease the tension with a smile and a shrug:

"I was never much for studying either. My mother couldn't get me to do lessons when we traveled."

With that, he finally succeeded in attracting Serena's full attention.

"Did you travel many places?"

"All over the South. My stepfather—he's dead now—he was an actor." Serena seemed genuinely interested:

"Oh, you must have seen such wonderful sights!"

He made a face. "Hotel rooms. Dirty theaters. Sooty railroad cars. Depots in the middle of the night."

"You're not being honest. I can't imagine anything more exciting than visiting different cities and towns. I want to travel one of these days. Travel—stay in fine hotels—"

She searched his face a moment. Did he? she seemed to ask silently. Catherine's quill went *tap* against the inkstand, then, quickly, *tap* again.

"What about that relative of yours in New York?" Serena wanted to know. "Did you ever visit him?"

"My second cousin once removed? No, I've never set eyes on Louis Kent."

"He's a wealthy man, though—didn't you tell us he's a wealthy man?"

"Very wealthy," he nodded. He'd been unable to gain her attention for so long, he wanted to keep it. The boast came easily: "'Course our side of the family—the Virginia side—has money too. My brothers and I will come into a lot of it when our father dies."

"You will?" She folded her hands under her chin, "You're not making that up?"

"Absolutely not." To convince her, he related how his father, the Reverend Jephtha Kent, had inherited a California gold claim and a subsequently formed mining corporation from Jeremiah's grandfather, a mountain man and prospector in the 1849 rush. Serena still acted dubious as he went on:

"Gideon, Matt, and I will come into equal shares when father passes away—although thanks to the war, I don't know what's happened to either one of them lately. Matt was always footloose—I expect he's taking care of himself, wherever he is. But I really worry about Gid. We're not sure if he's dead or in prison up north. If he's dead, I suppose his wife in Richmond inherits his share. But however it turns out, even a third of the earnings of that California company will be mighty handsome."

Teasing, Serena said, "If there is a California company."

Catherine exhaled, an abrupt, exasperated sound. "Serena, I don't know what to do with you. I've never heard you speak more rudely to anyone—with possibly one exception."

Jeremiah fought back another wave of anger.

"That's all right, Mrs. Rose. I'm used to doubters. Boys in the army called me a liar every day of the week. The truth is—"

He grinned in a disarming way.

"—I'm not bright enough to make up a story like that."

Catherine's eyes were warm as she responded, "Or malicious enough to try to deceive people. I believe you."

Serena studied her mother. Perhaps Catherine's conviction had persuaded her. She was more polite when she said:

"Why, I do too! I was only having a little fun."

"You have peculiar notions as to what constitutes fun, Serena. You have peculiar notions about a good many—"

Serena didn't let her finish:

"What are you going to do with all that money when you get it?"

Less angry now—though Catherine wasn't—he shrugged again, and replied honestly:

"Hadn't given it much thought. It'll be a long time before I see any of it. My father's in fine health, and I wouldn't wish him anything less—even if he is a damn Yankee."

That admission represented a change in his attitude that had taken place gradually over the past couple of years. He could still recall a vivid, ugly scene in a hotel room in Washington when Fan and his father had screamed at one another. Lamont had tried to intercede, and Gideon had wound up caning Jephtha unmercifully. Jeremiah had been terrified, understanding none of it.

Later, after Lamont's funeral, Fan had spoken to him and said Gideon and Jephtha were reconciled now—and that it had been Lamont, not Jephtha, who'd been responsible for the violent quarrel. She'd refused to explain further, and he'd never been able to learn more of the details. But her statements were an additional bit of proof of something suspicious about Lamont's death.

He sat up a little straighter, conscious of Serena watching him closely. He had her now! Even if she still wasn't wholly convinced about the California gold, she was at least treating him as if he were something more than a worthless boy.

Surrendering to an ugly impulse, he decided he'd fix her for all her previous slights. He shifted the position of his chair so he faced Catherine:

"I think we've talked enough about money. Maybe we should get to work on your list."

The older woman smiled, but in a tired way. "I suppose you're right. I've been avoiding it. I hate to think of why we must make a list at all."

The wine had definitely affected her speech. Slowed and slurred it. Lent it a despairing note. She inked the quill. Thought a moment.

"We must put some salt away. What little we have left."

She made a notation, then pondered again.

"Two barrels of flour."

She marked it down.

"I have two bolts of kersey in the sewing room. I wouldn't want to lose those."

"Heavens, no!" Serena exclaimed.

What a wretched excuse for a Thanksgiving dinner this had turned out to be! Of course, he admitted to himself a moment later, he hadn't exactly eased the situation by giving in to his impulse and turning his back on Serena. But he felt too embarrassed to shift the chair again.

While he watched Catherine Rose working on her list, he missed seeing the speculative look in Serena's blue eyes. She was no longer interested in her stepmother.

She was watching him.

ii

Late that night, unable to sleep, he lay with his hands clasped beneath his head, pondering the peculiar and venomous conversation between the Rose women.

All he could settle on as possible causes for their barely controlled animosity were two things. The first was Catherine's evident need for strong drink, coupled with the fact that she concealed the need from her neighbors and the members of the temperance society. The second was Serena's undisciplined behavior, which had apparently gotten her expelled from the young women's institute. Still, both reasons seemed too trivial to generate the kind of hostility that had crisscrossed the dining table.

He recalled certain other words of Catherine's. Serena had *"peculiar notions."* Could that possibly be a polite term for crazy? The girl's nature plainly included a violent, reckless streak. The blood he'd washed from the cuff of his nightshirt said as much.

Yet the underlying reason for the animosity between the two continued to elude him. Not that he much cared to probe for it.

Trouble was, the longer he stayed at Rosewood, the more likely he was to uncover it. The women were revealing more and more of themselves as each day passed. Perhaps the stress of living with the threat of Sherman's army made such a situation inevitable. He didn't like being in the middle of it. But he was.

Well, at least he'd scored a point or two against Catherine's bitchy stepdaughter. He was no longer quite so much of a child in her eyes.

His feelings about her were complex and upsetting. There was something damned dangerous about her. Yet the memory of her blue eyes and red hair kept him awake and aroused for almost an hour.

iii

During the next two days, Catherine put Jeremiah in charge of the heavier work called for by the Thanksgiving-day list. He was helped by a husky, companionable nigra named Leon; the one Serena had called on when she tried to whip a confession out of Price.

Jeremiah and the black man dug a pit behind the slaves' burial ground. There they buried the casks of salt and flour.

Next they loaded the plantation wagon with bales of cotton, the two bolts of kersey, and two more of denim cloth carried from the sewing room. Leon hitched mules to the wagon and showed Jeremiah a straggling track that led off into pine woods a quarter mile behind the little cemetery.

In a clearing far back in the woods they erected a lean-to of limbs and brush to protect the cache of cotton and cloth, to which they presently added two small barrels of molasses and a large chiming clock Henry Rose had presented to Catherine as a wedding present. Catherine had confessed she felt a mite ridiculous hiding an item of sentimental value such as the clock. But she had no basis for making decisions about what the Yanks might want other than reports received once or twice a day from the citizens of Louisville. They sent their nigras around the neighborhood to say that Sherman's army was indeed coming, and the general's order giving permission for his soldiers to *forage liberally* was being interpreted as permission to steal anything the invaders pleased.

Leon and Jeremiah tried to operate circumspectly on their trips into the pines. The big, innocent-eyed slave reported that Price seemed in extremely high spirits. When Jeremiah questioned him about any references Price might have made to a stolen Enfield, Leon allowed as how Price hadn't said anything directly about the musket. But he *had* been bragging that he'd be "fixed mighty good" if the enemy showed up at the gate by the highway. Jeremiah wished there were at least one weapon in the house besides kitchen implements and his knife.

He and Leon kept an eye out for Price whenever they drove the loaded wagon back into the trees. They never once saw the buck watching. But since the other nigras had observed the wagon's comings and goings, Jeremiah was sure Price was well aware of their activity.

Leon reported that something like a quarter of the blacks on the place were whispering about being free soon. A few more questions on Jeremiah's part revealed that a fierce split was developing at Rosewood. The more loyal nigras were being lectured by Maum Isabella until they promised they wouldn't assist the invaders in any way. And although the malcontents went about their duties as usual, they did so with a changed attitude. Leon summed it up:

"They didn't use to say nasty things about Miz Catherine, but they sayin' plenty of 'em now. And every other word, almos'—it's jubilee. Jubilee comin'—"

Did that mean only a celebration of new freedom? Jeremiah wondered. Or was it a code word that included reprisals?

Wherever he went on the plantation, he kept his sheathed knife in his boot.

iv

After the final trip back from the cache about midday on Saturday, Jeremiah was in the barn unhitching the mules when a long shadow fell across the matted straw on the floor. He turned; caught his breath—

Price was leaning in the entrance, arms folded.

"You and Leon sure been busy, mister soldier."

"Listen, Price! You know my name."

"Reckon I don't have to use it, though. Reckon I don't have to do anything you say with those Yanks so close. What you and Leon hidin' back in the pines 'sides cotton?"

"Go ask Mrs. Rose!"

The anger didn't ruffle the black.

"Oh, I doubt she'd tell me. Whatever you're puttin' away, I bet the Yanks find it. They goin' to find you too. 'Less of course you plan to hide out."

"Price, one more goddamn word out of you—"

A chuckle. "An' what? You get after me? You tear into me? Any time, mister soldier. Any time you want, you welcome to try."

He unfolded his arms, started away, then paused:

"Yanks gonna get you. Oh, yes, you bet they are." The brown pupils seemed to grow larger. "If they don't, I will."

"Price, how come you despise me so much?"

The forced calm in Jeremiah's voice brought a smirk to the other man's face. "Why, that's easy. You one of the soldiers been fightin' to keep me property 'stead of a free man."

"Bullshit."

Startled, Price raised an eyebrow. "How's that?"

"You heard. Here's the way I figure it. For you, being property's only an excuse. The day you brought me here, I saw how you scowled at the mama of that little girl who ran to see your turtle. I think you like people to be scared of you. Nigra, white, I don't think it makes a particle of difference so long as you keep 'em scared. I bet there's not one damn person in creation you do like—or would ever treat kindly. I met a couple of officers in the army just like you."

"Mister soldier, you think whatever you want. That won't change the way things come out 'tween us."

"Just how do you propose to fix me, Price? With my musket?"

The black put on a pious expression whose exaggeration was almost ludicrous:

"*Musket?* You still got a notion I stole *that?*" A soft, clucking sound indicated how pathetic he found the idea. "I don't need no musket, mister soldier."

He held up both hands, sunlight behind him shining between his fingers.

"Just need these."

He sauntered out of sight, his shrinking, distorted shadow lying at an angle across the straw at the barn entrance for what seemed like half a minute after he himself had disappeared.

# CHAPTER 8

## *With Serena*

CATHERINE ROSE had more than a thousand dollars in Confederate bills in her office. On Saturday, Jeremiah locked the bills in a trunk in the steaming attic, along with pouches of valuable papers: deeds; ledgers; the colonel's will. Downstairs, he returned the key to Catherine, who put it back on the ring with the others.

New padlocks had been hastily obtained from Louisville the day before. Jeremiah and Leon installed them on the doors of the gin house, corn cribs, and barns. As though locks could stop Sherman's men!

But doing something was better than doing nothing, especially when the highway had begun to show increased activity.

Poor farm families, slaveless, passed in rickety wagons, fleeing the county. A Home Guards unit consisting of twelve elderly men and four boys marched by. Eight horsemen wearing yellow-faced gray arrived—a contingent of General Wheeler's cavalry. As they watered their horses at the trough near the well they reported the situation was worse than anyone had imagined.

Sherman's sixty thousand were sweeping across the state on a broad front. In its wake the army left burned buildings, ruined fields, slaughtered livestock, and occasionally—one of the troopers whispered to Jeremiah—raped women.

The leader of the cavalrymen warned Catherine Rose to leave the plantation. She thanked him for his concern, said no, and sent the riders on their way.

ii

Late Sunday afternoon Jeremiah was on his knees in the sitting room, using his knife to cut a slit in the back of an expensive horsehair sofa.

Once the cut was made, Catherine started to hand him the family silver. He slid each piece through the slit and worked it down into the sofa's stuffing. Perhaps eighty or ninety pieces were jammed in before he pushed the sofa back against the wall.

He walked around in front and sat, deliberately letting his weight come down hard. The sofa clinked and jingled like some peculiar musical instrument.

"God a'mighty!" he sighed. "Any Yank sits here, he'll discover the silver right off."

"I'm hoping they'll be decent enough not to intrude into the house—" Catherine began, interrupted abruptly by a distant crackling.

Jeremiah dashed to one of the open windows, jerked the curtains aside, stuck his head out into the sunlight. He heard the crackling again.

"That's musketry!"

Catherine turned pale. She and Jeremiah rushed outside, joined a moment later by Serena, who appeared around a corner of the house. They stared at the lane, the highway, the fields beyond. The crackling was repeated a third time, but more faintly.

Jeremiah wiped sweat from his forehead and turned to Rose's widow: "Wherever they are, they're close. I'd better take the wagon and mules into the pines. Where's Leon?"

"I sent him down to the bottom to hide three crates of chickens."

"All right, I'll go alone."

"Let me help," Serena volunteered, startling him.

Although it was the Sabbath, the girl wore an everyday cotton dress. Catherine had decided not to waste time attending church services in Louisville.

The day was warm, with a languid, summery feel unusual for the end of November. A haze hung in the air and a sultry breeze blew. As Jeremiah scanned the blurred contours of the land to the north and west, he suddenly spied something that made his belly hurt.

He pointed. Serena strained on tiptoe. Finally Catherine saw it too. A thin, almost invisible streak of black smoke rising beyond the trees along the Ogeechee, an oblique mark across the reddening afternoon sky.

Catherine pressed a fisted hand to her chin. "Something's on fire."

"We'd better go right now," Jeremiah said. "I'll hitch the mules."

"You'll need help with that too," Serena said, surprising him again. She didn't seem the sort for physical labor. Her duties during the last couple of days had been limited to light tasks, including the gathering of pieces of jewelry, which Catherine had put into a small leather bag she wore beneath her skirt. The bag was fastened around her waist by a length of rope. Naturally Jeremiah hadn't seen the bag. Serena had described it.

He couldn't get over the change warm weather and tension had produced in the girl. Dirt smudged one cheek. Sweat rings showed at the armpits of her dress. Somehow, though, her untidy state didn't detract from her prettiness; actually seemed to enhance it by lending her a more human, less remote quality.

She dashed for the house. "I'll fetch a shawl. It'll be cool by the time we walk back."

Staring after her, Jeremiah again chided himself for his interest in the girl. The interest was even more foolish and harder to explain in the light of what he already knew about her temperament.

Maybe the attraction had nothing to do with Serena personally. Maybe it was just a normal combination of curiosity and inexperience with the opposite sex. Yet he doubted that. He found himself wondering how Serena's body looked, naked, beneath all those clothes.

Not just any woman's body. *Hers.*

He had difficulty dealing with his feelings about her. Turning his back on her at Thanksgiving dinner had compensated for earlier slights, and he'd tried to start off the next day fresh—as though nothing unpleasant had happened earlier. She too had behaved differently; had actually been cordial a few times. And when a mood was on her—a mood that prohibited cordiality—at least she didn't act contemptuous of him. He suspected one possible reason for her change, but preferred not to think about it.

He didn't exactly *like* Serena. Not in the way you liked a friend; a camp comrade. Yet he was attracted to her, even though caution suggested it was unwise. Caution, however, came from the head. His interest lay in another direction entirely. He felt an embarrassing stir in his groin when he thought of riding alone with her into the pines.

Catherine seemed to have no objection to their going off together. She was preoccupied, watching the smoke rise in the west:

"Damn them if they're burning private property! *Damn* them for making war on homes and farms!"

Surprised by her use of profanity, he offered another of his reassurances:

"We won't let them do it here, Mrs. Rose." But it was becoming more a hope than a certainty.

For a moment he forgot Serena, imprisoned again by the kind of despairing mood that had gripped him when Rose spoke to him just before he died. There was no honor in this scurrying around to hide family possessions. Hell, it was downright disgraceful!

He stared at the column of smoke and tried to convince himself it didn't mean what it seemed to mean. And he silently repeated his vow to stand up to the Yanks if they came, and demand they deal honorably with the residents of Rosewood.

iii

Bess and Fred, the mules, were balky. Jeremiah was glad to have Serena's assistance in hitching them.

She'd combed her hair, pinned her shawl to her bodice with a brooch, and put on cologne. He caught her scent as he maneuvered the wagon out of the barn. Serena closed the door, padlocked it, and climbed up beside him, sitting so close on the splintered seat he could practically feel her leg beneath her skirt.

He drove straight down the dirt track between the slave cabins. Beside one of them, Price rested in the shade. He surveyed the wagon without a flicker of expression. Jeremiah shook the reins to speed the mules:

"Damn it, why's he lying around as if he doesn't have a care?"

"He doesn't," Serena said. "The Yanks are almost here. Besides, what else is there to do except wait?"

"He would have to see us drive off! He'll know where we've hidden the wagon. He's probably found the cache already."

"Leon wouldn't tell him."

That relieved him a little. "You're right. And Leon's the only other one who knows."

"Leon's trustworthy. He's behaving himself too. Some of the rest are getting more and more sassy. In the kitchen just this morning, Maum Isabella had to slap Francy. She sauced me when I gave an order. I slapped her once myself for good measure."

She sounded pleased about it.

Serena began to hum. It took Jeremiah a few moments to recognize the melody. The way she speeded it, the hymn sung at her father's memorial service sounded more like a minstrel tune. Lord, what an odd one she was!

He reached down to his boot to make sure the sheathed knife was secure. The wagon rolled by the slaves' burial ground and back toward the dark privacy of the pines.

Once into the relatively cool shade of the trees, he began to feel increasingly nervous. The mules plodded. A fly deviled his cheek. He brushed at it several times, then tried a slap. The fly disappeared. All at once Serena stopped humming and leaned against him:

"Jeremiah."

"Yes?"

Softly: "I'm mighty glad you came from Atlanta."

The touch of her shoulder started his loins quivering in that embarrassing way. He squinted down the weed-grown track. "Is that right? I had a notion it didn't make a bit of difference to you."

"You were wrong. It does."

"Well, Miss Serena, you'll forgive me, but for a day or two, you surely didn't act like it."

"I was all upset! Because of Papa. I loved Papa more than anybody on this earth."

It might be true, he thought, but it didn't change the fact that she'd undergone an almost complete reversal.

"Besides—"

She slipped her hand between his elbow and his ribs, linking her arm with his. In the silence of the woods—silence interrupted by another far-off stutter of gunfire—he felt nervous and hot. Her cologne even masked the scent of the pines. The pointed firmness of her left breast pressed his arm.

"—we need a man on the place. Women just can't control a bunch of unruly niggers."

"Price is the one to worry about. When he wouldn't confess to stealing my Enfield, we should have locked him up."

"Or shot him," Serena said in a matter-of-fact way. He was stunned; he'd had the identical thought, but he wouldn't have spoken it to anyone.

"Too bad we didn't have another gun," she added.

Recovering, he said, "I'll keep watching him."

He had doubts about his ability to cope with the black on a man-to-man basis, though. He was rapidly regaining his strength. The bandaged wound on his leg troubled him less and less often. But he had no illusions about Price being a weakling. And he recalled the threat in the barn:

*"Yanks gonna get you. If they don't, I will."*

To impress her and reinforce his own determination, he added, "If any of those Yanks show up, we'll just have to talk to 'em straight and tell 'em we expect decent treatment."

Serena giggled.

"What's so blasted funny?"

"Sometimes you *are* priceless! You think Yankees'll act polite just because we ask?"

*I have to believe that. It's one of the reasons I'm here. Where I came from, there was no honor left. Not after your father died.*

"Yes, I do. They damn well better respect civilian territory. They will, Serena. I'll bet that every place there's been trouble, people have provoked them."

"Now you sound exactly like Catherine," she sighed as the wagon rounded a bend.

The mules flicked their ears to drive off the huge blue flies. The slow, lazy rhythm of the hoofs, the fragrance of her cologne, the isolation, and the feel of her breast touching his sleeve drove him into a state of almost uncontrollable excitement.

At the same time he felt uneasy; endangered, somehow. But it was a sharp, sweet danger, tinged with the lure of the unknown. Tense as he was, he wouldn't have stopped the wagon for a minute.

Yet he did stop it all at once, his tongue stuck in his cheek and his head cocked.

Serena frowned. "What's the trouble?"

He put a finger to his lips. Cold-eyed, he pointed off to the right. Whispered:

"Thought I heard something."

"Jack rabbits."

"No. Louder. Heavier."

They listened. He was sure he hadn't been wrong. But the telltale rustling of pine needles and the rattle of disturbed underbrush wasn't repeated. He hawed softly to the mules and set the wagon rolling again.

iv

Serena gazed at dusty bars of sunlight slanting between the trees:

"Getting late. It'll be dark before we're finished."

"Maybe not," he muttered. The notion of being alone with her after nightfall had become almost too nerve-racking to bear.

"Know something, Jeremiah? For a long time Catherine thought Price was the best buck on the place."

"She made a mistake."

A curt laugh. "Not her first. She always thinks the best of everybody. There was only one person she never thought well of."

"Who?"

"My real mama."

The words had an unforgiving sound. He let her go on:

"I heard Catherine arguing about it with Papa once. He said my mama was a lady, a private music teacher, and Catherine wasn't to forget it. But she said he was a liar. Said the kind of lessons my mama gave didn't take place on any old piano stool."

He nearly laughed, but was thankful he hadn't when Serena turned to look at him. Her blue eyes were smoldering:

"She called my mama a filthy name."

"What was it?"

"I won't repeat it. Why, you know a lady isn't even supposed to say she has legs. She has *limbs*. Once Catherine and I had a real fuss over that, too. But she did call my mama a filthy name."

He risked the question:

"Did she call your mother that name without any cause?"

"Makes no difference! She was my *mama*!"

Silence for a while. He'd overstepped. But Serena's anger was evidently directed at Catherine for the moment. Sounding melancholy, she continued:

"I've never even seen a picture of her. There was a picture in the house at one time, but it was burned. Papa said Catherine burned it. Believe me, Catherine isn't as pure and forgiving as she lets on!"

"I've never met a perfect person yet, Serena. You should be able to understand why your stepmother isn't wild about your father's first wife. When my mother remarried, my father felt the same way about her new husband."

"*But Catherine didn't have to use a filthy word!* I can't forgive her for that. Ever!"

She drew a deep breath.

"One of these days I'm going to pay her back."

The soft, quiet statement sent another shiver chasing down his spine. He recognized the cruelty in the words because he was tainted with a cruel streak himself.

Serena stared straight ahead. "Guess it must have been true about Mama. But Catherine didn't have to say it. That's the point—she *said* it."

"Did she ever say it to you?"

"Yes indeed. After I overheard the conversation with Papa, I marched right in to see her—she'd been helping herself to that wine she takes on the sly—and we went at it for the best part of half an hour. She called Mama that filthy name right to my face!"

"Well, I'm beginning to understand why you and Mrs. Rose don't get along too well," he said with a humorless smile.

Her teasing had a wicked undertone:

"Why, Jeremiah Kent, you're quicker than I thought!"

Stung, he retorted, "Thanks for such a kind compliment."

"Oh, I didn't mean to anger you."

She raised her head; pecked his cheek. Her lips felt warm and moist.

"Truly I didn't."

To cover his awkwardness, he batted at another fly buzzing near his ear. The pines were growing darker, suffused by the sun's deep red. It seemed too early in the day for sunset, he thought, though it *was* almost December. Back home in Virginia, there might have been a light frost by now.

Serena perked up a little: "I won't have to fret about Catherine forever, though. She'll go to her grave eventually and I'll be free of her. I'll have a good husband—"

He was relieved to have an opportunity to drop the subject of Serena's stepmother. In a lighter tone, he responded:

"Got one picked already?"

She shook her head. "But I know what I want. A man with some money. Money he's willing to use to make more money. Papa's father and grandfather had the knack. They knew how to buy up land. Increase the crop yields. Papa bought a little more acreage for Rosewood, but he was happiest just standing still. He kept the place almost the same as it was when he inherited it. I want a man with bigger ideas. One who won't be content sitting in an office going over books—or reading ghost stories for excitement in the evening. I want a man who can run Rosewood right!"

Jeremiah grinned. "You're talking as if it's already yours."

"It will be when Catherine dies—same as with that California gold mine you spoke about. With Rosewood and my husband's money, we'll be able to build a really big place. Travel, too. Into Savannah to the Pulaski House. Maybe to Europe. I'll find a man like that, I know I will. I know because I can offer a man a lot—"

She gave him an almost brazen smile.

"Rosewood and some other nice things. Provided he treats me right."

"I—" He was almost afraid to speak. "I think it'd be grand to treat you right. Take you places—I mean it'd be grand for that husband you're talking about."

Disappointment: "Oh."

"Now what'd I do?"

"Nothing. Guess I had the wrong idea."

"What idea?"

"For a minute I had a notion you might be talking about yourself."

He couldn't help blushing. "Oh, no. You're older than I am."

"But you've been to war! That ages a boy pretty fast I'm told."

He was at a loss to explain her sudden warmth except for one reason he'd been trying to forget: the Thanksgiving day conversation about how he and his brothers would be wealthy men when Jephtha Kent passed on.

He'd always been aware in a vague way that his father would leave him a considerable amount of money. But he'd hardly ever dwelled on the consequences of the inheritance; what he'd do with it, or how it could make him important to others. Now, for almost the first time, he began to understand.

With the realization there came questions:

How much money *would* be his? Thousands of dollars? Millions? He couldn't comprehend *millions*, except that it must be a devil of a lot.

It would be good money, too. Gold, not cheapened Confederate paper. *Millions!*

He was a bit overcome by the thought—then disgusted by the realization that he'd been right about the reason for Serena's changed behavior. He wanted to let her know he was aware of the reason. Something held him back; perhaps the way she squeezed his arm again as the wagon creaked deeper into the hazy shadow of the pines.

*Tell her you know!*

He faced her but still couldn't say it, overcome by the bold, almost inviting way she was gazing at him. Smiling—

Lord above, she was a beautiful girl! That was the problem.

Leaning near again, she whispered, "I imagine a boy becomes pretty experienced in a war, doesn't he, Jeremiah?"

"Y-yes," he said, not knowing how to respond to the obvious meaning of the question. "In only one day at Chickamauga, I learned how to stay alive."

She made a moue. "I meant experienced in other ways."

His tongue felt stiff. "Women—things like that?"

"'Course."

"Well, I suppose—yes, it's true," he lied. Aware of the immorality of speaking to a female about the unspeakable, he still blurted, "How about you?"

"Jeremiah, that's not a proper thing to ask a girl!"

But she was pleased.

Blushing again: "I—I was just curious."

"Decent young ladies don't do such things—and if they do, they don't discuss them!" Tormenting him with her sly smile, she peered down the track and thrust out a finger. "Isn't that your cache?"

Jeremiah squeezed his legs together to hide the stiffness, furious at her for leading him on, yet thankful at the same time that she hadn't permitted things to go further. Something in his mind kept warning him:

*Leave her alone. She's too deep. Too devious.*

*And she's not innocent—*

A part of him longed to believe she was. He was frightened anew by the intensity of that yearning.

"I said, isn't that your cache?"

He nodded, dry-lipped. He just didn't know how to handle a girl like Serena Rose.

The mules meandered into the little clearing, all but dark now. Awkwardly, he separated his arm from hers. Guided the mules to a stop:

"We'll unhitch 'em and tie 'em, and I'll fork out some of the fodder Leon and I brought in. Then you can give me a hand pushing the wagon out of sight."

He spoke very quickly to cover his flustered feeling. He looped the reins around the brake handle and climbed down.

Serena slid to the side of the wagon where he stood. She bent over, her bosom touched by dull red light seeping through the pines. She looked down at him, her tongue licking slowly over her upper lip.

She extended her arms:

"You'll have to help me."

He reached up, too eagerly. She stood, suddenly appeared to stumble or lose her balance—no accident, he was sure.

Crying out, she tumbled on top of him.

# CHAPTER 9

## *Red Sky*

THEY SPRAWLED on the ground. He started to roll away, his neck prickled by a burr, only to feel her hand on his chin.

She pulled him close; so close they were lying side by side, thighs touching. Her hand slipped to his cheek:

"Jeremiah, you listen to me. The day you showed up, I thought you were just a boy. I was wrong. You're a grown man."

Her mouth came nearer.

"If you want, you can kiss me."

He did—tentatively. All at once she pressed both palms against his face. With tantalizing slowness, she caressed his lips with her tongue.

Then she moved her body tighter against his, giggling again, this time because of the feel of his bigness.

"Here, *here!*"

She guided his hand; closed it on her breast. His fingers were clamped so tightly, he thought he could detect lace beneath her faded dress.

"Maybe I could give you lessons like the ones my mama gave. But you were in the army. I 'spose you don't need them—"

Another kiss. Harder; deeper.

"You've probably had lots of girls."

And another. Her wet mouth slid up over his cheek. The tip of her tongue teased his skin.

"You probably don't even like me much because of the foolish way I treated you the first couple of days."

They lay in almost total darkness. Over her shoulder, he glimpsed the mules' ears twitching away flies.

*Get away!* he thought. *She's all tangled up inside. About her real mother, and her stepmother—and she doesn't give a hang for you, it's that money she found out about—*

"Jeremiah, Jeremiah," she murmured, beginning to move her left leg beneath her skirt. The leg rubbed slowly, languorously against his. "Do you like me any at all?"

"A lot, Serena—a lot." The feel of her leg turned him so rigid he hurt.

"You're not fibbing to me?"

"No. No."

All at once he knew they wouldn't stop. Knew it as surely as he knew his name.

She'd had other lovers before; or at least there was reason for suspicion. The way she talked. The practiced touch of her hands. And he didn't want his first experience to happen with a soiled woman. Despite the way soldiers bragged, no decent man wanted that.

Yet something perverse in him refused to call a halt to the kissing and fondling. He wanted to discover how experienced she was. And answering that question would answer a larger one: How did a man behave with a woman? Any woman?

Her lashes were soft on his cheek as she clasped his wrist and tugged. Somehow her skirt had hiked up.

"You can feel me if you want."

He did, pressing hard against the cotton underclothes until she moaned. He almost yelled when she put her hand on him in a way he'd never imagined any woman would be so bold as to do. She kissed his ear, murmuring:

"You'd be a good husband, I'll bet. A fine husband."

He tried to comprehend all the implications of that astonishing word. They were too many and complex. And now wasn't the time. He flung a leg over her hip—

Instantly, she rolled her head to the side. He saw red light reflected in her pupils.

"What's wrong, Serena?"

"Just wait a minute."

"But I thought—"

"*Wait* a minute!"

Fury then: "Damn it, I thought you wanted—"

"'Course I do! I want it as badly as you! Just calm down a little! I noticed the sky all at once—"

She struggled to sit up. "What time is it?"

Still frustrated, he growled, "How should I know? I don't own a watch."

"Look over there. The sun's down but the sky's all red."

He jumped up, realizing what it might mean.

He ran to the west edge of the clearing. He could see little through the pines except the seepage of scarlet light that encompassed almost half of the hidden horizon.

Jolted back to his senses, he swallowed. "Serena—" He wiped his face. "That's not sun, that's fire."

"Dear God!"

She scrambled to her feet, knocking bits of weed from her skirt and raking two burrs from her red hair.

"Is it the soldiers?"

"I don't know. We'd better hurry back."

He was angry about the interruption. She sensed it, and raised her head to give him an almost chaste kiss on the lips.

"Yes, we'd better. I'm sorry. There'll be times later—"

"Will there?"

"If you want it."

*No, I don't! There's something tangled and wrong about—*

The loveliness of her face overwhelmed him:

"I do."

He slipped his arms around her waist for one more fierce kiss. Then they set to unhitching Bess and Fred, hurriedly tying them on long tethers and forking out fodder. Finally, shoving and straining, they rolled the wagon tongue-first into the brush.

They couldn't conceal all of it. The back still jutted into the clearing. Jeremiah pulled out his knife and whacked off pine boughs to cover most of it. He smelled smoke now, drifting out of the west.

He checked the lean-to where the household items had been stored, then caught Serena's hand and raced toward the track. They ran through the dark of the pines, stumbling in weedy patches, their faces lashed by branches not seen soon enough.

The smell of smoke grew stronger. The red glare in the night sky brightened.


ii


As they hurried up the lane between the slave cottages, he breathed hard, pain stabbing his chest because of the long run. His bandaged leg ached. Serena clung to his arm, barely keeping pace.

He grew aware of a stir and buzz on the porches of the cottages. An infant bawled. He heard a palm strike. The baby shrieked louder. He groped for Serena's hand and practically dragged her toward the house.

Probably not one buck, woman, or youngster was sleeping tonight. He sensed rather than saw them sitting or standing in small groups in the darkness—whispering and pointing at the glow in the west.

Twice he heard laughter. Some of the nigras weren't frightened at all. The red sky was a signal. *Jubilee!*

When he and Serena started across the rear piazza, a figure bolted from the shadows and ran at them. Serena screamed.

### iii

Jeremiah whirled her behind him—then breathed easier, recognizing Leon's hulking shoulders.

"Marse Jeremiah?"

"Not now, Leon."

"Yes, you got to listen! Price—he's gone."

"*What?*"

"That's right. Nobody seen him since just after you drove off in the wagon. He must of run away when he heard the Yanks was so close."

"We're better off rid of him." Serena declared.

Jeremiah gestured her silent. "Did you tell Mrs. Rose?"

Leon shook his head. "Didn't want to upset her. Things bad enough already."

He grimaced. "If we're lucky, Price is on his way to the blessed freedom of Linkum land."

"Marse Jeremiah, we ain't that lucky. I bet he's hidin' out in the pines, plottin' mischief."

A shudder rippled across Jeremiah's back. He tried to sound unworried: "Thank you for warning us, Leon. Come on, Serena. Hurry!"

### iv

They ran straight through the house and out to the drive, where he'd heard voices and glimpsed a spill of lamplight.

Holding the light, Maum Isabella looked surprisingly composed. So did Catherine. The same couldn't be said for the wispy woman in faded bombazine who was seated in the hooded chaise.

The woman swayed from side to side, sweaty faced and fanning herself with a kerchief. Jeremiah would have chuckled at the woman's expression, except that he knew she was fearfully frightened.

Next to her sat a haggard Judge Claypool. Two scruffy nigras, each lugging an old portmanteau, stood immediately behind the chaise. As Jeremiah and Serena approached, Claypool exclaimed:

"—not staying a moment longer!"

"Where are you going?" Catherine asked.

"Savannah. Nell has a sister there. If you have any brains, you'll get out too."

For a moment Catherine Rose didn't reply. She turned slightly, acknowledging the presence of Jeremiah and her stepdaughter. Her gray, fatigue-shadowed eyes remained calm until she noticed Serena's mussed shawl, dusty skirt, and tangled hair.

Catherine said nothing. But she gave Serena a steady, knowing look. Her face seemed to sadden, then firm again as she returned her attention to the judge:

"No, Theodore. We'll stay."

"I swear to God, Catherine—" The old man snatched his wife's kerchief and swabbed the perspiration glistening in the white stubble on his chin. The abrupt movement shifted his coat, revealing the holstered horse pistol. "—you have no idea of how many there are. Hundreds. Thousands! All around Louisville. On foot. On horseback. In wagons—the damn wagons are loaded with stolen furniture! Why the hell does an army need furniture? I saw soldiers carrying chicken coops, others leading livestock. They're taking everything! And some of the stragglers—why, you've never laid eyes on such scum!"

"Theodore," she broke in, "this is my home, I'd rather try to defend it than leave."

"Same thing that witless Clive Jesperson said ten minutes ago!"

"Clive Jesperson is right. If we leave, everything will be gone for certain."

"Well, it's your decision. But you'd better get rid of any wines and spiritous liquors because I hear the Yanks want alcohol almost as much as they want food."

"I'll take your advice, thank you."

"Ought to take all of it and *get out!*"

Claypool noticed Jeremiah watching him with disapproval. He blurted: "Nell's heart isn't strong. I'd stay, but I don't feel it's fair to risk—"

"We understand perfectly," Catherine put in, saving him from humiliation. She turned to the ragged blacks: "Floyd—Andrew—you look after Judge Claypool and his wife. Go on now, Theodore. We'll be fine."

Finally, Mrs. Claypool spoke:

"You're foolish, Catherine. Foolish! God be merciful over your mistake."

Claypool was almost incoherent with frustration:

"Isn't the Almighty she needs to beg for mercy, it's General Sherman! *Giddap!*"

He lashed the reins over the back of his horse, nearly tumbling his panicked wife into the drive as the chaise lurched forward and took the curve with its right wheels lifting off the fine-crushed stone. A moment later the chaise was rattling down the lane toward the highway, the two blacks with the portmanteaus running and puffing behind.

Jeremiah heard the gate open. Someone disturbed the bell rope. The bell tolled once. The mournful echo was a long time dying.

Slowly, the carriage noise faded in the broad band of darkness lying on the land. At the upper edge—treetop level—the darkness shaded from maroon to vivid scarlet. The light shifted constantly; glimmering feebly in one quarter of the sky; intensifying in another. Smoke blew, blurring the distant trees. The wind carried the stench. It came most strongly from the left; from heavy woodlands through which the highway curved tortuously before breaking into the open in front of Rosewood.

"It's the Jesperson place," Catherine whispered. "That's where the smoke is. Oh, poor Mr. Jesperson! He's worked all his life to build that little patch into a decent farm."

Jeremiah hardly heard. He was most concerned about the darkness. Unseen, the Yanks were approaching through it. Unseen, Price might be lurking in it.

*With that damn gun!* he thought, feeling for one ghastly moment just as terrified as he had when he'd first climbed toward Union marksmen at Chickamauga.

# CHAPTER 10

## The Prisoner

ON THE MONDAY MORNING following Thanksgiving, hundreds of miles to the north, Gideon Kent sat cross-legged among the all but silent Confederate officers who formed a ring around the single small stove in the barracks.

During the night the weather had changed. Severe winds out of the northwest had brought snowflakes whirling down on the island the local residents called Pea Patch. The wind speared through dozens of ill-fitting joints in the boards of the shed-like structure.

The barracks had been Gideon's home for six months. The sergeant in charge of this particular pen had lit the stove about half an hour earlier—nine thirty—after tossing in a handful of wood chips. One handful. And he'd done it smiling that unctuous smile Gideon had come to loathe:

"There, boys. Don't say Father Abraham doesn't care about your welfare. You'll be cozy all day and all night too."

A couple of officers had muttered obscene replies. But not loudly. By now, most of the inmates were well acquainted with the temperamental idiosyncrasies of Sergeant Oliver Tillotson. Staying safe in the state that passed for living was just slightly preferable to risking Tillotson's wrath.

The sergeant was always cheerful when he dispensed items necessary for mere survival. A few stove chips or the morning's ration of three hardtacks were presented as though he expected the prisoners to be grateful for his generosity, and by extension, that of the commandant, Brigadier General Schoepf.

Tillotson dealt harshly with complaints. Some said he patterned his behavior after the officer who controlled the island. This Gideon couldn't verify. He'd only seen Schoepf once, from a distance, as the commandant was entering the little Gothic chapel built, ironically enough, by the so-called chain gang: murderers, thieves, and deserters from the Union army who were kept at Fort Delaware along with the Confederate prisoners. Unfortunately he saw Tillotson every day except the Sabbath.

The stove's iron door stood wide open. Yet the heat did almost nothing to dispel the chill in the shed. Gideon's teeth started to chatter. He clenched them. It helped a little.

He'd wakened well before daylight, vainly struggling to find warmth by readjusting his one small, worn blanket. The blanket was folded so half of it cushioned his feet and calves and the other half covered them. But the blanket, now draped over his shoulders, and the grimy overcoat and the filthy clothing beneath, couldn't begin to restore heat to his emaciated body; not even with Tillotson's largesse blazing inside the stove.

The thin paperbound book he was attempting to read slipped from his stiffening hands. Around him he heard the Confederate officers speaking in quiet, resigned voices. Discussing what they always discussed:

How long the war would last.

How they were unlucky enough to be captured and sent to the most feared prison in all the North.

Their loved ones.

And escape. That was a truly laughable subject.

Ridiculous rumors circulated on the island at least once a week. Most sprang from the occasional issues of *The Palmetto Flag*, a pro-Southern newspaper published up the river in Philadelphia. *The Flag* was not permissible reading for the prisoners. But they heard from certain guards that it hinted more than once that the twelve thousand Confederate inmates might break out and seize the whole river corridor.

*Which twelve thousand?* Gideon usually asked himself when he heard the latest story. *Last month's? Or this month's?* The population of the island in the Delaware River was constantly changing. New prisoners arrived; former ones who hadn't survived the dirt and foul food and sporadic physical abuse were flung into pits in Salem County, over on the Jersey shore. When the air was clear, a man allowed up on the dikes could look out and see gravediggers preparing new pits. The work never stopped.

In Gideon's opinion, if the sponsors and writers of *The Palmetto Flag* wanted an insurrection, they'd have to plan and conduct it themselves. The prison population contained few men strong enough to fight anyone for longer than fifteen or twenty seconds; it required all of a man's depleted strength and mental stability just to endure from day to day.

Growing colder, Gideon gave up trying to read. He let his eyes drift around the circle. Did the other men feel as dispirited and miserable as he?

Most looked as if they did, though there were exceptions. Two officers on the opposite side of the ring, for example. Hughes and Chatsworth. They were disliked by the rest of the inmates of the pen because both had come to Fort Delaware with an ample, and unexplained, supply of Yankee currency. No doubt they had wealthy and influential relatives in the North. In any case, the two had quickly formed an alliance.

With their money Hughes and Chatsworth could solicit extra favors from Tillotson. They bought slivers of soap they refused to share. At the moment they were playing checkers with pebbles. Their board was a section of siding marked off with charcoal. They'd paid Tillotson fifteen dollars for the piece of lumber, and made no secret of it.

The two officers sometimes rented the board to others. But the price was high. Part of the day's rations of each man who wanted an hour's game. There weren't many takers—nor much cordiality toward the profiteers. Hughes and Chatsworth took turns sleeping with the board so it wouldn't be stolen.

Near Gideon were four men much better liked. John Hunt Morgan's brothers, one a captain and one a colonel, were playing euchre with Cicero Coleman, late of the Eighth Kentucky Cavalry, and Hart Gibson, who'd been assistant adjutant general on John Morgan's staff.

John Hunt Morgan was dead now; they'd heard that in October. The audacious cavalryman had raided into the North, been captured, then escaped from a prison in Columbus, Ohio, only to be shot down in a minor skirmish near Greeneville, Tennessee. Another loss of an able man that was creating a disastrous pattern for the South.

Morgan might have been luckier than the rest of us, Gideon said to himself, his closed eyes watering. The book slid out of his lap. For a moment he was too listless to retrieve it from the rank-smelling straw littered on the floor. His mind was drawn along a steadily darkening current of thought:

*Might have been better to go quickly, like Stuart, instead of this way, one miserable hour at a time.*

He stretched, hoping the movement would stir him out of his depressed state. He knew he shouldn't permit himself to think such morbid thoughts. He'd worked hard to survive on this damned island by remembering his wife and his small daughter—and his consuming desire to start a new life once he was free.

He'd made an effort to use the time in prison constructively. Use it to continue to make up for the abysmal lack of knowledge that was his constant burden:

*If I don't know how to read well, and write well—how to think well when I walk out of this place—I won't be able to support Margaret and the baby with anything except menial work.*

For them, he wanted to be able to do more than that. So whenever he could, he read. Old issues of *Leslie's Illustrated Weekly*, or pro-Union newspapers from Wilmington and Philadelphia. Sergeant Tillotson passed them out now and then, but always as if he were some blasted millionaire bent on good works and wanting everyone to appreciate it. Tillotson inevitably made it a point to indicate the columns and the engravings dealing with Union successes in the field.

Gideon wished for one of the papers or a *Leslie's* right now. He couldn't concentrate on the peculiar unrhymed lines in the cheaply printed volume Tillotson had grudgingly delivered to him the day before Thanksgiving. The book had been oddly wrapped in a triple layer of brown paper bound with an inordinately long piece of twine.

Except for short topical verses contributed to Virginia papers, Gideon had read practically no poetry during his boyhood and adolescence. He'd found the first few pages of the work called *Leaves of Grass* beyond him.

And he'd been brutally disappointed when *Leaves of Grass* was all Tillotson had handed him; just one slim volume with a short message from his father folded and inserted next to the title page. He'd been hoping for a good-sized shipment of books; hoping for it ever since early November, when he'd received an already opened letter written from the parsonage of the small Methodist church on Orange Street in New York City, where Jephtha Kent had again taken up his original calling.

In the letter, Jephtha had described how difficult it had been to locate his son.

He'd begun his search after a note from Lexington reached him via a route he preferred not to describe. Gideon supposed the route was across the warring lines. He'd heard there was still a good deal of illegal trading and smuggling going on. At any rate, Fan had informed Jephtha their eldest son was a prisoner. She didn't know where.

Former newspaper contacts in Washington made inquiries. They reported to Jephtha that Major Gideon Kent was incarcerated along with other officers, enlisted men, civilian political prisoners, and Yankee felons on the island located where the Delaware River took a sharp, almost ninety-degree turn toward the southeast, below Wilmington.

Gideon hadn't wanted his reply to be read. His request might be snipped out by the censor. So he'd answered Jephtha with the help of an overworked, prickly-tempered physician from the prison infirmary. The doctor voluntarily visited the barracks every few days, checking on the health of the inmates. He was one of the few Yanks at Fort Delaware who seemed to give a damn about the captives—and he usually went away in bad spirits, grumbling and cursing over what he'd seen.

Gideon had persuaded the doctor to smuggle a sealed letter off the island in his satchel and post it. The letter asked Jephtha for books.

Presently a second communication from Jephtha arrived. It said he'd attempted to gain permission to visit his son. The permission had been de-

nied. Still, Jephtha's Washington contacts might at least make it possible
for Gideon to receive reading material. He'd gotten his son's letter. But
he'd wisely phrased the statement about books as if the idea were his own.

Thus, on the day before Thanksgiving, Tillotson had brought Gideon
the volume of poetry. "A gift from that Copperhead father of yours, sir."
Tillotson mockingly addressed all the officers in the shed as "sir."

The note the censor had allowed to remain in the book promised that
Jephtha would pass along any information he might unearth concerning
Gideon's two younger brothers. Their welfare was part of Gideon's con-
stant burden of fear:

He feared for Margaret and little Eleanor as Grant's war machine maneuvered toward Richmond.

But he feared for Matthew, too, vanished on a blockade runner.

And for Jeremiah, who'd mustered in and had been shipped on the cars
to the Army of Tennessee.

God, he said to himself, blue-lipped and shivering, how long can a man
last, not knowing what's happening to his loved ones?

How long can a man last that way—in a place like this?

The pessimistic thought was again counteracted by shame. When
they'd shipped him north in a fetid boxcar, he'd vowed he'd live through
the worst the Yanks could offer. But he'd had no notion of how bad the
worst could be.

His normal weight was a hundred and sixty pounds. He guessed he'd
lost at least thirty of those pounds by now. Flesh had been steadily
stripped from his tall frame by the inadequate rations: three hardtacks at
nine A.M., and three more in midafternoon, plus an occasional piece of
moldy bacon or a gill of watery slop Tillotson, with a straight face, called
rice soup.

And water. God above, what water!

During the baking summer, the prison tanks had nearly gone dry due to
a lack of rain. A water boat had run up nearby creeks to resupply them.
But the unspeakable stuff that came gushing out of the boat's hoses was
tainted with brine; the boat hadn't gone upstream far enough to escape
the salty tidewater.

And whenever the hoses refilled the tanks, the influx stirred a hideous
sediment in their bottoms. Once Gideon had tried a cup from a new supply and vomited when he saw bits of leaves in it, along with the eye of a
fish and several white worm-like creatures writhing in the murky fluid.

Now he drank water only when absolutely necessary. He also avoided
the stomach-turning delicacies to which some of the other officers had resorted in desperation.

This morning all the circumstances of life in the prison seemed to come down on him with a ferocious pressure.

The shed was so frigid he could barely move. His hunger, his physical weakness, the roughness of his unwashed skin—and the bitterness he felt because his father had only been able to send him one book of incomprehensible poetry—stirred a rage in him that was almost overpowering.

He yearned to strike out. But at what? At whom?

His captors? Old Tillotson?

Futile.

But trying to survive in this pestilential place was proving futile too. All through August he'd watched men sicken and die as the sun broiled the alluvial mud of the Pea Patch. Overloaded boats had carried corpses stacked like cordwood to the Jersey pits.

He'd seen hysterical men turn on their guards, only to be beaten half to death, then carried away to the infirmary. Those men disappeared too. The infirmary was said to be run on a reasonably humane basis. But the injuries dealt out to those who rebelled were usually too severe for repair; punishment for guards who defended themselves was nonexistent.

*Margaret,* he thought, the water in his half-closed eyes turning to tears. *Margaret, I've been trying to pull through this. Believe me I have. But you don't know how hard it is.*

His right hand fumbled beneath his filthy coat. Pressed the pocket of his uniform blouse almost unconsciously. His fingers probed until he found the reassuring contours of the scrap of cloth in which he carried the little memento of his daughter. A lock of her hair; it had been with him since a few days after she was born. Some prisoners kept Bibles or Testaments. The precious curl from Eleanor's head was his religious token.

Touching it through the dirty cloth of his uniform, he wished for the impossible—a less hostile war. One in which the hatreds hadn't built so steadily, until they affected every phase of the struggle.

Mounting hostility between the warring sides was responsible for so many men being imprisoned in this wretched condition. When the North had begun organizing army units of runaway blacks, Jefferson Davis had decreed that any such soldiers captured, as well as their white officers, were not to be treated as prisoners of war, entitled to exchange. They were to be returned to the states from which the slaves had escaped, there to be punished under local laws. In May of '63, General Halleck had responded by ordering exchanges halted altogether. When Grant had assumed command, he'd made certain Halleck's policy was strictly enforced.

And after the war—what then? Tillotson bragged that he was a "hard peace" Republican, as opposed to the re-elected Lincoln, who favored more compassionate terms as soon as the conflict ended, as it surely would, with the South defeated. When that happened, wouldn't the hostilities linger?

Hell, what did he care? He just wanted to *get through it*; survive this time and this place by reading, learning, filling his head with words and ideas that might help him start again when—*if*—he were ever shipped home to Richmond.

*If* there was still a Richmond.

The Yankees wanted that city worst of all. Wanted it captured; even destroyed.

And Margaret was there.

The shed and all it represented had become unbearable to Gideon. Painfully conscious of his lack of strength, he staggered to his feet, then apologized to another cavalryman, Colonel Basil Duke, for bumping into him. Red, exhausted eyes turned his way when he broke through the ring of men huddled around the stove and lurched away. No one spoke.

He stumbled down the dark aisle between the pine bunks, pausing beside his own to slip the book of poems under the folded blanket. Then he moved on toward the end of the building. To an open doorway; Tillotson's lamp-lit cubicle.

With a hand that felt like granite, he gripped the jamb of the door, gulping less poisonous air, and savoring the heat from Tillotson's stove. Because it was enclosed by thin walls, the stove concentrated a fair degree of heat in the tiny room. Oilcloth had been tacked over two drafty windows.

Oliver Tillotson glanced up from a copy of *Leslie's*. He was about sixty, overweight, but no weakling even though he was far too old for combat. He wore a holstered Colt on his hip. In front of him on the desk sat a small, cheaply framed photograph of a dour woman and five adolescent boys in stiff paper collars and ill-fitting suits. Next to the group portrait lay the symbol of authority Tillotson affected—a stick cut from a walnut limb; a stick darkened and worn smooth by the pressure of Tillotson's pudgy fingers.

The stick was two feet long, perhaps three inches in diameter. Gideon had seen it used on two officers in the barracks. One had complained to Tillotson about his arrogance and refused to be quiet when Tillotson ordered it. The other had found maggots in a piece of bacon and turned on the guard, screaming; berserk. Both men had been beaten, sent to the infirmary, and never seen again.

As Gideon leaned in the doorway soaking up the soothing heat, Tillotson frowned. The sergeant had a red Saint Nicholas face, the effect enhanced by a neatly trimmed white goatee, white brows, and hair. There was a deceptively benign look about him even when he was annoyed, as he was now:

"You wanted something, Captain?"

Tillotson played games. He knew most of his charges by name and rank. But he pretended they were indistinguishable one from another. As, indeed, they usually were: unwashed, like Gideon; emaciated, like Gideon; their beards down to mid-chest, like Gideon's; their eyes half wild and half cowed, like Gideon's.

"I'd like permission to take a turn outside," Gideon said in a voice hoarse from the cold.

Tillotson appeared bemused. "Outside, sir? But it's wintry—"

"It's no better in the barracks."

"You Rebs," Tillotson sighed. He laid *Leslie's* aside. Picked up the walnut stick. Pointed at the family portrait. "When I go home weekends, I tell Ethel how you complain. You never seem happy you're alive rather than dead. My, it's puzzling."

"Is it, now?" Gideon breathed. "I'm certainly sorry you're puzzled. Would it help if I asked whether you eat a decent meal now and then? Or go to bed under enough blankets so you can sleep eight hours without waking?"

With his left hand, Tillotson stroked the end of the stick. "Careful, please, Captain," he said with a broad smile.

"Major. *Major* Kent, and you know it."

"No, you all look alike to me." Tillotson shrugged, his blue eyes maliciously merry. "Just like the niggers you people have penned up and maltreated for over two hundred years. Kent. Kent—oh, yes. Now I remember. Our dedicated reader. Preparing himself for better things when the war's over. You received a book from your Copperhead papa in New York."

Gideon almost swore; fought the oath back. Tillotson clucked his tongue; shook his head:

"I glanced at that material before I delivered it. Nonsensical stuff. Filthy! Ethel and her circle of women at church have discussed that poet. He should be prohibited. He should be arrested. You'll never qualify yourself for anything, reading such swill."

Tillotson was leaning forward, as if offering advice to a nephew of whom he was fond. All at once, sarcasm crept in:

"I suppose such material is all right for Rebs, though. Appropriate to your humbled station. Sweets to the sweet, but dregs to the dregs, mightn't we say?"

A vein beat in Gideon's temple. "I asked for permission to go out, not for a lecture."

"Oh, but you Rebs *need* lecturing." Tillotson smiled. "You must be taught not to complain so much. I can't fathom why you don't like it here."

"Well, it isn't exactly a vacation resort, is it?"

A hostile look on the Christmas face. "And I suppose you fancy our Northern boys are enjoying a holiday in those sinkholes down South? Libby? Andersonville? I suppose you think they're resorts compared to this? You don't know when you're well off, Captain!"

Gideon was seething:

"*Major.*"

Tillotson slashed the stick in a swift arc and struck the desk, *thwack.*

"Captain, you're vexing me with your disrespect. I have a position of authority to maintain."

"The only one you've ever had, I expect."

Three rapid blinks and Tillotson's mouth shaped into a surprised O told Gideon he'd scored an accidental hit. The prison was full of incompetents; men worthless elsewhere. He'd seen a fair number of the same kind in the Confederate army. In all ranks.

But even incompetents would strike out if someone wounded them:

"Hold your tongue! Remember you're speaking to the Government! In this barracks, sir, I am just as important as Mr. Lincoln. More! You'll never set your traitorous eyes on our President. You deal with him through me."

Another whack of the stick emphasized the last word. Then a smile crept back on Tillotson's jowly face. But there was spleen in it. The spleen of a man thrust into a position in which a whim, a change of mind, a word or two could preserve or ruin other men's lives.

"Am I clear to you, sir?" Tillotson asked. "When you walk in here, you are dealing with the *only legal government of this nation.*"

Gideon's forehead slicked with sudden sweat. The fat, arrogant turd! He'd like to take him by the throat and—

*No! Remember Margaret. Remember the baby. You've got to come through this whole. If you love them it's your duty to survive.*

He blessed the memory of his wife and child. Without its sustaining power in that moment when he looked at Oliver Tillotson basking in the warmth of his private stove, he might have tried to kill the man.

"I say, *sir,* am I clear?"

Gideon answered very softly:

"Clear."

"Then ask again. Briefly and respectfully."

A deep breath. "I am requesting permission to take a turn outside."

Tillotson waved the walnut stick. "Much better, sir. *Much* better. Go freeze if you wish. But please close the door. I neglected to do it, and I wouldn't want too much heat escaping into the shed. Brisk temperatures are healthy for you and your comrades."

"Certainly," Gideon answered. "Everyone out there is reveling in the healthful cold."

Another venomous glance. "I'm delighted." A jab of the stick. *"Close the door."*

With a hand tingling one moment and going numb the next, Gideon obeyed. Tillotson had already returned to his reading.

ii

He walked out of the shed, passing between two boys in blue capes. Each sentry's rifle was equipped with a bayonet.

The clouds blowing by seemed only a few hundred feet overhead. Snowflakes swirled down from them. The bite of the wind made Gideon feel even worse than before. Almost immediately, his teeth started to chatter again. He regretted his decision to venture into the open. The sights outside the barracks were even more depressing than those within.

Fort Delaware had been built on a treeless slab of ground several feet below water level. Stone dikes blocked out the river, obstructing the view of the Jersey and Delaware shores. The frozen mud was crisscrossed with ditches that oozed subterranean water on warm days. And the other sheds and fenced enclosures stretching around him were packed with gray men. Gray-garbed, gray-faced, gray-spirited.

Ghosts.

He saw the pale oval of a motionless and sorrowing face framed in the window of one of the barracks. Several young boys were tramping up and down in front of the privates' pen, hugging themselves, stamping their bare feet. When shoes wore out, no replacements were issued.

Over near the Delaware side, the chain gang labored. Sullen, murderous-looking men. The men hauled large carts full of stones used to repair the dikes. Teams of two men were roped to each cart like human beasts of burden. The work of each team was directed by a guard who sat atop the stones piled in the cart, unconcerned about adding his extra weight. Most of the guards were alternately swearing at their charges and shouting at them to pull harder.

Gideon weaved toward a group of officers crouched beside a breathing hole dug out of the mud. There were similar holes everywhere; he threaded his way between.

One of the officers turned to acknowledge his arrival:

"Hallo, Kent. Care to join the hunting party?"

Gideon's stomach flip-flopped. "Thank you, no."

"Fresh meat and rat soup if we're lucky."

"Jesus, stop," Gideon said, covering his mouth. He was feeling more nauseated by the moment.

There was a sudden flurry of activity around the hole. Exclamations of glee. Men hunching forward. The crunch of rocks on bone, then pulping sounds. One of the officers laughed, the snow-flecked wind whipping the sound away quickly.

Another officer, no older than Gideon but with a beard already pure white, held up the bloody and still-twitching prize—a plump, hairy water rat. One of the hundreds that infested the island and dug their runs under the hard surface.

"Shouldn't be so persnickety, Gideon," said the officer who'd spoken first. "Doesn't taste half bad once you're accustomed to it."

The white-bearded officer agreed:

"Like young squirrel, in fact."

But he'd seen cooked rat meat. White; sickeningly white. He turned away:

"Thanks kindly for the invitation. Another time."

"You'll get hungry enough one of these days."

The devil! Gideon thought, staggering on. Tillotson had been right. It was too blasted cold out here.

He noticed a subtle change in the air. Stuck out his tongue. Caught a droplet of water.

The wind had shifted. A mist was blowing upriver from the Atlantic. The snowflakes were turning to freezing rain.

Gideon wiggled his toes inside his cracked boots. Little sensation. None in one big toe. He was better off inside.

He hurried, but all it amounted to was an awkward limp not much faster than his normal walk. As he approached the shed, a man came shooting around the corner, leaning into the wind and holding his flat-crowned black hat on his head.

The man's long gray beard danced on his shoulder, whipped like the ends of the green and black plaid scarf wound round and round his throat and the collar of his shabby, loose-sleeved raglan.

Gideon stepped aside, but tardily. The leather medical bag in the man's right hand gave his leg a sound whack.

The man jerked to a halt; squinted.

"Kent! Very sorry. Can't see too well without my spectacles."

"Morning, Dr. Lemon," Gideon replied, without annoyance. Dr. Cincinnatus Lemon of Delaware City was the man who'd listened to his plea for books, circumvented General Schoepf's strict regulations about the frequency of outgoing and incoming prisoner mail, and posted the letter to Jephtha.

"Been meaning to come by and look in on you," Dr. Lemon said in a voice louder than normal. He was past sixty. His hearing was failing along with his sight. "Something I wanted to ask."

A sharp look at the barracks sentries. "But not here." He risked letting go of his hat to seize Gideon's arm. "Come along to my office."

Relieved to have an excuse to stay out of the barracks a while longer, Gideon nodded. When the two started away, one of the sentries called, "Just a minute, Reb."

Dr. Lemon spun. "Just a minute, nothing! I'll take this prisoner anywhere I please!"

"But, Doctor, he's not allowed out of sight of—"

"He is if I say so. Shut your mouth and go dry your ears."

The sentry reddened. "Where are you taking him?"

"Why, I plan to spirit him into my office, squeeze him into an empty chloroform bottle, and float him down to the ocean and home to Dixie. Come along, Kent!"

While they crossed the yard, Lemon complained:

"Damned cheeky farm boys. Farm boys and doddering old farts, that's all we have on this island. Sorry to say those categories include me. Kent, will you hurry up? I'm freezing what freely translates from the Latin as my arse."

iii

A crowded little room in one wing of the infirmary building served as a communal office for several full- and spare-time physicians attached to the fort. The office was nearly as untidy as Dr. Lemon himself. But it had a stove with plenty of fuel. Gideon sank onto a stool two feet from the open door and raised his hands to the blessed warmth.

Lemon flung off his hat, scarf, and raglan and dumped his satchel on top of them in a corner. While he fished for his glasses in his patched frock coat, someone screamed in one of the wards. Lemon winced.

"Your commander—Stuart—he used to sing a lot, didn't he?"

"Yes, he did. Why?"

Lemon's spectacles sparkled with the flames from the stove as he seated himself at a desk strewn with supply requisitions and patient reports. "I doubt he'd have been so cheerful about this cursed war if he'd heard the music I listen to all day."

Gideon massaged his hands. Some of the numbness was leaving. "I'm afraid I sang right along with him."

"Damn fools, both of you. Americans killing Americans. It hardly calls for a cheery serenade."

"You're right. I decided the same thing after First Manassas—with a little prodding from the young woman I married. We should have stopped the war long before it began. I guess no one knew how."

"They knew. Old men like me—they knew. Some of 'em, anyway. But *they* didn't have to march off to war and die. All they had to do was stay home, pound podiums, and spew slogans. No matter which side you're on, that's inevitably more popular than trying to stop the waste of human life. The filthy, immoral waste of God's gift—"

Veined hands brushed aimlessly over the accumulated papers, as though Lemon couldn't bear to pick them up. The doctor's shoulders were permanently stooped, his face weather-darkened and creased by deep folds and shallow wrinkles. "I'll tell you what I wanted—"

He stopped in mid-sentence, studying Gideon. The younger man thought there was rheum in the doctor's eyes. Lemon whispered:

"Uncanny."

"Pardon?"

Lemon jabbed an index finger between his glasses and his nose, ridding his right eye of the glistening water.

"I said uncanny. I can never get accustomed to your appearance."

Gideon tried to smile. "Pretty disreputable, I admit."

"Not what I meant. Mrs. Lemon and myself, we have seven daughters and one son. *Had* one son. You could be his younger brother. We lost him at Antietam."

"I'm sorry to hear it."

"You'd be even sorrier if you knew who shot him."

"Who?"

"One of the men in his own damn company. Mistook him for a Reb."

"Just about what happened to Stonewall Jackson."

"Just about," Lemon agreed glumly. "My boy took a wound in the chest from a round ball. It damaged too large an area of lung tissue. A round ball always does. A conical ball from a rifled piece would have given him a chance. Cleaner wound. Less tissue destroyed. Conical balls are worse in the abdomen, though. Usually perforate the bowel. The round ball travels more slowly. Often pushes the bowel aside without harming it. It *had* to be a round ball in the lung—from one of his own!"

He closed his right hand into a fist and stared at the desk.

In a few moments he composed himself sufficiently to eye Gideon again:

"I must say you do look hideous. Not surprised, though. Here—"

He shot out of the chair, opened one of the glass doors of a cabinet cluttered with bottles of pills and tinctures, fished behind them and brought out an amber flask filled with a dark fluid.

"This'll warm you up. Take a fast swig in case someone comes in."

Gideon unstoppered the bottle. Inhaled the almost-forgotten aroma of whiskey. He tilted the bottle and swallowed, twice.

"Thank you, Dr. Lemon." He handed it back.

"Hippocrates is no doubt applauding me from the beyond," Lemon said, ramming the bottle into its hiding place and slamming the cabinet door. The glass vibrated.

"I seldom get his congratulations any more. I'm a disgrace to the profession—because this place is a disgrace. Oafs like your Sergeant Tillotson keep sending me patients I don't want, lack the room to care for, and can seldom save after they're ministered to by our tender staff of keepers. I've protested to that damn Hungarian who runs the island. Think he pays any attention? *Pfaugh!*"

Lemon hurled himself back into his chair, the anger darkening his leathery cheeks. "Mad, this whole business. *Mad!* There had to be a more sensible way to set the nigras free!"

Gideon licked the inside of his upper lip, still tasting the whiskey. His stomach felt warmer. "I wish we'd found it," he told the doctor.

"At least some men such as yourself have a chance of pulling through. You're determined to get out of this infernal place with your bones and your sanity intact, and start over."

Gideon smiled wanly. Lemon had no idea how close he'd come to losing that determination.

"Which brings me to what I wanted to ask. Did Tillotson—"

A knock. Annoyed, Lemon snapped, "Yes?"

An orderly in a blood-spotted smock looked in.

"Oh—Dr. Lemon. I didn't know whether you were here." He cast a suspicious eye at Gideon.

"What do you want?" Lemon demanded.

"It's about Dunning. In the privates' pen—?"

Lemon sat very still. "The question in your voice is a damned insult. I remember every one of my patients. What about Dunning?"

The orderly fidgeted because Lemon's stare was so intimidating. "I—I found him this morning. Still huddled in his usual corner. But—"

"Gone?"

White-faced, the orderly nodded.

"God *damn* it!" Lemon roared, hurling the whole pile of papers from the desk with one sweep of his hand. The orderly backed toward the doorway.

"Get out. Get out! I'll sign the certificate!" Lemon shouted. The door closed quickly.

Lemon slumped. Presently he faced Gideon again:

"And do you know what I'll be forced to write down for cause of death? Nostalgia."

When Gideon frowned, puzzled, Lemon burst out, "Homesickness. Nostalgia! The boy was seventeen years old. For the past five weeks he's spent every waking hour sitting in a corner. No speech. Hardly any movement. When I speak—when I *spoke* to him, he behaved as if he didn't hear me, or even knew I was present. I paid one of those greedy incompetents in charge of his pen—paid him from my own pocket!—to force food down him. Wasted effort. *Wasted!*"

For a moment, Gideon thought Lemon might burst into tears—or destroy every paper and piece of furniture in the office.

He did neither, managing to calm himself again. He removed his glasses to polish them on a clean, worn pocket kerchief:

"You have your own problems. No need to share mine. But God Almighty! If only there'd been enough men of sense to shout down the fire-eaters *and* the worst of the abolitionist crowd. Well, what's the use of speculating? There weren't."

He resettled his spectacles on his nose. "It's the reading material I wanted to inquire about. I delivered the parcel to Tillotson. I've been derelict in asking whether that exquisite specimen of humanity gave you the books."

Gideon's ears were buzzing slightly from the warmth of the office and the sudden effect of liquor on his nearly empty belly. The last word brought his head jerking up. With difficulty, he focused his eyes on the hunched, shabby man at the desk:

"Books? I got one—"

"One only?"

"That's right. Poems by some fellow named Whitman."

"Damn!"

"My father sent *you* the package?"

"Why not? You said you mentioned my name and position in the letter I smuggled out for you."

"True, I did, but—"

"I expect he wanted to be certain the books reached you. I knew I should have brought 'em into the pen personally. Didn't take the time because I had to do three amputations that morning. But I guarantee there were more books than one. There were half a dozen. Books with meat in them. The sort of thing you said you needed to help educate yourself."

"How do you know there were so many?"

"The parcel had been opened and inspected before it was delivered to this office. The contents were listed on a form I had to sign. Let's see—"

An index finger *tap-tapped* a pile of papers.

"There was a second edition of John Bartlett's *Familiar Quotations*. A volume of essays and poems by Oliver Holmes. Reade's *Cloister and the Hearth*—that's a romance. Historical stuff, but not bad. There was Waldo Emerson's *Conduct of Life*. And your father even included *Parson Brownlow's Book* published two years ago. Brownlow's a hard peace maniac from Tennessee, but I expect your father thought you were man enough to hear what the shrillest anti-Southern voices are still saying. The Whitman was the final item in the package—you got none of the others?"

"None."

"That thief!" Lemon seethed. "That miserable shit of a thief. Kent, wait! Let me report it to Schoepf. Don't brace Tillotson yourself, you'll only damage your chances of getting out of—"

The slam of the door cut off the rest of the warning.

Gideon was barely conscious of the cold as he reeled into the open, his ears still buzzing and his stomach aching from the liquor. He crossed the yard in a limping run, understanding now why so much twine and paper had been wrapped around a single book.

One of the barracks sentries made a snide remark about Gideon's kissing the doctor's behind to obtain favors. He paid no attention. A larger anger occupied him as he lurched past the armed men. His blue eyes took on a glazed, almost demented look as he kicked open the barracks' door and, a moment later, Tillotson's.

iv

"See here, sir!"

The sergeant leaped up, *Leslie's Weekly* drifting to the desk in disordered sheets.

"Who gave you leave to crash in that way? When the door's closed, the order is *knock*."

"You're a thief, Tillotson," Gideon rasped. "You're a thieving Yankee son of a bitch."

Tillotson's pink face paled. His eyes darted, worried. Gideon swayed on his feet, dizzy from the cold and the alcohol, yet buoyed by his rage.

"I'll not stand for such profane, insolent talk from a prisoner," Tillotson warned, raising the walnut stick hastily plucked from beside the family photograph.

"You gave me *one* book! My father sent more. Where are the rest?"

Tillotson blinked. "The rest? I don't understand, sir!"

*"The rest of the books in the package Dr. Lemon delivered to you!"*

"Dr. Lemon?" The way the sergeant pronounced the name gave it an unclean sound.

"I just saw him."

Tillotson sniffed. "Evidently. Serving spiritous liquors to prisoners is against the rules of—"

"Shall I fetch him over here to repeat his story?"

Oliver Tillotson eyed the unsteady figure in front of his desk, calculating Gideon's physical strength—or lack of it. Then, surprisingly, he smiled:

"Not necessary. I expected this matter to come up eventually."

"So you admit it!"

"Why not, sir? You have no voice in what you receive and what you don't. The other books—decent literature, I might add—are safe in my house in Salem. Christmas is coming. The wages here—well, they're hardly adequate for a man with a large family. Every bit helps. I let you have one book, so let's not make an issue of the rest."

"I'm surprised you didn't steal them all!"

"Why, I wouldn't have anything by that Whitman in my home. He's notorious. A pervert, they say. We're God-fearing people. But my boys, now—they'll be delighted to find Reade and the Holmes book under the tree. 'The Chambered Nautilus' is a first-rate poem. First-rate!"

"You had no damn right—" Gideon began.

"I wouldn't make an issue of it, Major Kent," Tillotson purred, stroking the stick. "Leave this office immediately."

The order, and the insulting tone, shattered Gideon's control. Even as he circled the desk, he knew he was inviting reprisal. But he couldn't help himself—and hardly cared.

Before Tillotson could react, Gideon caught the sergeant's throat in both hands.

The obese man's eyes opened wide a moment, terrified. Then he lunged upward from his chair, pushing Gideon. He side-stepped, a wrenching movement—

*"Assistance! Assistance here!"*

Bellowing, Tillotson tore loose from Gideon's strangling grip. In the shed proper, Gideon heard raised voices—the other prisoners, wondering about the outcry.

Gideon groped for the sergeant's throat again, feeling perilously weak. Tillotson brought the walnut stick arcing toward the side of his head.

A moment after the impact, Gideon's legs buckled. His cheek raked the corner of the desk. He fell to his knees; clung to the desk top with both hands.

"Assistance!" Tillotson screamed, beating the stick on Gideon's knuckles.

*Damn fool,* Gideon thought as pain tore along his forearms. *Damn fool to lose your head when you don't have any strength left.*

The door burst open. The guards appeared, bayonetted rifles at the ready. Tillotson hit Gideon's knuckles again. Gideon let go of the desk, sliding sideways.

Tillotson darted around the desk and booted him in the ribs, twice. Gideon flopped over. Heard men running.

The sergeant's white hair was disarrayed. "Waldo, come in! Prentice, stay outside and close the door. If anyone tries to push by, use the bayonet. No matter what you hear."

The door shut. Gideon couldn't focus his eyes. He saw two Saint Nicholas faces, one lapped over another.

Tillotson crouched down, the stick in one hand. With his other he seized Gideon's beard and yanked.

Gideon's head jerked up, wrenching a neck muscle. Tillotson hung on, wet-lipped, panting. Gideon lifted his right hand. He could barely bend his fingers, let alone form a fist. Tillotson beat his hand down to the floor with two blows.

"Waldo, kneel on his belly. That's the way. Major Kent assaulted me. *Assaulted* me. Can you fancy that? It's necessary for us to discipline him. Oh, yes. Severely!"

The sergeant's figure loomed, distorted, as he rose and lurched to the open stove. He thrust the tip of the walnut stick into the flames. Almost instantly, Gideon smelled burning wood.

"Did you know Major Kent is a student, Waldo? A reader?" Tillotson's chest heaved; he was still out of breath from the surprise attack. "He hopes to improve himself. Wants to be ready to be welcomed back into the populace when the war's done. But he's also rebellious. Dangerously so. I've been too lenient."

The smell of charring wood grew stronger. Gideon saw a wisp of smoke curling past Tillotson's sweaty face.

"Too lenient," the big man repeated, smoothing his small goatee. Outside, Gideon heard a clamor of questions from the other officers, then the guard warning them he'd fire if they came any closer.

Tillotson was at last able to chuckle. "I believe we should make it somewhat more difficult for Major Kent to practice his rituals of self-improvement."

Terrified by a sudden suspicion, Gideon tried to struggle up:

"You sadistic, fat old—"

Tillotson drew back his right boot, then drove it forward, kicking Gideon's temple.

His head snapped over—violently. What little strength he had left drained away. He began to float in a kind of haze. Tillotson sounded far off:

"One more such remark, Major, and we'll make it impossible for you to study. Impossible. I trust that sort of lesson won't be required. Clamp your hand on his head, Waldo. Hold him still!"

Then Gideon saw it. The walnut stick. Its smoothly rounded end glowing red. An inch down, the wood smoked.

Tillotson dropped to both knees, adding his restraining hand to the guard's. Gideon tried to wrench his head away. Failed.

He felt the heat. He watched the red tip of the stick grow and grow, like the August sun doubling, tripling in size. Behind it, Tillotson's avuncular face glistened with sweat.

Gideon's hand moved unconsciously toward the wrapped lock of hair in the pocket of his blouse. He lacked the energy to reach it.

"You were very rash to assault me, sir," Tillotson scolded, slipping the heated stick between his wrist and the guard's.

The second after Gideon's left eyelid closed reflexively, the stick touched it.

Tillotson put weight on the stick. Gideon arched his back, the pain nearly unbearable—

The pressure lifted. His spine struck the floor. He gasped for one good breath; couldn't seem to fill his lungs. He was too weak to resist any longer.

Tillotson released his chin and used his free hand to carefully lift Gideon's left eyelid. The flesh of the lid was burned; stinking.

"Yes, indeed, you made a mistake, Major. As that fellow Poe wrote in one of his queer tales—no one attacks me with impunity. No one, sir!"

Panting, he jammed the stick against the exposed eye.

Gideon screamed.

# BOOK TWO
## *War Like A Thunderbolt*

# CHAPTER 1

## Enemy at the Gate

AS THE SOUND of Judge Claypool's chaise faded away, Catherine confronted Serena and Jeremiah in Rosewood's drive:

"It certainly took you long enough to hide the wagon."

"Got dark, ma'am," Jeremiah said quickly, to prevent an outburst from the girl. "Made the work of maneuvering the wagon a mite harder."

Catherine looked pointedly at her stepdaughter's bedraggled dress. "If that's *all* you did. Work."

Before Serena could retort, the older woman turned to Maum Isabella. "I expect we'd better heed the judge's advice. You and the house girls empty the sour mash jugs in the larder. Pour out every drop. The wines and cordials in the sideboard—get rid of those too."

At last Serena had a chance to retaliate:

"Even your favorite blackberry?"

"Everything."

"You mean to say you can get along without it for more than twenty-four hours?"

Catherine stayed calm. "I can. Go help the girls."

Serena's eyes mirrored the fire smearing the horizon. "That's nigger's work!"

"It's *our* work now. You *do* it."

"Blast it, I won't!"

Catherine stepped forward, digging her fingers into her stepdaughter's shoulder. Serena wrenched away. For a moment Jeremiah saw pure enmity in the eyes of both women.

But Catherine wouldn't be denied. She grabbed her stepdaughter again. Serena winced. Her right hand fisted. Jeremiah thought she might strike out.

Catherine stared her down. Maum Isabella stepped up to Serena's side and touched her gently:

"Come on, Miz Serena. The work won't take long."

"I'll be glad to lend a hand—" Jeremiah began. But Catherine shook her head:

"I want you out here with me. We've got to keep watch."

Serena's height gave her a certain advantage over her stepmother. But Catherine's will offset any physical difference between them. Catherine's will—and Catherine's eyes. With a disgusted exclamation, Serena flounced into the house. Maum Isabella followed, carrying the lamp.

Catherine walked a short way down the piazza. The distant firelight falling through the cypresses made a lattice of light and shadow on her cheeks. In a polite voice, she asked:

"Would you fetch a couple of chairs out here, Jeremiah? We might as well be comfortable while we wait."

He went into the house, hearing muttered complaints above the clink of glassware in the dining room. Serena rebelling—even as she did what she'd been ordered to do. As a kind of soothing counterpoint, Maum Isabella kept up a running patter of talk.

Jeremiah carried the chairs out one at a time, arranging them a yard to the right of the dark open windows of the sitting room. Catherine settled herself gracefully.

He took a place beside her, checking to make sure the sheathed knife was secure in his boot, and the hilt tugged up enough to be easily grasped in a hurry. Noticing Catherine's quizzical look, he explained:

"Just seeing to my knife. We may need it soon."

"You've been saying we wouldn't."

"I know. But the stories keep getting worse. Now there's that fire—I thought the burnings would surely stop."

Catherine's nod was slow; grave. In contrast to her firmness with her stepdaughter, she looked almost beaten now. Her shoulders slumped. She stared down the lane of live oaks toward the highway. Finally, grasping the arms of the chair as if to draw strength from them, she said:

"For the moment let's try to forget General Sherman. I sent Serena inside because I wanted to speak privately about another matter. One that's very important. To you."

Her faint intonation of warning set him on edge. Guardedly, he replied:

"What is it?"

He already suspected the subject and wished he were somewhere else. Her first sentence proved his suspicion was correct:

"It shouldn't have required so much time to hide the wagon."

"Mrs. Rose, I told you—the darkness was a handicap. We—"

"Spare me your fibs, Jeremiah," she broke in softly. "I'm not angry.

You're too young to know what you're doing. Or, rather, what's being done *to* you."

He bristled. His tiredness, and the tumultuous emotions Serena had aroused pushed him close to anger again. Catherine kept gazing at the red-tinged oaks while she continued:

"I dislike raising indelicate subjects. But I feel I must. I've noticed a change in Serena's attitude toward you. A very rapid and abrupt change. You don't lack intelligence. Surely you've noticed it as well?"

A nod admitted it.

"Do you know the reason for it?"

"I have an idea."

"Tell me."

"No, ma'am. You tell me."

"Isn't it obvious? She's discovered you're not a poor boy. In fact I expect you've more wealth—and if we survive this war—better prospects for the future than the half-dozen beaux Serena's had since she was dismissed from Christ College. No, please don't interrupt. I must say this while there's time. Young men in the neighborhood know Serena's character. Oh, she's charming to the eye. But those same young men—before they all went off to the army—Jeremiah, there wasn't one among them who called more than three or four times. Her behavior shocked them. I feel un-Christian saying this about my late husband's child. But—"

A shrug. He knew she wasn't telling the truth. She loathed Serena as much as Serena loathed her.

"—but it's for your own benefit. I was a teacher, you know. I've worked with young people. You think you're grown, but you're not, Jeremiah. You're still—unshaped. Malleable. You must understand one fact above all." A long sigh. "Serena is—not possessed of a stable temperament."

Catherine turned in her chair and gazed directly into his eyes:

"Do you understand what I'm attempting to say?"

He wanted to swear; wanted to curse her for speaking against the girl who'd roused such intense feelings within him. He restrained the impulse and settled for a deprecating laugh:

"Think so. But my own mother used to say as much about me."

Catherine shook her head. "I can't believe that."

"Oh, yes, ma'am. She did. She claimed my brothers and I all inherited what she called a cussed streak. We got it from our great-grandmother, a Virginia lady named Fletcher."

"Well, you don't strike me as cussed, as you call it. Just very young. Very susceptible to—"

Another pause. Somewhere inside, perhaps in the hall, he thought he heard a footstep.

"—to feminine ways."

Catherine leaned toward him.

"I'm deeply appreciative of what you've done for us, Jeremiah. Just your presence—a male presence—has been a great comfort. And the loyalty to my late husband that brought you here is commendable. But the moment the trouble's over—the moment the Yanks are gone and it's safe for you to travel, you must leave. I won't repay you by allowing you to become—entangled with Serena. You're a decent young man. But still—"

A gesture.

". . . malleable."

Suddenly there was a raw sound to her voice:

"I tried to raise her well! But Henry favored her too much. Overruled my discipline constantly!"

*Because you despised her real mother, and he tried to make up for it?*

He didn't utter the question aloud. But he was becoming convinced Catherine Rose was striking back at a dead woman through her child.

"I hope you do understand what I'm trying to say, Jeremiah. I'm worried that you'll allow Serena to—" Again she searched for words. "—to exert an influence you're too inexperienced to resist."

His resentment had become overwhelming:

"Ma'am, I'm fully old enough to look out for—"

She refused to let him finish:

"I won't be so rude as to subject you to questions about why you took such an unusual amount of time hiding the wagon. Or why Serena came back so disarrayed. Frankly, I don't need to ask. I simply want to beg you to leave as soon as you can. I've seen the way you look at her. She's a handsome girl, I don't deny that. But there are—depths to her that you can't begin to perceive after such a short acquaintance. She has traits in common with her mother. She's greedy. Lewd. She—"

The momentary compression of Catherine's lips pronounced final judgment even before she finished the sentence.

"—she is not moral." A whisper then. *"Not a moral person.* All the young gentlemen who called soon realized it."

Jeremiah exploded:

"Mrs. Rose, I can't believe you care so little about your own step-daughter!"

Catherine didn't take offense. "I told you I tried. For years! Finally I saw the truth I'd been attempting to avoid. That's why I wouldn't want Serena—associated permanently with a person I liked or respected. And I like and respect you."

One hand reached out, clasping his fingers. The pressure was intense.

"Leave her alone, Jeremiah. For your own sake."

The almost frantic clutch of Catherine's fingers repelled him. Without realizing it, he'd become Serena's partisan. It had happened, he supposed, during the frenzied kissing and fumbling an hour ago.

"Jeremiah?"

"What?"

"Give me your promise you'll leave when you can."

"No, ma'am, I can't do that."

"Why not?"

How could he confront her with the fact that she'd become suspect on several counts? There was her talk of Christianity and kindness coupled with her hypocrisy about taking wine. There was the old animosity toward Rose's first wife he'd learned about from Serena. And most of all, there was this quiet, venomous attack.

He couldn't explain those reasons. Much as he resented all she'd said, and knowing full well that Serena's new interest was most likely caused by the money, he still couldn't turn on Mrs. Rose. She'd treated him well. Perhaps she'd convinced herself she was still doing so.

"Jeremiah—*why not?*"

He was rescued when Catherine jerked around in her chair, to face the highway. Almost at once he caught the sound too. A lowing and bleating —out there in the darkness.

Then, muffled but unmistakable, the ragged rhythm of marching.

Catherine leaped up. "There's livestock on the road!"

"And men," he said, as she gathered up her skirts and ran along the piazza:

"If it's the Yanks, they aren't going to set foot on this property!"

All at once she was gone, dashing wildly down the lane between the live oaks whose trunks showed faint redness on their western sides.

ii

Jeremiah didn't follow her. He was too stunned and upset by her attack on Serena.

The lowing and bleating and out-of-cadence tramp of boots grew steadily louder. Finally he drove himself into motion. Left the piazza; took three strides across the drive.

"God *damn* her vile tongue!"

He whirled.

Serena stood in the main doorway.

iii

He might not have existed; the girl paid no attention to him. She gazed down the lane where Catherine had vanished. She was trembling.

Suddenly she riveted her eyes on his. He almost cringed at the hate he saw.

"I went into the sitting room to hunt for one last decanter."

She needed to say nothing more. He remembered the open windows not far from the chairs and the sound of a furtive footstep.

Serena's knuckles were white as she gripped the jamb. "You're not going to listen to her, are you? I'm not half so wicked as she wants you to think!" She beat a fist against the wood. "Sometimes I wish one of those Yanks would come around here and *kill* her!"

Jolted, he exclaimed, "My God, you don't mean that!"

She covered her eyes. "No. No. But—she makes me so blasted *mad*!"

She rushed forward. "Jeremiah, she's detested me since the day she married Papa. You know why? Because she detested my mama's reputation. She felt that having me around all the time soiled her—even though I never did anything to make her feel that way!"

The girl seized his shoulders. "If you listen to her—to those vicious stories she makes up—it'll ruin everything!"

Excited by her touch, he started to ask her to explain exactly what would be ruined.

Laughter—raucous male laughter—burst out down by the gate. For a moment he'd forgotten the strangers on the road. The laughter reminded him.

He spun, his heart hammering, just as Catherine's faint cry of protest rang out.

"I think the Yanks are here. I have to go."

"No. You wait!"

"Serena—"

"You *wait!* This is too important." Her urgency, and her hand, held him at her side.

"Jeremiah, you have to trust me. It's important to me that you do. I don't want you to think I'm the sort of person she says. 'Course I've flirted with boys. I admit it. Maybe I've even done more than flirt. But never anything truly wrong. Never! The rest—anything you thought I meant back in the woods—that was teasing. I'm not experienced." Tears glistened in her eyes. "That was all teasing. Dumb, idiotic teasing!"

"Can I believe you?"

"Yes—and I want you to—I do!" She pressed against him.

But he asked what needed asking:

"What's the reason, Serena? The money?"

"I'd be a ninny to say no. Any girl's anxious for a good catch. But that isn't the only reason. If you were eighty years old and rich as Midas, I wouldn't look at you. Not for a minute."

Relief flooded through him. She'd caught him off guard by being so candid about the inheritance. What lingered to bother him was her claim of inexperience. The implication of chastity. Did he dare believe that—much as he wanted to—after what had happened in the pines?

Catherine's faint cry sounded again. Someone had hold of the bell rope. *Clang!*

"Serena, I can't wait any longer!"

*Clang! Clang!* The bell raised echoes across the smoky countryside. He gave the girl a last anguished look and ran for the road. Ran toward the woman who needed his help. Ran from the girl he wanted against all doubt and reason—

*She is not moral.*

That was a damning accusation. But where did the guilt, the immorality really lie? Who had been honest about her change of heart?

Serena.

Who had belittled—condemned—the very child she'd raised. And done it secretly?

Catherine.

The balance tipped, heavily and finally, in favor of the girl who'd stirred fierce new longings with her mouth, her hands, her body.

His long tawny hair streamed behind him as he raced down the lane beneath the festoons of tillandsia. Ahead, he saw a lantern bobbing like an immense firefly. He glimpsed men and livestock. Heard an altercation growing louder and more acrimonious.

SHE IS NOT MORAL.

For an instant, he was unsure of his decision. Then, equally swiftly, he was ashamed of the doubt. Above all, he *wanted* to believe Serena.

And he couldn't flee—not later, and certainly not now. Directly ahead, where the lantern's yellow light paled in a sudden drift of smoke, he saw the boisterous Yanks.

iv

By the time he reached the closed white gate, Catherine had taken possession of the rope dangling from the bell post just inside. Two companies of scruffy, bearded men in Union blue had halted on the highway. The column of uneven ranks had come along the straight stretch leading out of the dense forest separating Rosewood from the Jesperson farm, which had evidently been torched. Thick, pungent smoke drifted from that direction.

In the cornfield on the highway's far side, a herd of about two dozen cattle and as many sheep milled. By the lantern's light, Jeremiah could just discern ragged drovers prodding the cattle into a steadily shrinking circle. The drovers' shouts and profanity were loud in the night air.

The soldiers outside the fence jabbered at one another in a guttural foreign language. Jeremiah supposed they must be some of the Dutchmen serving with the Northern army. Among the miscellany of arms they carried he spied several of the new Spencer rifles. The deadly repeaters held seven balls and could be fired every three or four seconds by a practiced hand. He'd seen one of the pieces, captured after Chickamauga. Lieutenant Colonel Rose had once remarked that the Spencer's rapid-fire capability would give the Yanks a final, decisive advantage in the war.

Some of the Union men had other, more unusual equipment with them; spades and axes, slung over shoulders or trailing in the dust. The lantern held by a burly sergeant with a bad complexion revealed the team and driver of a white-topped wagon stopped in the dark to the left. Some nigras clustered around the front of the wagon, clapping and joking. Jeremiah counted five—and was relieved that Price was not among them.

One of the nigras wore a top hat and an emerald-colored frock coat. The young woman with the group was gowned in shimmering orange silk. Undoubtedly the clothing had been stolen from a former master and mistress.

Beside the sergeant with the lantern stood two officers. One, the senior, was a square-faced, middle-aged man with mild brown eyes and a ragged uniform blouse. Hovering close to him, a younger lieutenant with a pointed chin eyed Jeremiah and whiped the heel of his right palm with the tips of his fingers. The nervous hand hovered beside the butt of his holstered revolver.

The older man addressed Catherine in heavily accented English:

"Captain Franz Poppel, madam. This advance party of engineers is widening and corduroying roads for General Sherman's army."

"You mean you're going to tear up the highway?"

"No, this road is adequate. However—"

"Road work isn't all you're doing!" Catherine exclaimed, pointing to the cornfield. "You're stealing livestock from civilians too!"

Poppel acknowledged guilt with a blush and bob of his head. The sharp-chinned lieutenant turned to her, eyes flinty:

"What we do is our business."

Poppel held up a hand. "Lieutenant Stock means we are under orders to forage according to our requirements."

The lieutenant refused to be silenced. "This your property, woman?"

"Would I be down here if it weren't?"

"Show a little more respect, if you please," the lieutenant snapped, taking two swift strides to the fence. He reached across, caught Catherine's upraised arm—her hand was still on the bell rope—and jerked it down against the top rail of the fence.

The rope danced. The bell pealed. The lieutenant levered Catherine's arm down harder:

"Else we'll teach you how."

"Stock!" Poppel exclaimed as Catherine's body twisted. She was in pain, but she didn't cry out.

Captain Poppel moved too slowly to get between his lieutenant and Catherine. *So this is what we're going to be up against?* Jeremiah thought bitterly, bending down fast to reach the top of his boot. He hadn't forgiven Catherine for her remarks about Serena. But she was still a woman.

"Secesh there—he's got a knife!" the sergeant cried.

The lantern began to swing wildly as the man retreated. Jeremiah's hand streaked up, the knife flashing light from pitted steel. Two long steps and he was at the fence.

His left hand shot out like a hook to catch the startled lieutenant by the back of the neck. The lieutenant's grip broke. Catherine scrambled away.

Jeremiah jerked the lieutenant forward. Off balance, the man fell, the side of his head slamming the rail. Jeremiah held the man's head against the rail with one hand, and with the other slid the edge of the knife against Stock's throat:

"You've mauled Mrs. Rose the first and last time." His voice was soft, but his mouth had set in that thin, cruel line.

Bent at the waist, the lieutenant tried to free his revolver with his right hand.

"Go on, get the gun!" Jeremiah whispered. He dug the knife-edge deeper. *"What's holding you?"*

A thread of blood began to trickle toward Lieutenant Stock's collar. There were alarmed exclamations from the ranks. Jeremiah was aware of a blue barrel aimed at his head. Then a dozen more.

"They fire," he warned Poppel, "your man's done."

Stock and the captain realized he meant it. Stock's hand dropped away from his holster. His eyes watered.

"Madam," Poppel exclaimed to Catherine, "beg your son not to provoke this kind of trouble!"

"He's not my son—" she began.

"Shoot the fucking Secesh!" a soldier shouted. Other men yelled agreement.

Sweating, Jeremiah held the knife steady against Stock's quivering throat. "Yes, feel free," he told Poppel. "I guarantee you'll lose one engineer. It's up to you."

# CHAPTER 2

## Invasion

"NO FIRING!" Poppel exclaimed, facing the road. "That is an order!" He spun to Jeremiah. "Let him go."

"So your boys can pick me off? No thank you."

Poppel swabbed his face with his sleeve. "What do you want?"

"Your promise," Jeremiah answered. "Not to touch this woman again. Not to harm this property or anyone on it."

"We intend to camp on your land tonight—" Poppel began.

"Inside the gate," Jeremiah said with a jerk of his head. "Under the trees. Nowhere else."

"Captain," Stock panted, "don't take orders from a goddamn *boy!*"

"This is my responsibility—not yours," Poppel replied. A nervous flick of his eyes toward Jeremiah. His tongue crept over his perspiring upper lip. Then he nodded.

"All right. Stock should not have mistreated her. I agree to the terms. We will camp on your land but will not intrude on your privacy. In the morning we will move on. We'll require provisions, however. Corn. Pigs."

"We're supposed to surrender our food just because you say so?" Catherine blazed.

Captain Poppel pointed at the ranks of men. Jeremiah saw the blue muzzles still poised. Saw hostile faces behind them. A nervous finger could blow him away—

"These are hungry men. We take nothing our orders prohibit us from taking. I will make certain no property is harmed. But I insist on provisions. And," he added to Jeremiah, "that knife."

Suddenly the strain wrenched his face. "Trust me! Else one of those men is liable to shoot you down."

"Can I rely on your word?" Jeremiah asked, searching the captain's face.

"On my word, and on this."

Poppel drew his own revolver. To his soldiers:

"After the young man gives me the knife, the first one who moves against him or the woman, I shoot. Now put the rifles down."

Grumbles; low cursing.

"*Put them down!*"

Slowly, the blue muzzles lowered. Jeremiah studied Poppel again, trying to assess the man's honesty. He thought he could trust him. It was a risk, but the alternative was far less attractive. Wounded or killed, he'd be no use to Catherine and Serena.

"Now let him go," Poppel said.

Jeremiah released the lieutenant's head and pulled the edge of the knife away from his bleeding throat.

The lieutenant's eyes were murderous. But before his fingers reached the butt of his revolver, Poppel cocked his:

"Hands down, Stock. We struck a bargain."

Stock fumed. Poppel extended his other hand.

"The knife now, young man."

He wanted to believe Poppel was decent; not lying. Catherine's expression seemed to urge him to cooperate. "I promise you will not be harmed!" Poppel cried.

"We—" Catherine's voice sounded unsteady. "—We'll rely on this officer's word, Jeremiah. Give him the knife."

He dropped the blade into Poppel's palm and stepped back. The captain exhaled loudly, relieved. His gun remained centered on a button on Lieutenant Stock's blouse.

"Very good. Form up the men, Stock." When the lieutenant hesitated, Poppel roared, "*Go!*"

Stock swabbed his neck with a bandana, pivoted, and stalked toward the grumbling soldiers.

"You wait till we leave!" a soldier shouted at Jeremiah and Catherine. "You'll be rooting around in ashes!"

Red-faced, Poppel whirled: "Be quiet! We do not burn private property."

"Then—" Catherine pointed shakily toward the heavy forest to the left. "—who fired the Jesperson farm?"

"Not my soldiers," Poppel replied. "With one or two exceptions, these are decent men. They have wives. Families. Homes of their own. I personally guarantee their good conduct. Unfortunately I cannot guarantee the manner in which this entire campaign is being waged. There *are* some units that act without restraint. However, mine is not one. Now may we come onto your land?"

Catherine sighed. "All right."

Poppel bobbed his head again, crisply. "We will camp under those trees. No one will enter the house except myself and my sergeant. I am required to search the premises for concealed arms and ammunition."

Out by the men, Stock shouted, "If that Secesh boy says different, we'll blow his damned head off."

The statement was meant more for the troops than Jeremiah. Shouts of agreement in German greeted it. Poppel whirled again, angry. The noise faded while Jeremiah stood with his hands clenched, hoping he hadn't gambled wrongly.

Catherine's eyes begged him for restraint. He decided threats couldn't really hurt him. What mattered was the captain's ability to exert his authority and enforce his pledge; there seemed no lack of such ability. The Dutchmen were all avoiding Poppel's fierce eyes.

Catherine stood back from the gate.

"Open it for them, Jeremiah."

Some of Jeremiah's tension drained away. In reply to Catherine's instruction, the captain murmured, "Thank you, madam."

Jeremiah reached for the pin. Despite Judge Claypool's reports of devastation and Poppel's remarks about disorderly troops, perhaps a little hope was justified after all. If men like Poppel proved to be in the majority, maybe the Yank march across Georgia might not be so savage and disgraceful as rumor said it was.

ii

He and Catherine stood back while a still-fuming Lieutenant Stock led the first soldiers into the lane.

Others followed quickly, spreading out beneath the oaks on either side. Poppel still had his revolver drawn as he waited beside Catherine and Jeremiah, alert to any signs of disobedience. There were sullen looks; angry remarks in German. But no attempted violence. Poppel's assertiveness and decency had taken the heat out of the situation. Under the trees, some of the soldiers were actually laughing.

The last of the men in blue passed. The noisy blacks started to follow. Catherine whirled to the officer:

"I insist you keep the nigras off the property!"

Poppel shook his head. "I can't do that, madam. They are free to go with us wherever they choose. However, I'll order them not to approach the house."

Flushed, Catherine watched the blacks going by. All at once her eyes opened wide. She recognized the yellow-skinned girl in the orange gown:

"Nanny? Nanny, why aren't you with Mrs. Hodding in town?"

" 'Cause I don't belong to Miz Hodding no more," the girl spat. "I belong to *me!* Linkum and Uncle Billy both say so!"

"You ran away?"

"*Walked* away! I'm free now."

"But Mrs. Hodding has no one to care for her. No one except you."

A shrug. "Too bad."

"Is she all right?"

The girl grinned. "Mighty fine. Last I seen her, she was sittin' in a chair in her parlor with a nice little round hole in her forehead."

Catherine swayed. "Oh, my God. Why?"

"She got bumptious with some of the sojers in town. Somebody took a gun an' fixed her. Wasn't me, but I wish it had been. Miz Hodding laid a rod on me plenty of times. She sold off my little baby boy when he only five! Wouldn't even let me name him Franciscus like I wanted. Made me call him Robert Rhett, same as some old Secesh up in Carolina she admired. She had it comin' to her." The grin reappeared. "You better be careful too."

Linking her arm with that of a laughing young buck, Nanny hurried on up the lane. Captain Poppel looked embarrassed. "There *have* been regrettable incidents."

"Do you really regret them?" Jeremiah shot back.

"Believe it or not, young man, I do. Admittedly, some on our side don't. Sometimes war becomes a handy excuse for behavior that otherwise would never be tolerated. Stock's a prime example. But I doubt every man in Confederate gray is above reproach either. However, I have given my word that no such incidents will take place here. Of course, you must continue to cooperate—"

"What choice do we have?" Catherine responded in a bitter voice as the wagon creaked into the lane and the soldiers flung themselves down among the trees, yawning and chattering in their foreign tongue.

### iii

By midnight the grass under the live oaks glimmered with dozens of small lights. The Union soldiers had speared their bayonets into the ground and stuck stubs of candles in the rings.

Catherine had permitted three of Poppel's men to take a pair of hogs from the pen, shoot them, and haul them down the lane. The dead animals had been hacked up by two of the Germans who knew something about butchering. The hogs were roasting now, on spits improvised from bayonets and branches.

The smell of roasting pork drifted up to the piazza. A couple of dozen of the plantation blacks had gathered in the driveway, awed by the sight of some of their own kind mingling freely with the Yanks. But Maum Isabella's presence kept the watchers in line. Several times, a stern warning prevented one or two from running down to join the visitors.

Catherine had returned to her chair. Jeremiah stood nearby, tense and tired. Just as he was wondering where Serena had disappeared to, Captain Poppel and his burly sergeant approached. The sergeant waited in the drive, eyeing a couple of the black women, while Poppel moved down through the shadows cast by the lattices.

"Madam?"

"My name is Mrs. Rose. You can at least be civil enough to use it."

"Of course. My apologies. I must trouble you for your keys."

"*Keys?*"

"Yes, I'm instructed to open any locked rooms, chests, cupboards, and the like. To conduct a search for those arms I mentioned."

"You took my knife," Jeremiah said. "We didn't have anything else."

Fatigue edged Poppel's voice with irritation:

"You will permit me to make that determination."

Catherine stood up. "I'll get the keys for you."

She vanished inside the house. Captain Poppel tried to be cordial to Jeremiah:

"What's your last name, young man?"

"Kent."

"A Georgian, are you?"

"Virginian."

"Then how is it that you're on this plantation?"

"Mrs. Rose's husband was my commanding officer. He was killed. When I was invalided out, I came to Rosewood to look after things."

"Praiseworthy," Poppel murmured. "Most men would have fled to wherever they could find safety. Where were you when you were hit?"

"Jonesboro."

"Come now, it's not necessary to be so curt. This is a dirty business, and I don't like it any better than you. I did not leave my own farm to wage war on civilians. Are you the only man on the place?"

"The only white man," Jeremiah responded, less testily.

"Well, it's good you are here. Some of the units following us—I did not care to be explicit in front of Mrs. Rose—they are totally out of control. Men are constantly breaking ranks. Running off to loot and—and other things. Stock would do so if I permitted it. May I ask whether there are any white women besides Mrs. Rose present?"

"Her stepdaughter."

"Is she attractive?"

"What the hell difference does that make?"

"Answer me, if you please!" Poppel erupted. "I am worn out and not in good humor. You caused me a considerable amount of trouble down at the gate—" He drew a deep breath. "I was merely asking the question to be of help. If the young woman is good looking, and other units stop here, there could be—difficulties."

Jeremiah let out a long breath. "Well, I'm sorry I blew off a minute ago. You seem to be sticking by your bargain."

An offended tone: "Did you think I would not?"

"I hoped you would." Fervently: "More than you can appreciate." Jeremiah rolled his shoulders forward. Twisted his head from side to side. Suppressed a yawn. "Lord, I'm tired."

"Quite understandable," Poppel nodded.

"Captain, considering what you said about more soldiers coming, maybe you could return my knife. It's all I have to defend this place."

"There's no *defending* possible, Mister Secesh," another voice interrupted in a laconic way. The heavy-set sergeant had strolled onto the piazza and was leaning against one of the lattices. Jeremiah heard wood crack. The sergeant didn't move, adding:

"Uncle Billy's going all the way to the ocean. We got this whole fucking state by the tail."

"That's quite enough, Meister," Poppel said. "Stay where I put you—in the drive!"

Scowling, the sergeant stalked off. When he was out of earshot, Poppel leaned close:

"I gave your knife to Stock. A souvenir to promote his cooperation. Have you ever led men?"

"No."

"Well, it is not entirely a matter of force and bluster. Sometimes you must drive them, but sometimes you must also appease them. I have learned that with difficulty. Now concerning your question—"

Catherine reappeared, key ring jingling. She'd evidently retired to remove the ring from the bag tied under her skirts. She handed the keys to Poppel and returned to her chair:

"Search all you want. Just don't touch personal things."

"I'll go with him," Jeremiah offered.

He'd spoken loudly enough for the sergeant to hear. The man exclaimed, "Hell, no. You got no say in this!"

Again Poppel's upraised hand stopped him:

"Meister, shut your mouth. He may come."

iv

For an hour the three ranged the house and surrounding area, Jeremiah holding a lamp while the sergeant guarded him with a drawn revolver and Poppel unlocked drawers in the office, trunks in the attic, and the new padlocks on the outbuildings. Presently Jeremiah grew less uneasy. Poppel was acting with great restraint.

In the attic, for example, he discovered the thousand dollars' worth of Confederate bills and the legal papers in the trunk. He examined everything, but replaced all the items carefully and saw that the trunk was once again locked. Again Jeremiah began to feel a touch of optimism. If Poppel proved to be the harshest officer with whom they had to deal, honorable treatment of the women of Rosewood might not be such a far-fetched idea after all.

Sometime after one in the morning, Poppel completed his search and dismissed the sergeant. The captain confessed to a thirst for coffee. He and Jeremiah headed for the house while the sergeant trudged back toward the campsite, where the little candles still flickered in bayonet rings, and loud voices sang a marching song:

> "*Hurrah, boys, hurrah!*
> "*Down with the traitor, up with the star!*"

In the kitchen, Jeremiah was surprised to discover Serena seated at the table, a cup of tea in front of her. The Union captain swept off his dusty campaign hat; even bowed:

"Madam. Franz Poppel."

"Miss Serena Rose, Captain," Jeremiah said.

"Delighted!" the captain said. Serena didn't reply.

"Where've you been?" Jeremiah asked her.

"In my room." A glance at Poppel. "Couldn't stand to watch any damn Yankees pawing through everything."

"Captain Poppel's been very decent," Jeremiah countered, moving around Maum Isabella who was tending the huge iron stove. A spicy smell rose from the oven. "You baking gingerbread?"

"That's right," the tiny black woman answered. "I figured that if we give the soldiers a little something extra, they might go away and leave us be."

"We'll go away in any case," Poppel nodded. "But I'm grateful for the kindness." His eyes rested briefly on Serena's profile. "There are many more men coming, however."

The girl looked at Jeremiah. But he was too weary to interpret whatever she meant to ask or imply. Poppel continued to shoot covert looks at her while Maum Isabella brought the coffee to a boil, poured a mug, and set it down on the table with a faintly insolent thud. Abruptly, Serena excused herself and left.

"I wonder if Mr. Kent and I might have a word in private?" Poppel asked the black woman.

Expressionless, Maum Isabella walked out. Poppel sat down. No one had offered him a seat before.

"That red-haired girl—she's quite handsome."

Jeremiah managed a smile. "I don't need a Yank to tell me that."

Poppel craned around, looking through the doorway leading to the front of the house. He took another sip of coffee, then leaned forward.

"Permit me to make you an offer, Mr. Kent."

"What kind of offer?"

"Kindly keep your voice down! Mrs. Rose—she is handsome but not young. However, that redhead—" Tired as he was, the captain could still sigh appreciatively. "Lovely. Now listen carefully. I was quite serious when I said there are undisciplined men with the army. And I cannot return your knife. However, in the morning, I will go up to the attic again. For one more search."

"You already searched it top to bottom!"

"Young man, are you witless?"

"I'm worn out. I don't know what the hell you're saying."

Another swift look toward the door. "Up in the attic, I can hand you a spare revolver I happen to have in my kit. You should keep it hidden. Because of that girl."

"I see. I'm sorry I was so thick."

"No matter." Poppel waved. "We have reached an understanding. I would not want anything on my conscience. Such as leaving you wholly unprotected, should other units pass this way."

He drained the mug. "I have two daughters of my own back in Missouri, you see. Sixteen and eighteen. If our positions were reversed, yours and mine, I hope you would do as I am doing."

"Yes, sir, I'd try."

"The attic, then. Tomorrow morning. But if you reveal a word of my offer to anyone, I withdraw it."

He stood, picked up his dusty hat, and clumped out of the kitchen. Belatedly, Jeremiah called after him:

"Captain? Thank you."

A slight hesitation in the captain's step showed the words had been heard.

v

At dawn, Captain Franz Poppel's woodcutters and road builders assembled on the highway while the drovers prodded the confiscated livestock to their feet in the field where they'd bedded for the night.

A portion of the white fence separating the plantation from the road had been smashed by the soldiers, but there was no other visible damage. Two more hogs were hauled from the pens, shot, and their carcasses trussed and flung into the white-topped cook wagon. Corn from one of the cribs was loaded next. Then Poppel staged his little show; announced a search of a corner of the attic he claimed to have overlooked. No help needed; he would see to it personally.

Alone with Jeremiah, Poppel slipped his hand beneath his blouse. He drew out a stained rag wrapped around something with the unmistakable contours of a revolver. He pulled the rag away, revealing the dirt-speckled gun.

"Take it, Kent. It's a rebel piece anyhow."

The attic was dark and warm; Jeremiah was sweating. Gingerly, he lifted the revolver from Poppel's palm.

The gun measured about thirteen inches, muzzle to butt, and had seen hard use. The feel of the metal sent a shiver up his back. For the first time since he'd awakened to find Price standing over him, he felt whole again.

"Where'd you get this, Captain?"

"I confiscated it at Resaca. From a dead man."

"Never seen one like it."

"Imported model. A Kerr piece, .44-caliber. We do not use them."

Squinting, Jeremiah examined the cylinder. "Five-shot. Four shots left."

"None in the chamber, of course. It's double-action, by the way. I am sorry I have no spare ammunition."

"Four shots are better than none."

"I advise you to hide it well," Poppel said.

Jeremiah pondered a moment, then began to roam through the attic's clutter. At every step he tested the planking by putting his weight on his right leg. At last, back in a corner, he discovered a loose board.

He knelt; tugged at one edge. The pegs had rotted. The end of the board lifted easily. He slipped the Kerr .44 down between the joists, then replaced the plank. As a further precaution, he moved a sheet-draped dress form from another corner to a point just in front of the hiding place.

"Excellent spot," Poppel observed. "I doubt any looter would trouble to rip up an attic floor." He started out.

"Captain?"

"Yes, Mr. Kent?"

"I'm honestly sorry for a couple of the things I said to you."

The captain smiled without humor. "Contrary to what you may have been led to believe, Mr. Kent, not all Northern men are ravening beasts. I only hope you have no reason to need that weapon."

vi

For two hours after Poppel's engineers had tramped on, Rosewood was relatively quiet. Jeremiah hoped the worst was over.

Catherine had retired to her room for a nap, complaining of being unable to sleep during the night. Serena had also vanished again. But he was too tense to rest. He sat in the kitchen drinking coffee with Maum Isabella, who told him tartly:

"Those bad-mannered Yanks ate every last bite of gingerbread without so much as a thank you. No, I take that back. One said it. One of the very first. He also asked for a plate and laid a coin in it. Nobody else paid, though. And a man at the end of the line picked up the coin, slipped it in his pocket, and walked out grinning big as you please."

"Well, we're still fortunate to have gotten off so light—"

Down at the gate, the bell began clanging.

vii

By the time Jeremiah reached the piazza, Catherine was at the foot of the staircase, rubbing sleep from her eyes. She joined him outside as horsemen came thundering up the lane. Blue-coated horsemen. Some of the coats were no better than rags.

Dust billowed behind the riders, making it difficult for Jeremiah to determine how many there were. Across the fields toward the river, he could see infantrymen moving. Hundreds of them, trampling the furrows. A long line of wagons stretched from the woods down the highway. The countryside was covered by men moving on foot and in the white tops; covered—like a land suffering a Biblical plague.

The cavalrymen reining up in front of Rosewood looked more like riffraff than soldiers. New riders arrived every few seconds, barely visible in the dust.

Their commander was a man in his late thirties, with sallow skin, thin arms and legs, and the beginnings of a paunch. His eyes were the color of dried mud.

Head on, his face resembled a pear, bulging below the ears. A half-moon of fat hung beneath his stubbled chin. He greeted Jeremiah and Catherine with a mocking touch of his hat brim, then addressed them in a nasal voice unpleasant to ears accustomed to mellower Southern speech:

"Your servant. Major Ambrose Grace of the Eighth Indiana, General Kilpatrick's Third Cavalry Division."

"The Kill-cavalry," Jeremiah said.

A purse-lipped smile twitched the major's mouth. "Sometimes we're complimented with that term, yes."

Suddenly, laughing men shied their mounts aside. Jeremiah groped for the support of one of the white pillars when he saw a black on a mule jogging out of the dust cloud. Catherine drew a breath, loud and sharp.

Price tugged the mule to a stop beside the commanding officer.

"This here's the place I was tellin' you about when I met up with you last night, sir," Price said. "Plenty of good things on this place—an' I know where every one of 'em is hid. I'll help you get 'em all," he added, reaching down to grasp the Enfield musket lying across his thighs.

A bit of red clay clung to the stock. The cartridge box hung from the black's rope belt.

"Damn you," Jeremiah said. "You had it after all."

Price's blue-black face wrenched into a chilling smile.

"Did you really think I didn't, mister soldier? Or that I wouldn't come back an' use it?"

# CHAPTER 3

## *The Bummers*

JEREMIAH TOOK A STEP toward Price. With his attention centered on the black man, he only heard the slither of metal on metal as Major Grace pulled his saber and extended his arm.

"Hold on!"

Jeremiah found himself blocked by the blade. The point touched his shirt. The major twisted the sword slightly. The point pierced cloth, pricking Jeremiah's chest.

With mock seriousness, the major added, "I can't have you threatening one of our most valuable informants."

Furious, Jeremiah yearned to reach up and knock the saber aside. But if he did, he'd probably be gutted on the spot.

Some of the cavalrymen snickered as he stood motionless. The laughter as much as called him a coward. Humiliated, he promised himself he'd get back at them—every one.

Catherine appeared more shaken than he'd ever seen her. Her voice was barely audible as she spoke to the slave with the Enfield:

"How could you do this? My husband always treated you decently. So did I."

Price's brown eyes brimmed with animosity:

"I don' call bein' kept as property decent treatment."

"But we always tried to take good care of our—"

"Your little bitch stepdaughter took care of me, all right," he broke in. "She took care of me with the whip, her an' Leon. They tried to make me tell about this here gun."

"They did no such thing!"

Price shrugged. "She never told you, that's all. Miz Serena, she ain't just mean, she's a sneak."

"You foul-mouthed bastard!" Jeremiah cried. Only Ambrose Grace's blade pressing into his breastbone kept him from lunging.

"That's enough," Grace said to him. To Price: "You mean to say there's another white female on these premises?"

"Yes, sir. Mighty fetching little piece, too. She might strike your fancy," the black added with a quick smile.

"Have to look into that," Grace murmured. Catherine fisted her hands. Jeremiah's belly hurt.

Grace gigged him again:

"Would you kindly step back so I can dismount? I'd like to conduct our business as politely as possible."

Jeremiah didn't budge. Grace frowned.

"Now see here, Reb. If you don't obey I'll have to split you wide open. That's a poor beginning for a friendly visit to this fine home."

"You aren't setting foot inside my—" Catherine began.

"We certainly are," Grace interrupted. "Else this young man's dead on the spot."

ii

Catherine drew a deep breath.

"You'd best do as he says, Jeremiah."

It was the surrender of Stock all over again—only this time the roles were degradingly reversed.

For a moment he was unable to think clearly. He wanted to snatch the saber and turn it on the snide, smiling officer whose unclipped hair straggled from beneath his hat to his frayed blue collar.

"Jeremiah!"

"No, Mrs. Rose. I'm not moving till we get a promise from this— *gentleman* that we'll receive honorable treatment. You especially."

The Indiana cavalryman looked thunderstruck:

"*Honorable treatment?* My God, you Rebs have brass! Fair treatment's what you'll get, boy. Fair treatment appropriate to your treason. You and your kind want to keep the niggers penned up till the trump of judgment blows. You tried to tear this nation apart to do it! You expect sweet forgiveness? Hasn't it occurred to you that you'll have to pay a penalty for your little adventure in rebellion?"

"We paid the price in the field. We're still paying it."

"Won't come close to settling the debt. And I'll dictate what happens around here, not you."

Grace exerted more pressure on the saber:

"Now either stand back or we'll dig you a nice grave."

"Jeremiah, *please!*" Catherine cried. "We'll report this man to his commanding officer."

Another burst of laughter from the lounging riders. Grace shared it, then said:

"Go right ahead. Lieutenant Colonel Fielder A. Jones. We haven't met up with him for three days." The major's eyes pinned Jeremiah. "What's it to be? I'll give you about five more seconds."

White-lipped and feeling the worst sort of idiot for thinking he could reason with such a man, Jeremiah retreated.

"Much better!" Major Grace slid his saber back in the scabbard and dismounted, asking Price, "Who is this pup? The woman's son?"

"No, sir. Some Reb who showed up a few days ago."

"Too yellow to stay and fight, were you? One skirmish and your hair turned white—typical of your side, I'd say."

Jeremiah's cheeks darkened.

"Price?"

"Yessir, Major?"

"You come indoors with us. We need your guidance to forage efficiently." He addressed a mounted corporal: "Burks, locate General Skimmerhorn—immediately."

Jeremiah didn't understand why some of the cavalrymen nudged one another until Grace explained to Catherine:

"General Skimmerhorn is our forager-in-chief. I believe he came from one of General Howard's infantry regiments. Quite a number of men have been wandering away from their units. Skimmerhorn and some others—ah —attached themselves to us. Up near Gordon, the local folk referred to them as bummers. I prefer to call 'em foragers. Skimmerhorn's turned out to be so excellent at supervising them, I gave him an unofficial promotion. Private to general."

Grace talked as though he were making light conversation at a social gathering. He reached for Catherine's arm to escort her inside. She pulled away, the mole beside her mouth stark black against her white skin.

Grace chuckled in a tolerant way, continuing:

"Have you heard what we did between Sparta and Gordon? The rebel plantations over there put up so much resistance, General Kilpatrick had us burn out every one of them. I trust the same thing won't be required here. Of course we can't display too much leniency. I'm not positive about Uncle Billy's whereabouts, but if he and his headquarters guard were to come jaunting along that road tomorrow or the next day, I'd surely want them to see signs of a job properly done."

The threat was stated in a good-natured way. Grace concluded:

"I sincerely hope you appreciate what you're involved in, ma'am. A military masterpiece. That's truly the only word for it—masterpiece. I predict people will marvel over it for generations."

Evidently Grace expected Catherine to agree. She was so dumbfounded, she couldn't even speak.

"Uncle Billy's a genius. No other general would have the nerve to cross enemy country."

"I'm delighted to be informed that what you're doing is a masterpiece," Catherine replied with a withering look. "Otherwise I might have reached a mistaken conclusion that it was something much less grand. Vile, in fact. Disgusting and vile."

"Oh, I can appreciate how it looks from your side. But try to keep my view in mind. That way, we'll have fewer problems. We surely don't want problems of the sort we encountered around Gordon, do we?"

Speechless again in the face of the smiling threats, Catherine turned and walked across the piazza. The major followed. He was distinctly bow-legged.

Price went next, giving Jeremiah a sideways glance of amusement as he walked by. The black's bare feet were caked with dried mud.

The other troopers began to dismount. Down by the highway, half a dozen men were using hatchets to destroy a section of the fence, ignoring the gate and creating a wider entrance for the canvas-topped supply wagons.

The dust raised by the cavalry horses was settling. Jeremiah was able to see the fields directly across the road. Men were still moving through them in ragged columns of fours. The lines stretched all the way to the woodlands on his left. Somewhere a regimental band blared the old South Carolina hymn tune that had been transformed to "John Brown's Body," and then, with new lyrics by some Northern woman, into the hated "Battle Hymn of the Republic."

On the fringes of the marching companies smaller groups of men drifted, keeping to no particular formation. Some of these men were breaking away and heading toward Rosewood, whose fence was now being systematically smashed a length at a time.

Jeremiah thought of the Kerr revolver in the attic. Much as he wished he had it right now, he didn't intend to go after it with Yanks in the house.

*I must save it,* he said to himself. *Save it until I can make every one of those four balls count.*

iii

In the sitting room, Price was plumping himself down in a wing chair as Jeremiah entered. The black drew up an ottoman and put his right foot on it. Tiny bits of mud fell on the embroidered fabric.

Price stared at Catherine to see whether she'd react. Though she was still furious, she didn't.

"Now, ma'am," Major Grace said, "we'll be requisitioning supplies and equipment from you."

Nodding in a weary way, Catherine said, "I've heard that speech before. Within the last twenty-four hours, in fact."

Grace's eyebrows raised. "Another unit stopped here?"

"Much better looking and considerably more polite than yours!"

The major's voice lowered: "The less of that sort of talk, the safer you'll be. Evidently I wasn't sufficiently clear when I made the point outside."

"You were. Go on. Just have the decency to avoid words like requisitioning. Say what you mean. Stealing."

"Call it whatever you damn please, we plan to take most of your foodstuffs. We'll leave a few kitchen implements, but we want all your cooking utensils. The War Department's so tight-fisted, we aren't issued any. We'll require every oven you have. Every skillet. Every coffee mill and pot."

"That's Sherman's idea of a military masterpiece?" Jeremiah fumed. "Robbing homes of *coffee pots?*"

Grace's eyes flickered angrily. "Don't feel sorry for yourself, Reb. You have no idea what war's really like. Georgia has no idea! You think the people of this state are faring badly? Wait till we reach the state that first fired on the Federal flag. We have orders to reduce everything to ashes. *Everything.* Believe me, South Carolina will be made to feel the sin of secession much more than Georgia—unless a lack of cooperation here forces me to provide a sample of what's in store for Charleston."

Alarmed, Jeremiah watched him stroll toward the horsehair sofa, still speaking harshly:

"I suggest you limit your antagonistic remarks and consider yourselves fortunate."

"*Fortunate?*" Catherine exclaimed. "Your gall is absolutely—"

Before the confrontation could grow any hotter, there was a diversion—Serena's sudden appearance in the hall, yawning:

"I was trying to nap but I heard a fearful—oh, my God!"

A single glance took in Price's foot on the ottoman, and Grace's uniform as he pivoted toward her. The major greeted her with an insincere grin:

"Good day, ma'am. I haven't had the pleasure."

He swept off his hat. His long, dirty hair began as a fringe midway down the sides and back of his head. Above, he was bald.

"Ambrose Grace. Major, United States Cavalry."

"My—my stepdaughter Serena," Catherine said with effort.

Grace licked his lips. His eyes slid to the bodice of Serena's dress. Jeremiah was barely able to stand still.

"Charming child. Lovely. We don't raise them one bit handsomer in Indiana. However—" A falsely rueful expression. "—we're here on business, not to be social."

Slapping dust from his hat, he sprawled on the horsehair sofa, which gave off a series of jingling sounds.

Grace sat upright, blinking. "What's this? A musical sofa?"

"'Spect they hid stuff in there," Price remarked. "Like I said, they been hidin' it all over."

"Let's find out, shall we?"

Grace rose and drew his saber. With two crisscrossing strokes he slashed the sofa's back. Catherine pressed her hand to her mouth as he reached into the opening and began flinging handfuls of stuffing and silver on the carpet.

Boots thudded in the hall. Serena darted aside as a man stomped in— the most appallingly unclean human being Jeremiah Kent had ever seen, or smelled.

"General Skimmerhorn reportin' for duty, Major."

"Just in time! Here's a trove for you."

Six more pieces of silver clattered on the rug.

Jeremiah couldn't take his eyes off the odd, hulking creature Grace had characterized as his forager-in-chief. If the bearded, broad-shouldered Skimmerhorn had ever belonged to a military unit, it was impossible to tell. He wore a bizarre collection of stolen and improvised apparel:

A black stovepipe hat. A coat stitched together from four contrasting sections of Oriental carpeting. Gray trousers with one knee torn out, and each leg decorated with the red stripe of the Confederate artillery. Cracked work shoes with the tips gone and grimy toes showing. In his right hand he held a gunny sack.

Under Skimmerhorn's coat Jeremiah saw a Navy Colt, and tied to his belt by thongs, two souvenirs of his work: a small skillet and a dead chicken with its neck wrung.

General Skimmerhorn gave Serena an appraising look, then turned his attention to his superior. Grace gestured:

"You may have all this silver as your reward for supervising the foraging."

"Yes sir—thankee!" Skimmerhorn crouched and began to grab knives and spoons and shove them into the sack.

Catherine rushed forward at the sound of boisterous men in the hallway. There were half a dozen, two in uniform, four in civilian clothing. They pushed and shoved to be first up the stairs.

"Where are they going?" Catherine demanded of the major.

"Why, to forage."

"They have no authority."

"Indeed, they do," the major slapped the hilt of his saber, "this."

The men vanished. Serena looked nearly as distraught as her stepmother. A few seconds later, there was a crash from the second floor.

At the back of the house, Maum Isabella cried out as a door splintered. The cry was followed by a horrendous clatter of crockery breaking.

"Now," Grace said to Price, "what else should we be searching for?"

"They's a clearing back in the pines where they put a lot of things. Mules. A wagon—"

"You followed us!" Jeremiah whispered. "It was you I heard in the brush!"

"That's right, mister soldier," Price grinned. But the smile didn't reach his eyes.

*He hates me and he's going to kill me*, Jeremiah thought. *He's liable to kill us all before this is over.*

Price described the contents of the cache in the clearing. When he finished, Grace asked:

"Catch that, Skimmerhorn?"

"Most of it," the forager replied in a phlegmy voice. He shoved the last pieces of silver in his sack, hawked, and blew a gob of spit on the carpet.

"We'll confiscate the cotton, kersey, and denim cloth," Grace advised him. "If the clock's fancy like the nigger says, I'll keep it for myself." Price didn't seem annoyed at being referred to as a nigger by the Union officer. "Could use a good clock in the feed store back in Vincennes. Turn the wagon and mules over to the wagon master. Mix some kerosene with the molasses. Oh, and don't forget kerosene in the well when we're ready to go."

"*Jesus!*"

Grace glanced at Jeremiah. "What's wrong, Reb? Did you expect us to leave you amply provisioned? You still don't understand Uncle Billy's style of fighting. He makes war for a double purpose—I've heard him say so. First he fights to gain physical results and second, to inspire *respect*. Respect for—"

Price snapped his fingers. "Major?"

"What?"

"Jus' remembered. They put salt an' flour in the ground out behind the slaves' graveyard. Two barrels of each. I can show you where."

"Excellent. Dig them up, General. Kerosene in those too."

"And mebbe a little piss to spice it?" Skimmerhorn asked, scratching his gray-streaked auburn beard with a hand on which an open sore glistened.

Grace shrugged. "You're in charge."

"I'll see to it." Skimmerhorn tipped his stovepipe and ambled out with the sack over one shoulder.

A man came clattering down the stairs and burst into the room wearing a lacy, ivory-colored gown over his uniform:

"Lordy, Major, lookit! First time I ever been a bride!"

"Absolutely stunning," Grace chuckled. Catherine lunged:

*"That's my wedding dress!"*

Grace shoved her back. "Union property now." He held her wrist until she realized she wasn't strong enough to break loose. When she ceased struggling, he let her go with another warning:

"Your outbursts are going to make this genuinely unpleasant, ma'am."

"It couldn't be any more unpleasant than it already is. You're *filth!*"

Grace turned scarlet. Lifted his hand to hit her, but managed to restrain himself. His voice shook:

"I personally am going to conduct the search for arms and ammunition. Give me your keys."

Catherine stared at him, her lips moving without sound. Grace raked a palm across his hairless skull. "Goddamn it, I'm losing patience! *Your keys!*"

"I—I have them put away in a private place. I'll have to retire to get them."

"What private place?"

Now it was her turn to redden.

"I said, *what private place?*"

"On—" Jeremiah could barely hear her. "On my person."

"Oh." Grace brightened again. "Well, this is wartime. We're forced to overlook the niceties. Get them out."

"Not in front of—not while everyone's—?"

There was sick disbelief in her eyes. Price giggled.

Catherine regained a measure of control:

"If I do, will you promise me there'll be no further damage to the house?"

"I can't offer any assurances. We'll definitely torch your barns, your gin house, and corn cribs. As to this building—" Another shrug. "No assurances."

"Catherine, you'd better give him the keys," said Serena, a warning note in her voice.

Grace sat down on the gutted sofa, crossing one leg over another, and studying the line of Serena's hip before he lifted his gaze to her face.

"You're not only a pretty child, you're intelligent." His glance slashed back to Catherine. "Ma'am, I'm waiting."

"Will you—will you at least allow me to turn my back?"

Grace sighed. "If you must."

Jeremiah couldn't stand this much longer. Hooting laughter, the crack of furniture, heavy running and jumping racketed from overhead. Each whoop, each crash, pierced him like an invisible bayonet. What a fool he'd been to think all the Yanks would be as decent as Poppel. He *deserved* the contempt of Grace and the rest.

At least he'd deserved it until this moment. Now all his illusions about humane treatment—decency—the rules of war were vanishing, replaced by a consuming, almost uncontrollable anger stronger than any he'd ever felt before.

His mouth took on that slitted white look. Through one of the piazza windows he could see tents being erected down by the lane, and cook fires blazing. In the drive, another band of blacks in confiscated finery clapped while three young women danced in a circle.

Catherine turned away from the men. She pulled up her outer skirt, then the underskirts of crinoline, corded calico and pleated horsehair. Finally, after much rustling and maneuvering, she dropped the skirts and turned back, tears on her cheeks.

She passed the key bag to Grace just as General Skimmerhorn appeared in the doorway:

"Got most of the foraging started, sir." He'd exchanged his gunny sack for a wicker-covered jug. He raised the jug and took a long drink. "Anything else we overlooked?"

Grace relayed the question to Price with a lifted brow and a word:

"Nigger?"

"A big buck named Leon, he carried three crates of chickens down to the bottom land near the river."

"Did he now! Well, we certainly wouldn't want any chicken dinners left on the table. General, another assignment for you."

Skimmerhorn drank again; scratched his crotch. His eyes slid to Catherine.

"All by myself?"

Grace laughed. "Need a guide, do you? Take her along. See that she's not mistreated, though. You know Uncle Billy's instructions—we're not to harm civilians."

He winked.

"Yessir," Skimmerhorn replied with feigned seriousness. "I'll be right nice to her."

They all understood; Serena, Jeremiah, and Catherine—who screamed and bolted for the hallway.

Skimmerhorn darted in front of her. Caught her around the waist:

"Here, woman, there's no call for that. I mean to treat you just fine— Christ!" he yelped as Catherine's nails raked his face.

The forager reeled back, three paralleled scratches oozing blood on his cheek.

Half crouched, Catherine resembled a trapped animal. Skimmerhorn's eyes narrowed as she tried to dart past him. The forager hopped to the right, then the left, blocking her. Finally, with a sharp outburst of breath —"Hah!"—he caught her arm and bent it back so she was forced to her knees.

"We're gonna have a fine time huntin' them hens, woman. You're right lively."

Jeremiah's control broke.

"*You sons of bitches!*" he yelled, charging straight at Skimmerhorn.

# CHAPTER 4

## *Serena's Plan*

PRICE KICKED THE OTTOMAN aside and stuck out his leg. Jeremiah failed to see it. He tripped, windmilling his arms as Serena lunged at Skimmerhorn.

The forager backhanded her across the face, sending her sprawling. Jeremiah had a distorted glimpse of the fall just as he recovered his balance. At least she stood up for Catherine when it counted.

He lowered his head and lunged at Major Grace, who had jumped between him and Skimmerhorn. Before Grace could draw his saber, Jeremiah struck him with his shoulder. The impact knocked Grace onto the gutted sofa. The momentum carried Jeremiah forward on top of him. He worked a knee over to the major's belly and bore down, pounding at the man's face with wild, hard blows.

"Get him off!" Grace howled, jerking his head from side to side to dodge the punches. Jeremiah lifted his knee, drove it into the officer's groin.

Grace grunted. Grimaced. Absorbed a glancing blow on his chin, then shoved. The two spilled off the sofa.

Jeremiah fell awkwardly, whacking his head against the sofa's corner. Dazed, he flopped on his back. He tried to turn over.

Price loomed, planting his muddy feet on either side of Jeremiah's legs. He raised the Enfield with the muzzle toward the ceiling, then smashed the butt into Jeremiah's middle.

With a choking cry, Jeremiah tried to twist out of the way and avoid a second blow. Too late. The stock slammed his belly again.

Again—

Price's face remained expressionless. But not his eyes. He put even more effort into the fourth blow.

Jeremiah rolled all the way over onto his stomach, retching. Grace careened to his feet and booted Jeremiah's temple, spitting obscenities.

Jeremiah's forehead dug into the carpet. His back heaved. He heard Catherine's cries as Skimmerhorn manhandled her out of sight. A moment later he had another impression of movement—Price, gliding out after the forager.

He struggled to raise his belly. Clutched it with his palms. That didn't ease the pain.

Growling one filthy word after another, Grace stamped on the small of his back.

Jeremiah yelled, his body driven flat. His vision grew more distorted. Fragmented thoughts went screaming through his head:

*God, it's no better here than with the army.*

*No decency left in this war.*

*Nothing but meanness.*

*Meanness and hate—*

In spite of his pain, his own hate was fierce and powerful. But it wasn't powerful enough to keep him from sinking into darkness.

ii

"Jeremiah?"

Barely conscious, he fought to speak:

"Mama? Mama, is that—?"

"Come to your senses! It's me."

He realized his mistake. Not Fan's voice. Younger. He'd been watching misty images of Lexington while consciousness returned.

He shifted his position slightly. He was still lying on a floor. Something pricked the underside of his left shoulder.

"Wake up, Jeremiah. You've been stretched out there almost two whole hours!"

Wetness on his shirt. At the spot where he'd felt the pricking. He reached for it with his right hand. Bits of glass fell from his sleeve, tinkling on the wood. When he attempted to sit up—an agony—something sharp jabbed his buttocks. His eyes snapped open.

"God! There's glass all over!"

Serena's face came into focus. Beyond her, outside the latched window of the first-floor office, a Union soldier stood guard.

With her help, he staggered to his feet, gaping at the carnage. The shelves were bare. Books were strewn everywhere. Some had been ripped in half.

The desk showed eight or ten fresh knife or sword scars. All the drawers had been pulled out and stamped to pieces. The chair had been reduced to kindling.

On the floor near the spot where he'd been lying, he noticed the small oil painting of Lieutenant Colonel Rose, out of its frame, and torn in half. In a corner lay the remnants of another frame, and nearby, the lock of Serena's bright red baby hair and the card, crumpled.

He stared, disbelieving, while the girl uttered a sad laugh:

"Aren't they kind? They started their search for arms and ammunition in here."

"What—" He licked the inside of his mouth. Massaged his bruised belly. His dizziness was passing. "—what time is it?"

"Two or three o'clock. I'm not sure."

The office was stifling. He started for the hall entrance.

"Won't do any good. We're locked in."

He leaned his back against the door, picked a long splinter of glass from his trousers, and surveyed the wrecked office again. He was disgusted—sickened—not so much by the damage as by his own failure to prevent it. He'd been unable to exert even the slightest moderating influence on the Yanks.

And after Poppel, he'd been encouraged. He'd really believed the Union soldiers might not be as bad as they'd been painted.

All at once the infuriating sense of failure was replaced by a sharp fear: What if they'd found the Kerr .44 in the attic? What if they'd decided to parade the dress form, as Catherine's wedding gown had been paraded? What if someone had accidentally discovered the loose plank?

He prayed they hadn't. Prayed he could get his hands on the Kerr piece before Grace's cavalry moved on. How pathetic to have thought even briefly that there was any other way to deal with the enemy.

Another memory jolted him:

"What's happened to your stepmother?"

"I don't know." Her voice was curiously flat. "That—what was the word? Bummer? He dragged her out. I tried to stop him. Grace caught me and put me in here."

"Then by now she's been—"

He couldn't say the rest.

"I expect she'll live through it."

Jeremiah's mouth dropped open. He couldn't believe the matter-of-fact way in which she'd spoken. Or the emotionless expression on her haggard face. Her dress was disarrayed; her hair too. But she seemed icily composed.

"My God, Serena, is that all you can say—*she'll live through it?*"

"Well, she will! May hurt her Christian conscience some, but it could be a lot worse. They could shoot her—they aren't going to do that."

He supposed Serena's fatalistic view was logical. But he also suspected there was another reason she wasn't particularly anxious about her step-mother's plight. Maybe she was even a little pleased.

Some of his shock must have showed. She cried suddenly:

"Jeremiah, they've *got* her! We can't do anything about what's already happened. Let's worry about what *might* happen. We've got to see the Yanks don't burn this house, or poison the well. They're going to fire the cribs and gin house, Grace left no doubt about that. But this building—"

Bitter, he broke in, "What the devil can we do about it?"

"I can talk to Major Grace."

"*Talk?*" He was thunderstruck.

"You heard me. Talk. I called the guard in the hall just before you woke up. Told him to fetch that no-good Yankee son of a bitch right away."

She tossed her head to rid her brow of a stray lock of scarlet hair. Some-how there was defiance as well as strength in the movement. Her smile grew sweetly vicious:

"'Course, I didn't use those words. I was polite—well, polite as I *could* be, considering what they've done." She seized his arm as he swayed. "You all right?"

"Yes." But he was having difficulty standing.

"You look awful."

"Another five or ten minutes, I'll be fine."

"That's all the time I expect to spend with Grace."

"Serena, what the devil are you fooling with him for?"

"Why, I'm going to beg him to leave the house alone."

He was startled, yet impressed by the calculating expression in her blue eyes. She went on:

"He put on a fierce show in the sitting room. Men have to do that—bluster some—in front of other men they boss around. But if I can get him alone—"

The thrust of her idea erased his appreciation of her calm:

"You've lost your damn mind! Before you came downstairs, *I* tried to reason with him and couldn't."

"Reason with him? I'll bet you sassed him and practically bit his head off. Right in front of his men, too."

A guilty look said she was right.

"I hate him as much as you do, Jeremiah. But I think he fancies me a little. He sure enough stared at me as if he did. Your tactics didn't work. Let me try mine."

Sarcasm in his voice: "You believe nice friendly words and smiles will have an effect on a man like that?"

"Might," she nodded. Then, piqued: "You have any better suggestions?"

"I suggest you forget the whole idea right now."

She stamped her foot. "What's the matter with you? Don't you understand Rosewood may be all we'll have left after these men move on? We won't even have Rosewood—or water fit to drink—if one of us doesn't do *something!*"

Her anger blunted his. He let another, deeper concern surface:

"But, Serena, that man—he's a bad sort. The worst."

"I know what you're saying."

"Do you? He could take advantage—"

"You think I don't appreciate that?"

She rushed to him. One hand touched his sweaty cheek.

"Doesn't it scare you?"

"'Course it does. But I want to save this house. And I don't want them to hurt you again. Considering the way you behaved, they might take a notion to do it."

Part of him responded to her sympathetic tone, but another part resented having someone else fight his battles. He stalked away three steps, crunching glass under his boot.

"I still say you're a damn fool."

"Now don't get all pettish just because you failed and I might not."

Stung by the truth, he swung around and glared.

"Jeremiah, it's not a case of man or woman, one better than the other. You tried—there's no shame in trying and being tromped on, two against one. This is our trouble—*ours*—together. While you get your strength back, I'll do what has to be done. At least make an effort—"

"What the hell happens if he starts to—to mistreat you?"

"Like the man who took Catherine?"

He nodded.

A small, sly smile curved her mouth, "I think I can handle him. I think I can make him do what I want and still keep myself out of a scrape."

There it was again; the maddening implication of experience.

"You're pretty sure of yourself."

The smile disappeared. She was upset by his reaction:

"I'm not! I'm scared to death. But I'm still going to try."

She glided close, letting him feel the contours of her body against his leg and aching chest. Her hand stroked his face again:

"I don't want to spend two seconds with that man. But I will if there's a chance to keep this house standing. It's all we have."

Softly he said: "You and Catherine—"

Arms around his neck. A light kiss on his mouth:

"You and I. Don't you see? I want something left for *us*."

"It's her house too."

Quick anger in her eyes was just as quickly hidden. "Oh, yes, I know it is! But I can't help thinking of you."

Another kiss; longer. Then she leaned her cheek against his shoulder. "I'm fond of you, Jeremiah. Fonder than you realize. We're going to be together when this is over. This house is going to belong to us." She pulled back, her eyes disarmingly wide. "Even if it takes some put-on sweet talk, with my knees banging together while I try to convince the major I believe he's a wonderful, kind man who surely wouldn't burn Rosewood to the ground."

"You—you won't do anything more than talk?"

"He lays one hand on me, I'll scream till they hear clear over in Louisville!"

Another change of mood; the sly look returned:

"Truly, I think I can handle that Indiana roughneck."

"And find out what's happened to your stepmother?"

"Yes, that too." She sounded less than enthusiastic.

For a moment he almost believed she possessed the feminine wiles to pull it off. But the plan still struck him as unacceptably dangerous.

The protest he started to make was silenced by the feel of her body tight against his. Sore and anxious as he was, she could still reach him. Convince him with a brush of her lips. With words that carried promises—

*We.*

*Us.*

"Actually," she said at last, "there's no guarantee the major will even answer my message. So you're worrying for nothing until—"

A hand rapped on the other side of the door.

"Until right now," he said with a grim smile.

Serena stepped to the door. Smoothed her hair.

"Yes?"

"Major Grace, ma'am." He sounded quite friendly. "I was informed you wished to speak to me?"

"I do. Will you please unlock the door?"

"If that Reb's awake, tell him to stand well back."

"Do it, Jeremiah."

When he hesitated, still tormented by fear for her safety, she clenched her teeth:

"*Do it!*"

He retreated to a corner, stumbling over ruined books.

"All right, Major."

The key rattled. From his vantage point, Jeremiah couldn't see the officer. Serena stepped out of sight behind the open door.

"Thank you for coming, Major. I'm anxious to speak to you because of the terrible things happening on this place. I want to plead with you to control your men. Not take such harsh measures. But I'd prefer to discuss it somewhere else, if we might. Privately?"

Jeremiah leaned his head against the wall and shut his eyes. How smooth and assured she sounded; in perfect control. He found himself admiring her nerve, and the ruthless way she went about manipulating Grace. There'd been an almost seductive lilt in her voice.

"Why, yes, Miss Serena. I believe I can spare a few minutes to listen to what you have to say. I must warn you, though. I'm not a man easily persuaded."

"We'll see. Shall we go to the sitting room?"

"By all means."

iii

The major took time to lock the door. His footsteps, and Serena's lighter ones, faded slowly. Then someone's weight made the door creak. The hall sentry, back on duty.

The guard outside the window remained motionless. Over the man's shoulder Jeremiah saw an ecstatic celebration in progress down among the slave cabins.

Young women danced in Catherine's dresses. One buck strutted with a torn Confederate battle flag draped over his head and shoulders like a shawl. Three of the foragers pursued a pair of girls across a ramshackle porch. The bummer in the lead had his hand up one girl's skirt, from behind, as they disappeared inside.

Crouching, Jeremiah rubbed at his chest where it hurt the worst. He gazed at Henry Rose's torn portrait.

The painted sections of the genteel, bearded face lay at right angles to one another. Broken apart—just the way everything at Rosewood was being broken by the actions of unprincipled men. Again he felt contempt for the pathetic soldier who'd tramped midnight roads, obeying an order; fulfilling a promise; believing he could fight honorably, meaningfully again on the plantation.

He did admire Serena's determination. But he was positive her scheme would come to nothing. Ambrose Grace would no more listen to her than he'd jump to obey an order from Robert Lee. North and South, dishonorable men had seized any excuse—nigra freedom; defense of their homeland;

punishment of the enemy—as a justification for indulging their worst impulses. The Franz Poppels of the world were rarities. Even Poppel himself had admitted as much by secretly giving him the Kerr.

He brushed glass aside. Knelt. Touched one of the ripped halves of Rose's image. His fingertip rested on the rough-textured paint that created a melancholy eye.

*I've failed you so far. But it isn't over yet.*

The yearning to race up to the attic became almost unbearable.

He drew deep breaths. His chance would come. Serena was bound to fail. The question was—how badly?

If she got through her interview without a physical assault by Grace, Jeremiah decided he'd bide his time. No more outbursts. No more foolish assaults when more than one man was present to beat him to the ground.

But if he heard the slightest alarm—a cry from her—then somehow he'd batter the damn door to pieces. He'd do as much as he could—go as far as he could toward the attic—before the sentry or one of the other Yanks shot him down.

Either way, the answer was his, not Serena's. The answer was the hidden gun.

He licked his lips, increasingly sure. He'd only stopped arguing with her because she was so adamant, and because she'd linked her plan with other plans for their future together.

He *wanted* the future at which she'd hinted. He realized that despite everything—including Catherine's spiteful warnings—he was falling in love with Serena.

Yes, there was a certain cruel edge to her personality. But there was a similar edge to his—sharpening moment by moment. To have denied her a chance to test herself—even though he felt she was foolhardy—well, it might have wrecked everything between them. She didn't want any protection—*or* any suggestion that she was a simpering female incapable of independent action. Maybe that's what had rankled poor Catherine so; she'd raised a child who didn't conform to the acceptable standards of feminine behavior. Jeremiah was glad she didn't conform. It made her a woman worth having.

He'd let her flirt and wheedle, and remain ready to act if Grace molested her. Even if Grace didn't, he was sure to reject her appeals. Then Jeremiah could step in. He knew how, finally. The only thing that would make an impression on the Union officer was the Kerr revolver.

*Impression—*

He laughed over the inadvertent aptness of the thought.

He'd make an impression, all right.

Three inches deep in the center of Grace's forehead.

# CHAPTER 5

## *Night of Ruin*

FIFTEEN MINUTES PASSED.

Twenty.

Jeremiah lingered close to the door, listening for an outcry from the front of the house. Once in a while he caught the soft sounds of the hall sentry shifting position. But that was all.

Growing more and more worried, he paced the office. He didn't hear anyone approach outside. He started violently at the quick, hard rapping.

He rushed to the door. Pressed his ear against it.

"Serena? Are you all right?"

She sounded shaky when she answered:

"Yes. He—he agreed."

"*What?*"

"I talked my fool head off. Flattered him—practically crawled for him. But he agreed to leave the house standing."

He couldn't believe it. She was more persuasive than he'd ever imagined.

"Did he try to—?"

"No. Seems there are a few rules General Sherman's pretty fierce about. His officers not harming women is one of them. Any man who's caught— well, I just got the feeling Grace wouldn't chance it."

"Serena, is anyone listening to this?"

"The guard's a ways down the hall. The major told him to stay there while I talked to you."

"But you're sure the house is safe?"

"I don't know how safe. There are men rampaging all over the place. But it won't be burned. Jeremiah, the major ordered me locked in my room for the night."

"Why not back in here?"

"Guess he's worried we might cook up some kind of trouble for him." A low laugh. "He doesn't know we've already gotten what we wanted. Now you stay calm in there. I'll be fine."

"I don't trust—"

"I tell you he's scared white about *any* of his troopers injuring women!"

"Doesn't make sense! He let Skimmerhorn—"

"Simmerhorn's not one of his men. He can always claim he had no control over him."

"He's a liar."

"'Course he is. But he's protecting himself."

"What did you learn about Catherine?"

"Nothing yet. Skimmerhorn isn't back. Maum Isabella promised to keep watch."

"Damn it, Serena, we've got to find out about her!"

"I can't! She sounded close to tears. "I've done all I could. Now you— you rest. Don't fret about me. Just remember—" She was moving away. "—we're going to be together soon. I love you, Jeremiah."

The unbelievable words left him open-mouthed. He banged a fist against the door in sheer surprise and happiness, overwhelmed by her unexpected success—and the whispered admission of her feelings.

A brief period of euphoria tempered his hateful feelings about Ambrose Grace, and distracted him from what was taking place outside. But before the night was over, he had spent a great deal of time at the window—

There, his hatred of Grace renewed itself, and grew stronger and stronger as the hours passed with no news of Catherine.


ii


All that Monday night he watched the systematic ruin of Rosewood.

The part of the property visible to him swarmed with the enemy, coming and going on foot and on horseback. Once darkness fell, cook fires were started wherever the Union soldiers and foragers pleased. With the fires lit, the activity outside took on the aspects of a nightmare.

Figures of horses and men became specters of flame and shadow. It seemed to him there were more stragglers in castoff clothing than blue-clad cavalrymen. Foot by square foot, the bummers devastated the expanses of lawn between the main house and the head of the lane leading to the slave cabins. They used sabers and ramrods to jab the earth and tear out slabs of turf as they hunted for buried possessions.

By torchlight, eight or ten bummers worked the slaves' burial ground in the same way, knocking over hand-hewn wooden markers and crosses of sticks and unearthing bodies—or parts of them. At one point Maum Isabella rushed at three of the men ripping up the cemetery. A spade glinted, swung by a pair of grimy white hands. The old black woman fell and crawled off into the dark before she could be hit again.

When digging up the grass and the burial ground yielded no treasures, forty or fifty of the enemy divided into two groups and staged a sort of sham battle with buckets of pine knots fetched from the woods. The knots were lighted and hurled at those on the other side. For a while the night sky was crisscrossed with arching traceries of fire and sparks.

Other men invaded the slave cabins, carrying out blankets, pans, or any other useful item. The few blacks who tried to stop them were knocked down, and if they resisted further, beaten.

A foul smoke from campfire garbage began to blur the scene, heightening Jeremiah's feeling that he was gazing through a window at hell.

His thoughts kept returning to Catherine. Then to Serena.

To what she'd said.

*"I love you."*

Those words foretold almost unimaginable happiness if he and Serena survived the night and the next few days.

Shortly after midnight, half a dozen cavalrymen converged on the three hog pens.

Two dismounted soldiers tore the first gate off its hinges. The horsemen milled just outside, revolver and rifle barrels catching the glare of the firelight. One pistol exploded. The hogs stampeded into the open, terrified by the snorting horses and whooping men. The office window shook from volleys of gunfire.

The sight of the dumb beasts falling, blood pouring from their snouts, bellies, brainpans made him turn away, nauseated. He listened to the shooting and the squealing for about twenty minutes, crouching in a corner with his hands clenched and his mouth a slit.

*Is this what Grace calls sparing Rosewood?*

### iii

He must have dozed. Daylight hazed by garbage smoke brightened the window as he roused to hear another urgent tapping from the hall.

The office smelled sour. In the night he'd been forced to urinate. Now his stomach hurt. He was starved.

The knocking came again. Louder. He stumbled to the door.

"Who is it?"

"Serena." Her voice sounded unnaturally faint and husky.

"What's wrong?"

"When I got up an hour ago, Grace let me out. Catherine still wasn't back. I got permission to go down to the bottoms. Had to sneak past three Yank camps to get there. I spent half an hour searching. I—I found her."

The last two words were so hoarse and full of anguish, he had a premonition about the rest. "How is she?"

Serena's voice broke:

"Half her clothes were torn off. She'd been dragged two or three hundred yards. She was all filthy with red clay. She—she's dead, Jeremiah."

He shut his eyes. "Jesus Christ in Heaven."

Somehow she managed to tell him the rest:

"About half the slaves have run away. But Leon's still here. I sent him to—carry her back. She was lying face down in the water. Drowned."

Suddenly the girl began sobbing: "She wasn't my mama—I never pretended to like her. But I didn't want anything like—like this—"

The words grew incoherent. His belly felt heavy as a stone. He pressed both palms against the wood.

"Serena? Serena, listen to me!"

The sobbing lessened a little.

"Did you tell the major?"

"Right—right away." Bitterness: "He's scared out of his wits. He kept saying he's only responsible for men directly under his command."

"It was that son of a bitch Skimmerhorn, wasn't it?"

"Can't be anyone else, can it? Grace questioned him. But he denied he killed her. Denied it over and over. The major's letting it go at that."

He closed his eyes a second time, but opened them almost immediately. There was no longer any doubt about what he had to do.

"Serena, get me out of here. Get Major Grace to unlock the door. Tell him I won't cause any trouble."

"I don't know whether he'll believe—"

"*Make* him believe it! You persuaded him last night—do it again!"

No response except faint crying.

"*Serena?*"

"I—I hear you."

"Get me out. *Any way you can.*"

"Y-yes. All right. I'll try."

Ten minutes later, the bald cavalry officer came personally to turn the door key.

## iv

"Kent—" Grace looked pale, far less assured than he'd been yesterday. "I assume Miss Serena told you."

"About Mrs. Rose? Yes."

"I deeply regret—"

"Shit."

"I do!"

"Because you may be in trouble with Uncle Billy Sherman? What a pity."

"Kent, listen to me! Skimmerhorn's given me his word he wasn't the one. He—took her, yes—"

"Against her will."

"But he didn't do anything more! She was alive when he left her. Someone else must have found her."

The man seemed genuinely terrified: "Look, Kent. Understand. In wartime, things happen that can't be helped."

"You could have helped. You gave him permission."

"I'll deny it. I'll deny it to heaven!" Desperate, he tried bluster: "General Sherman said it right, just before Atlanta. War's like the thunderbolt, he said. It follows its own laws. It doesn't turn aside even if the virtuous and charitable stand in its path."

*Sanctimonious bastard! How anxious, now, to ease his own conscience and avoid disciplinary action.*

"I doubt Sherman was referring to rape, Major. I doubt he was referring to murder either."

*Yet who besides Sherman had turned these monsters loose?*

All at once Grace's muddy eyes took on the look of a helpless boy. "I realize Mrs. Rose didn't stand in the way by choice. But the woman's *dead*. What's the use of arguing about blame?"

"None. So long as *you* aren't blamed."

"Kent, for Christ's sake!"

"All right," Jeremiah sighed, masking his feelings. "It's done. No more argument. I can't stand this damn room one minute longer. Just let me out of here and—"

He was interrupted by hysterical wailing from another part of the house. Maum Isabella.

Grace sniffed the rank odor of urine. "Under the circumstances—considering what's happened—the excesses—if you give me your pledge to cause no trouble for the next few hours I'll release you. We'll be gone by late afternoon."

Jeremiah's mouth soured. "How can I possibly cause trouble? What can I do against all the men you've got?"

He held up both hands. "I'm not exactly heavily armed. Just let me out. I need to eat something and use the privy."

He thought the plea might work. Grace was sufficiently upset—no longer the controlled, arrogant officer of yesterday. Blinking rapidly, the major studied him.

"If you pledge not to—"

"Yes," Jeremiah said, careful to sound beaten. "I give you my word. No trouble."

The major hesitated a moment longer. "Just remember—the guilt isn't mine. If you try to tell anyone it is, you'll never prove it."

"That I know," Jeremiah said, no longer lying.

Grace pivoted and moved unsteadily down the corridor, leaning a hand against the wall to support himself.

Jeremiah stood rigid in the open doorway. *You don't care that Mrs. Rose is dead. You only want to save your stinking Yankee skin.*

He clenched his fists but didn't move until Grace was out of sight.

v

Rosewood was a shambles. He discovered broken furniture everywhere. Feather pillows from the bedrooms had been ripped open, and their contents strewn like snow throughout the downstairs. Near the front entrance, someone had defecated. The stench was vile.

By the time he approached the door to the kitchen, he noticed his boot soles were sticky. Molasses had been spread all over the dining room carpet. Then corn meal had been spilled and ground in. The feathers were the finishing touch.

In the kitchen, Maum Isabella and the four housegirls wailed like demented creatures. They stood or knelt around the body of Catherine Rose laid out on the long butchering block. The body had been covered with a tattered blanket. Except for the face.

Jeremiah forced himself to approach the body. Stare at the livid bruises on Catherine's cheeks and forehead; the dried red clay in her hair. He didn't want to forget that face. Not until he'd done what must be done.

On her knees at the end of the improvised bier, Maum Isabella wrung her hands and rocked back and forth, tears running in the seams in her dark face. As he started to turn away, one of the other women screamed at him:

"Cry for her, Marse Kent. *Cry for the poor woman!*"

He shook his head. "It's too late."

His eyes looked feverish as he crossed the dining room with its sweet reek of syrup. Feathers stirring brought on a violent sneeze. His boots crunched the meal.

He checked the hallway.

Clear.

He stole up the staircase toward the attic. He found the wire dress form toppled over and bent beyond repair.

But the loose plank hadn't been disturbed.

vi

General Skimmerhorn was dippering a drink from the well on the rear piazza.

Two laughing, frock-coated bummers went trotting past on stolen horses. The neck of one of the animals was decorated with a shawl Jeremiah recognized as Serena's. Out of sight beyond the house, wagons rumbled. A blare of brass and riffle of snare drums kept cadence for the men beginning to march.

General Skimmerhorn noticed him half hidden by a lattice. The forager dropped the dipper back into the well. Droplets of water spattered his carpet coat when the dipper rope snapped taut.

Using his left hand—it was concealed behind the lattice—Jeremiah touched the front of his dirty linen shirt, making sure it bloused out sufficiently around his waist. Then he started toward the well.

Skimmerhorn brushed back the lapels of his coat so he could grab for his Navy Colt quickly.

"What you want, boy?"

"A word with you, General." He tried to sound appropriately cowed.

Skimmerhorn broke wind noisily, edging around to the well's far side. He was obviously wary of the lank-haired young man standing stoop-shouldered and motionless. Behind the forager lay one of the shot hogs, its entrails spilling from its belly and aswarm with crawling white things. The morning air was dark gray, heavy with humidity, and fouled by the fumes of smoldering garbage.

"If you come to talk about the woman, I'll tell you what I told the major. I didn't have nothin' to do with killin' her." Skimmerhorn scratched his beard. "I took her to the bottoms, right enough. Had my pleasure with her. Even got so het up, I clean forgot we was after three crates of chickens. Never did find 'em. She passed out 'fore I could ask her where they was. But I left her *alive!* And a long way from that water where I hear the girl found her."

"Face down." Jeremiah's attempted laugh came out as a snort. "She just crawled right on down to the water and drowned herself, did she?"

"What do you want me to say? Some women do queer things if they get mauled a little."

"Get raped, you mean."

"I didn't kill her! I ain't gonna stand and jaw about it!" He started away.

"Wait!" Jeremiah exclaimed, then added an appeasing word: "Please."

Skimmerhorn swung around, suspicious.

"I didn't mean to quarrel. Nothing's going to bring Mrs. Rose back."

"An' I didn't drown her—just you keep that in mind!"

Oddly, Jeremiah felt the forager was telling the truth. There was a desperate quality in Skimmerhorn's speech—an anxiety to absolve himself—that seemed genuine.

"Shit, boy, you seen the fields. There's hundreds of men movin' between here and the river. Any one of 'em could of done it."

"I know. If you say you didn't, I believe you."

"Well, that's a heap better." Skimmerhorn acted relieved. He settled his stovepipe hat on his greasy hair, a touch of his cockiness creeping back. "You're bein' sensible. Now is that all you wanted?"

"No, sir." Carefully he began the plea he'd rehearsed in silence. "After you go, we'll need some corn." He pointed to one of the cribs. "I'd like to ask you to bring some out. A sack or two—"

Skimmerhorn started to snicker.

"I can make it worth your while."

Skimmerhorn's greed overcame his caution:

"How? You got nothin' we ain't took already."

"You're wrong. There's something valuable back in the pines. One thing Price didn't see me bury."

A quick glance down the street between the slave cabins. Most of the blacks remaining on the plantation had disappeared indoors. Just one small boy was visible, seated on a slanting stoop in a forlorn posture and staring into space as if he'd been abandoned.

"Where is Price?"

"I dunno," Skimmerhorn answered. "He's been all over the place since yesterday. I 'spect he's struttin' around somewhere with that musket of yours. Listen, get on with it. What'd you bury?"

"A small sack. Mrs. Rose's jewelry."

"Jewelry! That a fact!"

"Look, General—" He tried to sound whiny; pleading. "—we've got to have at least a little corn to tide us over. You could take some out of one of the cribs before they set fire to them. I don't suppose they'll let me near the cribs." He eyed the soldiers guarding the doors of the buildings. Skimmerhorn's nod said his guess was correct. "But you can get in. If you hide two bags I'll show you the buried jewelry. Mrs. Rose doesn't need it any longer."

Skimmerhorn pondered the proposition. "How far we got to go to find it?"

"Only about half a mile into the pines."

The forager closed his hand on the butt of the Navy Colt. "Wouldn't be smart for you to play tricks on me, Reb."

"No tricks. We have to eat."

Another speculative glance at Jeremiah, and the forager made his decision:

"Find us a shovel and let's go. I'll take a peek in the sack. If it's good jewelry, mebbe I will fetch that corn. But I don't promise nothin' till I see the goods."

"That's fair," Jeremiah nodded. "All right if I come around the well?"

Skimmerhorn drew his Colt.

"Slow. Good an' slow."

Jeremiah nearly smiled. So far it had worked perfectly. He kept his voice appropriately apologetic:

"It'll take me a minute to turn up a shovel. Ought to be one down by the cabins. Then we'll be on our way."

General Skimmerhorn chuckled. "Goin' on a little treasure hunt. Right pleasing idea. Yes sir, right pleasing. You finally come to your senses."

*I did, General. Finally.*

"I know when we're whipped," he lied.

# CHAPTER 6

## Day of Death

JEREMIAH AND SKIMMERHORN walked toward the lane, the bummer two paces behind. Pretending to scratch his chest, Jeremiah loosened his shirt a little more.

A soldier standing guard by one of the cribs hailed the forager, wanting to know where he was bound. Skimmerhorn waved the Navy Colt:

"Little private errand. Be right back."

They went from cabin to cabin in search of a shovel. Each of the small houses had been stripped. Finally Jeremiah spotted the tool they needed lying near the edge of the burying ground. By now he was breathing so rapidly he was sure Skimmerhorn would notice the change.

But he didn't. The general was in good spirits, strutting and whistling "The Battle Cry of Freedom."

They followed the rutted track into the pines. The gray daylight barely penetrated here. The earth smelled dank. For a while the silence was broken only by the forager's whistling. Then he struck up a conversation:

"You know, boy, now that you've calmed down some, I can say I truly feel it's a pity about that woman. I wanted to enjoy her, an' I did. But I don't wish no female dead on account of me. Sure is a shame. Nobody'll ever catch the man who did it, I 'spose."

Jeremiah's shrug pretended weary agreement. *But someone will be punished for it.*

"Still," Skimmerhorn went on, "you an' that little red-headed gal ought to consider yourselves lucky. You'll be alive when we move on. The major says he don't plan to burn the main house."

"Miss Serena persuaded him to be lenient," Jeremiah nodded.

Skimmerhorn laughed. Jeremiah puzzled at the salacious sound of it.

"I'd love to have a morsel o' her persuasion." He nudged Jeremiah's elbow with the Colt. "She given you any?"

"I don't know what you mean."

"Persuasion!" A wink. "The sort a lively female dishes out when she's flat on her back."

"Flat on her—what the hell are you talking about?"

"You mean you don't know? Well, don't get testy about it. I figgered it'd be all over the house by now. She an' the major, they was locked up in her room most of the night."

Jeremiah nearly stumbled.

"I was hangin' around shortly before the men started killin' the hogs at midnight. The major come down in his trousers and undershirt to check on things. He got to braggin' some. Said that little girl went at it like an animal. A wild animal. They'd done it three times already—that is, if he wasn't lyin'—and he claimed she was ready for more. Starved for lovin'!"

Jeremiah's cheeks ran with sweat. His voice was barely audible:

"You're the one who's lying."

Skimmerhorn chuckled again, less friendly. "I ought to clout you for sass, boy. I'm givin' you gospel." He raised the Colt, barrel straight up, and planted his other palm over his heart. "Swear it! The major said he meant to try somethin' with her from the very first. But she got him alone in the sitting room and damned if she didn't beat him to it. 'Magine a girl that sweet-looking raising such a subject? Kind of shockin' even to an old rascal like me. It's the old saw about a book an' its cover, I reckon."

Jeremiah wanted to turn on the forager right then. Finish him. Stop the filth coming out of his mouth. But he didn't; he was suddenly haunted by the memory of Catherine's warning.

*She is not moral.*

He recalled his astonishment when Serena claimed to have persuaded Grace with words alone. He tried to deny that Skimmerhorn's story could be true. The harder he tried, the less he succeeded.

"Yessir, she practically begged him for it, the major said. She wouldn't of had to beg me! I'd have been up her skirts first time she flounced 'em at me!"

It was true. It had to be true. Why would the forager invent such a tale?

*And she'd said "I love you."*

His faith in her suddenly seemed even more pathetic and contemptible than his misguided belief that Yanks could act decently. His head swam. Everything was crumbling away. Crumbling into corruption; lies; dishonor—

And he hated Skimmerhorn all the more for having spoken.

The bummer halted, considerably less good-humored:

"Boy, you told me half a mile. We've gone that an' more."

"I must have judged it wrong. We're close."

Panicked, he searched the terrain ahead. Saw a break in the underbrush.

"There. Turn off to the right."

"I got fish to fry back at the house. More val'ables to pack up before we move on. Let's step lively."

"Yes, sir." Jeremiah quickened the pace.

He led Skimmerhorn to the spot where he'd glimpsed an overgrown path. He had no idea where the path went. And he was worried about the sound. They weren't sufficiently far from the plantation. But Skimmerhorn was impatient.

His head was hurting. Rage was mounting in him. Rage at the war. At Serena. And particularly at this man who'd destroyed an illusion with a few crude sentences.

He had meant to go a good distance along the overgrown path. But the pressure of his wrath grew too great. He stopped after a dozen steps. Here the path widened slightly. He pointed into the tangle of weeds and brush.

"Back in there."

Skimmerhorn bent forward, peering past him. While the man's attention was diverted, Jeremiah raised his hand from his belt buckle and undid two buttons on his shirt, covering the movement by swinging the shovel slowly up to his shoulder with his other hand.

"Lord, it's hot as an oven in here!" Skimmerhorn complained. He crouched. Pushed weeds aside with the muzzle of the Colt. "Don't look like a clump of sod's been turned in there for ninety-nine years." He started to rise and twist his head toward Jeremiah. "If you're shittin' with me, boy—"

Jeremiah's sweaty palm was already under his shirt. With his other hand he let the shovel fall. He drew the hidden Kerr before Skimmerhorn realized what was happening.

Skimmerhorn was fast, though. He pivoted on the toes of his boots, jerked the Navy Colt up with one hand, and punched Jeremiah's groin with the other.

Jeremiah reeled back, stumbling on the shovel. He lost his balance. Skimmerhorn fired from a crouch.

The underbrush rustled behind him, a kind of reptilian hiss, as the bullet spent itself. Only the fall had saved him. Before Skimmerhorn could aim and shoot again, Jeremiah fired.

The bullet from the Kerr blew away part of Skimmerhorn's right temple. He sat down hard on his rump. A spasm of his finger discharged the Colt a second time. The bullet buzzed away harmlessly.

Skimmerhorn swayed. His head lolled slowly to the right while a dark stain appeared between his legs. Blood poured down the side of his face, soaking his carpet coat, and reddening the needles on the branch his dead weight finally bypassed. The branch sprang back into place, flecking Jeremiah's shirt with scarlet.

The fingers holding the Colt clenched, then relaxed. Jeremiah wiped his mouth. Twisted toward the dirt track. Surely they'd heard the shots up by the house.

He thrust the Kerr in his belt and forced himself to approach the corpse. Insects were already clouding around Skimmerhorn's shattered skull. Sourness climbed in Jeremiah's throat as he pulled the Colt from the dead man's grip.

He straightened up and turned away, his face a study in confusion and pain.

*I love you.* She'd said that right after she'd whored all night!

He started to walk. In a moment he was running. Not toward the dirt track and Rosewood, as he'd originally planned. Not back to Serena, to protect her. Let her look after herself. She was quite accomplished at that!

He fled deep into the pines, where it was rank and dark. He thought he could escape her there. Escape the shattering memory of Skimmerhorn's words.

But he found he couldn't escape them—or the fury that shook him between spells of grief-stricken confusion.


ii


No one came hunting for him.

Or if they did, he failed to detect the sounds of a search. By nightfall he'd lost even a minimal concern about Serena's safety. He was pondering whether to leave—strike out for some back road and never see Rosewood again—when he noticed a red shimmer through the trees.

A light wind had sprung up, scouring some of the rankness from the air. Fire. Reluctantly, he left the little dell where he'd spent the day alternately gripped by a sense of total betrayal and an overwhelming hatred embracing the Yanks, the war, and *her.*

He didn't want to go back. The only thing that held him was the memory of Henry Rose.

Rosewood was the dead colonel's only monument. Jeremiah couldn't stand by and permit the house to burn. He felt it might, despite Grace's promises. He didn't trust the cavalry major. He had to go back. He had to discharge this last obligation to the man who'd saved his life.

When he reached the perimeter of the woods, he broke open the Colt, swore, and flung it away. General Skimmerhorn had fired his last two rounds defending himself.

He felt the Kerr under his shirt. Three bullets left.

He crept out of the trees and stole forward through the high weeds. When he reached the slaves' burial ground, he bellied down between overturned slabs and broken crosses, peering up the lane. The sky was bright red, the sound of the conflagration a roar.

Both barns had already burned. Little more than the glowing beams and rafters remained. As he watched, they crumbled and crashed inward.

The corn cribs were alight, but the flames were only beginning to eat through the walls. The smoky air had a strange tang. Roasting corn.

The gin house was on fire as well. It stood nearest the main building. The wind was blowing from behind it.

At the head of the lane between the cottages he glimpsed perhaps two dozen men and women silhouetted against the blaze. The nigras who hadn't run away. Then he caught his breath as he recognized a familiar figure beyond the slaves, standing at full height on the rim of the stone well.

He climbed to his knees, then began angling to his right, toward the cover afforded by the cottages on that side of the road. He saw no Yanks up by the house. Perhaps Grace had fired the buildings, assembled his men, and ridden on. But he thought he understood the confrontation near the house.

He crept to the porch of the last cottage. From that vantage point he could make out something metal-bright in the hands of the man standing guard over the well.

His own Enfield.

He crawled off the porch, hurried past the end of the cottage, and cut back to the left, running like someone possessed. As he ran, he moved further and further away from the cottages, so he could dash behind the first of the fired cribs standing at the extreme right at the head of the lane.

The crib's whole roof was burning. The wind was driving smoke and clouds of sparks ahead of it. Once the gin house was fully afire, the combined heat from it and the burning cribs would carry the blaze to Rosewood. For the moment he didn't give a damn about that. It was Price he wanted.

He kept running. His chest hurt. He tripped once, landing on his belly and cursing loudly. But the crackle of the fire covered the sound.

As he sped behind the second crib, the one nearest the highway, its burning side crumbled outward. He leaped wide. A splitting beam came down, nearly braining him. He slapped at sparks in his hair and kept running straight ahead into the dark. When he was opposite the front drive, he skidded to slow himself, and turned toward the piazza.

He searched the lane and the highway.

No tents.

No soldiers.

There was more fire in the sky, now in the direction of Millen. But the army had gone.

He lunged across the piazza, calculating his best point of attack. The larder—next to the kitchen. It led directly onto the rear piazza.

He opened the front door cautiously.

Darkness. Silence.

He dashed through the ruined dining room, and the kitchen where the lamps had been extinguished. Firelight through the smoke-stained windows outlined Catherine Rose's corpse. Candle wax had melted and rehardened at her head and feet.

He slipped into the larder. Even indoors, the heat was intense.

He pulled the Kerr from under his shirt. Outside he heard a voice he recognized. Serena's:

"Price, you've got to let us at the water!"

The man laughed. "No."

"But if we don't wet down the siding, it'll catch!"

"Let it!"

Three or four men yelled agreement. There was one fervent, "Amen!" Price had the Enfield. The blacks were either frightened of it, or siding with him.

Price's voice boomed:

"Let it burn, you white slut. You ain't giving orders to niggers no more. We're free people!"

Someone clapped. Another *"Amen!"* Then came a sound of scuffling. Maum Isabella's cry rang out:

"We're free to water the house down if we please!"

"No!" Price boomed back. "I ain't the only one who wants to see it burn."

"Yes, you are, you damned scalawag nigger. The rest of these so-called friends of yours are too scared—or too stupid—to know how mean you feel about Miss Serena and her poor dead stepmother. You stand up there with that gun, thinking you're some almighty angel—"

That amused Price:

"Ol' angel of death, Maum. Ready to shoot the first buck who comes close. Or the first woman."

"You're just as mean as the worst white soul-driver!" Maum Isabella shrilled. "Just as mean. *Twice as mean!*"

"Old woman," Price warned above the cries of protest and agreement, "you stay away. Else I'll drop you with this here."

Jeremiah hit the larder door with his shoulder and took two long strides across the piazza, the Kerr coming up in his right hand while his left steadied it.

Beyond the well, where Price stood with his legs widespread on the rim, menacing the half circle of slaves, Maum Isabella halted all at once. Her eyes popped at the sight of Jeremiah. Several of the other blacks saw him too. On his right he glimpsed Serena, her red hair limp, her face sooty.

He smelled the unmistakable aroma of wood catching fire. The wind was spreading a huge flag of flame from the gin house and the collapsing cribs, blowing banners of sparks against the end of the main building.

Jeremiah had a clear target: Price's massive body. The big buck saw the reaction on the black faces. He started to turn, just as a yellow-skinned slave pointed and yelled:

"Behin' you, Price!"

The yellow-skinned man hurled himself forward, perhaps in the hope of knocking Price off the well rim, out of danger. Both hands locked on the Kerr, Jeremiah aimed carefully; fought an impulse to let his rage drive him to a fast, inaccurate shot.

Price spun, sought his target, whipped the Enfield to his shoulder. Jeremiah fired.

The bullet took Price in the left arm. Drove him up on tiptoe as it sprayed blood and fragments of splintered bone like red needles in the firelight.

Price started to topple forward. The buck bowled into him, knocking him sideways off the well.

The slaves scattered, shrieking, as Price disappeared. Running toward the well, Jeremiah shouted:

"Maum Isabella, grab the Enfield!"

The yellow buck got it first.

Jeremiah was about six feet from the well when the buck's distorted face popped up on the far side. The man was trying to help Price to his feet. Maum Isabella darted toward them.

A bloodied right hand grasped the well's rim. Like some kind of dead creature rising from its grave, Price appeared, pulling himself up. Now he was using both his right hand, and astonishingly, his left, even though his left sleeve was soaked red and pierced by jutting pieces of bone.

Price's hate-filled eyes found Jeremiah. His face and neck glowed with sweat. A vein in his throat throbbed.

Jeremiah still had both hands on the Kerr. His forearms were trembling as he extended the gun. He nearly couldn't bring himself to look into those fiery eyes. Maum Isabella was darting and feinting at the yellow buck who jabbed with the Enfield's muzzle to fend her off.

*Why doesn't Price fall? No man is that strong.*

"Maum Isabella?" Jeremiah's voice had a cracked sound. *"Stand back!"*

Price's red hands gripped the well rim a moment longer. His eyes glowed bright as the blazing gin house. Then will and rage seemed to drain from him. He searched for Jeremiah again; found him. This time, his eyes seemed duller.

"Mister Jeremiah? You hit me bad. Leave me be now."

Jeremiah laughed. "Finally remembered my name, did you?"

"Please." Price lifted his gory right hand. *"Leave me be now!"*

A memory of Major Grace's remark about the thunderbolt darted into Jeremiah's mind. He glanced at Serena. Price uttered an almost plaintive cry as he watched Jeremiah's face change.

The yellow buck was still sweeping the Enfield in an arc to drive back three slaves—Leon and two others. But Maum Isabella had retreated. All at once he seemed to see Serena in place of Price. He wasn't frightened any longer. He felt quite different from when he'd defended himself against Skimmerhorn. He and the Kerr were welded into one—and there was joy in the thin curve of his mouth. He fired.

Price shrieked. The bullet blew a black and red hole in his tattered shirt just below the breastbone. The nigras screamed. Price fell.

The yellow buck was obviously unfamiliar with the operation of the Enfield. Jeremiah twisted at the waist, still holding the Kerr double-handed. The muzzle pointed at the buck's ear. The buck dropped the rifled musket and ran toward the dark at the front of the house. Maum Isabella flung a stone after him.

Screaming, milling, the remaining nigras didn't know what to do until Serena wheeled on them:

"Buckets from the kitchen! Hurry, damn you—Leon! Willis! Get a move on!"

Jeremiah stuck the Kerr back under his shirt, comforted somehow by the heat of the metal against his bare skin. He swabbed sweat from his eyes.

Serena quickly organized the nigras into a fire-fighting line. The stony smile remained fixed on Jeremiah's face as he walked around the well. Leon and some of the others began frantically passing buckets down a hastily formed human chain as two women—one of them Maum Isabella—worked the well's crank arm. To reach it, she had to stand on Price's body.

Jeremiah glanced down at the open-mouthed corpse. He felt no remorse. He could halfway admire Price now. The man had been vicious but in his own way, brave. A worthy adversary.

Jeremiah was proud of having killed him.

Serena rushed to him, pushing hair off her forehead. There was an odd, almost frightened light in her blue eyes as she gazed at his curiously amused expression. He ignored her for a moment, glancing toward the house. Some of the bucks were piling onto each other's shoulders to empty buckets and wet down the end of the building. Even though the barns, the cribs, and the gin house with its baled cotton and packing screw were gone, the heart of Rosewood would survive. It was the only memorial he could leave to the colonel.

But Henry Rose had been right there in the field hospital. War—Sherman's thunderbolt—was a destroyer. It destroyed hope. He'd learned the lesson; and it had transformed him.

Serena flung herself into his arms:

"Oh, Jeremiah, I thought they'd carried you off, or something worse—"

He shoved her away. Seized her wrist, his fingers biting so hard she winced. He dragged her toward the piazza.

"Jeremiah, let go! What's wrong with you?"

He paid no attention.

He pulled her through the larder to the kitchen, then flung her away. She caught herself on the iron stove, her eyes huge and terror-stricken as he stepped behind the block bearing Catherine's body. His mouth remained a bloodless line.


### iii


"Jeremiah, I don't understand why you're treating—"

"You whored for him."

"What?"

"*Whored!*"

"What are you saying?"

"Grace. *You whored for him.* Skimmerhorn said so. Before I shot him."

"You shot—?" Disbelief in her eyes.

"That's right. Back in the pines, this morning. Grace spared this house because you whored for him."

"Sweetheart—"

As she said it and started around the block, he called her the foulest name he knew.

She stopped, stunned. "Jeremiah, I—I had to!"

"You said you cared about me. You don't. I was taken in for a while, but now I know it's just the money you want, not me. You wanted the house too. And there's not a thing you won't do to get what you want, is there? Lie. Whore—"

"Don't keep saying that!" Serena lunged at the still body. "She called my mama that name. 'Whore,' she said. 'Whore, *whore!*'" She struck Catherine's waxy cheek. The pale head flopped over on the boneless neck.

Recovering, she pleaded:

"Jeremiah, I *had* to do what Grace asked!"

"He didn't ask. *You* begged. Skimmerhorn told me."

Caught, she started to say something else. But he saw the truth on her face. All at once her eyes looked crazed.

"Admit you begged him, Serena."

"Yes." She spat it again. "*Yes!* He was good, too. Almost as good as a lot of the others. Better'n you'd ever be! You're just a boy!"

"A dumb boy with money you wanted. Christ, you're as dishonorable as the rest. Catherine tried to warn me. But I was too stupid to listen. Well, I'm not going to stay here. You've got the house now. I wish your father or Catherine had it instead of you, but—"

A tired shrug.

"Nothing I can do about that."

Then, louder:

"You should have died instead of your stepmother."

"I'm *glad* she's dead. I'm glad some soldier whose name I'll never know caught her and drowned her. Maybe he raped her again before he pushed her in the water. I hope he raped her till it hurt. *Till it drove her crazy!*"

He shuddered. "You pretended to be very sorry when you thought you still had me fooled. You're good at saying one thing and doing another. Almost as good as the Yanks and Billy Sherman."

"*She called my mama a whore!*"

"I expect she was right," he said, and turned away. "Goodbye, Serena."

iv

He started toward the dining room. Heard her breathing quicken; then a sound he didn't recognize until she came rushing at him. The sound had been a drawer sliding.

He spun, his back against the wall. Saw demented eyes reflecting the outside fire; a butcher knife raised in her grimy fist.

She stabbed downward.

Weary as he was, the fear pumping in him gave him just enough quickness. He jerked his head to the side. The blade raked his cheek and snapped in half when it struck the door beside his head.

He caught her wrist with his left hand as she tried to cut him with the broken blade. Unaccountably, tears misted his eyes:

"She said you weren't moral. She never told me you were insane."

"Take your damn money! I don't care. I'll find someone else!" She was hysterical. "Someone who's rich and—and—" She was spitting at him; he felt the spray wetting his already damp cheeks. Her right arm shook. He had to push hard to keep the shattered but still lethal knife from his throat.

"And a man. Not a boy! Not a child! Not a baby. *Baby, baby, baby!*"

As she screamed he pulled the Kerr with his right hand and fired the last bullet into her stomach.

v

Dark woods arching over a dark road. Faint fire in the sky, in the direction of Millen.

He was running again.

He didn't dare do anything else. Maum Isabella had heard the shot and rushed in to find him standing over Serena's lifeless body. She'd cried one word:

"*Murderer!*"

Where would he go? He didn't know. But he had to get away.

Westward, that was the best direction. Out of the path of Sherman's army. As he limped along, it began to dawn on him that he could never go back to Virginia. The war would end; people like the Claypools would return to Jefferson County and ask how Catherine and Serena Rose had died. Maum Isabella would tell them, and one day, someone might come riding to Lexington to find him.

He had to flee a long way, long way. Never tell Fan what he'd done. Never give her the slightest hint. To keep from hurting her. And to keep from being found.

He'd tried to be honorable, and this was how it had ended. There was no place for honor in war. Or in the world.

God, how Serena had gulled him! And he'd been so willing! Not merely willing. Eager. He'd had warnings about her; hints of her deception. He'd ignored them, permitting himself to succumb to her charms— and her lies:

*I love you.*

The experience had changed him, he knew that. He'd killed three people since sunup and hardly felt any guilt.

That didn't alter his desperate situation; a situation he faced with relative calm until he reached a ford in a creek near the Ogeechee. He halted on the bank, overcome.

He sat down and wept for twenty minutes.

At the end, he glanced up, wiped his face, blinked at the stars, and thought:

*I'm sorry I failed you, Colonel. You told me war ruined people, and you were right. It ruins them because they don't understand how to fight and win. I understand now.*

He splashed into the ford, less emotional. He'd definitely head west. That was safest. Perhaps he'd go far west. Hundreds of miles away, he might be safe from the wrath of the unforgiving Yanks who'd keep the war going in their own way even after the South surrendered.

He paused in the middle of the ford, gazing down at his fragmented image in the water. He felt naked and incomplete without a weapon.

*Should have gone back for the Enfield.* It had been too dangerous with Maum Isabella screaming at him.

He'd find another. Steal one. Kill for one, if need be. The war had taught him a good many fine, valuable skills.

He kept gazing into the water. *There lies Jeremiah Kent. Served dishonorably in the conflict between the states; died; and rose again—*

Rose as a new man who understood the world and how it functioned.

Without honor.

Without honesty.

Without pity.

Jeremiah Kent. He probably didn't dare use that name any longer. What would he call himself?

He shifted his left leg. The water image rippled apart, no longer recognizable.

Straightening his shoulders, he stumbled up the other side of the ford, a last spill of starlight scattering on the white streak in his hair and his emotionless face before he disappeared into the wooded dark.

# CHAPTER 7

## "Let 'em Up Easy"

THE BOXCAR TRUCKS clattered. But not so loudly Gideon couldn't hear the pale artillery captain reading from the paper:

"'*After four years of arduous service marked by unsurpassed courage and fortitude, the Army of Northern Virginia has been compelled to yield to overwhelming numbers and resources.*'"

The artilleryman was seated with his back to the opposite wall of the car, about four feet to Gideon's left. Directly across the way, another Confederate—a Virginian, flanked by two more paroled prisoners—puffed one of the cigars he'd bought in the B & O depot. His face grew more and more disgusted as the artilleryman kept reading for the benefit of those nearby:

"'*I need not tell the brave survivors of so many hard-fought battles, who have remained steadfast to the last, that I have consented to this result from no distrust of them.*

"'*But feeling that valor and devotion could accomplish nothing that would compensate for the loss that must have attended the continuance of the contest, I determined to avoid the useless sacrifice of those whose past services have endeared them to their countrymen.*'"

"Shit," the Virginian said, and stuck the cigar back in his mouth.

The artilleryman twisted his head to the left, frowned at the source of the interruption and went on:

"'*By the terms of the agreement officers and men can return to their homes, and remain until exchanged. You will take with you—*'"

"Stop reading that!" the Virginian demanded, the cigar nearly bitten in half between his teeth. "It's over a month old—and every line says coward."

The artilleryman gave him a cool stare. "I wouldn't refer to anything written by our former commander as cowardly, sir. This is the first reprinting I've seen of his general order disbanding the army."

"Well, I don't want to hear it."

"Then don't listen."

"Some of us want to hear it," Gideon said. "Continue, sir."

The Virginian's look was hostile, the artilleryman's appreciative. The latter resumed:

"'—take with you the satisfaction that proceeds from the consciousness of duty faithfully performed, and I earnestly pray that a Merciful God will extend to you His blessing and protection.'"

The pale man faltered. He cleared his throat.

"With an unceasing admiration of your constancy and devotion to your country, and grateful remembrance of your kind and generous consideration for myself, I bid you all an—affectionate farewell.'"

Slowly, the artilleryman folded the paper; murmured:

"It's signed 'R. E. Lee. General'."

He let the hand with the paper fall between his knees. Because of the bad light in the car, Gideon couldn't be sure whether there were tears in the man's eyes.

None in the Virginian's, though. He shook his head. Growled another obscenity. He was in his early thirties, lank and sallow. He wore a torn linen duster over a farmer's shirt and trousers.

"Yella," he said emphatically. The soldiers on either side of him nodded tentative agreement. The artilleryman's head jerked up; Gideon almost expected a challenge. But the Virginian was too busy focusing attention on himself.

"One of Lee's own officers had the right idea. Said all troops still in the field should head for the hills. Keep the war going!"

The artilleryman shook his head, as if unable to comprehend such stupidity. He leaned back against the boxcar wall and shut his eyes.

"But, no! The gray fox wouldn't have it. Claimed the country'd take years to recover if the boys were in the hills, bushwhacking. I say what's wrong with that? Strikes me old Marse Robert was just plain tired of fighting. So he put on his sword, sashayed up to that farmhouse, and rolled over for Grant like a tame dog. Then he wrote *that* piece of sentimental swill!"

A stab of the cigar toward the artilleryman. There was no response. The pale soldier was dozing; or pretending to doze. He wouldn't waste energy on the Virginian.

Beneath the leather patch covering his left eye socket, Gideon felt an annoying itch. He fought the impulse to lift the patch and push at his upper lid. Instead he smoothed his long, tawny beard. He didn't know which was worse, the itch or the Virginian's ranting.

To watch the man, Gideon kept his head turned a bit to the left. For about a month after Dr. Lemon had rushed him to the prison surgery, administered ether, and removed his burned eye, he'd been unable to focus his good eye properly. Gradually, though, he'd trained himself to keep his head turned slightly at all times, so one eye took in almost as much as two had before. By now the habit was becoming unconscious.

Some of the forty Confederates in the car were still listening to the lanky man's remarks. But not all. Down at the other end, one boy in butternut rested his head on his forearms, his forearms on his knees, and wept without sound, imprisoned in some secret grief. Most of the other men either seemed indifferent to the Virginian, or like Gideon, resentful.

"Why, even my old chief, Colonel Mosby—" The man plucked the cigar from his mouth and cut a smoky arc with the stub held between his index and middle finger. The smoke whipped away toward a hole chopped in the side of the car above him. The hole let in flickering shafts of sunlight and fresh air. But not enough air to cleanse the car of the stench of dirt and sweat and wounds still oozing pus.

"—he disbanded the rangers last month. Voluntarily! I read about it right after I was let out. Couldn't believe it—John Mosby truckling to the Yanks for a parole! Said he was a soldier, not a highwayman."

The man spat into the straw between his knees.

"Wanted to get his shingle back up so he could practice law again. I'll tell you, I about puked. There weren't any tougher fighters than John Mosby's Partisan Rangers. We had less than two hundred men most of the time, and a lot of the boys tended their fields by day and rode by night. Even so, with Yanks all over the place, we had most of Loudoun and Fauquier counties under control. People took to calling the territory Mosby's Confederacy. Before I got trapped by some of Custer's men, Mosby was a regular fighting cock. Now, all of a sudden, he up and quits just like Lee!"

"I wish you'd quit, too," Gideon said in a weary voice. "The war's over."

Slowly the Virginian drew the cigar from his teeth.

"You speakin' to me?"

"That's right. What the hell good does it do to keep talking that way?"

"I'll talk any way I blasted please. They haven't whipped all of us yet. They haven't whipped Captain Leonidas Worthing!"

"Well," Gideon replied with a sour smile, "you just go right on fighting, then. But be good enough to do it silently."

The man in the duster surveyed Gideon's filthy overcoat; saw no emblems of rank. "Where'd you get on this train, soldier?"

"Major," Gideon snapped. "Major Kent of Stuart's cavalry. I got on at Baltimore, just like you."

Worthing absorbed the information. Gideon ranked him—though it really made no difference since Worthing had belonged to what was essentially a guerrilla group. It made no difference now that the meeting had taken place at Appomattox Station; now that the Army of Northern Virginia had surrendered and received General Order Number Nine; now that Fort Delaware had become a memory, though one Gideon would carry all his life.

There, Dr. Cincinnatus Lemon had summoned other guards, succeeded in breaking into Tillotson's office, and ordered Gideon rushed to his surgery table where he discovered the heated stick had penetrated Gideon's cornea.

For the sake of speed, Lemon had chosen to do an evisceration, rather than a relatively slower enucleation which took the whole eyeball and its connective muscle. "Damned medical professors can't make up their minds which is best anyway," Lemon informed him later. "We've been doing enucleations since '41, but the pedants still quibble, quibble, quibble!"

Lemon had widened the corneal opening with a scalpel, scooped out the contents of the sclera with an evisceration spoon, then repaired the cornea with silk sutures. Afterward, regular applications of mercuric chloride ointment prepared to his specifications kept the site of the operation clean.

Gideon had become despondent when he discovered he'd lost part of his vision. But Dr. Lemon waved every complaint aside, growling that it was an insult to his skill. It was Lemon himself who brought a hand glass and forced Gideon to look at his own face for the first time.

He was startled. The eyelids overlapped neatly; just a slight bulge suggested the empty sclera beneath. The eyeball itself, gristly white and lacking a pupil, was far from pretty. But the closed lids hid it well, and in a way not at all disfiguring.

As if he were discussing a choice of menu items, Lemon held a bedside debate with himself on the merits of a prosthesis versus a patch. He didn't care for the quality of available artificial eyes, and thus made Gideon's decision for him. It had to be a patch. Lent a man a certain air of dash and mystery, didn't Gideon agree?

Lemon's bristly good cheer was infectious. Gideon soon stopped thinking how unfortunate he was, and became thankful he'd pulled through. His spirits improved even more when Lemon arrived with word that he'd succeeded in getting Tillotson transferred to the most squalid and dangerous shed in the prison—the one housing the criminals from the Union army. All in all, Gideon would be eternally grateful to the skillful, kindly doctor.

But now he was impatient to get home to Margaret and Eleanor, and to begin piecing his life back together—though he had no idea how he'd do it.

That was what frightened so many of the silent men in the car, he supposed. How would they start again? Unless they hailed from family farms, what could they do to earn a living? The cities would be flooded with returning veterans as well as hundreds of thousands of freed nigras. Gideon was eager to start over, but fearful there'd be no place.

For the present, he drove that particular worry from his mind.

"So," Worthing said to him, mockingly, "you're another one who thinks we should have quit like we did?"

"We were beaten. What else could we do?"

Worthing leaned forward. *"Keep fighting."*

Gideon shook his head. "You heard Lee's order. They say he was sick of watching men die for nothing. When he lost the Petersburg line, he knew it was the end. He did the right thing."

"Not for me. You sound like Old Abe! Go home. Forgive. Forget. Those Republicans won't forgive *anything!* That Johnny Booth should have shot the whole damn pack of 'em, not just Lincoln."

If Worthing hoped for a response from the scathingly delivered remark about the dead President, he was disappointed. Gideon admired the way Lincoln had behaved during the last few days of his life. According to the papers, he'd gone to Richmond on a James River steamer less than forty-eight hours after Davis had abandoned the city and Lee had given up the Petersburg lines. Richmond's new military governor had asked Lincoln how to treat the people of the city and he'd replied, "If I were in your place I'd let 'em up easy."

Gideon would be eternally grateful for those words. Before he'd embarked on the trip back to Virginia, Dr. Lemon had voluntarily telegraphed Richmond for him; telegraphed Margaret and received a four-word reply:

*All well. Hurry home.*

She didn't know about his eye. But at least she'd survived the devastation of the city that Sunday in April when Davis and his cabinet had fled by railroad for Danville, the three trestles over the James burned and blown behind them. After supply and ammunition warehouses had been torched so they wouldn't fall into enemy hands, a large area of the city had been gutted by the spreading fire. That same night Admiral Semmes had blown up his pathetically small James River Squadron; shells in the magazines had erupted for hours, like an aerial display on the Fourth of July.

Presumably Margaret might have seen the first of the Federals coming into Richmond shortly after seven the next morning. They'd come from the east. Cavalrymen.

Black cavalrymen.

Maybe she'd even seen Lincoln himself walk all the way up from Rockett's Landing to the center of the city, accompanied by his son Tad and a small military guard. Nigras had poured into the streets to watch him pass. Clapped. Sung hymns. Even knelt in front of him. During that visit, he'd told the military governor to *"let 'em up easy."* On his way home, near City Point, a band on the presidential steamer had serenaded him. He'd called for "Dixie," saying with a smile that the melody was now Federal property. The whole nation's property.

And then he'd been shot in his box at Ford's Theatre.

Trying to keep frustration out of his voice, Gideon asked Worthing, "You plan to keep on fighting, do you?"

Worthing peered at the end of his cigar. "I expect I got to live just like anybody else. Before the war, I left Loudoun County to work on railroads all over the South. Surveying, grading, laying track—I'll get me another railroad job if I can. But I don't aim to forget what happened."

"And fight about it?"

"Should the occasion arise—" Worthing let the sentence hang, a smug smile on his face.

"You're a damn fool," Gideon said, turning away.

Worthing flung the cigar down and jumped to his feet. "Don't talk to me like that, you son of a bitch!" The butt smoldered in the straw, ignored as Worthing lurched across the car.

Men stirred in the gloom. Sleepers woke at the sound of an altercation—and at the slowing of the rhythm of the trucks. The B & O special was grinding to a halt.

Gideon shoved up from the floor, disgusted that he still had to keep on battling—and with one of his own kind. Other men, including the artilleryman, tried to step between them:

"No call for this, boys."

"We're all tired."

"It's been a damn long trip for all of us."

Worthing pushed and batted at the intervening arms. "I'm not gonna take any mouth from a coward!"

Gideon refused to be stared down. "All right," he sighed. "If you want to keep your war going, I'll accommodate you."

Someone stamped on the cigar and smoking straw as Worthing reached across the arms of the men trying to keep him separated from Gideon. The boxcar rocked to a stop. Worthing swayed, off balance.

The door rolled back, flooding the smoky interior with the sunlight of a May day in 1865. Gideon's right eye slitted against the golden glare. A gray-haired, heavy-set brakeman in a ragged blue Union overcoat leaned into the boxcar.

"Lads?" he shouted. "Time for a stretch!"

*Or a fight,* Gideon thought.


ii


The weeping boy never raised his head. Worthing glanced around to the brakeman:

"Why the devil are we stopping?"

"This here's Relay House. Switch point. 'Fore we go on to Washington, we got to wait for a train comin' from Annapolis with some more of you uncaged birds."

Gideon's eye adjusted to the brilliant light. He saw rusty tracks, and beyond, spring-green hills.

Switching his gaze back to Worthing, he said, "We can discuss our differences outside. More room." His tone unmistakably said he was prepared to do something besides carry on a discussion.

Worthing's unpleasant eyes scrutinized him, measuring his size and probable strength. Despite the patch on his eye, Gideon looked formidable.

The brakeman scratched a graying eyebrow. "What the hell's goin' on in there, boys? Don't none of you want a breath of air?"

A man with the right leg of his gray trousers pinned up at the knee maneuvered his padded crutch under his armpit. Steadying himself by pushing his left palm against the wall of the car, he hopped toward the door:

"I do. This place stinks to hell."

Gideon continued to stare at Worthing with one sun-touched blue eye:

"Well, friend?"

Worthing finally smiled in a contemptuous way. "Hell, I'm not gonna quarrel with a wounded man. Even a yella one."

"Don't worry about my sight."

"No, I don't fight cripples." Worthing pulled a fresh cigar from his duster; lit it as he stalked toward the rectangle of light. Gideon suspected Worthing had said one thing while meaning quite another. Even though one of Gideon's eyes was useless, Worthing had decided it might be an even contest. He probably didn't care for even contests.

Worthing shoved the man on the crutch out of the way. Someone snickered. Worthing's neck reddened. As he poised to jump down, he was blocked by the blue-coated brakeman standing close to the door. He booted the brakeman under the chin.

Several of the Confederates yelled in surprise and disgust. The gray-haired man sprawled on the gravel between the tracks. Worthing jumped down. Gideon knew he should stay out of it, but he was so sick of men like this—the Tillotsons for whom the war had become an end instead of a means—that his bad temper got the better of him. He shouldered past the artilleryman and the others who'd been attempting to prevent a fight. He hurled himself through the open door onto Worthing's back, driving him to the ground.

### iii

Grimy Confederates began to pour out of the long line of boxcars and stream toward Gideon and Worthing from both directions. But Gideon didn't intend to give them a prolonged show. He had the advantage, and he used it.

He dragged Worthing to his feet from behind; pulled Worthing around. The Virginian's stubbled face twisted in alarm. Evidently Gideon's strength surprised him. He tried to stab his freshly lit cigar against Gideon's cheek.

Gideon ducked, punched Worthing in the stomach to double him. Then, with his other fist, he delivered a hard chopping uppercut to Worthing's mouth. Worthing reeled back, blood running from a cut in his lip.

Some soldiers behind Worthing cushioned his fall. The Virginian tried to struggle free. Before he could, Gideon shouted:

"Put him in another car or I'll kill him."

The soldiers saw the intensity of Gideon's expression and dragged Worthing away:

"Come along, now."

"Come on this way, Cap'n."

"Ain't right that two who fought on the same side should go at each other."

Worthing protested, screaming curses from his bloodied mouth. But Gideon noticed the Virginian didn't make more than a token effort to escape those restraining him.

Panting, Gideon dropped his fists. His heartbeat slowed. He was quietly thankful the fight had been so brief; thankful Worthing had turned out to be largely bluster—at least against an adversary who could hold his own.

He walked over to the gray-haired brakeman who was still seated on the ground, looking baffled:

"What the hell did I do to that Reb?"

"He was mad at me, not you."

"Could have fooled me."

Gideon grasped the man's arm and helped him to his feet. "He hurt you?"

"Not much." The man worked his jaw back and forth. Smiled. "Thank you, soldier. Miller's the name. Daphnis O. Miller."

"Beg pardon? Your first name is—?"

"Daphnis." The man pulled a face. "Don't know what it means and never have. Sounds like it belongs to a woman. I think my mother made a mistake."

Gideon smiled. "Oh, I doubt it."

"You can, but I don't. It's been the curse of my life."

"Where are you from, Mr. Miller?"

"Jersey City. Got temporarily promoted from switchman to brakeman by the grand and glorious United States army. What's your name, young fellow?"

"Gideon Kent."

"Pleasure to meet you." Miller extended his hand.

They shook. In the simple greeting, flesh against flesh, Gideon suddenly found a small hope. The issue of an independent and sovereign South had been settled. If a Union trainman and a former Confederate officer could impulsively clasp hands, maybe the country could make a start at burying the animosities of three generations and healing the wounds of four years of carnage and bitterness. He felt a little more certain of it when several of the hundred or so Confederates taking the air outside the long train paused to apologize to Miller for Worthing's attack.

The paroled Confederates began to wander across the switch tracks and sprawl on a grassy bank. A balmy breeze warmed Gideon's unwashed face.

"Jersey City, you said. You're a fair distance from home, Mr. Miller."

"That's so," the brakeman nodded. "But they need us to run these prisoner trains—beg your pardon. Guess you ain't a prisoner any more."

"Take it you're a railroad man?"

"That's right. Where were you locked up?"

"Fort Delaware."

Miller grimaced. "Heard that was a hellhole."

"Compared to the fort, I expect hell would be a spa."

"A what?"

"Resort. Vacation place."

Gideon restrained a smile; the reading had helped. Dr. Lemon had somehow cajoled and threatened until Tillotson had returned the stolen books, which Gideon had devoured while he was recuperating in the prison infirmary. Now and again he tried a new, unfamiliar word; always with a bit of awkwardness, and always feeling he might be thought to be acting superior by the person to whom he uttered the word. But he didn't mean to sound superior. He simply needed to practice.

"What branch of service you from?" Miller inquired.

"Cavalry. Jeb Stuart's. I was captured at Yellow Tavern."

"Mighty fine outfit, the papers said."

Quietly: "That's understating it."

"Where's your home, Kent?"

"Lexington, Virginia, originally. Presently Richmond."

"Did you have a trade before the war?"

Gideon's stomach quivered. "No, none. I was too thick-headed to learn one. I'll pay for it now. I have a wife and baby to support. I'll have to find work."

In spite of the difficulties he faced in doing that, he'd made one firm decision in prison. Even if his father offered, he wouldn't accept so much as one dollar of help. The California inheritance would be his someday. But until it was, he meant to make his way on his own, hardship or no. If he didn't, he'd have no pride of accomplishment.

"Jobs are gonna be mighty scarce," Daphnis Miller observed as they started strolling beside the train.

"And not too many available for a man who's half blind, I suspect."

It was said with a smile, and no trace of self-pity. Yet the truth of his situation haunted him. What *could* a man do who was less than whole?

"Well," Miller chuckled, "you ever get desperate enough to work in a rail yard, come to Jersey City an' look me up."

"Railroading a rough business, is it?"

"Let's put it this way. A fellow who couples cars for a living and has both hands, all his fingers, an' two good legs is one of three things: Mighty quick, mighty lucky—or new on the job."

Gideon laughed. A whistle sounded eastward, the source hidden by the boxcars. The chug of a second train approaching grew steadily louder. Miller answered a hail from another brakeman up near the engine:

"Keep your pants on, Feeny, I'll be there. Kent, I truly 'preciated what you done. That Reb looked as if he wanted to tear me apart."

"He wanted to tear somebody apart. I don't think it mattered who it was."

"Damn job's gettin' as bad as workin' in the Erie yards. Well, so long. Thanks again."

"Mr. Miller?"

The trainman turned.

"Do me one small favor in return."

Miller's white eyebrow lifted, inquiringly.

"Don't say Reb any more. We're all Americans again."

Miller smiled in a sheepish way. "Guess you're right. Didn't mean anything nasty by it. But it's gonna take a while to get out of the habit."

He waved and hurried off.

Gideon leaned against the boxcar, fighting to keep his hand down. The blind eye itched again. The brakeman was right. Men on both sides would be a long time breaking the habit of using certain words.

*Reb.*

*Traitor.*

*Damn Yank.*

*Enemy.*

Men would be a long time forgetting.

iv

Presently, more boxcars were switched and coupled to the end of the first train. The whistle blew three times and the Confederates began to clamber back aboard the cars. Spirits had improved. There was a good deal of laughing and joking.

Gideon sank down in the place he'd occupied before. Miller appeared outside, spied him, and waved as he slid the door shut, leaving only the chopped hole to ventilate the boxcar as the train resumed its journey to Washington.

*So much to do,* Gideon thought. *See if my little girl even recognizes me. Doubt if she will.*

*Find a way to support Margaret.*

*Try to discover what's become of Matt and Jeremiah.*

*Visit my mother down in Lexington—*

For a moment the odds against successfully beginning a new life seemed overwhelming. Especially when he remembered Worthing and Tillotson. There were haters on both sides. They'd make Lincoln's idea— "Let 'em up easy"—difficult to turn into a reality. And with the Illinois President gone and his policies already being disavowed by many Northerners, the auspices were poor.

Indeed, they hadn't been too promising while Lincoln was still alive. Gideon had studied an account of the hysterical celebration in Washington two nights after Davis' abandonment of Richmond. Lee had not yet surrendered and even then, on a platform in front of the Patent Office, Vice President Andrew Johnson had roared to a howling mob that he would hang Jefferson Davis "twenty times." As for others who'd participated in the rebellion—Gideon could recall Johnson's chilling words almost exactly:

"*I would arrest them, I would try them, I would convict them, and I would hang them. Treason must be made odious! Traitors must be punished and impoverished!*"

So cried the obscure Tennessee Democrat, under fixtures specially arranged to blaze the word UNION from the top of the pillars of the Patent Office on the night all Washington shone with candle and gas illuminations to celebrate the fall of the enemy capital. Now Johnson was serving in the office Lincoln had still held on that evening when Johnson had shouted, "*Hang, hang!*"

Fortunately no one had expressed an interest in hanging Gideon. He was alive, and there was a wonderful, warm girl waiting for him in Richmond. He intended to devote himself to her and to their daughter; to giving them a comfortable, secure existence. He was done with war. Never again would he actively seek a fight, for whatever lofty principles. To that he'd made up his mind.

His thoughts kept returning to Margaret. They'd spent very little time together during the past three years, so each memory was just that much more vivid.

The sight of her. The feel of her lying close in the cool hours of the night. Her ardor as a wife—it sent a pleasurable thrill of anticipation chasing through him.

Somehow, no matter how formidable the obstacles, they'd overcome them together. Rebuild the life—the marriage—begun when he'd returned to Richmond after First Manassas. He felt more optimistic when he recalled the innate decency of Northerners such as Dr. Lemon and the trainman, Miller, with his words about looking him up in Jersey City. Miller obviously hadn't meant what he said; he'd merely been trying to express his gratitude in familiar terms. But at least he'd said *something*. It was encouraging.

Down at the end of the car, the boy in gray was still crying. His back heaved, but Gideon could hear no sound above the rattle of the wheels.

He smoothed his beard again, clambered up, and stepped over outstretched legs. Maybe there was something he could do to alleviate the boy's misery.

He knelt beside him. Laid an arm across the shuddering, butternut-clad shoulders.

"Son?"

Not even twenty-two years old himself, Gideon was calling this stripling son. But he saw nothing incongruous. He'd lived through enough struggle, enough perils, for three adult lifetimes.

"Son?" he repeated.

No answer.

"Any way I can help?"

Still silence. The boy didn't raise his head.

Gently, Gideon patted his back. After a moment the violent spasms began to subside.

Gideon remained where he was, neither speaking nor being spoken to, just moving his hand up and down, up and down, softly; an almost fatherly touch. Somehow it helped the boy.

The whistle on the Baltimore and Ohio engine shrieked. The boxcars clattered faster, carrying those wounded in body and those wounded in spirit on toward home.

BOOK THREE

*The Fire Road*

# CHAPTER 1

## *Escape to the West*

HE FIRED. RELOADED. Fired again. Every round seemed to miss.

The gray-faced men were cleverly hiding in the tangled second-growth timber fifty yards out in front of the log and brush breastwork. With startling abruptness, one or two would dart from cover, shoot, and jump back out of sight. He fired at one such marksman and an instant later, blinked. Where there'd been a target, there was nothing but the smoke.

Beside him, a boy no more than seventeen took a ball in the side of his face. The boy's shriek of pain turned to a whimper as he fell. The crackle of gunfire up and down the Union defense line quickly muffled the sound.

He squinted over the breastwork then, wondering whether the Irish Brigade of Hancock's II Corps had been sent into the tangled woodland known as the Wilderness, or into the nether regions.

Smoke billowed everywhere. Artillery rumbled like a storm in a sky he couldn't see. Not far overhead, tree branches formed a thick web that shut out most of the late afternoon light above, and intensified the light below: the spurting flash from rifle muzzles, the flickering light of large limbs and small twigs blazing and raining sparks.

Directly over him, a branch crumbled apart. A hot piece of charred wood dropped onto his neck. He yelped, jerked the trigger, saw a slab of bark fly from one of the gargoyle trees behind which the enemy lurked.

Even this deep in the forest, he could feel a fairly stiff breeze blowing. Somehow it failed to dispel the smoke, though it fanned the scattered fires. The Rebs kept sniping.

On his right, young replacements who'd joined the Brigade only weeks ago scrambled back as balls chunked into the crazily piled, hastily cut logs. One of the boys cried out:

"Mother of Mary! *She's catchin'!*"

The brush atop the logs a yard to his right burst into flame. Snapping, roaring, the fire raced both ways along the improvised fortification. More men of the Brigade leaped away. Out in the shifting red smoke, the Rebs howled in pain or in defiance and kept volleying.

The fire swept past him, not a foot in front of his nose. The intense heat drove him back. In moments, the entire breastwork was burning.

He heard a bugle call. The blare was suddenly aborted by a scream. Someone shouted, "Fall back! *Fall back!*"

Beyond the barrier of fire, the gray soldiers seemed to be on the move. He tried to find a target, then wiped sweat from his eyes with the back of a hand. He couldn't believe what he was witnessing.

Among the stunted trees, boys in butternut were advancing. Some had no weapons. In silence, they pleaded for mercy with outstretched hands. Minié balls smashed into their soiled blouses, piercing the fabric. No blood ran from the wounds.

He fought back a desire to scream and flee from this impossible battle taking place below the Rapidan. He clutched his rifle with both hands, as if gripping it would help keep his duty uppermost in his mind; keep him from running away.

The wall of fire rose higher.

Four feet.

Six.

From the other side, a woman called his name:

"Michael?"

He raised on tiptoe, risking death from the Confederate balls that had begun to whiz past again. A gust of wind tore holes in the flames. He saw her wandering among the gray men; saw her small, well-proportioned body with exquisite clarity in spite of the smoke. Her glossy dark hair had a scarlet nimbus. Her bright blue eyes reflected the glare of burning trees. Repeatedly, the advancing soldiers jostled her. They seemed unaware of her presence.

"*Michael?*"

A few Union soldiers were returning the Confederate volleys. Any second she'd be hit.

"Julia, go back!"

She didn't hear. Her head kept turning, her eyes searching for him.

He flung down his rifle, crouched, and ran at the burning breastwork. His left boot slipped on the body of a dead comrade. His leap was bad. He crashed chest-first into the sagging timber.

Fire scorched his ragged blouse. The last two metal buttons dropped off, their threads burned away. The pain on his exposed skin was hideous, but he bore it, scrambling up and over the collapsing fortification. By the time he cleared it, both his sleeves were afire.

He could still see her out there, helpless and unable to locate him. The gray men, pleading with their hands, continued to brush by.

"Julia? Here I am!" He waved his arms. The blue sleeves trailed fire. She'd come all this way to find him. He couldn't abandon her.

"Here, Julia. Here!"

A Confederate rifleman stepped from a turbulent cloud of smoke. Shot. Michael felt the ball slam into his belly.

Fire curled up his legs, filling his nostrils with the stench of burned leather. Another ball struck his left shoulder. She turned away in the red murk, shaking her head sadly. She started back to the gargoyle trees where the Rebel wounded flailed and bayed.

"Julia? Julia!"

Afire and hit, he began to topple forward. A third Rebel ball thumped into his body. Despairing, he continued to fall slowly; so slowly. At the impact of a fourth ball, he heard a deep, sonorous tolling.

He took another bullet in his left thigh. The bell tolled.

He took one in his right arm. The bell tolled.

Soon it was pealing without pause. It was the only sound he heard. It mocked his failure to reach the woman he wanted against all reason. It knelled his death in the Wilderness as he drifted face-first into a pit of dark where ground had been only a moment before.

ii

Someone jabbed his hip.

Terrified, he heard men grumbling. Sounds of motion above the bell's strident clang.

Michael Boyle's eyes popped open. He gasped loudly the instant he realized he'd been dreaming again.

He lay on his side in the cramped top bunk. In tiers of three, the bunks lined the walls of the eighty-five-foot railroad car lit at each end by a hanging lamp.

Moment by moment, the nightmare was fading. He searched for another familiar detail; found it in the pale rectangle of the charcoal drawing he'd tacked to the wall beside his head. Once he saw the drawing, he knew, finally and positively, that he was alive and whole.

Dry-mouthed, he scratched his crotch, wondering whether the cooties had gotten him at last. The bell beside the door at the car's end was being rung to wake the workers. Again he felt a jab on his hip.

He rolled over to face the aisle. The man who occupied the bunk below, Sean Murphy, stood on his own bed, his head on a level with

Michael's eyes. Murphy was fifty or thereabouts, robust, pie-faced, genial. He had surprisingly little gray in his curly, copper-colored hair and huge fan of a beard. He poked Michael a third time.

"Sleep all mornin', lad, and our boss'll be on your ass worse than he is already. Rise an' shine!"

"I'm coming," Michael growled. He sat up without thinking, banged his head on the wooden roof, and swore.

He swung his legs out of the bunk and jumped down among the other Paddies tumbling from their bunks with varying degrees of speed and ill humor. Murphy's bright blue-green eyes raked Michael's six-foot frame; noted the sweat rings under the arms of his long underwear. Murphy clucked his tongue.

"You must have had some night, Michael me boy."

"What makes you say that?"

"For the last hour 'twas all I could do to catch a few winks. You been tossin' and babblin' something awful. What was goin' through your head?"

Michael stepped on the edge of the empty bottom bunk, reached to the lower end of his own, and dragged out his faded flannel shirt, trousers, and boots. He dumped the clothing in the aisle, where he proceeded to dress amidst the buffeting of earlier risers already stumbling toward the end of the car.

He disliked having to answer Murphy's question. How could he admit he'd been dreaming of a woman who didn't belong to him and never would? A woman he'd come all the way out here to escape and couldn't? Guardedly, he said:

"I was back in the Wilderness. The last afternoon, when I got hit." Michael still bore a scar on his left hip. A Confederate ball buzzing in over the barricades had slammed him out of action—and out of the war.

"You dream of that every other night," Murphy sighed, helping Michael pull his galluses over his shirt. "That was two years ago, lad. Seems like you'd be forgettin' it by now."

He recalled the fire; the smoke; the feeling of forever being cut off from safety and sanity.

"If you'd been there, Sean, I doubt you'd forget it."

"But the war's over. I keep remindin' you of that."

Michael knotted a red bandana around his neck and finally managed a smile. He was a tall Irishman of thirty-six with fair hair already showing gray, a horizontal white scar across his forehead, and steady golden-brown eyes close to the color of the handle-bar moustache he'd grown since coming west. Like his hair, the moustache was gray streaked.

There was no flab left on him, either. He was spare and hard after eleven weeks as a rust-eater on what he and the other Paddies referred to as the U-Pay.

"Out of the way, I'm hungry," a man named Flannagan complained, giving Michael a shove. Michael stiffened. Double-chinned Sean Murphy laid a hand on his arm:

"Easy—*easy!* You're edgy as the devil this morning."

Michael let himself be restrained and took no offense. Murphy had become a good friend. Murphy was the man who'd persuaded him to leave the Chicago saloon where he'd been sweeping floors and tending bar. Together they'd ridden the cars west to the end of the existing rail lines, then traveled on to Omaha.

And Murphy's remark was embarrassingly accurate. Of late, Michael had found Louis Kent's wife slipping into his dreams with increasing frequency. No matter how far a man fled, apparently certain things could never be outrun.

He'd tried running once before, when he'd finally admitted how he felt about the spoiled and lovely spouse of Amanda Kent's only son. In a rage, he'd taken her at the family's country seat up the Hudson River from New York. The way he'd taken her amounted to rape. Almost immediately he'd realized it was more an act of lust than anger; he'd wanted her secretly for a long time. He'd enlisted in the 69th New York to escape the cause of his feelings, but found he couldn't.

After the Wilderness, the desire to flee had still been with him. But it was complemented by another drive, just as strong. He was sick at heart after seeing so much death. Weary of watching life and property being destroyed. He'd wanted an antidote; a feeling of accomplishing something; building something. So Julia had been one reason but not the only reason he'd left the Washington hospital as soon as he could, accepted his discharge, and headed for new country.

He'd spent a season in Ohio, planting and harvesting corn while Lee gave up to Grant at Appomattox, the bloodletting ended, and the Northern punishment of the beaten enemy commenced. Late in '65 he'd moved on to Chicago and held unsatisfying menial jobs in a packing house, a tannery, the saloon. During those months, the nation watched in astonishment as Andrew Johnson—"His Accidency, the President"—swung away from his pronouncements about hanging Southerners and began carrying out the conciliatory Reconstruction policies foreshadowed in Lincoln's 1864 inaugural.

In Ohio and Illinois, too, the memory of Julia stayed with him.

Then crusty widower, Sean Murphy, approached him in the Chicago saloon, and they became drinking companions and eventually friends. Michael listened with interest when Murphy spoke of leaving his poor-paying drayman's job for higher wages and cleaner work in the open air beyond the Missouri. There, the long-delayed transcontinental railroad was going forward at last. Michael decided to pack his few belongings and join Murphy and a number of other Paddies heading for the prairie.

The men went west in a spirit of hope, enthusiasm and pride, declaring that the Irish had built the Erie canal, a marvel in its day, and by God they'd build the century's newest and greatest marvel too—

"No denials, Michael?"

He forced himself from his reverie. "What's that?"

"I remarked—several hours ago, it seems—that you woke up nervous as an Orangeman in County Cork. Again."

Michael smiled. "Why, Sean, you should know moodiness is typical of an Irish fellow. Especially when he's throwing down a mile of rail a day, and working for a bastard to boot."

Murphy looked unconvinced. He headed up the aisle between the tiered bunks in the eight-foot-high car. He and Michael were now the laggards. Most of the other laborers had piled out the door at the end, where a rack of repeating Spencer rifles gleamed under the hanging lantern.

"I agree it ain't quite the soft duty I thought it'd be," Murphy said. "But thirty-five greenback dollars a month is a sight better than what I was earnin' haulin' kegs up and down Lake Street. Wait a damned minute, will you? Got to lace up my blasted boot again."

Murphy knelt. Michael scratched his groin and gazed at the rifles in the racks. Would they be needed against the Sioux or Cheyenne?

So far there'd been only four raids, each one over before Michael even heard about it. The pattern was always the same. He and the other men would be wakened late in the night by yells and the bang of Spencers. They'd tumble outside, rifles in hand, only to find the drovers who guarded the railroad's cattle firing futile shots into the darkness from which some Indians had come slipping silently to run off half a dozen head.

After the first theft, Michael and Sean Murphy had learned that information about the Plains tribes given them gratuitously in an Omaha saloon was false. They'd been told the hostiles never struck after the sun went down, fearing that if they were slain at night, their spirits couldn't find the way to the Indian equivalent of heaven. A drover guarding the herd explained the real reason Plains braves generally avoided nocturnal attacks: the gut strings on war bows grew damp and lost their tautness in the night air. Night thievery of cattle was commonplace, however, since it seldom required the discharge of even a single arrow. There'd been no casualties to the railroad men on any of the raids thus far.

But couriers galloping in from further west, where the grade was being prepared, had recently brought disturbing news about the Indians:

Early in the spring, peace commissioners had been dispatched by the Federal Government to attempt to arrange a treaty with the Sioux and Cheyenne. The tribes stood in the way of miners heading north toward the Big Horn Mountains—the Powder River country—where there'd been a gold strike.

The dispatch of the commission sprang from a shift in Congressional policy. Washington now thought it easier to buy peace on the High Plains than to fight for it. According to what Michael had heard, important chiefs of the Oglala and Brulé Sioux had journeyed to Fort Laramie to listen to the offer of one Mr. Taylor of the Indian Office:

The tribes would be given an annuity of seventy-five thousand dollars a year, plus firearms for hunting, if they'd guarantee the safety of whites traveling the Bozeman Trail to the new diggings. The negotiations had proceeded smoothly at first. Then they were abruptly ruined by the arrival of a Brulé chief, Standing Elk, who had encountered a column of white soldiers commanded by a Colonel Carrington. The soldiers were on their way to the Powder River country to build stockades.

Red Cloud, the most influential of the Sioux at the Fort Laramie parley, listened to the report of the army column with shock and anger. Offers of peace were being made even as soldiers tramped northwest to seize the disputed territory! Red Cloud and a great many other braves stormed out of the fort, promising war as repayment for the deception. So even though the U-Pay had experienced no serious trouble as yet, every man at the railhead knew circumstances were ripe for it.

"Broke the damn thing!" Murphy exploded. Part of a thong dangled from his hand. He stood up and stuffed the thong in his pocket. Michael turned away from the rifles and the gloomy thoughts they generated. Murphy returned to the subject of a few moments ago:

"I wanted to speak to you about the boss. I agree it's a damn shame we drew him as head of our gang—"

"I can't figure out how a Reb got such a good job, Sean."

"Corkle told me the fellow ran railroad construction crews in the South, before the war."

"I heard that too. But he's still a Reb, and this is mostly a Union outfit."

"All I can guess is, the Casements believe the only war they should fret about is a war with the calendar. They put experienced men where they can get the best use from 'em."

"Suppose so," Michael nodded. "All that's past is forgiven—or so you're always saying," he added with a wry smile.

"Well, we both understand I've been known to prevaricate on occasion," Murphy grinned. He remained in the door, intentionally blocking Michael's passage. "There ain't a hotter Southron at the railhead than the wretch we're workin' for—nor one who likes more to keep fightin' the late, unlamented war. Friend to friend, Michael, you're a mite too willing to butt heads with him on that subject—not to mention others."

"I have a reason. No, make it three."

"Such as?"

"He's a bully. He's a loudmouth. And he's a liar about the war. He won't admit fighting for the principle of states' rights was so much blarney. He and his kind may have fought well, but they were fighting for an immoral cause."

Here Murphy looked dubious; Michael's remark didn't reflect the conventional thinking of most Irishmen, who viewed blacks as an economic threat.

"Nigger slavery, y'mean?"

Another nod. "I also get sick of him claiming it's only the Northern factories that beat the South. He's partly right, but I'll tell you this. At the Round Tops, I saw no factories perishing, I saw Irishmen and Dutchmen. In the Wilderness I didn't see factories perishing, just Yankee boys."

"Well, have a care, Michael. He's no sort to fool with—and I've been wanting to remind you of it."

"I don't need reminders. I work with him every day. Thanks for your good thoughts, however. I'll behave. I'm through with fighting. I'm here to work."

"'An' they shall beat their swords into plowshares, an' their spears into pruning hooks—'" Murphy recited the passage with a merry smile. "'Neither shall they learn war any more'?"

"That's the general idea," Michael replied soberly.

"Book of Micah," the older man announced proudly. "Fourth chapter, third verse. See? I ain't the godless lout you boys are always accusin' me of bein'."

"But it's from the second chapter, fourth verse, of Isaiah as well as from Micah."

"What? It is?"

"Yes. And you left out the part about nation not lifting up sword against nation."

Murphy blinked. "My stars, I never took you for a Bible student!"

"It's the only book my mother owned when I was a boy in the slums. She died when I was seven, but she'd already taught me to read a few passages, and persuaded me to study it to learn moral behavior. When she passed away, and I went on the streets and worked on the docks, I kept a

Bible with me. For every moral lesson I took out of the pages, I saw two of the opposite kind happening in New York. But it was my principal teacher of decent English."

"And you're way ahead of me on the subject of the boss. Relieved to hear it." Murphy winked. "Certainly 'twasn't him you were thinkin' of last night. Along with the war, you had a gal on your mind, didn't you?"

Curtly: "No."

"Why, you did! You kept yellin' her name in your sleep."

Michael's face went blank. "You must have heard wrong."

"I'm positive I did not. Who is she, lad? Some Chicago colleen you never mentioned to me? Or one of them farm lasses you met down in Ohio?"

"Sean," Michael said, his smile affable but not his eyes, "we may be friends, good friends. But certain things are none of your affair. Quit swinging your clapper and let's go eat."

The younger man's expression had grown so grim, Murphy acquiesced without a murmur.

# CHAPTER 2

## *The Railhead*

THUS, AT DAWN on a Saturday morning near the end of August, 1866, Michael Boyle and Sean Murphy climbed down from one of the four cars standing with a locomotive coupled at the rear. Steam was already up on the 4-4-0 Danforth and Cooke wood burner named *Osceola*. The engine's cowcatcher pointed east along the single track.

*Osceola* and a quartet of double-sized boxcars comprised the railhead work train—the "perpetual train" as it was called by the Paddies who were pushing the line westward in an effort to silence doubters, lure more investors, and turn the foundering U-Pay into a success.

Dr. Thomas Durant, the vice-president and general manager of the Union Pacific, had in fact made a public commitment to finish two hundred and forty-seven miles of roadbed across the Nebraska Territory as soon as possible. Milepost 247 would be erected on the hundredth meridian. Until the meridian was reached, the line's charter to build and operate the eastern portion of the transcontinental railroad would not become official. So a growing number of ex-soldiers and day laborers from the cities were driving toward the meridian at a pace even the hardiest newcomers had trouble keeping up with at first. Michael well recalled the agony he'd suffered during his first two weeks at the railhead. Every night, he'd dragged himself up to his bunk, his whole body in pain.

Already there was noise and movement around the perpetual train. The sun had barely risen. But the light was bright enough to reveal a barren yet strangely beautiful ocean of grass, gently rolling, and treeless for as far as a man could see. The light burnished the greenish-gray buffalo grass and here and there illuminated radiant patches of purple pasqueflower, crimson wild geranium, and yellow prairie smoke.

West of the four huge freight cars lay the grade, prepared by gangs following the location stakes as far as a hundred miles in advance of the moving railhead. To the rear stretched the shimmering parallel rails, running a good two hundred miles to the Missouri River. Back past Fort

Kearney at milepost 191—the last real outpost of civilization, if a ramshackle infantry stockade and a collection of shanties could be called civilization. Back past the division point at Grand Island. Back past Fremont, only forty miles out of Omaha—or Bilksville as it was called by those who still considered the railroad a foolish venture destined to fail.

Fremont was as far as the rails had gotten by January of '66, even though Dr. Durant and other officials of the line had broken ground at Omaha almost a year earlier. There'd been poor progress until two men, the Casement brothers, had submitted a bid as subcontractors for track laying. Now the line was advancing at the rate of two rails every minute, four hundred rails every mile—and a mile of new track between sunup and sunset, six days a week. Michael found the speed astonishing—just as he found the sights of the prairie fresh and astonishing almost every morning. Today was no exception.

He stretched, beginning to throw off the lethargy of sleep and the memory of the nightmare. He drew in deep breaths of the cool, sweet air tanged with the smell of burning wood and the reek of valve oil from the funnel-stack locomotive. Men were hurrying from the two bunk cars to the dining car, second from the head end. The first car served as a combination office and kitchen.

A few late risers were rolling out of hammocks slung beneath the car where Michael and Murphy slept. Others were climbing down from tents erected on top. General Jack Casement's army of rust-eaters was growing week by week. Over four hundred men worked at the railhead now.

Smoke drifted across the paling stars, breeze-borne from vents in the roof of the kitchen. Michael thought he smelled fresh bread. He certainly smelled cow dung. To his left, five hundred head were rousing and milling, prodded by the drovers. The herd comprised the railhead's traveling meat supply; the four Indian raids had not cut into it substantially.

The lowing cows raised dust. But the Platte River, shallow, twisting and beginning to glow with sunlight, was still visible through the cloud. On the far side of the river characterized as "a mile wide and an inch deep," Michael could discern the ruts of the Overland Trail leading on to Fort Laramie and Oregon. Sometimes the road was noisy with freight wagons, or a stagecoach, or parties of buffalo hunters. This morning it was deserted.

But it had seen traffic during the night. He smiled at the sight of a couple of the transcontinental telegraph poles planted beside the trail. The poles had been pushed until they tilted to a forty-five-degree angle. Buffalo had passed, pausing to scratch off some of their shedding hump manes.

Michael and Sean Murphy trudged on toward the nearest line of men waiting their turn in the dining car. A similar line had formed at the car's other end. The morning bell rang at five thirty. In less than an hour, the first of the iron trains carrying a carefully calculated quantity of rails and ties, spikes and chairs would come chugging in from the supply base at Kearney. Then the work day—twelve hours or more—would begin.

The activity and numbers of men around the work train hardly suggested the difficulties the transcontinental line had encountered since the passage of the Pacific Railroad Acts. Michael knew a great deal about the Union Pacific's history. The supply trains brought newspapers as well as mail, and he'd become an avid student of the project.

The concept of a rail link between the oceans had been under discussion for years. Proposed routes had been debated in Congress and at the cabinet level for a decade. In the fifties, while he was Franklin Pierce's Secretary of War, Jefferson Davis had obtained surveys of several possible routes. But the start of the four year rebellion had interrupted the decision process, even though Lincoln by then had enough data on which to act.

In California a young engineer named Theodore Judah had located and mapped a feasible route through the Sierras. Other surveys, including those by the Union Pacific's new chief engineer, former U.S. Army General Grenville Dodge, had shown that the most practical route from the Missouri began at Omaha and ran toward the point where the Overland Trail joined the Platte.

Finally Lincoln had moved. He saw the railroad as a means of symbolically unifying the Atlantic and Pacific states and of solidifying the Union's hold on all the land between. Congress and the President had put the first Pacific Railroad Act into law in July of 1862, chartering two corporations: the Union Pacific, which was to build the line from the Missouri River, and the Central Pacific, which would begin eastbound construction at Sacramento.

The terms of the Railroad Act seemed ideal for attracting risk capital. The government had granted both corporations ten miles of land in alternating sections on either side of a four-hundred-foot right of way; ten miles in return for every mile of track laid. Resale of this land to settlers, it was presumed, would help finance the project. In addition, the Act had authorized Federal subsidies in the form of thirty-year bonds. The amount of the subsidy per mile of completed track depended on the terrain. On the plains, the rate was sixteen thousand dollars a mile. It jumped to forty-eight thousand a mile in the Rocky Mountains and the Sierras.

Control of the Central Pacific was in the hands of a group called The Big Four. The first of the quartet was California's governor, Leland Stanford. His partners were three merchants from the Sacramento Valley—a grocer and vegetarian named Mark Hopkins, and a pair of hardware mer-

chants, Collis Huntington and Charles Crocker. Their eastern counter-
parts were a group of businessmen led by Dr. Durant, a canny man who'd
abandoned medicine for a career as a railway promoter.

Despite the government's generosity, the sale of each corporation's
stocks and bonds had lagged because of the financial community's disin-
terest. No shrewd investor wanted to dump money into a railroad across a
wilderness when so much more could be made supplying war material to
the Federal Government. So a second Railroad Act had become necessary
in '64. Among its other provisions, it doubled the land granted per mile;
the two companies would eventually control over twenty-one million acres.

But even this failed to attract capital. By mid-1864, the Central Pacific
had laid exactly thirty-one miles of track. The Union Pacific's rails didn't
extend beyond the Omaha city limits.

Once more Lincoln had stepped in, this time primarily on behalf of the
Union Pacific. He'd sought the services of "the King of Spades"—Massachusetts Congressman Oakes Ames, who'd made a fortune from the
manufacture and sale of Ames Old Colony Mining Shovels. Lincoln
wanted Ames to put not only his money but his personal prestige behind
the line. Oakes Ames and his brother Oliver poured in a million of their
own funds, and attracted another million and a half—but it was still not
enough. War profiteering and skepticism continued to deter investors.

Michael had read a good deal about the directors of both railroads. He'd
also heard his share of gossip. Durant's crowd and The Big Four might be
greedy, but they were neither lazy nor stupid. They wanted the line built
not only because it might yield unprecedented profits, but also for the
sheer thrill of accomplishing an engineering feat of incredible magnitude.

There was mounting evidence, however, that the directors of the lines
were beginning to indulge in freebooting on a grand scale. Big Four director Huntington, for example, had scored a major coup with the subsidies.
It had been President Lincoln's responsibility to fix the place at which the
sixteen-thousand-dollar Sacramento Valley subsidy was replaced by the
forty-eight-thousand-dollar one for construction in the Sierra foothills.
Huntington had enlisted a friendly geologist who reported that the Sierras
actually "began" at Arcade Creek, twenty-four miles west of the point
designated in Theodore Judah's original survey. At Arcade, reddish mountain soil could be found mingled with the blacker dirt of the Valley. The
fact that the soil had washed down there was glossed over.

Armed with the "dramatic new findings," Huntington had launched a
campaign in Washington. Prompted by a cooperative congressman, Lincoln restudied his maps and accepted the Central Pacific claim—thus giving the line an additional two dozen miles at the considerably higher rate.

"Pertinacity and Abraham's faith," ran a wry report of the maneuvering, "removed mountains."

Dr. Durant recognized a major problem confronting the Union Pacific. A record of accomplishment was needed to attract capital and reverse unfavorable public opinion. *Accomplishment! Track laid!* The line wouldn't even be in business permanently unless the hundredth meridian was reached.

But slogans and rallying cries weren't enough to overcome the obstacles facing the U. P.:

First, every bit of equipment, food, water, and rolling stock had to be brought to Omaha by freight wagon or by steam packet from St. Joseph or St. Louis. The two nearest railroads east of the Missouri, the Rock Island and the Cedar Rapids & Missouri, both stopped a good hundred and fifty miles short of the river—as Michael had discovered when he'd journeyed west from Chicago. He, Murphy, and the other Paddies had completed the last stage of their trip by coach and on foot.

No bridge existed between Council Bluffs and Omaha. Anything arriving by wagon had to be ferried around the Missouri's dangerous sand bars. The line's very first Danforth and Cooke locomotive, the *Major General Sherman,* had been shipped in sections on a river boat and laboriously reassembled at its destination.

The Central Pacific had been luckier on a couple of important counts. The forested slopes of the Sierras provided all the hardwood the line needed to fuel its engines—and for ties. The Nebraska plains, by contrast, had no trees except the porous and unsatisfactory cottonwood.

The C. P. also faced no immediate threats of Indian trouble along its first miles of roadbed. But the line had to traverse mountains—blasting and tunneling through, or creating tortuous switchback cuts that wound around the peaks. Charles Crocker, the line's construction boss, had found a solution to the unwillingness of some men to risk themselves in such hazardous work. Crocker had begun to hire Chinese. The so-called Celestials proved to be first-class powder monkeys, expert at working with the explosives used to blast a path through solid granite.

Michael had read that not a few of the white men working on the Central Pacific hated the Chinese. But Crocker was delighted with them. They worked diligently, and had one appealing moral virtue their white brethren lacked: they drank nothing stronger than tea. Crocker's inspiration had been lauded in a toast that amused Michael: "To the Pacific Railroad—the only piece of crockery ware made out of China."

In spite of minor successes, such as Crocker's discovery of a work force that could plow through the Sierras without fear and without delay, Michael knew skepticism about the concept of a transcontinental line remained widespread. Even four short years before, the Union hero of the Georgia and Carolina march—the very man for whom the Union Pacific's Engine Number 1 had been named—had greeted the first Railroad Act with the comment that he wouldn't care to spend money on a coast-to-coast ticket to be used by his grandchildren.

Both railroads were drawing their share of press criticism, though for some reason roving correspondents treated the Central Pacific less harshly than they did the eastern line. Headquarters was reportedly still grumbling about articles by the editor of the influential Springfield, Massachusetts, *Republican*. He'd written that the job of laying track across the relatively level plains was "baby work." He and other Eastern pundits couldn't fathom why the Union Pacific was progressing so slowly—unless, as many said, it had been destined to fail from the beginning.

But now 1866 looked to be a watershed, thanks to the arrival of the Casement brothers, John S. and Daniel T.

Jack Casement had been brevetted to brigadier in the Union army. He was almost constantly at the railhead. Daniel remained in Omaha, calculating how many five-hundred-pound rails or chemically treated cottonwood ties were needed each day, or journeying out to the supply bases at Fremont and Kearney to coordinate the schedules of the iron trains.

To be accurate, the Casements didn't work directly for the Union Pacific. Nor did Michael or Murphy and/or any of the other rust-eaters. The actual work of building the road was contracted by a company called the Crédit Mobilier. In French the name meant movable loan. The Crédit Mobilier sold its services directly to the U. P. Some said its prices were never questioned.

That rumor tended to validate another Michael had heard about Dr. Durant and some of his fellow U. P. directors. It was said they also served secretly as directors of the subcontracting firm. If that were true, Michael saw no reason why a mile of track couldn't be billed at twice or triple its actual cost. One pocket, in effect, would pay another. In a cynical way he almost admired the suspected scheme. It would make thievery on a stupendous scale not only possible but easy.

In fact he'd reflected that such an arrangement might one day attract the interest, and money, of Mr. Louis Kent. Louis was at home among men willing to take not altogether legal risks for immense gain. One such venture—a trading company formed to do business secretly with the South during the early days of the war—had been exposed by Michael, Jephtha Kent, and the Boston banker, Joshua Rothman.

Jephtha had published a series of newspaper articles on Louis' company, Federal Suppliers. In those days Jephtha had been Washington correspondent for the Kent paper, *The New York Union*. But Jephtha had rashly warned Louis about the series prior to publication, hoping the matter could be settled quietly. Michael had told Jephtha that Louis would never dismantle a profitable business solely because of a threat, and he'd been right. Jephtha had been discharged from the *Union,* and Rothman had been forced to arrange for the articles to appear in Greeley's *Tribune.*

Michael's role had been that of a corroborative witness. Along with Rothman, he'd been present when Louis made his original proposal about setting up the company. Thus he was able to verify Rothman's statements in Jephtha's copy.

The company had vanished almost as quickly as it had arrived. Louis had suffered severe public embarrassment, though no actual prosecution had been launched by the government since the company was not in existence long enough to engage in a provably illegal act. If there had been a desire in Washington to prefer charges against Louis, Michael had never heard of it. After disconnecting himself from the Kent's long-time law firm, Benbow and Benbow—like the Rothman Bank, too scrupulous an institution for his taste—Louis had hired other lawyers. Michael suspected he'd sent one or two of them hustling to the capitol to distribute cash and make sure any contemplated government action was quashed.

Louis had also avoided substantial monetary loss simply because he'd planned to set up Federal Suppliers with funds that were not actually his. He meant to use the California gold money Amanda Kent had pyramided and left to Jephtha, her cousin Jared's son. That money would one day pass to Jephtha's three boys.

Rothman had balked at the proposal. He was chief steward of Amanda's California holdings, and refused to permit Louis to manipulate the accrued profits. Out of the conflict came Rothman's conviction that for the sake of the family's honor, Louis must be stopped—no matter where he finally secured his capital. He *had* been stopped.

Even though Louis had experienced no depletion of his personal fortune, the scandal was enough to earn Michael, Jephtha, and the banker the undying enmity of the young financier. That was another reason Michael had been glad to leave the East. He wasn't so much afraid of Louis as sick of him and all he represented. Rather, all he failed to represent after the Kent family had built its fortune and reputation through a combination of idealism and honest, unashamed enterprise.

Michael seldom thought about Louis any more—or any of the eastern Kents, for that matter.

Except Julia.

A vivid image of her face troubled him again as the line edged forward to the dining car. The image vanished when he became aware of someone watching him from a similar line at the car's far end.

It was the crew boss he and Murphy had discussed earlier. The Virginian, Captain Leonidas Worthing.

## ii

Worthing wore a straw hat and faded gray duster. A stump of cigar jutted from his teeth. He claimed to have served with Mosby's Partisan Rangers. There were a great many veterans in Jack Casement's little army, but few Confederates. And those few were generally rust-eaters like Michael himself. Worthing was the exception.

The light spreading over the Prairie lit Worthing's unfriendly face as men began to leave the dining car, their turn at the tables over. Worthing tossed away his cigar and elbowed his way to the head of the line. A workman objected. Worthing said a few words that made the worker flush and back away.

The Southerner turned his back on the man he'd intimidated. He stared at Michael again, tapping a leather riding crop against his faded trouser leg.

Lord, how Michael detested that swaggering oaf! Twice he'd protested when Worthing badgered some member of Michael's gang, which was only one of several gangs the Virginian supervised. One argument had nearly reached the point of violence. Then General Jack Casement had stepped in. Casement stressed cooperation. The work was arduous enough without personal feuds being added to the burden. But Leonidas Worthing didn't share Casement's philosophy.

Half a dozen Paddies came clattering down the steps. The car was emptying quickly. As Michael and Murphy moved forward again, they saw one of their crew walking toward them from the head end. Evidently he'd already eaten; he was picking at his upper gum with the point of a Bowie knife.

"Hallo, Christian," Murphy called, waving.

"Morning, lads." The young man nodded, wiping his knife on the sleeve of his old wool shirt.

Christian was lean and dark, with high cheekbones and straight black hair that reminded Michael of Jephtha. Christian admitted to being a Delaware Indian and hailing from Ohio, but that was all anyone knew about him. Startling blue eyes suggested at least one white parent or grandparent. Whether he'd been given his name as a symbol of a hoped-for religious conversion, or merely because it had a pleasing sound, was a mystery. But he was soft-spoken, well-mannered and mule-strong. He amused

Michael because he liked to sprinkle his conversation with words and phrases picked up from the Paddies.

"How's the beef?" Murphy asked him.

"Tougher than usual. Beans about the same. Potatoes overcooked. Boiled to mush, practically."

"Ah, that's plenty good enough for you, Chief," another man in line laughed. Christian took it in good humor:

"Don't sauce me, spud-grubber, or I'll utter my celebrated bloodcurdling whoop and summon the tribe to relieve you of your none too attractive hair." Less cheerfully, he leaned close to Michael. "I had the misfortune to run into himself as I was coming out."

"The captain?"

Christian nodded. "Keep clear. He's in a nasty mood."

Murphy sighed. "When is he not?"

"Nastier than usual, I mean. See you presently, lads." The Indian drifted away.

Murphy shook his head. "He talks prettier English than men born to it. Bet his old man was a missionary who went wild in one of them Ohio villages where the savages beat the drums an' dance nekkid all night."

"Sean, don't ever visit Ohio."

"I passed through Cleveland on my way to Chicago. Never seen the natives, though."

"The natives, as you call them, would sorely disappoint you. They don't beat drums, nor do their dusky daughters dance under the moon. In fact they don't have dusky daughters. They're just a lot of proper second-generation farmers and mechanics who hop after the coin six days a week and pray on Sunday."

"Just good Americans, huh?" Murphy said, grinning. Then he yelled at some Paddies who'd stopped to chat in the car entrance: "Will you kindly get your fannies down here so those of us still waitin' can have a chance at the elegant fare?"

"Oh, don't be in no hurry, Sean Murphy," one of the group called back. "You've no surprises waiting."

There were seldom surprises at mealtime. Though wholesome enough, the morning, noon, and evening menus were the same seven days a week, except when an occasional band of independent buffalo hunters rode in to sell a fresh kill. But the Union Pacific bread was always newly baked and warm, the coffee strong—and at the moment Michael was ravenous, perhaps because of the crispness of the air. It smelled of autumn.

He wondered if they really would reach the meridian before the first heavy snow. If not, the line would probably go under. Winter on the plains was reported to be brutal; he already knew construction would be halted during the worst months.

Finally the car entrance cleared, and the line moved faster. Michael followed his friend inside. A long table ran from end to end, with benches on either side. A little sunlight leaked through grimy windows, but hanging lamps were still needed.

Two Paddies on the far side finished their meals. To leave, they climbed on the bench and walked across the table, incurring the wrath of a cook's helper bringing in a fresh platter of beef and a wooden bucket of steaming coffee.

Other helpers with long-handled rag swabs darted in and out among the men who were scrambling to find places. Each tin plate was nailed down, only the coffee cups standing free. The helpers used the swabs to wipe each plate quickly.

Michael and his companion wedged in among the workers spreading out along the benches. Experience had taught Michael not to hesitate. He planted himself in front of a plate, grabbed a fork, and stabbed a slab of beef. Another fork from the other side narrowly missed his wrist.

He jerked the beef to his plate, then shoved his cup through a thicket of hands around the coffee bucket. He managed to dip out a full cup without spilling any. He lifted a leg over to the bench, ready to sit down, and felt a tap on his shoulder.

Across the table, three men grabbing handfuls of potatoes quieted suddenly. Sean Murphy, already seated, glanced behind Michael, then directly at him, with a look of warning. Michael's scalp prickled.

With deliberate slowness, Michael laid his fork beside his heaped plate. Then he put the coffee cup down. He turned to find Captain Leonidas Worthing pushing up the brim of his straw hat with his riding crop.

"Boyle, you've taken my spot. Move somewhere else."

It wasn't a request. It was a demand.

# CHAPTER 3

## *The Captain*

"BOYLE, I'M WAITING."

Leonidas Worthing said it with an insincere smile that revealed brown teeth. At the right corner of his mouth, a sore glistened. A little souvenir from one of the soiled doves of Omaha, perhaps?

Michael held his temper. "I see no place cards, Captain."

"True, but I decided to sit here so I can speak to Murphy about speeding up the work of your gang. Of all the ones I'm in charge of, it's by far the worst. Too many weak sisters." He left no doubt that he included Michael. "Fellows who'd rather bellyache than earn a day's wages honestly."

Michael knew what the Virginian meant by bellyaching: remarks he'd made over a pipe after working hours. They'd evidently reached the captain through someone who toadied to him. But the remarks were truthful.

Still getting no response, Worthing grew impatient:

"If you intend to dispute my right to this seat, Boyle, kindly tell me."

On the other side of the table, one man nudged another expectantly. Michael refused to be forced into a quarrel:

"Captain," he said quietly, "why is it you're always hunting excuses to fight?"

Worthing surprised him with a laugh.

"Because I believe in doing a good job!"

"And because you're not partial to Yanks?"

"If you expect me to be partial to your kind, you're a fool. I rode with Colonel Mosby, you know."

"Aye, so we've heard," Murphy sighed. "A score of times."

"But I never told you the circumstances of my capture, did I? I had the misfortune to lose my mount and get caught by some of General Custer's glory hunters. You know what those kindly fellows did before they loaded me on a prisoner train? They gave me a dose of their favorite punishment. Tied me to a wagon wheel. Arms over my head—" The crop shot up as he pantomimed it. "Legs stretched out. Then they gave the wheel a quarter turn. They left me hanging with the hub goddamn near breaking my spine. For fourteen hours! When I woke up on the train, I found I'd pissed and shitted myself like a baby."

"Jaysus, Captain," Murphy gulped. "I *was* attemptin' to enjoy my breakfast."

The Virginian paid no attention. "One of my fellow prisoners on the train said that when I was put aboard, I had spit—foam—all over my chin. I couldn't remember my own name for the best part of a day. Handsome treatment for an officer, wouldn't you say?"

Michael shrugged again. "I can't excuse it. But I wasn't there. I'm not to blame."

"Oh, yes." Worthing jabbed the crop into his chest. "You wore the blue."

"You're going to harass every Union man in this outfit just because you were treated badly?"

"*Harass!* Mighty fine word for a slum Irishman." Another jab with the crop. "Mighty fine!"

Michael's temper was heating. He seized the crop and pushed it down. "Of course I forget one fact. You don't limit yourself to harassing men. Last week you practically whipped that lorry-car boy to death with this thing. And merely because he was a little clumsy handling the horse. You surely didn't learn much from John Mosby, Captain. You didn't learn men work better when they're led, not driven. I suspect you're too stupid to learn anything so simple."

Livid, Worthing swung the crop:

"You damned high-assed mick!"

Michael's right hand shot across to catch Worthing's forearm. The dining car was completely silent.

There was a test of strength as Michael struggled to hold Worthing's arm steady. His face reddened. Veins rose thick on the back of his hand.

Worthing tried to wrench away. Michael held him. But his anger had subsided a little; he thought it best to bring the confrontation back into saner limits.

"Captain, if we keep this up—" A quick gasp for breath. "—we won't be ready to work at six thirty. What do you say we both try to forget the war's over?"

"Hell if I will!"

Michael's shoulder began to throb. He felt tension in Worthing's arm. The man was readying for another attempt to pull free. Already Michael had humiliated him, and he realized that he'd probably have to fight. God knew what trouble he'd land in with Casement for that.

Boots thudded on the steps at the west end of the car. The door banged open.

"General Jack wants all the crew bosses. Right away!"

Several diners grumbled and left their places. Michael weighed the risk, accepted it, and released Worthing's arm.

"That includes you, I believe."

He watched the crop, waiting for it to come slashing at his cheek. Worthing's hand whitened. Michael mentally gauged how far back he could jump and still throw a punch. The man at the door bellowed again.

"Worthing, shake a leg! The telegraph says the iron train's forty minutes late out of Kearney."

Eye to eye with Leonidas Worthing, Michael waited. Finally the ex-Confederate ran the tip of his tongue over his upper lip. The hand holding the crop relaxed and regained its color. The other crew bosses trooped out as the man who'd summoned them stormed forward.

"Dammit, Worthing, Casement said *now*, not Christmas!"

Worthing waved the crop. "Shut up. I'm coming." He inclined his head toward Michael's. "Wasn't good luck for you when they put you on one of my gangs, boy."

"Surprise me with something else, Captain. And don't call me boy again or I'll knock you down so you won't get up for a while. I answer to the name of Boyle."

Worthing reddened. Michael could see grins on the faces along the table. Sean Murphy's was broadest of all.

"Ah, who gives a shit what your name is?" The crop wigwagged; Worthing was trying to make light of his humiliation. "A mick's a mick. Except you—you're special. You've been headed for trouble since the day you climbed off the cars."

"I could give you a few reasons why." There was anger in Michael's eyes again; he'd had enough. "But I'd be wasting my breath."

"Reasons—" Worthing nodded, licking the brown stump of an upper tooth. "Lies you've been spreading around free and easy among your pals. That nigger. The half-breed I got stuck with—well, you remember one thing. There's a good forty miles or more until we hit the meridian. That's forty days. And you'll be working for me every damn one of 'em. I guarantee you won't feel like celebrating when we put down milepost two forty-seven."

He touched the crop to Michael's jaw.

"Before we get there, *boy*, I'm going to break your back."

## ii

Worthing spun and stalked to the door, shoving two workers out of his way. Michael barely heard the compliments directed at him. He was experiencing one of those shameful moments in which he wished he'd never met Mrs. Amanda Kent de la Gura. A good deal of her style—her refusal to be intimidated by those she considered in the wrong—had rubbed off on him while he'd worked for her.

But he'd joined Jack Casement's rust-eaters to find peace, not endless quarreling.

He sank down on the bench beside Murphy, staring with lusterless eyes at his plate of beef and cup of cooling coffee.

He had always been teased about his appetite. His belly seemed to have a limitless capacity—no doubt because he'd gotten so little to eat as a child. He never tired of cramming himself, and the enormous amounts of food he ate never added so much as one extra pound. But his earlier anticipation of breakfast was altogether gone.

*I'm going to break your back.*

"Lord, Fergus, did you hear that feller from the office?" a Paddy on the opposite side asked his companion. "First iron train forty minutes late. 'Spose it's Injuns?"

"Eat up!" Murphy urged Michael, who shook his head.

The man named Fergus shrugged. "The further we go beyond Kearney, the more likely it is. The Injuns don't like this railway cuttin' into their buffla grounds."

"But I thought General Dodge pacified the savages before he signed on with the U-Pay."

"It don't take 'em long to get *un*pacified these days," Fergus replied. "You heard what happened at Fort Laramie. Out this far, the only Injuns we got for friends are the one or two workin' on the line, and a few hang-around-the-forts. The buckos with the devil in 'em—ones like that Red Cloud—they don't pay any attention to what the tame Injuns say, do—or sign. Touch the pen, I mean. They can't write English so they just touch a pen to a treaty an' some clerk fills in their names."

Fergus' companion looked puzzled. "I dunno what you mean, hang-around-the-forts."

"That's because you ain't been out here long enough," Fergus announced in a smug tone. "Hang-arounds are Injuns who pitch their tipis near a post to trade an' beg for handouts. Liquor. Hot coffee with lots of sugar in it. Everybody back East thinks the Injuns are crazy for the alcohol, but a buffla hunter told me it's coffee with sugar they fancy most. Why, for years on the Holy Road—"

"What the devil is *that?*"

"You look at it every day! Holy Road's what they call the old emigrant trail across the river—just like this here's the Fire Road. The Injuns used to make a game of stoppin' wagons and askin' for sugared coffee as the price of lettin' white folks pass through."

"I don't know why we're gabbling about the red heathens," Sean Murphy put in, his words muffled by a mouth stuffed with beans. His cuff served as a napkin to catch the juice. "We've rails to worry about. Train'll more likely be an hour late, but we still have a mile to lay, regardless."

"We'll get it done," Michael said, more confident than he felt.

"Mebbe," Fergus said. "But I have a funny feeling it's to be one of those days that bust a man's privates."

*Or break his back?*

Michael drank a little of the tepid coffee. Tried to forget Worthing's threat. He forced a smile:

"Cheer up, Patrick Fergus. We do get paid this evening, you know. And with a start such as we've just had, the day can become no worse, only better."

But he was wrong.

# CHAPTER 4

## "A March as Glorious as Sherman's"

SEAN MURPHY'S PREDICTION proved accurate. The iron train pulled by the engine *Vice-Admiral Farragut* arrived an hour late. Not an auspicious beginning for a Saturday, the one work day Casement's men eagerly anticipated.

As soon as the day's work was over, gold or greenbacks would be handed out from the office car, and a man could spend the rest of the evening drinking, rattling dice on a blanket, playing euchre—whatever he fancied—with no fear that too little sleep or an aching head would hamper him next morning. Sunday was for sleeping, reading, writing letters, laundering and mending clothes, or taking a lazy dip in the Platte.

This Saturday, the men knew the evening's fun would be cut short. Late train or no, a mile of track had to be laid. Michael and Murphy drifted through the crowd watching the *Farragut* chug in from the east. They saw sour faces everywhere.

Michael also noted some longing glances directed toward an attraction that had been with the moving railhead ever since it passed Grand Island, a dusty little settlement populated mostly by German families hoping to build a future out of small farms or, as soon as the railroad lured more settlers, business establishments.

The attraction was an ordinary wagon. Drawn by two mules, it creaked along beside the advancing rails six days a week and stopped where they stopped each night. This morning the mules had not yet been hitched; were still tethered to the tailboard. What made the wagon of interest were two large barrels lashed to the side. A dipper on a chain hung from each. One barrel bore the name *DORN* in crudely painted white letters. The other said *WHISKEY*. There were two more barrels tied to the wagon's far side, and others stored under the patched canvas top. Beyond the wagon Michael glimpsed the large partitioned duck tent erected every evening.

He couldn't personally swear the interior of the tent was partitioned. But certain venturesome rust-eaters declared it was. On several occasions, these men—usually tipsy—had tried without success to get a midnight peek at a member of the family of the liquor merchant who'd lit out from Grand Island in an attempt to make money satisfying one of the vices tolerated by the U-Pay management—thirst.

Gustav Dorn, the bearded Dutchman who owned the rig and sold the whiskey, had a fondness for his own product. Michael had occasionally bought a half-dipper of forty rod from him. Dorn was always unsteady on his feet. He spoke broken English rendered nearly unintelligible by sips of his own stock.

At the moment Dorn was nowhere to be seen. His son, a plump blond boy of about fourteen, sat on the wagon seat, guarding the liquor and the nearby tent with an old but powerful Hawken percussion rifle. Casement's orders prohibited any liquor being sold until the day's quota of track had been laid.

As Michael watched, the tent flap lifted. The third member of the family appeared, carrying a coffee pot to a cook fire of buffalo chips. Why in God's name the German had brought his daughter to the all-male railhead was beyond Michael's comprehension. The only explanation he'd heard had come from the boy, via Murphy. According to Sean, Gustav Dorn believed his daughter was safer traveling with him than she would have been if she'd remained behind, alone, in Grand Island.

Dorn's daughter was seldom on display at the railhead. She only came outdoors to prepare meals for her father and brother. She spent the rest of her time in the tent, or in the wagon when it was en route between stops. Michael had also heard the girl was a religious sort and read the Bible a good deal.

He studied her while she hung the pot over the coals and poked them with a stick. As usual, she wore a man's outfit: trousers; a too-large woolen coat; a soft-brimmed old hat. Her hair was pushed up under the hat. That and the shapeless clothing virtually disguised her sex.

He'd never seen the girl up close. Some others had; she'd voluntarily doctored a few minor cuts or sprains, there being no physician in the work force. Her patients reported she was young and pretty, though not much given to friendliness. An understandable defense, he figured. One smile of encouragement and half the men in Jack Casement's crew would have stormed her tent with their pants at half-mast.

But the real deterrents to social intercourse—and attempts at another kind—were the Hawkens the family had brought along. On one occasion Michael had glimpsed the girl carrying one of the hunting rifles. He assumed she wouldn't have fooled with it if she were a novice at using it.

Without having met the girl, Michael admired her pluck. It took nerve to come to the railhead, even with protection. But he suspected Dorn's daughter couldn't be as pretty as described. Being the only female for a hundred miles could elevate plainness to stunning beauty in the eye of the lustful beholder. An objective analysis would probably reveal her to be a thin-lipped sort, cold-blooded, and disapproving of human weakness. No doubt she hoped to save her father's soul from eternal damnation, since he was engaged in a trade at odds with the precepts of the book she supposedly read for hours on end.

She was out of sight now—back inside the tent—and Michael's musings were cut short by a rising noise level that signaled the start of work.

With billows of steam and the squeal of drivers, the train of flatcars from Kearney pulled in behind *Osceola*. Foremen started shouting. From the disorganized crowd loitering on either side of the track, five-man gangs coalesced with surprising speed.

The gangs climbed aboard the flatcars and began unloading the day's supplies, starting with eight-foot ties of two kinds: stronger ones of oak or cedar, and softer, less durable ones of cottonwood impregnated with a zinc chloride solution to toughen and preserve them; the process was called burnetizing. Four treated ties would be laid for every harder one.

Wrought-iron chairs were manhandled off and piled beside the track, along with rails, fish plates for joining the rail sections, and casks of spikes and bolts. Then the *Vice-Admiral Farragut* began to back down the track, followed by *Osceola* hauling the four gigantic boxcars. Clanking and puffing smoke, the two trains withdrew beyond the stacked materials, leaving the western end of the track free.

Michael and Murphy started searching for the other members of their five-man gang as two lorry cars—lightweight four-wheeled carts—were lifted unto the track and loaded with the required number of ties, rails, chairs, fish plates, spikes, and bolts. The pair of Irishmen soon located a third—sour, sallow Liam O'Dey.

O'Dey was in his late twenties, but looked twice that. Unable to find work in his native Philadelphia, he'd left a wife and seven children ages six to fourteen. Somehow he'd hoodwinked his employers into thinking he was in good health. A consumptive cough said otherwise.

He dragged a news clipping from his pocket and showed it to Michael. "Ye'll have a fine laugh out o' this. It's from one of the papers at home. Me old lady sent it."

Michael scanned the type. Evidently the piece was an editorial, one of the few favorable ones he'd seen. O'Dey coughed, then pointed:

"See there? It says we're engaged in a 'second grand march to the sea!'"

Michael read the next lines:

Sherman, with his victorious legions sweeping from Atlanta to Savannah, must have been a spectacle no more glorious than this army of men a-march from Omaha to Sacramento, subduing unknown wildernesses, surmounting untried obstacles, and binding across the broad breast of America the iron emblem of modern progress and civilization. All honor, not only to the brains that have conceived, but to the indomitable wills, the brave hearts, and the brawny muscles that are actually achieving the great work!

"My," Michael said, smiling. "'Indomitable wills.' 'Brave hearts.' 'A march as glorious as Sherman's!' We've come into our own, lads. We're heroes just like the general."

O'Dey coughed again; spat on the ground. "At least we are to some pup of a scrivener who ain't been out here to see the filthy hard work for himself."

Murphy put in, "No doubt the writer's opinion will be sharply revised if we fail to reach the meridian before the heavy snows."

O'Dey crumpled the clipping and thrust it back in his pocket. "Bunch of twaddle," he said with his usual petulance. "Having Worthing in command, I feel more like one of the victims of Savannah than a conquerin' general."

"Ssst!" Murphy gestured. "Here he comes."

Worthing strode up to them, an angry glint in his eye. He waved his crop at the trio.

"Out where you belong—and snappy! Where's the nigger and the half-breed?"

A stoop-shouldered but powerful black man in his twenties slipped up to the rear of the group and waved the blue bandana he'd been using to swab his cheeks. The sun promised intense heat before the day was done.

"Right here's one, Captain," the black man said, winking at Michael to show that his toothy, truckling grin wasn't meant to be taken seriously.

"Find that scummy Indian. Get a move on!" Worthing pivoted away, heading for another of the gangs he supervised.

"Mornin', all," the black said as the four men began to trot toward the last pair of rails spiked down the preceding night.

"Morning, Greenup," Michael said. Greenup Williams was a freedman from Kentucky; one of about a dozen blacks in the work force.

"Captain sure does look thunderous today," Greenup observed.

"He and Mr. Boyle exchanged a few intemperate words in the dinin' saloon," Murphy informed him.

"That so? Well, let's hope everybody stays peaceable the rest of the day. I got a hankering to visit the whiskey wagon quick as I can."

O'Dey managed to sound gloomy even though gasping for breath:

"Captain Worthing will—no doubt have us—whistled out and too—weak to raise a dipper by the time we see sunset." He came to a halt as the others trotted on, cupped his hand over his mouth, and bent forward, coughing hard.

The three reached the last pair of rails. O'Dey straggled along a moment later. Down the line, Christian appeared, rushing to join them.

"Hey, Chief, you late," Greenup grinned as the new arrival dragged his galluses up over his shoulders.

Christian feigned annoyance: "Doesn't the Union Pacific permit a man to perform his natural functions in the morning?"

Michael spied Worthing striding along behind the Indian. He tried to warn Christian with a glance but failed.

Half a mile back, a cart boy led a work horse to the first lorry car. The boy was a towhead named Tom Ruffin. He'd run away from an Indiana orphanage to join the great enterprise. The boy tied the horse to the cart, then climbed on the animal's back.

Christian stretched a suspender and rolled his tongue in his cheek.

"No, on reflection I guess it doesn't. The only function that interests himself is the breaking of a man's spine. Or spirit."

"Christian—!" Michael began. By then Worthing had reached the Delaware. He jabbed the nape of Christian's neck with his crop.

Christian spun, one hand dropping toward the sheath of his Bowie knife. Worthing grinned.

"You're right about that, Injun. And I just put you on my list. Now shut up and get ready to lay some track."

Shoving Christian aside, he stalked by.

The Delaware fumed. Sean Murphy pressed a palm against his belly and bowed to the Virginian's back:

"Yes, sir, yer majesty, yer eminence."

Michael smiled. Greenup Williams laughed aloud. Worthing's head jerked. The back of his neck grew pink. But he didn't turn or break stride. He kept walking east, ready to signal the cart boy to bring the lorry car.

O'Dey looked unhappy. He seldom fraternized with the others and resented the bickering that frequently interrupted the flow of work.

Despite Worthing's threat in the dining car, Michael felt surprisingly devilish all at once. Sarcasm and laughter were weapons Worthing didn't understand, and against which he had no defense. *Your majesty. Your eminence.* He'd have to remember those.

By now Worthing had assembled all of his gangs. They were gathered along both sides of the last section of track. Worthing shouted and waved his crop. A half mile away, Tom Ruffin kicked the horse with his bare feet. The rope snapped taut. The cart was jerked forward.

Sparks shooting from beneath its iron wheels, the cart came rolling toward the waiting workers, the mounted boy hallooing and thumping the animal with his heels. As the cart neared the end of the track, men sprang forward, seized it, and dragged it to a halt. Two of the men shoved wooden chocks under the wheels while Tom Ruffin leaped down, quickly unfastened the rope and led the snorting horse off the roadbed.

Each of the waiting gangs knew its specific job. The moment the horse was clear, a second large group surrounded the cart. Pairs of men lifted ties, ran them out ahead of the last rails and lowered them to the hard-packed grade. Back where the supplies had been dumped, another cart boy was restraining his fretful horse and awaiting his signal. The rails went down at the rate of two every sixty seconds—no interruptions.

Worthing shouted a command. Other men beside the cart grabbed chairs, positioned them on the ties. Then, on Worthing's next order, Michael's five-man gang on the south side of the grade and another gang on the north converged on the cart.

Michael and Christian grabbed a twenty-eight-foot rail and began to haul it forward. The rail slid easily because the cart bed was equipped with greased rollers. As soon as the rail was halfway out, O'Dey and Greenup Williams took hold. Sean Murphy caught the tail end. Simultaneously, a second rail had been unloaded by the gang working from the other side.

At a fast walk, the five-man gangs carried the heavy lengths of iron over the new ties. Michael could already feel the first strain in his shoulders. By day's end, it would turn to pain.

Murphy shouted, *"Down!"* His opposite number on the other gang was only a moment behind with a similar command. Both gangs lowered their rails into the chairs waiting on the interspersed hardwood and cottonwood ties.

Men with notched wooden gauges jumped in, jamming the gauges down while Michael and the others in the two rail gangs kicked and shoved. Finally the rails were fitted tightly in the notches.

Meanwhile, the cart had been dragged off the tracks. Tom Ruffin re-hitched his horse and started back for more supplies.

Other men positioned the fish-plate joints and began bolting the new sections of iron to the old. Next, the spike gangs moved in with their mauls.

Workers crawled ahead of them, dropping spikes into holes, and scuttling on as the mauls came down. Michael continually marveled at the intricate timing of the operation. A careless spikeman could brain a spike handler if he swung too soon. But in all the time he'd worked at the railhead he'd never seen it happen.

The tie, chair, and rail gangs left the spikers behind and ran forward. In a moment the second lorry car arrived on the newly laid track. A new section of ties went down—and the process of removing the rails from the cart was repeated.

A familiar rhythm established itself while Captain Worthing stalked up and down, shouting, cursing and demanding that the various crews under his command go faster, to make up for time already lost.

ii

The morning advanced, the sun climbed, and Michael began to sweat. The labor was monotonous; mindless. But the five men on his gang had learned to work well together and took pride in their efficiency. Every man was important to the total effort. Behind the perpetual train, and interrupted only by the arrival of supplies, other crews would be finishing yesterday's track by shoveling and leveling fill between the ties.

South of the Platte an emigrant wagon packed with household goods rolled by in a haze of dust, the driver wigwagging his rifle. A woman and a small girl in sunbonnets waved.

No one broke the rhythm of work, but there were some shouts, inviting the older woman to pause for the night, and earn a pile of extra money. Michael was thankful the family couldn't hear the cheerfully filthy remarks.

Such raillery was common enough whenever the rust-eaters sighted a wagon with a woman in it. But the bawdiness upset Worthing. He considered any deviation from routine a violation of his authority. After the wagon passed from sight, Greenup Williams didn't help matters by starting to whistle "Marching Through Georgia."

"Better—" Breathing hard, Michael was lowering a rail on Murphy's signal. "—better pick a less partisan tune, Greenup."

"Oh, shoo," Greenup said, grinning. "I ain't no chained slave on the captain's little old plantation."

"True," Christian observed as the gauge men moved in. "But if himself would get it through his dumb skull that his side lost, we'd be a lot better off. But no, he—"

Suddenly Michael saw a long shadow behind the Delaware; then Worthing himself. The captain's gray duster was wet with sweat. Droplets glistened in the stubble on his cheeks.

"No singing, nigger," Worthing said. "And no remarks from you, either."

*Flick.* The crop stung the side of Christian's cheek. A spot of blood shone in the sun.

Christian nearly lost his grip on the rail. Michael felt a tearing strain in his shoulders as he absorbed an extra share of the five-hundred-pound weight. He braced the rail on his knee and got it to the ground without mishap.

Bent nearly double and trying to help, Christian said through clenched teeth, "Yes, *sir.*"

"Your eminence," Michael added, realizing too late that he'd let his temper slip.

With the rail down, the five men darted back to help those with the notched gauges. Worthing extended the crop; touched the bloody place on Christian's cheek; affected a sympathetic smile:

"Tickled you a mite harder than I intended."

Christian glowered, one hand perilously near the hilt of his Bowie. Worthing glanced at Michael, then back to the Delaware.

"Tell you what. You rest ten minutes. Yonder's the water bucket. Wash off that cut, and we'll let Boyle handle the head end of the next few rails."

Christian started to protest. Worthing fanned himself with his straw hat.

"Go on, Christian," he said. "Take care of yourself. Paddy Boyle's strong enough for a bit of double duty."

"Hold on, Captain!" Murphy exclaimed. "One man can't haul the front of a rail all by—"

"Be quiet," Worthing snapped. "Paddy Boyle can. Can't you?"

Suddenly Worthing's face twisted. His smile grew fixed and ugly. He jabbed the end of the crop into Michael's throat.

"Answer me, *boy.*"

It was all Michael could do to keep from tearing the detestable crop out of the Virginian's hand and using it on him. But he swallowed; backed up a step.

O'Dey yelped. Michael ducked, nearly brained by the backswing of a spiker's maul.

Alarmed, Sean Murphy and Greenup Williams pulled him down the slanting side of the roadbed, out of danger. Worthing kept watching as he put his wide-brimmed straw hat back on his head.

"You can do it—can't you, *boy?*" he asked. Every syllable carried insult.

"You're damn right I can," Michael growled, and turned his back, awaiting the next lorry car.

He saw Christian by the water bucket, slopping the contents of a dipper over his cheek. The Delaware's glance was sympathetic. Michael tried to ignore it—as well as the ache in his shoulder blades and the mumbled lamentations of O'Dey, who hated trouble.

"You drop any rails," Worthing called, "I'll see you're docked a week's wages. You hear me, *boy?*"

iii

When the cart arrived and the gangs moved in, Michael seized the rail with both hands and yanked. The other three men tried to give him as much help as possible. But the moment the length of iron was lifted free of the rollers, an excruciating pain shot through his shoulders and down his arms.

He staggered on the hard-packed bed; nearly stumbled over a tie. The noises of men shouting, horses neighing, mauls thudding, metal clanging became a torturous din.

"*Down!*"

Michael groaned as he bent, dropping more than lowering the rail onto the ties. He staggered back, his chest heaving and sticky with perspiration. He snickered in a humorless way at the thought of the Philadelphia clipping. He seriously doubted old Billy Sherman had ever enjoyed such a glorious drenching of sweat while conducting his glorious march. And the editorial writer probably kept himself comfortable in a saloon bar while composing his rhapsodic sentences about brave hearts and indomitable wills. The only accurate statement in the account was the reference to brawny muscles. A man needed those and, to deal with a Worthing, iron balls besides.

As soon as the rails were gauged and the spike men began hammering, he dragged off his shirt and flung it away. He unbuttoned his underwear, shucked out of the sleeve and pushed the top half of the garment down over his belt. Behind him he heard Worthing chuckle.

Michael reddened. He'd show Worthing he could handle two men's work—and do it without a murmur or a mistake. He'd take all the bastard could give—and more. By God he would!

Murphy sidled up; whispered:

"I can slip a word to Tommy Ruffin. Have him fetch Casement. You know—so's his arrival looks accidental."

Michael rubbed his palms over his sweat-slippery forearms. "Casement's in Kearney. Left yesterday."

"Then I'll get someone else."

"No."

"But—"

"No, Sean! Not on your sainted mother's life."

# CHAPTER 5

## Rage

TIME BEGAN TO DISTORT as badly as his vision. He seemed to have been alone on his end of the rails for a century, though the reality of it was undoubtedly more on the order of a half hour.

Intense pain had spread down the center of his back and outward, toward his ribs. His palms had blistered quickly. Despite several protests from Christian that he was feeling fine, Leonidas Worthing refused to put him back on the job:

"You rest a spell longer. Before he died, Old Abe said we're supposed to treat coloreds like white people. I assume that includes you right along with Williams." His tone was mocking as he continued, "You're due the same courtesy, the same—*watch it, boy!*"

Michael's hands had slipped. The front end of the rail thudded down. Only a clumsy stagger to the side kept his right boot from being crushed. He stood next to the rail, wiping his eyes and fighting dizziness.

"Ready to quit, Paddy Boyle?"

Michael drew a long breath and thought of Mrs. A, as he'd called Amanda Kent when she was alive. She wouldn't have truckled to anyone like Worthing. Or admitted she couldn't handle the work.

"No."

Another ten minutes passed. Ten more rails, each heavier than the last. Still Worthing refused to send Christian back to help.

The five-man gang on the opposite side of the roadbed kept working without comment, though Michael occasionally caught a commiserating glance directed his way. It didn't do a thing to help him regain his failing strength. But it hardened his resolve to suffer Worthing's punishment until he dropped.

Dimly, Michael saw towheaded Tom Ruffin kicking his horse along the line with a fresh load of supplies. He rubbed his bare, sweating shoulders. Deep in the muscles, fires seemed to be burning.

He gulped more of the hot morning air, readying himself for the next effort.

The cart arrived, lather dripping from the horse's flanks. By the time the ties were removed, Ruffin hadn't yet unhitched the animal. He was having trouble with the knotted rope. Worthing waved to his men.

"Keep going! Pull the rails off and the devil with the horse!"

Michael and his three companions moved in. This time the head end of the rail felt as heavy as the whole earth. Before it was three yards out from the rollers, the rough iron popped a huge blister on Michael's left hand. Draining water slicked his palm.

The rail slipped, banging down on the front edge of the cart. O'Dey and Greenup lost control. The rail slid forward, the end nudging the horse's rump.

The animal neighed and shied, tangling its hoofs between the ties. All at once the horse was tumbling sideways.

The other gang had lifted its rail clear of the cart. When the horse started to fall, they jumped back, and let the rail drop. The horse went down on top of it.

Michael's gang struggled to regain a hold on their rail; finally moved it out past the front end of the cart. But somehow, at that moment, O'Dey stumbled. The rail tore out of Michael's hands. The forward end struck the horse's thrashing hind legs.

The horse bellowed, pinned. Michael bowed his head, shaking with rage over the blunder.

Worthing stormed toward him.

"Now you've done it, you lout!"

The horse screamed again. Men came running from up and down the roadbed. Ruffin knelt by the frantic animal, then jumped away from its flailing front hoofs:

"Leg's broke, I think."

"You've cost us time, Paddy Boyle. Invaluable time." Worthing sounded pleased.

"Listen here!" Murphy exclaimed. "You were the one hollering for us to go ahead before the boy got the horse untied!"

"Nevertheless, that'll be two weeks' pay docked for Boyle. Maybe he'll even be rousted back to Omaha."

Michael wanted to plant a fist right in the middle of the Virginian's face. But he didn't. He was furious over the way he'd let Worthing maneuver him into responsibility for an accident—though he was convinced the man had planned to keep him working alone until a mishap occurred.

Tense, perspiring faces ringed him. Work had come to a stop. One man was running pell-mell toward the office car to report the incident.

Before Michael could say a word, Christian shouldered past him. With his back to Michael, the Delaware said:

"You're the one who deserves firing."

Worthing's crop whipped upward. Christian snatched it from his hand and sent it sailing over the frantic horse and the men beyond.

Worthing's cheeks reddened. Michael touched the Indian's arm.

"Christian, you don't need to take my part in—"

The Indian paid no attention:

"No one caused the accident but you, Captain. And that's what we'll tell General Jack when he's back from Kearney."

Murphy and Greenup agreed loudly. O'Dey remained silent. So did most of the other workers, not wanting to risk losing pay.

From the office car, a party of men approached on the run. Worthing tried to laugh away Christian's threat.

"You think Casement'll believe a mission-English Injun over a white man? I seriously doubt it."

"So do I," Christian smiled, startling the Virginian. "However, you don't qualify as a white man, or any other kind of man. The most appropriate word for you is animal."

Worthing's right hand shot under his sweaty duster, reappearing with a hide-out weapon—a four-barrel derringer Michael had never seen before.

"Jesus and Mary!" O'Dey squealed. Men scattered.

Christian reached for the hilt of his Bowie—but a moment too late. Exhausted and dizzy as he was, Michael managed to lunge forward and knock the Delaware aside just as the derringer exploded.

Worthing's ball hit Christian's right calf. The Delaware did a kind of jig step to the side, regained his balance, then collapsed on his right knee, clutching his leg, and wincing.

Michael's restraint collapsed, too. Head down and fists up, he went for Leonidas Worthing.

ii

He felt no need for niceties. He yanked Worthing's wrist to his mouth and sank his teeth in until he tasted blood.

That disposed of the derringer. He saw it wink and flash, falling, as he rammed his knee in Worthing's groin.

The Virginian doubled. Michael lifted his other knee. It caught Worthing under the chin, smashing him back onto the fallen horse. The animal's head jerked up, and it trumpeted its pain again.

Michael barely heard the shouts of encouragement from Murphy and Greenup as he dropped on Worthing's gut with both knees. He laced his hands together and began to pummel Worthing's head; chopping, brutal blows he seemed powerless to stop, even though he was incoherently ashamed of his anger:

*This is what I did in the war. This is what I came out here to balance with something better.*

Yet he kept striking harder. *Harder—*

Worthing's grabs at his forearms were ineffectual. Blood and mucus dribbled from the Virginian's nose. Michael's head hummed as his locked fists rose and fell, turning the Virginian's face to a smear of red.

Finally hands dragged him back. His legs crumpled and he fell over in a faint.

iii

"That all?" The very brevity of the question indicated how furious Casement was.

The cluttered cubicle in the front car of the work train was heavy with afternoon heat. Michael had wakened about three-quarters of an hour after the brawl. He still felt its effects in the aching sides of his hands, now purpling with bruises.

He'd cleaned himself up, pulled his underwear and shirt back on, swallowed some coffee, and been hustled under guard to Casement's office, there to be locked in until the construction boss arrived. Shortly before noon the preceding day, Casement had ridden alone to Kearney to straighten out some supply problems.

John Stevens Casement was no more than a year older than Michael; thirty-seven. He stood a scant five feet four inches with boots on. The boots didn't even touch the plank floor as he perched in his chair in front of a roll-top desk littered with survey maps, work rosters, and sheets of cost figures.

Plainly dressed in a wool shirt and old trousers, Casement had a tough, imposing aura despite his slight build; an aura enhanced by the brilliant red of his full beard and the piercing quality of his pale eyes. He didn't blink as he gazed up at Michael, who stood in front of him with his feet wide apart. Spells of dizziness and nausea were still making him wobbly.

"Yes," Michael answered, "that's how it happened." After a moment he added, "I do feel compelled to offer an apology. I had enough fighting in the army to last me a lifetime, and when I came out here, I vowed I'd done my last. I'm ashamed of the way I went after Worthing. I had to prevent him from shooting Christian, but I'm sorry about the rest. No, let's say disappointed. In myself."

Casement tented his fingers. Thought a while.

"I don't like it," he announced in his customary blunt way. "I don't like it one blasted bit, Boyle—even though I know you're telling the truth."

Michael blinked. "You do? How?"

"Did you think I'd fail to ask questions before I came in here? Murphy, Tom Ruffin, that freedman, Williams—even O'Dey—they all told it pretty much the way you did. How Worthing ordered the Indian off the job. Demanded your gang go ahead while the horse was still hitched. Everything."

His mind sluggish, Michael finally thought to ask, "How is Christian?"

Casement shrugged. "Flesh wound. Worthing's ball went right through his calf. No bone damage. He'll mend quickly."

"Where is he?"

"I asked the liquor peddler's daughter to clean him up and tend him for a few days. She arranged a pallet in her tent." Casement's mouth quirked. "Old Dorn may be a sot, but he's never too addled to ask for money. The daughter's a decent young woman. She'd have tended the Indian for nothing. But the old man stepped in with his hand out, and I had no time to haggle."

"Did you talk to Christian?"

"I did. He was coherent enough to support your story."

Michael said nothing. But he was relieved.

"I was doubtful about hiring Captain Worthing," Casement continued. "I made my decision on the mistaken assumption the war was over for all concerned. The trouble is, I can hardly afford to discharge even one man short of his committing murder. I've moved Worthing back to supervising the unloading of the iron trains. I don't suppose he'll be any more cooperative there, but at least you two will be somewhat removed from one another. You marked him up pretty fierce, you know," Casement finished. It didn't sound like a reprimand.

"Where's Worthing now, General?"

"Confined to his bunk. Raving like the very devil, I suppose. From now on you stay out of his way. Clean out of his way, understand? If he comes after you, I'll deal with him."

"I can't let other people be responsible for my quarrels."

Casement slapped a palm on the desk. A rolled map slid to the floor.

"You'll do what I say, Boyle, or you won't work on this line! The horse had to be shot. You and that fool Reb have cost me half a day. Half a mile of track!"

His chair squeaked as he swung around and pointed to a calendar nailed above the desk.

"Time—time! That's what you cost me. No one on this line seems to fully understand that we must operate like an army. We have an assigned objective—one that I fully intend to reach on schedule. But doing it requires discipline. The moment we lose discipline, we're courting failure. I made promises to Dr. Durant and the directors. I won't let a lot of damn squabbling disrupt this army, ruin my timetable, and turn me into a liar!"

He subsided, drawing a long breath.

"Any fighting will be done with those Spencers we carry. Do you know what I saw at sunup, riding back from Kearney? Braves on the horizon. Sioux, Cheyenne—I couldn't tell which. But there were two or three dozen. This railroad's just another invasion of their territory like the one that drove Red Cloud out of Fort Laramie in a fury. The Plains tribes are afraid of us. They're afraid of the locomotives, they're afraid of the telegraph wires—you can't blame them for fighting back. Especially after what's been done to some of them. Idiots like that Colonel Chivington massacring babies at Sand Creek two years ago—we even have to contend with things for which we weren't responsible! So if there's any fighting to be done, I want it confined to Indian raids. God knows no one will do that fighting for us. The army's still spread too thin out here. How long has it been since you saw any troopers gallop by?"

"Not since we passed Fort Kearney," Michael admitted.

And both men knew the Kearney fort was of little use in defending the railroad. It was an infantry, not a cavalry post. What few men the army had available were miles to the west, protecting the grading and bridging crews.

"Exactly. So I repeat, Boyle—any fighting will be done out of necessity, *not* to settle private feuds. I won't have a single man compounding our problems."

Quietly, Michael asked, "Does that mean you want me to quit?"

"No, dammit! Didn't you hear me say I need every hand? Why do you think I still tolerate Worthing's presence?"

"May I inquire as to how much pay I'm losing?"

"None—this time. But if you get into it with him once more I'll have your pay *and* your job."

"If he starts it—" Michael began.

*"You walk away!"*

Michael pondered; reluctantly shook his head.

"I appreciate your side of it, General. I want to see this line go through. So do most of the men. They'll say little about it—they'd be scorned as sentimental—but they're as anxious to reach the meridian as you. It's become a point of pride."

He looked Casement in the eye. "But I'm not sure I can pay the price you've set. As I told you, I had a bellyful of fighting in the Irish Brigade. On the other hand, I will not be trampled on."

He thought Casement was about to smile. He didn't. Instead, he said crisply:

"Entirely up to you. We understand each other."

"Yes, sir." Michael started to leave.

"Boyle."

Michael turned back.

"You tell another man I said this and I'll deny it to the gates of paradise. I wish you'd broken the back of that son of a bitch."

At last Michael grinned.

"I almost wish I had too, sir."

"Mind, now—" Another stabbing finger. "It has nothing to do with his former service—except that being on the losing side affected his attitude. If any man could have taken care of him, it would be one of Colonel Meagher's own."

Michael's grin widened. "That's always how we felt in the Irish Brigade. We could do the job when others couldn't."

Casement sobered. "But you lost your chance. Don't seek another."

Michael offered no assurances. He couldn't.

"Do you have any objections if I look in on Christian this evening, General?"

"I don't care if you look in on Satan himself so long as you avoid Worthing and help me lay a mile of track a day, six days a week. Now get out of here, find yourself a replacement, and take charge of Worthing's gangs."

A stunned look. "Take charge?"

Exasperated, Casement waved: "Someone's got to fill the man's spot! You're diligent. You know the routine. You're promoted. Until and unless you promote yourself back to Omaha."

Casement sat down, whirled his chair toward the desk, and immediately began to sort through the accumulated papers, the astonished Irishman already forgotten.

# CHAPTER 6

## *Jephtha's Decision*

STARTING SHORTLY BEFORE three in the afternoon, General Jack Casement personally took charge at the end of the track.

From the supply handlers, Michael had already dragooned a fifth member for his gang—a plump, bow-legged acquaintance of Murphy's named Artemus Corkle. And to the surprise of Murphy and the rest, Michael insisted on being a working supervisor. He handled the fifth position on the gang and kept an eye on the various other crews when he wasn't carrying rails.

He felt miserable; childishly weak after the brawl. But he drove himself, unwilling to surrender to the aches and dizziness. If he were to establish his authority, it had to be done at once, while the other gangs were still grateful Worthing had been removed.

The strategy worked. Casement watched with approval as Michael prodded and cajoled some spike men who'd gotten sloppy, never showing his fear that he'd pass out at any moment.

But Michael's performance was all that Casement approved. Although the noon meal had been shortened from one hour to twenty minutes, by the time the sun began to slant low over the prairie, setting the Platte alight with red ripples, not quite three-quarters of a mile of track had been put down. Casement grumpily called a halt. He murmured a word of congratulations to Michael, then announced there'd be no Sunday labor. But the lost quarter of a mile would be made up Monday.

Casement retired to his quarters, a scowl on his face. He wasn't the only one scowling. As the men straggled back toward the perpetual train, the Saturday night conversation was short on laughter and long on complaints. Business at Dorn's whiskey wagon commenced almost at once.

Normally, Michael Boyle loved the calm of the prairie evenings. The stark lines of the horizon were softened by the dusk. Lanterns on the work train shone like large yellow stars below the smaller, bluer ones glimmering in the purple arch of the darkening east.

The beauty of the Nebraska sunset held little attraction for him tonight. He was worn throughout from his effort to stay alert and on his feet during the seemingly interminable afternoon. He was tormented by pain in his hands, shoulders, and back. He was increasingly ashamed of having lost control and turned on Worthing. And he couldn't forget the captain was still at the railhead, his face pulped, and his authority destroyed. Sean Murphy had reported the Virginian was still lying in his bunk in one of the sleeping cars; not Michael's, fortunately. No doubt Worthing would soon be plotting retaliation—if he wasn't already.

Casement's charge not to indulge in further fighting rankled too. Michael wanted to do a good job of handling his new responsibilities. That was the sole reason he'd driven himself so cruelly all afternoon.

But if it came to a test of loyalty to General Jack—loyalty meaning turning the other cheek to the Virginian—Michael knew which way his decision would go.

At the evening meal he said little to his companions, Murphy and Greenup Williams. After a while they ceased their jokes about earning promotions with bare knuckles and let him eat in silence.

When their plates and cups were empty, the men walked to the office car and waited their turn at the paymaster's cubicle. Some of the rusteaters took all of their wages in greenbacks or gold. Others had part or all of their pay posted to their accounts. Michael chose the last alternative; he didn't plan to buy any whiskey tonight. He intended to sit with Christian —if Dorn's daughter would permit him inside the tent.

During the final hour of the workday, a combination payroll and commissary train had chugged in: two cars, a tender, and a locomotive whose engineer had decorated the top of his headlight box with spreading stag antlers. The train also brought mail. After having his wages marked down, Michael walked back to see whether there might be a letter from Jephtha.

To his surprise, he discovered two.

ii

In his bunk, Michael poured a little of his carefully hoarded tobacco into the bowl of his clay churchwarden, lit the pipe, and wriggled into a comfortable position for reading.

One of the two letters addressed in Jephtha Kent's familiar, boldly slanted hand was extremely thick. He opened the other, slimmer one first. It took him about a minute and a half to scan the message Jephtha had penned in mid-July.

Jephtha's first wife Fan had been prostrated by a heat seizure and had died two days later. Jephtha and his current spouse, the likable former proprietress of a Washington boarding house, were leaving next morning for the burial services in Lexington. Gideon, his wife Margaret, and their four-year-old daughter Eleanor were going too. Gideon was again searching for work, Jephtha noted.

That last disturbed Michael. Gideon and his family weren't having an easy time of it in New York.

Michael had never met Jephtha's three sons. Yet he felt a curious kinship with them due to his closeness to their father. In spirit, he might have been their cousin or half brother.

Of the three, he knew most about Gideon—because Jephtha had had more to tell. Previous letters written from Jephtha's small Methodist parsonage had contained a good deal of information about Gideon Kent's activities and attitudes since the end of the war.

Michael knew Gideon had been glad to see the conflict end. And he'd been fortunate that his rank of major excluded him from those classes of military men to whom Andrew Johnson's General Amnesty Proclamation of May '65 did not apply. Southern army colonels, navy lieutenants, and any officer trained at West Point or Annapolis who'd returned to the South to fight were still considered guilty of treason until personally pardoned. Had Gideon been a colonel at the time of his parole, he'd have been forced to seek the services of a new breed of legal specialists operating in Washington. The pardon attorneys or "brokers" could speed an individual application to the President's desk for a fee of $100 or $200. Even in making peace there was profit for scoundrels and opportunists, it seemed.

Michael knew Gideon had been dismayed at the South's defeat. But he'd accepted it—and considered that chapter of his life closed. He'd told his father he was ready to get on with the business of making a life for himself, his wife, and daughter. He'd even shown Jephtha a document he'd written out as a reminder. It was a verbatim copy of the widely publicized loyalty oath required of those who received individual clemency from Johnson.

Whoever took the oath vowed before God to support and defend the Constitution of the United States and to abide by the laws of the Union, including all proclamations dealing with Negro freedom. Various groups of noncombatant Southerners exempted from Johnson's general amnesty—postmasters, judges, tax collectors, even former Confederate government printers—had to swear the oath before they could again buy or sell real estate, apply for patents or try to recover their own land if it had been confiscated as enemy property.

Gideon hadn't been required to take the oath. He'd written it out as a private, personal declaration. Jephtha was delighted his son had returned to civilian life in a positive frame of mind, determined not to let the past, or his prison injury, ruin his future.

Despite the loss of his left eye, Gideon—at least according to Jephtha—looked handsomer than ever, even rakish with the black patch.

More important, he seemed to possess a new drive. Before the war he'd been easygoing; an indifferent student. The time in prison had made him realize he knew nothing except cavalry tactics. He'd decided he'd better settle down and try to learn a skill—or at least find gainful employment in some place where the economy was still thriving.

Considering the question of secession settled, and the country whole again, the place Gideon had chosen in preference to burned-out Richmond was New York.

Jephtha had used his connections in newspaper circles to get his eldest son a position as an apprentice in the press room of Gordon Bennett's highly successful *New York Herald*. Working for the *Union* owned by Louis Kent was out of the question.

Gideon's supervisors had reportedly praised his diligence and quick wits. But he'd quit quietly at the end of six months, unable to tolerate the confining indoor work. Reading the news in a letter, Michael had recalled hearing Jephtha once say his son was happiest outdoors, no matter what the weather. Gideon had taken a second job driving a wagon for a construction company.

The man who hired him evidently hadn't been concerned about his obviously Southern speech. That wasn't the case with the manager of the firm's wagon fleet. Gideon lasted exactly two days—discharged and replaced by a former Union soldier. The manager refused to pay wages to a "Southron traitor." And according to this current letter, Gideon had been unable to find another position. Michael wasn't surprised. The labor market was being flooded by returning veterans and newly freed blacks migrating from the South.

In previous correspondence Jephtha had confessed that he'd tried to offer financial assistance to his son. But Gideon had a stubborn pride and a determination to succeed by virtue of his own hard work. Provided anyone would let him work.

Margaret had evidently made a fine adjustment to New York, though. She liked the city, and had helped tide the little family through lean times by doing piecework for some of the better emporiums specializing in individually designed gowns for wealthy women. Gideon's wife was experienced in that area because of the time she'd spent in her aunt's Richmond apparel shop.

Jephtha had also remarked that Margaret had done a marvelous job of

creating a comfortable home in a small rented house in lower Manhattan
And she helped and supported Gideon in his effort to make up for his
lack of education through constant reading.

Naturally Jephtha regretted Gideon hadn't cared to stick with the print
ing trade. As a printer, he could have carried on the family tradition
begun with Philip Kent's founding of the firm of Kent and Son in Boston
—another business unfortunately still under Louis Kent's ownership.

But Jephtha was clearly resigned to Gideon's going his own way—if he
could ever find that way in a city glutted with Northerners and blacks
eager to take any job.

Jephtha and his son never saw Louis Kent socially. Louis despised the
elder Kent for his role in exposing the illegal wartime trading venture
And Gideon was a kind of living accusation that Louis had been a shirker
Undoubtedly Louis had paid the maximum fee—a trifling three hundred
dollars out of his millions—to exempt himself from the 1863 Conscription
Act that had sent mobs of poor New Yorkers into the streets for four days
to riot, burn, and hang blacks from lampposts as a protest against the war
and a draft lottery that only the wealthy could escape.

Actually, Michael was thankful for the rift separating Louis from his
relatives. Julia Kent was in his thoughts often enough as it was. It would
have been too painful if Jephtha's letters described personal encounters
with her.

The shorter letter closed with Jephtha saying that fifteen months after
the conclusion of hostilities, he still knew nothing of the whereabouts of
his two younger sons.

Always a poor correspondent, Matthew had last written his father early
in 1865, from Havana. Matt's skipper, McGill, had been preparing to take
his schooner *Fair Amanda* to one of the last ports still open to the Con
federacy—neutral Matamoros, across the Rio Grande from Brownsville
Texas.

That same, final letter from Matt had contained several of the charcoal
sketches he'd started making on his own, without formal training, when
he was much younger. Jephtha had mailed a drawing to Michael. It was
tacked up in the bunk.

He glanced at the sketch now. A sinuous black man, youthful but to
tally bald, dominated the foreground. He was wearing only a pair of rag
ged trousers and balancing a metal can on one shoulder.

The black's other hand was extended, as if he were pleading with some
one. His grin was infectious, his eyes merrily sly; the whole figure was
bent forward to suggest a subservience that was affected and hence not
degrading.

The lines of the figure were echoed in a few strokes suggesting a palm in the extreme background. Between the tree and the black was a smaller figure, a lighter-skinned gentleman in a white suit and wide-brimmed hat. He had a cheroot in his mouth and a small girl in his arms. In contrast to the controlled rigidity of the watcher, the black was all motion and suppleness.

Matt had signed the drawing *M. Kent,* and lettered a caption:

### MILK VENDIR & SUGAR PLANTER, HABANA-'65

Jephtha had often mentioned his second son's total inability to spell.

There'd been no further word of Matt since that final letter. Saddening, Michael thought with another glance at the picture. Not only had Jephtha perhaps lost a son, but possibly the world had lost a young man whose talent might someday have developed to an important level. Michael was no student of art. But he liked the composition of the drawing; the artful balance of line against white space. Matt's style had a crude vibrancy that, once seen, wasn't easily forgotten, or confused with another's work.

The final paragraph of the shorter letter was the saddest of all:

> *Of Jeremiah I know even less, and fear him dead. Many military records were either destroyed or lost when Davis and his crowd fled Richmond and carried their government into its brief exile. I am sure Jeremiah's regiment was in the Atlanta theatre, and that he was present in the ranks in the autumn of 1864. Beyond that point I have been unable to trace him. I suspect I will never know his fate— nor where he fell in the midst of the chaos attending Sherman's triumph in Georgia. To go to Fan's burial with that knowledge weighing on my mind is grievous, indeed. Thankfully, God's hand is ever present to lighten the burden.*
>
> *Hoping you are well, I remain*
>
> > *Faithfully,*
> > *Jephtha*

### iii

Michael turned his attention to the second, thicker envelope. The pages —ten or more, inscribed on both sides—had been written in early August, following Jephtha's return from Lexington.

There was pain in the very first paragraph. Lexington had reminded

Jephtha not only of the rift which had destroyed his family and deprived him of his itinerancy, but of the death of his good friend, General Thomas Jackson, at Chancellorsville. Michael already knew Gideon had been present when Stonewall had been accidentally shot down by men from his own side.

But there was elation in the letter as well:

> We were back from Lexington scarcely twenty-four hours when with the abruptness of a thunderbolt, we received a communication from Matthew—execrable spelling and all!
>
> In almost the final week of the war, his skipper did indeed run his schooner to the mouth of the Rio Grande, forty miles below Ma tamoros. Munitions from the schooner were put aboard the custom ary lighters for transport up the river. A ferocious squall struck with out warning and destroyed every one of the small craft, and drowned McGill and several crewmen. Matthew survived with se vere injuries, recovery from which literally required months. We had hardly absorbed the joyous news when, concluding an arduou trip overland from Texas, Matthew himself appeared on our door step!

Here Michael was so startled, he inadvertently sucked too hard on the churchwarden and drew smoke into his lungs. He coughed for almost a minute before he was able to resume reading.

> My son greeted us as if he had not been away for more than an overnight holiday. He then announced he was sailing for Liverpool where he is to marry a young woman with whom he fell in love dur ing his initial visit to the British Isles! For the first time since my re turn to the pulpit, I confess I availed myself of the medicinal bour bon Molly hides in the pantry.
>
> Matt's surprising liaison came about this way:
>
> While McGill was still skippering a steam blockade runner into Wilmington, the vessel was badly hulled by Federal cruisers, and sank. All hands gained the Carolina shore. Eventually McGill and Matt returned to Bermuda, then traveled to Liverpool to arrange for construction of a second steamer, which McGill financed from profits. The vessel was built at the Birkenhead Ironworks, across the Mersey from the city proper; the very same yard which launched Semmes' Alabama and several other Confederate raiders.
>
> The young woman to whom Matthew lost his heart is the daugh ter of a steam fitter employed by the Lairds, proprietors of the

Birkenhead Yard. Matthew first saw the girl there. He struck up a conversation with her at a mass meeting held in the city to express support for Lincoln's emancipation decree. Matthew had gone to the meeting to—as he put it—hear what the other side was saying.

The young woman, I might note, was an ardent foe of the slave system; and Matthew told me in a strangely disarming way that he soon concluded the "other side" was right. I do not think romance alone was responsible for his change of heart. He finally thought the matter through. He still kept on with his seagoing duties out of loyalty to his captain and the cause, however.

The name of the young woman is Miss Dolly Stubbs. If Molly and I may believe the photograph Matt showed us, she is a lovely, lissome girl with blond hair and a face that speaks of good humor, pertness, and determination.

Once Molly and I had recovered from the detonation of Matthew's "bombshell," I commented upon my son's long silences during the war. He looked bewildered and scratched his head in a rather absent fashion. He ignores clocks; he totally lacks a sense of the passage of time.

When I asked what exactly he had done while away for so long, his reply was characteristically vague and breezy. "Why," he said, "McGill and I ran guns in and we ran cotton out until a boiler explosion sent the second steamer to the bottom off Bermuda.

"Then we went to Cuba and McGill used his last money to purchase a sailing schooner to operate in the Gulf. In between all that I taught the Bermuda nigras and the Cubans and the Liverpool shipyard boys to play our version of baseball, when I wasn't sketching or falling in love. It was all damn lively. I had very few spare moments in which to write letters."

No spare moments in almost five years? The most sanguinary struggle in our nation's history "damn lively?" I must say Matthew is a unique boy!

Gideon and Matthew got along well during the five-day visit. It was altogether a happy reunion; they seem to like one another even after long separation.

But beyond a prompt marriage, I have no notion of what Matt's future plans may be. Nor does he. Hardy and outgoing, he is apparently content to travel wherever the winds of chance and his romantic alliance may blow. He will never be industrious like Gideon —who, by the way, is still unable to find work. But for the moment, Matt has no need to be industrious. His share of the profits from his various voyages was no small sum. He was handsomely attired in the *latest gentleman's fashions when Gideon's family, Molly, and I saw him onto the Liverpool steamer.*

*Once recovered from the excitement of Matt's visit, I returned to prayerful consideration of a matter much on my mind of late. I have not mentioned it to you before, and it is time I did.*

*I am no longer a young man, Michael. I have been giving considerable thought to the disposition of the California money. I would like to use a portion of it to re-purchase the Boston publishing house before I die.*

*Of course I know next to nothing about the book trade, only a little something about newspapering. But I would like to have Kent and Son back in the family, since the company is of small importance to Louis in comparison to the Union, his textile and steel interests.*

*Louis—need I tell you—has no grasp of the worthy purpose of publishing, nor any interest in it. Kent and Son today is in even worse straits than it was when it was the property of that blackguard Stovall. The firm has, in fact, ceased publication of conventional books altogether. Shifting with the tides of popularity and opportunism, it now issues nothing but cheaply printed fiction weeklies, which may be had for one of those new copper and nickel five-cent pieces the Congress authorized in May.*

*Even Rose Ludwig's novels have been stripped of boards and republished in gaudy paper covers. I am thankful Amanda's dear friend is no longer alive to suffer the degradation of her work by a man solely interested in profit.*

*Louis obviously hopes to duplicate the success of the Beadle firm by imitating their "nickel novelettes." To this end, he has discharged poor Dana Hughes, and replaced him with a staff of hacks. Do you wonder I would like to buy out such a pack of rascals?*

*The decision, of course, belongs to Louis—and I suspect he will turn his back on any overture I might make. I know his hatred of me. Still, imitators usually fail—and should this prove true with Kent and Son, greed might get the better of emotion. One never knows with men such as my esteemed cousin.*

*So I will watch the situation. I want the firm fully as much as I want my great-grandfather Philip's sword, his portrait, and the other family artifacts Louis keeps at Kentland with no regard for the tradition or the ideals they symbolize.*

*I honestly cannot say what I would do with the publishing company if I had it—beyond rehiring Dana Hughes at once. But I still dream of restoring it, along with the aforementioned heirlooms, to—how shall I put it? Clean hands. Honorable hands.*

*In the event such a purchase is ever possible, I propose to divide the ownership of Kent and Son equally between Gideon, Matthew, and you.*

The last word struck Michael like a blow. He started, spilling burning flakes of tobacco on his shirt. One left a hole in the fabric before he batted them out.

*Don't be astonished, Michael. You are more a Kent than Amanda's own son. Should acquisition of the firm ever become a reality, you would enjoy an additional security you well deserve. I say "additional" for good reason. Jeremiah is clearly gone for all time. Thus I can, in good conscience, transfer his share of the California wealth to you. I have so stipulated in a new will.*

iv

"God above!" Michael breathed. His hand shook so badly, he dropped the sheets.

He collected them hastily, then fumbled more time away putting them back in proper order.

Still stunned, he read the last paragraph again. He wasn't dreaming.

*Do not think this a rash act on my part. You were of inestimable value to Amanda. I know she loved you. After her death, it was you who raised Louis, and helped restore me to life when I fled Lexington, turned out of my own house. I owe you a great debt. The family owes you a debt. And you are as much a Kent as I.*

*Indeed, my vanity even makes me wish your last name could be ours, but that would be an affront to your parents. So you shall be a Kent in all respects except the name.*

Michael leaned back and closed his eyes. He tried to assess all Jephtha's decision could mean to him. How it would change his existence—for it certainly would.

But believing, *really* believing what he'd just read was still too difficult. He forced his attention back to the letter.

v

The rest was less personal; more philosophical—but no less charged with emotion.

Jephtha turned to the war's aftermath; mentioned the gratification he'd derived from the Constitution's Thirteenth Amendment, ratified only the preceding December. The Amendment had forever abolished the institution of black slavery. He'd also been heartened by the passage of certain other pieces of national legislation.

> It was a milepost on the march for human liberties when the Congress overturned Johnson's veto in February, thereby extending the life and enlarging the scope of the Freedman's Bureau, which can be of continuing service to the Southern Negro. The Radicals say Johnson used the veto to pander to the South's Democratic aristocracy. But any man who reads Johnson's record correctly will know the class he despises most, North or South, is the privileged class. He idolizes men who work their own land; his beloved "mudsills." The President's greatest fault, if it can be termed that, is perhaps a too-strict adherence to the Constitution. He felt the Freedman's Act could not be legal since the eleven Confederate states were not represented in the national legislature and had no voice in the act's passage.
>
> As you may know, Johnson likewise vetoed Lyman Trumbull's civil rights bill, which declared that all persons born in the country are automatically citizens, entitled to equal rights and protection under the law. Trumbull introduced the bill to negate the Supreme Court's Dred Scott decision. Here, too, the President hewed closely to his interpretation of the Constitution, maintaining that the matters covered by Trumbull's bill are solely the province of the individual states. He still insists the bill as finally enacted over his veto is another step—in his words, "a long stride"—to centralization and concentration of legislative power in Washington.
>
> To be doubly sure Johnson's view would not one day be declared Constitutionally correct by the High Court, many of the same provisions of Trumbull's bill were introduced into the Fourteenth Amendment passed in June and now being submitted to the states for ratification.
>
> The struggle between Johnson and the Congress has become a sorry, stained business—carried forward on both sides with mounting

*acrimony. As Mr. Voorhees, the Democrat, so aptly put it, the actions of Thad Stevens and his Radical Republicans serve notice that the war to restore the Union was an utter failure; the war is over, and yet the Union is rent in twain.*

Michael knew what Jephtha meant. The Omaha and St. Louis papers had told him a war of quite a different sort had been underway in the capital almost since the hour the bells tolled Lincoln's death. Some of the more extreme Republicans have supposedly hailed the assassination as "a godsend," assuming the new President would throw Lincoln's reconstruction plans into the dustbin and take a harder line.

They'd gotten a shock when Johnson began to implement policies dating all the way back to an 1863 formula for establishing new Southern governments after the war. At that time Lincoln had been willing to grant executive recognition to rebel states in which ten per cent of the eligible voters of 1860 took an oath of loyalty and agreed to support emancipation.

No such easy terms would satisfy the Republican extremists any longer. As a result they were at war not only with the President and the Democrats but with the more conservative members of their own party; a fierce and bitter war rooted in a fundamental dispute over the nature of the four-year military struggle.

In the papers, old Thad Stevens, the cynical and vituperative leader of the House's radical wing, constantly referred to the seceded states as "conquered provinces" whose future condition depended on "the will of the conqueror."

Johnson's position, and that of the more moderate Republicans, was simply that the Southern states had never seceded because it was impossible for them to do so under the Constitution. They were still states, to be dealt with accordingly. Jephtha mentioned Stevens:

*Though in his seventies, he possesses the unrelenting energy—and savagery—of a man half his age. He busies about Washington with his queer black wig askew and his club foot dragging, never bothering to deny press accounts of his liaison up in Lancaster with his mulatto housekeeper, Lydia Smith. He is aligning his forces for the coming battle to determine whether the President or the Congress shall dictate Reconstruction policy.*

*And a battle it will surely be. I am kept informed about it by occasional letters from colleagues. Twice in the past year I have been down to Washington in person. And Theo Payne, that good and downtrodden man who continues to edit the* Union *under Louis' direction, brings his brood to supper every fourth week or so—the only* evening of the month on which he is forced to remain sober!—so I am not unfamiliar with the conflict that may yet prove more harmful to the country than the war itself.

Payne told me the Washington war has even reached into the spirit realm! You do know there is quite a craze back here for nontheological séances purporting to put relatives in touch with deceased loved ones?

According to Payne, a Mrs. Cora Daniels of Four and a Half Street, Washington, recently spoke using the voice of a "Mr. Parker," one of the departed. "Parker" predicted Johnson would soon arrest many of the radicals, convene a "congress of Southerners and Copperheads" and force "patriots," such as Stevens, to retreat to another location—Ohio was mentioned—there to set up a rival Congress! The bizarre business ended with "Parker" stating we would soon be engaged in a second Civil War—this time largely fought on Northern soil. I trust I convey how tragic I find all of this. No one has hoped and prayed longer than I for an end to bloodletting. Now it appears we must have more, albeit brought about with different weapons.

Neither has anyone hoped and prayed longer than I for an end to the foul business of slavery. Yet now that it is accomplished, I wonder how smoothly the freedmen can be brought into the main stream of American society.

Even such a staunch Unionist as General Sherman has said that universal suffrage—the issue by means of which Stevens and his crowd means to force their control of Reconstruction on the President—may lead to "new convulsions" in the country.

Although I sometimes speculate as to how much of Thad Stevens' venom springs from the destruction of his Pennsylvania iron foundry by Lee's troops on their way to Gettysburg, I feel Stevens cannot be entirely faulted.

The new Southern legislatures established under the Lincoln formula showed an old face with their so-called Black Codes intended to control the behavior of the liberated slaves. Some of the Codes prohibit blacks from riding in rail cars set aside for whites. No intermarriage is possible without penalty of imprisonment. Parentless Negro children apprenticed under court guidance are subject to recapture, exactly like slaves, if they flee from cruel masters.

In these and similar laws I heard again the rattle of the chains. The rights of new citizens must be guaranteed—and chief among these rights is suffrage. But I have begun to smell a taint in the Radicals' espousal of it. I first caught a whiff last December, when I *sat in the House gallery and listened to Stevens challenge the administration.*

*He would keep the Southern states from any active role in government until the Constitution has been "amended so as to secure perpetual ascendancy to the party of the Union"—meaning, of course, the Republicans.*

*With cynical candor, he predicted that unless the Negroes were given the vote, the balance of power would swing to the Southerners and the Democrats. But if suffrage could be made universal, he said, there would "always be Union men enough in the South, aided by the blacks, to divide the representation, and continue Republican ascendancy." So, you see, it is not an honorable war, but one with a secret purpose. The "secret" becomes more blatant day by day.*

*You might also be interested—or dismayed—to know that many a Northern businessman has smelled the opportunity inherent in this immoral plan. One such is Louis. He has long been a notorious trimmer, pretending to favor first one side, then another, as seemed expedient. Now, however, he has declared himself not only a Republican like you and me, but a Thad Stevens Republican!*

Michael's mouth quirked in distaste as he drew smoke from the pipe, exhaled, and let the fragrance of the tobacco mask some of the fetid smell of the deserted car. Outside he heard a whoop from the direction of Dorn's wagon. He reminded himself that he owed Christian a visit as soon as he finished reading.

*I do not believe Louis has joined the Stevens' wing from humanitarian motives. He would be the last to welcome freed blacks at his dining table, no matter how much he prates about the wisdom of universal suffrage. I imagine he only sees the potential for power— the deliberate and pitiless manipulation of human beings that could assure Republican supremacy for years to come. No doubt he has allied himself with the cause in order to be on the winning side. The taint has crept even into our family.*

*Thus the war goes on. Different from the last, but no less furious. You would be appalled by the actions of politicians in both camps as they seek to influence public opinion by enlisting the support of popular war heroes. How ardently both sides court Grant!—though Johnson appears to have him in his pocket for the moment.*

*Second only to the supreme commander is Custer, the "boy general." His chief military talent seems to have been the ability to com-*

mit huge numbers of men to slaughter in order to secure commendations for himself and advance his career.

Yet he remains overwhelmingly popular. He was here late in March, attending lavish dinners at the Manhattan Club, and was constantly in the company of Democrats. He himself belonged to the McClellan clique whose political views divided and nearly destroyed the Army of the Potomac for a time, just as surely as did McClellan's own vacillations and presidential ambitions.

The Republicans, it is said, would like Custer in their camp—and never mind his views about the fitness of blacks for citizenship. On the subject of permitting Negroes to vote, Custer is fond of stating he'd "as soon think of elevating an Indian Chief to the Popedom of Rome." Can you doubt that the aim of some Republicans is not justice throughout the land, but absolute rule by their party?

Everywhere, in fact, there is much to dismay men of conscience. Davis is still in prison at Fort Monroe, facing indictment for treason. Lee—honorable, misguided Lee whom I also saw in Lexington at the time of Fan's funeral—is eking out a living as president of Washington College. Good neighbors who know his straits send bags of walnuts, potatoes, and pickles to his household table while Northern newspapers villify him as a "sinister conspirator"—this proud, torn, Christian man who refused a plea at Appomattox that he give his soldiers leave to take to the hills and woods and continue to fight as partisans. He told them to go home, admit defeat, build new lives. Yet he is labeled "sinister." Is this the "malice toward none" of which Lincoln spoke, and which Johnson is struggling to implement?

Still, I am not totally without hope. While the political war rages here in the East, there is a counterbalancing dynamism; a sense of our nation being only moments away from the dawn of a mighty age of expansion, if we can but keep the Union whole. Never, they say, has there been a period of such enormous industrial growth—or such visions of a prosperous, thriving land from sea to sea.

You are part of one of the remarkable enterprises that can bring those visions to reality. The transcontinental railroad will open the West to commerce and settlement in a manner undreamed of even a decade ago. Public land is there for the taking, a hundred and sixty acres of it available to any man, thanks to the Homestead Act.

Though we live in a troubled time, it is also a time of promise. I try to believe a spirit of healing, not hatred, will prevail. I try to have faith that even the schemes of a rapacious new class of moguls who care nothing for the human lives they exploit to see their facto-

*ries prosper—yes, and their railroads built—will, in the end, yield
blessings we cannot imagine.*

*Michael, forgive this long discourse written late at night. Poor
Molly despairs of my nocturnal ponderings and scribblings. But
there are not many others with whom I can share my deepest
thoughts.*

*I wish you good health and success in your courageous venture in
a part of the country foreign to you. From such willingness to strike
out in bold new directions was this country born—and, as I recall,
the Kent family founded!*

Slowly, Michael laid the churchwarden on his belly. He stared at the
last sheet in his blistered hand. The paper seemed to fade, replaced by
Julia Kent's blue eyes.

*Courage?*

*Bold new directions?*

*Jephtha, I'm glad you don't know all the truth.*

With effort, he returned to the brief conclusion.

*I look forward to any descriptions you can send of the exciting en-
terprise in which you are involved. May God bless and protect you.
Remember that from this hour, my revised will makes you a* bona
fide *member of the family to which, by word and deed, you have
belonged for many years.*

> *Your kinsman,*
> *Jephtha*

Michael was still touched and overwhelmed by Jephtha's act of generosity. All at once an idea came to mind. An important idea.

He gathered up the pages, folded them, and slipped both letters beneath his blanket. He jumped down from the bunk and quickly left the
car.

### vi

Two stragglers were all that remained at the paymaster's cubicle. Michael fretted impatiently while one received his greenbacks, and the balding clerk noted the wages of the second in a thick ledger. The clerk
yawned as Michael stepped to the counter.

"Give me the book containing the B's, Charlie. And your pen."

"What is this, Boyle? You've already received—"

"I know. But my name isn't listed properly."

"What?"

"Just ink your pen and give it to me."

Annoyed, the clerk handed him the pen, together with another ledger. Michael thumbed the pages. Located the correct line. He slashed a stroke through three words, hoping his dead parents would forgive him for abandoning Aloysius, which they had bestowed. His eyes looked wet as he wrote carefully.

He returned the pen and rotated the ledger so the clerk could read it.

"There. That's the correct version."

The clerk peered. "That's all you wanted? What the hell does it matter if we've got your middle name right or wrong? You're paid the save either way."

"It matters more than you'll ever appreciate," Michael replied softly. "Much more."

He turned and left while the puzzled clerk studied the drying ink that spelled out *Michael Kent Boyle*.

# CHAPTER 7

## Dorn's Daughter

MICHAEL STEPPED DOWN from the office car and breathed deeply. The air had turned cool and invigorating. His assortment of aches and bruises seemed less troublesome now.

The dark near the train was relieved by two torches stabbed into the ground at the corners of Gustav Dorn's whiskey wagon. Dorn himself was dispensing liquor from one of the barrels. He was a short untidy man with a gray-shot beard. His huge belly hung over his belt. He seldom smiled.

At the moment he had at least thirty customers lined up. Each drinker took the dipper from Dorn and swallowed whatever amount he'd bought while those waiting shouted for him to hurry. When the customer had finished, he went to the merchant's son a few steps away.

The phlegmatic-looking boy was perched on a small box behind a crate. His Hawken lay across his knees. The customer deposited his money on a tin plate lying on the crate. Occasionally the boy had to change a greenback or a coin. The rest of the time he paid no attention to the drinkers, staring out past the nearest torch in a joyless, vacant way.

As Michael walked closer to the wagon, one man who'd evidently passed through the line more than once spilled the contents of his dipper. Those waiting laughed and hooted. Dorn demanded payment. The worker refused.

Beyond the train, a cow lowed. Michael paused by one of the torches to watch the outcome of the dispute. Dorn spoke English badly but got his point across.

"You buy—you pay. Not my fault you sloppy."

"I'll be damned if I'll give ye a cent for somethin' I never tasted, Dutchie." There was humor in the customer's eyes, but testiness in his slurred voice. He wobbled around to get a judgment from those in line. "What d'ye say, lads? Am I fair or not fair?"

"Fair, fair!" a couple of his friends yelled.

Dorn snapped his fingers and barked German at his son. The stolid fat boy raised the Hawken. With a start, Michael saw the hammer was back, ready to fire.

Dorn looked smug as he tapped the customer's shoulder. The man batted his hand away. Excitedly, the workers in line pointed to the rifle. The drinker saw it and turned pale.

Torchlight shimmered on the Hawken's thirty-four-inch barrel. The St. Louis-made gun might be a good twenty years old, but at short range it could ruin a man with its .50-caliber ball. Dorn made clear that he intended nothing else.

"Shit with fair, Paddy. You pay. Now. Or my boy, he take the price out of your hide."

Grumbling, the man dug a hand into his pocket. He clenched his fist around the coin, then raised his hand as if he meant to hit the merchant.

Dorn retreated a step. "Klaus!"

The Hawken jutted forward across the top of the crate.

After another glance at the rifle, the drinker lowered his hand. He gave Dorn the coin.

The little act of extortion finally produced a smile from the merchant. He waved the man aside and brandished the dipper at the line:

"Next fellow! Step lively, hah? Got a business to run here."

The boy returned the Hawken to his knees, uncocked. Michael shook his head. The East had no monopoly on greed. And if the little scene he had witnessed was typical of the way Dorn conducted his trade, serious trouble was bound to erupt eventually.

He walked by the rear of the line, waving to acquaintances. Out in the dark near the end of the track, a fire of buffalo chips blazed. A group of Paddies sat around it. One started a song on an old concertina.

Michael recognized it instantly: "Corcoran to His Regiment," sometimes known as "I Would Not Take Parole." Corcoran had commanded the New York 69th at First Manassas, been captured, and imprisoned in Richmond. Paddies by the fire—men who'd never come anywhere near the Irish Brigade but were still proud of its record—bellowed the words.

> "Raise the green flag proudly,
> "Let it wave on high—"

The song conjured memories for Michael. Memories of smoke; thundering shells; wounded comrades begging for help as the ranks plunged past them. Bits of terrain he'd seen in Pennsylvania and Virginia—woodlands, hillsides—blended in his imagination like a mural by a deranged artist.

> "Liberty and Union
> "Be your battle cry!"

Sean Murphy lurched to his feet. Fists on his hips, he began to jig while the singers applauded in rhythm.

> *"Faugh-a-ballagh shout*
> *"From your center to your flanks—*
> *"And carry death and terror wild*
> *"Into the foeman's ranks!"*

*"Faugh-a-ballagh."* How stirring that Gaelic cry to clear the way had been during the early days; and how sadly futile in the weeks and months after Gettysburg, when the ranks were so disastrously thin.

Michael returned a hail from one of the revelers, declined an invitation to join them, and strode on. He wanted no more fighting—not even in memory.

Yet he'd gotten more of the real thing this very day. The railroader's music reminded him of the peace that seemed to elude him. The thrill of Jephtha's news was all at once blunted by a recollection of Leonidas Worthing.

Quickly, Michael looked behind him. His gaze encompassed torches at the whiskey wagon; the smudged yellow of the train's windows; the starry dark above. For a moment he'd been certain he was being observed. He saw no indication of it.

An uncontrollable gloom settled over him. He'd traveled thousands of miles to escape war, but as long as Worthing remained at the railhead, he was smack back in the middle of one. A lone man or a regiment—either could kill you.

Despite his gloom and nervousness, he forced himself to stand still while he relit his churchwarden. Then he hurried on to the Dorn tent.

ii

The tent stood a good twenty yards behind the wagon. A lamp inside made the front section glow. The rear was dark. He stepped to the flap and called softly.

"Hallo?"

"Who's there?"

"Beg pardon, Miss Dorn—is that you?"

The unseen girl laughed. "I've seen no other women in this godless place. I expect so."

A feminine silhouette appeared suddenly on the front of the tent. Unlike her father, she spoke without an accent.

"Who might you be?"

"The name's Michael K. Boyle."

"Oh, yes, Papa mentioned you." It was crisply said, with a faint edge of reproof. "The one who caused the trouble."

"The one who was on the receiving end of the trouble, if you don't mind! I had no hand in causing it." Not quite true. But the unseen girl had irked him.

"Well, it makes no difference," she replied in an airy way. "It was still ungodly quarreling."

That was two references to godlessness in a space of seconds. Disgusted, he blew out a puff of smoke. She must be a proper prude, all right.

He tried to control his annoyance:

"Whatever the cause, the result was the shooting of my friend Christian. I understand you're tending him?"

"That's correct. He'll recover splendidly."

"I came to visit him—which is pretty blasted difficult with this tent between us. Would you be so kind as to let me in?"

She ignored his sarcasm. "Are you alone?"

He had a good notion to inform her that a dozen wild-eyed rapists were hovering behind him.

"I am."

"All right, then. But your friend's asleep."

A hand lifted the flap. Michael ducked, starting inside, then stopped short. His mouth opened. The churchwarden fell from his lips. He caught it in time, letting out a loud, *"Oww!"* as his thumb accidentally jabbed into the hot bowl.

Licking his thumb and wincing, he didn't move. He was still thunderstruck.

A single lamp hung from the ridgepole. An open Bible lay on a stool beside an untidy cot along the left wall. To judge from the garments strewn on it, the cot belonged to her father or brother. The twin of the boy's Hawken was propped against an equally messy cot on the right—another male domain; a pair of patched trousers lay beneath.

Directly in front of him—no longer disguised by distance or a shapeless coat and hat—was the real cause of his surprise.

In one way, the workers whose hurts she'd tended had exaggerated. But perhaps to men of forty, a woman in her late twenties could properly be called young. Their other claim had been understated. She was more than just pretty. Without benefit of paint or furbelows, she was lovely.

iii

"For heaven's sake come in or go out, one or the other, Mr. Boyle," she
said in a sharp tone. She wore trousers of denim cloth tucked into heavy
boots, and a man's work shirt that fit tightly over large well-shaped breasts.
She had her father's square jaw but a more generous mouth and clear,
blue-gray eyes. Hair the color of summer wheat was drawn into a bun at
the back of her head.

Her skin had a sunburned coarseness—more noticeable on the backs of
her hands. The knuckles were red. Yet he found the weather-beaten look
curiously attractive. She had fine wide hips and smelled not unpleasantly
of strong soap.

"I'm afraid I'm not familiar with your first name—" he began.

"Is there any reason why you should be? It's Hannah. Now do you
wish to see your friend?"

She turned sideways, inadvertently drawing his eye to the curve of her
breast. When she noticed, her cheeks pinked.

"Mr. Boyle!"

He jerked to attention. "Yes?"

"He's behind the canvas partition. I don't think it would be advisable
for you to wake him up. Just glance in."

He didn't know what to make of the woman. She seemed to have more
than a touch of her father's stern temperament, and some of her remarks
would have been downright disagreeable had they not been tempered by
her smile and a pleasant voice. Her gaze was uncomfortably direct.

Michael shifted the pipe from one hand to the other. She gestured:

"You burned your thumb."

"Nothing serious."

"A burn is always serious for a man who works with his hands. You've
blisters, too, I see. I have some salve that would help. I'll apply it before
you leave."

"Truly, it's not necessary."

"Yes, it is. Women know more about such things than men. However,
I'd appreciate it if you'd extinguish your pipe." She smiled. "Smoking is a
wasteful, unhealthy habit."

"Oh, I see! Whatever you say, Miss Dorn." His tone was as tart as hers
of a few moments ago.

He stuck his arm outside, turned the pipe over, and shook the remaining embers and tobacco to the ground. When he faced her again, he surrendered to an ungentlemanly impulse and said:

"Do you consider smoking worse than drinking whiskey? Or selling it?"

Immediately he regretted the clumsy sarcasm. Instead of anger, it produced a look of hurt. She hid it by turning away.

"Though it's no affair of yours, I don't condone my father's trade, nor—" Softly: "—nor his own dependence on the product he sells."

She looked at him again. "But he *is* my father. My brother Klaus is very young. Someone must look after them."

"I didn't mean to imply—"

"That my father's a drunkard? He is. Don't the roughnecks in this camp know that by now?"

He was too embarrassed to answer.

"You see, Mr. Boyle, my father owns a small store in Grand Island. General merchandise. The store is failing because Papa's too fond of his whiskey to attend to its management or care about his customers. And he'll let no one help him, except in the most menial way. When he chose to try to make some extra money by temporarily closing the store, fixing up the wagon, and driving all the way out here to this hideous place, I had a choice. Let him take Klaus and bring harm to himself or both of them by provoking others with his brusqueness—railroad men are not so placid as farmer's wives, they say—or come with them. I'm afraid Papa's only the first of many who'll be following the tracks to take advantage of men's vices. Now if that satisfies your curiosity about my motives—?"

She spoke well, he was thinking. She was uncommonly well educated, or more likely self-taught.

"Miss Dorn, I didn't mean to pry—or annoy you with my tactless remark about the whiskey."

"That's all right. I just wanted you to know I was here for the sake of people, not profits."

The words carried an odd undertone. Pain?

He was at a loss to understand why she'd revealed so much in a few sentences—unless she'd contained a deep hurt for too long, and had no one but a stranger with whom to share it.

That gave him a little better insight into her character. She might be strong, but she wasn't marble. Not marble at all, he thought with another covert glance at her bosom.

He walked to the canvas partition and raised it at the divided center. Christian lay on a cot by the rear wall, snoring lightly. His dark skin tended to blend with the shadows in the unlit back section. But the neat white bandage on his right calf was bright in the lamplight falling over Michael's shoulder.

He was conscious of time ticking by. He couldn't prolong the visit much more, though for some unfathomable reason, to prolong it was exactly what he wanted. He was conscious of Hannah Dorn's fragrance—the clean, bracing odor of soap.

Finally he dropped the canvas and turned. She'd returned to the stool. The open Bible rested on her knees.

"Thank you," he said. "He looks fine."

A bob of her head. The wheat-colored hair glinted. "I fixed him soup. He took every drop. I also gave him half a dipper of Papa's whiskey to help him sleep."

"Oh, then you're not averse to drinking?"

"Mr. Boyle, don't bait me. Alcohol does have its purposes. Everything on earth has God's purpose concealed somewhere within it if you search hard enough." It was a quiet, rational-sounding declaration. He tried to detect a touch of the sanctimonious in it and failed.

He indicated the open book. "Are you searching now?"

"I do so whenever I can." She touched the page. "I was reading Second Chronicles."

He tried another smile. "I'm afraid my knowledge of scripture has shrunk to some memorized verses."

"Boyle's an Irish name. Are you Catholic?"

Damn, how direct she was! He'd never met such a woman.

"Are you?"

She smiled, enjoying the sparring. "Lutheran."

"Well, I am a Catholic—or I used to be. I've not been inside a church for a long time. Is my specific religion of importance?"

"Why, yes, it is."

"You dislike Catholics? You're not alone."

"I do not dislike Catholics. I asked for another reason entirely. We're isolated out here, among rough men. Those who profess any faith at all belong together. For mutual protection, wouldn't you say?"

She was still smiling. He did too. "I honestly couldn't offer a worthwhile opinion. My religion's like—like an object you carry out of habit but seldom use."

She met his gaze, then averted her eyes. He detected a tinge of color above the collar of her shirt. A point scored! Hannah Dorn wasn't quite so holy as she pretended. She was self-conscious with a man in her quarters.

"Well," she said, "at least you're honest. That's a virtue."

He touched the pipestem to his forehead. "Thank you kindly for the compliment. I'll be going along—"

He was totally unprepared for her next remark:

"If you're thirsty, I could warm some coffee."

The pink colored her throat again. He knew his earlier guess had been right. She had her religion, but it wasn't quite enough to counterbalance a certain loneliness. He wasn't sure he wanted any further involvement with such a curiously complex creature.

Torn, he hedged: "That would be very hospitable. But it's growing late."

"Not that late. I'd like some coffee myself. And I do want to attend to your hands. But outside. It's less compromising." The half smile was at her own expense. "I suspect I know what the men in camp are saying about me. Any woman who travels to a place like this—"

"You're wrong," he interrupted. He pointed to the Bible. "They say you're devout." His hand moved to indicate the Hawken. "And definitely not to be interfered with. You wouldn't believe how much that combination disappoints them."

She laughed; she had beautiful, regular teeth. The effect was dazzling.

"I do know how to use the rifle. Both of the Hawkens are loaded with the extra charges of powder hunters use to stop buffalo. I don't hold with killing, but I'm willing to wound the first man who tries anything improper. It's a matter of principle."

"Oh, of course," he murmured, straight-faced.

"Mr. Boyle, you're laughing at me."

"No, ma'am! You're just not—not what I expected."

"Please don't tell me what you did expect," she teased, "or our acquaintance will probably come to an abrupt end. I must admit I'm glad you stopped by. I don't often get to talk to anyone with some degree of education. It's a pleasure." Her eyes sparkled in the lamplight. "Even though you clearly have vices."

"Now you're the one who's laughing."

"So I am. Forgive me. Let's go out, shall we?"

Again she smiled, as if eager to establish at least a tentative friendship. He raised the canvas to allow her to precede him.

She left the Hawken where it stood, carrying a coffee pot in one hand and her Bible in the other. The two objects struck him as representing a contradiction. Warmth and reserve. But it was just that contradiction that made her intriguing—and, somewhat to his surprise, made him interested in knowing her better.

His eye fastened on the swaying curve of her buttocks. Delightful sight! Or it was until caution intruded:

*Have a care, Boyle. Don't broaden your interest to include wanting to know her in the Biblical sense or she's liable to blow your head off.*

*Wait. Not your head. She doesn't condone killing. No doubt she'd aim for a functional member more closely allied with your vices.*

*Bet she'd hit it dead on, too.*

The mere thought made him wince as he followed her from the tent.

# CHAPTER 8

## The Bible and the Knife

HANNAH DORN ASKED HIM to rekindle the fire with fresh buffalo chips stored behind the tent. As he went to fetch them, he recalled with amusement the first evening he'd been sent to collect them on the prairie.

He'd been at the railhead no more than two days. Sean Murphy had soberly instructed him to go to a nearby wallow and bring back any chips he found. "Wallow chips are the very finest," Murphy had assured him.

He'd returned with a huge load, carefully piled half a dozen together, and touched a match to them. He'd already been informed the chips ignited easily and produced a virtually smokeless fire.

By the time he'd struck ten matches, Murphy was laughing so hard tears came. Then he explained the joke played on greenhorns. Bison rolled in wallows to find relief from biting flies and mosquitoes. The mud that dripped from their bodies when they emerged formed unburnable but otherwise perfect counterfeits of real chips containing partly digested grass. Since that night, Michael had sent several newcomers to similar wallows; it was a sort of ritual of initiation.

He gathered the chips and walked back toward the fire, asking himself why he was interested in the company of Hannah Dorn when Julia was the only woman he really cared about.

*Perhaps I'm making it too complicated,* he thought as he rounded the corner of the tent. Hannah was placing a stool near the ashes. *I've been away from any sort of female companionship a long time. There's no sin in enjoying a bit of it—even though, for all of this lady's good looks, she's a strong, spiky sort.*

He didn't quite believe that assessment, though. Once or twice, Dorn's daughter had inadvertently revealed a softness—a vulnerability—beneath the shell of her religious conviction. He saw evidence of it again now—a noticeable uneasiness as she fidgeted with the lid of the galvanized tin coffee pot, peered down inside, replaced the lid, then lifted it again for another doubtful glance.

"It's the last of the morning coffee, Mr. Boyle. Very strong, I'm afraid."

"Couldn't be stronger than the poison they pour in the dining car," he laughed, dumping the chips.

Hannah used a thong to tie the pot's wire bail to a tripod improvised from three rusty iron rods. She dug matches from her pocket. Michael extended his hand.

She passed him two matches. Their hands touched. She inhaled softly at the unexpected contact.

He pulled his fingers back quickly. *Damned if I'm not as nervous as she!*

The chips caught almost instantly. Soon scraps of flame were tossing in the night breeze. He sat down cross-legged near her stool. Out of sight beyond Dorn's wagon, the workers had begun to sing again, this time "The Vacant Chair," a slow, mournful war ballad about a family's loss of a son. He turned his head to listen as a soprano voice soared above the rest. That would be Tom Ruffin, the lad from Indiana. One by one the older men stopped singing. Only the boy's voice was left—pure and almost painfully sweet under theNebraska stars.

"You were in it, then?"

Startled, he swung around. "What brought that to mind?"

"The look on your face when you heard the song from the war."

He tried to shrug as if the music raised no memories.

"Yes, I was in it. The New York 69th of the Irish Brigade. I was in it up until the Wilderness, where I took a wound." A bitter smile. "It was a struggle all the way. The fighting was enough to scare twenty years off your life every time you went in. And practically from the beginning, we never had enough men. After Gettysburg—we were only in sharp action on the second day—we had just about three hundred muskets left. We carried five regimental flags, every one supposed to represent something like a thousand soldiers. We tried to fight ten times as hard, as if we were a true brigade; but it was futile because so many had been lost along the way."

Studying him, she asked, "Were you proud of fighting?"

"Proud of killing other Americans?"

Michael's hand strayed to his moustache. An index finger smoothed the gold and gray hair as his eyes fixed on the fire.

"No. I came to hate it."

She was pleased. "As all men should who keep the commandments God gave Moses."

He grimaced. "I'm afraid my hatred of the war only appeared *after* I broke that commandment a number of times."

"How many?"

"Four that I saw for certain. Possibly more. I preferred never to be too sure."

His head lifted.

"On the other hand, Miss Dorn, I'd like to believe that when we *were* required to kill, we did it for a just cause."

"The Southern side thought the same."

"Admittedly."

"There should have been another way to settle the differences."

He sighed. "A great many men more clever than I tried to find one. For thirty years they tried. The differences were too strong. Too fundamental —ah, well. It's over."

But the memories weren't. Helpless, he was pulled back to a July afternoon of billowing smoke and blaring bugles. He heard again the incredible, earth-shaking bombardment from Seminary Ridge that had preceded the slaughter of Pickett's infantrymen as they advanced gallantly toward the clump of trees, only to be shot down, blown down, stabbed down—the highest cresting of the Southern tide, men called it. Michael's brigade had watched it from afar. His inner eye saw the gray-clad bodies tumbling, singly and in great masses, as other Irishmen—the Pennsylvania 69th of the Philadelphia Brigade—blunted the assault at Pickett's center.

He wrenched himself from the reverie.

"I do confess I took pride in our unit. The Union commanders put special faith in the Irish Brigade. Before an action, they'd ask, 'Are the green flags ready?' The flags were decorated with bright golden harps and sunbursts. A man could usually see the gold even in the thickest smoke. But by the end, there were too few marching behind the flags."

"Too few on both sides," Hannah agreed. "I've read that altogether four hundred thousand were lost."

"I've heard more than half a million, and perhaps the same number injured. No one will ever know for certain. Both sides kept shamelessly poor records. An officer I met in the hospital told me some Confederate units were still listed on the rolls when only six or eight from the original complement were left."

She sensed his distaste for the subject and shifted to a slightly different one:

"You said you belonged to a New York regiment. Did you mean the state or the city?"

"The city."

"It's your home?"

"Was," he nodded. He pointed at the dark bulk of the train. "That's my home now."

"Why did you come out here?"

He pondered the question. Should he be honest? Yes. But not entirely.

"Several reasons. To find work. Earn money—"

"Was there no work in New York City?"

"I could have returned to the docks, I suppose. I started there, as a longshoreman, when I was young."

She smiled, "Come, now. You're far from old."

"But getting there." His own smile faded. "When I left the hospital, I wanted a particular sort of work. No, better to say I needed it. Everywhere in the East, there are crippled men. Stumbling along the streets having left part of themselves in some damn—some bloody field or forest. It's too depressing a reminder of the price we paid to hold the Union together.

"I've read they're recruiting cavalry regiments for service against the Indians out here, and because so few able-bodied men are left, the Army's waiving many of its restrictions. The Plains Army will accept one-armed fellows, or men who've lost an eye. Men with a limp are welcome in the cavalry since a limp won't impair their riding. We'll be a nation of invalids for a generation. I hoped to see less of that on the railroad.

"But there's a more important reason I came to the U-Pay. I decided I'd done my share of destroying things. Property. Lives. I wanted work to balance that. I wanted to build, not tear down. The railroad's a worthy enterprise, even though many say it's controlled by schemers who aren't above bribing Congressmen to get it finished. But the heart of it's good, and important. Unfortunately—"

A rueful smile.

"—I haven't been entirely successful in my effort to get away from fighting. I allowed myself to be drawn into the scrape with Worthing. He deserved what he got, but I'm ashamed I was the one to dish it out."

She continued to study him without speaking. He'd experienced a strange release in describing his past. Unexpectedly, he found himself telling her most of the rest:

"I also left the East because of personal problems. Before the war, I was employed by a wealthy family. The Kents."

The name produced no response.

"I was discharged—rather, I did a thing or two which made it impossible for me ever to work for them again."

*Such as telling Louis I would not cooperate in his scheme to trade with the enemy.*

*Such as nearly raping his wife that very same night at Kentland, then finding myself smitten with her—*

He sat up straighter in an effort to clear his mind. For a moment Julia's blue eyes seemed to glow near Hannah Dorn's face. He blinked. The vision vanished.

"No need for you to listen to any more, Miss Dorn. It's a tedious story, full of mistakes and regrettable lapses into many of those vices you abhor."

"Why, Mr. Boyle, that almost sounds like an insult." But she wasn't angry.

"Please, I don't mean to mock your faith. I expect these times require more of it, not less. But as I suggested inside, I—just don't have any of my own."

"I don't believe you. Every man has something he wants to achieve."

"Yes. To lay a mile of track a day."

"I mean some goal he wants to reach."

"To get the job done. To reach the hundredth meridian, then see the Atlantic and the Pacific joined by the rails."

"And that's all?"

He nodded.

"What will you do when the railroad's completed?"

"I've no idea."

"That's a sad and aimless way to go through life, Mr. Boyle."

"In truth, it is. But it's better than making war."

His brows knit together. He was unsettled at the way this woman was drawing out confessions he'd never intended to make.

She lifted the Bible from her lap, stood up, and touched an index finger to the pot. She withdrew it quickly; the coffee was hot enough.

"At least you're better off than Papa," she said. "You have a goal to last you a while. Papa never thinks beyond the next dipper from the barrel. We had very high hopes when we came to America in 1850. I recall it well—I was twelve when we made the passage in steerage. I can still hear Mama talking before we left Hamburg about how grand the future would be. Better by far than what we were leaving."

She untied the thing with one hand and held the pot bail with the other. "There are two china mugs on the washstand, Mr. Boyle."

He walked into the tent, returned with the cups, and let her pour. She held the pot by the bail and the bottom, as if it weren't even warm.

Steam drifted from the mugs as she finished pouring and bedded the pot in the ash of the disintegrating chips. She accepted one of the mugs. Her eyelids dropped briefly as their fingers accidentally touched a second time.

He sat down again. "You came from Germany, you said."

She took her seat on the stool; stared into the mug. Spoke softly:

"Papa was the last of fourteen brothers. Fourteen men and not a girl among them to marry off. The family brewery couldn't support him as well as a wife. Eight of his brothers also had to make their way in other kinds of work. It was Mama's savings and Mama's insistence that brought us here from Hamburg. We got as far as Cincinnati. Papa tried the butcher trade. First working for a shop owner to learn it, then opening a place of his own. But as a young man, he'd gotten too fond of beer and spiritous liquors. The habit was fixed. In Cincinnati he abused his customers. Word soon got around. The business failed. Papa managed to make a little on the sale of the building, but it was nothing more than luck."

"And your mother?"

"Mama wore herself out raising my brother Klaus. He was born in '52. She also worked with the Cincinnati Negro railroad, helping blacks who'd escaped from Kentucky on their way to Canada. One night six years ago, she and two other women and I were giving food bundles to three runaway boys on the Cincinnati waterfront. We were set on by a farmer who'd rowed across the river to recapture the boys. There was no violence, just a good deal of rough talk. The farmer did brandish a gun, however. And Mama's heart was bad. She suffered a seizure and died that night."

"I'm sorry."

"It took Papa a year to recover, realize the butcher shop had failed, and sell it. We came from Cincinnati to Nebraska because Germans had settled here too. Papa set up the store in Grand Island, and within two or three months it was Cincinnati all over again. He drove customers away with his foul temper and his discourtesy."

"Yet you've stayed with him."

"I said it before—he's my father. And there's Klaus to look after. The strong man doesn't pass by the weak merely because the weak man's flawed. We're all flawed."

Her free hand came to rest on the dark pebbled cover of the Bible on her knees.

"Christ taught that."

With her head bowed, she drank, then resumed:

"Whatever happens to Papa, I'll stay in the territory. Mama's belief in America was justified, that much I've learned since I've grown up. And perhaps it's not Papa's fault that he isn't strong enough to take advantage of the opportunity this country affords. Nebraska is a good land. All it needs are good people who believe in God and hard work. In a few years Grand Island will have schools, and churches, and be as fine a town as any other. I'll stay—even after Papa's gone."

"You do have a strong faith," Michael said, hoping she understood it as a compliment.

She bobbed her head; self-effacement. He was conscious again of how lovely she looked with her face patterned by the firelight. But he still didn't quite know what to make of her odd combination of piety and vulnerability.

All at once Hannah set her mug between her boots and opened the Bible.

"Mama taught me to believe in three things, Mr. Boyle. Work. Cleanliness. And this book. I know some people would laugh at me for saying that."

He raised a hand. "Not I. Truly, I do wish I had things to believe in other than this infernal railroad. The family I worked for had such things. But they turned away from—never mind. Go on."

"There's little more to say—except one thing. I do believe what's in these pages. And I believe this country offers greater hope than any other land on earth. America will always be a blessed place if we abide by its purpose, and this book."

He looked dubious: "At the moment, I wouldn't classify the East as a blessed place. It's poisoned with hatred."

"No more so than here. That fellow you fought—how is he different from all those politicians tearing at one another? Or the businessmen the papers rail about? There's always wickedness in the world, Mr. Boyle. But we can turn away from it and enjoy the blessings of life here. We have guidance."

She patted the book. "I was reading something along those very lines when you arrived. Second Chronicles, chapter seven, verse fourteen—"

He was envious of the peace he saw on her face as she quoted without looking up the passage:

" 'If my people, which are called by my name, shall humble themselves, and pray, and seek my face, and turn from their wicked ways, then will I hear from heaven, and will forgive their sin, and will heal their land—' "

He wished he could believe her answer was the right one—and easily implemented. Their eyes met for a long moment. Then she succumbed to embarrassment. Resting her palms on the book, she gazed down at them. He was gripped by an impulse to stand, circle the fire, and touch her.

He didn't. If she knew that a certain tension below his belly was in part responsible for his feeling, no doubt she'd run inside the tent for the Hawken—

*What in the devil's happening to you, Michael Boyle?*

The answer was the same as before: a normal reaction to a long period spent without speaking to a woman more than casually.

But he tended to reject it. *This* woman was the one who fascinated him.

He tried not to deprecate her obvious faith in the words she'd quoted. But he couldn't help a touch of cynicism:

"That's a laudable message. Perhaps I should copy it and have it delivered to Captain Worthing."

"The man with whom you had the trouble?"

"Yes, have you met him?"

Distastefully: "No, but Klaus keeps me informed. Worthing is one of Papa's better customers. I hope you'll have no more to do with him."

Something prickled Michael's backbone.

*It isn't up to me.*

"I'd better not," he laughed. "General Casement warned me. Any more brouhahas and I'll probably be discharged."

"Let me say something, Mr. Boyle—and I beg you not to be offended by it."

He was on guard. "Go ahead."

"I believe a man finds what he seeks, whether it's trouble or peace."

"I fear it's not quite so simple."

"Not always. But in a general sense, yes."

"Well, it certainly hasn't worked in my case. I look for peace but don't find it."

"Perhaps you haven't looked in the proper spot."

"If you mean the Bible, you're correct."

"You might try it sometime."

"I wish I could—believing in what I was doing, I mean."

"That comes eventually. First there must be the intent."

He couldn't help feeling irked, and would have expressed the feeling if she weren't so sincere. He did make one admission:

"To a certain extent you're correct about finding what you seek. I could have knuckled under to Worthing. I refused."

"This is a difficult place. Among rough men, you'll always face such choices."

"And you don't face them in Grand Island?"

"Not as many." She smiled. "That's one of the few benefits of what people call the advance of civilization. In any case, before I go to bed, I'll pray Mr. Worthing won't force you into a situation in which you'll be tempted to fight again. If you do it will only make your unhappy feelings that much stronger."

His mingled amusement and anger faded when he realized she was utterly serious. Serious and concerned. He didn't know what to say.

The singing was over. The cooling air carried a winy tang. For no reason he could fully explain, sitting quietly beside Hannah produced a sense of calm he hadn't known in months.

The silence lengthened. He was acutely conscious of the woman's femininity. His body kept responding in a way she'd certainly find objectionable. He decided he'd better leave.

He drained his coffee—cold now—and contrived to stand up with a kind of twisting motion, so she wouldn't catch a glimpse of his trousers.

"Miss Dorn, I thank you for the company, the coffee, and the conversation."

"I enjoyed it, Mr. Boyle," she said with a little nod. "You're a sensitive and literate man."

"No, only a rust-eater," he laughed. "Your speech is finer. I'm wondering how you learned English so well."

"Mama. She believed that since this was to be our country, we should study the language, and its finest usage. Papa wouldn't but I did. I had no formal schooling here, mind, but I had great men for teachers. Shakespeare. John Milton. Wadsworth—"

She lifted the Bible. "And the translators who worked for good King James."

She laid the book on the stool as she rose, mercifully keeping her eyes on his face.

*Boyle, you're behaving like the worst adolescent!*

So he was. He couldn't help it.

Hannah Dorn walked around the dying fire. Her stride was long; determined.

"Wait here one moment. I still have a bit of doctoring to do."

Shortly she emerged from the tent with a small milk glass pot. The salve it contained had a foul color and a tarry smell. But it proved marvelously cooling as she spread it on his blistered palms and burned thumb. She rubbed vigorously until the salve was absorbed into the skin.

"Feels much better," he muttered, amazed anew at the reaction the feel of her fingers produced.

"I'm glad." She extended her hand.

After a moment's hesitancy—his palm was still slick—he clasped it. He squeezed a bit harder than necessary. She didn't seem to mind.

"I thank you again, Miss Dorn."

"The pleasure's been mine."

"Perhaps when Christian's awake tomorrow, I might look in a second time?"

The gray-blue eyes held his. "I wish you would." Then, with more animation: "A second visit might even result in a halfway peaceful Sunday with Papa. He's given up all hope of gentlemen spending more than a moment speaking to me. The Hawken and the Bible seem to get in the way. But I—"

She was forcing herself; wanting to say something and not quite able
At last she managed it:

"—I am not a shrew, I hope."

"On the contrary. Grand company! Sometime tomorrow, then—perhaps
late in the day?"

She teased again: "But there are no worship services to keep you occu
pied in the morning, Mr. Boyle."

"There's the Platte for taking a bath. If you were down wind of me
you'd understand why I'll be occupied for a while."

She laughed. "Fair enough."

He waved as he left, unconsciously beginning to whistle "Corcoran to
His Regiment" without a single thought of the song's significance.

ii

He walked by the whiskey wagon. The customers had departed. Klaus
Dorn was slumped over the crate with his plump cheek squashed against
his forearms and the Hawken on the ground. The whiskey merchant lay
against a wheel of his wagon, the backs of his hands in the dirt, his mouth
opening and closing. Spittle trickled from the corner of his lips as he
snored. The dipper on its chain swayed slowly back and forth in the wind,
inches from his lolling head.

A sorry sight, Michael thought, wrinkling his nose. Even at a distance
he could smell the liquor on Dorn. No wonder the girl retreated to her
Bible.

As he entered the darkened sleeping car and approached his bunk, Sean
Murphy whispered from the bed below his.

"That you, Michael Boyle?"

"No, it's Worthing come to lie in wait."

"Don't jest," Murphy grumbled. "Greenup ran into him earlier. He's
staggering about with a face dark as a rotten pudding. He's promising
things."

Michael laid his churchwarden up on the bunk and started to unbutton
his shirt. "What things?"

"Very ugly. You be on watch."

"I am."

Murphy sniffed. "Jaysus, you smell like a pill shop!"

"Miss Dorn gave me some salve for my blisters."

"Ah, yes, one of the lads did notice you callin' on her."

"Merely to ask about Christian."

"Took you an hour or more to ask, did it?"

In the lowest bunk of the three, Liam O'Dey stirred, then whined:

"Will you both shut your claps so a man can catch a wink?"

"Up your arse, O'Dey," Murphy replied. "Tomorrow's Sunday."

"I'm tuckered from Saturday!"

"Fiddledeedee. You've an entire day to relax and pursue your favorite activity, which is complaining."

The thought of Sunday pleased Michael as he dragged off his shirt and tossed it up beside his pipe. What an odd, flinty woman was Hannah Dorn! A rifle, a Bible, a tosspot father, a witless brother—and loneliness. Yet he was anticipating the day—anticipating seeing her again—as he hadn't anticipated anything in a long while. He'd have a bath, slick his hair, and drop by early in the afternoon.

The prospect made him chuckle.

"Ah, that's a dirty laugh if ever I heard one!" Murphy said. "What did the dear girl do after she doctored you? Admit you to the privacy of her quarters and give you a peek at her rosary?" The last word was juicily lewd.

"She has no rosary, she's one of the Luther crowd."

"Oh, God, don't mix with them!"

"Jesus and Mary, must we get filth an' theology blabbered all night?" O'Dey grumbled, thumping his mattress with his fist.

"Screw yourself if you're not too feeble, you sour old man," Murphy said, then let go with a loud, rasping fart to heighten the insult. O'Dey exclaimed, "*Agh!*" and thumped the mattress a few more times.

Again Murphy whispered, "I share but one thing with O'Dey downstairs. Exhaustion. Good night to you, Michael."

Michael's hands ached as he braced one against the bunks and used the other to pull off his boots. Undressing standing up was easier than doing it flat on his back. All at once it struck him that no thought of Julia Kent had crept into his mind for quite a while.

"I said good night, Michael Boyle."

"Good night, Sean."

Hannah's eyes glimmered in his mind. Part of the scriptural quote lingered too.

*If my people seek my face—turn from their wicked ways—I will heal their land.*

The second boot came off. He pushed his trousers down and pulled one leg free. A strained muscle in his thigh shot pain to his hip and calf. Too bad he couldn't get Miss Dorn's Biblical message to the Virginian. Worthing's land, the South, still wanted a deal of healing. Instead, it was receiving punishment. That was a big part of the man's trouble, Michael was sure. On the other hand, he might be letting his imagination run too free. Perhaps Worthing had been sufficiently chastened by the beating.

As he tossed boots and trousers to the bunk and started to climb up, he decided it was ridiculous to worry over the captain when he wasn't at all sure the man would take action. Though Murphy had mentioned threats there was a vast gulf between words and deeds.

At that exact moment he pulled himself so his head was level with his blanket.

*"Christ Jesus!"* he breathed.

### iii

"D'you say something?" Murphy asked drowsily from below.

Stricken speechless, it took Michael a moment to answer:

"Just blathering to myself."

His eyes remained riveted on the knife. A carving knife pilfered from the kitchen, by the look of it. He'd been unable to see it from the aisle below.

Someone must have come into the car earlier, while it was empty. His blanket had been hacked to pieces; left in tatters, with sections of Jephtha's letter scattered about. The knife had been driven into the mattress where Michael usually rested his head.

With a sweaty hand he pulled the knife loose and laid it on his clothes at the foot of the bed. He was shaking as he climbed up into the jumble of slashed wool and cut paper, calling himself the worst of fools for believing, even briefly, that Captain Worthing's enmity would confine itself to threats.

He hoped Hannah Dorn wasn't praying too hard. It was wasted effort. He would be forced to fight again.

# CHAPTER 9

## At Lance Point

SLEEP CAME HARD that night. Michael lay with his hands clasped beneath his head, struggling to disconnect his thoughts from the significance of the tangle of hacked blanket and ripped paper on which he was trying to rest. Trying and failing.

Worthing was determined to finish it with him—and to torment him with the realization that the reckoning would come unexpectedly, at a time of his own choosing.

Michael's eye wandered to the pale rectangle of Matthew Kent's drawing of the Havana milk vendor. For some reason the drawing had been spared; further proof, if he needed it, that Worthing wasn't entirely rational. A man whose violence was controlled would have destroyed everything in the bunk. Worthing had cut and slashed with such fury that he'd missed the picture. That worsened Michael's depression.

As did further introspection about his own behavior with Hannah Dorn.

He'd come whistling back to the car like some moonstruck swain, delighted by the possibility of a friendship. Now he had doubts about his breezy mood. Had it been a trick of his mind? Perhaps he'd unconsciously deceived himself about the whiskey merchant's daughter. Perhaps he was using her as an antidote for the altogether foolish longing for Louis' wife.

Images of Julia's nude body slipped in and out of his mind as he tossed and wriggled in the ruins of the bed. Images of a woman he could never have.

The uncontrollable desire humiliated him. It also cheapened and insulted Hannah Dorn. She'd treated with him in good faith, not knowing he wanted to be with her to attempt to submerge his feelings for another woman.

Ah, what a nasty, tangled mess it had all become!

He must have lain awake three or four hours before he dozed off, exhausted. Dreams of Worthing's face haunted him through the night.

When he drifted out of sleep again shortly after ten on Sunday morning, he felt no better.

Men were leaving their bunks one at a time, moving at a leisurely pace, and keeping their voices pitched low so as not to wake those still in bed. As Michael stirred, Sean Murphy whispered his name from below. He remained motionless and silent. He didn't reply to Murphy's second whisper. Or his third. Finally Murphy rose, pulled on his clothes, and left the car.

As soon as Michael was sure he wouldn't be disturbed, he unrolled an extra blanket tucked at the foot of the bunk, stood on Murphy's bed and spread the blanket carefully to conceal the havoc of Worthing's knife. He'd dispose of the cut cloth and shredded paper after dark. The knife itself he wedged between the bunk frame and the car wall; he'd get rid of it after dark, too. He never even considered showing it to Murphy—or reporting the incident to Casement.

Murphy hailed him as he entered the dining car. Michael couldn't refuse to sit with his friend. Greenup Williams arrived a moment later. It registered on Michael that both men had dressed with unusual care. Murphy wore his one white shirt and an old satin cravat. Greenup had donned his best work clothes and an ancient emerald-colored velvet jacket, somewhat too elegant to be owned by any rust-eater, white or black. Michael assumed the jacket had been given Greenup by someone for whom he'd once worked.

"I heard you tossin' most of the night again," Murphy said between swallows of coffee. He nudged Michael. "Thoughts of Miss Dorn keep you roused, did they?"

Michael shook his head.

Greenup laughed. "My, he's full of chatter today."

"Merely in awe of the splendid plumage of you fellows," Michael murmured.

"One of the boys who was shaving when I woke told me Mr. Stackpole and his wagon arrived in the middle of the night."

In response to Michael's blank look, Murphy amplified:

"Mr. Stackpole is one of the lads in the U-Pay Photographic Corpse."

"Corps," Michael corrected.

Murphy didn't take umbrage: "I needn't know how to say it, just enjoy it. Greenup an' me, we're going to have our pictures took. Spruce up and join us."

Michael knew the railroad had a small number of roving photographers whose wagons—traveling darkrooms—followed the tracks to create a pictorial record of the line's progress. Though the bulky cameras were in fairly wide use, Michael was still in awe of them. He found the science of photography one of the miracles of the century.

"I'd have too sour a mug and spoil the picture," he said with a shake of his head. When they repeated their entreaties, he continued to say no.

Finally Murphy shrugged and gave up. Greenup frowned—his first overt acknowledgement that he recognized something was awry with Michael. By then Michael was on his feet. He bid the two goodbye, picked up a week-old Omaha paper someone had left behind, and hurried back to the bunk car to razor his face and trim his moustache before going down to the river for a bath.

Much of the joy had been drained from the anticipated excursion. He was fleeing again. Fleeing his confusion over Julia and Hannah Dorn— and his worry about Worthing.

Outside the sleeping car, he did stop a few moments to observe Murphy, Greenup—and O'Dey, who had evidently incorporated himself into the portrait group without permission—fidgeting and posing near the short boxy wagon shrouded with black drapes. Inside, Mr. Stackpole could be heard grumbling and swearing as he coated his glass plates with whatever mysterious chemical mixture caused an image to form on them. In the dirt behind the wagon Michael noticed two padlocked wooden boxes of a sort he'd seen once before. Finished plates were kept in there after being chemically treated to fix their images.

Finally, Mr. Stackpole emerged to deposit his tripod on the ground. He returned for his large camera with brass lens ring. Stackpole was middle-aged and impatient, fussing loudly as he fastened the camera to the tripod. A small crowd was collecting. Quite a few men had dressed for portraits.

"All right," Stackpole announced finally, "let's have the first group."

He adjusted the black drape spread over the camera, then waved at Murphy and his two companions. "No, no, not there! Away from the shadow of the car!"

"Join us, Michael," Murphy urged again.

"No, thank you, I—" All at once he spied someone lounging up by the tender. Arms folded, the man was facing the crowd and the photographer. Cigar smoke trailed away from his mouth. He paid no attention to the workers swarming past him; Sundays, the engine and tender were uncoupled and turned over to those among the crew who fancied themselves marksmen. But all Michael saw was the distant dark blotch of one man's face.

Worthing's.

Watching him.

"No," he repeated, "I've need of a bath."

*And I've need to get away because I've come over a thousand miles and I haven't outrun Julia, or the fighting. I wonder if I ever will.*

"Come on," Greenup said to him. "It'll only take a min—"

"A bath, and that's that!"

The severity of Michael's tone brought a frown to Murphy's face. "Lad, what on earth's wrong with you this morning?"

"In place, in place!" Stackpole interrupted, manhandling O'Dey and Greenup to the spot he'd chosen. "I have a great many exposures to make while the light's good."

"Michael?" Murphy repeated.

"*No!*" Michael shouted, so loudly Murphy looked hurt. Michael spun away.

With the newspaper tucked under his arm, he walked rapidly toward the end of the track. But in his mind he was running. There was no escape. None, anywhere.

That truth rode his shoulder like an invisible hobgoblin as he cut across the tracks and quickened his step, fleeing toward the bank of the Platte.

ii

He walked almost a mile through knee-high buffalo grass on the north bank of the river. *Osceola's* whistle shrilled twice—a final summons to those who meant to go chugging east along the line, clinging to the tender, pilot, and running boards while they pinked at any buffalo in sight.

The sky was a muted blue, lightly hazed by thin clouds. A moderate wind blew out of the northwest, setting the long grass and patches of bright red wildflowers to rippling. Michael was conscious of the morning's surpassing loveliness. It eased his tension a little. He plucked one of the wildflowers and stuck it in the pocket of his shirt. The poppy bobbed in a jaunty way as he tramped along the bank.

The prospect of visiting Dorn's tent again was palling on more than one count. If he went to call on Christian and the woman, he'd be forced to speak politely to the thick-witted German. And he was in no mood to be polite. The memory of Julia had spoiled his happy feelings of the preceding evening.

What compounded his confusion was a new admission that, in spite of Julia, he *did* have a certain persistent desire to see Hannah Dorn again. She was attractive; intriguing in an odd way. A deep sort, that was the term for it.

Then he admitted another reason for his interest; one which surprised him. Though he didn't consider himself a religious man, he'd been stirred by some of her remarks last night.

He actually wished she were right. Wished solutions to problems were as simple as she made them out to be. What a blessing it would be if something so direct as a return to the kind of Christian behavior described in her Bible could indeed heal the country, tame the violence that erupted even at the reasonably well-ordered railhead, and overcome the widespread hate and corruption Jephtha's long letter had described. Although Amanda Kent had never been a practitioner of formal religion, her faith in certain principles reminded him of Hannah Dorn—and of his own woeful lack of convictions.

*I am a Kent now,* he reminded himself. *I had better get to work and find something to believe in. Something to work for again—*

The railroad was no longer quite enough. Especially not since he'd realized he had fled to it because it promised escape.

Which he hadn't found—

That brought him straight back to Worthing.

Caught up in his thoughts, he found himself at the edge of a grassless patch where half a dozen small cones of earth had been clawed out of the ground to form a village of what more experienced men on the U-Pay called prairie dogs. One of the curious, popeyed little creatures was sitting bolt upright in its hole, foreclaws raised, and quivering. It saw or at least sensed his presence and plummeted out of sight.

Michael carefully skirted the burrows so as not to disturb them. He returned the wave of a group of naked men splashing and wringing out laundry in the shallows to his left. He kept walking. He wanted privacy; wanted to be a good distance from fellow workers who might be anxious for conversation.

A rich, loamy smell rose from the sun-drenched earth. Clouds of huge grasshoppers buzzed near him. The land here was slightly more rolling. Ahead, a line of low hills made it impossible to see the far western horizon.

He stopped short of the hills and glanced back. The nearest bathers were a good half mile distant. He tossed the newspaper down and pulled a lump of yellow soap from his pocket. After tugging off his boots, he peeled away every scrap of clothing.

He flung the garments among the reeds at the river's edge, enjoying the feel of the sun on his bare spine and buttocks. He crouched in the shallow water and began to soap the pieces of clothing.

One by one he rinsed them and laid them on the bank to dry. He flipped the soap after them and returned to the muddy river with the paper.

He got to his knees, then stretched prone in the tepid water. It barely covered the lower half of his body. With his head up and his elbows in the mud, he studied a moving blur—bison—far in the south beyond two tilted, hair-covered telegraph poles. The wind blew puffs of dust from the ruts of the emigrant trail.

He turned to the paper to focus his mind on something other than personal problems. The leading story was a report on one of the featured speeches at the National Union convention in Philadelphia in the middle of the current month.

In '64, Lincoln and Johnson had run under the National Union banner. The President was again attempting to use it to form a coalition of Democrats and moderate Republicans opposed to the radicals. Republican Congressman Henry Raymond, founder and editor of *The New York Times,* had delivered the speech quoted—and done so at some risk to his career, the paper observed. As soon as the cheers of the audience faded and Raymond's remarks were reported to Washington, the capital began to stir with rumors that the traitorous Raymond would be removed from national chairmanship of the Republican party.

But evidently he'd been willing to accept that risk. In Philadelphia Raymond had unequivocally supported the views of President Johnson. He'd declared that, constitutionally, only the individual states could establish qualifications for the franchise; that the Southern states had never seceded and therefore had to be represented in Congress; and that the Fourteenth Amendment, worthy though it was, couldn't be ratified except by two-thirds of all the states—which included those formerly in rebellion.

According to the account, Raymond's speech had been no anti-Negro diatribe; not even a disguised one. The *Times* editor had declared slavery dead for all time and called for equal protection of the rights and property of every person, regardless of race.

But if Jephtha's letter was accurate, Michael mused, not even Raymond's sentiments about human rights would appease the radicals. Whether right or wrong about the Constitution, Johnson was flying in the face of important segments of public opinion. It had not gone down well early in the year when the President had confronted the noted black abolitionist, Douglass, at the White House, and calmly advised him that, in addition to violating the Constitution, immediate Negro suffrage would unleash a race war.

Michael was still unable to decide whether Johnson was courageously stating the truth, then and now, or revealing a prejudice against blacks. The article, however, only reinforced his disheartening feeling that Jephtha was correct about the ferocity of the new political war being waged by men not the least interested in the counsel of Miss Hannah Dorn's Bible.

Somewhat more enjoyable was a reprint of a piece by an eastern journalist named Bell. He had visited the railhead a few weeks earlier, and written a description of the track-laying operation. Its accuracy was pleasantly surprising, and its conclusion rhapsodic:

> It is a grand "anvil chorus" that those sturdy sledges are playing across the plains. It is in a triple time, three strokes to the spike. There are ten spikes to a rail, 400 rails to a mile, 1,800 miles to San Francisco—21,000,000 times are those sledges to be swung; 21,000,000 times are they to come down with their sharp punctuation before the great work of modern America is complete.

"Twenty-one million times, is that a fact?" Michael murmured. Impressive—though he couldn't swallow the notion that the "anvil chorus" was grand. Its performance was grueling, prosaic, noisy—and full of sour notes such as the outburst of a Leonidas Worthing. But at least reporters were beginning to write a few favorable items about the U-Pay.

A hail startled him. He rolled over. Saw tow-headed Tom Ruffin approaching briskly along the bank, a look of concentration on his face and a thick piece of cottonwood in his right hand.

"Good morning, Tom," Michael called back. "Heard you singing last night. Splendid!"

The boy stopped. "Thank you, Mr. Boyle."

Michael waved a wet hand at the grass Ruffin was studying:

"Lose something?"

"No, sir. Hunting a fool hen—or whatever you call it."

"I think the correct name is grouse, or maybe partridge. Not sure. But I haven't seen any."

"General Jack told me they were mighty delicious roasted. And so dumb you could walk up and brain 'em with a stick."

"So I've heard. Guess they deserve to be called fool hens."

The boy shielded his eyes and peered at the low hills ahead. "Might be some up that way." He waved and hurried on.

Michael rolled back onto his belly, forgetting Ruffin for ten minutes. Then, abruptly, a yelp—almost like an animal's bark—drifted from behind the hills where the boy had vanished.

He paid little attention until he heard the cry a second time. It was high-pitched and quickly muffled.

Michael raised his head. Not an animal at all, he realized. It sounded like Ruffin—in some kind of difficulty. Perhaps the boy had stumbled into a burrow and wrenched his leg.

He strode up the bank, wiped water from his legs and tugged on hi: trousers. Barefoot and bare-chested, he went running to the crest of the first hill.

And stopped, open-mouthed. In an instant, his heart was beating with frantic speed.

### iii

Evidently they'd come from the west. They must have ridden their large-headed, thin-legged calicos—the small but sturdy brown, bay, and white ponies Irishmen called piebalds—all but silently to the low place behind the screen of hills. He had an impression of considerable numbers of riders—thirty at least, every one of them armed with bows and deco-rated hide shields. Every one of them was watching him.

Most of them appeared quite large in relation to their mounts. That meant Cheyenne, didn't it? He'd been told the Cheyenne were, on the av-erage, taller than the Sioux. Out in front of the rest, a paunchy yet power-ful-looking warrior of about forty held Tom Ruffin under his left arm as if the boy were an empty meal sack.

The boy's heels hung down, kicking and making the warrior's calico skittish. The boy was prevented from crying out by the brown left hand clamped like a claw over his face. The Indian's right hand held a fierce-looking bow horizontally. The godawful weapon was eight feet long, at least—

And it was more than a bow, Michael saw suddenly. It had a pointed iron head. The head pressed the side of young Ruffin's neck. Wind flut-tered the feathers decorating the bow-lance.

Michael stood silent and stunned in the blowing buffalo grass, his frightened gaze taking in the dark cheeks; the nut-colored eyes; the hands gripping bows and shields; the animal-skin shirts with long twisted strands of hair knotted in the fringing. Scalp locks taken from their enemies—?

As he glanced from face to expressionless face, he found no friendliness. He shivered, all but certain several of the motionless horsemen were ready to reach for arrows in quivers slung over their backs. He knew that if he bolted to sound an alarm he'd be killed before he ran six steps.

And the nearest workers were half a mile away. Very faintly, he heard their shouts and splashing.

*So,* he thought with a mixture of terror and sadness, *it seems I've found another enemy.*

*And another war.*

# CHAPTER 10

## Hunter's Blood

SOME THIRTY MILES southeast of the railhead on a simmering afternoon in the same month, a handsome, twenty-six-year-old Oglala Sioux and his white companion found what they had been seeking for the better part of a week.

The Sioux, whom the white man called Kola, knew the search was over when his friend came scrambling down the side of the ravine to the dry wash where Kola had been told to wait with the rickety wagon. Two mules were hitched to the wagon. The wiry buffalo pony that was their common property was tied to the tailgate.

From the expression on his friend's face, Kola suspected the find was a good one. The young white man's dark eyes sparkled when the sun touched them beneath the brim of his low-crowned plainsman's hat. Like nearly everything else the partners owned, the hat had been stolen.

As always, the sight of the white man stirred a profound, almost religious feeling of affection within the Sioux. Only a few of the white's quirks bothered Kola. One was altogether minor, and by now almost amusing.

Six months earlier, the white man had found the Sioux brave half dead, beaten in most uncharacteristic fashion by the husband of a woman named Sweet Summer. In his pain, the young Sioux had tried to thank his benefactor. Again and again he'd pointed alternately to the white man and then to himself while repeating the word *kola* to indicate each was now a special friend to the other. The Sioux had had a regular *kola* during his boyhood years—Lively Cub, who'd taken the name Brave Horse after counting his first coups.

Although the white man soon came to understand what *kola* meant in a general sense, he took a fancy to the word. He preferred it to the Sioux's adult name, Clever Hunter.

"Kola, we hit some luck. There's a small herd lying down with their cuds, right up yonder." One of the white man's grease-stained buckskin gauntlets lifted toward the rim of the wash.

"How many, Joseph?" Kola asked in the badly accented English he'd learned hanging around the fort.

"Eighteen, twenty—" Joseph brushed a pestiferous fly from the long fair hair hanging over the back of his collarless flannel shirt. Suspenders held up his threadbare trousers. But his boots were sturdy.

"Couple of calves, too," Joseph added. "We'll let them go."

Kola shared his friend's happiness with a smile. Joseph was five or six years Kola's junior, but seemed older. He was lean, strong and, most importantly, trustworthy. At least he had never proved himself otherwise during their half-year association.

If Joseph tended to be somewhat more reckless than a Sioux, that was a peculiarity of his white temperament. Kola did not question it too deeply. The saving of his life by Joseph had been a sending of the gods. *Wakan.* Holy. Therefore an event of great meaning for the future. Shortly after their meeting, a night vision had confirmed it.

Occasionally Kola was disturbed by the pitiless set of Joseph's mouth when he fired one of their weapons. The Sioux killed to eat, and slew their enemies only when absolutely necessary. For honor, pleasure—and the preservation of tribal manpower—they preferred counting coups instead.

But Joseph was his *kola.* For that reason, and another even more compelling, the Sioux brave never spoke about disturbing aspects of his friend's behavior. The reason was Kola's certainty that Joseph was guided by his own inner voice.

Every Sioux heeded this most sacred and mysterious of all instructors. It told him where he must go, and how he must behave. It sometimes spoke when a man was awake, but more often it spoke through dreams.

Even the *winkte,* the target of so many warrior jests, did no more than follow the promptings of his inner voice when, as a boy, he chose to don women's clothing and face paint for the rest of his life. Thus every *winkte* —and they were numerous—was revered as well as scorned. A *winkte* was often asked to name a newborn so the child would never suffer sickness, for instance. Almost without exception, the inner voice of a human being was *wakan.*

So Kola believed that in all things, Joseph was only obeying the inner voice Kola would never hear, just as Joseph would never hear his. The belief made Kola forgiving of behavior he might otherwise have questioned.

The Sioux, a dark, supple young man wearing only a buffalo skin breechclout and moccasins with bull rawhide soles, glanced at the scorching sun which appeared to be sitting on the rim of the gully. The sun's glare threw the outline of his large sharp nose across one side of his face and created tiny shadows beside the two puckered scars in the hard flesh above his nipples. At eighteen he had committed himself to the religious frenzy of the gazing-at-the-sun dance, stamping and reeling for hours around the sacred pole until his zeal gave him strength to mortify his own flesh. The wooden skewers inserted under his skin by the shaman had torn free and fallen, bloody at the ends of the braided ropes attached to the pole. The twin scars were testimony to his courage.

The sun was a fearful and sacred thing to the Indian; another tangible sign of the presence of *Wakan Tanka*—the Great Mystery, the driving force and spirit of life which was in every place, every person, and every occurrence, though in ways not always discernible. This afternoon, however, the sun had a more practical significance:

"The time is late, Joseph. The buffalo will move soon to the night bedding place."

"Or find a larger herd," Joseph nodded. Kola had taught him that, in August, when the running season began and the bulls and cows grew impatient to breed, the animals tended to gather and migrate together in huge numbers—a thousand, two thousand—which made hunting more difficult. "We'll get them before they do," the white man continued. "I've already picked out the cow leading them."

Kola murmured a syllable to show the pleasure he took from his friend's confidence. In the spring when they'd first traveled together, Joseph had been unable to distinguish a leader in a herd of massive bulls, smaller cows, and their calves. Out of gratitude, Kola had taught him much. Kola did not hate white men with the ferocity of some of his race. He'd been around forts too long as a youth. And he'd been cast out from his own tribal group because of the wrath and influence of Sweet Summer's husband.

Joseph reached down to scratch his right leg just above the boot where he hid his skinning knife. "There are half a dozen bulls, the rest cows. Been through a grass fire not too long ago. Hides look burnt on the hindquarters where they've shed. Two of the bulls and two of the cows must have had their eyes ruined when they stampeded through the fire."

A scowl ridged Kola's brow: "Four of them do not see?"

"Practically sure of it."

The Sioux digested that. It made what they were about to do more difficult. The bison lacked good vision even when they hadn't been injured. But they possessed sharp senses of smell and hearing to offset the lack. Blind buffalo—common on the prairie—were even more alert to alien scents and sounds.

"Is there a hiding place where the wind is right?"

"Some brush. I have it all laid out."

Joseph spoke in a quiet, pleasant voice, slurring, and softening some of his words. Kola had encountered a few whites who talked the same way. Driving small herds of longhorn cattle, they had ridden up from the southern part of the land mass Joseph had frequently tried to describe for him, but whose immensity defied Kola's imagination. He was also unable to form more than a rudimentary mental picture of the fantastic collections of structures Joseph called cities, that the white man assured Kola were plentiful beyond eastern rivers Kola had never seen.

A happy curve relieved the severity of Joseph's mouth as he gestured to his companion:

"Let's unpack the guns."

A strong *kola*, this stranger who had fed and cared for him until he could walk and function again. A *kola* who handled white men's weapons well, although with a strange, almost possessive fondness.

Kola tied the reins of the mules and clambered into the rear of the wagon. He unwrapped the blanket and removed the three loaded rifles, along with a hide cartridge pouch. Kola noticed how perspiration appeared on Joseph's upper lip and a smile brightened his eyes at the sight of the trio of powerful buffalo killers.

ii

Conscious of the lateness of the hour, the two men still exercised caution in climbing from the ravine and working their way in a large semicircle to the brush from which Joseph would attempt to force the small herd into a stand. In fifteen minutes they were in place, both kneeling, the buffalo guns laid out side by side within easy reach of Joseph's right hand.

The equipment for the hunt consisted of three single-shot pieces: a rather battered Laidley-Whitney .50 caliber, and two fine Ballard .45s, all three capable of accepting the 70-grain powder charge required to bring down a rampaging bull. Kola didn't know where Joseph had gotten any of the buffalo killers. The white man was not talkative on the subject, except to say—usually with one of those mirthless smiles—that he wasn't the original owner of any of the rifles. Kola, however, had shown him how to use them on their proper targets.

The small herd rested about sixty yards away. The immense bodies were half concealed by the wind-blown grass. Great jaws moved slowly as the animals chewed the regurgitated grasses they'd cropped during their morning graze. Kola noted the tawny hides of the two calves nestling next to their mothers.

Joseph wiped a gauntlet across his wet brow and pointed. With a nod, Kola acknowledged and endorsed Joseph's selection of the presumed leader. Both the bulls and the cows had angry red hindquarters. Their winter protection—long, shaggy hair and thick, wool-like undercoats—had been shed or rubbed away. On the flanks of the resting animals Kola could easily discern scorch marks and large sores. At close range he would have seen many more sores; the bare hides attracted swarms of biting insects during the summer months.

Joseph held out his right hand. Kola passed him the first of the Ballards, then laid out extra cartridges from the pouch. The success of a stand depended not only on the witlessness of the buffalo but upon the speed and accuracy with which the hunter singled out the successive leaders.

Slowly, Joseph raised the Ballard to his shoulder. There was no sound except the faint murmur of the wind blowing from the direction of the herd. Joseph's hands lost color as he took a firmer grip and laid his cheek into sighting position.

All at once, in the ravine behind them, one of the mules brayed.

Not loudly. But the sound was enough to bring the cow leader to her feet.

The rest of the herd lumbered up. Kola watched Joseph's mouth go white and his eyes flick angrily toward the disastrous noise. Then Kola heard another sound from the same direction. The tinkle of bit metal—? He was almost positive.

He had no time to think of who it might be. The herd was starting to move. Joseph fired.

The lead cow bellowed, struck exactly where Kola had taught Joseph to hit. Behind the last rib, the point at which a bullet or an arrow would pierce and destroy the air sacs white men called lungs. Kola had not needed to teach Joseph how to shoot. He was an unerring marksman.

The herd grew frantic as the cow teetered and collapsed on her forefeet, shoulders heaving. A blind bull swung toward the source of the shot, then went plunging past the dying leader. Even nineteen bison with two calves trailing set up a formidable rumble in the ground.

Joseph never took his eyes from the running herd. His tension was betrayed only by the sweat rivering down his cheeks and neck. He thrust the Ballard to the ground. Kola slapped the second one into his palm. In seconds, Joseph was ready to fire.

But he held his shot while Kola swiftly and expertly reloaded the first rifle. Joseph was watching the fleeing herd. Letting them go far enough. Fifty yards. Seventy-five—

Suddenly a lumbering cow separated from the rest, veering north. The others followed. With the new leader identified, Joseph fired. A cry of pain, and she went down.

The buffalo kept running, widening the distance between themselves and the hunters. Soon the animals would be out of range of the Laidley-

Whitney Joseph held ready. But the pattern repeated itself. A new cow charged to the front. Joseph dropped her with a thunderous roar of the gun.

They waited. The critical moment—

A blind bull slowed and lowered his shaggy head.

A calf straggled to a stop.

A cow dashed on, then turned back.

After another few seconds, the entire herd, baffled by the loss of three leaders in quick succession, came to a halt. It was the classic stand every hunter hoped for if his timing and his luck were good.

A smile curled Joseph's mouth. He swabbed the filthy cuff of his shirt across his forehead. Then, with barely a sound, he climbed to his feet.

"It was well done, Joseph," Kola whispered as he finished loading the Laidley-Whitney. There was genuine admiration in his voice.

"Because I had a fine teacher. Now we can take our time. You'll have a nice feast tonight."

Kola could practically taste the savory brain and small intestine that would be left after the work of slaughtering. His mouth watered, and he thanked the holy spirits for bringing him into the presence of this white man. With a merry glint in his eye, he fell into the routine of loading and passing the buffalo guns to Joseph, who simply stood in place and shot the stupefied buffalo one by one.

Shadows lengthened on the baking prairie. The wind soon stank of blood and the contents of emptied intestines—to Kola the sweetest aroma on earth. As the last cow dropped and the forlorn calves wandered around the corpses searching for their mothers, the Sioux reminded himself that before he and Joseph moved north to the fire road, he must cut out and scatter the hearts of the dead animals so the herd would regenerate itself.

The echoes of the last shot went rolling away into the sullen red haze along the western horizon. Joseph relaxed, squatted down, and exhaled loudly. He laid the second Ballard on the ground.

"Well, my friend, there's the stake that'll keep us alive come winter."

Kola glanced at the dead buffalo. He was aware of the increasing slaughter of the herds upon which his people depended for food, clothing, shelter, horse gear, weaponry, religious objects—even the hair-stuffed calf-skin balls and netted hoops the children used in their games. No useful portion of the animal was ignored. Yet for a dozen summers and more, white hunters had been slaying buffalo in enormous numbers, and wasting most of the precious parts. Now here he was, doing the same. He wouldn't have done so except for the promptings of his inner voice which had told him he was destined to ride with Joseph. But as he eyed the dead animals, he couldn't keep a touch of disapproval from his voice:

"We will sell all of them?"

"Yes. All."

"Keep nothing for ourselves?"

"Kola, we can buy shirts cheaper than we can skin and sew them. We'll sell off the hindquarters to the Union Pacific at a dime a pound, just the way that fellow Cody's doing down south on the line's other branch. Further east, we should net a dollar and a quarter for every hide, two bits for every tongue. The people back east want fine quality lap robes and delicacies for dinner. If we don't supply them, others will. We'll have a stake and some profit left over—wait."

Kola saw Joseph's eyes dart past his shoulder. Back toward the rim of the ravine. He knew it must have been a horse he'd heard, because Joseph's eyes were wide as he grabbed for the Laidley-Whitney.

"No!" someone shouted. A loud, rough voice. "You're covered."

Joseph's fingertips hovered an inch from the buffalo gun. Slowly he withdrew his hand. His lips barely moved:

"Three of them. Where in the hell did they come from?"

"Nothing personal, y'know," the harsh voice called. "We just want those buffalo. Touch the guns and we'll blow you down."

iii

Joseph surrendered to the thieves without protest. Their leader announced his terms: they would relieve Joseph and Kola of the wagon, the dead buffalo, and the pony, leaving only the mules. Joseph accepted the statements with a resigned shrug. He even agreed to enjoy the hospitality of a cook fire laid at the rim of the ravine by the trio of tattered, foul-smelling white men. When Kola started to protest, Joseph laid a hand on his arm.

"Got to eat, don't we? Might as well be their food as ours."

Kola felt betrayed. He had never seen his friend so resigned—or so uncaring. By the time darkness fell, Joseph and the three other whites were seated around a chip fire in the cooling air—exactly as if they were long-time acquaintances.

To show his pique, Kola squatted several yards away. He was still astonished at the way Joseph had given up their guns and the animals whose sale would have kept them sheltered and fed when the snows drifted on the plains.

Sullen, Kola watched Joseph amiably accept a cup of coffee and a tin plate of beans from the leader of the thieves, a revolver-toting fellow with a cocked eye, a long, untrimmed gray beard, a gray military overcoat that reached below his knees, and a loaf-crowned hat with a five-pointed star cut out of the felt just above the greasy band.

"Thank you," Joseph said as he took the plate. Down in the ravine, the horses belonging to the thieves stamped and fretted. "I'll need something with which to eat."

"Use your hands," the leader smiled from directly across the fire. "I don't think it would be prudent to lend you a knife."

Kola frowned, trying to grasp an elusive thought hovering in his mind. He couldn't.

Joseph's eyes lingered on the leader's weather-beaten face. The leader was the only one of the trio who exhibited any sign of strength or character. The thief seated on Joseph's left was a shivering boy of seventeen or eighteen. He wore a forage cap, a sweat-stained shirt, a blue neck bandana, and a holstered revolver that looked much too large for his frail, nervous hands.

The thief guarding Joseph's right was a stubby man in a ripped blue coat. A gold ring shone in the pierced lobe of his left ear. Quietly, he began singing to himself:

> "Oh bury me not in the deep, deep sea,
> "Where the dark blue waves
> "Will roll over me—"

"No chanteys, Darlington," the leader said. "If you're going to sing that song, use the prairie words. You keep forgetting you're a landsman now."

"Not by choice, mate." Darlington concentrated on his beans.

The leader shook his head. "Sorry excuses for hands, aren't they?"

Joseph didn't reply. The man with the earring seemed irritated. He limited his protest to a glance. The leader added, "A man takes what he must."

"Including another man's kill," Joseph remarked with a frosty smile. "I'm sorry to say I don't consider that an honorable action, mister—?"

"Major," the older man broke in. "Major T. T. Cutright."

"Southern, aren't you?"

"Yes. I judge the same from your voice. Were you in the war?"

Joseph's lids screened his eyes a moment. Kola thought he saw something secretive glimmer there. But he immediately lost interest. He was still outraged by Joseph's cowardly acquiescence to the demands of the thieves who had ridden up behind them at precisely the wrong moment. As soon as the men were gone, he would separate from his companion. He thought he'd gotten to know him since the spring grass greened. Now he was discovering he hadn't. And Joseph's inner voice had abruptly turned him in a new, unacceptable direction.

"Last with General Hood," Joseph nodded in reply. "You?"

Cutright wiped bean juice from his beard with the sleeve of his gray overcoat. "I saw service, but I'd prefer not to say where. There was an unfortunate incident."

"What happened?"

"My commander was yellow. When he ordered a retreat, he took a ball in the back of his head. I was accused."

Joseph said nothing. Cutright laid his plate aside; reached for his coffee. "You haven't told me your name, sir."

"Kingston. Joseph Kingston."

Cutright sat up straight. "Kingston?"

"That's right. Something wrong?"

"Not exactly wrong, but—" Cutright looked a bit more wary. "I come from near Fort Worth. I heard of a Joseph Kingston who shot a crooked monte dealer there last winter, then murdered a peace officer who came to arrest him. That Mr. Kingston fled before he could be apprehended. There's a bounty on his head. Two hundred dollars."

Joseph's face took on a curious, stony quality. "I've never been in Fort Worth. Coincidence, undoubtedly."

Cutright uttered a short, wry laugh. "Undoubtedly."

Kola stared at his companion, suddenly struck by something he'd forgotten. It had been stirring in his mind ever since Cutright's reference to a knife. The thieves had taken the three buffalo rifles to add to their own stock of two. But they'd only subjected Joseph to a cursory visual search. They'd completely overlooked the hidden skinning knife.

All at once Kola grew warm. Could the undiscovered knife be the reason for Joseph's apparent cooperation? He fervently hoped so. Despite his bare flesh—he hadn't been permitted to go to the wagon for his shirt and leggings—his entire body felt hot.

Let Joseph be tricking them, he prayed. The meeting when he found me was *wakan*, and the dream afterward told me I would be his *kola*, and he mine, till the end of our lives.

"The wagon down in the wash belongs to you?" Cutright inquired.

"I'm the present owner, yes."

Cutright's cocked eye glowed as he inclined his head in a skeptical way. "Not quite the same thing."

Once more Joseph didn't answer.

"Your friend there. The Indian—"

"Call him what he is, please," Joseph asked quietly. "An Oglala Sioux. His name is Kola. It means special friend."

"Peculiar traveling companion for a white man."

Joseph shrugged again. "I found him on the prairie up north of the Platte. He'd fancied the wife of one of the leaders of an *akicita* society in his tribe. I've learned Sioux don't normally take offense when their wives crawl into the blankets with another man. They just throw the woman out of the tipi and cut off her braids—oh, and once in a while her nose—and that's the divorce. To do much more would give the woman more importance than she deserves. Apparently women don't count for much among the Sioux. Did you know they're even sent to live in special lodges when they bleed once a month? According to Kola, the men believe a woman in her cycle poisons a man's medicine and weapons."

Joseph drank a little coffee. "But as I say, most times a husband takes small notice of infidelity. To do otherwise would be like making a fuss over a dog pissing on the tipi. But there are exceptions to everything. Sweet Summer's husband was an exception. He not only divorced her, he waylaid Kola and thrashed him half to death. I came across him and nursed him back to good health. A dream told him we should ride and hunt together. Kola says the Sioux put great stock in dreams."

"Well," the man with the earring growled, "hope he ain't had too many dreams about sellin' off the buffla to the railroad. Those dreams are at five fathoms now, and don't you forget it."

Cutright frowned. "You needn't act so sour, Darlington. Mr. Kingston's being sensible about his state of affairs." To Joseph: "He ran the engine room on a Federal cruiser during the war. He's accustomed to bossing men around. But he isn't accustomed to the courtesies of the plains. Nor is Timmy there. Timmy's my wife's nephew. These days a man running cattle only gets the kind of help he can afford."

Joseph perked up. "Cattle?" He reached down to scratch his right calf. The bearded Cutright shifted his hand toward his holstered revolver, but Joseph's smile reassured him:

"Just a louse."

He kept on scratching the right side of his calf.

"Damn, they're pesky! You were running cattle?"

"Fifty head," Cutright nodded, relaxing again. "The most I could lay my hands on. Seems everyone in Texas is scrambling for longhorns to drive north. The restaurants and butcher shops back east want all the beef they can get."

"I don't see any sign of a herd—"

"No, you don't." Cutright looked glum. "I lost them about fifty miles south. They'd gone too long without drinking, and we came across some damn alkali water. I got my leader, an expensive steer named Crump, started exactly right. If my luck had held, he'd have stampeded them all right past the stuff. But he broke a leg and they went for the water before we could stop them."

"The alkali water poisoned them?"

"Yes, sir, Mr. Kingston, all but one. We've butchered and eaten it since. I should have brought more men with me, but times are hard. Rather than go home empty-handed, I'll now be able to make a little money selling the buffalo to the railroad. It's better than nothing."

"But it's also stealing."

Both Darlington and Cutright scowled. "You're not going to get contentious, are you, Mr. Kingston?" the latter asked. "I've a wife and brood of six back home. They're depending on me. A moment ago, you seemed sensible about the realities of the situation."

"I recognize the realities," Joseph agreed. "I'm just disappointed in a former Confederate officer's doing such a thing."

"Told you." The indifferent blinking of Cutright's good eye put a furrow on Joseph's forehead. "Hard times."

Joseph finally appeared to agree. One more weary shrug only heightened Kola's confusion. Had he been wrong about the skinning knife? If so, he was more determined than ever to abandon his cowardly companion the moment the gray-coated fellow and the others moved on.

Just then—unexpectedly—Joseph turned to glance at him. In the guttering light of the fire his dark eyes were oddly intense.

Kola pursed his lips, frowned, trying to signify he didn't understand whatever Joseph wanted to communicate. Joseph gave up. He turned to Cutright again.

"Wonder if I might have leave to stand?"

Cutright chuckled. "Lice still troubling you?"

"Too much coffee's troubling me." He poked a finger into his trousers above his groin. "I'll just step over there." He bobbed his head toward Kola and the starry dark behind him.

"All right," Cutright said. "Slowly, though."

He edged back the overcoat so he could reach the butt of his revolver. Six inches to the right of his knee lay the confiscated Laidley-Whitney. Loaded, as Kola recalled.

Smiling, Joseph rose, faced left, took a step, winced, and stopped directly behind the shivering boy wearing the bandana. "Damn!" Joseph cried again, crouching, and slapping his right calf as if another louse had attacked.

Cutright reached for his revolver but checked his hand when he heard the whack of Joseph's palm. He understood why Joseph had moved suddenly.

Seated directly between Joseph and Cutright, the boy started to turn. Joseph didn't straighten. His right hand dropped to his boot.

Cutright shouted: "Damn you, what—? Timmy, your gun!"

The Texas boy juggled the coffee cup from which he'd been sipping and made an ineffectual grab at his holster. Joseph moved with astonishing speed, slipping the skinning knife out of his boot and slashing a six inch gash in the boy's gun arm with a single continuous stroke.

The boy shrieked and flopped forward, eyes glazing. The contents of the cup splattered the fire and started it hissing and smoking.

"*Goddamn deceiving son of a bitch!*" Cutright screamed, the same instant Joseph yelled Kola's name.

The cry and the jerk of Joseph's head were signal enough. Overjoyed, Kola ran, leaped, and landed on the white named Darlington. He grappled for Darlington's drawn revolver. Joseph had already launched himself straight across the smoking fire, falling on Cutright with no concern for his feet being in the scorching coals.

The impact jarred Cutright. The revolver in his right hand thundered. Joseph jerked his head aside, just in time to keep from being killed.

Darlington's revolver exploded. Kola felt a rush of air near his shoulder as the bullet spent itself in the dark. Darlington was no match for Kola's strength and renewed faith. Kola clawed Darlington's face with one hand, dug the nails of his other into Darlington's wrist, and the revolver was loose.

Kola threw it away and jumped up. He stomped on Darlington's stomach. The man retched and grabbed his belly, rolling from side to side. Panting, Kola swung around.

Joseph had gotten Cutright's revolver out of his hand. He was standing with his left boot on the Texan's chest.

Cutright's hands were raised. The palms shone with sweat. Grimy fingers quivered. His good eye focused on the revolver Joseph was aiming down at him.

"Lord, Kingston, please don't—"

"Don't do what you planned to do to us?" Joseph's mouth was so thin, it appeared to be no more than a slit. "You don't think I believed your story about letting us go? You said you have a family near Fort Worth. And you'll want to do business up this way again, I presume. You wouldn't want Kola and me turning up to cite you for theft. You were going to kill us before you left."

Cutright's popeyed silence was confession enough. Kola crouched quickly beside the writhing Darlington. But there was no danger. The man was in pain, talking incoherently, and starting to weep.

Joseph remained with one boot on Cutright's chest.

"You're not going to shoot me—?" Cutright breathed. Kola burst out laughing. The Texan sounded like a man beseeching the holy spirits. "You gave up too quickly! You—you don't have the sand."

Joseph's smile was chilly. "I led you on, Major. You thought I didn't have the sand. That was your error and my advantage."

"You *are* the one from Fort Worth," Cutright wheezed. "Got to be."

"The two-hundred-dollar bounty would have been a nice extra profit for you."

"I swear, I didn't plan—"

"Shit. You murdered your commanding officer. Why should I expect better treatment?"

Joseph steadied the revolver and blew a hole between Cutright's eyes.

iv

Before Cutright's body had stopped its violent jerking, Joseph flung the revolver away. He picked up the Laidley-Whitney and motioned Kola back. From across the cook fire, he aimed at the screaming Darlington, who flopped over on his stomach and frantically started to crawl.

The buffalo gun boomed. Darlington skidded three feet forward, an immense hole torn through the clothing covering his backbone. Even Kola, who was accustomed to blood, averted his head.

Joseph laid the buffalo rifle beside Cutright's revolver. He sighed.

"Dishonorable men deserve to be treated in kind. Kola?"

The Sioux turned, momentarily frightened at the sight of his companion standing on the other side of the fire. Joseph resembled some demon risen from swirling smoke and tiny, licking flames.

Truly, Kola thought, this is a warrior to be feared more than any Sioux chieftain. He is so feared, his own kind offer money for his body. This is a great warrior indeed.

Kola couldn't tell whether his companion was saddened by what had occurred, or took pleasure from it. One moment Joseph's expression led Kola to believe the young white man had enjoyed killing the thieves. Then Kola thought he detected regret, or at least uncertainty, as Joseph looked at the moaning boy lying on his side with his head close to the embers. The boy's hair was smouldering.

"Pull the boy out before he burns to death. That hair stinks to hell."

Kola hurried to obey.

"Sit him up," Joseph instructed. "Slap him some."

Joseph watched impassively as Kola propped the boy up and smacked his face several times. Groggy with pain, the boy finally opened his eyes.

He recognized Joseph and Kola; then saw the bodies of his uncle and Darlington.

"Oh, my Lord!" He sounded sick as he seized his blood-soaked arm.

"No complaints," Joseph said. "You took your chances when you threw in with those two. You'd have stood by while they shot us. Probably even pulled a trigger yourself. Stand up."

Aghast, the boy exclaimed, "I'm bleeding to death!"

"Maybe. Maybe not. You'll find out after you've walked twenty or thirty miles."

"I can't walk!"

Joseph shrugged. "Your choice. Pitch me the knife, Kola."

"No, no, I'll go." The boy weaved to his feet.

"South," Joseph instructed. "If I ever see you north of the Republican River, you'll be dead for sure."

Red seeped between the fingers with which the boy clutched his arm. He glanced at Cutright again, then blazed, "You damn murderer! You could have left him alive!"

"Impossible."

"How can you kill like that?"

"I had excellent training, directed by Mr. Jefferson Davis. After you kill one or two, the others come easy. Now you better get out of here before I change my mind."

"I'll remember your name, Kingston. Swear to God. I'll remember it to the hour I die."

Joseph laughed. "Save yourself the trouble. By the time you're planted, I'll have had a peck of names."

"Someone'll find you."

"Someone will find *you*, stone cold stiff, if you don't start walking."

"I need food and water."

"No."

"At least a bandage!"

"All you get from me is a chance to save your conniving hide. That's more than you deserve. Now *walk!*"

The boy started off, wincing with every laborious step.

"Wrong way!" Joseph barked. *"That's* south."

Like a sleepwalker, the boy stumbled in an erratic half-circle and lurched in the right direction. Joseph watched until he was lost on the dark prairie.

Joseph jerked off his low-crowned hat and busily fanned himself, drying sweat that shone like grease on his forehead. The white man's next remark was intended to be conversational but had a strained quality:

"Now we can go ahead and take the buffalo up to the railroad. We're also three horses to the good. I'd call it a passable day's work."

Saying that, he turned away. But not before he astonished Kola with a sad, almost grief-stricken glance. With his back toward the Sioux, he added:

"A man should know better than to do a dishonorable thing like stealing another man's kill. *He should know better!*"

There was no regret in the last few words. Only anger.

Kola overcame the piercing fright produced by Joseph's unexpected ferocity. He realized again that he would never understand the man's unfathomable nature. But outwardly—ah, outwardly, Joseph was a *kola* of whom he could be eternally proud.

He let his awe and pride drive a yell of joy out of his throat. He circled the fire, stood over Cutright's body, and raised his clout, exposing his genitals to the dead man's staring eyes—his people's ultimate insult to a vanquished and contemptible enemy.

Joseph walked back to his coffee cup and picked it up. Before drinking he said in a casual way:

"We don't need to waste time disposing of them. The turkey buzzards will do it in a day or two. Besides, they don't deserve decent burial."

He tossed his head back and drank. A spurt of fire in the thinning smoke reddened the streak of white hair that began at his hairline over his left brow and tapered to a point at the back of his head.

# BOOK FOUR
*Hell-On-Wheels*

# CHAPTER 1

## The Cheyenne

MICHAEL BOYLE had seldom experienced the kind of
consuming fright he felt during those first moments when he stood rooted
on the summit of the low hill, trying to decide whether to run and attempt to warn the railhead. It was worse than the fear he'd suffered
charging enemy lines with the Irish Brigade. At least with the Brigade,
there had been others around him sharing the peril.

He was most conscious of the weapons arrayed against him. The short
hunting bows. The quivers bristling with arrows. The knives. The war
hatchets with shafts wrapped in bright red cloth and metal heads, not
stone.

The knife blades and hatchet heads meant the weapons were trade
goods, factory made. The Cheyenne—if that was indeed what they were—
had either bargained for them at forts or stolen them in raids.

He saw no revolvers or rifles. But he understood Plains Indians owned
few of those. Firearms which the Indians did manage to acquire were carefully guarded and used only on hunts or important forays against enemy
tribes. It was a small, hopeful sign.

He licked at sweat on his upper lip. The warriors remained motionless,
watching. The feathers in their sunlit black hair bobbed in the breeze.

The Indian holding Ruffin—the one with the immense bare belly—kept
staring too. A hint of a smile appeared on the man's thick-lipped mouth.
But the eight-foot bow-lance was rock steady. If Michael responded
wrongly, or acted precipitously, the iron head would pierce Ruffin's throat
in an instant.

One by one, other details registered. On all the calico ponies, plaited
horsehair was looped and knotted around the lower jaws to create both bit
and bridle from a single long strand. Quirts held by muscular hands rested
against naked thighs. The quirts resembled miniature whips—three
thongs of rawhide attached to a carved round of wood heavy enough to
deal a man a crippling blow.

About two-thirds of the Indians rode bareback. The rest, including Fatbelly, had hide saddles, little more than beaded pads. The leader's gear also included a blanket under the saddle, beaded bright yellow and red. Fringes hung from each corner of the square.

The big-bellied Indian bore scars on his shoulders and had pendulous breasts. The scars were in pairs. Michael recalled hearing a Paddy describe rituals in which Plains Indians pledged their lives to the protection of their people and the annihilation of their foes—and shed blood in self-mortification as proof of their intent. The scars as well as the leader's air of authority said he was the one with whom Michael had to deal.

Weary of Michael's hesitation, Fatbelly gigged the lance head deeper into Tom Ruffin's neck. A line of blood trickled. Ruffin's legs thrashed. Above the clasping hand, the boy's eyes pleaded with Michael.

Fatbelly raised his eyebrows. His forehead creased like a wrinkled hide. The lift of the brows asked an unmistakable question:

*What will you do?*

ii

Michael had no idea—except that he'd decided not to run and abandon Ruffin. In a voice as steady as he could manage, he asked:

"Do you talk English?"

Half a dozen of the braves—all in their twenties—snickered and whispered among themselves. One let out a low but frightening whoop, then spat over the ears of his pony. The fat-bellied Indian whipped the lance to the right, then thrust it over his head. The young men laughing at Michael fell silent. The smirks disappeared.

Fatbelly grinned in a disarmingly friendly way. Michael wasn't deceived. It would be foolish to trust the Indian—or regard him as a weakling because of his age, or his flabby breasts and stomach. The rest of him looked hard. The act of raising the lance had tightened huge muscles in his upper arm.

The Indian's smile grew wider, revealing brown gums studded with broken teeth. He nodded in a vigorous way.

"English," he said, garbling it so that it came out *Ang-lish*. The thumb of the hand holding the lance straightened, pointing at the Indian's chest. "English!" There was an almost childlike quality about the declaration.

When the Indian continued, he mauled the pronunciation of nearly every word:

"I have traded at white forts. But we are not Laramie Loafers—"

Some of the others understood and growled agreement.

"We do not come to bring war. We like black coffee that is sweet. We want to see the fire road you are making. No war, only see."

He widened his eyes, blinking several times. The illustration almost made Michael laugh, not in derision but genuine amusement. The fat-bellied man almost resembled a small boy—except for that bow-lance he'd quietly shifted back to Ruffin's throat.

"We friends." It came out *frans.* "No war. Just coffee." More blinking. "Just look."

Amusing as the Indian's enthusiastic declaration was, Michael remained wary. He'd heard tales of braves who had ridden up to a government fort to trade with perfect cordiality one day, only to return the next and launch a vicious attack. They were unpredictable as the plains weather, Casement claimed. So he didn't put much stock in Fatbelly's assertions. Though his heart was beating less rapidly, Michael kept a frown on his face.

"Very well. If you're friendly—"

Fatbelly's nod was again impatient. "Friends. *Friends!*"

"Then put the boy down."

The Indian cocked his head, acting baffled. Michael suspected the man understood more than he let on.

Michael resorted to gestures. A finger at the boy, then at the buffalo grass.

"*Down*. Let him go. Don't hurt him."

The Indian pondered. Shook his head:

"You are many. We are few. We keep him till we see the fire road and get coffee. Then we let go. Is not wise to believe all you whites say. You say friends, then you turn many guns against us."

Something ugly flickered in the man's eyes. His smile disappeared.

"Two summers ago it was so when Black Kettle camped at Sand Creek."

Michael winced; he knew the infamous reference.

In the autumn of '64, Indian raids in the Colorado territory had resulted in the organization of a Denver-based military unit of six hundred white men. The men—mostly riffraff—had been commanded by a fanatic Army officer named Chivington, who also happened to be an ordained Methodist minister. Chivington led his men to a nearby Cheyenne encampment.

Though not responsible for the raids, the inhabitants of the camp—Black Kettle's people—had feared reprisal and sought sanctuary from rising anti-Indian sentiment. The Army had proposed Sand Creek as safe territory. Black Kettle had moved there, even raising the Stars and Stripes on a pole—and then he'd watched Chivington's regiment of ruffians ride in. For

three or four hours, the whites had galloped back and forth, smashing tipi
and butchering close to fifty braves, women, and children.

"I had a sister there," Fatbelly said. "Sister?"

Michael nodded to signify comprehension.

"She never stole cows. Never cut talking wires—" A stab of the lance to
ward the telegraph poles across the Platte.

"—But her hair was taken. This hair—"

The lance lifted to touch his head.

"This hair too."

He lowered the lance to his groin.

"It was held up in a large place for whites who laughed."

Michael had no answer to satisfy the Indian's anger. He knew scalps of
Cheyenne children and the pubic hair of Cheyenne women had indeed
been paraded on the stage of at least one Denver theater following Chiv
ington's raid.

Michael was no expert on the confused policies and operations of the
Army in the West. But he did know officers assigned to the troubled territory during the war had generally been incompetents. The best men had
been assigned to the Union forces pitted against the Confederacy.

With men of poor quality in charge on the plains, it was no wonder decisions were poor as well. Such men didn't believe it necessary to locate
and punish the Indians actually responsible for a given act of murder or
arson. For effective control of what was termed the Indian problem, punishment of any Indian would do. Fatbelly's sister had evidently been one
of the innocents who suffered from such witless retaliation.

"No," the Indian grumbled, tightening his hand over Ruffin's purpling
face. The boy's eyes bulged. He looked ready to expire for lack of breath.
"We let this one go if we find no war. We let go after we drink coffee!"

The finality of it convinced Michael he'd better postpone further argument. He'd shaped a strategy for handling the situation, but before he
had a chance to implement it, Fatbelly barked at him again:

"Are you the fire-road boss?"

Michael shook his head. "I only lay track."

The Indian didn't understand.

"I work. *Work.*" Michael flexed his hands. Pantomimed lifting something. The Indian grunted.

"My name—"

Was that an unfamiliar word? Dry-lipped, he began again:

"I—"

A finger to his chest.

"I am called Boyle."

He repeated it.

"Bile," Fatbelly nodded. "I am—"

A rush of gibberish. Michael kept shaking his head. Finally the Indian went back to English.

"Guns Taken."

"Ah. Guns Taken." Michael's bobbing head indicated his comprehension.

The Cheyenne's grin returned. "Took three guns when I was ten summers. Three! From a white fort. I rode away fleet as the wind before they could close the gates and catch my pony. I was honored and became Guns Taken instead of Dog Barks, the name I was given at the hour my mother bore me."

There was enormous pride in the statements and the broad smile accompanying them. The innocence of the declaration relieved Michael's anxiety a bit. Almost made him like the fellow, in fact.

But it was dangerous to be lulled. Casement insisted the Plains Indians were not the primitive simpletons too many whites made them out to be. The Sioux and Cheyenne could be cunning. And volatile.

"Three *big* guns!" the Indian bellowed.

Michael nodded hastily. "Yes, yes, I understand." Evidently he hadn't acted sufficiently impressed. His failure wiped the smile from the Indian's face. Guns Taken thrust his lance at Michael.

"We go to the fire road. Now."

Knees pressing against his pony, the warrior started forward. Michael held up his hands.

"Wait."

He pushed his palms toward the Indian. Guns Taken's scowl deepened. Michael swallowed, wondering whether the man would fling his lance.

"Let me go first," Michael told him, mixing improvised pantomime with the words. "You stay here while I go ahead—ahead—so there will be no angry men. Let me speak to the boss of the fire road. It may take me a little while, so don't be alarmed. I promise to tell him you are not here for war. Then he will make you welcome."

Guns Taken shook his head hard. Michael's meaning was either unclear or the Cheyenne was again pretending. Tense, Michael went through it twice more, finally making the Indian understand he would precede the party and take whatever time was required to assure there was no trouble. He was not only concerned about Tom Ruffin's safety, but anxious for Jack Casement to get the men at the railhead firmly under control before the Indians appeared. He hoped he was doing the right thing.

Turning his pony, Guns Taken addressed the young men in his band. The Cheyenne spoke a swift flow of words Michael couldn't fathom. But gestures and expressions left no doubt about some of the reactions:

Complaints. Angry protests. Guns Taken silenced his braves with re peated shouts.

A couple of the Indians let Michael take the brunt of their displeasure The ferocity of their glances made him shiver.

But Guns Taken was in command. Michael was again encourage when the big Indian walked his pony forward three steps and gave a fina nod.

"You go. The boy stays till the fire-road boss says come in."

"No. I want the boy." With both hands he motioned to Ruffin, the the grass. "Let him down."

"You *go!* Boy stays." The dark eyes shone with a sad cynicism. "The there will be no guns fired to greet us. If there are guns fired, Bile—"

The smile reappeared, but it had a terrifying lack of humor. Th Cheyenne pricked Tom Ruffin's neck a second time.

"—the boy is yours. Dead."

The bargain was clear. *Jesus,* Michael thought, *why me in the middl of this?*

All the Cheyenne began to jabber, waving at him; impatient for him t leave. Guns Taken thrust the bow-lance at him a second time.

"Too much talk already! We thirst for coffee. *You find boss!*"

Michael started off, then paused. "Tom?"

Guns Taken uncovered Ruffin's mouth. In a surprisingly calm voice the boy replied, "What, sir?"

"Keep still and they won't hurt you. I'll be back soon."

Even with Guns Taken's hand clasping his face again, Ruffin managed a nod. The Irishman turned his back, crossed the summit of the low hill and broke into a run going down the slope. Despite Tom Ruffin's grit, Michael wondered if he'd see the boy alive again.

# CHAPTER 2

## Armed Camp

MICHAEL RAN with all his strength, plunging through the thick buffalo grass along the river. Sweat began to flick off his forehead.

He sped by the spot where he'd dropped his clothing and drew abreast of the first group of naked bathers laughing and enjoying a water fight. Wigwagging his arms, he yelled:

"Back to the train! There are Indians yonder. They have Tom Ruffin."

Up to his knobby knees in the water, Liam O'Dey scratched his testicles. "Ah, Michael Boyle, let's have none of your feeble jokes this morning."

Michael shook a fist. "It's no damn joke! I talked to them. If you stay here, the boy's liable to be murdered. Get moving!"

He spun and dashed on while O'Dey and his companions clambered up the bank for their clothes.

He stopped to warn three more groups, and sent a man from the last one running on down the river to summon in the others—a good hundred or so, strung out in the shallows for at least a mile to the east. Michael himself angled toward the perpetual train, waving his arms frantically again.

*Osceola* was pulling out. Armed men clinging to the sides of the locomotive and tender saw him coming. One poked his head into the cab. The engine stopped with a squeal and spurting of steam.

Michael went pounding around the edge of the beef herd. The disturbed animals began to low. Michael's shouts and arm waving brought two of the drovers charging at him. One brandished a long stick:

"Quit yer damn yellin' or ye'll stampede 'em."

"*Indians!*" Michael yelled, pointing west. The drover turned pale and crossed himself.

As Michael rushed on, noisy, half-naked men started streaming toward the train from points all along the bank. He reached the office car, vaulted up the steps two at a time, and ran along the narrow corridor. The door of Casement's cubicle stood ajar. Michael heard a voice he recognized.

"Either I get my job back from that mick, or I won't be responsible for what happens to—"

A bull-voiced Casement broke in: "You *will* be responsible or I'll ship you back to Omaha under guard. Worthing!"

Michael kicked the door open and grabbed the jamb with both hands, too upset to worry about the presence of the Virginian. Worthing pivoted toward him. His face was puffy and discolored. His left eye had swollen shut.

"Well!" he said in a nasty way. "The very mick under discussion."

## ii

Casement ignored him, eyes on Michael's sweaty face. Michael gulped air. He couldn't seem to get enough.

"What the hell's wrong, Boyle?"

"We have visitors, General. About a mile west. Thirty Indians. Cheyenne, I think."

"Merciful God!" Casement breathed. "That's all we need."

"Pity they didn't lift your fucking hair," Worthing said, touching a knuckle to the bloated yellow-blue mass of his left cheek.

"Let him talk!" Casement said. "You saw the Indians yourself?"

"I did. I had conversation with them. The head man speaks passable English. They captured Tom Ruffin. The boy had gone off to catch a grouse—"

In a few sentences he explained what had happened. At the end, Worthing gaped:

"You mean to say you let a pack of filthy savages hang onto the boy while you turned tail?"

Red-faced, Michael snarled, "The leader had a lance this long—" He flung his arms wide. "Square in Ruffin's neck. The head man said they don't want a fight, General Jack. Just sugared coffee and a look at the equipment. I said I'd come on ahead and guarantee there'd be no trouble. We won't get Ruffin back safely any other way."

"Ah, God," Worthing sighed. "I'd have *taken* him back."

Casement stamped over in front of the Virginian. Though the top of the construction chief's head only reached Worthing's chin, his anger was sufficient to intimidate the Virginian.

"One more word and I'll have you locked up."

The ex-Confederate's open eye glared. Michael heard men piling into the corridor, asking questions and calling for Spencers from the sleeping cars. Casement gestured.

"Shut the door."

Michael did.

"Now tell me. Do you think the hostiles were lying? Do they want their blasted coffee—or a scrap?"

Weary, Michael leaned against the wall and rubbed at the sweat on his belly.

"Hell, General, I'm no student of red men. One minute, the leader—his name's Guns Taken—struck me as a straight-out sort. Then I'd get a feeling he was saying one thing and thinking another. I can't honestly tell you whether they've come like children to a candy store, or are just pretending."

"A little of both, maybe," Casement said. "The fools in the Indian Bureau always make the mistake of thinking we're up against savages out here. That *was* your word, wasn't it, Worthing? Savages?"

Worthing seethed in silence as Casement went on:

"But they aren't savages. They've a society hundreds of years older than ours—and most are smarter than many an Army officer I've met. You won't see a Sioux or Cheyenne risking twenty men to rustle half a dozen cows, but some Army lieutenants would commit three companies to save one government heifer." Agitated, he tugged at his beard. "How are they armed? Any muskets or rifles?"

"None that I saw. They're carrying knives, hatchets, bows—and the head man has that devilish lance. It's all tricked up with feathers and a string for firing arrows."

Casement muttered a despairing obscenity. "Then he's a Bowstring. If so, they *are* Cheyenne." Noticing Michael's puzzled look, Casement explained, "The bow-lance is a characteristic of the Bowstrings, one of the Cheyenne warrior societies. It means the leader's no boy on a lark, but a man to be reckoned with. Did he harm Ruffin?"

"Gigged his neck and drew a little blood. More for my benefit than anything else, I think. But he said he'd kill the boy if there were any traps when he came in."

Casement turned away and pondered, palms resting on his cluttered desk. Finally his head snapped up.

"All right. The boy counts most. We'll pull every man off the engine, and issue a limited number of rifles. You go to the cooks, Boyle. Have them start brewing coffee. Gallons of the stuff. Pour on the sugar."

Worthing couldn't believe it: "You'll *permit* them to ride in here?"

"Exactly. I'll not truckle to them, nor let them think we're weaklings. That's why I want some Spencers in sight. But neither will I incite them."

"Jesus." Worthing still looked thunderstruck. "Our herd's been hit how many times? Three? Four?"

"We have lost animals, not men."

"But we should show 'em they can't get away with it!"

Casement shook his head. "We don't know whether these Indians are the same ones who stole our stock. To punish them as if they were is not only wrong, it's foolhardy. I'm not even considering Ruffin when I say that. Punishing the wrong Indians is the mistake Chivington made at Sand Creek. It's the same mistake the goddamn Army makes every day of the week. It's one big reason the trouble never stops!"

"This Guns Taken—" Michael put in. "He claims he lost a sister at Sand Creek."

Casement groaned. "Then we've double the worry. They're not only Cheyenne, but Cheyenne with a grudge."

"What fucking difference does it make if they're not the ones who drove off the stock?" Worthing fumed. "They'll see the beeves and be back to help themselves. I say stop 'em ahead of time!"

"Oh," Casement murmured, "you subscribe to the theory that all of their kind should be wiped out, do you?"

"As long as a single one causes trouble, yes!"

"Worthing, you're an ignoramus. *We're* the intruders. We're deep into the tribal buffalo grounds—the Republican herd's one of the largest in the West. They see the buffalo being shot by white men; they see their land being cut up by these tracks; they see innocent members of their race being punished for the depredations of guilty ones—I'll not compound the problems already created and risk losing men and time!"

Worthing stormed toward the door. "This is the goddamnedest outfit of yellowbellies I've ever seen. I'm going to get a Spencer and wait for—"

Michael was bowled aside as Casement lunged and fastened his hands on Worthing's gray duster. Before the taller man could react, Casement hurled him against the cubicle's outer wall. The planking vibrated.

Casement raised on tiptoe, cheeks red as his quivering beard.

"Captain Worthing, you have taxed my patience to the limit." A shake of the man's lapels. "*To the limit!* You lost the damned war, and I am sick to death of your trying to win it all over again by besting every man who strays across your path!"

Worthing's hands clenched. For a moment Michael was certain there'd be a fight. Then he recalled that the Southerner liked odds favorable to himself. But Worthing did fire a verbal salvo:

"I'll settle with you for this, Casement. You and the mick both. Count on it."

"I already received that message," Michael said. "In my bunk."

Releasing the Virginian, Casement missed the glance of venomous understanding between the other two. The construction boss wiped his hands on his thighs, as if he'd touched something unclean. He jerked the door open and confronted a press of men who bombarded him with questions:

"What's this about Injuns, Gen'ral?"

"Heard they got the Ruffin boy."

"A hundred of the heathen, someone said."

"Lads are breakin' out the Spencers—"

"You—" Casement grabbed the nearest man. "Go through the sleeping cars and issue a direct order from me. Twenty rifles out—no more! Have the gang bosses distribute them to men they can trust to keep their heads. The Indians may mean no harm."

Michael saw doubtful expressions as well as frightened ones. He was conscious of Worthing staring at him but didn't turn his head.

"At least they say they don't. They merely want coffee and a chance to examine our equipment. We'll take them at their word until they prove we shouldn't. You, and you—" Casement singled out three more men. "—you boys escort Captain Worthing to his car and keep him there."

Worthing began to swear. Casement paid no attention.

"Sit on him. Tie him. Bash his head in—I don't care. But he's not to be allowed outside or permitted to place his hands on a weapon. I'll not let one hothead bloody this whole camp."

"Come on, Reb," one of the appointed men said as the others closed in. "You just been to Appomattox all over again."

The cursing Virginian was manhandled out of sight. Michael wished Worthing's guards weren't so eager to show how much they disliked him— or so free with taunts about the South's defeat. They might only make the Virginian angrier and more reckless.

Casement began dispatching other men to round up the workers and have them assemble on the north side of the last sleeping car, where they would be hidden from any watchers Guns Taken might have sent to the hilltop. Michael worked his way along the packed corridor to the kitchen and called for fresh coffee from the startled cooks.

Within five minutes he was outside, and Jack Casement was preparing to address the growing throng around the steps of the bunk car.

### iii

Michael stood toward the rear of the crowd. Above the clamor of voices, he heard someone call his name.

He turned. Hannah Dorn was hurrying toward him, bundled in her shapeless coat. The floppy hat concealed her bright hair.

Her brother Klaus was with her, carrying his rifle. Then Dorn appeared from behind the wagon, buttoning his fly and belching. He looked unsteady on his feet. He too had his Hawken.

"Mister Boyle—" Hannah touched Michael's arm. In the band of shadow cast by the hat brim, her eyes widened in surprise and embarrassment.

It took her a moment to recover and ask, "What's the difficulty?"

"Surprise guests. Thirty Cheyenne—down there behind those hills. They've captured one of the lorry car boys, and—hold on." As he said the last words, he unconsciously reached across with his right hand and squeezed her forearm.

Then he too was struck by a realization that he was being overly familiar. He jerked his hand away.

Their eyes met again. He felt just as chagrined as she'd been a moment ago. Very nearly stammering, he added, "Casement—Casement will explain."

The construction boss spoke in a loud voice. At the announcement of the presence of Indians—the rumor verified—there were exclamations of astonishment and alarm. At scattered spots in the crowd, a Paddy demanded the intruders be met with volleys from the stored rifles. Casement shouted them down:

"Absolutely not! There'll be no shooting unless I give the command. They have Ruffin, and they may honestly mean us no harm."

"But General, we outnumber 'em!"

"That would be no consolation to any man killed or maimed in an unnecessary fight. Of course we outnumber them. We could storm out there and drive them off. But I doubt we'd see Ruffin with his scalp again."

Nervously, Michael glanced toward the blowing buffalo grass on the line of hills. Perhaps the Cheyenne were gone and Tom Ruffin was already dead. Contradictory images of Guns Taken flitted in his mind. He saw a guileless child, then a sly trickster. Which was the true picture?

He forced his attention back to Casement.

"We'll remain calm, keep all but twenty rifles out of sight, see exactly what they want, and hope they'll depart peaceably when they get it."

"You know what they want!" a voice burst out behind Michael. Hannah Dorn closed her eyes before she swung to look at Gustav Dorn.

Hannah started working her way toward him: "Papa, please. Let General Casement run things."

Even from eight feet away, Michael smelled the whiskey on the unkempt merchant. Dorn weaved on his feet as he flourished his rifle:

"You got shit in your head, Casement! It's more than coffee the red devils are after. It's guns! It's liquor—"

He brought the Hawken up to his chest.

"Sons of bitches touch my whiskey, I blow their heads off. You touch this gun, I do the same for you."

iv

"Papa, that won't help," Hannah pleaded. She took hold of the Hawken. "Put it down."

"Damn woman—*let go!*" Spit flecked Dorn's lips as he wrenched the rifle out of Hannah's grip. Michael felt a spurt of anger; started for Dorn. Casement yelled:

"Take that rifle away from him!"

Dorn began to back up, putting the Hawken on cock. A sharp intake of breath came from Michael's left—from Sean Murphy. Several Paddies scuttled aside, out of range of the weaving muzzle.

Licking at the corner of his mouth, Dorn dropped into a crouch.

"Nobody takes it. First who tries, I shoot."

"Dorn?"

The merchant swung toward Michael. The Hawken's barrel steadied, aimed at the younger man's belly.

"What's your two cents, Paddy?"

Michael extended his hand. "Give it up before you're hurt. The boy's life is more important than your liquor."

"Paddy, you stay away from me. I got a big ball ready for you if you don't—"

Michael took three more steps—a yard closer to the German—before he halted. He wiped his mouth. "Be reasonable, Dorn."

"You come on," Dorn interrupted, wiggling the Hawken. "You come right on, Mister Mick. As soon as you walk one step more, I shoot your goddamn thick head to pieces—*ahh!*"

He squealed as Hannah's fingers shot in from behind and clamped on his neck. She'd gone creeping around his flank while his attention was fixed on Michael.

Dorn lunged to the side, seized the Hawken's muzzle, and swung blindly. The stock slammed Hannah's jaw. *Jesus, it could go off!* Michael thought as the girl stumbled, her hat tumbling from her head. Bent low, he ran at the German.

He ripped the Hawken from Dorn's fingers and tossed it to a man who juggled it as if it were a poisonous snake. Dorn aimed a clumsy punch at

Michael's midriff. Michael jerked his belly back out of the way and used his longer reach to seize Dorn's ears. He yanked, hard.

Dorn staggered, shrieking obscenities. Men encircled him. Michael retrieved the Hawken and uncocked it. He noticed Sean Murphy had slipped up to the bewildered Klaus and relieved him of his rifle. He reached down to help Hannah to her feet.

"I'm sorry I provoked him. I'm sorry he hurt you."

"Oh—" Tears filled her eyes. Ashamed, she spun so he couldn't see. She snatched up her hat and whispered, "What does one more time matter?"

Her grief hurt him too, somehow. He wanted to reach out to her; comfort her.

Dorn thrashed and yelped as more men surrounded him. Michael wondered how Hannah Dorn's faith could withstand her father's behavior. All she believed seemed negated and made a mockery by the merchant's pathetic yet potentially lethal rage.

Almost ready to walk to her and risk humiliating her further by making her look at him, Michael was prevented by Casement calling for attention.

v

"Now that we seem to have things in hand, let's try to get through the remainder of the day without any casualties. It's up to you men—each and every one. I want no Indian Bureau commissioners descending on us to ask why we harmed innocent visitors."

*If indeed they're innocent,* Michael thought.

"I want to write no reports to General Dodge and the directors of the line, and more important, no letters to wives or sweethearts explaining how a good worker was needlessly slain."

There were still a few grumbles about Casement's lack of nerve. But most of the rust-eaters agreed with Michael's silent assessment: It took more courage for Casement to exercise restraint than it did to indulge the kind of hostility that made Dorn and Worthing such threats. General Jack's forceful voice overrode the last muttered objections:

"Our job is to save Ruffin, then lay track and reach the hundredth meridian as fast as we can. Remember that!"

Except for Dorn cursing among his captors, the crowd was still.

"Boyle?"

"Here, sir."

"Go tell the Indians to come in."

"Right away, General."

"And Boyle—"

Michael turned back. Three gang bosses had appeared behind Casement. All three had a pair of Spencers in each hand, and several of the tubular butt magazines in their belts. Casement indicated the weapons:

"Do you want one?"

Michael almost answered yes. He would have felt far safer. But he thought of Tom Ruffin. The sight of a rifle might provoke an impulsive stab of that bow-lance. One thrust was all it would take to kill the boy.

"No, I'd better go without."

Casement nodded, a thin smile relieving the severity of his mouth for a moment.

Heart hammering, Michael set off along a lane that opened in the crowd. The men had fallen so silent he could hear the whine of the prairie wind and the hiss of steam from *Osceola*.

# CHAPTER 3

# The Race

TWENTY MINUTES LATER, Michael returned to the railhead, a pale but unhurt Tom Ruffin by his side. Behind them, riding single file with Guns Taken leading the procession, came the Cheyenne.

Virtually every worker had turned out to watch. Hundreds of Paddies stood or sat in small groups. A few looked openly hostile, others anxious. But the majority were merely curious.

Approaching the finished track west of the perpetual train, Michael searched for the seven-shot repeating rifles distributed while he was gone. He spied the first two with the stock drovers. A wise precaution, he decided when he heard a burst of Indian talk. He turned to see a young brave point to the cattle and make a smirking comment to the rider behind. On the faces of several of the Cheyenne he saw undisguised envy.

His eyes moved back to the train. Most of the workers had gathered along the north side. He noticed one man still relaxing in a hammock slung beneath a sleeping car. No, not precisely relaxing; the barrel of a Spencer was visible.

Two men lounged beside their tent on the car's roof. The mellow sunlight of the mare's-tail sky set the barrel of another Spencer flashing.

The man holding the repeater shifted position. The flare of light vanished. But not before Guns Taken and his braves took note.

Closer scrutiny showed Michael the location of other rifles. Casement had arranged things well. The Spencers were inconspicuous but not invisible. The unarmed workers were aware of the guns. In front of a Paddy with a rifle in the crook of his arm, Liam O'Dey sweated and fiddled with his holy beads.

Casement came striding around the end of the nearest boxcar. He too carried a rifle, and had buckled on a holstered Colt. He stopped on the track, his red beard snapping in the breeze.

Along the north side of the train, Michael heard swearing. He craned to see the source—two cooks hurriedly setting planks on a couple of barrels.

A third man came scrambling down from the kitchen, rag-wrapped hands gripping the bail of a huge enamel pot trailing steam from its spout.

Casement's eyes darted to the boy at Michael's side. "He's fine, sir," Michael said quickly. "Guns Taken kept his word."

The track boss nodded and gazed past him as the procession halted. Guns Taken dismounted and walked forward with bow-lance in hand. His bare stomach quivered. Though the Indian was more than a little bowlegged and his huge melon of a belly looked soft, Jack Casement didn't relax.

Guns Taken stopped a foot from the construction boss. The Cheyenne's six-foot height and Casement's shortness presented a curiously comic picture. Guns Taken peered down at the smaller man with a guarded smile Casement didn't return.

Casement made the peace sign with his free hand. Guns Taken replied using the identical gesture. Casement's hand began to dart, point, describe fluid curves.

After a minute of the sign talk Michael didn't understand, Casement dropped his hand to his side. Guns Taken grunted in a way that seemed to signify satisfaction. Michael scanned the crowd again, finally located Hannah Dorn, her father and brother among a half-dozen men near the whiskey wagon.

Dorn appeared as truculent as ever. Three of those close to him carried Spencers. No accident, that grouping. Michael hoped the men guarding Leonidas Worthing were equally alert and well armed.

Again Casement spoke with his hand. Guns Taken answered:

"Yes, English. Talk English if you want. We are friends. Come only to watch how you build the fire road. Watch and drink sweet coffee."

Casement hoisted a thumb over his shoulder. "It's ready. Our present to you. We welcome a peaceful visit."

"First—" Guns Taken cocked his bow-lance toward a rail. "Show how these are put in the earth."

"No." Casement shook his head. "No, we are not working today."

Guns Taken didn't like that. He chattered to his warriors. Several scowled and grumbled. Michael saw hands tighten on quirts or reach toward knives. Casement saw it too. He spoke firmly to recapture the attention of the leader:

"This is a holy day for my men. A day of rest. They pray to God—" His swift-moving hand amplified the explanation. "—drink coffee. Sleep. Tend their clothing. Some ride the fire horse up and down the track—"

Guns Taken failed to understand the last word until Casement's finger indicated the same rail to which the Indian had pointed.

"Track."

"Uh. Track!"

"But there is no work on it today."

Guns Taken accepted the fact grudgingly:

"All right. Give us the coffee. Show us the fire horse."

Casement turned slightly. "Come this way."

The big Cheyenne didn't move. Back along the train, Michael noticed the photographer, Stackpole, readying his camera and black cloth with slow, cautious movements. Guns Taken glanced at the motionless workers. The small clusters looked almost posed. The Indian couldn't miss the rifles.

Michael thought the tall Indian's eyes lingered a moment on the whiskey wagon. *Lord, he can't read what's painted on the barrels, can he?*

Abruptly, the Indian stabbed the head of his bow-lance into the fill between two ties:

"Too many guns here."

"Not to harm you," Casement assured him. "Out here we must carry guns for our own safety. We have been raided at night. Cattle have been stolen—"

"We steal no cattle!"

"I am not saying you do." Casement's jaw thrust out. A touch of pugnacity sharpened his tone: "I have no way of knowing, however."

That displeased the big man. "Others. *Others!*"

"Very well, I believe you speak the truth," Casement replied, emphasizing it with more gestures. His hand kept moving as he started for the train. "Let there be peace while you examine—uh, see—the fire road. Come. Drink and see."

Guns Taken spent a few more seconds weighing the advisability of accompanying Casement to the side of the train where so many men were gathered. Some were still half undressed from their swim.

The Indian drew a deep breath, appearing to stretch himself an inch or two in the process. He looked not only taller but regal. His bearing was a declaration that he felt no fear among so many whites.

Moving with impressive grace, he returned to his pony and leaped onto its back in a surprisingly agile fashion. He raised the lance above his head. Still in single file, the Cheyenne began to walk their calicos toward the train.

Casement stood aside and beckoned Michael. The construction boss slipped the Colt from his holster, pressed it into Michael's hand and said in a low voice:

"Stay with me. You're one of the few I can trust to keep a level head. I assume you know how to use one of these?"

Guns Taken rode by. His shadow flitted across Casement's face. The

Cheyenne gazed straight ahead, not bothering to acknowledge the two white men.

"Yes, I've gone out on the engine pinking at rabbits once or twice."

"Let's hope there'll be no need for you to pink at anything else."

## ii

At the improvised coffee station, the cooks were busy filling tin cups. Stackpole approached with his tripod over his shoulder. He asked permission to take a photograph. The Cheyenne jabbered excitedly and shook their fists at the black-shrouded box.

"You've seen a camera?" Casement asked.

"At forts," Guns Taken nodded. "It is the box-which-steals-the-spirit. A part of a man is drawn into it and held captive there forever."

Casement controlled a smile. "Very well, no photographs." He ordered the camera removed by the crestfallen Mr. Stackpole.

Then he called on three workers to come forward and help him distribute coffee to the still-mounted guests. The Indians gulped the contents of the cups with lip-smacking pleasure. Michael eyed the group beside the whiskey wagon. Dorn was talking and gesturing; obviously resentful the Cheyenne were being so royally treated.

Guns Taken drained his cup. His bow-lance rested across his thighs. He thrust the cup down at Casement in an arrogant way.

Obviously irked, the construction boss nevertheless took the cup, had it refilled, and brought it back. Guns Taken drank every drop, then flung the cup on the ground.

"The fire horse!"

A bit testily, Casement said, "Right there it is. The engine is a regular 4-4-0 type. That is—" He pointed. "—four wheels on the front truck, four drivers, but no wheels beneath the cab. It weighs just under thirty tons, burns wood, and was named for a famous chief of the Seminoles, Osce—"

Bored, Guns Taken interrupted with a sharp shake of his head:

"No talk. Talk makes no sense."

"Then ride up and see the damned thing for yourself!"

Guns Taken was amused by the other man's losing his temper. This time his head-shaking was unbearably slow. He enjoyed making Casement uncomfortable.

"Show us the fire horse *running*."

Casement started to refuse, then thought a moment.

"All right. Boyle?"

Michael moved to his side.

"We'll take her a few miles down the track. You climb on the pilot board so they stay off. I'll ride in the cab. If they demand a demonstration, by God I'll give them one to remember."

Michael trotted to the head of the engine, scrambled up on the platform of the cowcatcher, and squatted down while the Cheyenne walked their ponies closer to the locomotive. Their eyes grew huge at the sight of the hissing contraption with a smoke plume drifting from its funnel stack.

Casement mounted to the cab and barked orders to the engineer and fireman. Suddenly the whistle blasted. A calico reared, nearly upsetting its rider.

Another Cheyenne grabbed for his hatchet, yelped something that must have been a curse and flung the weapon.

Michael ducked. The hatchet clanged off the front of the engine not far from his head. He tightened his trigger finger just a little. Casement leaned out of the cab:

"Guns Taken, keep your braves quiet! That's the sound the fire horse makes when it's ready to run."

The whistle screamed again, joined by the clanging bell. The Indian ponies shied. Guns Taken clapped his free hand over his mouth, his eyes round as a child's again. The bell kept ringing as the engine lurched forward.

The Indians scattered to both sides of the track. Michael felt wind against his face as he squinted at the braves trotting along beside him, awed by the slow *whump* of the drive rods and the grind of the wheels. The ringing bell was interrupted by a third howl of the whistle that brought alarmed looks to several dark faces.

That fear wasn't good, Michael thought. Fear could lead to anger.

In a moment he was proved right. One of the braves kicked his pony and raced up beside the cowcatcher, shaking his bow and screeching at the iron monster starting to spew sparks along with the smoke.

*Osceola* was gathering speed, its rods moving back and forth with a steadily accelerating beat. The front truck rattled. The huge driving wheels squealed on the rails. The brush of the wind against Michael's face became a push. Twenty yards ahead, Guns Taken flourished his bow-lance, kicked his pony, and went charging east beside the track.

His braves howled and followed, racing on either side of the right of way. The ponies raised dust that blew in Michael's face and started him coughing.

The Indians rode hard, waving hatchets, quirts, and bows and uttering cries of scorn. The engine fell behind. The yelps and barks grew jubilant as the braves increased the distance between themselves and the fire horse.

Abruptly, Michael felt the engine lurch. The rhythm of the rods began to quicken.

He shot out a hand to grip one of the vertical bars by which a man could hold his place on the cowcatcher. The locomotive swayed around a slight curve, gaining speed again. Plainly Casement meant what he'd said about a demonstration. Politeness was one thing, defeat that suggested weakness quite another.

Clanking and rumbling, *Osceola* moved steadily faster. Spark-filled smoke streamed from the stack. Swaying from side to side as he clung to the bar, Michael thought he heard the engineer call for more wood. He definitely heard the wood crash into the firebox. Within seconds, the locomotive began to close the gap.

The Cheyenne looked over their shoulders and started flogging their ponies with bare heels. Their cries of pleasure became cries of outrage.

Michael's bones throbbed as he knelt on the pilot board. He was all but blinded by billowing dust. Chuffing and thundering, the locomotive drew up opposite the slowest rider.

*Osceola* passed the Indian and, moments later, another. He shook his bow at Michael.

The engine caught up with four more Cheyenne on the other side. Their mounts were already lathered. They fell behind.

A cacophony of rattling, clanking metal beat against Michael's ears. The engine swayed more and more violently. The whistle screamed, and the bell never stopped ringing. Michael's hand was white on the bar.

Soon, half the Cheyenne had been outdistanced. After another half mile, only Guns Taken remained unbeaten. He rode bent forward over his pony's neck. He kicked the game animal without mercy and kept glancing back at the puffing monster. The Cheyenne's spine and shoulders glowed with sweat.

The engine noise was like a cataclysm shaking the earth. The point of the cowcatcher drew up even with Guns Taken. The warrior's mouth worked, but the roar drowned his cries as he urged his mount to greater and greater effort.

To no purpose. Inexorably, *Osceola* began to pass him.

Through the dust, Michael had a last glimpse of the Cheyenne's face turned toward his adversary. Tears or sweat shone beneath his enraged eyes.

Bell jangling, whistle bellowing, the locomotive left him behind in a cloud of smoke, sparks, and drifting ash.

iii

With a yowl of iron, the engine began to slow down. The bell stopped ringing. Michael exhaled and slackened his hold on the bar.

Over the next half mile, *Osceola* ground to a halt, jerked into reverse, and began to chug backward toward the railhead. Without any warning, Guns Taken was there beside the track, his bow-lance clutched in his right hand.

He sat absolutely still as he watched the locomotive go by. Wind blew smoke from the stack and gusted it down into his face.

Sparks made his pony sidestep, start to rear. Guns Taken jerked on the plaited hair and gave the animal half a dozen vicious kicks until it stood quietly again. Then he jerked the bridle and began to follow the engine back toward the work train.

One by one the other Cheyenne appeared on either side of the cow-catcher and fell in behind their leader. On each sunlit face Michael saw mingled fear and fury.

The Indian procession trailed *Osceola* at a distance of about a quarter mile. Not one brave spoke. Michael wondered at Casement's wisdom in demonstrating the engine's speed. It was never good to humiliate an enemy. He'd learned that from Louis Kent and Worthing, among others.

The Cheyenne jogged slowly after the locomotive, their eyes brimming with the hatred men reserved for a conqueror whose power they had come to feel at a cost of great pain and lost pride.

iv

When the engine braked, Michael jumped down. He thrust the Colt into the waist of his trousers and ran back to join the sooty-faced Casement climbing from the cab.

"I don't believe our visitors took kindly to losing, General."

Casement ignored the Irishman's rueful smile and shrugged in what amounted to a callous dismissal.

"I didn't intend that they should. Maybe if they're sufficiently impressed before they depart—"

"You mean frightened."

"Call it what you please. I hope I've persuaded them to leave us alone."

Michael inclined his head. "Look at the head man."

Guns Taken was riding past the engine, scanning it as if it were a thing of filth.

"He doesn't enjoy being whipped."

"But he has been. That was my purpose. To whip him. Peaceably but positively. Don't forget, Boyle—" Casement's glance said he wasn't overjoyed to have Michael question his actions, "—our objective is still to get the line through with a minimum of trouble. If their pride has to take a licking before they realize they can't stop us, so be it. I didn't order Charlie to open her to full throttle just on a whim."

Michael let the matter drop, though he still had doubts as to whether intimidating the visitors had been wise. Guns Taken gave the locomotive a last withering look. There was no longer any pretense of friendliness on his face as he jabbed the bow-lance at the boxcars.

"Show us those, white man."

The Cheyenne didn't miss Casement's faint smile. "Certainly."

The sullen Indians dismounted. Casement ushered the first of them into the second bunk car, Michael's. The construction boss hadn't lost all sensitivity to the perils of the situation. Captain Worthing was in the other car.

Michael waited at the steps, letting the Cheyenne climb up and enter one at a time. None of the Indians uttered a sound. An almost eerie silence had descended on the camp. In Worthing's car, someone yelled.

*Christ, keep a tight hand on that fool!*

The last brave passed him, intentionally stumbling, and driving an elbow into his ribs. Michael's hand jerked toward the Colt but he kept his temper. He met the Cheyenne's defiant gaze calmly and motioned for the Indian to precede him.

When he had, Michael grasped the handrail and went up the steps, fervently hoping Casement could conclude the visit and get the Indians away from the railhead before their anger exploded.

# CHAPTER 4

## Slaughter

IN THE BUNK CAR it very nearly did.

Guns Taken hovered at Casement's elbow, leading the line of braves down the aisle. The Indians stared but remained silent.

At the end of the car, Guns Taken paused beside the partially empty rifle racks. From his position at the rear, Michael heard the Cheyenne leader say something in a quarrelsome tone. The exact words were lost because the others blocking the aisle started growling agreement.

Gradually the hubbub diminished. Michael caught Casement's firm, "No."

"White man—"

"No. Absolutely not."

The line moved again. The Cheyenne shuffled out of the car. Michael drew abreast of Casement, who was still stationed beside the racks. The red-bearded construction boss whispered:

"The big one's really hot now."

"Why?"

"He wanted some of these rifles, gratis."

Outside, Guns Taken stood beside the roadbed, both hands on his bowlance. His braves had gathered behind him. The track boss went down the steps. Michael started to follow, then snapped his head around at the sound of ferocious thumping in the adjoining car.

Several of the Cheyenne heard the noise. Hands dropped to the hilts of knives and hatchets. But there was further disturbance.

Guns Taken shook his lance at the car just vacated:

"You show us something else."

"What?"

"Show that the men of the fire road are truly friends. Give us—" He held up his left hand, the fingers spread. "—this many guns."

Casement said quietly, "I've already told you the guns belong to the railroad."

Guns Taken thrust his fingers close to Casement's nose. The smaller man didn't blink.

"*This many!*" Guns Taken insisted.

"No, and that's final."

Michael eased the Colt into his hand. The mood of the confrontation was growing ugly. All along the train, watching workers were stirring, anticipating trouble—

More temperately, Casement went on, "We have welcomed you peacefully. We have shown you the strength of the fire horse. We have poured sweet coffee."

Guns Taken spat on the ground to show what value he placed on everything Casement had mentioned. The moment produced an unexpected ambivalence in Michael. He admired the audacity of the Cheyenne leader. It took courage to make demands in the face of vastly superior numbers. At the same time, he felt sorry for Guns Taken and his braves. In the masses of white men—and the humiliating speed of the locomotive —the warriors had glimpsed their coming defeat. Perhaps even their extermination.

Once more the construction boss resorted to sign language along with words:

"I am deeply sorry Guns Taken is angered. We wish only friendship. But we cannot give away rifles which might be turned against us."

Guns Taken thrust his bow-lance into the shoulder of the roadbed, raking a long gouge in the gravel. He whirled and addressed his braves. Muttering, they followed him back to the ponies. While the Indians mounted, more cursing and thumping erupted in the other sleeping car.

Re-forming his braves into single file, Guns Taken began to ride out the way he had come in. He maneuvered his pony close to the front ranks of the workers, forcing them to fall back. A few didn't want to, but the more prudent prevailed. The potential troublemakers were virtually dragged out of the way.

Michael and Casement followed the procession on foot. Michael observed the heightened tension—the scowls, the whispers—among the men, and despite good intentions, fell victim to it himself.

The hoofs of the ponies plopped in the silence. Puffs of dust blew away in the breeze. Guns Taken gazed down contemptuously at the Paddies he passed.

All at once he reined his pony to a stop opposite the whiskey wagon.

Dorn's half-dozen guards stepped closer. The merchant was still fuming. Behind him, Hannah stood white-lipped, her hat in her right hand and her wheat-colored hair glinting in the sun. Her eyes remained fixed on her father.

Guns Taken pointed the bow-lance at one of the barrels.

"We drink water before we go." He rubbed his palm across his throat. "We have a great thirst."

Casement strode forward. "That's not water. You can't—"

Guns Taken paid no attention. He climbed off his pony and started toward the wagon. Casement caught up, snagged his arm.

"Guns Taken, the answer is no."

The last word ignited the Cheyenne's temper:

"No, no!—I have heard *enough* no!"

He shoved Casement away. Dorn cursed and took a step. Three of his guards caught and held him as Hannah pleaded for him to restrain himself. Then, without warning, Guns Taken lunged and rammed the iron head of the bow-lance into a whiskey barrel.

ii

Wood cracked and split. The Cheyenne jerked the lance-head free, wonderment on his face. The odor of the pale brown liquid spurting to the ground was unmistakable.

The other Cheyenne identified it too. They began to murmur and gesticulate. One laughed.

"Goddamn you, let go!" Dorn puffed, trying to free himself. "If that red bastard steals—"

"Papa, be still!" Hannah cried.

Guns Taken drove his bow-lance into the barrel again, increasing the size of the hole.

Chortling, the fat-bellied Indian squatted and put his mouth to the spouting stream of forty-rod. Dorn broke loose.

Casement called a warning. Men tried to catch the merchant, failed. He was halfway to the crouching Indian when one of the younger Cheyenne flung himself from his horse. Michael saw metal flash.

The young warrior ran with astonishing speed. Over by the train, a Spencer came up—too slowly. Dorn fastened his hands on Guns Taken's neck. The younger Indian uttered a piercing yell and drove the blade of his trade hatchet at Dorn's forehead.

Bone cracked. Dorn shrieked and staggered, the hatchet buried in the front of his skull. Blood trickled down both sides of the blade and into his eyesockets.

iii

"*Papa!*" Hannah screamed, running to help him.

Dorn fell against the wagon, dying on his feet. The blood poured down the folds beside his nose to his white-streaked beard. The young brave turned on Hannah, ready to fight barehanded. Michael jerked his Colt level but the girl was in the way.

He dropped the revolver and flung himself between the Indian and Dorn's daughter. Casement shouted something he couldn't hear. A Spencer blasted from the roof of the office car.

Had Michael not caught Hannah's waist and dragged her down, the rifle ball would have hit her. It thwacked the wagon bed a second after Dorn's guards scattered.

Michael sprawled on top of Hannah as Guns Taken scrambled to his feet and dashed for his pony. Hannah screamed again, hysterical now.

Lying on top of her thrashing body, he heard the hammer of boots, confused yells and curses, then a second explosion. The ball plowed a furrow a foot from where he had pinned Hannah to the ground.

He twisted his head to look. Through a tangle of mounted Cheyenne, Michael glimpsed Leonidas Worthing on the sleeping car steps. The Virginian levered a spent cartridge out of the breech of his rifle. His gray duster was torn, his face marked by cuts. Behind him, two of his three guards staggered into view. Both were badly bloodied.

The guards tried to jump Worthing. He eluded their hands, leaped down from the platform, and aimed at the Indians milling around Guns Taken to protect him while he vaulted to the back of his pony.

Casement was directly in the line of fire. He flung himself to the ground. The ex-Confederate blew a Cheyenne off his horse. Blood pattered on the ground next to Michael and Hannah. The shot unleashed pandemonium.

Two rifles roared. Another Indian shrieked. Michael jumped up, retrieved his Colt. A Cheyenne was aiming an arrow at Casement, who was climbing to his feet. Michael fired.

The Cheyenne toppled sideways off his pony. Michael winced at the sight of the gaping wound in the Indian's belly.

Guns Taken kicked his pony and went racing away toward the end of the track. Here and there a Spencer banged. But Casement's judicious placement of the guns now had an unexpected consequence. Those with the weapons were so spread out, and so many men were milling everywhere, the rifles couldn't be used effectively. Drifting smoke from *Osceola* and dust raised by the Indian ponies only compounded the problem.

Virtually unmolested, the rest of the Cheyenne swung westward and galloped after their leader, who obviously knew they stood no chance, and refused to squander more lives in a futile fight.

Casement was on his feet now, wigwagging his rifle:

"Let them go. *Let them go!* Someone see to the Dutchman."

"Stand aside, you damn coward," Worthing yelled, appearing behind Casement and clubbing at him with the stock of the Spencer.

Casement dodged. Worthing bellowed, "I'll get one or two more be-fore—"

Casement beat Worthing's arm with the muzzle of his Spencer. The bloodied, demoralized men who'd permitted Worthing to escape goggled from the bunk car steps.

Casement avoided a second blow from Worthing's rifle. The dust thick-ened. The last two Cheyenne leaned down from horseback with amazing suppleness, snatched up their two dead, and went racing away toward the trackless grade.

Michael and other men were rushing to help Casement. But not quickly enough. The Virginian's third blow glanced off Casement's tem-ple and knocked him down.

Michael ran faster. Worthing saw him coming. Something uncontrolla-ble had taken possession of Worthing. The Cheyenne were out of range, but he still wanted a target. The Spencer muzzle shifted through a quar-ter of a circle, aimed at Michael.

Worthing's eyes glowed with perverse joy. Michael flung himself face forward in the dirt as the rifle thundered. The ball hit Dorn's wagon and sent splinters flying.

"Pack of cowards!" Worthing bawled. "Wouldn't have happened if you'd listened to me. You, Boyle." He peered through the dust. "You're the one responsible."

He aimed for Michael again but couldn't get a clear shot. Too many men were hurrying to Casement's aid. They pulled up short as the muzzle of Worthing's rifle menaced them. On his knees, Casement groped for Worthing's leg.

Worthing had to concentrate on the closer adversary. Again he seized the rifle by the barrel. Started to bring it down stock first on Casement's head.

Lying prone with his gun hand extended and his view all at once unim-peded, Michael yelled Worthing's name. The man in the duster didn't hear. Or if he did, he was too angry to care. He bashed Casement on the top of the head.

Casement cried out. Once again Worthing found Michael and leveled the rifle at him. *God forgive me,* Michael thought, and pulled the trigger.

The Colt boomed and bucked. Two men who had almost succeeded in reaching Casement took headers in the dirt. Michael's shot caught Worthing squarely in the chest, bulging his eyes and hurtling him backward.

Sick, Michael leaned his cheek on his forearm.

*It's the war again. In another place, another time, but it's the war all the same.*

*I was a fool to think I could ever escape.*

### iv

The railhead was in total confusion. Men were running; shouting. The one on the roof of the westernmost car fired vainly after the retreating Indians. It was too late. The last riders disappeared beyond the low hills near the river.

The sunlit air smelled of blood, powder, the excrement of dead men. Michael wobbled to his feet as a black face emerged from the drifting dust.

"Greenup? Look after General Jack."

The black and Sean Murphy reached the construction boss just as he struggled to a sitting position, blinking and coughing. A patch of lacerated scalp gleamed redder than Casement's hair.

"I—I'll be up in a moment." Casement gasped. He pushed with his hands, finally managed to stand. "How many are—hurt?"

"*Catch him!*" Greenup cried as Casement collapsed.

Sean Murphy and the black started to lift the fallen man. "Don't!" Michael warned. "Not till you see how badly he's injured."

He spun to a couple of Paddies who had crept forward to examine Worthing's corpse. One wore a torn shirt. Michael had seen him behind the Virginian on the bunk car steps. He shook the Colt in the man's face.

"How the hell did that lunatic get loose?"

"Jumped us," the man panted, wiping his nose with the torn shirt's tail. "Fought like a catamount."

"Thanks to you, he did almost as much harm as the Cheyenne."

"But we couldn't help—"

"Shut your goddamn mouth!" Michael pivoted away.

He was growing sick at his stomach. He tasted sourness in his throat. Quiet began to settle all at once. A final rifle shot crashed and echoed.

In the silence, Hannah cried out.

It wasn't a scream. It was lower; a hurt, guttural sound. He flung the revolver away, turned and saw her crouching beside her father's body.

She was trying to touch him. She rocked back and forth on her heels, her fingers an inch from the cloth-bound shaft of the hatchet. Young Klaus leaned against a wagon wheel, crying.

Michael forced himself to walk.

"Miss Dorn?"

No response.

"Miss Dorn, come away. We'll take care of him."

She raised her head and looked straight at him. He might have been transparent.

Suddenly her hand closed on the red-wrapped shaft. She wrenched the weapon out of Dorn's skull. "Jaysus, she's gone daft!" a man yelped.

Stunned workers watched Hannah clamber to her feet, a strange moaning sound coming from her clenched teeth. The hatchet dripped red onto the worn toes of her boots.

She seemed like some tortured animal, staring around the ring of astounded faces. Michael stretched out his hand.

"For God's sake, Miss Dorn, give me—"

With a wailing cry, she turned and dashed to the wagon. To the one liquor barrel left unbroken.

Both hands on the hatchet handle, she swung the weapon in a lateral arc, smashing the wood.

She struck a second time.

A third.

The staves cracked. Liquor gushed over her trousers. Still she kept swinging, trying to find something to destroy—something to blame for the corpse on the ground behind her.

Michael edged closer. "Careful, lad!" Sean Murphy called. "She may turn on you."

"We can't let her do herself harm."

He shot his hands out, seizing her wrist.

She wrenched, trying to tear free. The hatchet head grazed his left thumb, drawing blood.

God, she was strong. Strong and wild with grief.

Desperate to avoid the slashing head, he pressed her wrist with the nails of his right hand. While she shrieked at him to let go, the hatchet slipped, plopping into the slime of mud created by the spilled liquor.

He wrapped one arm around her waist and dragged her against his chest. She struggled, but he held fast.

She kept crying. The reaction to the killings struck him then. He began to shake, almost as badly as she was shaking. He fought to shut out sounds. Klaus hiccuping as he attempted to control his crying; Casement protesting feebly that he was fine.

Gradually Michael's trembling passed. He stood with both arms protectively closed around Hannah Dorn, asking himself whether the price of anything valuable—the price of Union, the price of freedom for the blacks, the price of a mile of track a day—always had to be *this*. Had to be war. A big war or a little one, with identical, inevitable endings—

Savagery. Blood. Loss. Suffering.

*She came so far,* he thought as he wrapped his arms tighter around her shuddering body. *I came far too. Neither of us found a whit of peace.*

His heart broke for her. Again this morning, the faith she professed had been made to seem worthless. He lifted a hand to stroke her hair.

It failed to calm her very much. She kept sobbing and shuddering. An anonymous voice clamored out of his memory:

*"Jaysus, she's gone daft."*

He didn't doubt that for a short time she had. What frightened him now was something far more important. After what she's seen, would she ever be rational again?

Without realizing how it had come to pass, he discovered the answer mattered.

Mattered desperately.

# CHAPTER 5

## "To Every Purpose Under Heaven"

A GRIM-FACED JACK CASEMENT sat propped in his bunk in a tiny cubicle adjoining his office. It was shortly past seven that same evening. Michael had been summoned.

Casement looked uncomfortable in his bulky nightshirt. Lengths of bandage were wrapped around his head. He directed his visitor to a stool with a quick, almost irritable gesture.

Michael sat down. Waited. A ceiling lamp illuminated half of Casement's face. He gnawed his lower lip. Changed position. Grimaced:

"Boyle, you were right."

"Concerning what, sir?"

"Humiliating the Indians. Letting the engine beat them. It was my decision, and it was a bad one. If I hadn't mishandled the situation we might have gotten them out of the camp with no casualties."

Michael shrugged in a tired way. "Why worry now, General? It's done."

"It certainly is not! I'm obliged to tell General Dodge. More important, I'll have to write a report for the directors. Frankly, I'm thinking of falsifying it. If I put the truth on paper, I'll be trumpeting to the world that the line's run into more difficulty—exactly the sort Dodge predicted. In Omaha, he told me privately we'd be lucky not to lose a man for every mile of track laid west of Kearney."

Michael said nothing. He liked the hard-driving little man too much to encourage such questionable behavior.

He wondered exactly what Casement wanted of him, then decided the construction boss would let him know when he was ready. He kept silent while Casement yanked his nightshirt over his pale knees and shoved at the bedding to raise himself.

"Don't you see, Boyle—if anything gets into print concerning what took place this afternoon, Dr. Durant, Dix, and the rest of the officers will have an even harder time attracting capital. God knows the job's difficult enough already. Now personally—" He covered his mouth, coughed. "—I don't give a damn what people say about me. My brother and I are merely contractors. We can push the line through whether we're pilloried in the press or not—"

A pause. Then a sardonic smile quirked Casement's mouth.

"No, I'm lying to you. I do care about my reputation. I've always despised being a small man. That's why I want to build part of the biggest damn construction project of this century. But it *is* the truth when I say I'm not thinking solely of myself. The more trouble reported to Wall Street and Washington, the more the line's in danger of collapsing altogether."

His eyes pinned Michael. "The next two months are crucial."

Michael felt compelled to be honest:

"I don't see how it's possible to suppress what happened today."

"It's possible for six or eight weeks. That's all I need. All the line needs —nothing in print until we pass the hundredth meridian. Of course the men will talk. They'll talk to the supply train crews. But rumors in Omaha are one thing, newspaper stories quite another. I've already taken one step to forestall problems. I've telegraphed headquarters saying I'll permit no more journalists at the railhead till we reach the meridian."

"I realize the meridian's an important goal. But what difference does it make whether the story's spread before we get there?"

"Because—" Casement hesitated. When he resumed, he sounded almost conspiratorial. "Because Dr. Durant has informed me he's planning a mammoth rail excursion."

"A what?"

"A trip out here on a special train, to celebrate the line passing the meridian. Keep that to yourself. Otherwise I'll get a second-best effort out of the lads. All they'll be thinking of is a celebration—and they'll crucify me if they learn they won't be taking part."

"Can you tell me any more about this excursion?"

Casement's sour look suggested the whole scheme was an irritant.

"Yes. Durant telegraphed the details last week. Even though the Federal acts don't require us to reach the meridian until next year, we *have* to reach it before winter. As you know, the line's charter is unofficial until we do. But that's not half so important as the cash problem. If we go one more year without a big infusion of capital, the line may wash right down the drainpipe. So the good doctor has come up with this"—an annoyed wave—"this publicity party! The purpose is to impress invited guests from New York and Chicago. A hundred of them, perhaps more. Reporters. Potential investors. Foreign nabobs. The military. Members of Congress— maybe even Andy Johnson himself. It's the same sort of holiday that Central Pacific arranged last year for Schuyler the Smiler."

"Who?"

"Schuyler Colfax, that Republican trimmer from Indiana. Speaker of the House."

"Oh, yes."

"It's evident Durant means to stage something ten times as lavish as the Central Pacific excursion. He's already purchased the Lincoln car—the armoured one built for Abe in sixty-four. Only time the poor devil traveled in it was when he went home to Springfield. Dead. Anyway, Durant's cleaning out the till to make the trip a success. My God, the man's a gambler!"

"I've heard railroad promotion requires that kind of temperament," Michael smiled.

"He has it. He's putting thousands into four new coaches being built in the Omaha shops right now. When the excursion train arrives, there'll be every kind of lawful diversion you can think of—and no doubt some unlawful ones to boot. There'll be fireworks. Lectures on phrenology. Demonstrations of horsemanship and Indian tactics by Frank North's tame Pawnee scouts. Picture takers all over the place—food catered by that high-priced Kinsley outfit in Chicago—and Rosenblatt's Band of St. Joseph and the Western Light Guard providing the music."

"Sounds like quite an investment."

"Quite a risk, you mean. I've wired Durant I won't permit the festivities to interfere with work. But I know he needs the excursion to attract cash. A press account right now, describing an Indian attack, will practically guarantee its failure."

He scrutinized Michael. "Do you understand why I'm considering a falsified report?"

"Now I do."

"I suppose I'm also fishing for advice."

"And for someone to ease your conscience by endorsing a fake story?"

"Mr. Boyle, some men would boot your ass for that remark." But he was smiling.

Michael wasn't. "I'm just trying to establish what you want of me. Is it advice on whether to lie?"

"Don't be presumptuous. Besides, there's no way to lie about two dead men. I'm talking about a—" He tilted his hand back and forth, a gesture of equivocation. "Call it a coloration of the facts. It can be done. I won't have to account to Worthing's kin. I had the employee records brought in a while ago. The departed captain listed no relatives except a distant cousin in Mississippi. The Dorn girl, though—with her father murdered, she could make trouble for us."

He scratched his nose. "Suppose I put nothing really damaging on paper. Suppose we just had a camp altercation—reported as such."

Casement studied the other man, awaiting a response. When he got none, he prodded:

"The difficulty is still the young woman. Have you seen her?"

"Yes. About half an hour ago, I called at the tent to offer my sympathies."

"Does she intend to stay here?"

"No."

"I didn't think so. When she goes home, she's liable to talk. Word could reach Omaha—"

"That's true."

"Goddamn it, Boyle, give me some facts! How *is* Miss Dorn? How's her state of mind?"

"About what you'd expect it to be. It's obvious Dorn wasn't the most admirable parent in the world. But he *was* her father."

"Is she calm?"

"Under the circumstances, I'd say she's quite calm."

"Resentful? Does she blame the railroad?"

"Not that I'm aware. She's humiliated because she fell to pieces. And of course she's hurting."

*Nor is she the only one.*

He bent forward. "General, I'd like to ask a question. May I have leave to quit the gang?"

"*Quit?* You may not! I need every man."

"I meant only for a few days. I expect the Dorns will be leaving for Grand Island as soon as possible. The boy's doing all he can to look after his sister, but he's hardly old enough to provide adequate protection on the trip. Someone should go with them. Armed."

"Someone who could urge her cooperation along the way?"

Casement's flinty stare told Michael the terms of the bargain had been proposed.

"Yes. Considering what you've said about the importance of the next six or eight weeks, it wouldn't bother my conscience to do that."

Casement scratched his beard. "How far do you propose to travel with her?"

"As far as Kearney. East of there, she and her brother should be relatively safe. Cooperation aside, General, I believe we owe Miss Dorn that protection. She's tended men who were injured."

"You don't have to remind me. She's a fine person." He pondered. "All right, you can go."

"I'll need guns. A Spencer. Several magazines of ammunition. A re volver."

"I'll sign the order tonight. Now. What does Miss Dorn propose to d with her father's remains?"

"Why, remove them to Grand Island, I suppose."

"I don't want that body seen by anyone in Grand Island. Any half-wi ted mortician who's been out here more than thirty days could guess wha sort of weapon killed Dorn." Casement's voice grew sterner; more bus nesslike. "Talk to her again this evening. Tell her the corpse will putref before she gets it to Grand Island. Tell her a burial here will be muc easier on her than riding home with a decomposing body. Since—"

Again he hitched himself higher in the bunk.

"—since I don't intend to be lying here much longer, I recommend w bury Dorn and Worthing at dawn. I'll read the service."

"All right, let me see what I can do. I wonder, though—"

"Wonder what?"

"Do you think you should be up quite so soon?"

"Tomorrow is a work day. We have Monday's track to lay—and the bal ance of Friday's. I'll be up."

Michael rose. "Very well. I'll speak to Miss Dorn immediately."

"And tactfully. Tactfully!"

"Of course."

"On your way out, fetch me a pen and some paper from the desk. I'l write your gun requisition—and begin drafting my report. A friendly visi by a few Cheyenne—"

His mouth twisted. Michael detected guilt in Casement's eyes.

"—following which, a quarrel developed amongst the men. Worthing and Dorn were the casualties. It's the eastern money I'm thinking about The meridian. The excursion—"

His eyes almost pleaded for understanding.

"Yes, sir," Michael answered, feeling weary as he stepped out of the lamplight to the adjoining office. He rummaged on Casement's littered desk.

*It's the eastern money I'm thinking about.*

*It's winning the war I'm thinking about.*

Always, the object was to win, no matter what the cost in lies, o human lives, or human misery. For him, the price was growing too high

Perhaps great enterprises automatically meant conflict. The saving of the Union, the binding together of the oceans with iron cords—perhaps each required a warlike attitude for success.

And clearly Casement wasn't entirely happy with what he had to do even though he wanted to see the line go through.

Michael understood human motives and human progress were seldom pure. Amanda Kent, whose ruthlessness had sometimes tarnished her idealism, had taught him that. So he didn't scorn Casement too much as he delivered the paper and pen before saying good night. He too believed the line should go through.

But he didn't know how much longer he could fight this different but still sanguinary war. He didn't know how much longer he could pay the personal price of constant struggle and no peace.

ii

The canvas-wrapped bodies of Gustav Dorn and Leonidas Worthing lay side by side between two shallow trenches dug near the right of way. Despite the unpopularity of both men, death demanded respect; almost the entire camp had turned out to stand silently under the vast, cloudless sky sprinkled with paling stars. A clean, sweet wind blew out of the northwest. To the east the treeless prairie was reddening.

Michael stood across the circle from Hannah Dorn. She'd proved cooperative—more accurately, indifferent—about Casement's scheme, and agreed to be evasive about her father's death when she returned to Grand Island.

She looked tired but composed. She'd put on her shapeless coat again. Her hat hung from her right hand. Her left rested on her brother's shoulder. He was trying not to cry. Hannah's eyes, a little shinier than usual, betrayed her own grief.

Casement read from Hannah's Bible. She had selected the passages.

"'To every thing there is a season, and a time to every purpose under the heaven:'"

Michael's head was bowed just far enough to permit him to watch her. His red bandana snapped in the wind. Away in the east he heard the hoot of the iron train, rolling in early. To his left, Sean Murphy scratched his armpit, then blushed when Greenup Williams and Christian, propped on a handmade crutch, both noticed.

"'A time to be born, and a time to die; a time to plant, and a time to pluck up that which is planted:'"

He believed he knew why Hannah had asked Casement to read from Ecclesiastes. After Sunday's almost senseless violence, she needed reassurance that there was a divine reason for one of those lumpy canvas sacks; a reason why a man who had tried to find a place in a new land had failed and perished.

As far as Michael was concerned, drunkenness and a vile temper were

the causes of Dorn's death. He sought no other explanation, and certainl
found no hidden purpose in the event; not even while listening to word
from the holiest of books.

"'*A time to kill, and a time to heal; a time to break down, and a time t
build up;*'"

Casement sounded uncomfortable with the sonorous language. Michae
lost track of the next few verses, pondering earlier ones.

A time to kill. A time to heal.

A time to break down. A time to build up—

From First Manassas to the Wilderness, he'd seen the killing and th
breaking down. He'd come out here not only to escape the memory o
Julia but also to have a hand in building something worthwhile. Now h
was utterly disillusioned. The price of helping to build the U-Pay wa
confronting a Leonidas Worthing. The price was more killing. The price
was another war.

Maybe that was the way of the world. The only way.

Dear Lord, what a hateful idea! He yearned to believe it wasn't true
But every scrap of evidence accumulated during the past few years said i
was.

His earlier enthusiasm about his unofficial adoption into the Kent fam
ily was gone. He had no idea as to how he'd use the money he woul
some day inherit. In fact he had no interest in it, because there was n
longer any hope of discovering personal peace, or a way to conduct his lif
that didn't involve brutal struggle.

Still, he had to do something. This battleground was surely no worse
than another he might stumble into if he were stupid enough to repeat hi
earlier mistake and again flee in the hope of finding a calm haven.

There was none.

"'—*A time to love, and a time to hate; a time of war, and a time o
peace.*'"

A lie, he thought. God have mercy on me, but that last is a lie.


iii


Casement's pause was a signal to the men he'd chosen earlier. Michael,
Artemus Corkle, Sean Murphy, and five others stepped forward. Four of
them handled each of the canvas bags. They lowered the bodies into the
trenches with great care.

Michael picked up a shovel from a pile brought to the grave site late in
the night. The whistle wailed in the east. A pillar of smoke rose on the
brilliant red horizon.

While Casement turned to the New Testament, moistening his thumb nervously on his tongue several times, Michael and the others began shoveling dirt into Dorn's trench. Casement sounded hoarse as he resumed, reading this time from one of the Gospels. St. John, Michael thought it was.

"*Jesus saith unto her, Thy brother shall rise again. Martha saith unto him, I know that he shall rise again in the resurrection at the last day.*'"

*Chunk*, a shovel of dirt landed on the sack. Michael heard a soft outburst of sobbing from Klaus Dorn and glanced up as Casement continued to read. Hannah was watching Michael with a curious expression whose meaning he couldn't interpret well.

For a few moments he didn't hear Casement's words. Hannah's look had captured him. There was pain in it. But there was doubt too.

Did she believe what Casement was quoting? Her faith was strong. Or had been. Was it still? Somehow he hated to see her tested so severely. Her faith was her whole way of life.

"*Jesus said unto her, I am the resurrection, and the life; he that believeth in me, though he were dead, yet shall he live.*

"'*And whosoever—*'"

The whistle screamed. Hannah's head turned, her eyes furious at the intrusion.

But the supply train wouldn't stop. The work wouldn't stop. Otherwise men—and women—would grieve too long. Accomplish nothing. Permit a bitter sense of futility to drain them of hope, as Michael was drained. He inverted his shovel, *chunk*, full of impotent anger all at once.

"'*—whosoever liveth,*'" Casement repeated, louder because of the whistle, "'*—and believeth in me shall never die.*'"

Slowly he closed the book.

"Amen."

Michael flung one more load of dirt into the trench. The canvas was nearly hidden. Sean Murphy leaned on his shovel handle and crossed himself. Michael found his own hand rising, making the holy sign he'd traced so infrequently since his childhood. In his heart and mind, a strange, unexpected prayer stirred.

He prayed that Hannah Dorn, a decent woman, would not grieve too long, or have her faith destroyed as his had been.

iv

When the trenches were covered, men set crude wooden crosses in place. Michael walked to Hannah and Klaus.

He waited until a small group of workers had offered their shy, clums
condolences and melted away into the larger crowd Casement was leadin
toward the train. Finally the last man, Christian, hobbled off. Michae
stood awkwardly silent, his shovel canted over his shoulder and his necker
chief fluttering in the breeze.

"What is it, Mr. Boyle?"

To his relief, she was dry-eyed; her pain was contained.

"Whenever you're ready to go—tonight, tomorrow—"

The whistle of the iron train interrupted him. Hannah spun again, sun
rise reddening her eyes. She crammed the floppy brimmed hat on her hea
and gazed with loathing at the smoke plume.

At last her features smoothed. "The sooner I'm away from this despica
ble place, the better I'll feel."

"I can't say I blame you."

"You don't like it either?"

"After yesterday? Not much. I think I told you I came out here becaus
I was sick of fighting, and all I've done is fight."

"Leave."

He sounded as he felt—despondent:

"And go where? Where will it be any different?"

She looked at him sympathetically. He was ashamed of revealing hi
weakness; his nakedness of soul. He turned away and laid the shovel on
the earth.

Thankfully, she forgot his inadvertent admission when the whistle bel
lowed again. Over its noise, her voice turned hard:

"I'll have the tent packed and the mules hitched in half an hour."

# CHAPTER 6

## The Coming of the Godless

AT TWELVE-MILE INTERVALS, special crews following the railhead had erected pine-jacketed water tanks beside the track. The sun was setting that evening when Michael, Hannah, and Klaus made camp in the shade of one such tank. It resembled a primitive wash tub on thick timber legs, and looked incongruous on the rolling prairie; an ugly intrusion of civilization.

While Michael and Klaus unfolded and raised the tent, Hannah laid a fire to heat coffee and broke out jerked beef and biscuits. Michael was using a stone to hammer a peg when he heard a creak of wheels south of the right of way. He dropped the stone and shot out his hand.

"Klaus. The rifle."

Hannah hurried to his side. "What's wrong?"

Still crouched, Michael put the Spencer beside his boot. "As yet, nothing."

A wagon drawn by mules rolled through purple shadows on the east side of a round hill. A tarpaulin had come unhitched on the rear of the wagon's bed. As the wagon creaked into the glare of sunset light, the breeze flapped the tarp and revealed slabs of black-speckled meat.

An Indian clad in a hide shirt and leggings drove the mule team. Beside the lead wheel closest to the track rode a lean white man on a wiry pony. He was in his early twenties, wearing a threadbare flannel shirt without a collar and trousers held up by suspenders. Long hair visible under his plainsman's hat shone fair in the sunset.

Michael breathed faster. The two men took note of the campers but made no sign of greeting. The white man's saddle was equipped with what looked like a handmade leather scabbard divided into two sections. The stocks of a pair of buffalo guns jutted from it. The Indian had a third rifle on the seat.

Wagon and rider soon passed close enough for Michael to note the white man's gaunt, high-cheekboned face. It was curiously familiar. He was sure he'd seen it before, but didn't know where. Maybe the man looked like a Union soldier he'd met briefly and forgotten.

The black specks proved to be flies swarming on the raw slabs of meat.

"I thought they were hunters," Michael nodded.

"Is that buffalo in the wagon?" Klaus wanted to know.

"Appears to be. Notice the bundle of hides there at the back?"

"Are they going to the railhead, Michael?" Hannah asked.

"I assume so. Probably to sell the meat."

Klaus looked disappointed. "They're not going to stop."

"Just as well," Hannah told him. "They're carrying too many guns for honest men."

Michael scratched his moustache. "Odd combination, a white and a Sioux. At least the other one's chunky enough to be a Sioux."

"Sure don't look friendly," Klaus murmured, just as the white man jerked two fingers to his hat brim to acknowledge their presence. Then he booted his mount and sped west raising dust.

The Indian whipped the mules with the reins. The wagon rapidly grew smaller. Michael still felt he'd seen the white hunter before. But he couldn't pinpoint a time or place. He relaxed and forgot about it when the travelers disappeared, leaving only a haze to mark their passage.

Presently the three sat down to eat. Michael kept the Spencer within easy reach. He'd also fetched a borrowed Colt from the wagon and buckled the holster belt around his hips.

Klaus munched a biscuit, drank some coffee, yawned, and said good night. A moment later the lantern Hannah had hung inside the tent went out.

Twilight was rapidly deepening into darkness. Hannah clasped her hands around her knees and gazed at Michael through the tatters of flame. Her strained expression finally compelled a response.

"Are you feeling any better, Miss Dorn?"

"Better than I was this morning. By the way, you're perfectly entitled to call me Hannah."

"Thank you. I've been concerned about you. You've said so little all day. I know your father's death wasn't easy to bear."

"I'll bear it. I believe the words General Casement read from St. John."

"I admire your conviction—as I think I noted when we first talked."

"Then you've no faith in life after death?"

"Let's say my view on that is more a question than an opinion."

"But you aren't without a belief in something. You *will* be going back to the line?"

"Yes. For want of anything better to do."

Hannah swept off her hat and laid it on the parched grass near the fire.

"Do you know what I was thinking about while we drove?" He shook his head. "The passage from Ecclesiastes. I believe those words too. I believe there must have been a reason for Papa's death."

Although the theological waters were growing a bit deep, Michael said, "You mean some purpose to it?"

"Exactly."

He was dubious: "What is it, then?"

"Why, I—I don't know." She glanced away. He had the feeling she knew the answer but was unwilling to reveal it. Spots of color in her cheeks reinforced the suspicion.

"Tell me, Mr. Boyle—"

"Fair's fair. If I'm to call you Hannah, you must call me Michael."

An appreciative smile. "All right, Michael." The sound of it was pleasing. "I'd like to know a bit more about you. Did you leave a family to come west?"

"Only my adopted family. The Kents. I believe I mentioned them."

"Yes. They were people you admired—"

"Some of them."

"Have you ever been married?"

The question was so matter-of-fact, he was stunned. Why the devil would a woman who'd just lost her father be interested in such a subject?

"No, never," he answered. "There is—was—a woman, but she—ah. Best we forget it. May I have more coffee?"

She poured with a steady hand. He was conscious of the intimacy of the fire, and of the handsome curve of her full bosom beneath the shabby coat that grew taut when she leaned forward.

He heard a rustle and a series of rapid thumps south of the track. Possibly one of the huge plains jackrabbits bounding by. All the red light had leached from the west. A thousand stars shone, but none quite so bright as the blue-gray eyes of the woman close to him.

*How lovely she is by firelight.*

"You seemed upset a moment ago," Hannah said as she returned the pot to the coals. "I didn't mean to intrude in a delicate area."

He waved. "No intrusion. I just prefer not to discuss the woman."

"Why?"

A sadly cynical smile. "If I told you the tedious truth, it wouldn't enhance my already low standing in your eyes."

This time her smile was disarming. "Your standing is not low at all, Michael. What is the truth?"

Lord, she had a way of digging into a man!

"I joined Meagher's Irish Brigade to escape an altogether sordid situation. If you must know, I coveted another man's wife—which I believe is definitely frowned upon by the Bible."

The coffee tasted as bitter as his mood had become. He shouldn't be revealing his past to a virtual stranger, yet he was. Perhaps he was like Casement discussing his report. Perhaps he secretly wanted a judgment about the degree of his guilt. Against all good sense, he kept on:

"The relationship was, in fact, adulterous. Which makes me a violator of more than one commandment, does it not?"

Asking for scorn, he got none:

"Christ says all men can be forgiven. Did the woman love you?"

"No."

"But you loved her."

"I wanted her. I don't know if it was the same thing as love."

"Do you think of her a great deal?"

He started to lie; changed his mind.

"All the time."

"Does she write you?"

"Never. She doesn't know where I am. Or care."

A long silence.

"When you've finished your work out here, are you going East to look for her?"

"She's still married."

"That isn't quite an answer."

*Sometimes I want to go, but—*

"The answer is no."

"So the truth is, you didn't come out here just to compensate for what you did in the war. You were running away."

"Hannah Dorn," he exclaimed with a sharpness leavened by a smile, "you can't be interested in my personal life at a time like this!"

"Oh, yes," she nodded, smiling too. One of those dazzling smiles that softened her sternness and made her look so beautiful. "Every man, every human being, has something of interest to tell. But I'm sorry if my questions offended you."

He stretched out, leaning on his elbow. "Not at all. It's just that my story's—well—it's entirely in the past."

"What about your future?"

"Beyond the railroad, I have none. Time we changed the subject. Will you and Klaus be staying in Grand Island?"

"Yes. I'll take over the store and run it as best I can. The store is part of the reason I was thinking so hard on Ecclesiastes all afternoon. Perhaps God meant Papa to die so I could do something about the chaos he made of the business."

He would have laughed, except that you didn't laugh at someone bereaved and groping for answers. Softly, she continued:

"Perhaps I can turn it into a profitable enterprise, then do something for Klaus. Papa never permitted Klaus to think about attending a college. Papa didn't consider education worthwhile. I do. If the store succeeds, I might be able to send Klaus East for a year or two—"

Another smile. "You've maneuvered me into talking about myself."

"I'm interested in your plans," he said, meaning it. "Maybe the terrible business yesterday will mean the start of better times for you and your brother."

"In certain circumstances, that's entirely possible."

She was staring at him again. He couldn't understand why she acted embarrassed.

Abruptly she scrambled up, snatched her hat, and walked toward the tent. Her cheeks were pink again. But her voice held no trace of emotion:

"I'd like to rest now. Will you be comfortable out here?"

"Quite comfortable."

"Good night, then."

"Good night, Hannah."

The tent flap fell. He was unexpectedly depressed not to have her still with him, sharing the fire's warmth; sharing deep feelings it was a relief to speak aloud at last.

## ii

Quickly, though, puzzling questions intruded. Why in the world did she want to know about his past and his future? And why had she suddenly grown so nervous about the drift of the conversation?

He had no idea. But he was positive she'd been probing his background for a reason.

He left the Spencer near the fire and walked to the wagon a few yards from the tank. Starlight glinted on the rails. Somewhere a wild bird warbled. The tethered mules twitched their ears and snorted as he approached.

The liquor barrels, two sound and two broken, had been stripped from the wagon and left behind. He reached over the tailboard and found the small canvas bag in which he'd packed a fresh shirt, his razor, his churchwarden, and tobacco. He lit the pipe and strolled in a wide circle so Hannah wouldn't catch a whiff of the immoral smoke. As he puffed, a frown deepened on his forehead.

*Blast it, that woman wants something of me. What is it?*

*And why the devil do I care all at once?*

He could find no adequate answer for either question, even though he asked them endlessly as he sat on guard beside the fire all night long.

### iii

They started east at sunup. Michael tied his red bandana around his forehead because it promised to be a hot day. About eight, they spied a peculiar caravan coming toward them. Two open phaetons, dilapidated but serviceable, following the track.

The first carriage was piled high with portmanteaus, crates, and what appeared to be folded canvas. The driver, a bearded, vacant-eyed young man, had a buck-and-ball shotgun resting across his lap.

In charge of the second phaeton was a man of quite a different sort. About forty; heavy-set; red-faced. Points of a scraggly moustache hung below his jaw. He wore one of the short untapered sack coats that had been introduced about ten years earlier but were still considered cheap and ostentatious in some circles. The color of the one-button coat matched that of the thin brown lines forming large checks on the man's gray trousers.

A black silk cravat spilled over the top of his red velvet waistcoat. His hat, cocked at a jaunty angle, was hard brown felt with a red band and a crown shaped like half a melon. An English hat. Michael didn't know the correct name. It was sometimes called a bowler, after the hatter who'd designed it, or a derby, after the earl who'd adopted it and given it social approval. He'd seen many of the hats back east.

While the first phaeton continued on, the flashy gentleman reined in his plodding team. Beside him, a pale, coarsely attractive girl fanned herself with a lace handkerchief.

The girl was barely Klaus' age, but she was dressed as if she were twice that. Her wrinkled bloomer frock was orange-dyed organdy. Matching Turkish pantaloons showed beneath the short skirt. A black velveteen bodice, tight on her large breasts, had been repaired several times. The ribbons dangling from her wide-brimmed straw hat were frayed at the ends.

In the second seat, also facing forward, sat two other women, thirty or thirty-five. One had a faint moustache and a heavy scattering of pockmarks on her cheeks. All three females looked uncomfortable in their heavy, gaudy clothing.

The fellow in the melon hat smiled. But his dark eyes had the warmth of lumps of unlit coal. Again Michael had encountered someone he thought he'd seen before, and again he couldn't recall where.

"Good morning, friends," the man said. "Brown's the name."

The man swept off his hat and tipped it. Before he set it back on his hairless head, Michael saw a bruise and a diagonal white scar on the sunburnt scalp. Recognition came instantly.

"Could I trouble you to tell us whether it's far to the railhead?" Brown asked.

"No, it isn't." Michael was conscious of Hannah sitting stiffly beside him. Brown's three traveling companions surveyed her clothing and unpainted face with amused looks. Back in the bed of the wagon, Klaus was goggling.

"You'll make it before dark," Michael added.

"Thanks kindly. We're anxious to get there and set up."

"And get these goddamn hot clothes off," the young girl said. Brown's glance made her cringe.

The pockmarked woman laughed. "Nancy's always eager to go to work."

Hannah clenched her hands in her lap. Brown turned, his smile fixed but his eyes furious.

"Alice, be so kind as to keep your language decent."

The woman looked as terrified as the girl. She swallowed and lowered her eyes as Brown said to Hannah:

"Very sorry for the impropriety, ma'am." To Michael: "I'm positive we've run into each other before."

"We have."

"Where?"

"A card palace in Omaha. You won a big pot and were in a generous mood. You bought everyone at the bar a stein of lager."

Brown snapped his fingers. "That's it. You were standing right next to me. Going out to work on the line."

"Correct."

Brown's smile changed again, growing unctuous. "Still there?"

"I'll be returning in a day or two."

"Then perhaps we'll have the pleasure of renewing acquaintances. When we do, I'd appreciate a favor."

"Such as?"

"Such as your confining your remarks about our first meeting to what we just discussed. My winning that pot. Buying a round. Forget the rest."

He spoke in a casual tone. No one would have construed his remarks as a threat—unless they'd seen his eyes.

Michael shrugged in a noncommittal way. Brown looked less than pleased.

By now the young girl was paying attention to the Irishman. He was mortified when she smiled and let her gaze range up his legs to his groin. Then she looked him in the eye and slowly licked her painted lower lip. He could feel Hannah's shoulder tremble with tension.

"Safe journey to you," Brown said. "*Hah!*" He flicked the reins to start the team.

iv

Turning, Hannah watched the phaetons bounce along westward. When she spoke, her voice seethed:

"I knew Papa would only be the first."

Michael shrugged again. "With a project as big as the railroad, you must expect enterprise of all sorts."

"*Enterprise!* Godless people, that's what they are. That Brown looks absolutely vicious."

"He is."

"He hinted about something that happened in Omaha—"

"He has quite a reputation there. The night we met, he proved he deserves it."

"Is he a sharp?"

"What's a sharp, Hannah?" Klaus asked.

"A gambler."

"Among other things," Michael nodded. "He was referring to an incident that took place shortly after he stood everyone to drinks. He was caught cheating at stud poker."

"Who caught him?"

"A poor fat fellow from the U-Pay roundhouse. Brown had bilked him before. He was watching for hidden cards; he claimed he saw them. With some friends urging him on, he swung a punch. Brown charged around the table bellowing about his honor. He half killed the U-Pay lad with his head."

"His *head?*"

"Didn't you see the scar and the bruise when he took off his hat? The barkeep called him Butt Brown. Butt, two t's. Apparently he can well nigh destroy a man with his fists and his skull. The U-Pay chap lasted half a minute. Brown would have left him dead or crippled if others hadn't intervened. Before I left Omaha, I heard Brown has killed at least four men."

Hannah shuddered. "Filth. And Papa wanted to mix with them. Do business just as they do—" Klaus was tugging at her arm. "What is it?"

"Who were those women? Do they work for the railroad?"

Michael wanted to laugh but felt it wiser to refrain. "My boy, they certainly do. At least that's their intention. In polite company, Mr. Brown's damsels are known as soiled doves."

"If you please, Mr. Boyle! He's not old enough."

"Not *old* enough? I disagree! If he goes East to school, or even if he remains in Grand Island, I'm sure he'll see more and more of such women. You'll have to explain eventually."

"Explain what?" Klaus insisted.

"He said eventually!" Hannah snapped.

"Mr. Boyle?"

"No, Klaus. I bow to your sister."

"Thank you." She was still simmering. Klaus sighed and crawled to the rear of the wagon.

Michael picked up the reins and set the wagon in motion. "For weeks we've been hearing there would be sharps and whor—uh, persons of questionable moral character coming out to set up tents and travel with us."

"And you'll soon be back among that kind!"

The rancor in her voice made him caustic:

"I take it you disapprove of card playing along with tobacco?"

"I do."

Irked, Michael craned his head to make certain Klaus was occupied. The boy was glumly staring at the dust cloud left by the phaetons.

"Tell me, Miss Dorn. Do you also disapprove of what's discreetly referred to as congress between men and women?"

She whirled on him. "Are you trying to make me out a prude, Mr. Boyle?"

"Inquiring! Merely inquiring!"

"Evidently you think I'm a prude because I believe in the Bible?"

"Some say the two go hand in hand."

She stared straight ahead again. "I admit I despise women of the kind that aroused such curiosity on your part."

"*Curiosity?* Dammit, I was only being polite!"

"That young slu—young woman had something on her mind besides social intercourse."

"What the hell is this? Why do I have to answer to you?"

"You don't. But you're too fine a man to squander your life among—" She bit her lip. "I've said too much. I'm sorry."

He let out a long breath. "The fault's mine. I had no right to mock your beliefs."

"I shouldn't have expressed them so tactlessly. I know the Lord said to forgive women like that. I try—but I hate the way they cheapen one of God's finest gifts! Sell it, like a measure of flour—"

He was still sufficiently piqued to say, "This fine gift you mention—you speak of it only in the abstract, I suppose?"

A quick look over her shoulder; Klaus was paying no attention.

"If you mean have I slept with a man, I have not. But I talked at length with Mama on the subject. Crude as Papa was, she said he still brought her a great deal of—Boyle, you're blushing! Who's the prude?"

A smile softened the retort and broke the tension. He laughed, then raised a hand.

"Guilty. You took me by surprise. You take me by surprise quite often."

"That," she declared, "is because people are not books containing just a single page to be understood in one quick reading."

He chuckled. "No, I'm certainly discovering that's true of you."

"You might think me disinterested in—the topic you brought up. On the contrary, I'm not. At the proper time, in the proper place, my husband won't find me wanting. He'll find me inexperienced. But—not without ardor. Not without—oh, *fiddle!*" she cried, utterly flustered.

The exclamation caught Klaus' attention. "Hannah, I never heard you cuss before."

"I was not cursing!"

"But you came close." He was grinning.

"*You be still!*" A whisper. "We mustn't discuss it any further."

"All right," he agreed, even though he thought turn-about only fair play. Last evening she'd asked a good many personal questions, for a reason he was just beginning to guess—with considerable discomfort.

*Or am I a conceited oaf? Flattering myself?*

He thought it wise to try to lighten the conversation. He rolled the tip of his tongue in his cheek. "Actually, you need have no fear about my virtue when I go back to work. I don't patronize women such as Mr. Brown employs. Nor am I particularly fond of gambling. In fact I have no intention of honoring Brown's request. I'll warn my friends about him. No sense in them squandering their wages and betting against a man who wins nine times out of ten. I watched him that night. He lost on an average of once every twenty minutes. For the sake of effect, I don't doubt."

"You see? That only proves the railhead's an ungodly place and will obviously grow worse. There are better and safer places a man could spend his time."

"What places?"

She didn't answer.

"What places, Hannah?"

"If it isn't clear to you by now—"

Her lips pressed together. "Never mind."

Angry at herself, or him—or both—she pointed east.

"Drive faster."

He did. His wild suspicions hadn't been so wild after all.

At first he was astonished. Then he was touched. But that mood quickly vanished. He knew how a forest animal must feel coming across a hunter's iron trap directly in its path.

He'd have gotten angry all over again if what she wanted hadn't been so upsetting.

# CHAPTER 7

## *The Vow*

NEXT MORNING HANNAH left Klaus asleep and came down from the campsite on the edge of Kearney to see him aboard the westbound supply train.

Full daylight was still a good half-hour away. Only two lamps glowed in the improvised huts and unpainted plank buildings that straggled along the north side of the river opposite the old infantry stockade.

The air was chilly. Pungent wood smoke drifted back from the locomotive as Michael approached a stake-sided flatcar loaded with rails tied down with heavy rope. There were four such cars between the tender and two boxcars at the end of the train.

He'd spent the night outside the tent again, wrestling with cold blankets and sleeplessness. He felt edgy and tired as he laid the Spencer and canvas pouch on the stacked rails. When he turned back, Hannah took him by surprise. She leaned forward and gave his cheek a quick, chaste kiss.

He was speechless for several moments. Then all he could do was blurt, "Why—thank you, Hannah Dorn."

She ignored the forced levity in his voice. "You've been very kind, Michael. Despite all you say about being irreligious, you're a good and compassionate man. I apologize for my temper when we met that Mr. Brown. You're not like him. It was shameful of me to imply that you are."

"I appreciate the compliment, but it isn't necessary."

"It is. I don't want you believing I'm nothing but a prude."

He caught her nervous hands between his palms. "Believe me, Hannah, no one faults you for your principles, least of all me. God—uh, heaven knows I could use some of my own."

She glanced toward the locomotive. Sparks rose and vanished above the stack. "I hardly slept last night." She covered her eyes. "Oh, I'm such a clumsy, graceless person. I don't know how to do this."

"Do what?"

"Tell you—" He felt her hands tighten within his. "You'll laugh."

"No."

Her eyes caught starlight. "Last night, I—I prayed for hours. There *is* a purpose for everything. Even for Papa being struck down as he was— Michael," she interrupted herself, "where will you go when construction's shut down?"

"I suppose I'll stay at the winter camp, wherever that may be."

"Stay with all those sinful people?"

"What else should I do?"

In a quick burst of breath, she said, "Come back to Grand Island. I can make the store succeed if I have a man to help me. I told you I prayed. I repeated the words from Ecclesiastes over and over."

Her speech grew less breathy; became soft and direct:

"I know now Papa's death came so there'd be room for another man. You were meant to take his place."

Once again he couldn't speak. He was shaken to the center of his being. He'd already concluded this might be the reason behind yesterday's questioning—not to mention her flirtation with the subject of sex.

He tried to pierce her air of certainty with another little laugh.

"Miss Dorn, permit me to say with all politeness, you're touched in the head."

"No, I'm not. You're a man looking for a place, Michael Boyle. God has revealed it."

Hostile all at once because he felt threatened by her confidence, he exclaimed, "Not to me! My place is up the line, pushing those rails to the meridian. Do you realize I'm thirty-six years old? Before I'm too blasted feeble to do anything but sit in a chair and look back at all my mistakes—all the years I spent taking human life—I want once—*once!*—to know I've done something worthwhile. *Something!*"

"Do it, then. But start back before the snows are too deep for travel."

"You're the damnedest woman I ever met!"

"I would appreciate your not cursing. This is too serious."

The whistle tooted. One of the train's two brakemen waved his lantern from beside the last car.

"Come back and help me build a good store. Then another. Those godless people will keep moving west, chasing the easy money. The territory will soon be ready for civilized things. Where we live, we'll help build a town. A fine, decent one."

An impulse to say yes swept over him. He fought it.

"No, Hannah."

"Why not?"

"I can't, that's all."

"*Why not?* Am I unattractive?"

"You're very attractive. But—"

He was unable to finish. Honesty would only hurt her.

But she'd been hurt already. A tear sparkled on her face. Angrily, she wiped it away.

"You don't think you could ever love me? I don't expect you to love me now, Michael."

"Hannah, stop!"

"You love that other woman."

"No," he lied. "But I like you too much to pretend I feel anything more."

"Love will come. Give it a chance. Give *me* a chance."

She flung an arm around his neck and kissed him on the mouth with unmistakable passion. He felt the sweet curve of her breasts against his body, then her tears on his face.

With her mouth still close to his, she whispered, "I've love enough for both of us. Come back."

"And if it didn't work, and I left again? I'd hurt you worse than I'm doing right now."

"I'll accept the risk."

He shook his head. "I would never subject you to that kind of uncertainty, that kind of—"

The whistle howled.

He seized two of the stakes and hauled himself up to the rails. The train lurched forward.

The trucks began to click slowly. Spark-filled smoke gusted around him. Through it, he heard her call, "Before the snow!"

The smoke cleared. As the last car passed she stepped to the center of the track and waved.

*Damn!* He didn't love her. Better to hurt her again, this moment, than subject her to prolonged pain. He shook his head in an exaggerated way. She couldn't mistake the finality of it. Yet her head remained unbowed and she blew him a kiss, as if she were supremely confident.

ii

He sat down on the stacked rails and watched her figure shrink in the starry dawn. Soon she was a speck against the widening band of red-gold on the eastern horizon. Then she was gone.

He tried to excuse himself for hurting her by summoning anger.

*"I'll be damned and double-damned. That queer, Bible-reading girl did bait a trap as if I were some woods animal!"*

The anger didn't help. He almost wished he could have jumped right between the trap's jaws. She was a fine, handsome woman. But he didn't love her enough.

*Love?*

To the best of his recollection, it was the very first time he'd thought the word in connection with his unexpected fondness for her. He *had* lost his heart just a little, without realizing it. But what he felt for her wasn't enough to make him change his mind about returning to the railhead.

The iron train gathered speed on the Nebraska plain. Far to his right, a herd of shaggy buffalo swept down from a ridge, trampling the earth loudly enough to be heard above the train's roar. Flickering light from the firebox reddened his cheeks as he stood up and faced west, one hand on a stake, his feet braced wide apart. The change of position didn't help clear his mind of the confusion.

*That woman is mad!*

*No, in her own way, that woman is as strong as Amanda Kent.*

*Handsome, too.*

*And not nearly so pious as she pretends.* He well remembered the fervent feel of her mouth.

He tried contempt.

*Outrageous, the way she picked a husband! "God's made a place!" Fancy such nerve!*

*She wouldn't say it's nerve, she'd say it's faith.*

*And would it be so bad a place?*

*I cannot go there under false colors!* About that, he was adamant.

Yet he was beginning to loathe himself for having hurt her so badly.

The buffalo veered off and vanished in the north. The train swayed. He gripped the stake tightly to keep from being hurled off.

The points of his moustache and the ends of his bandana flicked against his face. He peered through the smoke and specks of soot but never saw the vast prairie rushing by.

*That's all I do, hurt or kill others.*

*That is all I ever do.*

iii

Some eight miles further down the track, with the sun clear of the horizon, he was startled from his bleak reverie by a series of piercing blasts from the whistle. He recognized the signal; the train was stopping.

On the roof of the last boxcar, the brakeman who'd been sitting with his legs dangling over the side struggled to turn the horizontal wheel. Its vertical rod applied pressure to the primitive brakes.

Iron squealed back there, then up front, where the other brakie worked the wheel on the first flatcar. He leaped to the second car as the couplers crashed and the cars began to shunt against one another, slowing down with the kind of erratic jerking that frequently caused a break-in-two on a downgrade.

The front brakie pointed to the south. Michael clambered to the top of the rails as the train came to a standstill. Near the river turkey buzzards wheeled and darted at the ground.

A queasy feeling fluttered his stomach. Where the carrion birds swooped, patches of buffalo grass shone bright red.

iv

He jumped down from the flatcar, his Spencer cocked. The fireman had another, the engineer a third. The two brakies—boys working their way up from yard switchman to engineer—were unarmed. They followed the older men, looking as bilious as Michael felt. Suddenly he smelled the blood stench.

"Appears to be a body lyin' out there," the fireman said, swallowing. The men started running. The noise sent the buzzards flapping away.

Michael's mouth was dry as he began to glimpse white and red lumps strewn along the bank. "More than one body."

"No horses—" the engineer muttered.

"And they'd have been on the other side of the river if they was travelin' in a settler's wagon," the engineer put in. "Buffla hunters, mebbe? Chasing that herd we seen?"

They were a quarter mile south of the track now. Michael nearly stumbled on a foot-wide rock all but concealed in the waving grass. He glanced down.

"Oh, Mother of God."

On the rock lay an ear cut from a human head. Blood was drying brown in the breeze. Beside the ear rested an eyeball, a crushed white globe with a dark spot—the pupil—turned up to the light.

One of the brakies turned around and staggered back toward the tracks, coughing up vomit and slopping his trousers.

They found the remains of what they calculated to be four men. At first Michael thought two of the victims might be the pair he'd seen at the water tank the preceding evening. Then he knew he was wrong. None of the flesh was brown. And he spied no wagon tracks.

There was little doubt the men were hunters, though. Scraps of deer-skin shirts and pants were scattered everywhere. Not one body was whole.

A mutilated head rested against another stone. The ears were gone, and the nose. The point of the chin had been worked off with a knife or hatchet. The hair had been lifted, and a pit opened in the top of the skull so the brain—or part of it, slimy gray and fly covered now—could be removed and placed beside it. Michael could barely stand to look.

"Injuns?" the fireman asked.

"Yeah," the engineer said. "It's the way they work when their tempers are up. I seen something similar once before."

Wherever Michael stepped, he found more evidence of the massacre. Amputated feet. Arms chopped at the shoulders. Entrails twining through the grass like lifeless red snakes. Mutilated genitals had been placed on what remained of a torso. One head covered with gashes still had part of an arrow jutting from the mouth. The arrowhead had been driven up behind the upper teeth and the shaft broken at midpoint.

Tears in his eyes, Michael finally lurched away from the carnage. He was trembling.

Who had done it? Guns Taken and his Cheyenne? It made little difference. The remains were mute proof of the savage level to which the coming of the railroad had raised the war between the whites and the Plains tribes.

A conference was held, well away from the site of the massacre. The engineer would report to Casement, and ask for a work crew to come back, pick up the remains, and search for identification. "We stay here any longer, we'll be late to the railhead," the engineer said. It was an excuse, but Michael was thankful for it.

Soon the train was headed west again. The memory of what he'd seen beat at Michael's mind. The trembling returned. He was almost pitched off the flatcar before he closed both hands on one of the stakes. Jumbled images spun past his inner eye.

The trees of the Wilderness bursting afire.

A splendid green banner tumbling toward summer grass, its wounded bearer trying to hold it aloft, failing, and weeping as he stained the silken sunburst with his blood.

Pickett's line, human wheat scythed down slowly in the powder haze of a steamy July afternoon.

Worthing's face when Michael's bullet hit him.

The dismembered bodies of men who must have known fear, love, hope, laughter, and who had found death by following the twin tracks of what purported to be civilization—

Clutching at the stake, Michael cried, "Enough!" Cannon thundered in his brain. All the hurt men of the endless wars seemed to wail in chorus. *"Enough!"*

The rear brakeman shouted something he didn't hear. Slowly, he gained control of himself. He wiped his tear-tracked face with the back of a hand.

It wasn't sufficient for a man to cry out against the struggles that rent the land. A man had to do something more than curse bloodletting when he too was responsible for it—

A man had to do something to defy and defeat what he detested. Amanda Kent had taught him that long ago. He remembered the family motto. Take a stand. Make a mark.

Seated again, he gazed at the sky.

*If you're there, listen to me.*

*Never again will I knowingly hurt another person the way I hurt Hannah Dorn.*

*Never again while I breathe will I lift my hand against another human being, no matter what the provocation.*

*Never.*

v

At the railhead, Adolphus Brown was supervising the raising of a large tent. The girls were already inside, setting up cots, hanging canvas partitions, and uncrating whiskey bottles. Brown's half-witted young helper, Toby Harkness, swung a sledge to peg the last guy rope.

Although it was barely daylight, the feisty little construction boss, Casement, had already called on Brown to inform him his presence would be tolerated because Casement realized the men required certain diversions. But Brown was under orders not to open for business until the end of the work day. Something else was on Brown's mind at the moment, though.

Toby leaned on the sledge, grinning. "All done. Butt? I said all done."

"Oh. Good. Now hang up the sign the way I showed you."

"Boss, what's chewing on you this morning?"

Brown fanned himself with his hard felt hat. *Going to be a sonofabitching hot day.*

"Boss?"

"That Paddy we encountered driving out here."

Toby scratched his beard. "Hell, he seemed pretty harmless."

"Depends. He knows me from Omaha. Some of the others here might also. They could talk. Discourage trade."

"We got the place to ourselves!"

"Not for long. I know of three gents who'll be arriving with their outfits inside of a week. In a month, there'll be a small city of tents following the line. We could end up sucking the hind tit."

"Because some mick shoots off his mouth? If any of them do that, I'll talk to 'em. They don't listen—" Toby caressed the handle of the sledge. "I'll talk a little louder."

Adolphus Brown felt a burden lift. He clapped his derby on his scarred head and laid an arm across the younger man's shoulder. "Toby my boy, you know what I'm thinking almost before I think it. That's why I admire you."

Toby smiled in a way Brown found hilarious. The lout had all the brains of a sparrow. Brown managed to keep a straight face as Toby declared:

"Nobody ever admired me before I met up with you."

"That was their mistake."

"I promise you, Butt. Those micks get in our way, I'll fix 'em."

"And do a splendid job, too," Brown grinned as they strolled toward the tent entrance. Inside, Nancy and Alice were bickering like ruffled hens. He must keep his patience. By sundown he'd have them on their backs, with their attention focused on the only spot where a woman's attention belonged.

"Yes, sir, a splendid job. I can count on that as surely as I can count on a winner when I need one."

He jutted his hand toward Toby's face. The sleeve garter and attached elastic worked perfectly, popping the spade ace into his fingers as if it had materialized from the air.

Toby giggled like a child, grimy fingers over his mouth. "Lordy, Butt." He giggled again. "Not out here where everybody can see."

Brown pointed toward the dining car. "Everybody's in there, stuffing. Getting ready to bust their asses and lay a mile of track quick, so they can pay us a visit. You get busy with that sign."

"Yes, sir," Toby said in an almost worshipful way.

Brown hid the card in a slit in his red velvet waistcoat and entered the tent whistling. Toby was a crackerjack. Stupid but a crackerjack. Any Irishman who flapped his mouth about Omaha would regret it.

# CHAPTER 8

## *Meridian 100*

"*DOWN!*"

On Michael's signal, the five men lowered the rail. About two and a half feet of it projected beyond a splintered board stuck in the earth beside the right of way. Faded white numerals were painted on the board:

247

The moment the rail touched the ground, Sean Murphy whirled to the crew on the other side of the grade. "Beat you!" Disgruntled, they placed their rail as Murphy wigwagged his arms and bellowed in the direction of the perpetual train:

"It's done! We're past!"

Voice after voice took up the shout. A mass insanity seemed to seize the hundreds of men strung out at the railhead this crisp afternoon, the fifth of October.

Christian, fully recovered, put his hands on his waist, bent backwards, shut his eyes and wailed, "Whooo-*aaaah!*" Artemus Corkle—permanently on the crew now; Michael had replaced the complaining O'Dey—ran down from the right of way, performed two quick somersaults, then raised himself on his palms and proceeded to walk with his legs in the air, bleating like a calf.

"*WHOOO-AAAAAAAH!*" Christian howled again. Jostled by screaming men, Michael accepted a maul from one of them.

"Take a lick, Boyle. Someday you'll want to show this place to your grandchildren."

With a melancholy smile, Michael hammered the spike twice. He passed the maul to Murphy, who was laughing and crying at the same time.

The shouting intensified, spreading eastward, picked up by hundreds of throats. The engineer of the locomotive behind the perpetual train doubled the noise by blowing the whistle and ringing the bell.

In five minutes, all work had come to a stop. Greenup Williams snagged Michael's waist and hand, danced him around in a circle, then cupped his mouth and yelled at the western horizon:

"We done it, Charlie Crocker! You listenin'? Meridian one hundred! We'll be all the way across the plains while you're still sitting on your behind in those mountains!"

Guards atop the cars of the work train fired their Spencers at the sky. North of the train, men and a few women poured from a disorderly collection of tents, the ever-growing movable town that packed itself into wagons and buggies every day or so, following the railhead. Someone had christened the tent village Hell-on-wheels. It was appropriate, Michael thought. All sorts of riffraff had been attracted to it, exactly as Hannah had prophesied. Sean Murphy was fond of telling the more recent additions to the work force, "The place is fast becoming civilized, several men having been killed here already."

Michael had already had a run-in with one of the tent town's citizens—Harkness, the dull-witted young man, who worked for Butt Brown.

Harkness had caught Michael alone one September evening when he was returning from a chat with the drovers. He demanded Michael stop talking to new workers about Brown's curious habit of winning against all opponents.

Patiently Michael explained that he never sought opportunities to discuss Mr. Brown. Though he didn't admit it, the fact was he'd only volunteered information to a few close friends. The rest of the time he merely answered newcomers' questions honestly. He put Harkness on notice that he'd continue to do so.

Evidently trade at Brown's Paradise was already suffering because Harkness replied with threatening language. He emphasized his warning by repeatedly jabbing a finger into Michael's chest.

Michael's temper flared. But he suffered the rest of the tirade, and a few more jabs, without resorting to his fists. He meant to keep the pledge he'd made on the car from Kearney.

Toby Harkness departed with a smirk on his face, apparently convinced he'd been dealing with a coward. Michael had already accepted the fact that such opinions would be the price of fulfilling his vow—

Now Michael watched Butt Brown slip a pepperbox derringer from his waistcoat and begin shooting over his head. Further up the dirt street between the tents and the train, he suddenly spied the white buffalo hunter and his Sioux companion.

In August, the two had already been gone by the time he returned to the railhead. Now they were back, strolling and enjoying the celebration. The white man waved his plainsman's hat once or twice, and tipped it to a soiled dove in front of Brown's Paradise. Even at a distance, a white streak in the hunter's fair hair stood out clearly.

Michael assumed the pair had brought in another load of buffalo meat. He was still convinced he'd met the white man during the war. He made up his mind to inquire.

A troop of the cavalry now guarding the workers on a full time basis galloped by, the men no more than blurs in their dark blue blouses and light blue, yellow-striped trousers. Sabers swinging in crazy arcs, they went pounding west, screaming as enthusiastically as the Paddies. Their bugler blew the charge.

*Meridian one hundred.*

It was a goal every man had concentrated on for months. With the goal reached, Michael had to confront the reality of the next phase of his life: more grueling, lonely work of the same kind. He didn't like the prospect very much.

He did feel a sense of pride in having helped push the line this far. As of today, the Union Pacific's charter was official. The eastern skeptics would be silenced, and perhaps the line would begin to attract the investors it needed. Within ten days to two weeks, Dr. Durant's much publicized Great Pacific Railway Excursion train would be chugging out of Omaha bearing its select group of government dignitaries, military officers, and potential stockholders. Jack Casement was undoubtedly already sending a telegraph message to Durant, informing him of the day's accomplishment.

Meridan one hundred. He was proud of having been part of the effort.

Yet something was lacking. He felt disconnected from the revelry, and unenthusiastic about the work ahead. The unease wasn't new. It had been with him ever since the trip to Kearney. He'd grown moody and uncommunicative. Sean Murphy had commented on it several times.

A man came charging from the office car, repeating his news as he ran: "No more work! General Jack says we can take the rest of the day an' have a good time!"

More cheering. Michael started for his quarters, his face composed but not his spirit.

Men waved and screamed with renewed fervor when Casement appeared on the steps of the office car, a jubilant smile on his face. The rifle fire grew almost continuous, the roar of the Spencers proclaiming the victory and challenging anyone within earshot—God Himself, up in the hazy autumn sky—to accomplish something more wondrous.

It *was* a triumph, and Michael knew it. Why, then, did he feel so remote from it?

Because he constantly remembered the price paid in blood to achieve it?

Remembered the dead men, including the four butchered hunters who had never been identified?

Or was it because, of late, he found Julia Kent's face frequently and disturbingly replaced in his thoughts by that of Hannah Dorn?

ii

After supper he walked from the dining car to the row of lamplit tents where rowdy men were already plumping down their wages for overpriced whiskey, a chance to beat a professional at three-card monte, or a quarter hour with one of the fourteen or fifteen soiled doves inhabiting the portable town.

He passed Brown's Paradise. A reveler staggered out. Before the tent flap fell, Michael was gratified to see no other patrons inside. He had nothing personal against Brown. But he figured the new men arriving every day or so should understand the risks of visiting the establishment.

At the rear of the narrow lane between Levi's Bird Cage Saloon and Tidwell's, his destination, he spied a wagon parked in the semidarkness. A tarp-covered wagon, with a black-haired man rolled in a blanket on the hard ground beneath.

He recognized the white hunter's Sioux partner. The Indian cradled a rifle close to his chest while he dozed.

Inside Tidwell's, the only railhead establishment selling general merchandise, a cheerful, overweight man slapped his hands on the plank counter.

"How do you do, sir. Bucyrus Tidwell's the name." He rolled a gold-plated toothpick from one side of his mouth to the other. "Help you find something?"

Michael surveyed the hand-labeled jars, bottles, and boxes on makeshift shelves. Everything from calomel to cartridges. He tugged his churchwarden out of his hip pocket.

"I need some tobacco."

Tidwell hefted an amber jar and carried it toward the balances. "Got some choice Virginia. Six bits." His smile widened. "Per ounce."

"Per *ounce?* You're joking."

Less cordially, Tidwell said, "I know my own prices."

Michael was observing the sums chalked on the jars and boxes. He'd never been in Tidwell's before. Disgusted, he said:

"And you haven't set a fair one on anything. Your profit looks to be three or four hundred percent."

Tidwell shrugged. "Costs a lot to have freight forwarded here."

"Not that much."

"There also ain't no comparable store between here and Kearney." Tidwell's smile returned, an arrogant half-moon. "You want to walk there for tobacco, feel free."

"Damn gouger," Michael growled, pivoting away. "I'll go without."

"Do that, you cheapskate Papist!"

Michael broke stride, fought his anger, then walked on. He batted the tent flap aside with a savage slap.

### iii

Jeremiah Kent lay on a blanket-covered cot located in a second, smaller tent directly behind Brown's Paradise. He'd discarded his clothes on the dirt floor, anxious to satisfy himself with Nancy. Now that they'd finished a romp, he was content to relax a bit, taking pleasure in his own nakedness—he'd bought a bath at The Tonsorial—and in hers as she lay straddling him. He barely felt her weight.

A lamp, trimmed low, rested on a crate in the corner. Hanging canvas separated the crowded nook from two similar ones in the tent. Beyond the canvas to his left, one of the other whores was puffing and moaning while her customer growled a continuous stream of profanity. Peculiar way to enjoy a woman, Jeremiah thought.

Nancy tightened her spread legs against his. Where the roughness of her hair brushed him, he felt himself stir. Languorously, he fondled the globular breasts bobbling above her chest. His thumbs worked slowly on the brown tips. She had her palms braced on the cot so he could touch her that way.

"Honestly didn't think you'd come back, Joe—"

"I like my full name better, hon. Joseph."

"All right, Mister Joseph," she laughed, moving one hand to stroke his cooling forehead and the white-streaked hair above.

"First time I called on you in August, I told you I'd be back."

"Is it me you like, or just any ol' gal?"

He lifted his head to buss her lips. "You."

A shudder rippled down her back. She squeezed him harder with her thighs. Then she rested her head on his shoulder.

"I'm glad that friend of yours didn't come in with you. Butt won't let us take none of his kind. Nor niggers, neither."

"Kola knows that. He goes to see Miss Gold Tooth, down the line."

"Us girls up here won't even speak to that disgusting old whore. She'll take anybody—" Suddenly she kissed his throat. "Oh, Joseph, you're so damn nice!"

He chuckled. "You don't have to deliver the speech your boss taught you."

"He didn't tell me to say it," she breathed. "It's good with you. With all the others—'specially those blasted Irishmen—it's just work."

"I'm flattered. But I'd say 'all the others' is overstating it. This place appears to be crying for trade."

"It is. Butt's mighty upset."

"Since there's no line waiting, he won't care if we have another go—"

"Yes, he will! He's mighty strict about the clock. You only paid for one time. Fifteen minutes. We used that already."

The anxious words faded into a murmur of pleasure as he reached behind her and started to rub her bare buttocks.

"Joseph, Joseph—you're a sweet boy. But we don't dare. Butt would have my hide."

"I've got your hide, Nancy. Gonna keep it a while, too."

There was a more pronounced stir in his groin. Quickly she shifted her pubis, lowered herself, and moaned as she felt the rigidity.

"God, you just melt me," she whispered, kissing his ear, his eyelid, his cheek while his thumbs pressed harder against her breasts. "You got a mean look sometimes, but you're sweet and easy on a girl—must be the Southron in you. Were you in the war?"

"Yes."

"D'you ever meet up with that old Reb, Davis?"

"In a manner of speaking. You might say Mr. Jefferson Davis was responsible for teaching me some of life's most valuable skills."

"What'n the fire's that mean?"

"Never mind," he laughed, pulling her head down.

She wriggled. "Sweet, we *got* to think of the time. If you don't pay—"

"Be quiet," he said, affably but firmly, and kissed her.

She gave up without protesting and kissed him back, her mouth open, and her tongue darting. Now she was moving her hips, raising them and lowering them faster each time. A faint sound—not next door, outside—distracted him. He opened his eyes.

Over her shoulder he saw a distorted shadow cast on the canvas by an outdoor lantern.

"Hey in there, Kingston."

"Shut up!" Roused now, he clutched Nancy's perspiring back.

"Your time's up."

"Oh, it's that damn pea-headed Toby—" Nancy panted. Jeremiah thrust. "Oh. *Oh.*"

The shadow stirred. "You don't put your pants on, Kingston, I'm comin' in."

Jeremiah stopped the movement of his body, raging because he'd just slipped comfortably into the girl. The silhouetted arm of the proprietor's assistant moved toward the opening in the canvas. Jeremiah dropped his right hand beside the cot. Seized the Ballard that laid atop his clothes.

"Boy, if you set foot in here, I'll blow you all the way to the river."

The silhouetted arm dropped. "But you got to pay again."

"After."

"No, before. It's Mr. Brown's rules."

"Hell with his rules. I'll settle up later—" Jeremiah's voice acquired a harder edge. "You better skedaddle because I see your shadow just perfect against the lantern. Leave us alone or I'll put one through you with this buffalo gun. Not even your own mother'll recognize you."

Quickly, the shadow shrank and disappeared. In the next cubicle, clothing rustled and the whore said in a monotone, "Oh, that was sure sweet, thanks a lot."

Jeremiah relaxed, shifted his right hand back to Nancy's hips and returned to more pleasurable pursuits.


iv


Adolphus Brown was in a vile temper. He leaned his elbows on the board resting on two barrels and surveyed his clientele. One miserable Paddy, passed out on the floor.

For the first time this evening, two of the girls were occupied in the annex, but the third was still alone. He'd already taken a turn up and down the street. He knew his competitors had more customers than they could handle.

Brown pulled a tarnished pocket watch from his waistcoat, snapped it open, and checked the time. Toby came rushing in.

"Butt—"

"Those two finished with Alice and Nancy?"

"Yes, sir—that is, Alice got done on the dot. But that buffla hunter told me to leave. He'n Nancy, they're goin' at it again."

Brown's eyes clouded. "I assume he paid you—"

"No, Butt. He—he said he'd shoot me if I went in to collect."

Brown slapped his palm on a worn deck lying on the board. "I'll have that bitch for breakfast!"

Toby fingered his beard. "Ain't her fault. That Kingston's an ornery sort."

Brown's glance was scathing. "You mean he has enough sand to scare you off? I thought better of you, my boy."

Humiliated, Toby stood speechless. Brown started to say something else, but then Liam O'Dey slipped inside the tent. With a jerky swipe of his hand across his mouth, he hurried to the counter.

"This one on the house, Mr. Brown?"

"Why in shit should it be?"

"Well, sir, because—"

Nervously, O'Dey glanced at the entrance.

"—that time before, you asked me to keep my ears cocked. I'm still doin' it."

"You said it'd be a pleasure, seeing as how Boyle tossed you off his gang."

"That's right. Not ten minutes ago, I overheard that bastard speakin' with four of the greenhorns who arrived yesterday. He was next door to Tidwell's, outside, and I was inside—he didn't see me slip in behind him. He wasn't bothering to keep his voice down, either. He told the greenhorns he couldn't advise them about any of the places except this one, where—"

O'Dey touched the deck.

"—where he said the railroad bibles are not straight."

Brown cursed, grabbed the deck, and flung it. Cards fluttered down. Toby was wide-eyed.

Gaining control, Brown jerked his hat off, mopped his scarred pate, and settled the hat back on his head. "Toby, you'd better go see that loudmouth again. Guess your first call made no impression. This time you must talk louder—unless, of course, the customer we were discussing watered your guts too badly."

"No, Butt! I just didn't want to go into the dark against a man lugging a hunting rifle—"

"I'll handle him," Brown nodded, grabbing a bottle of Overholtz cut with Platte River water. He shoved the bottle into O'Dey's white hand.

"Two swallows."

O'Dey drank greedily.

"Now get out."

When he was gone, Brown motioned Toby to his side. There was a pathetic eagerness in the young man's eyes.

"We can't fool with the mick any longer, Toby. Waited too damn long already."

He frankly feared reprisals from Casement if one of the workers was seriously injured. But as things stood at the moment, his choices were to take a risk or pack up and leave.

"Watch the Irishman till he's alone," he cautioned. "Be sure no on
sees you."

"It'll be easy, Butt," Toby said, bobbing his head. "First time I brace
him, he wouldn't raise a hand. He's yella."

"Well, you talk to him in your most persuasive way."

"Loud, Butt?"

With a steady gaze, Brown said, "As loud as you know how."

"Yes, sir!"

Toby scuttled from the tent. Brown jerked out his watch again, noted
the hour and minute, and thrust it back in his pocket. He stalked to the
entrance, muttering and kicking strewn cards. By God, he was through
letting pious micks ruin his trade, and randy itinerants take advantage o
him!

Before stepping into the street, he paused to consider his strategy. He
pulled out the four-barrel derringer, removed the shells and returned the
pepperbox and the shells to separate pockets. He left the tent smiling.

v

In the dark behind the annex tent, Toby frantically rummaged among
empty crates in one of the unhitched phaetons. He was ashamed of the
way he'd disappointed Butt. Ashamed and anxious to make amends.

He hadn't told Butt the real reason he'd balked at entering the annex
though Butt had guessed it. Toby had seen the young, soft-spoken hunter
once in August, then again this evening. Both experiences had left him inexplicably frightened.

He didn't frighten easy, either. But there was something vicious about
Kingston's eyes. They were worse than his employer's eyes, even when
Butt was boiling mad.

He found what he sought. A handle broken from a spike maul. Thick
enough and stout enough to beat a man to death in three blows.

With the maul handle clutched to his side, he slipped deeper into the
darkness as Butt Brown stormed out of the main tent and headed for the
entrance to the annex. Nancy's wordless voice came through the canvas,
uttering cry after strident cry.

# CHAPTER 9

## *Kingston*

"MR. KINGSTON?"

The voice pushed at the edge of his mind, barely audible because of Nancy's outcries and the roar of his own breath. Her nails dug, then scraped his back. Bodies shuddering, they reached the end together.

"Mr. Kingston, this is Brown."

"Oh, God," Nancy panted, limp on top of him all at once. Jeremiah whispered for her to be quiet, then shifted his head away from hers. Clearly delineated on the front canvas, he saw the motionless silhouette of the stocky man in the melon-shaped hat.

"I hear you," he said as his breathing became more regular. He slid his hand down to the Ballard.

"Believe there's been a slight misunderstanding—"

Jeremiah blinked. Brown sounded friendly.

"Might we discuss it a moment?"

"Go ahead."

"No, I mean out here."

Jeremiah ran his tongue to the corner of his dry mouth. Despite Brown's puzzling cordiality, something smelled of danger. Far in the distance, drunken men sang a sad Irish ballad. A revolver banged. A woman laughed, shrill as a crow's caw.

"Toby should have known better than to interrupt," Brown resumed. "The lad's not too heavy upstairs. You're welcome to Nancy's company for as long as you want to enjoy it, provided you pay in advance. Trade's light this evening—I'll even set you a special all-night price." A pause. "Mr. Kingston?"

"Still listening."

"Oh, good. Gentlemen can always reach an accommodation. If you'll step out, it'll only take a moment. I'm not armed."

Nancy's mouth was tight against Jeremiah's ear:

"Joseph, I think he's fooling you. He always carries a hide-out gun. And he doesn't do favors—"

"Kingston?" the voice prodded. The shadow jerked toward the adjoining cubicle. "Alice, stay there!"

The woman next door complied without a murmur. Jeremiah heard her return to her customer and quietly urge him to remain where he was.

"Pardon me for doubting you, Mr. Brown," Jeremiah called, "but during the celebration this afternoon, I distinctly recall you shot off a pocket gun. I wouldn't care to hold a conversation with that gun somewhere about."

A chuckle. "You're quick, Mr. Kingston. I do have the gun. It's empty. Check it."

The shadow bent. The canvas stirred. An object slid in the dirt beneath.

"There. Proof of my good faith."

"I tell you something's funny," Nancy breathed. "Isn't like Butt to surrender his weapon."

There was a smile in Jeremiah's voice: "Maybe he *is* anxious to have me stay the night. As he said, business isn't all that grand."

Naked, he stole to the front partition. He located the pepperbox and examined it against the glow from the outside lantern.

"Empty, all right," he called.

"Then if you're satisfied, come out. As soon as we agree on the price I'll leave you alone."

Jeremiah debated. What if Brown had a second gun? A hidden knife? Nancy suspected it.

Still, she might be inordinately cowed by the man. And he *would* enjoy a whole night at a bargain rate.

"Mr. Brown?"

"Here, sir."

"Be right with you soon as I put my pants on."

"Excellent!"

He struggled into his trousers, shushed Nancy's next warning, then patted her hair.

"Gonna be all right, hon. We'll have a fancy time right till the cock crows."

He left the Ballard beside his hat and returned to the front. "Stand back two or three paces, if you please, Mr. Brown."

The shadow shrank. Jeremiah raised the flap. Brown stood at the far edge of a pool of butter-colored light between the main and secondary tents. Quickly Jeremiah eyed the other man. Smiled.

"You don't mind if I'm cautious? Show me the linings of your coat. Spread 'em wide."

Brown looked annoyed, but did as Jeremiah asked. No bulges or unexplained slits were visible. He gave a satisfied nod and left the tent.

"Didn't mean to talk so sharp to your boy—" He dug in the pocket holding the bills from the sale of the latest kill. "How much will that be for all night?"

Brown had his hat in his right hand and was mopping his pate with the other. He dropped the hat, shot his arms forward, and caught Jeremiah's ears. "Damn cheating Reb!" he cried.

Brown jerked Jeremiah's head forward and simultaneously lowered his own. The top of his skull hit Jeremiah's face like a log ram.

Angry and dazed, Jeremiah backstepped. Brown released him. The impact of Brown's blow multiplied the images he saw. Blood began to trickle from his nose.

He'd never come up against a man who fought in such unorthodox fashion. He didn't know what to expect. He staggered to the side, hands hunting a support. Brown sidled forward, lunged for his shoulder.

Jeremiah managed to elude the grasping hands. He put his left foot behind him. His bare sole came down hard on a sharp stone imbedded in the ground. He teetered, off balance. Brown lowered his head and charged.

He butted Jeremiah just above the belly. With a grunt, Jeremiah reeled over and slammed on his spine, conscious of Nancy outside the tent, her soiled wrapper clutched to her breasts.

Butt Brown landed on top of him, both knees in Jeremiah's midsection. Jeremiah's vision cleared just enough to give him a sharp look at the saloon keeper's face. At very least, the man meant to maim him.

"Nancy, the rifle!" As he called to her, the edge of Brown's hand chopped his throat. He gagged.

A second, even less clearly defined figure appeared behind the young prostitute, then scampered away. Alice's customer.

Brown had Jeremiah's ears again. He lifted Jeremiah's head and pounded it against the ground.

Then again, *slam*.

Jeremiah threw a punch. It grazed Brown's jaw but did no damage. Brown's lips peeled back. His nose shone with sweat. Blood smeared Jeremiah's mouth and chin. He nearly fainted when Brown rammed his head down a third time.

"Think you can come in here—" Brown bashed his forehead with a heavy fist. "—high-assed and snotty and break my rules? *No, sir!*"

A knee bore into Jeremiah's crotch, the pressure excruciating. Brown had taken him by surprise. The advantage had belonged to the stocky gambler ever since. Brown's face was dark as a beet, his eyes pitiless.

"*Rifle—*" Jeremiah croaked as Brown chopped his throat again.

Nancy hesitated. Brown's knee jerked, digging. Jeremiah almos screamed from the pain in his groin.

Once more Brown resorted to ear pulling. He tugged Jeremiah's head up and snapped his own head forward. The scarred skull loomed, shooting straight at Jeremiah's eyes.

He managed to wrench onto his side. Brown had meant to knock him out with a butt to the forehead. He absorbed the blow on his ear. His head rang.

He wedged his hand between his body and Brown's. Found the man' belt buckle. Hoisted with all his strength and succeeded in hurling Brown off.

When Jeremiah reached his feet, he wobbled. Blood and mucus contin ued to drain from his nose. His head and his testicles hurt unbearably Where was Brown?

He found him, indistinct in the lantern's glow. The saloon keeper wa disheveled but steady. He lowered his head. Ran at Jeremiah.

Something hard jabbed Jeremiah's side. He saw a flash of metal, caugh hold and yanked the Ballard away from Nancy. He dodged clumsily twisted, and booted Brown's behind. The kick and the momentum o Brown's charge hurled him to the ground. His jaw snapped hard agains the dirt. Jeremiah's first advantage.

He pressed it. Using the Ballard as a club, he swung down from straigh overhead. He broke the stock on Brown's skull.

Brown yelled. Jeremiah hurt too much to stop or be merciful. The Ballard barrel seemed to fuse with his hands as he kicked Brown's ribs.

The stocky man retched; flopped onto his back. A hand brushed Jere miah's forearm.

"Leave him be, Joseph! He's whipped."

Nancy's words made no impression. Both pride and body had been in jured too badly. He knelt on Brown's waistcoat, the positions of a few mo ments ago reversed. Gripping the Ballard at muzzle and breech, he shoved it down like a bar across Brown's throat.

The man's eyes popped. Fingers groped for Jeremiah's face. He straightened his arms. Pushing. *Pushing—*

Brown couldn't reach him.

He laughed at the sudden and pathetic fright in the saloon keeper's eyes. It took only a few moments more to cut off the man's air supply Brown's discolored tongue shot between his clenching teeth. His body arched three times, each spasm less violent than the one before. Then he collapsed. Jeremiah didn't lift the rifle for another thirty seconds.

When he staggered to his feet, he was still shaking with rage directed mostly at himself. The saloon keeper's treachery and wild fighting style had nearly cost him his life.

Alice lifted the tent flap, took one peek at his red smeared face, and darted back inside. He realized Nancy was weeping.

"Joseph?"

"What?"

"Is he—?"

"Yes."

"I gave you the gun just so you could scare him off!"

He barely heard. His rage subsided, replaced by a forced calm. This unexpected turn changed the situation completely. He had to flee—without delay.

"Hand me my clothes, Nancy. Appears I won't be seeing you for a while."

Nancy stood with the wrapper fallen away from one reddened nipple. His eyes fixed on her wet face. For a moment weary despair swept over him. She was actually sorry the crazy bastard was dead! And terrified of him because he'd done the deed.

"I said I want my clothes, goddamn it!"

Nancy rushed inside. His heartbeat was slowing. He stepped to the edge of the annex, glanced toward the main street. Against the smoky glare of lamps and the bulk of the train, men passed back and forth, making so much racket the scuffling had gone unheard.

That gave him a margin of time. He'd wake Kola, hitch the mules, and be rolling across the prairie in fifteen minutes. Kola would have to drive. He felt too groggy.

Nancy brought his hat, boots, shirt, and long underwear. He held out the Ballard.

She wouldn't touch it.

His fondness for her was swept away by disgust. Were all whores like this? Miserable with their pimps, and just as miserable without them?

He laid the rifle on the ground. Used his shirt sleeve to swab some of the mucus and blood from his mouth and chin. Then he climbed into his drawers, donned his shirt, and pulled up his suspenders.

"Joseph, you didn't need to kill—"

He pointed the Ballard at her exposed breast. "Don't go soft on me, hon. What do you think he meant to do to me? Now listen. You stay in that tent half an hour before you fetch anyone to look after the body."

His dark eyes held pinpoint reflections of the lantern. His lips thinned to little more than a slit.

"If anybody comes chasing me sooner than half an hour, Nancy, I promise I'll see you again. Someplace. I won't be coming for your services, either."

"God." A shiver. "You aren't the kind of man I thought you were."

"I can say the same about you. Brown was a no-good, reckless—"

*"He took care of me!"*

"You expect me to stand still and let some dishonorable son of a bitch jump me and put out the lights? No, ma'am! Get inside!"

He jerked the Ballard at her. She reacted like a startled rabbit, hurrying to the sanctuary of the tent.

"Half an hour—no sooner!" he called. Unsteadily, he walked toward the rear of the annex.

For a moment he felt sick at his stomach. Why did it always end the same way?

*Because you enjoy doing a man to death. Don't deny it. You started to enjoy it the moment you pulled the trigger on Serena Rose.*

All right, he *had* taken pleasure from watching Brown's last moments. But the gratification had been costly. It created a whole host of new problems.

He'd have to change his name again. He probably should have changed it before he reached the railhead. That Texas boy he'd foolishly spared was no doubt raising a halloo down south. Searchers might come this far north. They'd discover Joseph Kingston had come this far as well.

Fuzzy-headed and still in pain, he staggered on. He passed three more gambling establishments and pulled up short. In the leak of light from the street, he spied Kola's empty blanket beneath the wagon.

And two men, one unfamiliar, squared off against each other.

They saw him. It was too late to run.

ii

A few minutes earlier, Michael had decided to satisfy his curiosity about the stranger before returning to the bunk car to turn in.

He cut between Tidwell's and the packed, noisy Bird Cage. At the rear of the tents he stopped, disappointed. The blanket beneath the wagon had been abandoned. The Indian had evidently gone off to search for his friend.

As he turned to retrace his steps, the corner of his eye caught movement at the far edge of the saloon tent. A shambling figure appeared around the corner.

Michael's stomach spasmed. He recognized Butt Brown's bearded helper. The young man carried some kind of club.

Toby slouched through the shadow cast by the Bird Cage. "Hullo there, mick."

Michael drew a deep breath. Had Brown's helper been following him while he strolled? There could be no other explanation for the young man's abrupt appearance.

"Butt sent me to see you."

"A few weeks ago, you and I said all that was necessary."

"Thought we did," Toby agreed. "But we hear you're still spoutin' off about Butt."

"The way I answer questions about your boss is my affair." Michael tried to act relaxed as he swung to the left, in the direction of the main street. "Good night—"

He heard the hiss of air as the maul handle came down. He sidestepped, but not soon enough. The handle slammed his right shoulder.

He lurched; dropped to one knee. Toby jumped in front of him, grinning.

"Plan to give you a few more like that. Then maybe you'll plug your mouth. Don't you make it too easy on me, though. Robs it of all the sport."

Quietly, Michael said, "I'm not going to fight you."

"Yes, you are."

"No."

"Damn coward, that's what you are! I knowed it the first time we met up."

Toby Harkness had shifted to a position directly between the mercantile and gambling tents. Michael's path was blocked.

He climbed to his feet and forced his hands open; they'd fisted almost without his being aware of it.

"Stand out of the way."

Toby hawked and blew spit on his trousers.

"All right," Michael said, his anger bubbling so fiercely he could barely contain it. He pivoted a hundred and eighty degrees. "I'll take another route."

He wrenched his head as the maul handle whistled in from behind. Despite his quick move, the wood clipped him alongside the ear. His hand shot up to cover the side of his head. Toby giggled.

Anger shone in Michael's eyes. "Back off! I'm not going to fight."

"I told Butt you was yella." Toby poked Michael's cheek with the smoothed end of the handle. "Yella from tip to toe."

Michael jerked his head out of the way, narrowly avoiding the next thrust. He refused to shout for help. But neither would he answer Brown's thug in kind.

*Just stay calm. You knew one day it would come to something like this.*

"Yella dog, yella dog!" Toby chanted. The handle gigged Michael beneath the eye.

Toby gave the wood a twist, then stabbed it into his midsection. "Ain't you gonna howl for me, Mr. Yella Dog?"

*"You witless bastard!"*

"Hey, the dog can bark! Bark some more—" He took a shuffling step. "Come on, let's hear a yelp."

Toby smacked the handle lightly against the ear he'd already hit.

"I said yelp!"

The handle struck Michael's temple.

*"Yelp!"*

He brought the handle down on Michael's right shoulder.

A pitiless inner voice spoke the truth of it. *There is no way out of this unless you go after him.*

He wanted to do it. The desire was like a dizzying drunkenness.

Growing incoherent, Toby rammed the handle into Michael's belly. "You yella mick fucker! *Act like a man!*" When Toby spit this time, the moist gob landed beside Michael's nose.

He cursed and surprised Toby by fastening both hands on the maul handle.

*Don't!*

He was too enraged to heed the cautioning voice, or care about the vow. He tore the handle out of Toby's fingers. The younger man was startled; slow to react. Michael raised the handle over his head, his clenched hand white.

Eyes on the length of wood, Toby began to retreat.

*DON'T!*

With a slashing outward motion, Michael flung the handle. It turned end over end, clattering against the wagon. He turned his back on Toby— perhaps the hardest thing he'd ever done—and started to walk.

He felt neither victorious nor proud of himself, only ashamed.

He heard Toby run for him, heavy boots scuffing the ground. He turned. Toby dug in his heels a couple of feet away. A smile crept back on his oafish face.

Slowly Toby flexed his fingers.

"What the hell's going on?"

The white man with the streaked hair lurched out of the dark, a rifle in

one hand, hat and boots in the other. The white man's sleeve was marked
with blood. So was his face.

Toby recognized the stranger, who paused behind Levi's Bird Cage.

"Where's Kola? Where's the Indian?"

"I don't know—" Michael began.

"You—" Toby sounded less confident; started edging toward the fallen
length of wood. "—you fold your hand, mister. My confab with this here
mick is private."

The hunter glanced at the maul handle. "And one-sided, from the look
of it. I'd suggest you light out of here, boy. If the Irishman takes you, no
one will shed a tear. You've lost your number one backer."

"What—what d'you mean?"

"You'll find out presently. Just break this up and get going."

Toby seemed to see the blood on the hunter for the first time. "Did you
do somethin' to Butt?"

"Shut up and *move!*"

The hunter walked away from the hard-breathing young man. He
tossed his hat and boots onto the wagon seat. Toby dashed for the maul
handle. He got hold of it just as Michael called:

"Look out for yourself, mister!" The hunter pivoted at the waist.

Swung with Toby's full strength, the handle landed athwart his temple
and knocked him backward. He floundered against the wagon wheel, stabbing the split stock of his rifle into the dirt to prop himself up. Toby
kicked the stock. Reflected light from the tent street shone in the hunter's
eyes as he crashed to his knees, hurt but refusing to quit.

Toby reached for the hunter's hair. "What'd you do to Butt?" With an
almost regretful expression, the hunter fired the rifle from his hip.

The spurt of light blinded Michael a moment. The reverberating roar
silenced the clamor in the Bird Cage. When he opened his eyes, he no
longer saw the slightest remorse on the hunter's face.

Bucyrus Tidwell popped into sight between the tents.

"Who's out there?"

Toby uttered a series of whimpers. Dropped the maul handle. Leaned
his forehead against the wagon and clawed the side with both hands.
Then, with a lazy slowness, he slid down until there was no more wood to
lean against.

He fell face first on the rumpled blanket. Where his chest had rubbed
the wagon, a wide swathe of red glistened like new paint.

Almost instantly, men were shouting and clamoring around Michael.
He barely saw the hunter collapse on his side, not unconscious but laboring to breathe. Blood had begun leaking from the man's nose. His eyes
closed.

"What the hell's the row?" Tidwell boomed, just as the Sioux, rifle in hand, came slipping into sight at the far side of the Bird Cage. He saw his fallen friend, ran to him, knelt, then glanced up with furious eyes.

"Who did this?"

Michael shoved through the growing crowd, ignoring shouted questions. He pointed to Toby.

"He did part of it. The youngster was after me. Your friend came along, the boy went for him, and your friend took him out. I don't know who bloodied him."

As if there weren't pandemonium enough, a woman began to scream. Down in the direction of Brown's Paradise, Michael thought. The direction from which the hunter had come.

The Sioux cradled the white man's head in his lap.

"Joseph? Joseph, do you hear? I woke and could not find you. I went searching—"

"That's all we need, more goddamn Injun trouble," someone complained.

"There won't be any," Michael said. "He's the white man's partner. The white man helped me."

The keening scream was joined by a second one. Michael walked over to the Sioux, who watched him with suspicion.

"Your friend's hurt. He needs attention. You want to pick him up or shall I?"

The Indian saw half a dozen drawn revolvers in the mob spilling from the lane between Tidwell's and the saloon. Out in the street, a man yelled:

"Fetch General Jack!"

"We stay here—" the Sioux began.

"No," Michael said. "I think he'd better rest on the train until this is cleared up."

The Indian stayed motionless. A revolver cocked, loudly.

"You'll be safer somewhere else!" Michael insisted. "Some at this railhead don't like any Indians but dead ones. Did you say your partner's name is Joseph?"

"Yes, Joseph Kingston. He is my *kola*. My sworn friend."

The name meant nothing. Undoubtedly he'd been wrong about having seen the white man before.

"Well, now he's mine too," Michael replied. "You can trust me. Let me have your rifle so some drunken idiot doesn't take a potshot at you. Come on, give it to me."

Doubtful, the Indian searched Michael's strained face. Then he complied.

"Pick him up and bring him along to the train. We'll put him in my bunk."

# CHAPTER 10

## A Matter of Truth

STRANGERS MURMURED in a half-lit dark. They spoke English, but the accents were not his own. Some of the voices carried a Yankee harshness. Others had a certain lilt he'd first heard at the railhead. Irish talk.

Jeremiah came fully awake. His groin, his nose, and his forehead throbbed. When he grew conscious of his surroundings, fright dried his throat.

He was boxed in a bunk; prisoned below, above, and on the right. Only when he floundered over on his side facing the amber light did he see no wall.

His eyes focused on the man who'd almost taken a beating at the wagon. A slender Paddy with a weathered face and brown eyes flecked the color of the lamps in the—

Bunk car, that's where he was. The place was rank with the odor of unclean bodies, abuzz with conversation. About him, he presumed.

He was resting at the top of a tier of three beds. The Irishman with the graying hair and mustache stood on the lowest one, trying to pull up the blanket while Jeremiah pushed it away.

"Easy, lad," the Irishman said. His voice had an echo. Or was that only in Jeremiah's head?

His upper lip felt tender when he explored it with his tongue. Someone had washed his face. The sense of confinement—of threat—intensified.

"Easy, now. You're safe. You've been looked at. Jack Casement knows a bit of field medicine. Nothing's wrong with you except you've got a bashed nose and a bushel of bruises."

"Where's my rifle?"

"The Indian has it."

"Where is he?"

"Sitting down here." The Irishman motioned to the lowest bunk. Jeremiah couldn't see Kola. "No harm will come to him. By the way, my name is Boyle. I've learned yours is Kingston. You needn't speak if it hurts too much. But I want to thank you for what you did."

The golden brown eyes picked up lamplight. A sadness touched the stranger's face as he went on:

"The boy's being wrapped for burial. I hate to see him dead, but under the circumstances I've no call to quarrel. Do you want some broth? One of the cooks is willing to—"

"I want out of here."

"Afraid that isn't possible as yet. Casement plans to speak with you. Meantime, you should rest."

"*I want out of here!*" Jeremiah sat up too quickly, knocking his head on the plank ceiling. Despite his determination, his bones seemed to lose their stiffness. He lay down again, breathing hard.

The light of the car lanterns shimmered, then began to compress, squeezed between layers of darkness. The Irishman touched him.

"Would a drink of whiskey help?"

The panic of enforced confinement still gripped him as he lost consciousness.

ii

*—sorrysorrysorrysorry—*

"What? What did you say?"

"I said—"

It was the Irishman again, barely perceived as Jeremiah's sleep-clotted eyes came open. The man was still standing on the lower bunk. Evidently time had passed. Some lamps in the car had been extinguished. His aches weren't quite so painful.

Outside, cannon fire rumbled. Then he realized it was a distant prairie storm.

"I said, I'm sorry to wake you. Jack Casement insists on seeing you right now. I tried to persuade him to wait until morning. But he's exercised about all the trouble tonight."

"No objection," Jeremiah said. He was grateful. He didn't want to stay penned in this smelly prison any longer than necessary. Out in the stormy dark there were dead men crying his name. He needed to be away before the living heard.

He clenched his teeth. Started to swing his legs toward the edge of the bunk. The pain wrenched his face.

"Take my hand," Boyle offered.

"No. Stand back."

He hadn't realized how difficult it would be. He struggled until he was on his belly with his legs hanging over the aisle. When the Irishman steadied his elbow, he jerked his arm away resentfully.

He muttered an apology. He wasn't himself because of the confinement, the sense of being entrapped by unfamiliar faces, dim ovals in the equally dim wash of yellow light. Wriggling into position to drop to the floor, he glimpsed Kola with the Ballard. A reassuring sight.

He saw a rectangle of paper tacked to the wall near the head of the bunk. Some drawing of a nigra carrying a—

His eyes opened wide. A guttural sound rose in his throat. He was unable to control the tears of astonishment.

"Joseph?" That was Kola.

"Kingston, what's the trouble?" The Irishman.

"Nothing!" he said louder than he intended. "Brown almost kicked my balls off, you know. Hurts a bit."

He blinked, clearing his eyes. But it wasn't so easy to rid himself of the surprise and anguish that had torn him like a bullet when he saw two words below the drawing's caption.

*M. Kent.*


iii


Who was the Irishman? Where had he gotten the picture that was unmistakably Matt's? He wanted to ask, but wouldn't until he was in better control of himself.

Fortunately there were distractions. The effort to walk; Kola supporting him; the Irishman hovering.

They reached the platform between cars. Wind battered his face. Northwestward, a white light flared and spread on the horizon, soon followed by a prolonged roll of thunder. A cloud of dirt carrying bits of grass and other debris went sailing by. Beyond it he glimpsed men laboring to keep one of the tents from falling.

"What time is it?" he asked Boyle.

"Something after three in the morning."

"Bad blow coming."

"Fast," Boyle replied, holding the next door. "This way."

Jeremiah had seen but never spoken to Jack Casement. He was no man for trifling, that much Jeremiah knew the moment he was ushered into the office. Casement was fully dressed, fully awake, and unfriendly.

"Boyle here is pleading you're too banged up to be on your feet, Kingston—that is your name?"

Jeremiah confined his answer to a nod.

"I overruled him. I want tonight's business settled. I have already talked with an Alice Peaslee—do you know a woman called Alice Peaslee?"

"One of Brown's whores."

"Yes. Nancy Dell, the female who caused one of the incidents, is apparently too distraught to speak to anyone."

Casement tipped back and forth in his chair. It squeaked. Even when he sat all the way forward, his legs didn't touch the floor. His glance was nearly as fiery as his beard.

"Alice Peaslee satisfied me that her employer, Adolphus Brown, attacked first."

Relieved, Jeremiah said, "That's correct."

"Two men are dead, however. Brown and his boy of all work."

"Toby came at me with the handle of a sledge. He—" Jeremiah located Michael leaning in a shadowy corner. Thunder pealed. "—he was all over this gentleman. When I suggested he stop, he turned on me."

"You found it necessary to shoot him?"

"At that moment—" Jeremiah shrugged. "Yes."

"Well, you were apparently provoked on both occasions, and Boyle supports the second part of your story. The prostitute confirmed the other part. So I have no cause to detain you. Butt Brown was one of the worst influences in this camp, if there can be any degree of difference between men of his stripe. But I don't want your kind at the railhead either, Mr. Kingston. I don't want murderers here."

"I defended myself!"

"In the first case, apparently you did. The boy is another matter. I want you to take your wagon and your Indian friend and get out. Immediately, and for good."

"Sir," Boyle protested, "you should at least let him rest a bit mor—"

"Immediately," Casement repeated, and swung his squeaking chair to face the desk. He reached for a pile of papers and within seconds was immersed in them. There was no appeal.

iv

Michael helped Kingston and the Sioux hitch the mules. The storm was coming rapidly. Swollen clouds were visible overhead whenever the lightning flashed.

As soon as the wagon was ready, Kingston ordered the Indian to drive to the end of the track and wait. A few moments later, still moving with a lack of steadiness, he led his buffalo pony in the same direction.

"Walk with me a moment, Mr. Boyle."

Michael was puzzled by the hoarseness of Kingston's voice. He didn't know what to make of the hunter. The man was neither illiterate nor constantly rough-spoken. But there was a remote, unfeeling air about him that made Michael thankful Kingston wasn't his adversary. The man seemed able to keep his head while bearing a great deal of pain.

They struggled against the wind, passing behind the tent town. Half a dozen of the canvas structures had been struck in anticipation of the thunderstorm. The rest flapped and tilted toward the east, their poles creaking, their guy ropes whining. Only the Bird Cage showed a lamp.

"Devil of a shame you're turned out so soon, Kingston. Casement has not quite forgotten he's no longer commanding or disciplining Union soldiers."

Kingston laughed in a curt way. "Was he an officer? I suspected."

The buffalo pony shied as they passed the last tent and took the wind's full force. Kingston held his plainsman's hat on his head as they labored toward the grade. Another lightning burst revealed the buffalo guns bobbing in the handmade saddle scabbard.

"I have a question for you," Kingston said.

"What is it?"

Kingston opened his mouth, then hesitated. The question Michael heard was not the one Kingston meant to ask, he thought.

"Why did you permit that boy to maul you?"

"I don't know whether I can explain. I was in the war—"

"Yank side, of course."

Michael nodded. "From your speech, I'd guess you were on the other one."

"Yes, I was. Go on."

"I grew sick of the fighting. I journeyed out here to get away from it and didn't. I had to kill again. I won't bore you with the story, but I promised myself I'd never fight again."

"Think you can stick by such a decision?"

"I can try."

Kingston grunted, then dabbed his sleeve against a thread of blood below his purpled nose. When he spoke again, it was with a wry sadness.

"I admire your determination. I didn't find the war a pleasant or uplifting experience either. But when I came out of it, whole in body if not exactly whole of mind, I made a different choice. I decided I'd never let any human being best me in a fight for my life. Nor would I suffer the behavior of dishonorable men. Your position has its merits, though. I'd urge you to stick by it—"

What the devil was this? Michael wondered. Something close to sadness had crept into Kingston's voice.

Or was he merely imagining that, deceived by the noise of the raging wind?

No, it wasn't imagination. He saw that when the lightning illuminated the prairie again. The rails shone like streaks of iridescent fire, leading beyond the meridian marker to the wagon, the restive mules, the motionless Indian. Kingston's eyes were wet.

"—because if you do, you stand a chance of being a happy man. Don't let any bastard chivvy you into changing your mind."

"Toby nearly did. He kept calling me a coward."

"Not surprised. But I've had a taste of each kind of life. In many ways, yours demands more courage—"

Kingston's voice broke. He pivoted away. Michael squeezed his eyes shut against the blowing grit. He couldn't fathom why this young man who killed so easily seemed eager to counsel him. He was taken by surprise when Kingston seized his arm.

"Where did you get the picture?"

"What?"

"The drawing in your bunk. Where did you get it?"

"Why, from the artist's father."

"Do you know him?"

Michael was alarmed by the intensity of the question. Kingston's fingers dug into his sleeve. Puzzled and annoyed, Michael pulled away:

"See here. I hardly consider this an occasion for discussing—"

"Goddamn it, answer me! Do you know the artist's father?"

"Yes, I know him."

Lightning lit heaven. Thunder shook the earth.

"He's my father too," Kingston said.

"Jesus Christ, that's it," Michael breathed. No wonder he'd missed the obvious. He'd been looking in the wrong direction.

"What are you talking about?" Kingston said.

"Your face. It's like Jephtha's."

v

Kingston—or Jeremiah Kent, as he announced himself to be—repeatedly refused to answer Michael's questions about his past. He wouldn't explain how he'd gotten from Georgia to the railhead, or why he was traveling with a Sioux and calling himself by another name.

Hoping to break through the stubborn barrier of refusals, Michael told him Jephtha Kent believed his youngest son to be dead.

"In a sense that's true, Mr. Boyle. Now what do you know about my brothers?"

Still shaken, Michael described Matthew's survival of the blockade and his marriage, then Gideon's unsuccessful struggle to find a place for himself in New York City, where Jephtha was preaching.

"So both of them came out alive. I'm glad. Is my mother well?"

"She—she died this past summer."

A glare of lightning showed Michael the other man's bent head. Jeremiah made no sound.

"King—Jeremiah—blast! I can't get used to calling you Jeremiah—"

"Don't. It isn't my name any longer, just as Kingston won't be after tonight."

"You've got to tell me where you've been! How you got here—"

"No, Boyle. I refuse. But what about you? I don't recall hearing anyone speak of you. What's your connection with my father?"

Hoping cooperation would engender more of the same, Michael explained. Jeremiah nodded from time to time, and said when Michael finished:

"Well, if my mother ever mentioned you before I left Lexington, I've forgotten. I'm happy to hear my father's alive."

"He'll be happy to learn you are, too."

"You're not going to tell him."

"Of course I am! As soon as pos—"

Jeremiah interrupted with a shake of his head. "You won't tell him a thing unless you want to hurt him."

"Good God, it wouldn't be fair to keep this news from—"

Michael stopped. There was a measure of truth in what the younger man said. Which truth had priority? He thought of one way he might answer that:

"There's a circumstance which could change your mind. You surely recall the California money—"

"Amanda Kent's money? Yes."

"When Jephtha concluded you'd been killed, he decided to will me your share. He adopted me unofficially into the family—in my bunk I have his letter explaining why."

"What you've just said proves he did the right thing. You could have kept the information to yourself. You're a proper Kent, all right."

"Well, I'd never surrender that part. But the inheritance is yours. It doesn't belong to me any longer."

"It certainly does. Consider it your reward for never informing my father, my brothers—anyone—that we've met."

"You can't ask—"

"Not ask. Demand."

"You expect me to keep it from Jephtha forever?"

"Unless you don't give a damn about him, yes."

Michael's composure was shattered. Too many shocks had piled one onto another. His eyes started to fill with angry tears:

"I can't do it!"

"You can and will. I saved you. For that, and for the money—you owe me. Use the money to give yourself a decent life. Buy a home when you're done working out here. Marry a good woman. Raise a family—" Mockingly. "You *can* find use for the money, can't you?"

"Why—" Suddenly Michael saw a possibility, and felt guilt. "—of course. But it would be wrong to—"

"The decision isn't yours."

Up where Kola waited with the wagon, one of the mules brayed. Jeremiah gripped Michael's arm again, gently this time.

"To convince you my father mustn't know, I'll say this much. I was in Texas for a while. I got into a difficulty. Unfortunately, it's become hard for other men to bring me down. And hard for me to let them."

Michael asked himself whether he'd lost his senses. There was a crusty, almost arrogant pride in Jeremiah's voice.

"By the time I left Fort Worth, they had a bounty on my head. By now I expect there's a second one."

"Why?"

"Not important. But I think you'll read about Joseph Kingston in some paper, and fairly soon. When you do, Kingston will be long gone. I'll have another name. Now do you understand why I don't want my father or my brothers to know how I'm living?"

He reached for the double scabbard. Touched one of the buffalo rifles. "I plan to keep living the same way for a good many years."

Michael shuddered. Jeremiah's eyes softened again.

"So you're welcome to the inheritance. I could never put it to use."

"You could travel. Europe, the Orient—you could live well."

"Hell, I haven't even begun to see this country. Besides, I've no head for managing money. The war left me with somewhat limited talents."

"The money could funnel through me. Jephtha need never find out."

Jeremiah pondered. Cocked his head, smiling a little. "Tempting—" The smile disappeared. "But there might be a slip."

"It's unfair to ask me to keep silent. It's damned unfair, and it's wrong!"

"Perhaps. But you'll do it. Your opinion doesn't matter. My father and brothers are the only ones who count in this."

Michael uttered a sigh of frustration. Swiped his forehead with his palm as if his head hurt. "Oh, I suppose—" His voice strengthened. "I suppose sparing them is the honorable thing, but—"

"Honorable?" Jeremiah broke in. "I hadn't thought of it that way." He touched his hat. "I'm grateful you put it in such a light."

Michael felt a splash of rain on his cheeks. Lightning showed him great tumbling clouds directly above; the storm's leading edge, sweeping over the railhead.

Jeremiah lifted his foot to his stirrup. He grunted as he hauled himself into the saddle. The rain intensified, blurring, then hiding the wagon waiting out beyond the unfinished track.

"Do I have your promise you'll keep silent, Mr. Boyle?"

Drenched and confused, Michael hesitated. Suddenly Jeremiah's pony reared. He lashed it with the rein until all four hoofs were on the ground. He jerked one of the buffalo guns from the scabbard. He pointed the rifle at Michael's head.

"This piece may misfire because of the downpour—" He was shouting to be heard. "—but if that's the case, I'll deal with you another way. Since you've abandoned fighting, I should have no trouble. I want your promise or I'll see you dead right here."

The rain roared in the silence.

"Boyle?"

Michael lifted his head. "All right. For his sake."

The thin-lipped face jerked in what might have been a smile. Jeremiah slid the rifle back to its place.

"Now say it again. I want to hear the promise given freely."

Not knowing whether he was right or wrong, Michael said, "I promise."

"I'm obliged. I urge you to get out of this damn place while you're still in one piece. Use the money. Amount to something. Find a home and stay there. I'll tell you something about being able to go home. It seldom seems important until you can't do it."

He turned the pony's head. "Goodbye, Mr. Boyle."

"Jeremiah!"

The younger man fought to control the fretful animal.

"Would you have shot me if I hadn't given my word?"

"Yes."

He kicked the pony and galloped west beside the right of way, quickly lost in the rainstorm.

## CHAPTER 11

## A Matter of Faith

BY THE TIME MICHAEL reached the sleeping car, he was soaked and exhausted. But Jeremiah's words denied him rest.

*Get out of this damn place while you're still in one piece.*

*Amount to something.*

*Find a home and stay there.*

The line was past the meridian. He'd helped accomplish that much. But the cost was high.

Killing Worthing.

Watching Dorn and two Cheyenne braves perish when it might have been prevented.

Finding the remains of the massacred hunters.

Being instrumental in Toby's death.

Important as the railroad was to the country, he could never again separate it from violence and suffering.

Jeremiah's face kept intruding as he changed to dry clothes. He barely heard O'Dey's whined complaints about his noise.

He grieved for Jeremiah, by turns callous and considerate.

He grieved for Jephtha too. And Matt, and Gideon. Still, a painful lie about an unknown grave would be less hurtful to them than the truth—

All at once he rebelled against the burden he'd accepted when he gave his word. But the rebellion lasted only a short time. Amanda Kent had never insisted a man or woman should feel no sorrow or anger. She had insisted sorrow and anger must never keep a man or woman from the right course. He'd keep his promise.

He took down the drawing of the milk vendor and studied it by the feeble light of the one lamp still lit at the end of the car. Instead of the figures on the paper, he saw Jeremiah's eyes. An old man's eyes, aged by distrust and deceits and acts of rage. He and Jeremiah were different, yet in one way they were alike. In the flawed mirror of Jephtha's youngest son he at last confronted an image of what he was—and might become.

He hoped to God he possessed the will to keep his vow. He prayed he'd never reach the point where he would be capable of emulating Jeremiah's curious pride in killing another human being. He didn't think so.

Yet between himself and the hunter there remained a fearful bond. They were both rootless. Both running. Jeremiah had little choice. He did. And he'd come to understand the folly of flight. It was time to seek a hope of peace, however tenuous, some other way.

He laid the drawing up at the head of his bunk and walked forward through the dark train. The only sound was the pelt of rain.

Fortunately Jack Casement was still awake.

ii

Before the first supply train arrived, he went out to the end of the track. It had occurred to him the Kents were collectors of mementos of their common past. He had become a Kent. He wanted a souvenir of his work on the transcontinental line.

The storm had obliterated footprints and wagon tracks. He crouched in the driving rain and scooped a handful of mud and crushed stone from between two ties. He used his soggy bandana to wrap it, tying a secure knot.

When the bandana's contents dried out, he'd hunt up a box for keeping them. Some day, years from now, he might be able to open the box and discover time had erased recollections of decidedly unromantic sweat, tortured muscle, and dead men, leaving only a single fine memory of having lent his hand to building the greatest marvel of the age.

iii

The boy's alarmed voice brought Michael up short at the rear corner of the unpainted building. The front of the building had shown no light—not surprising since the hour was close to midnight. With the exception of two pine board saloons down near the right of way, Grand Island's business establishments and small homes were dark.

The empty supply train whistled twice as it chugged onto a siding. The whistle had a forlorn sound in the drizzle. The rain had lasted nearly sixteen hours.

On the dark, roofed back porch, Michael thought he saw the unmistakable outline of a Hawken. Aimed his way.

"Only me, Klaus."

The boy scooted to the edge of the porch. "Mr. Boyle?"

"Yes. May I come forward?"

"Sure." The Hawken's butt plate thumped on wood. "You're back from the railhead?"

"So it appears." Michael flexed the cold, stiff fingers curled around the staff to which he'd tied his bundle of personal belongings and an oilskin tube with the drawing carefully rolled inside. "Up a mite late, aren't you?"

"We stay on watch till the saloon crowd settles down. We've had three break-ins lately."

"Ah."

Michael glanced at the slit of light beneath the back door.

"Your sister's awake, then?"

"Yes, sir." The boy thumped the door, then pushed it open.

"Hannah? Guess who's here."

iv

Klaus stood aside as Michael climbed the three creaking steps, grateful to be out of the wind and damp. He stepped into an immaculate but crowded room dominated by a massive iron stove. Curtains partially concealed two beds in alcoves. Unfinished shelves held jars and boxes of staples. In the center of the pegged floor stood a large table that had seen hard use. On the table were a flickering lamp, ledgers, scribbled slips of paper, and an open Bible.

Hannah had been seated with her back toward the porch. She rose as Klaus shut the door from outside. Her joyous smile reached deep into her blue-gray eyes.

"Michael!"

He noticed she was wearing a faded gingham dress. It flattered her figure. "Hello Hannah. I imagine you're surprised to see me."

"No, I've been expecting you, though I wasn't certain when."

He caught the clean soap fragrance of her skin. "I can't believe that."

Still smiling, she walked to a shelf and drew down a milk glass jar containing something dark. She set the jar on the table.

"See for yourself."

He lifted the lid. Inhaled the aroma of pipe tobacco.

"I'm afraid it's dry, but it's all we had in the store. I've ordered more."

He laughed. "My God. You do have cheek!"

"Faith."

His weariness started to slough away. Gazing into her eyes, he experienced an unfamiliar and wondrous sense of calm.

"Are you hungry?" she asked.

"Ravenous!"

"Before I fix you some food, I must say something. I know you have that other woman to think about. I won't blame you if you do. For a while," she added, teasing just a little. "I plan to keep you too busy, and too happy, to bother with her for very long. Now what would you like to eat?"

"Coffee will be enough—but not yet. I want to say something as well. I have a bit of money I didn't mention before—"

A *bit* of money! God above, that insulted Amanda's memory, and Jephtha's goodness. He'd never be able to overcome a sense of guilt at having taken the inheritance from its rightful possessor. But circumstance and Jephtha Kent had dictated that he have it. He wondered how he'd tell Hannah he'd probably be rich as Croesus before he died.

Conscience-stricken, he realized why he wasn't telling her now.

She was waiting for him to finish. "Um," he said, collecting himself. "The money. I believe I can draw on it. I thought—I thought it might help buy goods. Put the place in order." His smile had grown almost shy.

"That's wonderful, Michael. In Kearney I saw a piece of property ideal for a store. We needn't limit ourselves to just one."

*We?*

The audacity! He burst out laughing again.

"I don't know why you're so amused," Hannah said in a cheerfully tart way. "You look wretched. Sit down. Rest. We'll discuss the store later."

"Hannah—"

"Coffee will be here in just—"

"*Hannah.*"

She turned.

"I must be fair to you. I must warn you."

"My, that sounds forbidding." She hurried on to the stove.

"Please listen! I've resigned from Casement's crew. I've come back. But the thing is—"

Exhaling, he thumped the bundle on a chair.

"I don't know if—ah, *damn!*"

He faced away from her.

"Are you trying to tell me you're uncertain about whether you'll stay?"

"Yes, that's it."

She walked back from the stove with a soft rustling of underskirts. He peeked over his shoulder. Her hair and eyes glowed in the lamplight, but it was that astonishing smile which truly illuminated her face.

"I just don't know, Hannah."

She picked up the jar of tobacco and set it close to the Bible. Lord, what a lovely sight she was! How peaceful it seemed in this plain room—

"I do," she said, and put her arms around his neck and kissed him.

# BOOK FIVE

## *The Scarlet Woman*

# CHAPTER 1

## Meeting With a Mountebank

BE CAREFUL, Louis Kent thought as he poured brandy for himself and his guest. Forget the man's nautical pretensions and his air of butcher-boy innocence. Remember his reputation. He could be baiting a pretty trap.

Louis stoppered the decanter. His swarthy hand was steady. Only his black eyes betrayed his tension, shifting to the left to see what his visitor was doing.

The man's fat legs straddled the hearth. His stubby pink fingers were locked behind his back, exactly as if he were on the bridge of one of those steamships he fancied. He was studying the objects above the marble fireplace of Kentland's overheated library. A servant had kindled the fire while Louis and his three guests had dined on boned squab.

Slender and erect, Louis lifted the crystal snifters and swirled the brandy. The huge Neo-Gothic house he'd built to indulge his unlamented former wife was utterly still this January evening in 1868. All the help had retired to their quarters on his instructions. Just after arriving, Louis' male guest had whispered that sending the servants away might be advisable. Once business was disposed of, the gentlemen could then enjoy themselves in privacy.

Upstairs, one of the women laughed. Louis was startled by his body's sudden and pronounced reaction. The little ballerina brought along for him was equally as vapid as Mr. Fisk's inamorata, an actress named Josie Mansfield. Neither woman had uttered an intelligent sentence during dinner.

Intelligence was not a quality Louis Kent demanded or even found desirable in a woman, however. Fortunately most women lacked it. He knew from experience that pretenses in that direction merely led to trouble.

Still, the companions of Mr. James Fisk, Junior, were particularly witless. Fisk didn't seem to mind. During the meal he'd repeatedly tickled Josie Mansfield's chin, which sent the other girl into convulsive laughter. The dark-haired, pale-skinned, and voluptuous Miss Josie saw nothing improper about tickling Fisk right back—in front of a relative stranger. She'd also bussed Fisk's cheek several times, and called him Sardines, which nearly forced Louis to retire and throw up.

Now the ladies had gone upstairs to bathe. Quite against his will, Louis found himself vividly recalling the little blonde dancer whose "professional" name—Nedda Chetwynd—was almost as ludicrous as her lack of social graces. Miss Chetwynd had clearly been brought along as a bribe. He had no intention of availing himself of the gift until he spied the trap or, if there was none, struck a bargain.

Yet the trill of feminine laughter had aroused him. Annoyingly, he found himself perspiring. His olive forehead glistened as he continued warming the snifters.

There'd been a January thaw. Fog drifted past the stained-glass windows at the end of the long, rectangular library. No lights showed outside. Kentland stood on the bluffs of the Hudson near Tarrytown, well separated from neighboring estates. The isolation was appropriate for a chat involving polite treachery.

He had to be wary. A mistake, even a wrong inflection, might cost him everything. The stakes which had brought Mr. Fisk to Kentland were immense.

Fisk fingered his yellow curls and smacked his lips as he surveyed the various articles on display. A scabbarded French sword hung above the mantel. Immediately below was a polished Kentucky rifle.

On a bookshelf to the left of the hearth stood a small green bottle containing a thin layer of tea leaves which would soon be a century old. A stylized version of the bottle still appeared on the masthead of Louis Kent's lucrative newspaper, *The New York Union*, and served as the colophon of the Boston printing house to which he no longer devoted much attention.

In a corresponding nook on the other side, the gaslights glared on the glass front of a display case with wooden ends. Inside the case, a slotted velvet pedestal held a tarnished fob medallion. In front of the pedestal lay a small circle of tarred rope.

The sword, rifle, and bottle had all been accumulated by the founder of the family, Philip Kent. Philip's second son Gilbert—begetter of Louis' mother, Amanda Kent—had struck the medallion, incorporating the tea bottle symbol and adding a pretentious Latin motto, *Cape locum et fac vestigium*. Gilbert had given the medallion to Amanda's cousin Jared, who had also acquired the little bracelet. It dated from the 1812 war. The tarred cordage had come from the frigate popularly known as *Old Ironsides*, on which Jared had served.

With another smack of his lips, the man the press liked to call Jubilee

Jim completed his survey. He was a red-cheeked New Englander with a sizable paunch that Louis found reprehensible in one so young. Fisk was thirty-three, two years older than his crony, the melancholy Mr. Gould of the Wall Street brokerage firm of Smith, Gould, and Martin.

At thirty, Louis Kent was trim, handsome, and urbane. His father's Spanish blood showed in his coloring and the Latin cast of his features. Two more dissimilar conspirators could hardly have been found; Mr. Fisk looked deceptively soft and jocular. He enhanced his aura of good-humored innocence with his wardrobe—tonight dark blue trousers and a sea captain's jacket aglow with brass buttons and dripping with gold frogging.

It seemed improbable that this man who had once hawked tinware in the Green Mountains and shoveled up manure in Van Amburgh's Circus was a power in the American financial community. Outwardly, Fisk deserved the opprobrious description uttered by the influential minister, Harry Ward Beecher: "The supreme mountebank of fortune." But Louis Kent wasn't deceived by catchphrases. He knew that behind the clown demeanor there lurked something far more substantial than a mind bemused by ballerinas and braid. Men who allowed themselves to be lulled by Fisk's facade usually paid dearly.

Louis didn't intend to find himself suddenly included in that group—no matter what sort of trap Jubilee Jim was baiting.

ii

"Fascinating collection of trinkets," Fisk declared. A pudgy hand rose to twist the points of his Napoleon III moustache. "Have some significance in the family, do they?"

"They did at one time." Louis handed him the brandy. "I should have gotten rid of them long ago. The sword, the rifle, and that tea come from my great-grandfather."

"The mean-looking fellow whose portrait's in the drawing room?"

Louis nodded. "He collected them before or during the Revolution. Apparently he found some inspiration in them that I fail to perceive."

To begin convincing Fisk that he was the right sort, he added, "I'll stand with Sam Adams."

Fisk gulped the brandy as if it were water. "What'd he have to say?"

"That there wasn't a democracy in the history of the world that had not eventually committed suicide. I assume he meant common people were uniformly venal and gullible. I agree. I don't noise it about, though. I pre-

fer to take advantage of it while stump speakers divert the rabble with
fairy stories about the goodness of democracy and humankind."

Fisk waddled to a chair. "Careful, now. In the Congressional elections a
year ago last fall, you were a pretty hot stump speaker yourself."

Louis flicked a bead of sweat from his lip. The man was beginning to
test him.

"God forbid that you should ever find me standing on a stump, Mr
Fisk."

The visitor didn't smile. "You addressed certain dinner parties. Quite a
few, Jay reminded me."

A deliberate thrust, Louis decided. *Jay* was a name men feared. It was
vital he not seem intimidated.

"Certainly," he snapped. He sat down opposite the fat man. "I waved
the bloody shirt just as all good Republicans did. The objective was to
pack the Congress, and we achieved it. This fall we'll get that drunken
tailor out of the White House and elect someone more amenable to friendship with business. General Grant, I hope."

Fisk meditated. "Andy may be out sooner than the fall. All I hear from
Washington is talk of impeaching him. Thad Stevens and his Congressional crowd want his scalp."

"Johnson was a fool to defy the Tenure of Office Act by trying to
remove Secretary Stanton from the War Department."

"Still can't see why old Thad's so hell bent on impeachment, though
Andy was whipped last year when the military reconstruction bills put the
cork in Lincoln's bottle of sweet forgiveness. The five military districts
down South will soon be filled with twenty thousand Federal soldiers. Including some nigger militia, I'm told. I 'spose you're in favor?"

Louis smiled and ignored the obvious bait. "Mr. Fisk, I don't give a
goddamn what happens down South unless it helps national elections
come out the right way."

"Helps the industrial and financial sector?"

"Exactly."

"You aren't all wild to promote nigger freedom?"

"Only when it serves the purpose I mentioned."

"You aren't thumping to get 'em treated just like white men?"

"Absolutely not. They aren't."

Louis drank too much brandy then. It scalded his throat. He was having a devil of a time convincing Fisk. The inquisition irritated him. He
supposed it was the price of gaining the man's confidence.

He hadn't done so yet:

"Don't mean to doubt you, Mr. Kent. Just trying to establish where you
stand. You *have* been pretty closely identified with the Radical Republi-

cans. You were quoted all over the East Coast before the sixty-six elections—"

Fisk leaned back and closed his eyes in a drowsy way. " 'Every unregenerate rebel calls himself a Democrat.' "

Louis' hand constricted on the snifter. The foxy bastard knew his speech by heart!

" 'Every man who murdered Union prisoners—who invented dangerous compounds to burn steamboats and trains—who contrived hellish schemes to introduce yellow fever into Northern cities calls himself a Democrat. In short—' "

Fisk's eyes popped open. His lips curved into a cupid's bow smile.

" '—the Democratic Party may be described as a common sewer and loathsome receptacle.' " Fisk sipped. "You were quoted, Mr. Kent."

Louis gave it right back:

"I arranged it, Mr. Fisk. For public consumption. Hell—" He waggled the snifter. "I stole most of those words from Oliver Morton of Indiana. I think it's intelligent to be on the right side at the right time. But I never permit politics—or what the public perceives as my politics—to interfere with business. I chatted with Mr. Gould at that dinner for major shareholders—"

"Made a good impression, too," Fisk admitted.

Louis concealed his excitement. The offhand remark partially answered a question he'd been pondering for the past five days—ever since he'd received the note from his guest written on the gold-embossed stationery of Fisk & Belden, Stockbrokers. The note had requested a confidential meeting.

Louis had sent a reply via messenger, inviting Fisk to Kentland. But he hadn't been sure whether Fisk had acted independently. Now he suspected he hadn't. That made the visit twice as important. It also meant he was swimming with two sharks instead of one.

He pressed his advantage:

"Mr. Gould and I discussed a bit of politics. He said that in a Republican district, he's a Republican. In a Democratic district, he's a Democrat. In a doubtful district, he's doubtful—but he's always for the New York and Erie Railroad Company. That's been my position ever since I started acquiring Erie shares three years ago."

The fat man's eyes grew curiously opaque as he heaved himself up from the chair. "Damn fine brandy."

Louis jumped to take the empty snifter. He prayed Fisk would overlook the perspiration he felt on his forehead. He sensed a watershed had been reached. He hoped he hadn't said the wrong things.

iii

While Louis poured with a hand less steady than before, another squea
of laughter drifted from the high reaches of the house.

"Your comments are helpful, Mr. Kent. Don't mind saying they've in
creased my confidence in the outcome of this discussion. With millions up
for grabs, confidence is important."

Louis shuddered with relief. Fortunately Fisk didn't notice. He had ar
eye cocked at the library's arched ceiling. The woman upstairs was stil
laughing.

"Time we got down to issues," he said abruptly. "The ladies migh
grow impatient if we dawdle too long. I keep my wife Lucy up in Boston
but I don't do it solely to free my schedule for business transactions!"

He winked and snickered like a boy with a lewd secret. Louis gave him
the snifter. "Many thanks."

Fisk walked to the stained-glass window and peered at the fog. Louis
used the opportunity to whip out a linen handkerchief and wipe his brow.
He had the kerchief hidden when Fisk turned.

"I think you know the situation, Mr. Kent. In the next couple of
months, the favors of the dear old Scarlet Woman are going to be fought
for like the very devil." The Scarlet Woman was the Street's term for the
Erie. "That's why Jay and I decided to approach you now."

There it was. The suspicion confirmed.

Fisk's eyes lost any semblance of cordiality. "Just where are you going
to stand when the war's declared?"

Louis didn't want to appear too eager. He shrugged.

"On the winning side, I trust."

"All very well to generalize, but I traveled up here for specifics! The
first test is right around the corner. Through the board members he con-
trols, the Commodore wants us to cancel our rate reductions on freight.
He'd like us to go back to charging the same as his Central Line." Fisk
licked his lower lip. "But to do that would only settle the dispute *his* way.
I hope you don't object to candid remarks about the Commodore, sir?"

More bait. Louis decided not to take the whole piece. He knew the information Fisk was after, but withheld it.

"Not at all. I'll be even more candid. The Commodore may be seventy-
two years old, but he still wants to gobble any competition that confronts
him. That's always been his style. We both know he's after absolute control of the passenger and freight business between here and the Great
Lakes." Carefully Louis revealed a bit more of his feelings. "Christ knows

where the foul-mouthed old vulture found his passion for railroads so late in life."

It was working. Hearing the word vulture, Fisk had almost smiled. He put in softly, "Same place we all did. In our pockets."

"He swallowed up the Harlem and Hudson lines. Then he got hold of the New York Central but he still wasn't satisfied. Now he's bought into the Erie and aims to fix the rates."

Fisk's eyes looked tiny and piercing. "And with the Erie in his pocket, the game's won. Everyone but the Commodore comes out a loser."

"I don't propose to be a loser, Mr. Fisk. He's not going to win."

"You sound as if you're offering guarantees."

"You know I can't do that. I don't have a majority position with the Boston group. I do have large holdings, however. The group listens to me. I can offer a substantial degree of advice. And I'm willing."

A genuine smile then. "Capital!"

Louis tried to contain his excitement. To be allied with the two shrewdest and most powerful men on the Street not only meant unbelievable opportunities for profit, it meant prestige. He'd been jockeying toward this goal for months. Fisk's note had abruptly opened the door. Coming so close was almost dizzying.

He feigned a thoughtful, sober attitude:

"But before I say anything further, I must tell you I do *not* fully understand the current situation. I need a clearer picture."

"You just said you're pals with Elbridge and Jordan!"

"But not privy to every one of their secrets. Or those of the Erie board."

Fisk pondered. "All right. I assume you're aware Mr. Elbridge of your group was Vanderbilt's hand-picked president of the Erie?"

"Of course. I was getting at the current relationship of Drew and the Commodore."

"Strictly business," Fisk snapped. "Vanderbilt and Uncle Dan'l used to play cards together, but that's over. So is any pretense of friendship. Ever since the Commodore started acquiring stock, he's been very exercised about Uncle Dan'l's fondness for using Erie money as if it were his own."

Louis nodded. On the Street, Drew was sometimes called the Speculative Director. He'd literally purchased the job of Erie treasurer by means of loans he'd provided when the road was foundering. Fisk went on:

"Dan's tapped as much as sixteen million to operate in the Street. So when Vanderbilt said he wanted Uncle Dan'l off the board last fall, your friend Elbridge jumped through a hoop."

"And you and Mr. Gould were somehow spared."

Fisk had no comment. Louis didn't pursue the matter. He'd be foolish to insist on knowing how that little rescue operation had been arranged.

"But Vanderbilt reneged—" he prompted.

A vigorous nod from Fisk. "On his own. There was no consultation with your group, was there?"

"None."

"Thought so. Vanderbilt didn't consult anyone, just forced his position on us through the board members he owns. The truth is, he got scared. He thought Dan Drew might be more dangerous out of sight with his shares and his money than he would be at our table. The rest of us agreed. So back on the board he came."

"Not everyone agreed," Louis said. "Frankly, those of us in the Boston group considered Vanderbilt's sudden reversal a sellout."

"Even Elbridge?"

"Yes. I'm still puzzled, though. Follow me a moment, if you will."

He felt like a man on a rope that spanned an abyss. A wrong step and he was through.

"Vanderbilt removed Drew from the board, then brought him back. You and Mr. Gould are allied with Drew. It's possible all three of you could still be allied with Vanderbilt."

"Mr. Kent," Fisk purred, "if that were true, would I be here?"

"You could be testing the opposition."

Louis' audacity brought a grudging chuckle from Fisk. "You're shrewd, just like Jay said. But it's tit for tat, sir. Elbridge of *your* group was Vanderbilt's tame dog."

"No longer. Not since the sellout."

"Are you speaking personally, or for the group?"

"Well, Elbridge and Jordan and the others—I suppose it's conceivable the Commodore could placate them somehow." He put the offer in plain sight. "Provided someone in the group isn't actively working to prevent it."

"Such as yourself?"

"Draw your own conclusions."

"No, sir. I want it said plain. Are you ready to sell the Commodore out? Form another alliance? Influence your group to stand fast against him?"

"If the reward is sufficiently generous."

"How generous?"

Louis' fingers curled against his palms, pressing hard. His gaze remained locked with Fisk's.

"I had in mind a seat on the board. A directorship."

Fisk didn't react. Louis was sure he'd asked for too much. Overstepped—

Then Jubilee Jim's laugh boomed.

"That's a coincidence, Mr. Kent. Jay sent me up here to offer you just that."

CHAPTER 2

## The Tame Dog

"WELL, SIR? DO WE HAVE A BARGAIN?"

Louis wanted to give Fisk an immediate yes. He was more than willing to be bought; he was eager. But he didn't want the man thinking him too compliant.

"We're very close."

Fisk's smile disappeared. "There's something else?"

"I'd like a further clarification of your connection with Vanderbilt."

"There is none!"

"I'm sorry, but there's Drew. You and Mr. Gould are again closely associated with that hymn-singing old robber."

Blandly, Fisk said, "Dan Drew brought Jay and myself onto the board last October. Since then, we have never been disassociated. But as I indicated before, the friendly relationship between Drew and the Commodore has been dissolved."

"Does the Commodore know?"

Fisk's grin was sly. "He will before long. Don't be too concerned with appearances, Mr. Kent. When you've gained a bit more experience in this sort of thing—"

Tact prompted Louis to let the deliberate slur pass without reply.

"—you'll learn that only two things matter. How much stock you control, and whether you're in a position to influence the price."

The fat man was right, of course. In the last decade, the Erie line from Jersey City to Buffalo had been a speculator's dream. After insinuating himself as treasurer, Drew had repeatedly used his position to advantage. His biggest and most spectacular killing had been in '66, when he'd played his favorite role—the bear.

Erie stock had been trading at a relative high of ninety-five. Bemused by false hopes of a price rise, the bulls had agreed to buy shares from Drew which they assumed he did not as yet own. They believed the old man was mistakenly gambling that the value of Erie shares would fall.

But Drew hadn't been gambling. He'd known exactly what he was about. He quickly manipulated the price of Erie downward from ninety-five to fifty by dumping twenty-eight thousand units of unissued stock along with other shares resulting from conversion of roughly three million in Erie bonds. Something like fifty-eight thousand shares all told deflated the price just as Drew had planned. It had come out later that he'd amassed the secret hoard of stock and bonds as security for one of his loans.

The bulls were trapped. Because of their prior commitment, they were forced to pay ninety-five for shares worth fifty. There was no regulatory agency to even wag a finger. Those not involved laughed—enviously. Those who'd been caught recalled too late the caustic maxim of the Street: "Dan'l says up, Erie goes up. Dan'l says down, Erie goes down. Dan'l says wiggle-waggle, Erie bobs both ways."

Louis himself would be in a position to participate in such a coup if he gained a seat on the board. It all depended on the outcome of this conversation. Three factions were involved. One was Vanderbilt, who wanted the freight rates fixed.

The second faction consisted of Drew and his newfound friends, Gould and Fisk. They wanted to dominate the line for precisely the reason Louis hoped to ally himself with them—the profit that could be milked from stock manipulation.

The third group, membership in which had brought Louis to the threshold of this stunning opportunity, was nominally led by the Boston money men John Elbridge and Eben Jordan. They sought control of the Erie not only to jiggle its stock, but also to shore up one of their own projects, a planned but as yet unfinished feeder line called the Boston, Hartford, and Erie. In the spring of the preceding year, the backers of the B. H. & E. had arranged a subsidy from the state of Massachusetts to help complete the line. In order to make the funds flow, an ever larger sum had to be raised from outside sources.

Louis remained on the offensive. "I'll grant what you say is true, Mr. Fisk. There's still one thing I don't understand."

Fisk fiddled with a curl. "I thought I was asking the questions tonight. But go ahead."

"I'm flattered you and Mr. Gould chose to approach me. Still, it would be more logical for you to go straight to one of the Boston board members."

"Jay'd be happy to," Fisk said blithely. "Then we wouldn't need you at all. I'm the fly in the ointment. Old Eben and I don't get along."

"I've heard that. But Jordan's close-mouthed on certain subjects. I didn't know whether it was a fact or a rumor."

"Fact. During the war, he and I had a falling-out. I was arranging cotton deals for him. The son of a bitch decided my expenses were running too high. He discharged me. You were into cotton yourself, weren't you?"

That was a sore point:

"I intended to be. My second cousin had different ideas."

"Who is he, some Government busybody?"

"No, at the time he was a reporter. Today he's a cheap-jack Methodist preacher. He lives in the city. He, my mother's Irish clerk, and that Jew banker, Rothman, decided my little venture was immoral. They spilled the whole story to the press."

"Must have missed the item. Probably appeared when I was working the Western Theater for Eben."

"Well, I was out of cotton before I got in."

"The luck of the game, Mr. Kent. I spent my cotton days in Memphis. Dealt with some first-rate gentlemen of the Confederacy through a charming go-between. Little actress. Hot piece, she was."

Fisk's pink lips curled in a smile of pride.

"Never got caught, either. I was giving Eben all the goddamn cotton he could mill. He delivered Jordan Marsh blankets to the Army and cleaned up. But he got scared by some prying from Union headquarters. He used my expenses as an excuse. Know what he handed me in severance pay? A measly sixty-five thousand dollars. I haven't any cause to be friends with Mr. Eben Jordan. Actually, I think Jay and I will ultimately be glad we had to deal with you. You strike me as our sort."

*Our sort.* Louis couldn't resist a moment of self-congratulation. Both Fisk and Jay Gould were giants on the Street. To be accepted as their confidant was a supreme accolade.

He decided it was time to abandon the pose of reluctance. He helped himself to a perfecto from an inlaid box. He lit up and sniffed the fragrant smoke.

"Thank you for saying so, Mr. Fisk. You've answered my questions."

"Hell!" Fisk cried with a flamboyant gesture. "We're getting on well enough to drop the courtesies. Let's make it Louis and Jim."

Louis smiled through a veil of smoke. "Happy to, Jim."

"Do we have a bargain?"

"We do. I'll exert every effort to see the Boston group sides with you and Mr. Gould."

"Your efforts have got to be discreet until the directors meet and the Commodore's men actually put a motion to fix freight rates on the table."

"No one will ever hear about this meeting. When the motion's made, I feel confident it will go down."

Fisk's chubby lips quivered. He was pleased.

"As soon as that happens, the directorship's yours. 'Course, holding a

board seat won't be all roses. When the Commodore's motion *is* defeated
he'll know he has a scrap on his hands. Jay and I reckon he'll try like hell
to capture a majority position in the stock so he can merge the line into
the Central or let it die altogether."

"I'm prepared to fight," Louis returned quietly. "I'm confident we'll
win."

Fisk laughed again. "Jay's going to be fond of you, Louis."

"I'm not in this for compliments. When you spy a money machine, you
don't turn your back. I've done well with my steel interests, the spinning
works in Rhode Island, the newspaper, and everything else I own."

"Jay likes the notion of your having that sheet. He's always been a
keen student of using publicity to his favor."

"I've only lost one money machine in all my career. That cotton-trading
company."

A memory of Julia disturbed him. In her own way, hadn't she been
such a machine? Deliberately acquired to improve his social standing and
thereby gain him introductions to men like Vanderbilt, who could and did
suggest investment opportunities? He'd lost her too.

The loss was even more humiliating than the collapse of Federal Suppliers. He could comprehend how that company had been ruined. The
reason for the destruction of his marriage still eluded him. He continually
fell back on the easiest explanation. Julia had lost her mind.

"I guarantee we'll use the paper to advantage, Jim. In fact, to get what
we want, I'm not averse to using any means available."

Fisk slapped the arm of his chair. "Louis, you're a fighter! I'd heard
that. Takes a man with nerve to ride in General Lee's Left Wing. Jay
did."

Louis preened. The term referred to gold speculation, which he and
others in the North had engaged in profitably during the war, ignoring
Washington's pleas that the currency must be kept sound.

The perfecto tasted better by the moment. He'd really done a good evening's work. Aligned with the winning side in what the Street was already
calling the Erie War, he could conceivably wind up increasing his net
worth five- or tenfold.

Abruptly, the euphoric mood disappeared. Fisk had a mild frown on his
face. He scrutinized Louis while he scratched the front of his ostentatious
jacket. Then he stunned the other man:

"I surely hope we can trust you."

"My God, we have a bargain! Why would you doubt—?"

The tiny eyes never blinked.

"I believe at one time you were pretty thick with Vanderbilt yourself."
Fisk was demanding the information Louis had held back earlier.

"Correction." Face darkening, Louis jumped up. "My former wife's father, Oliver Sedgwick, was thick with Vanderbilt. That's how I became interested in the speculative side of the railroad business. Sedgwick's dead. And I haven't played whist at Vanderbilt's house since I divorced Julia a year ago."

*Liar. She divorced you.*

"Reassuring," Fisk murmured. "Jay will be heartened. Uncle Dan'l will be heartened.—" The fat man relaxed again. "Hate to say it, but in many ways old Daniel's a simpleton. Robs the road six days a week and sings hymns at St. Paul's on Sunday to salve his conscience. He's wild to build more seminaries and have them named after him. Jay and myself, we have no such ambitions. We're in this and everything else to make money—and by Jesus have a good time doing it!"

Fisk thumped his snifter down. Louis' tension drained away. He could appreciate why the hostile press had little good to say for the proper and happily married Gould, but tinged its columns about the "railroad pirates" with grudging admiration of Fisk. Unless you peered closely into his eyes, or paid strict attention to what he said, the man had a bumptious likability which the yellow curls, plump cheeks, and luxuriant moustachios only enhanced.

Gould, by contrast, struck many people as downright sinister. Even now, Louis could see him vividly. It was not a comforting image.

Fisk's partner was barely five foot six inches, with a tubercular cast to his features. He wore a full beard to conceal what he must have considered a weak face. But Louis had come to judge men by their eyes. Gould's lacked any trace of human emotion. Coupled with a murmurous voice and a habit of rarely speaking above a confidential whisper, he inspired respect and sometimes terror among his adversaries. As should any man who'd earned his first million dollars by age twenty-one. At a recent dinner gathering of holders of substantial blocks of Erie, Gould had differed with one of Drew's opinions, and imperiously overridden his objections. Afterward, old Drew had whispered to Louis in a shaken voice:

"That man, Kent—that man's touch is death."

Remembering, Louis shivered. He didn't intend to get on the wrong side of Mr. Jay Gould. To do so would not only be unprofitable but downright dangerous.

ii

"Glad we've settled things," Fisk said as he lumbered to his feet. He rubbed his hands together and bounced on his toes. "Disreputable and shabby as she is, there's still gold in the Scarlet Lady's drawers. And you're right, no sensible fellow surrenders a money machine. I was wiped out twice in the Street right after the war. Uncle Dan'l came to me needing cash to tighten his hold on the Erie. I helped the old fool unload his Stonington Steamboat Line—God, I love those boats. Must own a line myself one of these days. I'll make it the fanciest the world's ever seen. Marble and mirrors in the saloons! Caged canaries singing in every—well, never mind that. Let's just say I made a smart move getting next to that pious cow drover. You made the same kind of move tonight. We don't have a thing to worry about."

Louis looked faintly cynical. "Except Commodore Vanderbilt's brains, his thirty millions of capital, and the gentlemen he keeps in his pocket. Judge Barnard of the Supreme Court fifth district, for example. Vanderbilt can spew out injunctions the way the Treasury turns out coins."

But Fisk had clearly tabled such concerns for the remainder of the evening:

"Let's fret about that when he starts doing it. Right now I feel good about the whole operation. 'Course—" A shrug. "I always feel good working with Jay. He's got the brains and I've got the brass." He laid a pudgy arm across Louis' back. "You'll see. You're one of us now."

Louis was faintly repelled by the odor of sweat oozing from his guest's collar and cuffs. Fisk bubbled on:

"We should join the ladies, don't you think? Oh, but before we do—"

A soft hand closed on Louis' arm. He was again jolted by a change in Fisk's tone.

"Maybe it's not necessary to say this straight out. Still, we shouldn't have any misunderstandings."

"No, we shouldn't," Louis agreed, disturbed by the glint in Fisk's eyes. "Do we?"

A shrug. "Not so long as you keep one fact in mind. Jay and myself, we call and play the tune. I'm an easygoing fellow—"

Louis doubted that, but said nothing.

"But Jay always wants to be firmly in command. No interference. No arguments. Nothing said or done to muck up his plans or embarrass him."

"In other words, if I'm a tame dog—"

"That's a pretty harsh way to put it, Louis." Fisk smiled. "But a good one. If you ever cross Jay by choice or by accident, you, not Jay, will come out hurt. That's why I threw in with him. He's been a scrapper since he was a little tad helping his pa tend cows on the family farm up by West Settlement. I don't believe Jay's pa thought very much of him. Too frail. Kind of disappointed the old man, Jay did—one boy among five sisters. From the start, I think Jay wanted to show his pa—maybe the whole damn world—that a thick arm doesn't count for as much as a smart head. People say there's sharp blood in Jay's veins, too. Jew blood. His great-grandfather led militia in the Revolution, only his name was Colonel Abraham Gold. The family started calling itself Gould around 1800. There's a lot of reasons Jay's a fighting cock. No man's ever bested him that I heard about."

The fat man's tongue worked across his lower lip, leaving a gleam of saliva.

"No man," he repeated. "Old Charles Leupp tried."

Louis had never met Leupp, but he was familiar with the story. Leupp had been a respected New York leather merchant who prided himself on personal integrity. He'd bought a sixty-thousand dollar partnership in a Pennsylvania tannery Jay Gould had acquired before he was of legal age. The original tannery partner, Zadoc Pratt, had seen the enterprise thrive under young Gould's managerial ability. But profits appeared skimpy. When Pratt accused Gould of diverting funds for private speculation and doctoring the books to cover his deceit, Gould's reply was reportedly a sardonic smile and a shrug.

Gould offered to buy Pratt's interest using money obtained from Mr. Leupp. The second partner was mulcted just like the first. Leupp discovered Gould had used his name and his capital to effect a corner on hides. Confronted again, Gould admitted his crooked behavior. Threats of legal action merely made him laugh. And he was unmoved by claims that he'd soiled Leupp's good name. Nothing moved Jay Gould save the prospect of a success achieved by speculating with huge sums of money—preferably other people's. He wished Charles Leupp good luck if the firm were dragged into bankruptcy. Leupp went back to his New York mansion, contemplated his dishonored status, and shot himself to death with a hand gun.

The point of the reference wasn't lost on Louis:

"I know what happened to Leupp. You can assure Mr. Gould I won't oppose him, or embarrass him in any way."

Still, Fisk's oblique threat was hard to swallow. He disliked hearing the truth when it was couched in a phrase such as *tame dog*. He tried to remember the main chance; the millions to be made milking the Erie.

"Just wanted you to understand," Fisk nodded. "No pussyfooting between partners, eh?"

He slapped Louis' shoulder. "Time to frolic! Did your butler send up the champagne?"

"He had orders. Three bottles to each room."

Louis opened the door, relieved to escape the stuffy library. Gaslights flickering in the entrance hall cast a bloated shadow of Fisk against the wall as the men strolled to the opulent staircase and started for the second floor. Fisk rambled on with other anecdotes complimentary to his partner. They walked down a long corridor to an intricately carved door. When Fisk opened it, Louis saw the dark-haired young woman standing before the blaze in the hearth. Her body was barely concealed by a thin gown.

Josie Mansfield hurried forward. "Sardines, I thought you were going to leave me by myself all night!"

"Be with you in a moment, Dolly."

The actress remained near the door. Fisk's voice grew a shade heavier. "I said I'll be with you in a moment."

Josie slipped out of sight. Fisk was unsmiling.

"Anything bothering you, Louis?"

His chin lifted. "Yes." In spite of the dictates of good sense, he blurted, "I don't care to be called anyone's tame dog."

"That's what you are, though. Bought and paid for."

He chuckled. It had a hard sound.

"Being a tame dog isn't so bad, Louis. When the rest of the world's freezing and starving, tame dogs stay warm and well fed. Keep that in mind. Keep Charles Leupp in mind, too."

He reached up to loosen his black sailor's cravat. He was still smiling as the door closed.

# CHAPTER 3

## *The Portrait*

LOUIS DIDN'T BOTHER to knock before entering his own rooms farther down the hall. He surprised Nedda Chetwynd, who was blonde, dumpling-cheeked, twenty-one, and eminently forgettable.

She sat naked in bed, her breasts coyly covered by the silk sheet. She'd already opened one of the champagne bottles in the silver stand. One hand clutching the sheet, she used the other to sip from a goblet. Her smile was hesitant.

He didn't return it. Why should he? The girl meant nothing to him. He was sure Fisk had given her explicit instructions, and promised her a handsome present afterward.

He scowled when his body responded to the girl's nearness. He hated to dignify her that way. He reminded himself he was experiencing a reaction solely because his encounters with women had grown less and less frequent during the past year. The press of his personal affairs kept him too busy and, often, too tired.

He stripped off his coat and cravat, then reached up to trim the recently installed gas jet near the oil portrait of Julia. He spun away and attended to the other ornate fixtures around the room, conscious of the girl watching him as she drank champagne in a revoltingly noisy way.

Ah, well. No point fretting about her manners. She'd serve her purpose and he'd never be forced to see her again.

Although the walls between the upstairs rooms were thick, Josie Mansfield's high-pitched laugh was loud enough to catch his attention. Then came a great bullish bellow from Fisk. Almost at once, the bed in the adjacent room began to creak. The rhythmic noise quickened with astonishing rapidity.

"I'll be with you in a moment, my dear." He didn't glance at the girl as he said it.

He stepped into his dressing room, closed the door part way, and began to remove the rest of his clothing. Even in the smaller chamber, the racket of Fisk's bed was audible.

He had to admit some of the man's crude ways repelled him. On the other hand, Fisk definitely was not stupid. Despite the remarks about tame dogs, Louis vowed not to think badly of his new partner. Fisk had given him exactly what he wanted. A directorship was nothing less than a mandate to steal from the poor old Scarlet Woman.

In the past couple of years, the Erie had become notorious because of its directors and its condition. The press, with a few notable exceptions which included the *Union*, constantly decried the line's lack of service to the public.

The hope of such service was, of course, pathetic. "Twin streaks of rust" was a popular term for the Erie and it was a fitting one. The line's seven hundred-plus miles of track were ancient and dangerous. Its rolling stock was a disgrace. Collisions and derailments took place almost every week, as did injuries and loss of life. Just after New Year's, another switchman had been permanently crippled in the main yards in Jersey City.

Many journalists and labor radicals persisted in spreading the ludicrous idea that the Erie directorate had a responsibility to its passengers and employees. Such esteemed "thinkers" as Charles Francis Adams the younger, the son of Lincoln's war ambassador to Britain, seemed to believe the burgeoning American rail system was somehow intended to benefit the public. If Adams and men like him had had any appreciation of the realities of life, they'd understand that damned few miles of track would have been laid anywhere in the nation if the entrepreneurs hadn't cared more for their purses than for people. The sole function of a railroad was to make money for the insiders. And the only railroad men admired on the Street—and secretly admired by the dim-witted masses, Louis was convinced—were those who understood a line's purpose and acted accordingly.

Now he was one of those men. Or he soon would be. The more he thought about it, the more he was convinced he'd been foolish to object to Fisk's bluntness. He could and would submerge his pride and self-esteem to make sure he did nothing to embarrass or irk Messrs. Drew, Fisk, and Gould.

The reward would be well worth it.

ii

He donned a silk robe, dimmed the gas, and returned to the bedroom. Nedda Chetwynd wiped champagne from her chin, still smiling her fatuous smile.

"May I call you Louis?"

He shrugged. "If you wish." He was growing impatient. Why had he even bothered with the robe?

He knew. That damned painting. He forced himself to glance at it. As always, the pale blue eyes seemed to mock him.

Fisk's trollop helped herself to more champagne. Louis found himself continuing to stare at the porcelain face on the canvas. The picture generated feelings of humiliation and hatred. Why had he kept it?

In a slurred voice, the blonde girl asked, "Is that the lady to whom you were married?"

"That is indeed."

"She's pretty."

"She was until she lost her mind."

Miss Chetwynd almost spilled her drink. "You mean she's locked away?"

"She should be. She got mixed up with that idiotic woman's movement. She began complaining she was being used like a household object. That's a woman's primary function—to be used—"

Louis sat down on the edge of the bed. He pushed the sheet away and fondled the girl's nipple.

"To give pleasure. In the kitchen, or here."

The stupid slut could only giggle.

"The next thing I knew, Julia was equating herself with the niggers."

Astonishment: "With the—?"

"You heard me. Niggers. She's always despised them, but overnight they became her sublime symbol! If the niggers are free, she said, why should women be denied voting and property rights? That's one argument Mrs. Stanton, Mrs. Stone, Susan Anthony, and the rest of that deranged crowd use to justify their bizarre ideas. The moment my wife took up with those harridans, the result was inevitable."

Louis was talking quietly and for his own benefit. There was a certain relief in speaking aloud in an attempt to sort out the incomprehensibilities of the recent past.

Not that he was having any luck. His troubled and vaguely baffled expression was genuine. Although he'd listened to dozens of Julia's tirades before she'd departed in December of 1866, he still could not understand her reasoning—or what had changed her in a period of three or four years from a demanding child to an adult with a frightening degree of independence.

As far as he could recollect, her complaints about being used dated all the way to '61, shortly after the disastrous meeting at Kentland when Boyle, Rothman, and his mother's mulatto mine supervisor from California, Israel Hope, had refused to endorse the formation of Federal Suppliers.

Something had happened to Julia that spring. Exactly what, he couldn't guess. Nor would she speak of it when he questioned her. Whatever it was, it had been the start of their difficulties.

She'd begun mentioning the Irishman, to whom she'd never paid more than the most perfunctory attention before. Sometimes she was warm in her praise of Boyle's stand about Federal Suppliers, or of his character generally. At other times—in a totally contradictory way—she spoke his name with what amounted to barely suppressed anger. Louis had tried to laugh off that particular paradox by telling himself she was being typically feminine. It didn't work. "Typical" femininity was precisely what Julia was shedding in slow, inexplicable, and horrifying stages.

Her complaints about being "used" dated from the spring of 1861 as well. So did her resistance of her husband's intimate advances. She'd moderated her crusade briefly in '62; that was when their only child, Carter, had been conceived. The calm was short-lived. Somehow Julia had heard gossip about Louis' involvement with a salesgirl from a Manhattan shop. The war had resumed.

By the time she left him, taking their four-year-old son—no loss; Carter was a vile brat who constantly wanted Louis' attention—Julia had become a model of calm, rational determination. Terrifying!

He'd commissioned her portrait for one of their earliest anniversaries. Many times since '66, he'd come close to ordering the painting burned. Yet he hadn't done it.

Perhaps the picture served as a cautionary warning. He'd already taken a silent pledge that he'd never become entangled with another woman. A woman was like a bad investment: too many unpredictable and therefore unacceptable risks. He was willing to undertake risks of the kind to which he'd committed himself by sealing the pact with Fisk. At least that type of risk offered a chance of profit. With a woman, the best you could hope for was to maintain status quo.

No, he was through with anything other than casual relationships with members of the opposite sex. Perhaps he kept the painting to strengthen that resolve.

Nedda Chetwynd was watching him in a puzzled, almost nervous way. He feigned a smile, plucked the goblet from her hand, and tossed it to one side without looking. The glass broke, tinkling.

He stood up and removed his robe. For a moment he wasn't the least self-conscious about standing naked in front of Julia's portrait. He rather enjoyed it.

He peeled the silk sheet away, disappointed in the smallness of the girl's breasts. But her stomach was plump and pink.

She simpered at the reaction in his loins. But she let out a cry when he pulled her out of bed.

Belly to belly with her, Louis gave her a quick kiss. She was practiced. Her tongue licked languorously while she reached for him with a caressing hand.

He pushed it away. "One more thing about my former wife, Miss Chetwynd—"

"Oh, do call me Nedda!"

He tried to hide his disgust. "Very well. Nedda. I should just like to observe that my wife's, ah, problem was essentially a simple one—"

*Liar.* To the hour he died, Julia's notions would remain aberrations, and the reason for them a mystery.

"She failed to understand where a woman belongs."

He took hold of Nedda's shoulders. The pressure of his grip made her wince. All round eyes and red round mouth, she gazed at his hugeness, then at his face.

Softly, he said:

"Let's find out whether you do, shall we?"

# CHAPTER 4

## The Man in the Burned Shawl

THE FEBRUARY TWILIGHT softened the raw look of the cottages along General Wayne Street in Jersey City. Gideon Kent stood by the parlor window, his good eye narrowed as he studied the black clouds billowing in from the northwest.

*Snowstorm coming.* After nearly two years he could recognize the signs. Raised in Virginia's temperate Shenandoah Valley, he still wasn't accustomed to the Northern weather. Seldom in his boyhood had Lexington received more than an occasional powdering of winter white. Up here, bitter winds blew for days at a time, and snow piled into loaf-like drifts that were slow to melt. Since autumn he'd already endured three such storms. Tonight there was obviously going to be another.

The thought had only a marginal connection with his own safety. He seldom fretted about that any longer, although Margaret worried a good deal. The threatening sky reminded him vividly of Augustus Kolb. It had snowed the night after New Year's, when an accident had destroyed Kolb's life in a few seconds.

The memory called up a second one. He thought of the man to whom he'd listened a couple of hours ago, down at the Diamond N Lager Palace.

Because of the man's reputation, the Diamond N proprietor forced him to convene his discussion group in the saloon storeroom. Even now Gideon could smell the sawdust and see the visitor's lined, exhausted face. The weary yet somehow spirited eyes. The powerful-looking hands resting on threadbare knees as the Philadelphian leaned forward to exhort the nine switchmen from the Erie yards. They had gathered to see what if anything they could do for Augie Kolb and his family.

"You can do nothing," the man told them, "unless you organize. That's the only way we've made gains in the Iron Molders' International."

"We ain't mechanics, Sylvis," a man named Cassidy complained. "We ain't skilled like your journeymen."

The emaciated man plucked at the shawl he wore over his thin overcoat. The shawl was virtually in tatters, pierced by black-edged holes. Sylvis claimed that for every foundry or cluster of foundries he'd organized into a local, he could count a hole burned by molten iron. There were dozens of holes.

"Makes no difference," Bill Sylvis replied. "The principle's the same. Single-handedly you can accomplish nothing of substance or permanence. United, there's no power of wrong you can't defy. I want you to think about that. And think of Kolb's wife Gerda. She's related to a man in our Philadelphia local. He asked me to take the train up here and talk with you."

Gideon was sitting cross-legged in a corner at the very back of the group. He'd only come because Kolb had been a friend. He had little interest in meeting a radical like Sylvis. So he was surprised when he found the man and his message commanding his attention. He was prompted to speak up:

"I suppose it's the same principle General Stuart taught us."

Sylvis craned his head. "What's that? Who spoke?"

"Reb Kent back there," said one of the others, though not unkindly.

Gideon raised his hand. "During the war I rode with Jeb Stuart's cavalry. He taught us to stick together in the field. The more of us there were, he said, the safer we'd be—and the greater the chance we'd be able to execute our orders."

Bill Sylvis nodded in an emphatic way. "That's it exactly. In Kolb's case, an appeal by a few men will probably accomplish nothing. But if a number of men—all the men in the yards—join forces and strike, they can effect a change. We learned that in the Molders. It's a lesson I travel ten thousand miles a year to promote."

A friend of Daphnis Miller uttered a glum chuckle. Miller had been pessimistic about the value of the conclave. He was out in the saloon proper, swilling beer. There was no question about the value of *that*.

Said Miller's friend, "We raise our heads out of the trench, we'll bring change, all right. We'll bring a flock of damn niggers or greenhorn immigrants to the yard. The bosses will replace us!"

Rather than disagreeing, Sylvis nodded in a grave way. "That is the great weapon the employers hold over us. We must find such a weapon ourselves."

"There isn't any."

"Oh, yes, there is. It's so obvious we overlook it. I did for many years, and even now I hesitate to express the idea publicly. It wouldn't be popular. But it's inescapable. If labor is ever to win a lasting victory, it must include everyone in its ranks. *Everyone.* The skilled will have to combine with the unskilled. I suppose that means women will have to be admitted to labor organizations. Black men too."

The quiet statement brought an uproar of protest. Sylvis raised a hand. "I didn't come to that conclusion easily. I know laboring men think of unions as the purview of the skilled trades. And I once believed the nigras were a threat to every white fellow who sweated for a living. But I've begun to change my mind. The Negro is no longer a slave, but neither is he free." The intense eyes shone as he scanned the troubled faces. "Neither are *you* free. We're slaves together. We must put off our slavery together."

"It's been tried!" objected a burly switchman named Rory Bannock. "Five years ago, twelve railroaders got together out in Detroit to start the Brotherhood of the Footboard. They wanted post-mortem benefits for widows of men killed on the job. They had to meet in secret for fear they'd be fired. Whole business never amounted to anything."

"I expect it would have if they'd stuck with it," Sylvis countered.

"Don't be too sure. Boys on the B & O wanted to approach one of the bosses with some complaint or other. They were discharged just for askin' for an appointment!"

Sylvis' eyes had a melancholy cast. "I never said the struggle would be easy. It hasn't been in the Molders. But when you organize—"

"We organize ourselves out of a job!" Bannock exclaimed.

Most agreed. Loudly.

"I agree solidarity isn't without its risks—" Sylvis began.

Cassidy gestured. "Let someone else take 'em. I got six kids."

Sylvis looked disappointed. So did the switchmen. They'd hoped Sylvis would recommend some quick and simple plan for securing financial assistance for Augie Kolb and his brood. Instead, he was speaking of abstract matters. Wage slavery. The union movement. A long-range strategy instead of a short-term panacea.

Gideon sat frowning, barely aware of the racket from the saloon. The objections notwithstanding, he suspected the soft-spoken Philadelphian might be right. At the First Manassas, he'd learned the value of standing together. He'd taken a few men off on his own and damn near gotten shot to death by a dying Yankee.

He wanted to help Augustus Kolb's family. But Bill Sylvis poured bitter medicine. He was realistic about the possibility of firings if demands were made. He'd upset and disappointed the switchmen. His candor about eventual mingling of the races in the labor movement hadn't helped either.

Gideon Kent and every other man in the storeroom needed their jobs.

That was the difficulty which brought the meeting to a swift and inconclusive end.

ii

All the way home, Gideon had been unable to get forty-year-old William Sylvis out of his thoughts. Now, at the window, the approaching snowstorm again reminded him of the chief officer of the strongest of the nation's fledgling trade unions.

Sylvis was well known among working men. He'd personally built the Molders into a network of over a hundred and thirty-five locals. He'd held sometimes reluctant iron workers off their jobs and won a major settlement with the foundry owners who'd staged the famous Albany Lockout of '66. He constantly promoted the formation of worker-owned cooperative foundries as an alternative to the existing iron and steel establishment. And he was being mentioned as a potential president of the National Labor Union, a relatively new association of workers' assemblies, union locals, reformers, and eight-hour leagues pushing for a shorter work day.

Still, the price Bill Sylvis had paid for his achievements was quite apparent. He'd been shunted into the anonymity of a storeroom because even small businessmen considered him dangerous. His clothes were hardly better than rags. His health looked none too good, either. At the meeting he'd declined all refreshment, saying he had a persistent stomach condition. He'd worn himself out—and, Gideon had read, kept his family in poverty —for the trade union cause.

In fact Sylvis had looked fragile and almost forlorn when he left the meeting and walked into the dark day with only his thin overcoat and that burned shawl to protect him. Gideon could still see the ends of the shawl fluttering like bullet-pierced flags.

The image vanished as he chafed his hands to warm them. The cottage parlor was dingy and frigid. The ancient floral wallpaper had a sooty tinge. Wind whistled through gaps in the siding.

The old walnut clock on a rickety table chimed half-past five. Gideon couldn't wholeheartedly admit Sylvis was right. To do so would compel a man to think of taking the next logical step. Like the others gathered at the Lager Palace, he wasn't prepared to do it. Times were too hard; work too scarce.

From the kitchen came the sound of Margaret starting Eleanor's bath. In the midst of the splashing, she called to him:

"Gideon? Your supper's ready."

"I'll be there."

But he remained at the window, his gaze fixed on the ruts of frozen mud and the shabbily identical houses straggling toward the river. His next door neighbor, Daphnis Miller, said the only way a man who enjoyed his beer could find his way to the right bed after imbibing was to count cottages starting at the corner.

Miller was a generous man. In less than half a year's time, he'd also become a good friend. Last summer, after being discharged from three successive jobs because of his Southern background, Gideon had recalled meeting the trainman at Relay House. In desperation, he'd ridden the ferry to Jersey City.

He'd expected Miller to be long gone or, if he were still employed, to have forgotten him. Certainly he'd have forgotten his casual invitation for Gideon to look him up if he ever needed employment.

On all counts Gideon had been wrong.

Miller had introduced him to the superintendent who hired switchmen. Gideon's infirmity had produced a gale of disbelieving laughter.

But the superintendent hadn't turned him down flat. Despite depressed economic conditions and a scarcity of jobs in the industrial East, few men were hungry enough to risk themselves working for a line as disreputable as the Erie. Even so, Gideon had found it necessary to plead his case for almost fifteen minutes:

He was strong. His tall frame and wide shoulders attested to it. He'd regained most of the weight he'd lost in prison.

He was agile. He'd been a cavalryman during the war.

He'd had to argue heatedly about his eye, though. He thumped the superintendent's desk and informed him he could march into any Army recruiting office and sign up instantly for one of the new regiments of Plains cavalry. If one-eyed men were acceptable to General Hancock or young General Custer—a soldier Gideon tried not to hate for leading the Wolverine horsemen who'd killed Beauty Stuart—then dammit, they should be acceptable to the Erie Railroad! Coupling cars couldn't be any more perilous than facing a band of rampaging Sioux Indians.

The superintendent remarked wryly that Gideon might be surprised, but agreed to give him a try. The man's expression said he didn't expect Gideon to last long. That only increased Gideon's determination to succeed.

The work *did* prove as dangerous as Miller had suggested on that afternoon at Relay House. A man was killed or injured every few weeks. Gideon constantly had to soothe Margaret's anxiety, reminding her he'd finally found employment that would keep him out in the weather, which he liked. Except, of course, during these blasted Northern winters.

Besides the appalling toll of deaths and injuries, the other discouraging element in the young family's situation was the move across the river in August of '67. It was necessary if Gideon planned to work steadily. During the cold months, ice drifting in the river made ferry service undependable at best.

Moving to Jersey City sharply limited their chances to see Jephtha and Molly. But Gideon and Margaret bore the new isolation without complaint. Finding a cottage for rent adjoining the Miller place helped. Daphnis Miller became not only his friend but his mentor. He willingly showed Gideon the tricks of the switchman's trade, and arranged for the younger man to be assigned to his own shift—dusk to dawn. Tonight, Miller would come along as usual about six-thirty, and the two would set out on their half-hour trudge to the yards.

He decided he mustn't tell Margaret about listening to Bill Sylvis. Luckily he'd made a second stop while he was out of the house. It would explain his absence.

He didn't want his wife to think he was flirting with a cause which might lose them what little security they enjoyed. In truth he wasn't. After the war he'd sworn he would never again fight for any so-called lofty principle such as state's rights. Mere survival was struggle enough. He worked a twelve-hour shift for the magnificent sum of one dollar and a half per day. Mr. Greeley's *Tribune* estimated an average family needed $10.57 per week to meet minimum expenses. Only Margaret's sewing enabled the family to reach that figure.

Nevertheless, Gideon and his wife repeatedly refused the gifts of food and clothing offered by Jephtha and Molly. Occasionally—and this was one of the occasions—he wondered if he'd been a lunatic to tell his father he wanted no financial help. A word to Jephtha, and he, Margaret and Eleanor could enjoy a secure life. Eat decently. Inhabit an adequately furnished home over in Manhattan.

He sighed. Independence surely had its price. Was it fair to ask Margaret to continue to pay it? Pride was fine, but it couldn't fill stomachs, or refurbish worn-out wardrobes.—

*Stop*, he thought, irked with himself. He shoved a hand through his long light-colored hair and blinked his right eye to clear it of a speck. He'd made the decision. He'd stick by it; build a future with his own labor and his own wits—even though he frequently felt the latter were still pitifully inadequate.

He was doing something about that, however. Every night. Every spare moment. His goal wasn't unrealistic. Many men were self-educated, including Sylvis. The Philadelphian had told the saloon gathering that his family had hired him out for farm work when he was eleven. He'd taught himself to read because he could afford no other teacher. Later in life he'd struggled to master extremely complex material because a grasp of it was essential for a union organizer. Sylvis had mentioned names that meant nothing to Gideon. Adam Smith. David Ricardo. Karl Marx.

He rubbed the sleeves of his flannel shirt. Lord, it was cold! His bladder felt full. But he had no desire to tramp out to the privy in the howling wind. The threatening sky continued to remind him of Kolb.

During the last blizzard, Augustus Kolb had gone to his switchman's job, had slipped on an ice-covered rail, and been crushed between shunting cars. Before midnight, a sawbones had removed both legs at mid-thigh. He would never work again.

And all Kolb's pregnant wife and two small children had received by way of compensation was a flowery note of sympathy written by some high-living, faceless Erie nabob.

*"You can do nothing unless you organize."*

"Gideon? Your food will be cold!"

"Coming."

iii

He trimmed the parlor's one kerosene lamp to conserve the fuel. As always, he kept his head turned slightly to the left while using his hands. The flame spurted once, throwing a quick highlight on the black leather patch covering his left eye socket. Then darkness claimed the room.

The bedroom was cold on the parlor side, warmer near the kitchen. The iron stove radiated welcome heat. As he headed for the lighted rectangle of the doorway between the rooms, another remark made by Sylvis slipped into mind:

*"Until you have a union, they'll take advantage of you. There are only two classes in the United States. The skinners and the skinned."*

The statement reminded him of his second cousin once removed. He'd never met Louis Kent. Jephtha detested him and, though related, never saw him. But Gideon often read about Louis in the papers. He was a major stockholder of Erie. On a night like this, he certainly wouldn't be shivering and shaking in his fine new mansion on Fifth Avenue, or his palace up the Hudson.

Again Gideon scored himself for envy. He didn't want wealth handed to him. But he did feel men such as Louis should display some responsibility when an employee was maimed for life.

Ridiculous to expect that, though. Louis was one of the skinners. Even before he'd met Sylvis, Gideon had begun to realize gentlemen such as Mr. Louis Kent lived at the expense of others. While Kolb's wife, heavy with child, tended him and probably cried herself to sleep because of the family's predicament, Louis Kent occupied himself with parties, voyages to Europe, and financial manipulations Gideon didn't begin to understand.

He'd tried, certainly. He read every available newspaper account of the current struggle for control of the Erie. None made much sense. He was still hard put to differentiate between "bulls" and "bears," and utterly failed to comprehend what a "pool" was, or a "combination," or a "corner"—

"Gideon Kent, what are you doing out there?"

"What? Oh—" He hadn't realized he'd stopped four paces from the kitchen.

"Why are you standing in the dark? What are you thinking about?"

*"You can do nothing unless you organize."*

"Nothing important," he said, submerging a pang of guilt and hurrying to her.

# CHAPTER 5

## *The Family*

HE STEPPED into the warm kitchen, lifted from his pensive mood by the sight of his wife and daughter.

Five-year-old Eleanor stood fidgeting in a washtub. Kneeling beside the tub, Margaret whipped a piece of nappy toweling called a rubber around the little girl's pink rump.

Eleanor Kent was one of the delights of Gideon's life. She was a happy, sturdy child with her mother's dark hair and eyes. Now, though, she was frowning:

"Papa, she's taking the skin off me!"

Gideon chuckled as he sat down at the old table where a plate of stringy beef and boiled potatoes awaited him. "She knows best, Eleanor. That hair brush—" He pointed to the bristly object lying beside a lump of homemade soap. "—does a lot more than warm you up."

"I'm too hot now, Papa!"

"Stop that. All the doctors say children need a good scratching after a bath. Makes the blood run properly."

"I don't care," Eleanor declared, "the scratch brush hurts like the devil!"

"Please don't use that word, Eleanor," Margaret said, delivering a light swat through the rubber she was using to dry the child.

Margaret Marble Kent was Gideon's age. Nearly twenty-five. She was a slender but full-bosomed young woman with pretty features marred only by a stubby nose she despised. Gideon had met her in Richmond at the start of the war. He loved her deeply and had never regretted his decision to marry her.

She was a strong-minded person and not timid about letting others know her convictions. An embroidered motto on the kitchen wall typified that characteristic.

*A NEAT, CHEERFUL HOME*
*KEEPS SONS FROM BECOMING FAST AND*
*DAUGHTERS FROM BECOMING FRIVOLOUS*

The sight of Margaret jogged Gideon's memory about the present he'd bought after leaving the meeting. He rose, walked to the cupboard, pulled the parcel down, and hid it behind his back.

"Eleanor, kindly stop wiggling like an eel!" Margaret brushed a loose lock of hair off her forehead. She laid the rubber aside and started to drag a heavy nightgown over her daughter's head. From within the folds, Eleanor answered in a muffled voice:

"I will if Papa sings a song."

"Papa must eat his dinner before it turns to icicles." She lifted the child from the tub. "The weather's abysmal, Gideon. They should close the yard when it storms—why on earth are you looking so smug?"

He bounced on the soles of his cracked boots, the small package concealed behind his back. "Got a surprise for you."

"A surprise?" She jumped up, smoothing her stained skirt. "Is that where you went after you woke up? To buy something we can't afford?"

"Didn't cost me all that much," he fibbed. "You'll have to pay for it, though."

Eleanor scampered to him and tugged the leg of his heavy corduroy trousers. "Papa, will you sing?" He slipped a hand around her head, fondling her hair.

"In a minute. First your mama and I must make a little exchange."

He rattled the paper with his other hand. He leaned forward and kissed Margaret, then revealed the parcel and bellowed a kind of fanfare.

Margaret looked increasingly pained. "Whatever it is, we definitely can't afford it. I'll return it."

"Impossible. I already got my kiss. You have to take it."

He pressed the parcel into her red-knuckled hands and picked up his daughter. She giggled while he pulled out the chair and plumped her on his knee.

"Any favorites, Miss Eleanor?"

Arms around his neck, the little girl continued to wriggle. "'Yellow Rose.'"

"Fair enough." He began to jog her up and down in rhythm as he sang in a strong baritone.

> "Where the Rio Grande is flowing,
> "And the starry skies are bright—"

Eleanor joined in, her voice clear and sweet:

> "She walks along the river
> "In the quiet summer night."

Eleanor jumped down, planted her fists on her hips and hopped from foot to foot—her version of dancing. Gideon clapped and kept singing.

> *"She thinks if I remember*
> *"When we parted long ago,*
> *"I promised to return,*
> *"And not to leave her so!"*

Booming the last words, he seized Eleanor's waist and hugged her so hard she squealed.

"For heaven's sake don't encourage her!" Margaret said. "Ever since three, she's been the most incurable show-off I've ever seen."

"You told me children always show off at age three."

"It's supposed to stop."

Gideon had to admit his daughter was unusually outgoing. He said wryly:

"Perhaps the Lord sent us an actress who'll support us in style when we're old."

"An *actress*? I hope not! I want no child of mine in a scandalous profession like—"

"Margaret, I'm teasing."

"What's an actress?" Eleanor wanted to know. She had no difficulty with the word; she'd learned to handle complex words and sentences long before most children of a comparable age. "Is it something nice?"

"An actress is a disreputable person who displays herself and—never you mind!"

"Go ahead and open the present," Gideon prompted.

Still looking perturbed, Margaret unwrapped the brown paper. She uttered a little gasp of delight when she discovered a small, wrinkled lemon and a large brown egg.

"Gideon, how much did you pay for these?"

"Doesn't matter."

Margaret gazed at the purchases as if trying to decide whether to continue the discussion of cost or just enjoy the unexpected gift. She did the latter, bending down and tapping Eleanor's cheek.

"Stand aside and let me kiss him again, miss."

She put her head between her daughter's and Gideon's and pressed her mouth to his. "You're a foolish spendthrift. But I love you for it."

"Well, God—uh, heaven knows—" he corrected as Eleanor clapped a hand over her mouth and rolled her eyes. "—a woman who works as hard as you deserves something nice once in a while. The *Tribune* says all the fancy young ladies whose broughams dash up and down Fifth Avenue beautify themselves with egg and lemon. If it's proper for society girls, it's proper for you, Mrs. Kent."

"I've read it truly does work wonders," Margaret said, carefully placing the egg and lemon between Gideon's plate and a book lying on top of a copy of *Leslie's Illustrated Weekly*. A subscription to the popular periodical had been one of Jephtha's and Molly's Christmas presents.

"Softens the skin," she added. "I could use that. The cold weather makes mine rough as bark."

"Always feels fine to me," Gideon grinned. He stuffed a frayed napkin into his collar and began to eat. "I wanted you to have something for yourself."

"Even though we haven't the money."

"Let me worry about the money. Time in this life is short, Margaret. I've been thinking a lot about Augie Kolb—"

"Is that what kept you standing like a statue in the bedroom?"

He nodded. "I wondered if Augie had ever bought his wife a present. He should have. Now he's crippled, and he'll never earn another half-dime—" He flung his fork on the plate. "It's damned unjust. Augie sweated eight years for the Erie. But now that he can't work, Mr. Louis Kent and the rest of the muckamucks have forgotten him. Something should be done to remind them."

"You sound like one of those trade unionists."

He looked away hastily, fearful his face would reveal his guilt.

"Thinking of Louis just about ruins my appetite. Don't let it ruin the present."

"It couldn't! Oh, Gideon—" Her eyes misted a little. "You *are* utterly foolish sometimes. But I can't get angry with you." She touched the lemon. "I'll try this tonight. You're supposed to scoop the pulp out, then beat the egg white and let the lemon peel sit in it. The oils mix. The lemony white whisks away all the wrinkles."

Quietly: "I'm giving you those a lot faster than you deserve. I've forced you to live like this."

She squeezed his hand. "You know I never quarrel with anything you decide after we talk it over."

"Including the decision not to ask father for money?"

"Yes, including that. You make me very happy, Gideon." She leaned closer, her breast touching his arm and creating a familiar, comfortable warmth. "Especially when you indulge that Virginia gentleman's temperament and buy presents."

She kissed him again, her lips lingering. Eleanor sighed and let her attention wander elsewhere.

Gideon forked a chunk of boiled potato toward his mouth. "I know I didn't make you happy by taking the yard job."

"I only fret when the weather's bad. You told me most of the other men never show up on a night like this. You could stay home."

"Shades of Richmond! 'Don't ride off with old Jeb, Gideon.'"

She flushed. "I'm sorry."

Soberly, he said, "I didn't mean to tease so hard. Truth is, I'd like to stay home. But I'd have to say I was under the weather, and I've never been much good at lying. Besides, we need the money."

Perched on a stool, Eleanor was rubbing her bare toes together. "What about the book, Papa? I want to hear some of the book."

"Oh, dear!" Margaret exclaimed. "I got so excited over the present, I forgot the child's feet—"

She rushed to the bedroom and returned with coarse woolen stockings. Gideon listened to the whine of the wind. The cottage creaked. A roof shingle tore loose and went rattling away. An arduous twelve hours lay ahead.

But before he left, he still had the pleasure of the evening ritual.

Margaret finished forcing the stockings on Eleanor. The little girl looked eagerly at her father. She didn't understand half the words during a reading, but they fascinated her because they fascinated him.

"All right," Gideon smiled. "We'll have the book in just a minute."

ii

Margaret brought him a hot cup of coffee from the claw-footed stove. Jephtha and Molly had ordered the stove installed as a surprise present when the couple moved to Jersey City.

While Gideon sipped, Eleanor raced to a corner to pick up a wire carpet beater. She pretended to capture imaginary insects in an imaginary net. Margaret emptied the woodbox and fed the kindling into the stove.

When he picked up the book he noticed *Leslie's* cover engraving for the first time. The engraving was a composite of three oval portraits. One of the men pictured, squint-eyed and narrow-lipped, was considerably older than the others. A decorative ribbon beneath his picture identified him as *Drew*.

The plump, sleepy fellow with the luxuriant moustache was *Fisk*. The third, sporting a fan shaped beard so large it concealed his cravat, was *Gould*. The cover was captioned:

### AT WAR WITH VANDERBILT—
### THE ERIE TRIUMVIRS

Gideon had never seen likenesses of the men who were part owners of the line for which he worked. He studied them avidly. He was especially fascinated by Gould. If the portrait was accurate, it created a deceptive impression. The infamous Mr. Gould looked about as dangerous as a poverty-stricken clerk.

Margaret finished at the stove and sat down. Eleanor swatted another invisible insect. She fixed her luminous brown eyes on her mother, who turned to a page marked with a slip of lace.

"Oh," Margaret said abruptly, "you mustn't forget to tell Daphnis what we discovered about his name."

Gideon nodded. "I won't."

She began to read aloud from the collection of President Johnson's public speeches. The book came from Jephtha's parsonage library.

"'The tendency of the legislation in this country is to build up monopolies—'" She glanced at her husband. "Monopolies?"

The ritual reading had begun two years earlier, prompted by Gideon's desire to familiarize himself with America's history and the flow of political and economic thought to the present day. It was Margaret who'd first suggested that she read aloud in the evening. She'd pointed out that Andrew Johnson had learned the same way. In his tailor shop in Tennessee, he'd paid men fifty cents an hour to read to him while he cut cloth and stitched seams.

She'd begun with the Declaration of Independence and the Constitution. Her patience and good humor had eased him through the first weeks in which many of the concepts made only a dim kind of sense. Now he'd progressed far enough so that he enjoyed the challenge of a question, and the chance to show his mastery of an idea:

"Monopolies are groups—small groups—controlling a type of business."

Margaret nodded encouragement.

"They usually agree privately to fix their pricing."

"What do you call a man who does that?"

Gideon rubbed his forehead. God, there was so much to know. He dredged up the answer.

"Monopolist?"

"Yes." Her smile heartened him. "The practice itself is monopolism."

"Ism," he repeated. He smiled. "As in Vanderbiltism."

She laughed. "I don't think it's in the dictionary, but it's apt." She returned to the book. "Build up monopolies—here we go. 'The tendency of legislation is to build up the power of money. To concentrate it in the hands of the few. The tendency is *for* classes, and *against* the great mass of the people.'"

"Sure is true of the Erie," he observed. "The directors run it for themselves, not the passengers. Workers don't count for a hoot either. The directors should remember what happened to old King George."

"But the law doesn't provide for railroad passengers to have any voice in running a line. Or laboring men, for that matter."

"Maybe the law's wrong. Maybe the Erie directors see to it. Maybe things should be changed."

Margaret was staring at him in a curious way.

"What did I do?" he asked.

"Nothing. You just sound like one of those trade unionists again."

He realized she was right. It disturbed him. "Shoot, I was only thinking out loud."

He started at the sound of a fist hammering on the back door. He opened the door to admit Daphnis Miller and a blast of wintry air.

Eleanor let out a screech as the air hit her. Miller lurched as Gideon slammed the door. Gideon's neighbor was bundled in a patched Union Army overcoat. A woolen cap covered his ears and forehead. A scarf was tied around the lower half of his face.

"You're early, Daphnis," Gideon said. Closing the book, Margaret looked almost as disappointed as her husband.

The scarf muffled Miller's voice. "Gonna be a hard tramp to the yards. Sleet's been comin' down like sixty for the last fifteen minutes."

Miller flicked droplets of water from his gray brows. He weaved to the range, extending hands encased in several pairs of mittens. "Real bitch of a night—oops. Beg your pardon, ladies."

Gideon started into the bedroom. He smelled the beer with which his neighbor had fortified himself.

"Maybe they'll cancel most of the runs, Daphnis," Margaret said.

"Not unless she drifts too bad. Gid, you better fetch an extra pair of mittens if you got 'em."

"I haven't," he called, returning with the ragged Confederate greatcoat he'd brought home from Fort Delaware. He put it on, donned his forage cap, stretched a muffler over the top of his head, and knotted it under his chin. Margaret raised on tiptoe to kiss him.

"Don't take any needless chances."

He patted her arm. "I won't." He was concerned about Miller, who had apparently continued to imbibe after coming home from the Lager Palace. In Miller's household, necessities were often sacrificed to pay for alcohol. Gideon religiously avoided drinking before going to work. Beer or spirits slowed response time. To survive in the yards, you had to be quick.

"Bolt the doors when I leave," he said to Margaret.

"I thought I'd go over and help Flo with her laundry."

"Mighty kind of you," Miller mumbled. "Those four youngsters can sure dirty a bale of clothes."

"Take Eleanor with you," Gideon advised. "And when you come back, lock up again. There are too many men out of work wandering around."

Bristling a bit, Margaret said, "Gideon Kent, I'm perfectly capable of looking after myself!"

He grinned. "I know. I keep forgetting. See you in the morning."

"Either that," Miller wheezed, "or a representative of the Erie will bring condolences."

Margaret flared: "That's a poor joke, Daphnis!"

He looked blearily contrite. Gideon hustled him to the door, then bent down to hug Eleanor. As he straightened, Margaret flung an arm around his neck.

"Be very careful."

"Will be. Promise." To Eleanor: "Whose girl are you?"

"Yours!" She blew him a kiss with both hands.

He tugged the door shut behind him, almost reeling in the blast of wind that howled through the tiny back yard. Miller waved his arms, losing his balance on the steps. Gideon caught him and held him steady. With his toe he tested the exposed edge of the porch. Slippery as glass.

The sleet was freezing wherever it hit. He didn't blame Margaret for worrying. He was worried too.

CHAPTER 6

## *The Accident*

THE WHITE WORLD of the storm dimmed lamps in distant cottages and drove stinging sleet against Gideon's exposed upper cheeks. The wind blew with such force, he felt as if a huge man were trying to push him back at every step. Before he and Miller had completed half of the two-mile trek to the yards, he was laboring for breath.

Ruts in the deserted streets were rapidly filling with a treacherous accumulation of frozen snow. It crunched under foot. Gideon knew it would cling to the metal of the cars they'd be coupling. Cling and freeze.

Miller's gait continued to be erratic. But he kept up a nonstop conversation, another indication that he'd drunk too much. Several times Gideon yelled, "Can't hear you!" Miller simply kept talking.

It seemed they'd been trudging for hours. Suddenly Miller yanked his arms, then jammed his face close to the scarf covering Gideon's left ear.

"You promised—more'n two weeks ago!"

Gideon shook his head. He had no idea what Miller meant.

A switch engine whistled in the murk. They were close to the yards. In spite of the weather, service hadn't stopped.

The older man shook his arm doggedly. "Gid, you *promised!* You said you were readin' that fairy story book at supper—"

He understood what his friend wanted. Margaret had urged him to mention it and he'd forgotten. "Myths," he bawled back. "A book by Bulfinch."

"Bull what?" Miller almost took a tumble. Gideon grabbed Miller's overcoat and helped him right himself. They leaned into the wind again "Finch. *Finch!*"

Months ago, Miller had begun badgering him about his first name. The railroad man's parents had been illiterate farmers in the Mohawk River Valley. Few people with whom Miller came in contact were conversant with anything but the daily papers. He'd appealed to Gideon to help him discover the origin and meaning of Daphnis.

So on Jephtha's last visit, Gideon had asked him for any book which might contain the answer Miller sought. Jephtha had located a volume on his shelves and posted it to Jersey City. This was no time to discuss it, though.

"Come on, Gid!" Miller sounded peevish. "Tell me what the book says."

They turned a corner and started down a dark street of warehouses next to the yards. At the end of the street, the light box of a slow-moving locomotive glared. The buildings shielded them from the worst of the wind; conversation was easier.

"How much beer have you had today, Daphnis?"

"Plenty. I said, *plenty*. Knew it was gonna be a pistol of a night. Now what'd you find out?"

A gust of wind blurred Gideon's answer.

"You won't tell me," Miller growled. "It's a woman's name. My mama gave me a woman's name. I always knew it."

"She did not. It's a perfectly proper man's name. The original Daphnis was a Greek shepherd."

Miller's grumbling told Gideon he couldn't hear. Cold and irritated, Gideon roared:

"Sheep! Daphnis herded *sheep!*"

"That the honest to God truth?"

"Yes."

"My daddy kept some sheep—tell me the rest."

Gideon coughed. His throat was growing raw. "Daphnis played music on some kind of pipe or flute. He fooled around with a—" He could see the word. *Naiad*. He wasn't sure how to pronounce it. "—a girl who lived in the water all the time."

"You say they were Greeks?" Miller cried. "Like the Greeks comin' off the boats with the Slovaks and the Dutchmen and the Jews? The kind of Greeks you see at Castle Garden and Wards Island?"

"No. They weren't real people. It's just an old story. A legend. Now keep quiet till we get in where it's warm."

He doubted he'd ever be warm again.

ii

They cleared the line of warehouses. To the left, between switch tracks, haloed lamplight shone from the shack belonging to the yard superintendent. The locomotive he'd glimpsed was chugging in the other direction, already hidden behind eight white-roofed freight cars.

They hurried toward the shack. Miller chuckled.

"Well, by God, I finally found out I wasn't named for any silly female —Gid, I truly thank you. First time we met on that prison train, I knew you were all right."

Gideon laughed, practically pushing his friend toward the shack. As a result he nearly lost his balance. Every exposed surface in the yards was covered with ice.

Miller blundered against the door, yanked it open, and careened inside. Gideon followed. The corner stove created a welcome island of heat.

Water dripped from the coats of both men. Miller slumped on a bench and appeared to study his mittens. "Named for a damn Greek sheep herder. D'you fancy that?"

The night superintendent, a short balding man named Cuthbertson, sat at a desk in front of a board. The board displayed the numbers and departure times of a dozen trains. Chalk lines had been run through all but two.

Cuthbertson jerked a foul-smelling black cigar out of his mouth. "Hallo, Gid. Who's your mush-mouthed friend?"

Miller's watering eyes blinked above the scarf. "Cuthie, kiss my sheep."

Cuthbertson looked dour. "You been puttin' in too much saloon time, Daphnis. Again."

"He's just tired," Gideon lied. The wind rattled grimy windows. The icy crust of a four-inch snow build-up glittered on the outer sills.

Gideon sat on the bench and dragged the muffler away from his mouth. His lips and chin felt numb. So did his fingers and feet. He peeled off his soggy mittens and hung them on the stove's open door.

"What's the situation, Cuthie?"

The superintendent pointed to the board. "All the passenger runs are canceled. We got two freights to make up, starting with the eight-thirty for Albany." Those were probably the uncoupled cars Gideon had seen as he approached.

"Maybe I could work with someone else," he suggested. "Daphnis could rest and handle the second train."

"I ain't got anyone else!" Cuthbertson snapped. Despite his perpetually brusque manner, he wasn't a bad sort. Just overworked, and hampered by inferior equipment. "We been hit by another of those mysterious plagues. Happens every time it snows."

"You mean nobody else reported?"

"Nobody."

Gideon's frown deepened. Four switch crews of two men each usually worked the shift.

"I can't wait to hear all the touching tales," Cuthbertson snorted. "Chilblains. Flux. A sudden call to visit a sick friend. I know who *that* is.

The barkeep at the Diamond N. Oh, we'll have a grand session of lying tomorrow!"

Melted snow trickled off Gideon's boots and formed little pools around his toes. The superintendent jerked his head at Miller and raised his eyebrows. Miller didn't notice. He was still contemplating his mittens and mumbling.

"Sure, we'll get it done," Gideon said in reply to Cuthbertson's silent question. His eye drifted to the open stove. In the flames he saw Augustus Kolb. The man had been thirty-one at the time of the accident.

Cuthbertson lit a second cigar from the stub of the first. "You don't exactly seem the soul of cheer tonight."

"Oh—" Gideon untied his scarf, took off his forage cap, then his mittens. He used his fingers like the teeth of a comb, raking snow out of the hair around his ears. Cuthbertson was waiting for an answer. "For some reason I've been thinking a lot about Augie Kolb today."

Cuthbertson nearly took his head off. "Why?"

Irked by the reaction, Gideon retorted, "I just have." He noticed the superintendent's face. "Cuthie, what's wrong? Something is. Tell me."

Cuthbertson exhaled a cloud of smoke. "They found Gerda early this morning."

"Gerda Kolb?" A nod. "Where?"

Miller's chin had dropped onto the lap of his overcoat. He snored softly. After more prodding from Gideon, Cuthbertson said:

"One of the youngsters found her in the shed behind their cottage. She used strips from a blanket to hang herself."

### iii

"My God. She was expecting!"

"Don't you let on I told you! I got orders from the headquarters in Manhattan. Ain't to be no reports of accidents in the papers. The bosses are gettin' whipped plenty hard enough over this stock war. I hear Vanderbilt's after a majority of the shares, and Gould wants all the favorable publicity his side can get. With him and his chums playin' their games, it don't help to have engines derailed and switchmen's wives doing themselves in—"

Cuthbertson stopped, peering at the end of his cigar. He pressed his chest as if his digestion were upset.

"Why would Gerda Kolb kill herself?" Gideon asked. "She had Augie to care for. Two boys to support. A child on the way."

A weary shrug. "I 'spose that's the very reason. Too many mouths and no money. You know the line didn't give Augie one cent after the accident."

"What'll happen to the boys?"

"I guess they'll take to the streets. Steal. It's that or starve."

"Jesus. You'd think someone high up would have the decency to pay them something."

"Why, no," Cuthbertson said. "High up, they got more important matters to think about. Meaning no disrespect to any relative of yours," the superintendent added sarcastically.

Gideon waved. "I don't know a thing about Louis Kent except what my father and the newspapers tell me. I gather Louis is the kind who wouldn't spend a dime to put flowers on his mother's grave—damn it, Cuthie, we ought to *force* the line to do something for men who die or get hurt!"

"Go right ahead. Call on your cousin! You might start lookin' for another job at the same time."

"Job or no job, someone's got to stand up for people like Augie's widow and kids."

"Not me. I like my three squares and a roof over my head." The superintendent rose. "You and Daphnis better start making up the eight-thirty. Provided you can get him on his feet."

"Daphnis—"

Gideon prodded the older man. Miller snorted. He shifted sideways on the bench, slow to rouse.

Cuthbertson lifted the angled lid of a storage box. He pulled out a pair of yard-long clubs of hickory wood.

"You boys want these? The links and pins may be froze pretty bad."

Miller was awake. "Listen, Cuthie. As long as I've been with the Erie, I've never used the staff of ignorance. I don't propose to start now."

"How about you, Gid?"

Gideon shook his head, settling his cap and retying the scarf. The brakeman's clubs were helpful in coupling cars. But experienced men considered using one to be an indication of inferior skill and a lack of confidence. Cuthbertson tossed the clubs back into the box and slammed the lid. Out in the storm, a whistle blew twice.

"The lads are waitin' on you," Cuthbertson said.

Gideon brought two lanterns from the corner. He stuck a twist of straw into the stove and used it to fire the wicks. He handed one lantern to Miller, who almost dropped it before he worked the bail over his arm.

Bundling up, Gideon was still upset by the news of Gerda Kolb's hanging herself, killing her unborn child in the process. It wouldn't have happened if the line compensated men for injuries and provided post-mortem benefits for widows. He thought of Jeb Stuart.

*Stay together. Press right on toward the objective—together.*

He saw the burned shawl of Bill Sylvis.

*Organize.*

Like Cuthbertson, he didn't really want to lead the way into what would inevitably become a storm of conflict and controversy.

Still, he couldn't escape one truth. Until *someone* led, the problem would never be solved.

Miller lumbered to the door and jerked it open. The storm tearing through the yards drove the imaginary one out of Gideon's mind.

iv

They tramped toward the switch locomotive, the glowing lanterns hanging from their arms. As they negotiated the ice-covered ties on the track beside the eight boxcars, Gideon shouted that he'd take the first; the one to be connected to the switcher's tender.

The wind garbled Miller's reply. He slipped again; almost fell. Gideon realized wearily that he might have to couple the entire train by himself. With the link-and-pin system, switchmen usually handled alternate cars.

Gideon wigwagged his lantern at the engineer leaning from the cab. The sleet slanted through the backwash of the headlight like tiny silver arrows. "'Bout time, you damn lazy clods!" the engineer shouted. "Let's get her together!"

"Blasted thing—" Miller was struggling with the lid of the link box between the first boxcar and the adjacent track. "—she's stuck tight."

Gideon beat on the lid with his fist. Ice cracked. Pieces rattled on the frozen cinders of the roadbed. He wrenched the lid. On the third try he got the link box open.

He checked the iron drawbars on the tender and the boxcar. To his relief he saw the bars were on the same level. He reached into the box for a link—a hoop of iron thirteen inches across—and two iron spikes.

There was about a yard of working space between the cars. The minute he forced the link into the horizontal slot of the tender's drawbar, he knew this would be no simple job. Ice clogged the slot. The link wouldn't seat properly.

He set his lantern down and began chipping at the ice with one of the pins. Then he used both pins to hammer the link home.

He positioned a pin over the opening in the drawbar. More ice kept it from falling. He pounded with the other pin. Finally the first pin dropped, securing the link to the bar.

Gideon stepped from between the cars and waved the lantern. "Back 'er up!"

The engineer retreated into the cab. Gideon averted his face from the wind as the drivers reversed. Slippage on the rails produced a sound like a scream.

The fireman clambered down, swearing loud enough to be heard above the storm. He flung four buckets of cinders and sand on the rails. Abruptly, the wheels found traction. The tender rolled backward. Horizontal wooden beams that served as car bumpers crunched under the impact. Gideon was lucky; the force of the collision drove the link into the boxcar's drawbar. The pin dropped without difficulty.

"I'll take the next one," Miller called. His lantern bobbed as he fished in the link box. The flickering light revealed a gooseneck in his glove. A gooseneck meant the drawbar of the second freight car was not at the same height as that on the first. It was a perennial problem with rolling stock; there were no uniform manufacturing standards.

Gideon followed his friend and waited tensely while Miller wedged the gooseneck into the bar of the first car. Miller stepped back to signal the switch engine. He slipped. The engineer interpreted the sudden jerk of his lantern as a signal. Gideon barely had time to drag the floundering man to safety before the cars crashed together.

"Too damn close, Daphnis. Let me do it—"

He pried the pin out of Miller's mittened hand. The older man snatched it back.

"Listen, Gid. You been treating me like a baby all night. I knew how to do this job 'fore you were a pup!"

Reluctantly Gideon let Miller have his way. It took the older man five minutes to seat the pin in the icy slot. Above the moan of the wind he heard the engineer hectoring them for taking so long.

"Keep your britches on!" Gideon shouted. "We're going as fast as we can!"

His right hand was growing numb again. The wind had intensified, hurling the mingled snow and freezing rain almost horizontally. He managed to couple the third car fairly fast; the drawbars were parallel.

Miller ran past with the link and pins for the next one. Again Gideon followed him, fretting. Miller stepped into the four-foot space between the cars. He had trouble with the link:

"Lord! The slot's solid ice—"

"I've got an extra pin. Let me in. I'll work on it."

He stepped to the edge of the boxcar. His boot skidded. He lost his grip on the pin. Without thinking, he bent to retrieve it as Miller again attacked the slot.

Doubled over, Gideon realized his error. The lantern on his arm had dipped.

The drivers squealed. Sparks shot from the cindered rails. He heard a chuffing, loud as doom.

Standing up, he inadvertently smashed the lens of his lantern on the corner of the car. He reached for Miller's bent back:

"Daphnis, get out of there!"

The cry went unheard. But Miller felt Gideon touch him. He swung around, his eyes angry. The train was shunting backward.

Miller saw the end of the forward car moving. He tried to jump to safety. The toe of his boot caught on a tie. Gideon had hold of Miller's overcoat. Trying to regain his balance, Miller jerked too hard and lurched the other way.

The bumper beam of the forward car closed the gap and thudded against the one behind. Daphnis Miller was pinned at the waist between them.

v

Time seemed to stop. Gideon heard bones crack. Miller's lantern went out.

The older man's upper body was twisted toward Gideon and projecting from between the cars. Not twelve inches from Gideon's eyes, Miller's face contorted. His hands scratched Gideon's sleeve as he hung there and screamed.

The scream faded. Miller's eyes bulged. He slumped forward. His head slammed Gideon's chest.

"Daphnis!"

Gideon seized his friend's head, tore off the scarf, and slapped his cheeks in a wild, irrational effort to strike life into the body bent at the waist like a cornhusk doll. Terrified, Gideon went floundering toward the locomotive.

"Go ahead! *Ahead*, damn it! Miller's caught!"

He heard the consternation in the cab. He couldn't tell whether it was the engineer or the fireman who shouted:

"You signaled! I saw the lantern—"

"Just go ahead so we can get him free!" Snow mingled with tears in his good eye. "*Just go ahead!*"

## vi

When the cars separated, Daphnis Miller was dying.

Gideon caught him as he fell and dragged him to a spot between the tracks. He was nauseated by the wet feel of Miller's overcoat. Not the watery wetness of snow; something sticky, welling from hidden ruptures in Miller's body.

The engineer and fireman bent over the switchman, stricken speechless. Snow whitened Miller's coat. It turned dark as blood soaked it.

Gideon ran like a man pursued.

*I didn't think.*

*I should have put the lantern aside; I saw Daphnis make the same mistake.*

*I SHOULD HAVE DONE THE WHOLE TRAIN MYSELF!*

"Cuthbertson!" He almost fell into the shack. "Cuthbertson, hurry up! Daphnis has been killed."

"Oh Lord, almighty—" White-faced, the superintendent ran for the door without stopping for a coat.

## vii

Daphnis Miller resembled a fallen snowman by the time Gideon and the superintendent reached him. The fireman had located a lantern, but Gideon wished he hadn't. The diffused rays illuminated Miller's contorted face. Life had gone out of him at a moment of extreme pain. His mouth was open. Unmelted snow lay on his tongue. Sleet spattered his distended eyes.

"My fault," Gideon said, struggling out of his gray overcoat and kneeling beside the body. He flung off his scarf and cap. He was unable to hold back his tears.

He'd seen men perish in wheatfields and forests. He'd seen them sabered, shot, blown apart by artillery fire. Terrible as that was, he'd never been shaken as profoundly as he was now. His hand stretched out to close Miller's hideous eyes, and he wept his rage and shame:

"Oh, Daphnis, goddamn it, this is my fault."

"Quit it, Gid," Cuthbertson said. "He was tipsy when you come to work. Tipsy and half asleep."

"But it was *my* lantern—oh, hell, it's too late."

Full of self-loathing, he covered Miller's body with the Confederate overcoat. He cried into the palms of his mittens.

"Listen, Gid," Cuthbertson said gently. "I take a big share of the blame. I should have ordered him to stay inside the shack till he sobered up."

"His mind wasn't on it." Gideon talked to himself, and the storm. "He had a lot to drink today, but he was happy. He finally found out what his first name meant." The tears dried up but the pain consumed him. "Jesus. *Jesus!*"

Even the engineer seemed moved: "Kent, don't take on so. Accidents happen."

"Happen all the time on this rotten line," Cuthbertson agreed.

Gideon's head jerked up. The leather patch was white. His good eye glared.

"I know. I know what happens afterward, too. Nothing."

The fireman didn't understand. Gideon's finger stabbed toward the body.

"Miller's my neighbor. He has a family, just like Augie Kolb. A wife. Four youngsters—"

Cuthbertson batted snow from his eyes. "Who's going to tell them?"

"I'll tell them. I'll tell them I killed him."

"Gid, you didn't!" Cuthbertson protested.

"They're not the only ones I'm going to tell. I won't see his children starve to death or his wife go to her grave like Gerda Kolb."

Cuthbertson tried to shush him.

"Cuthie, if you'll take him back to the shack, I'll couple the rest of this goddamn train."

"Sure, Gid."

Snow flecked Gideon's light hair. He twisted his scarf in his hands, the wind-raw skin under his right eye wet again. He thought of Louis Kent. His face grew ugly.

He bent his head and whispered a promise to himself:

"Once I tell them, they won't forget, either. I swear before God they won't."

# CHAPTER 7

## *Call to War*

"CAN'T YOU SLEEP, DARLING?"

"No," Gideon said.

She shifted her head close to his and tucked her forehead against his chin. Her hair smelled of the harsh homemade soap.

The bed creaked as she changed position and brought her right leg to rest on his thigh. The warmth of her body was comforting. But it couldn't banish the images of Daphnis Miller's corpse, or Flo Miller's worn face changing from disbelief to hysterical sorrow when he stood at the door of the neighboring cottage in the blustery dawn following the accident.

All the heat of the kitchen stove had dissipated. A chilly dampness clung to the rooms; warmer temperatures had arrived twenty-four hours after the storm hurled by and swept out to sea.

Gideon slid his right arm around Margaret while he folded his left under his head. The noise roused Eleanor in the truckle bed. Margaret tensed.

When the child settled down, she said, "You haven't had a decent rest in three days."

Nor had he reported for work at the yards.

"Is it Daphnis?"

He worked his head around and kissed her, but it was done in an absent way. "Don't fret about me. I'll be fine."

"Fine! Gideon Kent, we've been married long enough for me to know when you're fibbing. Tell me what you're thinking."

Silence.

Rain began to patter the roof. In moments it built to a downpour. A familiar dripping started in the parlor.

"I'd better set the pail out."

She tugged him back. "Not until you say what's on your mind."

"I don't want to upset you, Margaret."

"Do you think I can sleep, or keep my mind on the house, or help Flo get ready to go upstate for the funeral when you're in such a state? Refusing to eat? Sitting in the parlor till all hours with the lamp out? Barking at Eleanor?" A forgiving caress of his face. "Say it."

There was a peculiar blend of anxiety and relief in finally doing so:

"I have to go after them."

"The owners?"

"Yes. I'm going to get money for Flo, and for Augie Kolb."

She pondered that. Said gently, "You know what the outcome will be."

"They'll say no?"

"You won't get close enough for that. No one in a position of authority will even talk to you."

"They might."

"If they did, the answer would still be no."

"Cuthbertson said the owners are dead afraid of any bad publicity right now."

"They'll accept bad publicity rather than meet demands that could set a precedent."

"Goddamn it, Margaret, I know the chances are slim. But I've got to try."

"I didn't mean to anger you. I just want you to be realistic."

"I know. I'm sorry." He hugged her. The drip in the parlor quickened. Eleanor turned again, muttering.

"You'll lose your job, won't you." It wasn't a question.

"Yes. That's why I've been reluctant to say anything."

"Gideon, you know I'm willing to stand by you when I think you're right."

"Do you this time?"

"Your idea may be right. But it's hopeless."

He tried to sound more confident than he was. "Maybe not."

"Your father would be glad to give you enough money to keep Mr. Kolb and Flo secure for the rest of their lives."

"It wouldn't be the same. It'd be charity, not something deserved. The Erie *owes* those two families!"

"You're doing this because you feel guilty about Daphnis—"

"In part. I think I wanted to do it for Augie before Daphnis got killed. I kept trying to deny it to myself. The accident tipped the scale, that's all."

"You realize it's almost like going to war again? You said you never would."

He nodded. "A man changes his mind, Margaret. Circumstances change his mind." The exhausted face of Bill Sylvis drifted past his inner eye. "Daphnis was kind to us. When he died, he was almost as close to me as I am to you. Have you ever been close to someone who died violently?"

"No."

"Well, it's ugly. Ugly and dirty and sad beyond belief. Last month Cuthie was reading one of those Beadle novels. Some tale about Army scouts in the West. I looked at a column or two. Three men were killed in as many paragraphs. The author knocked them down like ninepins. There was no hint of pain. Nothing about the foulness when a dying man's functions fail. The writer made it clean and—and trivial. The deaths shocked no one. Left no one hurt. Undoubtedly the author's never seen men die either. A real human being can't be forgotten so easily."

"It's still a lost cause, Gideon."

A short, sad laugh. "I expect. But I fought for one of those before and survived. The thing is—I have no choice."

"Well," Margaret murmured, "it's decided. We can go to sleep."

"You're not against it?"

"I can't say I like it. But I suspected it was coming."

He rumpled her hair; tried to tease:

"Aren't you going to caution me not to canter off with Beauty Stuart because I'll get hurt?"

"No, Gideon. I've learned something about you and your family. The Kents have a tendency to go wherever they must, and hang the consequences. Just the other night, when everyone else stayed home during the storm, your conscience sent you to work with Daphnis. Even when I think about what might happen this time, I can't help feeling proud of you—"

She kissed his cheek. "Where will you start? The superintendent of the yards? The general manager?"

"They only take orders. I'll start with the people who can make a decision. I don't know any of them. But I have a connection with one."

Astonishment: "You don't mean Louis?"

"Why not? They elected him a director last week. It was in all the papers."

"He'll give you no special treatment. He despises your father. And you've never even seen him."

"Even so, I'm closer to him than to any of the others. I know where Louis lives. Father knows what he looks like. I must fix that damn pail—"

He disentangled himself, climbed out of bed, barked his shin on a post of the truckle bed and almost woke Eleanor. The rain pelted harder as he groped his way into the kitchen.

*She's right,* he thought as he lugged the pail to the parlor and placed it beneath the leak. *She's too loving to insist you abandon the idea, but she knows you're a damn fool. She knows it as well as you do.*

It had simply come down to a choice between doing nothing or making an effort. He had no great hope of success. But without making an effort, he'd never sleep well again.

ii

His tension and the river's choppiness combined to unsettle his stomach when he rode the ferry to the foot of Courtland Street next morning. Margaret had emptied her jar of kitchen money to provide him with a dollar and a half for boat fare and trips on the horsecar lines. He walked to the parsonage on Orange Street.

The study in the house next to St. Mark's Methodist Episcopal Church reeked of cigar smoke. But there was no cigar in evidence when Jephtha Kent opened the door, just the haze of his secret vice.

"Gideon!"

"Hello, father."

"I thought I heard the bell."

"Molly let me in."

Gideon entered the cozy, book-lined room. Outside the window, the narrow walkway between the parsonage and the church proper looked dark as twilight.

"I hardly expected to see you in town during the week," Jephtha said.

*He looks old,* Gideon thought with a touch of astonishment. In not much more than a year, Jephtha would be fifty; his long, straight black hair had a generous streaking of white. Age had softened his gaunt features. But many of his flock said he still resembled a red Indian.

"There's nothing wrong with Margaret or the baby?"

"No, they're fine." Gideon sank into a chair in front of the littered desk. He coughed.

A flush crept into Jephtha's gaunt cheeks. "Stuffy in here," he muttered as he raised the window. The sudden rush of air set the smoke moving and only made it doubly noticeable.

Self-consciously Jephtha sat down. His desk was strewn with sheets of notes for a sermon. He stacked some of them on top of an open Bible and picked up a large, stiff rectangle of paper that Gideon hadn't noticed before.

"Look what the morning post brought. A photograph of the new store. It's their fourth."

Absently Gideon took the photograph, which showed an unfamiliar man and woman posed in front of a frame building with plate-glass windows and a large signboard:

## H. & M. K. BOYLE
## OF CHEYENNE

An unconscious jealousy crept over him as he stared at the brown-tinted image. He'd never met Amanda Kent's clerk, Michael Boyle, to whom his father had willed Jeremiah's portion of the California wealth. He knew Jephtha loved and respected the Irishman. Yet he'd always felt it somewhat unjust that family money should be given to Boyle, no matter how strong Jephtha's feelings.

Still, he and his father didn't agree on everything. Since he was entitled to no voice in the decision, he'd never mentioned his reservations.

"I tell you, Gideon, that wife of Michael's must be a clever woman. They've already trebled the money I advanced them, paid the principal back with interest, and wherever they open an establishment along the railroad, they can't keep up with the volume of business. There's a letter somewhere—" He rummaged among the notes. "They'll be coming east in the spring to buy merchandise."

Suddenly Jephtha's dark hands ceased shuffling the papers. He noticed the look of strain on his son's face.

"I'm sorry," he said. "There is something wrong, and I'm rattling."

Gideon drew a deep breath. "I need some information about Louis."

"*Louis?* What on earth for?"

Gideon explained. Jephtha leaned back in his chair with his fingertips touching beneath his chin. When Gideon finished, Jephtha asked immediately:

"Do you know what you're doing?"

"Hell, yes!"

He fell back in the chair, embarrassed by the outburst. "Margaret and I have already discussed the certainty that I'll lose my job. Let's not waste time on that. I'd like to know what cousin Louis looks like."

"Easy enough," Jephtha said, and described him in a few sentences. Gideon felt uncomfortable. Jephtha's face had grown expressionless, showing neither approval nor disapproval. "Where do you plan to see him, Gideon?"

"I intend to try his home first."

"I'll ask you again—do you know what you're doing?"

"If you mean to say I'm a fool for trying to wring money out of the Erie for those two families, I know it. I must try anyway."

"Even though you're asking for the impossible? Generosity from men

who have no concern for the welfare of others? That hypocrite Drew. Fisk
—an out and out libertine. And Gould—possibly the worst of the lot. Pious
and proper in his personal life—a positive maniac on the subject of keeping it above reproach. I sometimes wonder if his wife deceives herself or is
simply ignorant. Propriety at home and piracy everywhere else, that's
Gould's style. I know a few pale imitators in my own congregation," he
added with a sad chuckle. "As for Louis—what can I tell you that you
haven't already heard? Before Amanda died, she feared she'd set him a
bad example. She was a wonderful woman, but in that respect she was
right. She failed with Louis. He's venal, self-centered—and the last person
on God's earth who deserves to possess the family heirlooms. He has as
much human kindness as his newfound partners in fortune, which is to
say he has exactly none. He doesn't even share Gould's virtue of maintaining a decent home."

"Do you know where he spends his time when he's away from Fifth
Avenue?"

"I've no idea. I would imagine he belongs to a club or two. The Erie
headquarters downtown would be another possibility. Since this amoral
stock war began, the papers say the directors gather there every day or so."

Gideon sighed. "I'd best begin with the Fifth Avenue address. From
there I'll trust to luck."

"You'll need plenty," Jephtha said in a sober way. "Despite Mr. Gould's
concern for editorial opinion, how the public feels generally doesn't affect
those men. Of course if Gould's wife saw a story saying he was chasing
another female, you'd see him deny it oftener than Simon Peter denied
the Lord. Still—"

A glint of amusement lit Jephtha's dark eyes. "We might be able to
singe some trousers in that crowd."

"We?" Gideon shook his head. "You aren't going to be dragged into
this in any way."

"Perhaps I'll choose to be! I'm in sympathy with what you're attempting, Gideon. I suspect it's futile but that doesn't make it unworthy. So
consider it a family endeavor. I might be able to help you from my pulpit.
It's been a long time since I've given my congregation a good teeth-rattling
sermon on some public issue. Everyone's agog over the affairs of the Erie.
Post-mortem benefits for Erie laborers might be an ideal subject—and who
knows? Gould might be sensitive just now."

"I'll keep that in mind," Gideon promised. "Meantime, I'd best be
going—"

Jephtha leaned forward. "Are you sure Margaret's in full agreement
with this course?"

"Yes. She's not enthusiastic. But she'll go along."

"Even if by some miracle you should win a small concession, you realize it wouldn't be the end. Rather, it would be just the beginning."

"What do you mean?"

"You'd be a marked man. Reprisals might be attempted. Certainly no business of substance on the East Coast would give you even a menial position—if that. Any future you hoped to find in commerce would be wiped out. Consciously or otherwise, you're behaving like some of the most hated men in America."

"You mean the trade union people?"

"I do."

Gideon bristled. "Everyone keeps throwing that in my face. I'm no damned unionist!"

"You are when you concern yourself with death benefits for laborers." Jephtha held up his hand. "I'm not objecting. In fact, I'm proud of you. We haven't had a good cause in the Kent family for quite a while. Perhaps it's time we did."

He circled the desk and gave his son's shoulder an affectionate squeeze. "Before you launch off, come along to the kitchen. There's hot tea on the stove, and Molly's baking bread. It should be ready soon. You look as if you could stand a bit of nourishment."

Gideon reached across with his right hand and clasped his father's fingers. "I've already gotten a good portion. Thank you."

"Just remember my offer of a sermon." Jephtha opened the study door. "A trade unionist. Imagine that. Your poor mother's probably whirling in her grave."

"Father, I do not see myself in that role at all."

Jephtha turned, his eyes intense. "I believe you. But you see, I don't count. Anyone who threatens the status quo, no matter how humane and sensible the reason, is usually accused of being a radical of the most extreme sort. Perhaps it doesn't happen without cause. Perhaps any time you *do* threaten the status quo, you *are* a radical. You're in good company, however. When your great-great-grandfather Kent fired his musket at Concord Bridge, he upset the status quo with a vengeance. But he was right. So are you. In the end, nothing else matters."

He clapped Gideon's shoulder and preceded him out of the study, walking with an exuberance Gideon wished he could match.

### iii

For five cents, a car on the Sixth Avenue Railroad took him nearly to the end of the line. Shortly past noon he approached the portico of the handsome house Louis Kent had built at upper Fifth Avenue and Fifty-fifth Street.

The city was spreading north; all the way to Central Park. Property owners around Madison Square, a highly fashionable address just a decade ago, bemoaned the growing commercialization of the area. Louis had done more than bemoan.

A stiff-backed manservant informed Gideon that Mr. Louis Kent was out for the remainder of the day. The brief and one-sided conversation ended when the great carved door slammed without Gideon having an opportunity to state his name or his business.

He clacked the knocker again. The servant appeared at one of the window lights beside the door. He motioned Gideon away, then disappeared. He didn't respond to the third knock.

Gideon went down the drive, out the gate and south along the rain-drenched avenue. A farmer from the open country above Fifty-ninth Street was driving a dozen squealing hogs in the center of the street. He gave Gideon's gray overcoat a suspicious examination. Head bowed, Gideon paid no attention.

Where should he go next? The only possibility was the one his father had suggested—the Erie headquarters located on the Lower West Side near the line's Pier 15 ticket office. He turned west to catch the Sixth Avenue horsecar again.

By early afternoon he was loitering in a dim cul-de-sac opposite a handsome, cupolated building housing the railroad's general offices. Trash bins at the mouth of the cul-de-sac shielded him from direct observation. A second floor overhang provided protection from the weather. But he still felt wretched in his soggy coat.

A half block west, the Duane Street pier jutted into the river. A great steam liner belching smoke from its funnels went churning toward the ocean, the British ensign hanging limp in the rain. Gideon bent his leg and braced the toe of his right boot against the brick wall. He opened the copy of the *Union* he'd purchased. At the end of fifteen minutes he decided he might have gambled correctly. Expensive carriages began to pull up in front of the headquarters, depositing well-dressed gentlemen who hurried inside.

Employees came and went as well. The traffic was observed by a couple of wide-shouldered men lounging on the porch. They had the look of toughs, but they tipped their derbies deferentially to the new arrivals.

A handsome victoria approached along Duane Street. Its calash was folded down to shield its passenger from the rain. A young man of about thirty climbed out. Gideon only had a glimpse of him, but the man's age

and swarthy skin convinced him it was Louis Kent. No one else fitting
Jephtha's description had shown up.

*That man is my relative,* he thought as he stared at the gilt-lettered
doors through which Louis had vanished. A curt laugh helped him overcome a curious sense of awe. Gradually, Louis began to assume more
human proportions.

Despite his fine clothing, he'd looked perfectly ordinary. The same applied to the rest of the visitors. At long range, their wealth and power lent
them an—Olympian, that was the word he wanted—an Olympian aura.
But they were men exactly like he was. They could feel pain and fear. If
he remembered that, he'd have a useful weapon.

Soon the last of the gentlemen went inside. Gideon had counted eleven
in all.

To pass the time, he began to leaf through the paper. He found the
usual collection of lurid material—a staple of the *Union*—including an account of a train robbery in the Nebraska Territory:

### UNION PACIFIC LOOTED!
*Armed Bandits Conduct Daring Raid
Near North Platte!*

The dispatch was a week old. It described the theft of a payroll from a
supply train by an unidentified white man and his Indian confederate.
The robbers had stopped the train by piling three frozen buffalo carcasses
on the track. They'd gotten away safely and Dr. Thomas Durant had announced a substantial reward for their capture.

On the next page he came across the editorial drawing. It made him
smile. A huge loathsome octopus with a wizened human face imprisoned
six anguished maidens in its tentacles. The octopus was captioned *Vanderbilt* while each of the suffering females had the word *Competition* lettered
on the hem of her gown.

Eventually the rain slacked off. He finished the paper as the street
began to darken. His empty stomach ached. He had no timepiece, but he
guessed the conclave had already lasted about three hours.

One of the toughs lit gas lamps beside the office entrance. The other applied a match to kindling in a metal drum at the curb. One by one the
carriages returned, including the victoria.

From the direction of the river a poorly dressed boot boy appeared, carrying his homemade shoe stand. He scrutinized the waiting vehicles, the
fine horses, and the well-dressed drivers congregated around the blazing
barrel. The boy set up shop by squatting on his box. One of the guards

made a half-hearted attempt to shoo him away, but he paid no attention. The guards returned to scrutiny of the street and their diamond rings.

In another few minutes the doors opened. The gentlemen who'd been meeting started to emerge. One thwacked his silk hat on his head angrily. Several were arguing. The fire helped Gideon observe faces. Earlier, he'd seen almost nothing but the backs of heads.

If he recalled the *Leslie's* cover correctly, the round-faced chap was Jim Fisk. He looked sleepy and phlegmatic. Gideon searched for Gould but couldn't find him in the crowd.

The doors opened again. Louis emerged, followed by an old fellow with unkempt gray hair and a choleric countenance. The gray-haired man negotiated the steps with arthritic caution, planting his drover's boots carefully. His cranky high-pitched voice carried across the street:

"You come here and listen, Fisk!"

The portly Fisk ignored him and escaped into a brougham. Gideon heard him call instructions to his driver as the carriage clattered off.

The old man—Drew, he recognized—was suddenly blocked by the boy, who addressed him in heavily accented English.

"Black your boots, sir? I'll do a fine job."

Louis stepped up, grabbed the boy's shoulder and flung him aside. Old Drew, still seeking someone to listen to his complaints, chose Louis. Above the racket of departing vehicles, Drew exclaimed:

"Ain't going to Ludlow Street for you or any of the rest of these sharps!"

Louis turned his back rudely and jumped in the victoria. The door slammed. The vehicle shot away across the rain slicked cobbles. The opening where it had been standing gave Gideon a clear look at Daniel Drew. Furious, the old man crammed a battered cowman's hat on his head and headed for his own carriage.

In moments the entire curb was deserted. The bootblack picked up his box, heading east. The toughs disappeared inside. Gideon heard the rattle of a bolt on the gilt doors.

"Young fellow!" He stuffed the paper in his overcoat and ran.

The bootblack's pinched face showed suspicion as Gideon approached. The suspicion intensified when a gusting flame in the barrel showed the boy the color of Gideon's overcoat.

"I don't shine no boots for Rebs."

"That man who shoved you—" Gideon slipped two coins into the boy's hand. "Did you hear him speak to his driver?"

The boy examined the coins as if they were tainted. But he pocketed them.

"Might have."

"Did he say where he was going?"

"Someplace on East Twenty-seventh."

"Did you catch the number?"

The boy's eyes had an old, weary look. He stuck his hand in his pocket and rattled the coins, almost tauntingly. Gideon found another ten-cent piece and held it up in the firelight. The boy repeated an address.

"Is that someone's home?"

The boy sneezed and wiped mucus from his nose. His smirk said Gideon, not he, was the naive stranger.

"Everybody knows Mrs. Bell's Universal."

"I don't. Is it a saloon?"

"Whorehouse. Too rich for you."

The boy strolled away. In the distance an omnibus bell clanged.

Gideon debated. East Twenty-seventh Street was across town; a long car ride. By the time he arrived, Louis could well be gone. Still, he might have a better chance to see him at a brothel than he did at the Fifth Avenue mansion.

As he started east on Duane, the rain began again. He clenched his teeth to keep them from chattering and put his hands in his pockets. Five cents bought him warm chestnuts from a pushcart vendor. The hunger pains abated a little.

But the food did nothing to warm him as he trudged on. The rain fell harder. It promised to be a long, cold night.

# CHAPTER 8

## At the Universal

IN A PRIVATE second-floor parlor of Mrs. Hester Bell's establishment on East Twenty-seventh Street, Jubilee Jim was having a bath. If Louis had ever witnessed such a bizarre scene, he couldn't recall it.

The parlor's walls and ceiling were covered with mirrors. On a dais in the center of the carpet sat an oversized zinc tub topped with imported marble. A mirrored door led to a bedchamber. Mrs. Bell also provided a piano for patrons aesthetically inclined.

The club's blind black musician was working downstairs at the moment. The arpeggios of a classical piece drifted to the parlor, interspersed with restrained feminine merriment. The door to the hall was bolted on the inside. After the formal board meeting had broken up, Fisk had insisted on a private conference. He refused to go anywhere but the club; Miss Mansfield was suffering her monthly indisposition.

Louis sat at a small marble table next to the wall opposite the bedroom. Across the table was the small and sallow Jay Gould. An obligatory glass of lager stood beside his pale hand. He resembled a church deacon transported to hell against his will.

Wherever Louis looked—right, left, or overhead—he saw Jubilee Jim submerged to his chest in perfumed water and surrounded by a constantly changing mosaic of bare buttocks, dark-nippled breasts, and black hair. Fisk had a sea captain's hat cocked on his yellow curls. He was being tended by a pair of Oriental girls. Chinese, Mrs. Bell said. Neither was more than eighteen.

The Universal Club employed girls of eleven nationalities—plus two men, a Portuguese and a West Indian mulatto, who catered to a small segment of the clientele. Mrs. Bell guaranteed none of the employees could speak English, thus assuring their discretion. A cadaverous fellow named Dr. Randolph acted as club manager and translator; he'd been a professor of languages at a New England academy for boys until his dismissal on morals charges.

Fisk, a regular at the Universal, had brought Louis there for the first time three weeks ago. Louis had heard of the place before that, of course. But it took a man of Fisk's status to gain him admittance as a customer.

He wished the meeting had been arranged for another location, though. Somehow the sight of the naked young women bothered him; reminded him of the little dancer, Nedda, whom he thought he'd forgotten.

Giggling, one of the girls refilled Fisk's champagne glass. The other girl, kneeling on the tub's far side, was vigorously bathing the fat man. At least her arm was immersed to the elbow, and her unseen hand appeared quite busy. Fisk's face was a study in simple-minded bliss.

Louis cleared his throat. Gould said:

"Jim, you've inconvenienced me by insisting we traipse over to a place like this. Let's get on with the business."

"Jay, my friend—" Fisk tilted his glass, drank, and smacked his lips. Some of the liquid dribbled down his chin. "The trouble with you is, you're too starched. Too blasted starched."

He winked at Louis. "I always tell Jay there's one big difference between us. I have more trouble to get my dinner than to digest it. He has more trouble to digest it than to get it. Enjoy yourself for a change, Jay!"

"My idea of a good time is to be home with Helen and the boys."

"All right," Fisk pouted. He jiggled the forearm of the girl bathing him. "You wait in the bedroom."

The girl blushed, unable to understand. Fisk waved the champagne goblet:

"In there. Vamoose! Scat!"

The two retired, rumps jiggling. The mirrored door closed. With a pallid hand Gould pushed his beer glass toward Louis.

"You may have this if you want it. I haven't touched it."

"Jesus, what an old stiff neck!" Fisk heaved himself out of the tub, snatched a towel, and began drying his genitals. He wrapped the towel around his paunch, sat on the marble tub rim, and wiggled his pink toes. "We do need to have a talk, though. I think Uncle Dan'l's losing his nerve."

Gould shrugged, unexpectedly tolerant.

"When a fellow passes seventy, he's bound to be less than steady."

"Oh, shit on that, Jay. The Commodore's three years older than Dan and *he* hasn't lost his nerve. He's busy as a flea on a hound. He's out to corner Erie shares, keep us from issuing any more, and use his majority to shovel in a whole new board of directors next month. Unless we prevent it."

Louis knocked back the rest of his champagne and reached for the bottle in its silver stand. "We took action to prevent it this afternoon. Jay's inspiration solved our problem."

He said it with genuine respect. Gould had remembered an antique printing press stored in the basement of the Erie offices.

Louis hoped the press was the answer to the difficulties they'd encountered in the past few weeks. The war was intensifying. After the vote on rate fixing had gone against the Commodore thanks to Louis' efforts, the old man had realized the Boston group was abandoning him. He'd issued a terse order in the Street: "Buy Erie and keep on buying."

While his brokers piled up shares, he took steps to prevent Gould's faction from doing the same. Just two days ago, his captive State Supreme Court judge, had issued an injunction preventing the Erie from paying Drew interest or principal on an outstanding loan of three and a half million dollars; money that could have bought shares. Judge Barnard had separately enjoined Drew from speculating with a sizable block of stock still in his possession.

That had been the gloomy picture until the afternoon's gathering of the board—from which the Commodore's men had lately absented themselves. In his most confidential manner, Gould had pointed out that despite the injunctions, the Vanderbilt group had failed to plug up an escape hatch—a complex New York state law permitting issuance of new shares when one railroad acquired another. A few weeks before, the Erie had secretly purchased the moribund Buffalo, Bradford, & Pittsburgh line just in case injunctions were forthcoming.

Now it was necessary to invoke the law to legalize a new float of bonds convertible to stock. Following Mr. Gould's quiet but stunning mention of the old printing press in the basement, a vote had been taken authorizing ten millions of such bonds.

Louis had helped draft the language for the minutes. In outrageously straight-faced sentences, the directors had declared the move was being made because of an *urgent and distressing report* from the line's general manager. He was pleading for funds to repair the Erie trackage, *where,* the minutes now read, *it is wholly unsafe to run a passenger train at the ordinary speed. Broken wheels, rails, engines, and cars off the track have been of daily, almost hourly occurrence for the past two months.*

It looked marvelously official. But the three gentlemen at Mrs. Bell's knew the worried general manager would never see a penny of the income from the new issue.

Louis chuckled. "By God, it *is* a brilliant move—churning out bonds in the basement."

"That's the spirit I like to see!" Fisk exclaimed, jumping up. The towel fell away, but he paid no attention. He capered like an overage cherub.

"Just give me enough rag paper and we'll hammer the everlasting tar out of that old mariner from Staten Island!"

"Of course," Gould thought aloud, "the Commodore will soon know we're simply dumping more shares on the market."

"And he'll go after them," Louis agreed. "It's no strain on his bank account. He still has thirty millions to play with."

Fisk waved that aside. "After we've swallowed eight or nine million of his money, maybe he'll realize he's throwing it down a sewer." Warming to the subject, he practically pranced. "We can print bonds faster than his brokerages can buy 'em! Ink's cheap. White paper's cheap. If we can make Vanderbilt pay us fifty or sixty dollars for little pieces of paper that haven't cost us two cents, it's good night Commodore!"

"Unless he moves against us in the courts again," Gould warned.

"I'm more worried about Uncle Dan'l," Louis put in. "Jim's right—I think he's going soft."

That sobered Fisk dramatically. "Yes, Drew's the real reason I wanted us to meet. If we lose his vote, we're hulled and sunk. He has enough influence on the board to stop us from running the press. And he's scared. Jay, you saw how he turned white when you proposed the printing scheme. Danny still wants to win, I think. But the question is—how badly?"

Jay Gould didn't answer immediately. He sat like a meditating ascetic, his mournful eyes probing places beyond the ken of his companions. Finally he roused.

"I agree, Dan's a queer case these days. It may be senility. Or perhaps he's just gotten too fond of endowing seminaries and preening in his pew at St. Paul's. Business and religion are oil and water. Whatever the reason, he's forgotten that."

Fisk agreed vehemently: "When he voted for the bond issue this afternoon, his hands were shaking."

"And he tried to hector me about the idea afterward—" Louis began.

"I suppose all he can see is a cell at Ludlow Street," Gould said. "He'd be devastated to have his pious reputation soiled by a term in the clink."

"Well, Christ," Fisk laughed, "I don't want to see the inside of the lockup any more than he does. But as Dan himself used to say, if a cat wants to eat a fish, she's got to be willing to wet her feet. We're going to print the bonds as fast as possible. While we do, it's up to each one of us to keep pounding at Dan. Keep reminding him we can't win any other way, and this way, we're sure to win. Every time we dump shares, the price'll drop. Vanderbilt's hirelings will jump in and spend like Midas. The price'll go up, then we'll crank the press and drive the market down again. We'll have him dizzy and half broke if we stick to it!"

"I'm in agreement," Gould said. "We must all work on Drew. Bolster his nerve."

"I'll take him to lunch at the Union Club tomorrow," Louis promised.

"A good start." Gould's almost colorless lips curved in a tiny smile barely visible between his moustache and beard. "You've already proved your persuasive powers are considerable, Louis. Just don't utter the word injunction to Dan. It terrifies him. However, I do think it's probable Vanderbilt will get another one to prevent us from running the press."

"That's another point on which we have to agree," Fisk nodded. "What if it happens? Do we stop?" He barely paused. "I say no."

Louis pondered. The prospect of lengthy court proceedings—even an arrest—was unappetizing. But he didn't dare offend Fisk; he was in too deeply.

"So do I," he said.

Gould said, "I'm wondering how long we can keep Vanderbilt from realizing what we're up to."

"Mmm." Fisk scratched his jowl. "Today's the nineteenth. I'd guess a week. Maybe two."

"We can take a hell of a lot of his money in that time," Louis said.

"But how do you vote on stopping, Jay?" Fisk prodded. "I'd like it to be unanimous."

Gould's face showed no hint of hesitation. "It is. We go straight ahead until the constables bring an injunction to the doorsill. Then we'll figure out our next move."

"If there *is* an injunction," Fisk said, "Uncle Dan'l will quit."

"*Want* to quit," Gould corrected. "Again it's up to us to prevent him. Remind him that if he buckles, he'll not only be unable to shower endowments on churches, he'll be a ruined man. We must keep cautioning Danny that jail is bad, a tarnished reputation is worse, but being ruined is worst of all. *Ruined* is the key word. It's better to risk Ludlow Street now —or hell in the hereafter—than be ruined. Deep down, Drew knows it."

The balding financier's eyes were brightly thoughtful. Louis shivered. Gould was an absolute wizard, not only of share manipulation but of the forces that motivated men. In the contemporary vocabulary there was no word more potent than ruined. Men would risk almost anything rather than be labeled with it. So would women—although to the female sex, ruin meant a loss of something other than wealth.

Louis began to feel less anxious. Fisk too seemed relieved. He lifted one flabby leg into the tub and lowered himself. "Knew we'd see eye to eye. We'll go ahead." He belched, adjusted his nautical cap, and used an index finger to dribble perfumed water into his navel. "And, between us, we'll keep Danny's pecker stiff when it droops. Every one of us is responsible."

A glance at Louis. It said he was being tested again. He still didn't enjoy the full measure of confidence Fisk and Gould had in one another. But they'd handed him another chance to prove his worth. He wouldn't neglect it.

Out in the hall, someone knocked.

Gould jerked upright. "Confound it, Jim, we issued explicit orders."

The words carried an edge of concern. Louis strode to the door.

"Who's there?"

"Mrs. Bell," a basso voice replied. "That you, Mr. Kent?"

"Yes. We said we weren't to be interrupted."

"Well, sir, I'm afraid you'll have to be," the woman retorted. "We have a peculiar situation downstairs. Some fellow's asking for you."

Louis' stomach knotted when he heard Gould's sharp intake of breath. Fisk began to burble outraged questions.

"Tell him I'm not here, for God's sake!"

"He knows you are. He's polite but he's insistent."

Louis turned. As he pointed to the bolt, his nervous eyes queried the other two men. He got a curt nod from Gould, unlocked the door, and admitted a massive woman in a brocaded gown.

"Why didn't you have Dr. Randolph get rid of him?" Louis demanded.

"Because," Mrs. Bell shot back, "he says his name's the same as yours. He says his name's Kent."

## ii

Jay Gould stormed toward them.

"Louis, what the devil is going on here?"

Stunned, Louis lifted both hands. "Jay, it's a damned mystery to me. How old is this man, Mrs. Bell? Forty-five? Is he wearing shabby clothes, like a parson's?"

Hester Bell shook her head. "He's shabby, all right. But I've never seen a parson in a Confederate overcoat. The boy's in his twenties. Partially blind. That is, I assume so. He wears a patch—"

One of her ringed hands touched the powdered skin below her left eye. She added:

"He says he won't go till he speaks with you."

"Blast it, I knew we shouldn't have come here!" Gould cried. "Who is he, Louis?"

"I don't know!"

"You've talked about your cousin, the preacher. I've never heard you mention any other Kents."

Louis began to perspire. Even Fisk no longer looked cordial.

"Reverend Kent has a couple of sons," Louis explained hastily. "I've never met them. I had no idea any of them were in New York. They're Virginians."

"Frankly," Gould murmured, "I don't care who it is. Someone knows you're on the premises—and may know I am too. I have a reputation to protect."

That amused Mrs. Bell.

"About the same kind as a Kansas rattlesnake's."

Gould went livid. "I'm referring to Helen and my sons. I sent my carriage home. You get that blasted Dr. Randolph to whistle up a hack. Send it to the entrance by the back stairs right away."

He snatched up his overcoat, stick, and gloves. Mrs. Bell sighed:

"I'll do the best I can. It's still raining. May take a little while."

Gould's eyes reflected the gaslight like chips of burning coal.

"It better not take longer than two or three minutes or I'll speak to Bill Tweed, and then all the cash on the Street won't help you keep your doors open."

The warning was softly spoken. But Hester Bell looked terrified. Gould turned his wrath on Louis.

"I don't care what personal matters have brought your relative here, but you damned well—" He thrust the gold head of his cane into Louis' chest. Louis turned red but held his temper. Gould was in an absolute fury; that was plain from his use of profanity.

"—damned well better get rid of him, and not let on you're here for any reason except pleasure!"

Fisk came flopping out of the tub like a white whale. "It's all damned puzzling. Smacks of one of the Commodore's tricks—sending some fellow around to spy on us. You came in your own rig, didn't you, Louis?"

His voice was unexpectedly weak:

"Y—yes. Straight from the headquarters."

"Was there anyone hanging around when you left?"

He tried to recollect. "Just the other board members. Oh, and a boot boy."

"Did you give this address to your driver?"

"Of course."

"Loud enough so the boy could hear?"

"I honestly paid no attention."

He began to feel increasingly threatened. Cornered, Fisk and Gould stuck together. In a space of seconds he'd again become an outsider—and all because of some damned act of carelessness he couldn't remember! His voice trailed off in a lame way:

"I suppose it's possible."

"Well," Gould snapped, "you've created a devil of a mess."

*"Jay, I'll take care of it!"*

The black eyes were those of an enemy. "I know you will."

Gould swept by, turned right in the corridor, and disappeared down the back stairs. Louis shivered again.

"Get out of here, get out, for Christ's sake!" Fisk exclaimed. He shoved Louis into the hall, and Hester Bell after him. The door slammed. The bolt rattled in its socket.

Louis' stomach was hurting fiercely now. If he had needed to be reminded of the stakes for which the Erie War was being fought—or the way an ally could be abandoned at the slightest hint of trouble—the last few minutes had done it.

"Mrs. Bell, are you sure this fellow said his name was Kent?"

"I'm not deaf. He said it."

"Is he armed?"

"Not that I could tell."

He thought quickly. "You have a back parlor downstairs, don't you?"

"Yes."

"Private?"

"Quite."

"Show him in there. I'll be down in three or four minutes." He reached into his pocket, pulled out a clip containing greenbacks and gold certificates. "There's a hundred for your help."

Hester Bell slipped the money down her bodice. But she'd turned on him too:

"I don't want any scrapes here, Mr. Kent. I pay off too many policemen —and through them, the Boss himself." She meant the man to whom Gould had referred—William Tweed, who virtually ruled the city through his control of the Tammany Society and the board of supervisors.

"I'm paying you to help me *avoid* a scrape!" Louis countered. "Are your two roughnecks in the house?"

"At night they're never out of the house."

"Have them stand by near the parlor."

"All right." She started away, then swung back. "Mr. Kent, I can be almost as vindictive as little Jay. If you've brought personal quarrels into my club and are trying to pretend you don't know anything about it—"

*"I don't!"*

"You'd better be telling the truth," she smiled, picking up the train of her dress and hurrying toward the main staircase.

*Damn* her! Where did the madam of a brothel get the gall to speak to him that way?

He knew very well. She was an intimate of Jubilee Jim—he was tight with Gould—and Louis had only been lately admitted to their confidence. If he bungled again, he would be out.

Tormented by worry, he paced the upper hall until he judged three minutes had passed. Then he wiped his palms on his trousers and started for the front stairs.

# CHAPTER 9

## *"I'm on Top, Ain't I?"*

THE TINTED GLASS BOWLS of the hallway gas
jets cast a watery aquamarine light. Gideon paced back and forth in the
entrance of the parlor to which Mrs. Bell had led him. The room opened
off the long, narrow corridor at a point midway between the front foyer
and a vestibule leading to a back door with an elaborate stained-glass
window.

About ten feet back of the parlor and perhaps six feet from the vestibule, there was a large dark recess in the opposite wall. The well of a rear
staircase, he suspected. He kept his eye on it. He had no idea where Louis
would appear—or if he would. But for several moments now, he'd had an
eerie feeling that someone was lurking in the recess. Hesitating there—
perhaps hoping he'd desert the hall.

Could it be his cousin?

The presence of the unseen observer only heightened his fear and uncertainty. He'd brazened his way into the Universal Club by using Louis
Kent's name and pretending a familiarity that didn't exist. Now he wasn't
sure how to proceed. He was beginning to think he was foolish indeed to
believe he could stand up to one of the directors of the line—or even speak
his mind in a coherent way.

He was uncomfortably conscious of the fetid stench of his wet overcoat.
He must look a sight. Certainly he looked out of place in this quiet, elegant corridor where blue light shimmered.

A faint squeak by the back stairs. He was virtually certain someone was
there. He turned and walked into the parlor—but not far.

He heard the footsteps distinctly. Two long strides took him back to the
hall. A short man with a walking stick was hurrying toward the vestibule.
He darted a look over his shoulder.

Gideon's heart pounded. Recognition was instantaneous.

The bearded man averted his head and rushed on toward the stained-
glass door. Afterward Gideon never knew where he found the courage—
better, the idiotic audacity—to go charging down the hall in pursuit. Per-

haps it came from an unconscious realization that he'd never again have such an opportunity.

"Mr. Gould?"

The short man broke stride. Gideon's mouth went dry.

"Mr. Gould, wait. You're one of the men I want to see."

The man hesitated. Then he turned around. Gideon almost winced under the impact of the piercing dark eyes. The cover of *Leslie's* had sprung to life.

He hadn't realized Gould was so small. Five foot six or seven inches. The financier spoke softly, but with more than a hint of strain:

"You've mistaken me for someone else, sir."

"No, I don't believe—*wait!*" Gideon lunged for Gould's arm as he started away.

Gould panicked. Wrenched out of Gideon's grip. At the front end of the hall, footsteps quickened to a run:

"Let go of him!"

Someone seized Gideon's shoulder; flung him against the wall. Pendants on the gas fixtures tinkled.

"Jesus, Jay, I'm sorry. Are you all right?"

Dots of color appeared above Gould's beard. In the stairwell Gideon glimpsed two heavy-set men watching. Where had they come from?

There was confusion on Louis Kent's swarthy face; Gould's anger seemed chiefly directed at him. Gideon forced himself to say, "You'd better listen to me, Mr. Gould—"

The short man ignored that, giving Louis another furious glance before starting for the stained-glass door again.

"—unless you'd care to have it noised about that you frequent whore-houses."

Jay Gould stood absolutely still, his head tilted back slightly. When he turned, his lips barely moved.

"Is this your relative, Louis?"

"Jay, I've never seen him before! I don't know—"

"*Will you stop repeating my name like a parrot?*"

Gould glowered past Gideon's shoulder. In the front foyer, two round-eyed girls ducked out of sight. Suddenly Gould stalked to Gideon and pushed him toward the parlor.

"In there! I don't discuss *anything* in hallways!"

ii

Gideon tried to walk calmly, straight to the center of the parlor. Louis, distraught and sweating, fumbled at the sliding door. He couldn't seem to locate the handle. Gould thrust him aside and closed the door with a thump.

Two trimmed gas jets cast a blue light much weaker than that in the corridor. Gould seated himself at one of the marble tables, his gloved hands planted on the head of his stick. Louis leaned against the door, breathing noisily.

"Identify yourself," Gould said.

"My name is Gideon Kent."

"You *are* this gentleman's cousin?"

Gideon could barely nod. He tried to remember the financier was as mortal as he. The remark about a whorehouse, a sudden inspiration prompted by Jephtha's comment on Gould's personal life, had given him Gould's attention. He must take advantage of that.

"Mr. Kent and my father are actually second cousins—"

"State your business."

Gideon's voice steadied. "I'm employed in the Erie yards over in Jersey City." Louis inhaled sharply. "I'm a switchman. Since the first of the year, two men—friends of mine—have been in serious accidents while on the job."

He was perspiring. But he dared not stop.

"One lost both legs. The other was killed, just this week. Both left dependents. Families that now have no income. They did your work, Mr. Gould. I want—"

On an impulse, he doubled the figure he'd had in mind.

"I want twenty thousand dollars for each family."

"*Twenty thousand?*" Louis gasped. He started to snicker. A gesture from Gould cut it off.

"Let me correct one thing you said," the financier murmured to Gideon. "You *were* employed by the Erie line. As of tonight, that connection is severed."

"Of all the lunatic demands—!" Louis exclaimed.

Astonishingly, Gould chuckled. His black eyes remained fixed on Gideon.

"You have brass, Mr. Kent. I'll give you that. But in all sincerity, I must tell you that your cousin's word—lunatic—barely covers it. No railroad, including the Erie, pays money to those who are killed or injured while on duty. The risk is a condition of employment. You're very foolish to think otherwise." He leaned forward. "Unless you're some sort of union rabble-rouser. But we have no union that I'm aware of."

"Perhaps it's time you did."

Louis started to slide the door back. "This has gone far enough. Let me whistle up the boys—"

Gould's raised glove checked him. "I want to hear the rest."

"I've said my piece, Mr. Gould. Except for this. You make plenty of money from the Erie. A fortune, I've heard. You can afford something for the families of two men whose lives were wiped out while they were working to fatten your bank balance."

"Of course I could afford it," Gould agreed. "You're not speaking to the issue. You completely misinterpret the purpose of a business—or the purpose of employees." His voice dropped; he became the weary father dealing with a slow child:

"Any employee of the Erie line must look after himself as I do for myself. Employees are parts of the machinery of the Erie, nothing more. Sound business policy dictates that when a part is ruined, money be spent for a new one, *not* on trying to salvage a useless one."

Gideon was thunderstruck. "Parts of the machinery? That's how you regard human beings?"

"Exactly."

"In—" He forced himself to speak up. "In this case it's going to be different."

"Merely because you ask?"

"Yes."

"Well," Gould said with another shrug, "you're quite wrong. Your friends mean nothing to me, and I daresay any other astute manager would feel exactly the same." He wagged the ferrule of his stick under Gideon's nose. "I do admire your nerve, Mr. Kent. But your thinking is pitifully naive. Good evening."

*Parts of the machinery.* That was the sorry truth of it, Gideon had no doubt. Nor would Jay Gould change his position or bend even a little. It was evident in the brisk way Gould started for the sliding door; it was evident from the relieved smile on Louis Kent's face. The momentarily annoying gnat had been killed.

Terrible discouragement swept over Gideon. Louis and Gould would laugh for years over his clumsy demands.

As Gould approached the door, Gideon noted a glint of perspiration on his forehead. *By God, I did unsettle him a little!* It was enough to drive him to one last gamble:

"I thank you for listening to me, anyway. Your decision will be announced Sunday. Along with an account of when and where you made it."

Jay Gould's balding forehead gleamed as if it had been oiled. "What do you mean—announced?"

"Just what I said. I'm not alone in this effort. Your comments will be

repeated from the pulpit of St. Mark's Methodist Episcopal Church on
Orange Street."

"That must be his father's church," Louis said.

Gould whispered, "Mr. Kent, your father surely would not make reference to a place like this in a sermon."

"On the contrary. He's a very forthright man."

"I am here on *business!*"

Somehow Gideon managed to laugh. "I'm sure you are, sir."

Gideon was conscious of Louis' having moved around behind him, to
his left. He was hidden by Gideon's limited field of vision. He heard
leather scrape the carpeting, turned his head and saw Louis start for him:

"We've had enough from you—"

"*Stand where you are and shut your damned mouth!*"

Gould's shaken voice stopped Louis like a child's marionette whose
string had been jerked taut. Gideon was almost delirious to see the little
man so badly out of control. He prayed he could keep his voice steady another five seconds.

"Perhaps you should bring your family to St. Mark's on the Sabbath,
Mr. Gould. Perhaps your wife would be interested in learning where you
conduct your affairs."

The parlor was still. A classical melody drifted from the front of the
club. Gideon caught the creak of a board in the corridor. Undoubtedly the
two men from the stairwell. All Gould had to do was summon them and
Gideon was done for.

"Jay, it's a damn bluff!" Louis insisted. Gould didn't even glance at
him. Gideon couldn't fathom what had happened to his cousin. Louis
seemed to sag, lose confidence. He stared at Gould like a worried boy
who'd failed to please his parents.

Gould swallowed. Ran his tongue over his upper lip. "Yes, I suspect it
is a bluff. But I don't intend to find out. I don't intend to have Helen find
out."

Gideon felt dizzy.

"Mr. Kent, you or your representative may call at my brokerage tomorrow. There'll be a draft waiting. In the amount you specified. The draft
will be drawn on The Bank of Commerce in Nassau Street. It will bear
the name of an account holder who is unfamiliar to you. There will be no
way for you to link the money with the New York & Erie, or with me. If
you try, you'll be laughed at. Are you willing to accept those terms?"

Gould's voice was quiet. Yet Gideon was still terrified. He managed to
nod. The small dark eyes locked with his.

"I'll say it again. You have brass. Jim Fisk has brass. I have a touch of it myself. Always have. When I was a boy, I had one good friend. Twice as tall as I am. We used to wrestle. Most of the time I'd beat him. A fellow my size—that's unlikely, eh? But you see, I wouldn't beat him fair. I'd use every trick I knew. He'd complain, but it didn't bother me. Know what I'd tell him? 'I'm on top, ain't I?' You're on top for the moment, though you're not entirely responsible. This—gentleman—"

A scorching look at Louis.

"—smoothed your path without intending to do so. Nevertheless, I admire any man who comes out on top by using whatever means he finds at his disposal. That's not to say you'll ever be on top of Jay Gould again."

He smiled. Gideon's mouth was bone dry.

"I'll pay you what you demand—once. But I won't forget the way you forced me to do it."

He pointed the stick at Gideon's face.

"I promise you, I won't forget."

He started for the door. Louis hurried to his side, but before he could speak, Gould slashed the stick against Louis' arm.

*"Get out of my way!"*

Gideon's cousin stumbled aside. Gould poked the ferrule in the handle of the sliding door. The door rolled back, and Jay Gould scurried off in the watery blue light.


iii


Louis gaped at Gideon as if he were some creature on exhibit in a menagerie; beyond his comprehension. The heavy-set men glided into sight in the hall. For a moment Gideon was positive he'd never leave the Universal Club on his own feet. Then Gould called from down the hall:

"Let him go, boys. If anyone fixes him, it'll be me."

The rear door closed. The men eyed one another. Gideon took advantage of their hesitation and started to walk.

Speechless with anger, Louis watched him pass. Gideon turned right. Moved with feigned calm toward the foyer of the brothel. He listened for the sound of a rush, but it didn't come. He kept his hands thrust in his pockets so the girls and a couple of male patrons in the front parlor wouldn't see him shaking as he passed.

In the parlor, the blind black musician lifted his fingers from the keys. Sniffed:

"Old wool coat. Don't belong in this place."

Hester Bell opened the front door and held it, eyeing Gideon with a curiously awed expression. He stepped into the rain and closed his eyes briefly as he walked down the steps. Now his legs were shaking.

When he was out of sight of the entrance, he ran.

# CHAPTER 10

## Casualty of War

UNDER JUBILEE JIM'S none too friendly scrutiny, Louis jammed the last of the greenbacks in the cheap suitcase. He handed the suitcase to the burly guard who rushed it down the stairs and outside.

Louis looked wan in the March sunlight slanting through the high windows of the Erie office. Fisk and Gould were treating him as if he were hired help, not a partner.

"That's the lot, Jay." He leaned against the side of the great iron safe, empty now. Gould finished scanning some papers, shoved them into the stove, and asked:

"You made an accurate count?"

Louis started to reply, then realized Gould hadn't been speaking to him. Fisk's brow furrowed at the attempted intrusion; he answered the question:

"Twenty-eight suitcases. All but two are already gone in the first hack."

"How much in total?"

"Six millions. For God's sake, will you hurry up with that damned paper shuffling?"

"I'm done," Gould said, reaching for his expensive tweed overcoat.

Jay Gould had sent a messenger to upper Fifth Avenue to summon Louis. By the time Louis had arrived on Duane Street at a quarter to one, all the headquarters employees had been sent home. One guard occupied the porch, admitting no one without permission of Gould or Fisk. The other guard toted the suitcases to a hack as fast as Louis and the fat man could fill them.

Gould had spent the time sorting through documents, retaining a few in a valise, burning others and discarding the rest on the floor. The large office looked as if it had been struck by a paper blizzard.

"How's Daniel holding up?" Gould wanted to know.

"He's out there blubbering like an infant. He don't like the idea of running to Jersey. We won't get the chance if you don't shake a leg. I have

boys waiting at the Cortlandt Street Ferry to act as a rear guard, but unt
we reach the terminal we're fair game."

Gould remained unperturbed. "Have you booked a hotel?"

"I sent Chad to Jersey City right after we got the news from court. He
arranging for suites at Taylor's. I'm also having three cannon sent over s
Vanderbilt can't surprise us. We'll be snug by dark—*if* we get out of here

Louis decided he should take encouragement from having been aske
to help with the clean-out. Gould wouldn't have dispatched the messenge
if their alliance had been permanently damaged. The thought took th
sting from the way they'd ignored him the past hour or so.

The abandonment of Duane Street was the result of the latest in th
series of bizarre moves and counter-moves in the struggle for dominance c
the Erie.

Gould's scheme to use the basement printing press had worked exactl
as planned. In fact it had worked so well that the thousands of share
dumped in the Street had depressed not only the price of Erie but those c
other issues. The papers had started screaming about an "Erie Panic."

Naturally Vanderbilt had caught on to what was happening. Suprem
Court Judge Barnard had enjoined the line from issuing any more stocl
Gould had immediately paid for a counter-injunction from anothe
member of the bench. Then Vanderbilt retaliated with still more court o
ders, placing the line into receivership and ordering the arrest of key direc
tors for stock fraud. The last decree had been handed down late tha
morning.

Now the six million in the suitcases—the money earned by the base
ment press—was going out of the jurisdiction of New York law, togethe
with Messrs. Gould and Fisk. Louis had overheard the two discussin
reorganization of the line as a New Jersey corporation. In Jersey, Vande
bilt would have difficulty exerting his influence. Of course, the reorganiza
tion remained strictly theoretical while the planners were still in Mar
hattan.

"You go along, Jim," Gould instructed. "I'll be there shortly."

With a baleful glance at his huge pocket watch, Fisk vanished down
the stairs.

A tug hooted on the river. Dust motes moved slowly through pale sun
beams. It seemed unthinkable to Louis that a carriage-load of deput
sheriffs might be clattering toward Duane Street this very moment. I
seemed nearly as unthinkable that weeks had passed since Gould had me
Gideon Kent and surrendered what amounted to pocket change to sav
himself from a potential scandal. In all that time, Louis had not heard a
syllable of reproof from the financier.

Of course, Gould had been frantically busy with Erie affairs. On severa occasions Louis had tried to invite Gould to his club for a drink, an expensive dinner—and an apology. Each time Gould had brushed him aside. Finally Louis had attempted to apologize after a board meeting, only to have Gould walk away. He was beginning to think Gould might have accepted the defeat and put it behind him in the face of more pressing problems.

Louis started to don his coat. "You needn't do that," Gould remarked quietly. "You're not coming with us."

"*Not coming?* What about the warrant?"

"You're not named. Just Drew, Jim, and myself. I've checked. Even if you were included, my original statement stands. You're not coming with us to Jersey City."

"Then why did you call me down here? Why in hell did you let me help and think I was still part of it—?"

He stopped. Gould smiled at his discomfort. He knew the answers:

"You did it so you could build me up to this. You son of a bitch!"

"I'll overlook that," Gould murmured as he tugged on leather driving gloves. His voice was so muted Louis had to strain to hear. "If there's name-calling to be done, I'd say I deserve first crack. When you were approached to help guarantee a favorable vote on the freight rates, I believe Jim made it clear I'd tolerate no objections to my decisions. Nor would I think well of any man whose actions intentionally or inadvertently subjected me to personal embarrassment. You nearly cost me the love and respect of my wife and children, Louis. You nearly saw to it that an announcement was made from a pulpit, a *public* pulpit, that I frequent houses of ill repute."

Sweating, Louis exclaimed, "For Christ's sake, it was Fisk who insisted we meet there!"

"But it was you who led that cousin of yours to Mrs. Bell's."

"How many times must I tell you, Jay? I had *no idea* he was following me!"

"Carelessness is not a virtue in a businessman, Louis."

The dark eyes bit into him like augers. "Once we're safely in New Jersey, there will be a vote to remove you from the board of directors. Danny, Jim and I are authorized to act as an executive committee and do that, you know. I trust you enjoyed your brief career with the Erie. You'll never have a similar opportunity if my word means anything."

"You just used me for the freight vote, is that it?"

"I use whoever it's expedient to use. That's how I stay on top. Some of the people I use remain my friends. Some don't. You fall in the latter group. You can't be trusted."

"*Jay*—" Louis groped at him.

"Don't touch me," Gould whispered, and walked out.

ii

The hack careened through darkening streets. "I don't like this," Drew complained from his seat beside one of the guards. "I don't like being carted off to Jersey, away from my church."

The guard tactfully ignored the outburst. He continued to stare out the window, his hand curled around the butt of a pistol.

"You'll find another over there," Gould assured the old man. "Just remember there are no regular services in the Ludlow Street jail."

"Vanderbilt's sure to send bullyboys after us," Fisk said. He actually sounded pleased. "The hotel's near the waterfront, y'know. I think we should have a shore patrol. Three or four lifeboats carrying men we can trust. We'll call it the Erie Navy and Coast Guard. What do you think, Jay?"

Gould pursed his lips in distaste. "Before you start playing admiral, I want you to attend to another piece of business. It pertains to that young man who milked me for forty thousand dollars."

He shifted his eyes quickly to indicate the suffering Dan Drew. "I needn't go into it now, though."

"I'll see to it whenever you're ready," Fisk promised.

Soon the hack rattled up to the Cortlandt Street Ferry Terminal. A dozen slum roughnecks Fisk had recruited and sworn in as Erie detectives were already unloading the suitcases from the first cab. As Fisk hoisted the last two bags, Drew again complained about leaving New York. Fisk hustled him toward the entrance:

"Listen, Danny, I plan to send for Miss Josie soon as I can. Say the word and I'll have her bring a parson to keep you company."

Gould lingered in the windy March twilight. When the last of the suitcases disappeared inside the building, he approached the guard who'd been riding with him.

"Biggs, I want you to do a chore after we've gone."

"Yes, sir?" The taller man smoothed an index finger along his moustache. He had to bend to hear the next.

"I want Louis Kent hurt."

"Badly?"

Gould nodded. His dark eyes looked almost benign. "I leave the means to you. But I don't want to be connected. Ever."

Biggs smiled. "Got you." He touched his derby.

Jay Gould's head lifted in response to the shriek of the ferry whistle. Smiling, he hurried into the terminal.

iii

Barely awake, Gideon scratched his nose. Not only had he forgotten to extinguish the lamp in the kitchen, Margaret had forgotten to damp the stove and save the wood.

He could have ignored the stove. But the light was a problem. He'd have to get up.

He yawned. He was exhausted. He'd spent the day working for a farmer out in the county west of Hoboken. Helping the farmer tend his hogs. For fifty cents. When he'd come home, he'd been too weary to do what he'd been meaning to do for days: drop down to the Diamond N. See who was there from the yards. Speak to them—

No, exhaustion wasn't the only reason he hadn't gone. He was sure they'd reject him, out of fear.

But he'd already recognized that there'd be scores of rejections before he achieved even one success. Why was he letting potential defeat incapacitate him?

He knew that too. The moment he stepped inside the Diamond N and uttered what was on his mind, he could never turn back—

Hell. It was too taxing to think about right now.

The coverlet rustled. He propped himself on his elbows; squinted. Eleanor peeped over the edge of the bed.

"Papa? What's burning?"

He awoke instantly.

Eleanor coughed. She began to whimper as Gideon prodded Margaret's hip.

"Margaret, get up. The place is on fire!"

His lethargy was gone. The glow in the kitchen was brightening to a blaze. The smell he'd mistaken for stove wood grew heavier. Smoke began to drift in the bedroom.

He heard a crackling in the parlor. Margaret was stirring, but slowly, God almighty! There were flames near the front door as well—

"Eleanor, run to the window. Open it!"

He rammed his hands under his wife's body and lifted. Her eyes flew open.

The flames shot around the frame of the kitchen door, eating the thin walls, the old paper. Margaret saw the fire as she hung in his arms.

Gideon was having trouble breathing. *Why was the cottage going up so quickly?* Then he smelled a telltale odor mingled with the smoke.

Eleanor struggled with the sash. "It's stuck, Papa!"

"The blasted snow and ice—let me at it."

He set Margaret on the floor. He could feel heat on his bare soles now. He fisted his hand and drove it through the curtain and the glass. A piece nicked his wrist. Blood sopped the cuff of his nightshirt.

He picked up a chair, battered the most dangerous shards out of the window frame. "Come here, Eleanor. Hurry!" He had to shout above the mounting roar.

Trembling, she let him lift her to the sill. She jerked suddenly, frightened. Glass slashed her instep. She screamed and fell back into Gideon's arms.

That cost them precious seconds. When he'd quieted the child, the fire was covering the wall by the window. It had spread the other way too, along the wall behind the bed. Red reflections glared in Margaret's eyes.

He hooked his bloodied hand around Eleanor's waist and dragged her to his shoulder. "Hold tight to my neck." Margaret clutched his other arm.

"Why is it burning so fast, Gideon?"

"Because it was set! We have to go out the front."

He dragged his wife to the parlor. Fire ran along the baseboard moldings. The smoke was so thick he could barely see the front door. Before they reached it, a barrier of flame confronted them.

His eyes watered. The hem of his nightshirt began to smolder from stray sparks. "Hang on, Eleanor. Margaret stay close to me. We'll have to go through."

The fire glowed on the leather eye patch. There wasn't even time to tell her he loved her. He lowered his head and ran at the rising wall of heat and flame.

iv

The wine from Delmonico's blurred his sight; aroused him, too. Yet it did nothing to ease the monstrous feeling of loss.

He had come so close. Cooperated. Played the tame dog—and he'd been within reach of the very top rung of the ladder. Then, because his second cousin's son had been clever and nervy enough to follow him to Mrs. Bell's, it had all come undone.

Financially, he wouldn't suffer. He'd taken maximum advantage of his tenure as an insider, selling certain issues a day or two before a dump of new Erie stock depressed prices on the Street, and buying others advantageously when the prices bottomed out. He'd more than doubled the paper worth of his investments in only a couple of months.

But the real cost of that profit had been the dismissal from the board.

Never again would men at the highest levels of the financial community deal with him as an equal—or as a man worthy of confidence. He had been deemed unworthy by Jay Gould.

He knew it was being talked about on the Street and in the clubs:

*Gould got thick with Louis Kent for a few weeks. But he dumped him. Gould's a piratical son of a bitch, but there's no shrewder man. Must be something wrong with that Kent fellow.*

The divorce from Julia had cost him his friendship with Vanderbilt. The Erie fiasco had cost him the friendship of Vanderbilt's foremost peers. He was well aware of how the Street would describe his situation:

*Kent may still have his money. But for all practical purposes, he's ruined.*

Clinging to the wrist strap of the victoria, Louis tried to fix his attention on the squalid street. An almost stygian blackness enveloped it. The damp air smelled of garbage and the river. It was a filthy neighborhood, only a block from the Bowery. The victoria was proceeding slowly while Louis' driver searched for an address.

God, he hoped she was there. It was past midnight. It had taken him two days to locate the address through a theatrical agent. He didn't know what he'd do if she were gone. He couldn't stay by himself one more night.

She still meant nothing to him. But it had become impossible to sleep or even think rationally in the mansion on Fifth Avenue. He was sick of going over and over his failure. What if? *What if—*

To come after her this way was an admission of weakness. He didn't care. The solitude of the mansion was unbearable. The solitude contained too many specters. Too many reminders of how close he'd come to absolute preeminence on the Street, in America—the world.

"Believe this is it, sir." The victoria swayed to a halt. "Not a very savory location. Do you wish me to wait?"

"No. Pick me up at eight in the morning."

He stumbled to the curb, stepped across the corpse of a cat and climbed the steep steps as his carriage rattled off. He was peering at the tenant's board when the hollow *clop-clop* of another carriage horse caught his attention.

The hack was coming from the direction of the Bowery. His own vehicle was already out of sight. But he was too drunk to give the slowing cab more than a glance.

He struck a match. Among the cluster of dirty cards he found one reading *N. Chetwynd.* He heard a door close softly as he noted the number on the card. The match went out.

All at once he realized a man was coming up the steps. His responses

were sluggish from the prolonged evening of drinking; he'd had virtually
no food.

"Hallo, Mr. Kent."

The voice was unfamiliar. A tic started in his right cheek. He was still
facing the tenant's board, slightly bent. Panic spread through him and he
started to turn:

"Wait. I'm not—"

His grunt interrupted the sentence. Then he shrieked from the pain of
the knife rammed into the lower quarter of his back.

v

Gideon could still smell the smoke. Not the same kind of pungent tobacco smoke lying heavily in the Diamond N. The acrid smoke of charred
siding; burned cloth; ruined upholstery.

He spied Rory Bannock leaning on the mahogany bar.

"Evening, Rory."

"Gid! Jesus, boy, we heard you got burned out last night."

Gideon noted the ornamental clock. A quarter past five. Soon Bannock
would be leaving for the night shift. He slid a coin across the bar and signaled for lager.

"Yes," he said, "there's nothing left of the cottage. It's the landlord's responsibility, but what little furniture we owned is gone. I barely got Margaret and Eleanor out soon enough."

"Heard the fire was set."

"That's right."

"Coppers catch anyone?"

He shook his head. "Whoever poured the kerosene ran away the moment it was lighted."

Bannock winced. "You got an idea who done it?"

"No," Gideon lied. He knew very well. A man who had met his demands but who had not forgiven him. A man who was living down at
Taylor's Hotel right now, delighting the New York press with his armed
guards and his cohort's rowboat navy.

It was impossible to prove, of course. But Jephtha's warning about retaliation had been correct. Oddly, once Gideon's loved ones were safe and
the shock of the fire had passed, he was almost pleased that Gould had
seen fit to respond as he did. The fire had finally given him the courage to
make his commitment.

"Anyone could have done it," he said before he sipped from the stein.

Bannock drained his. "There are a lot of hungry men wandering around these days. Hunger and failure can drive a fellow to crazy things."

"You're out of a job, aren't you, Gid? Cuthie said so."

"He's right."

"The Erie giveth and the Erie taketh away," the other man remarked with a sour smile. "Speakin' of giving, has anyone learned who sent all that money to Flo Miller and Mrs. Kolb?"

"No. I suppose it was some charitable person in New York."

"Didn't know there was any charitable persons in that town. Guess it doesn't matter who's responsible, though. The families are deserving."

"So are the families of men who are still alive, Rory. Your family. You deserve some things too. Better wages. Shorter hours. Things the Erie'll never grant you unless you demand them."

"Ah, that Sylvis stuff again," Bannock grumbled. "Spare me."

*For the moment.*

"You're the one I fret about," Bannock went on. "I hate to see you down. I never said this before, but you're a helluva good lad, Gideon."

"That's quite a compliment." He smiled. "Especially from a Yankee."

Bannock waved. "A witless Philadelphia mick, you mean. Let's have no more of this Yankee business, eh? The war's been over for three years."

*That war. Another's beginning.*

Bannock leaned on his forearms, boozily cordial. "Me and the missus, we talked about you being bounced out of the yards. Now there's this fire —how will you get by?"

"I don't know. But we will."

Sheltered temporarily at the Miller cottage, he and Margaret had already discussed the future and agreed on what Gideon had to do. He planned to keep on working at whatever jobs he could find. But first he had a job here.

"Anyway, Rory, that's not what I came to discuss."

He still had an opportunity to retreat. He was pledging himself to a mission that would make him a—a pariah, that was it. Fine word.

He'd be a pariah to a great many respectable people. Yet the work needed doing. Unless someone took the first step, it would go undone. Responsibility couldn't be shrugged aside. Most of the Kents had believed that for generations. He would not be an exception.

He dug his last coin out of his pocket. "Let me buy you another beer, Rory." He grinned. "That way, maybe you'll listen to what I have to say."

Standing straight and speaking calmly, he added, "I want to talk with you about the necessity of starting a union in the yards."

Epilogue at Kentland

# The Lifted Sword

THAT SPRING OF 1868 was a season of war. After almost forty-nine years on the planet, the Reverend Jephtha Kent was beginning to suspect there was no season that was not.

The fiercest struggle was being waged in Washington. The Congressional radicals had succeeded in charging President Johnson with violation of the Tenure of Office Act and other deeds of misconduct. Johnson's impeachment trial had begun in mid-March. How it would end, no one could say. A close outcome was predicted.

If the radicals won, they would have won it all. Under bills they'd sponsored, military governors enforced the law at bayonet point throughout the South. Jephtha had watched the steady and deliberate expansion of Republican power, and at the same time, seen his worst fears about manipulation of the black vote confirmed. His ardent Republicanism was waning.

Closer to home, the so-called Erie War had diverted the public's attention for months. For a time, Fort Taylor—Jim Fisk's name for the Jersey City hotel serving as the line's temporary headquarters—had received national attention. Daily press dispatches had provided thrilling accounts of bulls and bears locked in combat. No detail was ignored. Mr. Fisk's mistress was interviewed. Members of his navy of thugs were interviewed as they rowed up and down keeping watch for a Vanderbilt flotilla. Anonymous "confidants" were interviewed, and they described everything from the breakfast served Mr. Gould in his suite to Dan Drew's worsening tantrums; he feared affairs of his church were foundering without him.

No Vanderbilt flotilla had appeared from Manhattan. The Erie directors had escaped the enemy's wrath, but at a cost of exiling themselves from the nation's financial center. Finally Gould had packed some valises. Containing close to a million in cash, it was reliably stated. He'd hustled to Albany to end the stalemate by wooing the Black Horse Cavalry. The Cavalry was a group within the New York legislature which made no secret of its willingness to sponsor and support any desired piece of legislation—so long as the price was right.

The Commodore's men had rushed money to Albany to counterattack. But Gould's ante was the highest. An act permanently legalizing conversion of bonds within the state passed both houses. Now Vanderbilt faced a threat of endless issues of Erie stock—and a skillful publicity campaign to which Gould had turned his attention.

The newspapers had started carrying Gould's warnings to the citizenry: A new predatory animal was abroad in the land! Beware the archmonopolist! Jephtha couldn't recall hearing the term before, but Vanderbilt made a vivid prototype.

In the face of Gould's carefully orchestrated campaign, one paper inexplicably reversed itself and began to praise the Commodore. It took Jephtha four days at the end of March to learn, through a member of his congregation active in the Street, the shocking reason *The New York Union* had changed its editorial policy.

While not openly hostile to Vanderbilt, other papers found Mr. Gould and his gratuitous warnings to be good copy. Why, Gould cried, the villainous Commodore would soon swallow so many firms and rail systems that his whim would dictate the very price of a loaf of bread on the commonest table! Blithely disregarding the source of the charges, some molders of opinion were demanding that Vanderbilt's power be checked. They never specified how it should be done.

Recently there'd been a development to indicate that the peculiar war might be limping to an end. Faced with the law legalizing the Duane Street printing press, and already poorer by close to ten million dollars, the Commodore was said to be sick of the struggle. The member of Jephtha's congregation with Street connections claimed Vanderbilt had invited Dan Drew to call on him, to patch things up. If that was true, the Commodore had run up the white flag for perhaps the first time in his life.

The Erie War had its comic aspects, but the seething struggle in the South had none. That tragic situation was creating hatreds that would last a generation or more.

Northern politicians continued to flood into the region lugging their despised carpetbags. With the cooperation of the so-called scalawags—Southerners who turned their backs on their own people in order to ally themselves with the Northern power bloc—the invaders were capturing control of state and local governments. The military governors encouraged it.

Private citizens of the lately defeated Confederacy had other battles on their hands. They hurled charges of shiftlessness, impudence and outright criminality at the freed blacks. Some had begun a guerrilla war to cow the Negro.

The war's military organization was an innocently conceived social society founded by a group of bored veterans around Christmas, 1865. In a law office in Pulaski, Tennessee, the veterans had created a secret fraternity called the *Kuklos*, after the Greek word for circle. Someone had added *clan* to reflect the area's Scotch-Irish heritage, and the whole thing had been transmuted to a spreading network of night riders whose aim was to discipline and sometimes punish blacks.

The clan was operating in most of the South these days. The pranks of its members had taken on an ugly tone. The illiteracy of most of the blacks was played upon. A favorite trick of the colorfully robed and hooded clansmen was to surround a Negro cottage at night and, in sepulchral voices, beg for drinks. The mounted visitors would claim to be dead men who hadn't tasted water since perishing at, say, Shiloh Church.

When water was offered, almost endless quantities of it appeared to vanish magically through the mouth slits of the hoods. Jephtha had read the trick was performed with a tube and concealed rubber bag, but few of the victims knew that—or were sufficiently calm to think it out. One had died of a heart seizure early in April. Even the former Confederate cavalryman, Bedford Forrest, who at first had vigorously supported the clan's activities, was reportedly disenchanted by growing excesses.

Jephtha refrained from condemnation of all Southerners, however. He felt the North should set its own house in order first.

The scorned greenhorns pouring off the immigrant boats from all sections of the Continent were being crowded into slums and manipulated to the advantage of industrialists, who used the threat of immigrant labor to beat off the demands of trade unionists. Gideon had allied himself with the unionists. He was struggling to start a small organization in the Erie yards. Jephtha respected and admired Gideon's dedication. But he had no illusions about his son's future. Gideon had merely exchanged one war for another.

Blacks remained an even more despised minority in the North. Jephtha needed to go no further than Forty-fourth Street and Fifth Avenue to be reminded of that.

Every time some pastoral chore took him by the spot, he recalled four simmering days in July of '63. Right after Gettysburg, New York had fallen into anarchy as rioters—mostly poor whites—protested the Federal draft.

Blacks had been beaten; hung from lamp poles; had kerosene poured in their wounds, then lit. Even children had not been spared. The Colored Orphan Asylum at Forty-fourth Street and Fifth had been surrounded by a howling mob of three thousand. Fortunately soldiers had arrived to shepherd two hundred Negro children and the staff to safety. Afterward the mob had rampaged through the orphanage. One frightened black girl was discovered still huddling beneath her bed. Jephtha would never forget reading the account of how she'd been beaten to death. Until such incidents were forever banished, the North had no right to be sanctimonious.

The '63 holocaust had resulted in the burning of more than a hundred buildings and in the deaths of as many as two thousand civilians, soldiers, and police. No one would ever know the exact total. Once Federal troops had quelled the worst of the violence, a pundit had jeered, "This is a nice town to call itself a center of civilization!" Five years later, Jephtha wearily decided the same could be said of the nation. The great war had won freedom for the Negro, but there were few signs it had won equality, or even acceptance.

In view of his calling, Jephtha was always ashamed when he felt so pessimistic. He tried to remember that no era in human history had been free of the passions fed by ignorance and greed. Certainly Christ's had not.

But the nation had been created to offer a shining hope of liberty; justice; *change*. Occasionally Jephtha felt progress in America was unconscionably slow, if not altogether absent. Sometimes he wondered whether Jeremiah had gone to his grave for nothing.

With his faith and his wife Molly to help him, Jephtha had learned to accept the pain of realizing his youngest son was gone. Every six months or so he still dispatched a letter to a friend in Washington and requested another search of the Federal casualty records. No new information had ever been forthcoming. The day and place of Jeremiah Kent's dying were apparently forever hidden. Jephtha only prayed the death had not been meaningless.

In brighter moments, he knew it was not. The slave system was gone forever. The country was expanding at an unprecedented rate, and a much more worthwhile war was being won in the West. The Central Pacific and the Union Pacific were annihilating time and distance. In mid-April the Union Pacific had reached its highest elevation above the sea, Sherman's Summit at 8,248 feet, and had begun laying track on the Wyoming downgrade.

Out there, in land abounding in the free space in which men could build new futures, thousands were doing exactly that. Michael had done that with his mercantile enterprises. His letters said he had found deep satisfaction. He didn't use the word peace, but Jephtha knew that was what he meant.

Perhaps Matt too had found his version of the same thing. His enthusiastic letters, crammed with sketches, said he and his wife Dolly were enjoying their splendid poverty in Paris. Matt's surprising inclination toward drawing was finally receiving some direction through exposure to great museums and the ferment of the city's art colony.

Spring weather usually banished the worst of Jephtha's pessimism, and it was no exception this year, even though he had lately been forced to resort to spectacles for reading, and his knuckles and knees hurt a great deal of the time. When he heard an item of gossip from the Wall Street attorney who belonged to his church, his spirits positively soared.

He had resigned himself about purchasing Kent and Son, Boston. It struck him as an unattainable goal.

But something else he coveted just as shamelessly might not be unattainable. The Monday morning after he heard that, he set out for Tarrytown.

ii

Outside the little office, sunlight glowed through rustling trees. "Yes, sir," the agent said. "We are the authorized representatives."

He cast a dubious eye at Jephtha's rumpled black suit. "It's quite expensive."

"But it *is* for sale?"

"Most definitely. The owner has been confined to St. Luke's Hospital in the city, as perhaps you know."

Jephtha nodded.

"A ruffianly attack by street thieves, we've been told."

Jephtha said nothing. He'd heard the same thing in March.

"Mr. Kent is paralyzed," the agent went on. "He may never regain the use of his lower body. He is divesting himself of several properties."

"Does your price include the furnishings?"

"It does."

"Everything? Every last book? Every item of bric-a-brac?"

The agent frowned. "May I ask why that's so important to you, Mister—?"

"Kent."

He said it quietly and watched for the reaction, which was pronounced. He continued:

"I don't want my name mentioned. That's a condition of my offer. If you violate it, you've lost a commission."

"Are you related to the owner?"

"Distantly. I don't wish to be identified with the sale for personal reasons. Attorneys will act in my stead. I'll meet the price, whatever it is."

The agent had a stunned look.

"But only if all furnishings are left intact. Are you willing to proceed on those terms?"

An unctuous smile curled the agent's mouth. "Of course. Buyers in this price category are not numerous. I'm sure everything can be arranged to your satisfaction."

iii

On the seventeenth of May, Mr. Patrick Willet, contractor, sat in his wagon in the driveway of Kentland. It was a brilliant morning, breezy and full of the sweet smells of living earth and foliage. Just the preceding day, the eleventh article of impeachment had failed to gain the needed two-thirds majority in the Senate. The margin of defeat had been one vote.

Mr. Willet wasn't thinking of that sensational news today, though. He was in a state bordering on euphoria. The reason was his prospective client, the estate's new and somewhat unusual owner—a shabby-looking but clearly wealthy minister from the city.

The gray-haired cleric's last name was the same as that of Kentland's former tenant. Willet had mentioned the coincidence but had received no explanation. He didn't press for one. The potential fee was too important.

The Reverend Kent had contacted him a week ago. Willet had eagerly agreed to drive him out from Tarrytown when he took possession of the property. He was inside doing just that. The front doors were open on darkness and a smell of dust.

Mr. Willet cut a piece of tobacco from his plug and slipped it up next to his gum. It might be a while until he was summoned. He'd gladly wait. He'd wait till judgment for an opportunity to earn the huge sum which would accompany a major alteration.

He was startled when the Reverend Kent appeared in less than five minutes.

Kent was carrying the portmanteau he'd taken into the house. It bulged now. And, curiosity of curiosities, the preacher had a scabbarded sword and an old rifle under his arm.

Kent put the carpetbag on the drive, then the rifle. He walked from the shadow of the portico to the sunlight. Almost reverently, he drew the sword a third of the way out of the brass-tipped scabbard.

Willet scrambled down and peered over the other man's shoulder. The sword had a handsome ribbed grip and a pommel shaped like a bird's head.

Kent noted the contractor's interest. He raised the sword a little higher.

"It's a French infantry briquet. Given to the founder of our family by the Marquis de Lafayette, before the Revolution."

"Handsome," Willet murmured. Kent slid the blade back into the scabbard and as he did, the hilt caught the sun and shot off a star of light. The minister's dark eyes gleamed.

Fellow's crying! the astonished contractor said to himself. There was certainly no accounting for the queerness of parsons.

That was demonstrated again as Kent carefully laid the sword, rifle and portmanteau in the back of the wagon, then inserted a key in Kentland's front door.

"Here, Reverend!" Willet exclaimed. "Aren't we going to have a look inside?"

"No, Mr. Willet. I have the things I came for, with the exception of one painting in the drawing room. That will have to be crated and removed later. The other mementos are going to my oldest son. He's in a line of work I doubt you'd approve," Kent added with a smile. "You being the proprietor of a business, I mean."

"What's your boy do?"

"He's a labor organizer."

"You're right, I don't approve," Willet shot back. "Fellows like that upset the equilibrium of society."

"Society needs upsetting every generation or so, Mr. Willet. Peacefully, of course. Otherwise things that need changing are accepted without question."

Willet sniffed. "If you don't mind my asking, sir, how did your son become involved in such radical work?"

"He's not a radical, I assure you. Perhaps he'll become one. He'll certainly be called one. To answer your question, let's say a passion for causes runs in the family."

Willet was mystified when Kent glanced at the house and added, "Certain branches of the family."

The contractor wanted to enlighten Kent with more of his views about the union movement. But he was beholden to the man, so he changed the subject:

"Well, sir, if we're to examine the place, you oughtn't to lock up."

Kent climbed to the seat. "You can give me your estimate on the way back to Tarrytown."

"Reverend, I can't estimate repairs without seeing—"

"Wait," Kent interrupted. "I'm not hiring you to make repairs."

Willet's brow shot up. "But I thought—"

The minister shook his head. He studied the sun-drenched façade, smiling in a curious way.

"I never said I wanted alterations, or that I was planning to live here. I'm going to pay you to tear Kentland down."

"*Tear it down?*"

"Yes, Mr. Willet. Every last stone."

# *Afterword*

Apologies are due to readers of The Kent Chronicles for the unusually long delay between this volume and the preceding one. The summer of '76 brought a twenty-fifth wedding anniversary, and an extended vacation that probably should have been spent at the typewriter but wasn't. Contrary to rumors that continue to drift in from parts of the country as widely separated as Maine, the Florida Keys, and Big Sur, California, the author is (as of now, anyway), alive, well, and working to complete the next book in much less time than it took to bring you this one.

Several people who have contributed to the success of the Series have yet to be mentioned in these notes. So here's a hearty thank-you to John Rutledge, the gentleman who so capably directs the Pyramid national sales staff. John's not only a first class marketing man, but a fine companion on autographing trips; his good humor can even turn a bumpy ride on a jammed Eastern shuttle into a pleasant experience.

Belated thanks are also owed to former Pyramid art director James McIntyre, who supervised the cover concept for the Series, and to Herb Tauss, the talented artist who created it and continues to execute it so beautifully, book after book.

JOHN JAKES